Chocolate House Treason

Chocolate House TREASON

A Mystery of Queen Anne's London

David Fairer

Matador
9 Priory Business Park,
Wistow Road, Kibworth Beauchamp,
Leicestershire. LE8 0RX
Tel: 0116 279 2299
Email: books@troubador.co.uk
Web: www.troubador.co.uk/matador
Twitter: @matadorbooks

ISBN 978 1838591 045

British Library Cataloguing in Publication Data.
A catalogue record for this book is available from the British Library.

Typeset in 11pt Adobe Jenson Pro by Troubador Publishing Ltd, Leicester, UK

Matador is an imprint of Troubador Publishing Ltd

For Jane Stabler

The Prologue

KENSINGTON PALACE, 28 JANUARY 1708

THE SWISH OF satin and creak of whalebone ceased. Two angry women faced each other across the wide drawing-room, their eyes locked in a single blazing stare. Each was transfixed. The old magnetism between them was still powerful, but now it was working as bitterness and distrust. Neither would relinquish her gaze, and so they stood motionless, held together by an invisible force – the Queen and her subject.

During the interview there had been a lot of tossing of heads and flicking of fans, but gradually their circling of the room had become slower and more wary – and now there was only silence.

The one detectable movement was a hand clutched around a necklace of pearls that hung generously over layers of lace and golden silk. The fingers pressed and rubbed them like a rosary, until suddenly the thread broke. Like tiny firecrackers popping and jumping on the parquet floor, the pearls slid in a cascade to freedom, running in every direction, slipping under the furniture, hurrying towards the door. One of them, as if it acknowledged a lost intimacy, began rolling slowly up to the other woman's embroidered shoes, where it came to rest.

The figure looked down, but held her ground. Across the room those regal eyes were now red and glistening. The remaining loose pearls were being gripped with whitened knuckles, and the bosom pulsed quickly as the reluctant words finally came, almost sobbing:

'I am still your poor, faithful Morley… You know this well enough!'

'No! I see that my years of devotion are nothing to you. All my care for your interest is to be set at nought!'

'I am more tenderly yours than I can express…'

'Ha! You say so – but you talk just as you write – professions of love only! You are distant and stubborn, and every day you grow colder. That deceitful interloper has wound herself into your affections. She plays with you – but you refuse to see it!'

The other figure held her pearly fist resolutely to her breast, and straightened her back.

'How dare you talk so? There was a time when you spoke kindly to me. My beloved Freeman always had licence to tell me her mind freely. But now all I have is your contempt. You presume too much on our friendship!'

'No, no – you are no more the friend…'

Mrs Freeman's flaxen head bowed for an instant – it was a cursory gesture –

'… You have dwindled to a Queen!'

In the silence, Mrs Morley suddenly became the statuesque monarch. She raised her head – very like the profile on her new coinage – and delivered a magisterial reply.

'Yes, God be praised, Queen of *Great Britain*. At last the nation is united – and *I* embody that unity. Let it not be forgotten! I am its nursing mother… though alas, it is all I *can* nurse now…'

The majestic fist rose and hung in the air, before the fingers released their grip and let the five remaining pearls slip away. They made a last pathetic stuttering sound on the floor, and the grand room seemed suddenly empty and cold.

Punch's Theatre, Covent Garden, 28 January 1708

Meanwhile, a couple of miles away in a large well-appointed room in the south-eastern corner of Covent Garden's piazza, a theatrical entertainment was in progress. Here a wooden figure hardly three feet high, wearing a gold-painted crown and a sweeping velvet robe studded with artificial pearls, was strutting across a diminutive stage. In one hand the puppet-queen held an exotic fruit, and in the other a metal rod which she beat against her breast. The voice was high-pitched and distorted to a whine.

'Aaaah! Mrs Church-*ill!*'

After a moment of shocked silence, a ripple of laughter swept through the audience. Glances betrayed embarrassed amusement, and paper fans trembled in outraged delight. This was disgraceful – unheard of – *treasonable!*

'Alas! Alack!' the little figure wailed, 'what will become of meeee... ? How can I bear your scorn? I swear yoooo shall always be my favourite! – of all the Duchesses in London, yoooo are my precious jewel! My *Marlborough!* My *sceptre!* My... *pineapple!*'

The royal manikin struck the tin sceptre against its head, while the other hand lifted up a miniature fruit instead of the orb of state. The audience gasped at the blasphemy. On the far side of the stage, in an answering gesture, the second female marionette, tiara'd like a duchess, raised a hinged arm and shook it angrily.

'But you have betraiiied me, *Mrs Stuart!* Must you *toy* with my affections? Do you think me made of *wood?...* Am I nothing to you... but *a puppet??*'

At the Seven Stars in Covent Garden, Punch's Theatre was putting on a fine show. The place was packed with discerning men of the Town, coffee-house wits, and a good crowd of the female *bon ton*, who were enjoying a satirical afterpiece featuring the latest conflict in the political world.

Suddenly from offstage a wheezing voice was heard.

'Your Majesssssty!! My preciousss *Anna!* My Ssssaint! Do not let that vicioussss... Duchessss... distresssssss you!!'

To delighted applause, a heavily panting Mr Punch pranced onto the stage, led by his protuberant belly, his large nose dipping down toward the big ruff that circled his neck. A golden chain dangled from his shoulders and in his hand he carried, instead of his usual heavy stick, a white staff of office... It was Robert Harley in burlesque!

At once, the figure in the Duchess's tiara cried out in terror: 'Ah! *Harley* is come! Help! Help! Where is the *Junto* when I need them??' Her jaw bounced from its invisible wire. 'Where is my beloved *Sunderland?* Help me! Help me!'

From the other side of the stage, a second be-robed figure with a rabbit-fur collar and a similar white wand entered, its head carved into the likeness of the Earl of Sunderland. A few moments later, the wooden Harley and the wooden Sunderland, the nation's two Secretaries of State, were indulging in energetic sword-play, their white staffs cracking against each other.

While the two puppet politicians fought in heroic fashion, the two women shook one another's heads until the tiara and the crown both rattled to the ground. The duels then became one as each pair struck out at the other. The Queen and Harley yelled *Down with the Whigs!* and *The Junto to the Devil!* while the Duchess and Sunderland screamed *To hell with the Tories!*

and *Jacobites to the Pit!* Much fun was being had on both sides, and very soon the polite audience began to mimic their insults. Within the room, amused murmurs grew into loud derision, and treasonous cries began to echo round the walls.

Thursday

29 January 1708

Chapter One

It is often said that a widow of substance can do pretty well anything she likes, and certainly Mary Trotter was beginning to settle into the idea quite happily. She was recently a widow, and fairly substantial, and as the thought of her new-found independence struck her she leaned over the coffee-house bar, spread her hands, squared her shoulders and took a deep, satisfying breath.

Over to her left a crackling sound came from the fireplace, the cavernous heart of the coffee-room, where a large cauldron was simmering contentedly above the flames. Ranged along the edge of the grate was a miniature parade of pots and jugs, their spouts gesturing elegantly, all eager to do their duty. In front of her, around the long oak tables were huddled a few assorted hats and wigs, with sometimes a face visible beneath, and from time to time they nodded or shook, or dipped behind a paper. A general hum of conversation rose and fell, cut suddenly by a mocking laugh before subsiding again into a lively buzz.

The room was heady with bitter-sweet fumes of coffee, tea and chocolate, flavoured with a mingled glow of orange and cinnamon. Each intake of breath brought a hint of exotic spices edged with pungent exhalations of tobacco. The atmosphere was, she thought, an oddly masculine brew. It was both comforting and acerbic. On this freezing winter morning the coffee house was a welcome refuge, but also a place where news and ideas might break the peace at any moment and where combative minds could assert themselves.

Widow Trotter allowed her eyes to close as she inhaled the wonderful concoction. But what began as a sigh of pleasure ended with a slight shudder. She felt proud and delighted, yes, but also a little apprehensive of how this new challenge would work out. All the responsibilities of the Good Fellowship Coffee House were now hers. It was like being captain of a ship: this place, for good or ill, was her little kingdom.

'Split me, widow!'

The voice, a gruff whisper, was near, and her opening eyes took a moment to focus themselves. A face swung towards hers. There was a disconcerting twinkle in its look and acrid mundungus on the breath.

'Day-dreaming of your new-found riches, my lady? Do you feel the Peruvian ore running through your fingers?'

A rough hand lifted itself before her nose with surprising delicacy, the splayed fingers rippling as if touching magic dust.

'Ah, Mr Cobb, I see only dirt and drudgery. Tables to be cleaned, dishes to be washed, the fire to be tended…'

'But widow, *widow* – what a musical sound that is! – you need slave no more. The house is in good order and your friends continue in your interest. Now we are yours to command. We are your knights and you are our *chatelaine*.'

The constable liked to think he had a polite way with words.

'Elias Cobb, you are becoming dangerously poetical.'

'But your fancy must surely give birth to new ambitions? Let me be the man-midwife to your thoughts!'

The prospect was an uncomfortable one. Widow Trotter changed her ground and spoke quietly to him.

'My *thoughts,* Mr Cobb, are on why the Watch are here at such an early hour...'

She nodded in the direction of a table in the far corner where two partly-muffled figures sat quietly, trying not to look across the room toward her.

'... The evening is the time for you and your friends to gather. Is there some business afoot?'

He brought his face close to hers, and spoke low.

'These are uneasy times, Molly. You are an astute woman and have sniffed us out!' And even closer: 'We have a little matter to settle this morning. Pray don't be alarmed. It will be achieved smartly – and without violence, I assure you. We shall execute our task *sans peur et sans reproche.*'

The constable's Covent Garden French had its own unique charm. With a slight nod of the head he turned to face the company. His voice was suddenly loud and jovial.

'Ah widow! Your virtues commend you. This house is in the best of hands!'

There was a murmur of assent from the table nearby, and two dishes and one glass were raised in her honour.

'Peter!' Widow Trotter called out, catching the mood. Her young coffee-boy, smart in his green livery and apron, a little brown bob-wig on his head, stood to attention. 'Supply all my friends! Let each in the room have his order – at the house's expense. On this freezing day you all need warmth and comfort. Mr Trotter may be here no longer, but I assure you his spirit of conviviality will still preside!'

A cheer welled up. One of the tables resounded to a beaten hand. A snatch of song emerged. Somewhere a glass shattered. Peter Simco the coffee-boy stood rooted to the spot. Uncertain where to turn, his face twisted round more quickly than his wig, leaving it tilted precariously.

'Anon, gentlemen! In order please!'

The room was suddenly busy, and a smiling Elias Cobb made his way back to the far corner. He settled into the seat by his two partners, facing the room, his eyes directed away from the coffee-house door but aware of its location.

At another table a dark-haired young man, free of the encumbrance of a wig, was looking at the door repeatedly and with some apprehension. He nursed an earthenware dish of coffee, and in his right hand a sheaf of papers was folded discreetly before being slipped down into a deep side pocket of his coat. From the other pocket a watch emerged, not for the first time, and was consulted with a slight furrowing of the brow. He moved a pewter plate to one side, now wiped clean of its toasted cheese. Again the doorway was checked. He toyed with a spoon.

Within range of his arm was a much-thumbed copy of *The Daily Courant* and he reached over for it half-heartedly, knowing too well what to expect. There would be nothing about politics: no mention of the latest drama in parliament; not a whisper about the poisonous relations between Queen Anne and the great lords of the Whig 'Junto' who challenged her power; not a hint of the party strife that was bidding to pull the new nation apart. Indeed there was utter silence on anything in this mighty metropolis – and certainly no news from elsewhere in the land. The young man gave an audible sigh as he scanned the page.

No, on this cold January morning the newspaper delivered into this little corner of Covent Garden the freshest reports (merely two weeks old) from Naples, Leghorn, Budapest and Vienna. Here were the movements of foreign ships and regiments, the parading of princes and dukes – an endless slow-motion story of naval preparations, troop levies, commissions and diplomatic manoeuvrings. He groaned inwardly at the pompous folly of it all. This was European conflict as a distant chess-game, played out across the continent while everybody waited for the spring when the big fighting would resume. Nations politely at war! And the patrons of the Good Fellowship could keep track of exactly how the European envoys and generals were comporting themselves. He could almost see the stars glinting on their uniforms... But what of Westminster and the seat of government a mere mile and a half away?... Nothing! That was a world apart. It might have been the Indies.

The young man was sinking into an irritable mood when his face suddenly broke into a smile: in the far column of the paper, as if in wicked parody, was an advertisement for the *Alexipharmicon*, a remarkable panacea for ills of every kind – 'The greatest *Antidote* in the World,' it read, 'against all poisonous and malignant Diseases whatsoever, the most infallible Medicine in the Universe.' The potion was to be had exclusively from Mr Spooner at the Golden Half Moon in Goodman's Fields. It was expensive – half a crown a bottle – but how very much cheaper than war!

He threw the paper down. Beyond it lurked what was clearly a badly-printed pamphlet. The title-page was packed with bold capitals proclaiming *A Modest Vindication of the Present Ministry, Evincing That We are not in such a Desperate Condition as has been Lately Insinuated.* He reached across for it casually, anticipating a few minutes of amusement. But as he picked it up he saw something underneath. It was a sheet of paper covered in writing – verses by the look of them. Many manuscripts found their way into that room, and this one may have been handed round or possibly left there by an aspiring wit.

The single page was written in a flowing hand, but strangely the lines were untitled and unsigned. The young man read them through and liked what he saw: unlike many of the squibs that landed on these tables, this one had some elegance. It was a satiric sketch, but graceful in manner. It didn't attack its victim but amusingly patronised him:

He practised vices of the lighter sort,
Coffee and tea, tobacco, wit, and port…

He gave another glance at the door as it opened; but the rush of cold air brought in a figure he didn't recognise.

In disappointment he put the manuscript down and took up the pamphlet again, and began leafing through it. The 'Preface' declared that *A Modest Vindication* was 'humbly submitted to the Judgment of all Impartial men' – and indeed its humility was embarrassing. He couldn't help but read on, a smile spreading across his face. 'Flattery I know is nauseous,' the author declared, 'and therefore I shall not undertake the difficult task of enumerating the manifold blessings with which gracious God has been pleased to crown the administration of a pious and grateful Queen, committed to the care of an able and a faithful Ministry…' There was much more of this pretentious stuff. He laughed to himself. In such an age who could *not* be a satirist!

He wearily turned the pages. The hack was working at full stretch, throwing predictable phrases into the pot and stirring them. But on page twelve things suddenly changed. He noticed a thin, folded sheet of paper squeezed in between the leaves. He extracted it and flicked it open. These were more manuscript verses, but their style could not have been more different. This poem was signed 'Bufo,' and the lines were written closely on both sides in a small, spiky hand, incised in deep black ink:

Ah H - - - - - s*! Satan's double-dealing imp,*
Foul Wharton*'s cully, mighty* Somers*' pimp,*
In Spencer*'s service like a rat serves fleas,*
Sign of our body politick's disease;
Whore of the Junto…

The great Whig lords! – and under their own names!

As he read the dangerous words he felt another rush of chilly air. Two men entered, visibly shivering. They were both wigless: one was older, plainly dressed and with a large leather wallet hanging from his shoulder – clearly a man of business – and the other was a tall and willowy youth, the familiar face he'd been looking for. He beckoned to them, and without reading any further instinctively pocketed the piece of paper. At the corner table, the three figures conversing in hushed tones shifted slightly but remained in their seats, discreetly noting the performance.

The pair came over towards him, and he rose to greet the visitors. The older man chose his ground in deliberate fashion while the younger turned and gave a sweep of the arm.

'This, Sir, is my friend, Mr Thomas Bristowe.'

At this introduction Tom inclined his head slightly as the figure in a plain brown suit appraised him with a critical eye. John Morphew, publisher, was a man of shrewd instantaneous judgments:

'Ah yes, our lovesick *Celadon*. How does your heartless Delia, Mr Bristowe? Still unresponsive to your "tim'rous flame"?'

Tom winced and began to redden. *The Myrtle Garland; or, Celadon's Plea*, his single venture into print, had been an auspicious début. The pastoral lyric was taken up by the Town, set to music and performed at Spring Gardens and in polite drawing rooms; but now the poem was being hawked in a satirical parody by the street balladeers. His graceful opening, 'The passing wind receives my sigh; / I know that my sweet Delia's nigh,' had become 'The passing wind, my mighty fart, / Can never reach sweet Delia's heart.' And it got much worse.

'Be assured Mr Morphew, Tom has put those lines *behind* him!'

His friend laughed at his own wit. Tom looked at him murderously. Will would die for this.

'Have no fear, Mr Bristowe, Mr Lundy tells me you have abandoned the lyric strain and have now turned to satire?'

They sat down and he beckoned the coffee-boy.

'Yes indeed, Sir. I have the piece in my pocket. Will told me you might wish to see it. It is substantial – in imitation of Juvenal.'

John Morphew's eyes narrowed slightly.

'A dangerous model in these times, Mr Bristowe – though perhaps a welcome relief from the polite Horace, I'll grant you. But not too much *savage indignation* I hope?'

Tom Bristowe looked momentarily dark and serious.

'The Roman poet is indignant only about human nature and its self-delusions.'

'From that I take it you are a young man entirely free of them?' said the publisher in a tone of genial amusement.

'I have my share, no doubt – and especially at this moment.' He glanced ruefully at Will.

'Tom wants to set the world to rights. But that is our youthful prerogative is it not, Mr Morphew?'

'Ah, Mr Lundy: *prerogative* is a very troublesome word – best steer clear of it. But I shall be happy to take a look at your poem, Mr Bristowe. I trust there's nothing in it that will deliver you to the pillory? You will recall how poor Joseph Browne has suffered that fate for just eighteen injudicious lines. "The Country Parson's Honest Advice" turned out to be too *honest* – another word we must be careful of!'

From her station behind the bar Widow Trotter watched the group with particular interest. They were now chatting easily. The tall young man's hands were expressively active, and Tom's face was animated, his melancholy brow noticeably lifted. She liked her handsome new lodger – a welcome addition to the place – and it was good to see him bringing his friends here. She had begun thinking that under her new regime she would try to draw in a set of younger faces and some new ideas with them. The old regulars were dear to her, as they had been to her late husband, but the place had become predictable. The 'coffee-house politicians' occupied their favourite long table and met each day to set the usual antagonisms in motion – a predictable parody-warfare of Whig and Tory.

Until the barrel of prunes put an end to him, Henry Trotter had run the Good Fellowship Coffee House like his club. Her husband had been a genial soul: he had greeted all comers with an open countenance and was happiest playing the guest himself, sitting down with friends and forming his own circle. For thirteen years the 'Good Fellowship' – the name was its character – had stood for conviviality and good humour, both of them welcome things.

But this was a new age. Now the name seemed to her distinctly outmoded. Not only that, but it lacked urban style. She searched for the right word: it was too naive?... too obvious?... jejune?... If only there was a nice monosyllable that would catch the full idea. It was just a bit ------' (perhaps she should invent a word for the purpose?). She was feeling restless. The place needed to have more of that confident mixture of elegance and adventure which she could sense all around her in London. The capital city of the new nation was freshly-minted and humming with life, and so too – she couldn't help but think – was 'Widow' Trotter with her own new title that signalled a degree of power and independence. She thought of the future, and part of her craved an adventure of her own – something that would break the coffee house's comfortable routine and catch the current of the times...

An inner voice was beginning to whisper *be careful what you wish for,* when her musings were cut short. She noticed the two watchmen slipping out of the door, and Tom was signalling to the bar in excitement: there was evidently good news, which he would share with her in a moment. At the table, the publisher was placing Tom's sheaf of papers in his wallet and shaking hands – a good sign! The two friends thanked him, and the man took his leave, acknowledging her with a polite nod before the door closed. Across the room Elias Cobb was also rising from his seat.

Tom and Will looked at each other for a second in silence, before Will gave a whoop of glee and aimed a happy punch at his friend's shoulder.

'I can see it now, Tom! "LONDON: Printed for John Morphew near Stationers-Hall." In grand folio, perhaps – and with handsome ornaments?'

Tom risked a smile and took a deep breath.

'But will I ever be anything other than Celadon? No-one will let me forget it.'

'Trust me, I prophesy that after thirty years the joke will have worn thin, and the memory fade. You shall be seated here, a magisterial fifty-year-old in a large armchair, holding court to your admirers. Whatever the fashion for wigs, yours will be bigger and shinier and more curled than anyone's. And with a laurel wreath on top of it.'

Will's gaze was directed three inches above Tom's head, transfixed by the dream of fame.

'And you, Will, shall be presiding at Westminster Hall, the laws of England in your keeping. You will be Justice personified, a wise counsel and far-sighted legislator. You will right your father's wrongs, and make the Law a humane institution.'

'Ah, my father! You're not the only one with something to live down…'

Will's shoulders tensed spontaneously as if the very thought was a weight on him.

'… But you must introduce me to your extraordinary landlady.'

The two of them strode towards the bar, where Widow Trotter was beaming in anticipation, though her mind was momentarily distracted – Elias had slipped outside. But her attention was at once fixed on the two young men who now stood facing her, side by side. They were an attractive, though very distinct pair. Will was tall and slender, with longish light brown hair and what she could only think of as a mercurial countenance, alert and quick-eyed; beside him Tom was darker, rather more stocky and determined looking, with a saturnine face that suddenly unlocked itself in a bright smile. For the briefest instant, placed together like this, they struck her as a diptych of temperaments, each asking to be weighed with the other.

Tom made the introduction.

'Mrs T – This is my good friend William Lundy, Esquire, of the Middle Temple.'

The formality was quickly dispensed with as her nod returned his. She hesitated.

'I take it you have hopeful news, Mr Lundy? But perhaps I shouldn't congratulate Mr Bristowe *just* yet?'

'Not yet, Mrs Trotter; but Tom's star is distinctly rising. After all, he has now left Grub Street and installed himself in Covent Garden – exchanged a lonely garret for Good Fellowship and more salubrious quarters. Unless of course you've hidden him in the attic among the rafters?'

'He is exactly where he belongs, Mr Lundy – deep in the cellars with the coal and the stores. I only allow him out for meals, when he has to adjust his eyes to the light.'

'Perfect for his subterranean muse!'

Before the tone descended further into burlesque, she shifted the topic.

'And what about you, Mr Lundy? I take it you lodge in the Temple? A pretty wild place by many accounts.'

'Hundreds of young men with little to occupy them, Mrs Trotter, and sadly lacking those civilising touches that only the ladies can give.'

'He means that it's much like Oxford, but with even more distractions – and no Proctors patrolling the taverns. He insists that he visits Covent Garden in order to be *civilised*. But you mustn't tell his father that!'

'I was going to ask, Mr Lundy. You are studying the Law – are you perhaps... ?'

'The answer is yes, Mrs Trotter, I confess. "Hemp" is my father. He is determined that I enter the profession, and as long as he maintains my allowance I'm happy to accommodate him. Though it's hard having a name that is not wholly your own, either to make or mar.'

Although the word 'notorious' would be an exaggeration, Mr Justice Oliver Lundy had a formidable reputation. At the Old Bailey sessions, 'Hemp' Lundy (a tribute to his affection for the rope) made many a jury quail and many an accused grow visibly pale. House-breakers and light-fingered Drury Lane whores especially could expect no quarter. Will was only too ready to change to a more comfortable topic – though not perhaps for his friend.

'Tom's father, on the other hand, is admirably indulgent, letting his son loose in London with no profession at all. Just the harmless pastime of poetry. He invokes the Muse, and she comes at his call. No hard books to pore over, no endless note-taking in Westminster Hall, no threat of the attorney's office hanging over him. Instead he sits and dreams in elegant couplets, exercising his fancy rather than his judgment – I, however...'

'... have more than enough imagination for both of us, Will – and an unstoppable lawyer's tongue! Can you hear him, Mrs T? This fellow has it in his naturals. If he doesn't entangle you in his flow of words then he'll trap you in your own. Believe me,

Westminster Hall is Will's natural home, and he knows it. And for all his moaning he longs to make a figure there some day.'

Widow Trotter could well imagine it. Will must look very fine in a gown, although the hair would have to curb its enthusiasm under a periwig.

'And what is Mr Bristowe's world, Mr Lundy? It seems to be a more uncertain one.'

'No no, Mrs Trotter, far *less* so, indeed. You see, the *Church* is waiting...'

At once Will's features became composed and his voice took on a mock sonorousness.

'... but the young man *does not heed the call*. At this time when the Church is in danger, and he might become such an ornament to it, he resists the summons...'

She could easily understand it. Tom Bristowe did not strike her as someone who would be content with being ornamental to anything.

'... But he can only hold out for a few more months, and then it will claim him. He will measure himself for the cloth. Dr Bristowe, Prebend of Winchester, will insist.'

'I've promised my father, Mrs T. I have a year to prove myself in the literary world, or else it's the Church. Six months have already elapsed.'

This was said without animation, indeed with a glumness that brought their conversation to an uncomfortable halt. Neither young man seemed to have anything more to say. Widow Trotter beckoned them to sit down and signalled to Peter Simco, who marched up brightly.

'Sweet chocolate for the two gentlemen, Peter. And buttered toast with nutmeg and sugar. They both have something to celebrate!'

Her tone was cheery, but her mind misgave her. The Watch had evidently settled their *little matter*. But to what result? She glanced out of the window, not with any purpose but in the knowledge that the answer was certainly outside.

The matter had indeed been resolved briskly. In less than two minutes after he left the coffee house, having turned left in the paved court and emerged from under the arch into the busy thoroughfare of Drury Lane, John Morphew, with his coat wrapped tightly around him and his wallet heavy, had found himself confronted by two stout men of the Watch, who blocked his path, spoke roughly, and reached out to him. As he turned instinctively, the solid hand of Elias Cobb stopped him in his tracks. The publisher slipped slightly on the icy ground, and as his body swayed he found himself helped with disconcerting suddenness and ease into a hackney coach that stood but a yard away. The door clapped, and without a word the vehicle moved off instantly, swinging on its loose springs with the four occupants pressed up against each other, their wintry breath shrouding them.

In the warmth of the coffee house, the toast and chocolate had done their work. Tom and Will were relaxing and talking about poetry, and specifically about satire. Tom remembered the papers he'd been reading earlier – they were something Will would appreciate. Two such different little poems: one elegant and polite, written with good-humoured irony, and the other something savage and bitter – and in these times potentially seditious, to be passed around only with extreme care. He needed to read more of the thing. But as he reached down into his pocket, there was nothing there. His hand found only the empty lining.

Chapter Two

'THIS IS NOT an arrest, Mr Morphew, merely an invitation – though I regret it has lacked the usual proprieties. However, Elias Cobb has a very polite way with him, and we like to employ him for any business that requires some delicacy. He is surprisingly lettered, with none of the sourness of an ill education. I hope your journey here was not too distressing?'

The publisher wondered if he ought to thank this pompous fellow for arranging it all so thoughtfully. One thing he was oddly grateful for: to know how it might feel to be a pressed sailor or a kidnapped servant suddenly snatched away from everything familiar. But the man's geniality was far from reassuring: it made him feel mocked and excluded even as he was being soothed. They were both seated, although his own chair had been placed a demeaning distance away as if to make him more available for scrutiny.

'We wish simply to have a conversation with you, to hear your thoughts and find what way they are tending. We would hope perhaps to offer something that will be of benefit to you – and to us.'

'To be bundled by force into a hackney-coach is not a good beginning.'

'Again, I apologise, Mr Morphew, but I hope you'll understand that to announce myself at your shop would broadcast something you may wish to keep to yourself. Any public encounter would create gossip and might damage your reputation.'

'I hope my reputation is in my own hands, Sir.'

'I can assure you it is. We must see that it remains unsullied.'

The irony was hard to gauge. He was annoyed by the man's cuffs which twitched unnecessarily. They flapped again as he reached for a file of papers on the desk beside him and began leafing through them in silence. At once the easy sociability was suspended, and the man's concentration was intense. His head was lowered and the finely-brushed wig hung down in lavish curls either side of his chest. With a slight grunt he began reading quietly to himself.

John Morphew tried to think quickly. Beyond a door in the far wall he detected a hum of conversation but could make nothing of it. He knew he was in Westminster, just off Whitehall, and had been delivered to a modest side-door in an alley that issued out into St James's Park. It was not his usual part of town. But this was clearly a government building and he had been ushered into an untidy wainscoted office. A wall of shelves was occupied by ledgers, boxes, and groups of hide-bound volumes which from his seat he could not identify. He had not been arrested, but all this suggested he was someone of interest to the Ministry. Was he facing a threat, or an offer? Possibly both. It was obvious that the interview had a purpose and he would be expected to play his part.

The man lifted his head and the scene resumed as if there had been no interval. But the mood seemed different.

'You are in large part – I don't speak disrespectfully – a 'jobbing' printer. You print to order, take commissions irrespective of party.'

'I have also begun to commission work myself.'

'Indeed you have, Mr Morphew. To state things briskly: the line is sometimes hard to draw between what you are paid to print and what you choose to print...'

The conversation was progressing with unsettling haste and the tone was becoming more firm and direct. The man drove on with his point.

'... Nevertheless, although the intellectual property may be another's, by setting your name to it you are publicly responsible. It is an obvious point that I don't need to labour.'

The man smiled disconcertingly. If this was a threat, it was being politely made.

'Of course – but you must know that if I enable others to speak, I do so without prejudice.'

'No prejudice, I grant, but... a *predilection* is very clear...'

The word came after a slight pause; it was savoured, as if some hidden vice were being exposed. There was a further pause for effect, and then the thrust.

'... You are Harley's man.'

'I am the Queen's man, Sir.'

'Ah, of course – as are we all, Mr Morphew!... But I am wondering if you equate the two. Do you consider Mr Harley's enemies to be Her Majesty's enemies?'

'I hope I steer a middle way between extremes, avoiding the malice of both parties.'

His questioner threw himself back in his chair, and fought to suppress a laugh.

'Ha! You speak like Harley's puppet – that is his very own jargon! You have been reading too much of Mr Defoe's *Review*, Sir – in a moment I shall hear you talk of the *Golden Mean of Peace and Moderation*...'

He recollected himself, and at once softened his tone.

'... Forgive me, Mr Morphew, I do not mean to mock – a man has a right to a political opinion. But we are becoming concerned. What issues from your shop betrays more than moderation. It hints at something dangerous.'

The picture was rapidly clarifying. He was evidently being courted. In a rough way no doubt, but courted nonetheless. His services were being sought. There was an element of bluster in the man's responses, perhaps designed to draw him out; but it suggested he would at some point be made an offer. How choppy the sea would become before he was thrown the cork was impossible to say.

'You say you are the Queen's man, Mr Morphew. And indeed you celebrate the Queen with genuine fervour.'

He lifted up a printed half-sheet, which he held suspiciously at his fingers' ends.

'It seems you worship a *sacred* Monarchy. You speak of Her Majesty as a dazzling goddess who drives her golden chariot across the sky, eclipsing all human achievement: *Majestic Anne, in Glory's chariot drove*... This is quite a performance.'

'The poem on the Queen's Birthday is not mine, Sir.'

'It is yours Sir. It is anonymous. It comes from your presses. It is sold by you. It is subscribed with your name.'

His voice took on a formal, distinctly mocking tone:

'*When dazzling* Phoebus *gilds the hemisphere,*
Each fainter light submits, its Rule foregoes,
Nor dares its bright antagonist oppose...

– This is a glorious vision in which all *opposition* is suppressed. What a painterly picture! Why, it is veritably... *baroque!*...'

The man spoke the French word with obvious distaste.

'... It is worthy of a ceiling at *Versailles!* Is this the monarch you wish for? A divinely-appointed tyrant lording it over the earth? A Sun Queen to match the Sun King?'

'It is a celebratory poem. There is poetic licence in panegyric.'

'But this is popular stuff. A halfpenny half-sheet hawked about the streets.'

'They were printed months ago, lame verses at best – merely ephemeral. They had their moment, and no revolution in the nation's affairs has come about.'

'But they are part of a drip, drip of ideas, Mr Morphew. You claim such innocence; but you and I know what you are about. You are serving Mr Harley's ends. He attacks the *rage of party*, but only in the hope of forming a party of his own. He uses his newsmen, pamphleteers, spies – and poets – to attack Whig and Tory alike, merely to wind himself into the Queen's favour. The man is ruthlessly ambitious. I am telling you nothing you cannot see with your own eyes.'

'You speak like a politician yourself, Sir. Are you a party man? I think you are.'

'At this moment no-one is above party, Mr Morphew. We must simply be honest and direct.'

'You are making a great deal out of a few hobbling verses.'

'Well let us see where they hobble next!'

He lifted the sheet to his face and continued to read aloud.

'Across the globe shall ANNA *spread her beams,*
Obscuring modern, past, or future themes.
The greatest hero shall resign his claim,
And Marlborough*'s self stoop to his mistress' name.*

They are wretched lines, but the point is clear. Our great Marlborough must be humbled. The victor of Blenheim and Ramillies is to be put in his place! You drive a wedge between the Queen and the Duke, exalt one to belittle the other. Once again I hear Mr Harley's voice. The puppet squeaks with the voice of his master… Do you wish the war to end, Mr Morphew? Are you content to let the French have Spain, leave Holland vulnerable, and let our trade – the lifeblood of the nation – drain away? Are you one of Harley's peacemakers?'

'I would endeavour, Sir, to *keep the unity of the spirit in the bond of peace*. I recognise your own Whiggish phrases – the words of strife and dissension. I hear a voice behind yours: Lord Sunderland's is it not?

The man was disconcerted, but only for a moment.

'I have to admire you, Mr Morphew. You have brought us to the kernel of the business sooner than I expected. Your composure is admirable – though I must take care not to flatter you.'

'I would not welcome it, Sir. But perhaps you will allow me to ask where I am, who you are, and what you want from me? I take it I am not about to be charged with sedition and dragged off to Newgate?'

'Certainly not. I apologise for having omitted the initial courtesy of introducing myself. I am Thomas Hopkins, Secretary to the Earl of Sunderland. Your surmise was correct. From this I take it you have not visited the Cockpit before?'

'No, I've not had that privilege. Am I here at the behest of the Secretary of State himself?'

'Lord Sunderland has indeed interested himself in you. His fellow Secretary of State is already your protector, I think?'

'Mr Harley is not my keeper – though he is a man I admire. I may have printed some pieces from that source, but I am not *Harley's man*. This dissension between the Earl and Mr Harley is deplorable – the endless plotting and counter-plotting can only comfort the nation's enemies. But you already know my views I think, and my comings and goings too. You were evidently expecting me at the Good Fellowship Coffee House this morning. I take it you have a "friend" in my shop to keep you informed?'

Under-Secretary Hopkins swung his hands onto his lap and smiled.

'There are many people with whom we have channels of communication, Mr Morphew. Yes, your pressman John Emmet is one of our links among the booksellers. He told us you were going to take delivery of a new satire this morning, and such a thing is naturally of interest to us. Any ambitious satire, especially by someone unfamiliar to us, awakens our curiosity. We like to know what is in the air – before it becomes substantial.'

The publisher felt an angry blush rising. Emmet was his trusted confidant – or he had thought so. The implications were shocking and he was unsettled by the casualness – as if being a spy were the most natural thing. Here was a man who evidently took all this in his stride.

'Is John Emmet in your pay? I know there are informers everywhere, but do you keep watch on a mere *jobbing printer?* Can no-one be trusted now?'

'It's not a case of *trust,* Mr Morphew. In the current climate we can only repose trust in what we *know* – and it is the duty of government to know as much as possible. Our enemy is secrecy, not openness. The word "spy" is quite wrong. We need to know of anything that might unsettle the public mood or encourage disaffection and despondency. It is our responsibility.'

'And so... private letters are opened, conversations reported, rumours set going, false news mixed with true. The Ministry foments the deception. It is public honesty that suffers.'

'Have a care, Mr Morphew. I can see you are becoming heated.'

'No Sir, I simply wonder at your assurance. You people are on guard against satire, and yet you delight in fictions and satires in your turn – so long as they serve your ends.'

'But satire also exposes vice to ridicule, *with sharpened pen to scourge the offending age...* But please, Mr Morphew, let us leave such sparring to the coffee-house wits, who will endlessly debate but never settle the issue.'

Thomas Hopkins seemed very much at ease, as if refreshed by the skirmish of words, and he now leaned forwards with an amused gaze. The man really was an extraordinary performer.

'It may interest you to know, Sir, that your satire is being honoured with a reading at this very moment, in the next room – by my fellow Under-Secretary. It is, after all, distinctly his province. Mr Addison's judgment weighs more than anyone's in literary matters.'

The publisher's blush was suddenly returning at the thought of such distinguished critical scrutiny. If young Tom Bristowe only knew what eyes were scanning his verses at this moment!

'Mr Addison hopes that you might remain in touch with us. At this critical time in public affairs we would wish to be alerted to anything that might be about to cause a stir. I appreciate you are a man of principle. We are not wishing to *buy* you, Mr Morphew, but we want to remain friends and perhaps put some business your way. There is an *offer* Mr Addison would like to make which would do distinct honour to your reputation.'

The publisher was stumbling to reply. He had no sense of what was coming his way. If the interview was intended to disorient him, it had succeeded.

And at that moment, as if a stage drama were unfolding precisely as rehearsed, the far door opened tentatively and another man half-entered the room. It was a face he recognised. It was pale, and the mouth was slightly discomposed. Mr Under-Secretary Addison stood at the threshold, consciously not stepping into the room. Thomas Hopkins rose and went over to his colleague and there was a hushed exchange. He could not make out the words, or whether they concerned himself, but both men looked alarmed. The atmosphere was tense.

After a short interval Addison withdrew, and the moment the door closed Hopkins rounded on the publisher. His look was one of controlled anger.

'It seems, Mr Morphew, that you may after all be spending the night in Newgate!'

The publisher choked momentarily and suddenly felt how dry his mouth was. Something very bad was happening. He looked round instinctively for an escape route, but the door behind the desk swung open again and Elias Cobb strode in. For the first time Morphew noticed a pistol tucked into the constable's belt. He half rose from his chair, but relapsed back as Elias's solid frame moved towards him. Hopkins spoke brusquely:

'You must be questioned further, and this time with no pretence of politeness. You will have to explain yourself, and if you do not satisfy us fully then you will be put in the strong-room while we decide what to do with you.'

'But this is outrageous...'

'Save your protests. You are in a dangerous situation, so weigh your words carefully. If we do not have the complete truth from you, we shall have no compunction in using the full rigour of the law – and that will crush you!'

Hopkins turned to Elias.

'You will need to remain here, Mr Cobb – and not only for the sake of your pistol. I think you may be able to help clarify matters. Please draw up that other chair for Mr Addison.'

The constable went over to a large oak armchair and lifted it like a wicker basket.

'You are not a magistrate, and this is not a court. I have every right to remain silent.'

'I did not take you for a fool, Morphew. Saying nothing will merely implicate you...'

He fixed the publisher with a look directly between the eyes.

'... I don't think you realise the credit we are giving you. The situation is serious, and Mr Addison and I will have to take you into our confidence. There may be no other way.'

Once again things were realigning themselves strangely. He thought it better to say nothing until he understood what was going forward. Elias Cobb brought up a small table alongside the second chair, and then stationed himself by the door. Hopkins had left the room and Morphew remained alone with the constable, both of them still and silent, not meeting each other's eye. The awkwardness was palpable.

After a long ten minutes Hopkins returned with a thunderous look on his face, accompanied by his distinguished colleague. Joseph Addison was the slighter figure and seemed apprehensive as he placed a bundle of papers on the table. The two men settled into the chairs and adjusted their wigs. It was an oddly formal procedure, almost an improvised board of inquiry, and it occurred to him that Lord Sunderland's two Under Secretaries must have constituted themselves like this on other occasions. But there was no-one taking minutes.

He was expecting Addison to take the lead and found himself staring at the great man of letters as he raised a delicate pair of spectacles to his eyes and peered at one of the pages. It was an intimate close-up. Could this really be the poet of *The Campaign* – that rousing celebration of Marlborough's triumphs? In imagination Addison could capture the heroic slaughter of Blenheim, but here he looked fastidious and vulnerable. His full, light brown wig touched his left temple, and there was a slight hectic on the cheek.

But it was Hopkins who spoke.

'This morning, Morphew, you entered the Good Fellowship Coffee House at near a quarter before ten. What were your movements earlier?'

'I walked there direct from my lodgings, some twenty minutes.'

'You live in Salisbury Court, off Fleet Street?'

Morphew took this as a statement, and merely smiled to himself.

'You did not visit your premises by Stationers' Hall?'

'No, that would have been out of my way. I walked straight from home and did not make any other call.'

'So, at the coffee house, by prior arrangement, you met a Mr Bristowe, and there you collected some manuscripts from him...'

Hopkins looked round at the constable.

'... You can confirm that this transaction took place, Mr Cobb?'

'I can, Sir. He arrived with a Mr Lundy, a young friend of Mr Bristowe's. The pair talked with Mr Morphew for some little time before the material was handed over.'

Hopkins turned back to the publisher.

'What exactly did Mr Bristowe give you?'

'A poem – some ten or a dozen handwritten sheets. The one you've been reading. I'm afraid I have not yet been able to examine it.'

Addison glanced at his colleague.

'To which poem are you referring, Mr Morphew?'

'I don't understand. I allude to the imitation of Juvenal's Thirteenth Satire. It is entitled *Crime and Punishment*.'

'But what of the second poem? Was this from the same source? Or was it already in your possession?'

'Is there a *second* poem? I was expecting only one. Nothing else was mentioned to me. Perhaps Mr Bristowe handed it to me in error? As I said, I've been given no chance to overlook the papers.'

Hopkins broke in impatiently.

'Your wallet has been emptied, Morphew, and besides the Juvenal we retrieved a private letter – a most *feeling* letter, I might say – various bills and memorandums, a short inventory... and a further most unpleasant item: a copy of verses of the most disgusting and treasonous character – a poem that belongs amongst the piss and dirt of the gutter – from where you may have retrieved it?'

'I don't know the piece to which you refer.'

'Come, come, you've been found out. You are evidently in the market for sedition.'

'You speak in riddles. I know nothing of it.'

'This guileless innocence will convince no-one. You've set your name to some inglorious sweepings in the past, but we are now wondering how many anonymous scraps have come from your shop…'

'But this is—'

'Scurrilous things, dropped in alleyways, stuck on bog-house walls, hawked by boot-blacks and slipshod prentices…'

'This is fantasy—'

'This is not fantasy, Morphew – this is pen and ink!'

Hopkins seized the thin sheet of paper and shook it.

'You were scurrying home to your shop with *this*, and by tomorrow a new seditious libel would have been on the streets – and with no trail back to your press. A few dozen copies run off overnight, ready to do their work on the morrow. In this case the sedition is indistinguishable from *treason!*'

He struck the paper with the back of his hand. In the pause that followed, the word reverberated like an alarm bell. Morphew broke the silence.

'Show me the paper.'

Addison looked nervous, but Hopkins, who was rapidly overheating, immediately thrust it at him. The publisher saw its import at once and noted the opening invocation.

'*Ah H—s!*'

Morphew looked up at his interrogator, who responded darkly.

'Yes indeed. Two syllables. *One name.*'

Hopkins's outrage could now be explained. The publisher looked the piece over. The words were almost cut into the paper, little incisions of hatred. Yet at one point he struggled to hold back a smile as he read:

A hackney Crew who trade on War's alarms,
And build their Mansions as they scant our Arms.

Queen Anne was also mentioned – not in a derogatory way, but her majesty was tarnished by the poem's distinctly unwholesome air.

'I have to say I've not seen this before, nor do I recognise the hand... But *Bufo*...'

'*Bufo*... the name is familiar to you?'

Hopkins leant forward eagerly. In response, the publisher hesitated, realising that this was a decisive step.

'Yes... Two days ago John Emmet showed me a printed handbill subscribed with that name. Strong, accusatory rhymes much like this – it was a *caricatura* of the Duchess of Marlborough, alluding to her power over the Queen and her ambition of bringing in the Whigs.'

'And where did Mr Emmet lay his hands on this handbill?'

'He told me he found it dropped outside my shop.'

'Dropped? And so he simply picked it up and brought it in to show you?'

Hopkins and Addison exchanged a meaningful look.

'I saw it in his possession and enquired about it.'

'This really is an odd coincidence, Morphew...'

Hopkins's voice took on an ironic tone.

'... In recent days *Bufo*'s trashy libels have twice found their way to you – and entirely by accident.'

'I see the import of your questions. But if you think I'm responsible for printing the handbill, then ask John Emmet. He knows of everything my presses produce.'

'But such a little thing could be secretly composed and run off within the hour by a practised hand – a few dozen copies merely – just enough to scatter around and set rumours and speculation going.'

'But why would I risk such a thing?'

'No doubt you would be well recompensed by Harley – a valuable supplement to your official work.'

'But ask John Emmet. He and I discuss everything. He would have told you of anything suspicious – he was evidently overlooking me and my business.'

Once again Hopkins and Addison exchanged glances.

'Indeed so. In fact, Mr Emmet brought that very handbill to us yesterday. That was when we learned of your interest in Mr Bristowe's satire.'

This was worse and worse. Had Emmet made some accusation against him? And if so, for what motive? Morphew's anger, hitherto reined back, was tugging at him. Thanks to Emmet he had been kidnapped and brought in for questioning, and was now in danger of being accused of sedition – or something worse. The dark stink of Newgate was coming nearer by the moment. But it was all so flimsy and circumstantial – mere accident and coincidence.

Hopkins had settled back in his chair. Addison took up the questioning, but in a different tone.

'What do you know of *Bufo*, Mr Morphew?'

'I know nothing beyond some gossip I've heard – that a street-hawker on Ludgate Hill has been arrested for selling a two-penny pamphlet attack on the Whigs – *Bufo's Magic Glass*. And before you ask, I have not seen it. Only the title-page. It was arousing curiosity.'

'That was no doubt the intention, Mr Morphew... It is a mock-prophecy of the most treasonous character reflecting on the state of the nation – a vile piece of Tory propaganda against Lord Sunderland and his friends. On Tuesday we were able to seize a bundle of copies before they could be circulated. How many were printed we do not know. Where did you hear this gossip about the hawker?'

'In a tavern nearby – the Cross Keys.'

'You did not see a copy being handed round?'

'No, I did not. Only the hawker's hat. It was being exhibited to much glee. The title-page was stuck upon it. People were speculating on what the pamphlet might contain.'

Hopkins intervened:

'You paint a ludicrous picture. But what you say is reassuring. It seems that very few, if any, copies have escaped our net. I take it you will instantly deny being involved in its printing?'

'I know nothing of it, or its contents.'

'It is a disgraceful defamation of Her Majesty's advisers, especially those with Whiggish principles. A contemptuous libel on the Junto lords! Undoubtedly it comes from Harley's office. The hawker insists the things were left for him secreted behind a broken wall. Did you hear any speculation about the identity of this *Bufo*?'

'No, I did not.'

'Come, come, did you gather nothing?'

'I have no grounds on which to speculate.'

'Again you give us this front of injured innocence! We know you have links among the Grub Street hacks...'

Addison cut his angry colleague short and spoke quietly, shaking his head.

'No, Hopkins, this *Bufo* is not some low-life hack. The verses have a clever snap to them, and a cunning naivety. But their content is more than defamatory. It hints at corruption of the blackest dye and expresses contempt for our very constitution – and for the Queen's authority.'

Addison ended with a fastidious shudder, a sense that some ultimate boundary had been crossed.

Hopkins remained undeviating:

'In your wallet, Morphew – among Mr Bristowe's pages to be precise – we have just found a fresh sample of *Bufo*'s nasty verses – *handwritten*. This is the key, and we must make use of it. In only three days this malcontent has made himself known, and matters are becoming critical. The man is working to undermine the State, and as yet we have merely glimpsed what he might unleash.'

Hopkins straightened himself in the armchair as if conscious of settling into a magisterial role.

'You of course remain under suspicion. Something of what you say has been helpful, but we are justified in thinking you know a lot more. You clearly need time to recollect and ponder the situation you are in. And in order to encourage this I would ask Mr Cobb to lead you to our strong-room, where you will be kept until things are clearer. We do not want you to disappear into the alleys of the city. Our local roundhouse is too public, so you must be grateful we are not adding to your embarrassments by dispatching you there with the whores and drunkards. You are forcibly our *guest*. How long you remain so depends on how matters develop over the next twenty-four hours.'

'But you have no right to detain me. I'm a free man. It's clear that you can't decide whether I'm a suspect or a helpful ally.'

'At this stage you are both. That is why you will continue to be our guest. Such a compromise reflects the nature of your position. Mr Addison and I still hope you will be our friend...'

The publisher was being allowed his dignity, and in the politest way possible the invisible chains were attached.

'... And I think, as a matter of urgency, we need to know more about this satiric young man who is fascinated by crime and punishment, and who takes the scurrilous Juvenal for his mouthpiece.'

Addison interjected: 'The hand-writing is very unlike; but in places there is a certain swagger and rhythmic confidence in the style that might be thought similar.'

'Certainly, this Mr Bristowe has some urgent questions to answer,' said Hopkins, 'and the Good Fellowship Coffee House demands our attention. The place may be a nursery of sedition, and if such treasonous materials take their rise there, we must needs find the source.'

Addison nodded silently, indicating assent. But in that small movement John Morphew caught a degree of uncertainty, a momentary glance into the middle distance that was more ambivalent. It was an aroused curiosity, tinged with fear.

Elias Cobb was motioned forward, and the constable led Morphew out of the room to his unfamiliar lodging. He would not be in physical chains – at least for now. The door slammed behind him, papers were gathered up, and the tribunal came to an abrupt end. But not to a conclusion. For each of the three men some matters had been clarified, but the conversation had raised further uncertainties. By the time he entered the strong-room, Morphew's imagination had begun playing with his senses: there was the smell of treason in the air – or was it the stink of Newgate?

Chapter Three

EVERY COFFEE HOUSE has a character of its own, and its mood shifts from hour to hour. In the late afternoon of that same day, Thursday, January the 29th, 1708, the Good Fellowship appeared to be at peace with itself, a refuge for men who had dined well and who wished to be easy and reflective. Even the fire burned more quietly in their presence, and the water in the cauldron steamed silently as if not wanting to disturb their thoughts. Along the bar, a row of lit candles was in readiness for customers to collect as they entered, and as a further encouragement to relaxation a teapot and several fine blue china dishes were on display. But the calm was deceptive. In the coffee house this was a time for some serious and more hushed talk. In a short while the room would echo to the cut and thrust of wit as men arrived ready for their evening entertainments, but just now things were more intimate. A few older heads came together over the candles as reports were compared and thoughtfully weighed, and confidences entrusted or breached. The gathered news of the day was being digested along with dinner.

It came from all directions to Covent Garden, strategically placed between London and Westminster. Over in the east, inside the walled City, much of the day's business had been transacted. The merchants and money-men bustling at the Exchange had done their deals, and people had got wind of the latest schemes for making and losing fortunes. Down by the Thames, the favourable easterlies had brought in ships with secret packets reporting events in Europe and news to be hurried over to Whitehall. The sailors' own accounts, sometimes travelling even more quickly, spread through the taverns along Fleet Street and the Strand. Wedged together in the city wall, those close neighbours, Newgate gaol and the Old Bailey, offered fresh supplies of sensation for the street vendors and balladeers, and a promise of spectacular justice on the gallows at Tyburn. Out westwards, across the elegant squares and terraces beyond Covent Garden's piazza, the polite world was bringing new scandals to the market from St James's and Piccadilly. An incident at the palace *levée* or in St James's Park came post-haste along with the hackney coachman or the sedan chairmen. Court intrigue and political gossip were bundled together, and what a servant overheard at a toilette in Pall Mall could reach a Drury Lane bagnio within the hour.

During this lull in trade, the staff of the Good Fellowship seized the chance to occupy themselves. In the coffee-room Widow Trotter was attending to the shelves by the door, tidying papers and pamphlets, and arranging the selection of books. They lent the place a touch of sobriety, she thought, and reminded the livelier clientele that this was a place where knowledge and thought still had a foothold. Peter Simco was sorting out the long clay pipes in the storage chest and carefully refilling the snuff-box with Spanish snuff. Old Ralph, who helped out in return for a free snack of coffee and the occasional brandy, was sweeping the muddied floor ready for a fresh sprinkling of sawdust.

Beyond the door in the rear wall, there was purposeful activity in the kitchen, where Mrs Dawes had just placed two chicken pies in the oven and was now checking the venison pasties that would be sliced cold later in the evening. Alongside her, Jenny Trip was humming to herself while grating spices for the speciality drinks of the house. And down in the cellar the brawny Jeremy was broaching a quarter-cask of madeira. The whole place was devoting itself to comfort and stimulation.

At this hour of the afternoon there was hardly more than a handful of customers, and all but one seemed comfortably occupied. The exception was a dark-suited figure in the corner of the room who from time to time crossed and re-crossed his legs and struck the table sharply with his knee. With an intake of breath through his teeth he leaned forward over a sheet of paper, a quill active in his fist, and propped his head on his hand, pushing his peruke up from his forehead. He emitted an occasional sigh, and on a couple of occasions took a turn about the room for no other purpose it seemed than to measure out his steps across the floor. His eyes when lifted from the paper appeared to be focused on some distant prospect beyond human ken. Mr Bagnall, author of *The Shoe-Buckle*, was in the throes of poetic composition.

Further along the room, two young men were intent on their game of backgammon. Both carried swords at their sides and wore smart new suits, not decorative but sober and expensively tailored. Alongside their dishes of coffee were two small glasses of *usquebaugh*, which at this time of day were serving to encourage a mellowness of spirit. Six months ago, one of Henry Trotter's shrewd ideas had been to mark the Union of the two kingdoms with the sale of North Britain's national drink, and so the two young adventurers could recall the land of peat and heather in the midst of this alien city. After only a fortnight in London, Gavin Leslie and David Macrae had already arranged some private lessons to adapt their Scotch tones to something more acceptable to English ears.

At the table closest to the fire, three Good Fellowship regulars were talking quietly, and under a circling plume of tobacco-smoke the occasional shaking of a wig and twist of a brow told their own story. Every so often an emphatic phrase emerged from the background murmur: 'A new nation indeed!'... 'A Tory plot!'... 'losses and disgraces'... 'French mischief'... 'bullied out of our own seas...' Samuel Cust, Jack Tapsell, and Barnabas Smith were all facing difficult times. Sam Cust's share in his Jamaican sugar estate was bringing little but grief, and with the uncertainty of the convoys the Atlantic trade was virtually at a stand. The war was dragging on, and it was coming uncomfortably close. Even the English Channel (the name was now an embarrassment) was at the mercy of French privateers, and the Tapsell wine business and Barnabas Smith's enterprise in exporting good English woollen cloth were both suffering. Portugal and even Holland were becoming out of bounds, with naval escorts hard to secure; and across the south coast fully-laden merchantmen cowered in port for weeks on end, even months, waiting for a safe passage.

Jack Tapsell had brought with him the latest unsettling news from a coffee house in Exchange Alley.

'The boldness of it – off Brighthelmstone! – a *dozen* French ships on Tuesday night, out in the bay, bobbing around like a bunch of fine fellows at the King's Head. They say on a gust of wind you could hear 'em toasting King Louis' health – and destruction to Albion!'

'Off Bright'on!'

Barnabas Smith, a Sussex man himself, groaned and pictured his damp bales of cloth rotting in Shoreham harbour.

'Worse, my friend, I have it that they sent boats into Newhaven. Tried to steal a vessel but couldn't get her from her mooring – so they plundered and burnt her.'

Barnabas's groan became a stifled cry. Over the backgammon board apprehensive glances were exchanged. Bagnall's knee received another blow.

Jack Tapsell's voice remained a little above a whisper.

'The Exchange was seething like a wasp's nest, I can tell you. What will it be next?... '

He leant further forward and spoke with resonant authority.

'... It will be the Papists – King James across the water. That's their plan.'

Barnabas Smith nodded heavily.

'The French are up to something, certainly – gathering their forces. Is it true they have sixty battalions assembled?'

'Aye, that and more – the report has not been contradicted. They say the Dutch packet was delayed for a secret express from Paris. Before the summer, mark me, we'll have the invasion. It will be *Scotland,* no doubt of it!'

Sam Cust readied himself to speak: 'But surely, with the Union...'

'The Union be damned! – We'll not have true *union* till the traitors are rooted out. The Scots! What a bloody country – Covenanters and Papists! Kill a king, and import a king – and entirely free of duties!'

Barnabas grinned at his friend's dark wit.

'Jacobites...'

Silence fell. The terrible word slid slowly down onto the table, where it lay between their dishes of coffee. They contemplated it in silence for a moment, then each drew on his pipe, finding in the smoke a warmth and bitterness that spoke eloquently for them.

Throughout these exchanges the two young Scotsmen played on slowly and with less concentration than usual. With some tut-tutting Gavin brought the last of his men home and shook his head.

'Davie! You're so ready to be beaten, there's scarcely any triumph in conquering you. But you'll take your revenge?'

'No indeed – another time. My head's aching. I cannot concentrate. Do you hear them? *Scot, Jacobite,* and *traitor* in the same breath.'

'Dinna mind their blether, Davie...' He checked himself: 'Let them worry away.'

'Is that the new motto of the Leslies? No longer *Grip Fast* but *Let It Go?*'

'A neat cut – you have me there! But don't bring trouble on us. They're still getting used to us. Remember what we agreed.'

'But can't we talk with them?'

'No, we'll sit here and be good-humoured. We shall give a lesson in civility to our new compatriots. And to mark our polite nonchalance, David, we shall *take a dish of tea.*'

Gavin spoke the words with a clipped elocution.

'Boy – over here! A pot of your best *Bohea* if you please.'

Peter responded to the summons with delight and began the tea-making ritual at the bar. He took pride in the practised way he worked. After all, tea-making was an art that called for precision and elegance, and the young apprentice handled his materials with care. Since Widow Trotter had instructed him in the business he regarded it as a trust, and a sign that his role in the coffee-room was more than servile. He helped set the tone of the place. Peter moved to the cauldron and turned the small tap, draining off into the exquisite teapot just the right amount of water. Gavin and David watched him approvingly and began to loll slightly, consciously assuming a more easy manner.

In contrast, Mr Bagnall was becoming increasingly tense, muttering to himself in a strangely rhythmical way, as if conjuring a spell. Suddenly he gave a start and with a flurry of his quill, which squeaked like a scurrying mouse, the paper before him began filling up with remarkable speed. The three regulars watched with a combination of wonder and amusement. Jack Tapsell got to his feet and walked over to the poet, who continued to write fervidly.

'Whoa there, whoa! Your Muse is at a gallop, Mr Bagnall! What has put your brains into such labour?...'

He peered down at the poet's papers and picked up one of them.

'... What's this I see? "Public Virtue: An Epistle to the Right Honourable Robert Harley, Esq."... Is this an encomium, or a *satire?*'

Jack beamed at the company.

'It is a poem on the times, Mr Tapsell, and the taxing duties of public life. I naturally address it to a man who is helping to guide the new nation along a difficult path.'

'*Taxing duties!* Ha! Ha! Yes indeed – duties and taxes – you've found a most poetical subject! And what do you make of our *new nation?* – Harley's precious Union? *Great Britain* indeed! I put it to you, Sir, that all it unites is an old corruption with a new. All the old Court jobbery and Tory place-seeking – only now we're swamped by ambitious Scots panting for their share. Is this your gist, Mr Bagnall? Am I writing your poem for you?'

'You're not, Sir. My *gist,* as you term it, is very different. I'm offering some humble advice, that is all; I stress the need for public probity, and how manners in private life can set the tone for the whole nation.'

The Tapsell impatience was mounting.

'Nation? Nation? That damned word! – we hear of nothing else! And the *Union,* Sir – that's the biggest *job* of all... But I have to admit, perhaps it's better to have the *northern tribes* governed from Westminster, and not making their own arrangements with our enemies. At least they're here, where we can keep an eye on them!'

'And *they* can keep an eye on *you,* Sir!...'

David Macrae swung round. He had heard quite enough:

'... I think you should sit down with your friends, finish your pipe, and not overheat yourself.'

'And who are you to offer advice, young man? What leaky boat has brought you to these shores?'

'A Third Rate of sixty guns, Sir, of *our* Royal Navy.'

'Worse and worse! – so we now have Scotch stow-aways!'

'Give your tongue a rest – it's clear your insults are as unbaked as your politics.'

'My politics, Sir, are for good old English Liberty. In this country a man may speak his mind.'

'Or he may be a noisy *crack-fart*.'

'Well well! Very elegant indeed. The politeness of the *peat bogs!* Best go home where you belong, Sir!'

David sprang to his feet, and Gavin after him. He grabbed his friend's arm, which moved ominously to the hilt of his sword.

'Go up! Go up, Davie! Let's be awa.'

But David Macrae pushed him off. Barnabas Smith was up from his seat and jumped forward to stop Jack Tapsell's hand swinging towards David's face. The sword was nearly out. Bodies reeled awkwardly, and coats and hands swirled about. Behind them on the swaying table the Chinese porcelain teapot, still hot, with its finely interwoven design of flowering shrubs in a terraced garden, had a last proud moment and poised itself on the edge, before falling to the stone floor and shattering into a dozen pieces.

The sharp crack drew everyone's attention. The warm liquor spread at their feet and the china crunched under a boot. In that moment of respite Widow Trotter, who had heard the sudden commotion from the kitchen, was in the middle of them. They instinctively drew back.

'Gentlemen! You are disgracing my house. This is not a tavern!'

She looked them up and down.

'I had not thought to see my guests brawling like ragamuffins in an alley. Mr Tapsell, you shame yourself.'

He lowered his head. She turned to Gavin and David, who suddenly felt like naughty schoolboys.

'And you, young sirs – you were made welcome here. I hoped you would make friends, not enemies. In this place there are many arguments, and a lot of buffeting of opinions and ideas – but we don't come to physical blows. People here lash with their tongues, not with their fists.'

'I apologise, Madam,' said Gavin, 'we must learn not to be so easily provoked…'

He looked at David, then at the floor.

'… I'm afraid your bonny teapot is the biggest sufferer, and we shall of course make reparation for it.'

Within a minute Peter Simco was on his knees carefully picking up scattered fragments of blue and white porcelain. He had always taken delight in the teapot's large looped handle and domed lid, both of which were still intact, but the body with its delicate exotic scene was no more. Ralph's sweeping-brush finished the job, and the coffee-room was soon tidy again.

Widow Trotter tidied up the human pieces. She sat her customers down, ordered a round of coffee and sweetmeats, and ensured that proper introductions were made. Jack and his friends discovered that the two Scottish invaders were not French spies or Jacobite plotters, but reasonably sound gentlemen with acceptably Whiggish credentials. The fact that Gavin's distant relative, Lord Rothes, was a notable Williamite, and that David's uncle captained a man-of-war, completed the reconciliation. Indeed it began to look like a basis for much future banter and raillery.

Throughout the course of the squall, Laurence Bagnall looked on from his corner seat. Far from being disquieted by all the commotion, he found its dynamics fascinating; and by the time calm had returned and the atmosphere of the coffee house restored to good humour he had composed several well-shaped couplets arguing that national disputes were simply coffee-house squabbles writ large – storms generated in a mere teacup.

Chapter Four

NEAR SIX O'CLOCK on that same frosty evening John Emmet walked at a good swift pace towards Covent Garden. The importance of his errand drove him on, and with his head slightly bowed he ignored every distraction. At this hour the place was readying itself for the adventures of the night, and on every side there were things to distract him, the exotic and mundane together. As he hurried by a candlelit doorway a female figure stirred and raised an elegant hand, rustling her silk manteau in invitation. Just a few paces further on, a fatty aroma surged up his nostrils and a pie-seller cried loudly into his ear. To his left, a heavy basket of pears was thrust at him, grazing his elbow, and the old woman's shout was harsh: 'a farthin' for some fine fruit, yer worship?' He was no stranger to the locality, and in the normal course of things he would be strolling around here at his leisure; but on this occasion Emmet's mind was on other matters.

His customary alertness had not deserted him, and with each twist and turn he felt the Covent Garden night pressing in. He squeezed past a group of figures huddled round a brazier of glowing coals, struck by a sudden intense heat that tasted of acrid smoke and roasting chestnuts. Striding past the open window of an alehouse he caught a warm beery smell and heard a tenor voice exploring a tune, not altogether successfully. A snatch of laughter was cut short by an angry cry. More ominous sounds, almost non-human, emerged from a huddle of young men gathered under a street lamp, which encouraged him to quicken his pace even more. Fortunately the evening was young and their nocturnal sport only beginning.

For a shortcut he decided to turn into a narrow side alley and was instantly plunged into darkness. It was all the blacker for the contrast, and he was momentarily blinded. The smell of piss was hovering here, and the paving underfoot was uneven and slippery. He felt his boot slide on something thick and clinging, and he realised he had kicked on a soft bundle of some kind; but he pressed on, not daring to investigate what shape it might be. Fortunately a few moments later he saw a link boy striding in his direction, the flames of his torch dancing on the shiny brick walls. The passageway narrowed further, and he was dazzled for a moment as the torch passed by his shoulder. A giggling couple walked arm in arm, and in their wake a sharp oily smell made his eyes sting.

It was a relief to turn northward into the open thoroughfare of Drury Lane; but at once Emmet's scurrying figure was swept up in the throng of people who blocked him at every turn. Along the pavement within the line of posts the crush was severe, but to venture beyond that protective barrier was foolhardy. Sedan chairs hurtled with disconcerting speed, and the chairmen rarely swerved to avoid a slow-moving walker. Carts delivering market produce at this late hour shuddered on the cobbles, and creaking coaches with their blinds drawn threaded their way through the confusion to the sound of cracking whips.

On this particular night any progress was being frustrated by a large funeral hearse, heavily draped and beribboned, which swayed as it fought its way up the street. The six horses, their black ostrich feathers bobbing wildly, tried to maintain a stately pace, but were repeatedly blocked. Each time the lavish equipage halted, groups of dark figures holding tapers above their heads crowded up behind, less like a formal procession than a swirling mob. On the pavement, elegant gentlemen unaccustomed to being cramped for space doffed their hats precariously, and stylish ladies attempted a nicely judged lowering of the head. But graceful movements were hardly possible. Pent up between the side wall and the cobbled roadway, the harassed pedestrians pressed even more closely together. Swords scraped against legs, and what began as a dignified walk turned into an untidy *mêlée*.

Emmet cursed himself for choosing this route when he should have known how busy Drury Lane might be. As he repeatedly side-stepped around people he was being pulled away from the wall, and his frustration mounted. He worked his way back again, and was at once enveloped in a pool of deep shadow from a narrow alley to his left. Vinegar Yard was a place he recognised; but tonight he found himself struggling past it towards a small illuminated opening further up the street that was sucking in groups of people. Here the roadway was almost blocked by stationary carriages and sedan chairs, each attempting to deliver its occupants to their evening entertainment. The passage formed an insalubrious entrance to the Theatre Royal, which hid itself behind a frontage of houses, ensuring that its besatined patrons lost a little of their pomp in the transition from coach to box. All around, the vendors' cries competed for attention, offering posies, sweetmeats, handkerchiefs, bundles of dried lavender – everything a theatre-goer might need for the occasion.

Emmet made his way against the flow, and after a further struggle across Russell Street, which involved an encounter with a speeding wagon, he was able to cover the final hundred yards more briskly. It was with relief that he turned left into Red Lion Court, where a blessed stillness took over.

As he walked under the arch, the noise of Drury Lane was instantly muffled and only a single sedan chair was making its leisurely progress towards him. A coronet on the door marked it as a private vehicle whose occupant valued an even-paced life and a calm stomach. Here a lantern bracketed to the wall lent much-needed light, and further on a pair of oil-lamps shone out, their posts set behind the iron railings that skirted the alley. And there on the right, at last, was the Good Fellowship Coffee House. The flickering of candlelight along the ground floor was distinctly cheerful, and the building appeared well settled into its foundations. The highest of its three storeys bowed slightly over the paved yard, which gave it a venerable air; but the rows of sash windows presented a more modern appearance. In the centre, solid oak door-posts were surmounted by a lamp of crystal; alongside it a painted sign showing a plump smiling gentleman with a pipe completed the welcoming picture.

Within a few moments, a grateful John Emmet was in a warm room that was humming pleasantly. It made him crave the tang of coffee, and he immediately made for the canopied bar at the far side. Standing behind it was a bright-eyed young woman in a loose gown, her head dressed with a tall tiara of lace. A sparkish youth held her in rapt conversation, and as she glanced around the room the ruffle at her throat changed shape, and the pink lappets hanging on either side of her face swung in accompaniment. Jenny Trip's ability to mix the barmaid and the Persian princess was a real asset, and Widow Trotter was too sharp a businesswoman not to exploit it at a time of day when stray young bloods were abroad. The older regulars too enjoyed her teasing ways. But on this occasion Jenny's hypnotic charm was broken as the new customer, penny in hand, leaned across the bar towards her.

'You have a Mr Bristowe lodging here?'

Jenny was jolted by the directness of this. Her young admirer, like a musician hearing a wrong note, looked at the small intruder with obvious annoyance. Jenny touched him reassuringly on the hand before turning to give Emmet her brief attention.

'Indeed, Sir. He is the gentleman over there reading.'

She pointed to a young man with his back to the room, clearly absorbed in a book. Emmet nodded a silent thanks and placed his penny on the bar. He snapped his fingers at Peter and beckoned for a coffee. A moment later Tom was aware of a figure by his side, making to sit down. He was a trim, precise-looking man, but seemed to be sweating slightly, his hair cut close.

'You are Mr Bristowe, are you not?'

'Thomas Bristowe, yes.'

'I'm very glad to meet you, Mr Bristowe.'

Emmet held out his hand and smiled a piercing, intense smile.

'I am a colleague of John Morphew's – John Emmet is the name.'

'Mr Emmet?' Tom responded warmly: 'Of course. I know the name. My friend Will mentioned you. I understand you were instrumental in Mr Morphew's hearing about my work? For that I have to thank you. In fact, only this morning he was seated at this very table.'

'That is why I am here, Sir. Forgive me for interrupting your reading, but Mr Morphew cannot come himself. I am merely the messenger.'

He gave a little modest nod. Tom brightened at what this could mean, and he found himself responding with embarrassing eagerness.

'Has he read my poem already? I know what a busy man he is.'

Emmet was now seated, and Peter Simco appeared by his side to pour the coffee. Holding the dish in one hand, Peter lifted the pot high with the other, and performing a well-practised turn of the wrist let the liquid cascade down into it. Emmet noticed that Tom's own dish was empty and signalled for Peter to refill it. The manoeuvre was repeated for Tom with especial dexterity.

'Mr Morphew is well disposed to your piece, Mr Bristowe. In fact he has sent me to inquire what other verses you may have. He is considering producing a poetical miscellany of shorter pieces in the satiric vein.'

Tom looked thoughtful for a moment.

'He said nothing of that this morning – but of course he hadn't sampled my work...'

He paused. Once again he felt his tone was wrong – it sounded as if he assumed the Bristowe genius would be immediately recognised.

'Exactly. He already knows your lyric gift, but thinks you have a strong satiric talent too – one that could match Matt Prior's.'

Tom looked immediately sceptical; but he met Emmet's smile. Was this man the angel or the tempter?

'Please don't exaggerate, Mr Emmet. I have a sober sense of my own shortcomings as a poet. I think I'm making progress, but I'm only an apprentice as yet. Forgive me if I appear uneasy – *When Flattery sooths, and when Ambition blinds...*'

'I'm sorry, Mr Bristowe – it is I who must apologise. You cast me as the false *Achitophel,* and I'm properly admonished. But what I said was kindly meant. We want only to encourage you. Too many young poets in this age are pushed down and ignored.'

Tom sipped his coffee, and replied a little sourly.

'Some rightly so! But I take your words in the spirit they are offered. I must admit the suddenness of this has surprised me. Can I take it you might wish to publish my poem?'

Emmet enjoyed the generous moment, and in replying he felt a surge of power – what it might be like to use this power for good.

'A contract will have to be drawn up advantageous to both parties. But I'm sure this can be negotiated...'

Tom was speechless, and Emmet warmed to his role of interested patron.

'... Have you been writing any more satire? Are you leaving Juvenal behind to speak in your own voice perhaps?'

'I hope I've helped Juvenal speak through me. Naturally it's hard to lodge in a coffee house and not pen a few things – But I've been doing this in a desultory way so far. Disconnected epigrams and portraits, nothing more – nothing appropriate for a published collection I'm afraid.'

'Do you perhaps have anything of that kind you could show me?'

'I have a few little things in my desk; but I'd be ashamed to let you read that stuff. I would prefer to work up a few of them into something a little more ambitious and extended. Might I do that and let you see the result? That would certainly be an encouragement.'

'Our age needs its satirists. Sharpen your quill, Mr Bristowe! – but *direct* it also. Random spleen is of no use to anyone.'

Emmet laughed, and Tom smiled in response. He sensed a sharp ironic mind behind Emmet's words, and this intrigued him.

'I promise to lash the age with all the power I can muster. After all, it requires little invention to put our crimes and vices into verse!'

Emmet looked around him at the well-filled tables and the papers scattered over them.

'I would think this place must be a repository for some fascinating scraps and improvised pieces? I don't expect the Good Fellowship to rival Will's, but do you find anything of interest – or *quality* rather – left here? It's clear you spend much of your time in this room.'

'It saves on fire and candles. My own room can be chilly, and I find I like the convivial atmosphere. Though when I have a book in my hand I can shut it out well enough.'

Emmet pressed on with his point.

'Mr Addison uses Will's as his *Lyceum*, and that place is a very library of fine new writing – it has been so since old Dryden's time. I just wonder if the Good Fellowship has anything of that kind. Are there wits who leave their pieces here, perhaps?'

'Yes, one or two. Laurence Bagnall favours us often, and finds the coffee-room conducive to writing. He insists it's to escape the demands of his wife – but we all know it's because he has fallen out with Mr Addison! Bagnall is someone who writes easily amid the buzz of conversation. Indeed he sometimes appears to be putting all our doings into couplets.'

'Yes, I know of Mr Bagnall of course. A man of wide-ranging poetic talent – very much suited to the miscellany!'

'Though at present he's penning something considerably more ambitious – an *Epistle to Mr Harley*, no less. On *public vices* and *private virtues*.'

'I'm interested to hear of that. I'll tell Mr Morphew, if I may.'

Tom realised this Emmet might be a useful man to keep in touch with. He took another drink of coffee.

'There is little verse left here of any quality. But as it happens, this morning I found something that struck me as stronger and more witty than many such things. It was a satiric portrait. I couldn't think whose it might be, since there was no name attached.'

As Tom spoke these words, Emmet's whole body flickered into life. The man leaned forward and clasped his hands together. Tom noticed how large they were – for someone smallish – and the arms were solid as tree trunks.

'That sounds just what I'm looking for! Did you not recognise the writing?'

'No, and I didn't take it up. It may still be here. I'll look for it later when the place is empty. I suggested to Mrs Trotter only yesterday that we might keep a box in the room to deposit anything that deserves preserving. These things are so ephemeral, but just occasionally a piece is worth a second reading. I seem to remember one couplet of it...'

He paused, frowning, and Emmet gave him his full attention.

'... *His vices of a lighter sort, / Tobacco, coffee, wit, and port...*'

Emmet looked disappointed.

'... But I'm doing the piece an injustice, and have misremembered it. They were well-turned *penta*meters.'

At that precise moment Tom recalled the second paper with its angry railing verses. But something made him hold back. The thing was street stuff, not for a published miscellany. And it was a dangerous libel, not the usual political squibs. He said nothing. But the thought brought another idea to mind.

'The Mutton-Chop pieces are generally a sad collection.'

Emmet showed renewed interest.

'*Mutton-Chop?* I'm afraid I don't understand.'

'They are a small dining club that take the upper room here for their celebrations. They gather every fortnight, on Wednesdays. Mrs Dawes roasts excellent mutton, and they end up carousing around a bowl of Jenny's punch. She has an expert hand with the spices...'

Tom looked over at Jenny Trip, who was now offering snuff on the back of her hand to the young gentleman still stationed at the bar. He could hear them laughing.

'... The Mutton-Chops are a lively set – only seven or eight of them, but they make enough commotion for twice that number. By midnight their toasts have been celebrated many times over, and there's usually a jumble of verses left behind. Most of it has to be swept away the next day, but some finds its way into the coffee-room. Last night they were very boisterous – my room is above theirs.'

Emmet smiled.

'Another excellent reason for passing the evening down here!'

'I did indeed – and the ever-generous Mrs Dawes supplied me with a cutlet of my own.'

'But are the Mutton-Chops' politics as turbulent as their behaviour? Do they toast the reigning beauties – or do they perhaps raise a glass *elsewhere?*' Emmet's eye twinkled knowingly.

'It's the usual Patriot exuberance. They are high-flying Tories to a man.'

Emmet balanced his dish on his thumb and took a sip of coffee.

'Is that the complexion of this place generally, would you say?'

'No, no. The Good Fellowship is a political mash-tub. We have more than our share of solid Whigs too – all for the war, trade, the stocks, toleration, and occasional conformity! There is also the Universal Grumbling Party, of course; a sprinkling of *True Believers*; and inevitably a few *State-Enthusiasts*.'

'*Whig* plotters, are they?'

'I think they rather come here as a relief from their intrigues and cabals.'

'And no doubt you have a handful of *Jacobites* to balance them out?'

'As I said, this is a miscellaneous house. The result tends toward moderation. Mrs Trotter is careful to cultivate that wherever possible.'

'Ah, the Widow Trotter. Is she not here this evening?'

'She is marketing in the piazza, but should be returning soon.'

'Paying *moderately* I hope?' Emmet's humour sounded a little sly: 'Do you share her zeal for moderation?'

'A contradiction in terms, Mr Emmet! Mrs Trotter does not admire zealots of any kind, and nor do I.'

'That's reassuring, and I think Mr Harley – and Mr Defoe – would approve. You take the *Review* here I assume?'

'Most certainly – but other papers too, of all complexions. Widow Trotter has little patience with coffee-house politicians. But why are you asking this?'

Tom was becoming uncomfortable with the topic, and Emmet sensed it.

'I apologise for seeming to interrogate you. I merely ask because it occurs to me that you might like to pay *Will's* a visit, if you have not already done so? It is, after all, only a short stroll away. The very place for aspiring poets! It has of course become somewhat Whiggish since Mr Dryden's time, and its political cast may deter you. Like Mr Bagnall, you may be uneasy with *Kit-Cat* politics and resist being thought one of Mr Addison's circle?'

Tom began to feel uneasy.

'I have respect for Mr Addison as a writer. Perhaps I may venture there, but not until I feel I can hold my head up. And I value my independence.'

In response to this, Emmet's tone became more avuncular and encouraging.

'Please do consider adventuring to Will's. Ambrose Philips is much praised, and Doctor Swift is now seen there since he is back from Ireland.'

But Tom was unresponsive. There was an awkward pause. Emmet's neck arched inelegantly as he peered over Tom's arm.

'What book do you have there?'

Tom presented the volume to him, opening it at the title-page: *Cyder. A Poem in Two Books*.

'Ah, the *other* Mr Philips! I have seen it advertised. A simple poem about apple-growing, is it not?'

'If you think that, Mr Emmet, then you are not the sharp man I take you for. The writer celebrates fruitful *Union* – the benign art of *engrafting* – marrying a new scion to the old stock. And the result of that union is delicious – the fruit of a *Stuart peace!*'

Tom articulated his words with a precision that was slightly taunting. Emmet recoiled a little – this was no political innocent. Perhaps the young man had discovered as much about his questioner as his questioner had learned about him. He tried one last push.

'You and I know that John Philips is seen by many as the Tory antidote to Mr Addison.'

'And yet, the great Tonson – Mr *Kit-Cat* himself – publishes it! The world of letters is a republic, Mr Emmet. The greatest writing goes beyond party.'

'We see eye to eye on that. I happen to know that Mr Addison approves the poem – even though its author is an Oxford Tory and Mr Harley sponsors the book.'

'We are certainly living in confusing times, Mr Emmet.'

It was clear their conversation had run its course, and both parties knew that driving things further might entangle them in something more disputatious. Each was unwilling to carry it beyond this point, and they finished their coffee together.

But as he savoured the bitter smack of the final drop, Tom recalled the buoyant spirit in which their talk had begun and the joyful news about his poem. Its publication could make his reputation; and although he felt this Emmet was something of a sly character, he knew he ought to be grateful and end their meeting on a warmer note. The result was an exchange of pleasantries and an agreement that the conversation had been profitable on both sides.

Emmet left the Good Fellowship satisfied that his mission had been a success. Outside the door he turned to the right, and muffling up against the biting wind that now whistled through the alley he walked in the direction of Bow Street, from where he hoped to find a hackney to carry him swiftly to Westminster. There would be no more walking the streets for him tonight, at least not until he had conveyed his report at the Cockpit. Mr Hopkins would surely be interested to learn more about the Good Fellowship and those who frequented it, and to hear news of Bagnall, Widow Trotter, the Tory Mutton-Chops, and of course Thomas Bristowe. This was a young man with decided views and a satirist's eye. For the most part he had kept a tight rein on his tongue; but Emmet had heard enough of it, and seen enough of that earnest and intense face, to sense how Tom's eloquence might run him into danger. Juvenal had left his mark.

Chapter Five

IN THE COFFEE house, Tom didn't have long to wait before Widow Trotter returned from her marketing. Instinctively she paused in the doorway and her eyes took a rapid survey of the room. Like a skilled general she noted the disposition of her forces: how her customers were grouped, who was busy, who lounging, and whether any new faces were evident. She was pleased to see that with young Jenny in occupation the bar resembled a shrine with a little knot of votaries gathered before it. As always, Peter was performing delicate feats with the coffee pot; and, as so often, Jeremy was dawdling about the place in suspended activity, waiting to clear, waiting to carry a message or run errands, waiting to stoke the fire. He did lots of useful things, but still spent too much of his time between jobs, hovering over the tables.

'Jem!' She called him over. 'More logs! And we shall need two chairs from the upper chamber. The Captain is sitting by the door, so place one for him by the fire. I don't want him to catch cold. And after that there are things to collect from the market.'

The slouching Jeremy perked up and began to co-ordinate his limbs for action. Beneath the mop of hay-coloured hair his hang-dog look became almost purposeful.

'Directly, Mrs Trotter!'

One thing her eyes immediately picked out was Tom, who had turned round from his book and was looking over with a remarkably bright countenance. A few moments later she was half-seated on the bench beside him hearing the wonderful news of John Emmet's visit: how *Crime and Punishment* had been accepted, and how the publisher's associate saw a future for him as a denizen of Will's Coffee House, mingling with writers of the highest reputation and fashion.

'Of course, as a regular at Will's I shall have to look the part. I believe I must have myself measured for a fine new coat – one with twice as many buttons – and I shall order some shoes with red heels. And I must learn to nod under a wig in a sagacious manner, like this...'

He placed a finger alongside his chin and moved his head gravely up and down as if attuning his mind to the wisdom of the universe.

'I am convinced already, Mr Bristowe. Fame will come naturally to you.'

'And it would be good to polish up some useful phrases – *this is vastly clever*, or *here is no ordinary genius*, or *Sir, these are tolerably neat verses*. At Will's, you know, every poet has to be a critic too.'

'And you will be a most judicious one.'

'But have no fear, I shall not forget my former friends, Mrs Trotter.'

'There will always be a slice of toasted cheese waiting for you here, Mr Bristowe – to remind you of your weeks of struggle.'

They laughed simultaneously, and Widow Trotter was reassured she would not be losing her talented young lodger quite yet.

'That publisher must have a high opinion of you. It's been managed with remarkable haste. He clearly thinks your poem will take the Town by storm and wants to claim you before any rivals can step in. When do you see him to conclude matters?'

Tom paused slightly.

'I didn't arrange a meeting with Mr Morphew – perhaps I should have settled this.'

'Then you ought to call at his shop tomorrow. Strike while the iron is hot.'

'But somehow, Mrs T, my mind misgives me. Things are moving on so rapidly – it's as if Fancy is leading me into a magic garden. I need to pinch my legs.'

'Yes, but tomorrow perhaps. Enjoy a few hours of wild delight first – they offer themselves so rarely…'

Tom appreciated her combination of practicality and indulgence. There was genuine concern in her face too.

'… However it is, you need to find out where you stand, and think sensibly. Your Mr Morphew is a man of business, remember, not a patron.'

'You're very wise, Mrs T. But such a task, as you say, is for tomorrow.'

'Your friend Mr Lundy will be delighted.'

Tom suddenly realised that in his slightly giddy state he had let Will slip from his mind. It was thanks to him and his contacts among the printers that all this had come about.

'As it happens, Mrs T, I'm dining with Will tomorrow. I shall tell him the good news over the roast beef in Middle Temple Hall.'

'Good – that will be the perfect chance to celebrate in style!'

Widow Trotter rose to her feet. 'I must about things. But all this talk has set me thinking again.'

Her voice was suddenly quieter.

'It looks like your future is taking a new turn. Well, over recent days I've come to the conclusion that the Good Fellowship should take a new turn also. I'd value your opinion.'

Tom's interest was caught, and he replied with eagerness, though in slightly hushed tones.

'You have plans for this place, Mrs T?'

'They are not to be spoken of yet; but the widow has ambitions too!'

'I'm eager to hear more.'

'Then sup with me at nine – if you're free to. I would not interfere with any of your arrangements.'

'I have only one, and that undertaking will be fulfilled by then. I intend to indulge myself this evening – with a *five-shilling* luxury...'

Widow Trotter's eyebrows rose at least half an inch. The delights of Covent Garden came at all rates.

'... I've decided to lay out a full crown, and surrender myself to Mr Small. A hot steam bath, a heavy sweat, and a cold plunge are just what I need.'

'When I said *wild delight*, Mr Bristowe, I wasn't thinking of the Hummums. But I'm sure the place will supply something of that kind. That's a properly extravagant thought.'

'Your suggestion put it in my head.'

'I hope to see you at *nine*, then, thoroughly doused and purged!'

Widow Trotter left Tom to his reading and began taking her rounds about the coffee-room. In his chair by the fire, Captain Roebuck was now comfortably settled into one of his stories about the Flanders campaign of '92 and had found an attentive listener. He was pointing to the bullet which was deeply embedded in the heavy leather wallet that hung from his waist. All these years later the old wallet continued to be the talismanic protector of his manhood and a rebuke to anyone who dared speak ill of the Duke. As a mark of his allegiance, the lump of metal now formed the centrepiece between two carved mottos, 'BX 1704' and 'RX 1706'. The Captain hoped for an addition to these emblems, although a further Marlborough victory would undoubtedly mar the symmetry.

Symmetry of a combative kind was in evidence at the table nearby, where volleys of accusation were cutting through the air to right and left. The respective characters of a Low-Church Man and a High-Church Man were being fiercely debated. The two disputants were head-to-head, and the contemptuous phrases took on a life of their own. *Trimming hypocrite* stood its ground against *Papist fanatic*; then *worldly compromise* fought it out with *tyrannical authority*; a few moments later *cant* warded off *empty ritual*; and *crafty, sly, and insidious knave* exchanged rapid blows with *seditious, factious and violent spirit*, until finally the only figures left on their feet were *villainous double-dealing* and *subverting the constitution*, who battled themselves to a standstill and eventually came to terms over a shared venison pasty.

Further along the table, a subtle thread of gossip was being spun by three elegant figures who had spent the day skirting the drawing-rooms of St James's. A chance conversation in the park, followed by an encounter at White's, had served only to confirm that *matters at Court* were reaching a crisis. They had heard it whispered on good authority that the newly-married Mrs Masham was now fully installed as Her Majesty's *confidente intime*. Indeed, so *intime* was their friendship that the barrier between the closet and the bedroom had been… *violé*. The Duchess of Marlborough's indignation at her supplanting was venting itself in terrible rages audible through the tapestried walls of the palace; that Mr Harley now saw his opportunity, with his cousin Abigail having the ear – more than the ear! – of the Queen, to pursue his grand plan of ousting the Whigs. It was hardly to be spoken of…… As the men's operatic scenario began to take shape, pungent grains of snuff scented with bergamot heightened the delicious shock of the idea; and their expressive manipulation of the finely-chased silver snuff-box, which moved from hand to hand like a precious secret, seemed only to emphasise the delicacy of the matter, the necessity to handle the thing most carefully.

Tom returned from the Turkish *hamam* in the Little Piazza impoverished but glowing with health and spirits; and at nine o'clock prompt he walked through the kitchen to the back parlour of the Good Fellowship with a brisk step and no little appetite. Widow Trotter liked to keep the parlour as a refuge where she could read in private or deal with the accounts. During the course of the day, the steaming kitchen was a communal area with everyone taking their hurried meals whenever they could, but at this time of the evening she liked to have her own supper in the calmer surroundings of the wainscoted parlour. Newly painted in a pleasing pale green and with mirrored sconces on the walls, it was the nearest the Good Fellowship came to elegance. On the oak sideboard, alongside various ledgers and neat piles of bills and invoices, were a pair of silver-rimmed glass decanters, several crystal wine-glasses, and on this occasion a substantial round cheese, a small loaf, and a plate of cold meats.

Widow Trotter scooped up one of the decanters and two glasses, and invited Tom to sit down at the half-opened table.

'This new madeira is excellent. On a cold January night there's nothing better for celebrating good news. So let's drink a toast to your future fame and fortune!'

The two glasses were charged and lifted.

'I don't want to provoke the gods, Mrs T. So please can I offer instead: *To poetic success, and whatever meagre reward it may bring me!*'

'A cautious sentiment, but just as heartfelt I'm sure!'

The glasses clinked, and the hesitant toast to potential fame was drunk. The sweet wine was appropriately heart-warming.

'You speak of *the gods*,' Widow Trotter continued, 'but perhaps it's your father who needs to be placated? Will this win him round, do you think? Will he begin thinking of you as a poet rather than a clergyman?'

'He has always insisted it's possible to be both. But, to tell you the truth Mrs T, I dread the thought of a country parson's life. I'm terrified of those endless days in deepest Wiltshire. I picture myself sitting in my ancient rectory writing admonitory sermons, and turning my hand to hymns and devotional verses. The only distractions will be a snoring housekeeper and the birds scuffling in the eaves.'

'No, I don't think a life of rural retirement would suit you at all.'

'The highest I could aspire to would be poetic meditations on the rural scene. You know the kind of thing: – "Sweet *Monkton!* loveliest village of the dale, / Where sheep and cattle wander o'er the vale" – all that muted pastoral stuff.'

'Certainly that doesn't sound like your voice. But I don't suppose a parish priest could write satire?'

'Not in a country parish. But a well-connected place-man might attempt it – someone who lived the high-life in London while a village curate performed his duties. How easily he could denounce pride and luxury! But I would hate that even more – a priest only in name! Hypocrites shouldn't write satire.'

'You paint a chilling picture – it's as if you have somewhere particular in mind.'

'I fear I do.... I've not told you about my Wiltshire cousins, have I?'

Widow Trotter was immediately intrigued. She had a nose for a good story, and on this occasion it would also satisfy her curiosity. Since his move into the Good Fellowship ten days earlier Tom had said little about himself. She had heard only briefly about his time at Oxford, and of his father in Winchester, and he had alluded to 'the old Squire' in a way that suggested this might be his grandfather. But not much could be pieced together. This was clearly the moment for her to replenish their glasses.

'It could be said, Mr Bristowe, that you never know a person until you know something of his family.'

'Well, I hardly know where to begin. But to be as brief as possible…'

Widow Trotter pushed the full glass towards him encouragingly.

'It would be helpful to have the *larger* picture, perhaps, if the situation is a difficult one.'

'It does have some complications, Mrs T, and I suppose I owe you a little more.'

'Tell me everything you think I should know. And if you're seeking advice, then I'm always happy to give it!'

Warmed by the second glass of madeira, Tom began telling her about the Bristowes and the Pophams. He knew that family trees, although fascinating to some, were extremely tedious to others, and so he gave only a rapid sketch (he was one of those who found them tedious).

'The living has been promised me by my uncle Jack. It's a country parish, Winterbourne Monkton in Wiltshire, and is in the gift of the Popham family. My Aunt Anne, my father's sister, married John Popham of Monkton Court. It's a lovely old house – if you have a fondness for ruins – the kind of crumbling edifice you're forced to share with a huge family of mice and an overworked tom cat. The gallery of disreputable Pophams glowers down at you while you eat.'

'The place sounds romantic,' said Widow Trotter, whose taste in reading as a child had extended to stories of fair damsels and barons bold.

'Yes, it's like something out of Spenser's *Faerie Queene*. And yet the Pophams are a busy, modern family. Monkton Court may look like the retreat of a crusty Tory squire – more suited to my old grandfather! – but my uncle now finds himself in the polite world, although a countryman's heart still beats inside him. Nevertheless, he has plans to knock the place down and build an elegant pile with a pediment and a balustrade – and urns along the top.'

'That would be a shame. What would happen to the mice?'

'They would all troop to the rectory. There's plenty of room there, and lots of creaking floorboards to hide under.'

'But you say you've been *promised* the living? Has it all been arranged within the family?'

'Yes. They want to do the best for me. You see, my uncle Jack was devoted to my aunt – and I was too. I used to stay at Monkton during the summer and became almost one of the family. Cousin Frank is the same age as me, and we used to wrestle each other, climb trees, and rob birds' nests. But my aunt died when we were twelve, and my uncle was deeply affected.'

'Does your uncle have any other children?'

'Yes, two of them. There's cousin Lavinia, who's now seventeen, and young Wilmot, who is behaving very badly at Winchester College – where my father attempts to keep watch over him.'

'It sounds like your two families are really one.'

'Yes, but matters became complicated when my uncle re-married.'

'Ah! Is this a case of the *wicked stepmother?*'

Widow Trotter imagined herself turning the page of an old storybook to find a woodcut illustration of a fearsome crone.

'No, no – there's no wickedness involved. Considerable pride and frivolity, yes – but no malice. I'm afraid the match has not proved easy for either party. Aunt Sophia, you see, is twenty years his junior and is very taken with London society. She lives almost permanently at their house in Pall Mall and regards Monkton as a horrid wilderness. She would *like* to make a figure in the country, but for that she dreams of having a miniature Chatsworth transplanted to Wiltshire. My uncle very much wants to please her, but the old house has precious memories for him.'

'A Chatsworth? My goodness, Mr Bristowe! I hadn't realised you had such relations. Your uncle must be a very rich man!'

'The new Monkton would be *miniature*, I assure you – though Aunt Sophia's aspirations know no limits. But if I tell you that her name used to be Sophia Doggett, you'll realise that the Popham family money has only recently materialised.'

'Doggett's *Bank?*' Widow Trotter seized her half-full glass of madeira, trembling slightly, and supped some more.

'My aunt naturally thinks the money is truly hers, and that she should have a say in how it's spent. My aunt is very good at spending money.'

'If her dowry was so large, she'll expect more than pin money.'

'Yes, I sympathise. But poor Uncle Jack has never been fond of the metropolitan life. To placate her he's managed to procure himself a position at Court; but I know he's uneasy about it. He refuses to let it be a sinecure.'

At the word *Court,* Widow Trotter suddenly realised she was still holding her glass firmly against her chin.

'Your uncle is a Courtier??'

She couldn't conceal her surprise, and her voice made the whole idea sound incongruous – after all, Tom himself was the most uncourtly of characters. In response, he hesitated and looked a little embarrassed.

'I can see you have a picture in your mind, Mrs T – all satin, powder, sword-knots, bowing and scraping.'

'Don't disappoint me, Mr Bristowe, please! You're not going to tell me he sits behind a desk in an office?'

'No, no. Have no fear – he's no dull clerk. Uncle Jack does indeed have a desk – a large one – but he also has an array of embroidered suits in various colours, enough for a dozen birth-night balls!'

She brightened at the glittering image that was beginning to form.

'Dressed like a lord! You evidently have what they call "connections"!'

Tom blushed slightly, but couldn't help smiling at his landlady's ability to be impressed and amused at the same time.

'Oh Mrs T. You've wrung it out of me… He *is* a lord…'

Widow Trotter breathed out long and audibly.

'… Viscount Melksham. He's the Queen's Deputy Treasurer.'

'Well well well! Mr Bristowe, you've certainly been keeping that secret. I hope you don't feel too ashamed of so grand an uncle. You mustn't blame him – after all, somebody has to treasure Her Majesty. And he's only a deputy!'

Tom was relieved at the satirical tone. It made him feel more at home.

'Yes, that's one comfort. It helps to lessen the shame. Though I'm afraid the person he deputises for is *extremely* grand – the Duchess of Marlborough, no less.'

'Worse and worse, Mr Bristowe! You'll be telling me next that he runs the Queen's finances.'

'You are unerring, Mrs T. You clearly know how to worm out a scandal. Yes, I confess it. The *Privy Purse* is the Queen's private account. The Duchess is the Keeper.'

'Then that must make him *Deputy Keeper of the Privy Purse* – an admirably quaint title! – From a *palace* to a *p*…'

'Please! Mrs T! Poor Uncle Jack has to endure a lot of jocularity. He doesn't wish to be in the public eye, and all these matters of place, titles and distinctions he finds rather wearing.'

Widow Trotter was momentarily checked. Before the banter could deteriorate further Tom pulled himself up short and determined to return to the business in hand.

'... You've deflected me! I'm afraid I'm wandering from the matter of the *living*...'

She was only too happy to turn her curiosity in that direction. This really had been a productive conversation.

Tom gathered himself.

'... Over recent years my uncle has encouraged me to think of the living as mine, and my father has been happy with the arrangement. The present Rector is an old gentleman who longs for the day when he can retire to a cottage on the estate and live out his days with only a small garden to tend. So you see, everything is waiting for me to step in as soon as I take orders. My father and my uncle have been more than generous in letting me have time to consider – a full year, as you know.'

'I can see you're being placed under pressure – by yourself as much as by your family.'

'Yes, I do feel obligated. Family ties are important to me. And I know Uncle Jack would be greatly reassured to have me settled in the living: it would be a reminder of happier years. I'm really very fortunate to be offered such a comfortable life – but it's not the life I want.'

'And so you've made a bargain about establishing yourself as a poet.'

'Yes, and if I fail in that, then I'll have no other course but to take orders and become a reverend gentleman.'

Tom was now looking very glum. Widow Trotter offered him a cheering smile and a little more of the madeira.

'That makes today's good news even better! It looks like you're beginning to succeed. What a fascinating story. A happy ending does seem to be approaching.'

'I hardly dare think it is. But today has been very encouraging, and it makes me determined to work even harder.'

Widow Trotter stood up and gave Tom a plate.

'I think you need something more substantial to sustain you – especially if you're to hear about my plans for the Good Fellowship.'

'My dear Mrs T! I'm sorry. You've been so patient. I've been sitting here chattering about family affairs, while you have important news to impart!'

'Thoughts rather than news at this stage. But like you, I'm determined on the direction I want to go.'

At the sideboard Tom suddenly remembered how hungry he was and helped himself liberally. They both settled once more at the table, and Widow Trotter decided that a little more madeira might be welcome. In response, Tom raised his glass again.

'I think we need another toast – to your own plans. Can I propose we drink to the future glories of the Good Fellowship?'

'Ah!...'

Widow Trotter paused and looked down, with no little dramatic effect.

'... I think we might postpone that until I've told you what my ideas are. You may think them misguided. In fact you may want to toast their overthrow! But let's eat while I ask your advice.'

Over the cold meats and cheese, Widow Trotter explained that she felt the Good Fellowship, for all its solid virtues and homely comforts, had become a little set in its ways. The place seemed to her to lack something of the *modern* style.

'I look around the coffee-room and see much that pleases me: a set of characters with a variety of opinions and concerns; a deal of good humour and strong debate, with a nice portion of gossip and scandal mixed in. All this is welcome. But I feel something is missing. The place needs a seasoning that will add zest to our entertainment.'

'But things are perhaps starting to change? Jenny is attracting some young admirers.'

'Ah yes, the *oglers* – I'm pleased to see that. And I hope they'll draw in a few of their friends also. And you, Mr Bristowe, are more than welcome to bring your friends here. I was very glad to meet Mr Lundy this morning, who seems to be a young man of genuine wit and eloquence.'

'Yes, he has qualities well suited to the *bar*.'

'I want to encourage the younger set. I'm not thinking of fops and fribbles – though a light sprinkling of them would be amusing – but men of *ideas*. People of thought and taste, with a literary turn, who might come here for stimulating conversation. I want to encourage people to converse freely – be more *inquiring*. Do you follow my drift?'

'Wholeheartedly, Mrs T.'

Tom was struck by his landlady's eloquence. It was as if she were living her vision.

'I don't like to see people set in their ways and hugging their prejudices. But *innovation* has now become a bad word, and there's a lot of fear and suspicion abroad. We ought to be thinking of ourselves as a new nation, should we not? Looking to the future? Only this afternoon two smart young Scotsmen paid us a visit, and very quiet and polite they were too – until they tangled with Jack Tapsell and his Whiggish friends. They were taken to be Jacobite invaders and had some lively taunts to endure. I'm afraid they sailed unthinkingly into the rocky shoals!'

'I hope a shipwreck and loss of life were averted?'

'Narrowly, yes. However, we shall need a new teapot.'

'From what you say, I take it that Mr Bagnall doesn't entirely meet your requirements?'

'I'd like him to be a little more sociable. He tends to settle himself in a corner and just scribble away. He's a man of few words – except on paper.'

'I agree it would be good to attract other writers here, men of knowledge and philosophy.'

'And perhaps men of some fashion too. The world is becoming *polite*, Mr Bristowe, and I want to attract people who will help to polish each other – rub away their rough edges. There's so much dissention and party violence in the air.'

'So you're bent on *Reformation*, Mrs T?'

'Too dangerous an idea! No, I'm looking for a change in character. I can't help thinking that infusing a new style into this place would give it fresh life. The Good Fellowship finds it hard to rise above its name. The place is very… I don't know how to express it… very… *1690s*…'

Tom smiled at her strange turn of phrase, but understood exactly what she meant.

'… In other words, I want to drag the Good Fellowship into the *Eighteenth Century*.'

On that climactic note, as if to emphasise the decisiveness of the sentiment, Widow Trotter chewed off a substantial piece of cheese, which proved larger and more obstinate than she expected. She coughed and reached for the madeira.

Tom admired the rhetorical flourish and the genuine force of what she was saying. It was as if the widow was speaking out for the first time.

'Was this something your husband resisted, perhaps?'

'I did exchange views with Mr Trotter from time to time. But I was happy enough for the place to reflect his character. He was a convivial soul, and he valued his independence. Mr Trotter was always proud of being a Freeholder – unlike most of our neighbours in the Garden we're not the Duke of Bedford's tenants – and this makes matters much easier. There is no lease, and any change is in my own hands.'

'Did he leave any specific provision for you?'

'No, Mr Bristowe… You see, it was all extremely sudden. One moment he was striding confidently through the piazza, and the next… crushed under a barrel.'

'That's terrible, Mrs T. I'm so sorry.'

'Well, it was a memorable death – and a stylish one. An over-hasty delivery wagon turned too sharply, and shed its load on him. It was a barrel of prunes…'

Tom looked simultaneously shocked and sympathetic.

'… They were top quality *Bordeaux* prunes. The very best – shipped over from France…'

Tom hardly knew what to say.

'… In fact, in commemoration we now offer our own *Aromatick* as one of the specialities of the house. It consists of wine, prunes, and sugar, flavoured with cinnamon, and is quite popular. An excellent, soothing liquor. The barrel is still far from empty.'

Tom hurriedly filled his mouth with bread. The conversation paused for a moment while both of them took stock. It was clear that each was determined to get hold of life and find an independent path.

'I think your ambitions are admirable, Mrs T. Have you given thought to how you can achieve them?'

'I've begun to make plans, and this is where I'd be glad to have your ideas – and your support. The coffee-room needs to be smartened up and new-painted, with some overdue refurbishments: a convenient letter rack, a set of elegant pegs for gentlemen's hats, one or two better paintings I think, and a large mirror by the door… that sort of thing. And in place of the earthenware coffee-dishes I intend to buy a set of Chinese porcelain. A shipment is soon expected at the Exchange, and I've put in an order. These things should enhance the appearance of the coffee-room, and encourage more polite behaviour.'

'They will certainly refresh the place. The Good Fellowship will be given a new lease of life!'

'But alas, Mr Bristowe, the *Good Fellowship* will be no more...'

Tom was a little startled and confused.

'... What think you of... the *Bay-Tree?*'

Tom paused while he played the name over in his mind.

'It's very different, Mrs T! But it makes a good sound. And I like the picture it brings to mind. You could place a small tree by the door, and weave a laurel garland from it for your very own poet *laureate?*'

'I'm not sure I should encourage Mr Bagnall's pretensions! But I do want to hint at aspiration and achievement. My plan is to preserve the old name by making the upstairs chamber the *Good Fellowship Room*. That will help the Mutton-Chops feel at home, don't you think?'

'You have the wisdom of Solomon, Mrs T! *The Bay-Tree* will be one of the most stylish coffee houses in Covent Garden.'

'Ah! well, not *exactly*...'

Tom was once again nonplussed. It was clear that Widow Trotter already had a full campaign strategy. He could only stay quiet and listen, slightly awestruck by the confidence with which she was setting out her plans.

'The place is to become the *Bay-Tree Chocolate House*.'

Widow Trotter smiled broadly, sat back in her chair, and silently raised her glass, in which a small amount of liquor remained. Tom lifted his own glass to meet hers, and nodded.

'The name has an excellent ring to it. You will make the place *bran-new* as they say!'

'Do you approve?'

'You have my full support, Mrs T. I'm sure you'll go about this very carefully. It would be a shame to lose any of the customers you already have.'

'Yes, I'll have to be circumspect. But the *chocolate house* will I hope have a new spirit infused into it. I want it to remain a place of many voices, and the coffee-room will still be the *coffee-room*. But the house's new name will signal that men of polite tastes will be welcome. I intend to add to the speciality drinks, and offer certain delicacies from day to day. Mrs Dawes is more than willing to play her part. Pies and pasties will still be popular, no doubt, but other tastes will be catered for.'

The conversation paused, and for a moment the pair contemplated their lives in silence. Each saw the challenge that was approaching, and neither was going to drift calmly along the current. Retirement and ease were not for them.

The meditative interlude was an extremely brief one. There was a heavy knock at the door before Jeremy pushed it open and occupied the threshold.

'What is it, Jem?'

'It's Mr Cobb wishes to talk with you, Mrs Trotter. He says it's something you need to hear. He's lowering like a thundercloud.'

'Then I'd better see him at once. I'm sorry Mr Bristowe, perhaps you'll slip away? – it sounds a little ominous.'

'Please, Mrs Trotter. Mr Cobb says that if the young gentleman Mr Bristol is in the place then you and he should both hear what he has to say.'

Widow Trotter and Tom looked at each other with apprehension.

'This sounds like a serious summons. You had better show him in here, Jem. And bring us three coffees.'

Chapter Six

THE GRIM FROWN that Elias Cobb brought with him into the parlour changed the atmosphere in an instant. The decanters and wine-glasses still sparkled with the firelight, and the candles flickered in the mirrors, but as soon as he appeared Widow Trotter saw that something was not right. There was to be no good cheer. Aware of the niceties, she gestured him to take a bite of supper. He was about to wave it away, but the cheese did look very good, and so politeness and the need to collect his thoughts got the better of him. He took the proffered chair and sighed as he sank into it.

'Ah Widow, what a dangerous and deceitful world we inhabit!'

'You surely see more of it than many of us, Mr Cobb.'

'Indeed I do, indeed I do. Not a day passes but I encounter it. And today has been no exception.'

Widow Trotter filled his glass from the decanter of claret, and there was an awkward pause while a supper-plate was set before him and supplied with food. The constable was not his usual brisk and voluble self, and she detected some uneasiness as he glanced over in Tom's direction. The pause allowed her to raise a question that had been picking at her during the day.

'I've been puzzling over your little appointment here this morning. You and your friends slipped away so quietly. Are you able to speak of it, or was your mission a secret one?'

'It was a routine task, albeit one that required discretion. But as events unfolded…' He glanced at Tom again, who was by now looking distinctly apprehensive. '… I found myself involved – as a witness.'

'Is that what brings you here, Elias? Jeremy implied you had something urgent to say, and that my lodger, Mr Bristowe, may be somehow concerned in it.'

'Indeed so. But I'm in some embarrassment. I came here with the intention of keeping you informed – but it's all damned difficult. I should not be here at all. It's a plaguy ticklish business altogether.'

'This hesitancy is most unlike you, Elias. You and I are old friends, and any confidences will of course be kept. If it concerns Mr Bristowe, I'm sure we can keep things between ourselves.'

Tom felt he had to speak.

'I don't know why you need me here, constable, but if it concerns me, then I'd be grateful if you'd speak squarely. You can do no less.'

Elias Cobb looked squarely, and spoke squarely.

'You're in trouble, young Sir, no doubt about that.'

Tom was alarmed at the directness.

'What trouble? Is it something I've done? I don't recollect anything.'

'It's for what you *may* have done – and for what you *may yet* do.'

'This is riddling…'

Tom looked across at Widow Trotter for some explanation. It was clear that she was intrigued.

'I've known Mr Cobb for many years, Mr Bristowe, and have rarely seen him embarrassed like this. The constable, you should know, is a man with many interests and responsibilities, official and unofficial. I suspect this affair has some connection to his less formal activities... I think you should start from the beginning, Elias.'

It was obvious to the constable that not only had he approached the *brink*, but had stepped over it, fallen into the water, and now had no choice but to strike out boldly for the opposite bank.

'You had an appointment with a printer here this morning, did you not? And gave him some papers?'

Tom swallowed involuntarily.

'Mr Morphew? Yes I did – but you make it sound suspicious. There was nothing secretive. I had arranged to show him a poem of mine in the hope he might agree to print it. In fact, I've since heard that he's willing to do so.'

'You've been in communication with him since this morning?'

'Yes – indirectly. His pressman called with a message for me.'

It was now the constable's turn to look uneasy.

'You have had a visit from John Emmet?'

'Yes, earlier this evening. He told me the good news. And he was interested in my future plans. It's all very encouraging. In fact I'll be calling on Mr Morphew tomorrow morning to discuss arrangements.'

'In that case you'll have a wasted journey...'

Elias did not want to sound over dramatic, but he hesitated slightly. And as he did so, the parlour door opened and a tray of coffees appeared. The pause added considerably to the revelation of the moment.

'... You see, the printer is in custody, and has been so since my men arrested him this morning.'

In Tom's brain there was a sudden crash that was almost audible. So many questions pressed in at once.

'*Arrested?* What has he done? Where is he now? Why did John Emmet say nothing of this? How could he have had time to read my poem?'

'He hasn't. We had a hackney waiting for Mr Morphew when he left the Good Fellowship. He has been under guard ever since.'

Tom put his head in his hands and sank lower in his chair. For Widow Trotter things were beginning to slip into place.

'Mr Bristowe, I think this evening's visitor must have had other reasons for calling on you. I think our Mr Emmet was sent from the Cockpit... Thank you Jem, just leave the coffees on the tray.'

The sheepish Jeremy half-bowed, and hesitated awkwardly by the door.

'The coffee-room is very busy, Mrs Trotter. Peter and Jenny are finding things hard...'

'Then give Peter a hand, Jem. But be careful. Remember what I told you – *elegance at all times*.'

'*Elegance*, yes. I'll do that, Mrs T. Have no fear.'

He managed to close the door behind him, and the three of them were left pondering the situation. Thanks to the interruption they all had a moment to think, and each began to sketch out an idea of the fuller picture. It was Widow Trotter who spoke first.

'At whose behest did you arrest Mr Morphew? Is someone pressing him for a debt?'

'No, the thing is much more serious: he is suspected of sedition. The Ministry have been taking an interest in him, and I was asked to arrange for his collection this morning. It was not an arrest *de jure*, you understand – more an invitation he was not expected to decline. It was quite a routine matter. I didn't think it was important.... But then they found the paper.'

'What paper was that?' Tom was curious.

'It was a treasonous poem attacking the State. They found it on his person.'

'*My poem?* I can't believe this. O mighty Juvenal! Are men yet afraid of you? They are such fools! What a perfect satire this is on the Ministry!'

'No, it was another poem – a short thing scribbled on a single sheet. They found it with your other verses, Mr Bristowe.'

Suddenly things began to make sense. He didn't know whether to be relieved or slightly disappointed.

'No, that wasn't *my* poem, Mr Cobb, it was a paper I found in the coffee-room here. It must have become jumbled with mine, and poor Mr Morphew pocketed them both. The old Juvenal and a modern Juvenal – one interleaved with the other!'

Tom's fragile poetic ambitions may have been collapsing all around him, but he appreciated the witty idea of the two texts rubbing along together: an ancient sedition and a new. There was hope for satire yet.

'Mr Bristowe, in telling you this I may be compromising myself. I was present at part of Mr Morphew's interrogation at the Cockpit and am undoubtedly breaking a confidence...'

He placed one hand flat on the table and began moving it slowly from side to side.

'... As Mrs Trotter has said, my role as an officer of the Law can be said to be an informal one. Here in Covent Garden I have charge of the Watch, but that is a little business of my own: the men are in my employ and I organise them as a body. But I also have some wider interests. I find it valuable to communicate with the Ministry. They consider me a useful pair of eyes and ears, and it's helpful for me to know something of what is going on – to have notice of any trouble that may be in the air. The arrangement is not a regulated one – I'm not in their pay – but it works well enough.'

'Mr Cobb is a very *necessary* man, Mr Bristowe.'

The constable turned to Tom.

'I have come here to alert you – both of you. I've known Mrs Trotter for many years – Henry Trotter and I were apprentices together – so I can place trust in anyone she trusts. And you in turn, Mr Bristowe, will have to trust me... I want to know the drift of your conversation with John Emmet, and any further information you may have... But first you both need to know what has been happening.'

Elias raised the dish of coffee to his lips and savoured the bitter unsugared concoction. Then he spoke quietly, as if he were in danger of being overheard.

'During this morning's questioning it was evident that Mr Morphew's pressman has been spying on him. It appears he may be implicating the printer in some dark doings. The Ministry are worried, and something important is stirring. People at the highest level are involved.'

After that mysterious introduction, the constable gave a brief account of Bufo's libels and how the voice of this anonymous accuser was suddenly making itself heard.

'I detect some panic. Perhaps the Ministry knows something that makes Bufo's accusations especially dangerous. They seem afraid that a co-ordinated attack is about to begin – one that goes beyond exposing corruption and threatens the Constitution itself. The matter is of great urgency for them. So, you see, your little piece of verse is important. They now have a paper in Bufo's hand and they know it originated in the Good Fellowship.'

'So they suspect that Mr Morphew is Bufo's printer?'

'Yes, Mr Bristowe, indeed they do... And they now suspect that you yourself may be Bufo.'

Tom's eyes widened.

'Of course – they must think I wrote those verses. But I assure you I found the paper concealed in a pamphlet here in the coffee-room. The bit I read was denouncing the Whig Lords and naming names – it was angry abuse rather than an expression of grievances – though I saw only the opening lines.'

'You didn't think to read further? That's hard to believe.'

'I was interrupted. Mr Morphew arrived at that very moment and I crammed the thing in my pocket.'

Elias looked at Widow Trotter, who allowed herself a guarded smile:

'I think you can be assured Mr Bristowe is not using the Good Fellowship as his headquarters for a pamphlet attack on the State.'

'I didn't suspect that at all, Mrs T. But you both need to know how things stand. Every hour might bring a new revelation.'

Tom was hesitant. There was another question he needed to ask.

'What about my own poem, Mr Cobb? Was that taken from Mr Morphew?'

'Taken, and read – but you will be relieved to know that nothing excessively libellous was found in it. There was no naming of names. However, Mr Addison did detect a similarity of style with Bufo's verses.'

'Mr *Addison?* He has read *my poem?*'

This certainly counted as a revelation, but it was a doubtful one. A piece of news that should have lifted Tom's confidence to the skies was weighed down by the thought that his verses were being scrutinised for seditious libel. His poem had met the great Joseph Addison's eyes, but they were evidently narrowed by suspicion while he read it. The image was an unsettling one.

'It was Lord Sunderland's Under-Secretaries, Mr Addison and Mr Hopkins, who conducted the interview.'

'Then it's clearly important,' said Widow Trotter. 'Did they send this Mr Emmet to report on us?'

'It would seem so. He must have been dispatched urgently.'

Tom's face took on a rueful expression.

'Thank you, Mr Cobb. I now know what a fool he's made of me. I was stupidly distracted by hopes for my poem – bewitched by his flattery. The man showed great interest in my writing, but an even greater interest in the Good Fellowship. I was most informative. He wanted to hear about who comes here, and of what party, which papers are taken, what poems left. Of course, I now see it was my own interrogation. How naïve I was!'

'He seems to be a deceptive customer altogether. You were not to know this.'

'But alas, I told him so much – and he told me so little.'

Tom was forced to re-live the conversation by giving a brief account of what he and Emmet had discussed. It was reassuring that Mrs Trotter seemed to approve of what he'd said.

'You gave him a fair account, Mr Bristowe – although I'm a little concerned that word of Mr Bagnall's poem will have reached the Ministry.'

'Yes,' said Elias, 'there's great suspicion of Mr Harley and his friends in Lord Sunderland's office, and Mr Bagnall's verse letter may place him under suspicion too.'

'I'm afraid I was altogether too voluble. My tongue ran away with me.'

Widow Trotter looked at her two friends and spread her hands on the table. 'Well, what do we do now? Is there indeed *anything* to be done?'

The constable weighed his words.

'After Emmet's report this evening, they may be about to bring Mr Bristowe in for questioning. But I would not advise taking cover – on the contrary. The best policy is honesty. You have nothing to hide – I would like to say *nothing to fear*, but we cannot tell what machinations are afoot.'

'But we can surely do something?' said Widow Trotter, who was indignant that her little kingdom might be threatened with invasion. 'Can we not do some investigating ourselves?'

The constable smiled at her. Mary Trotter had always shown an active interest in his line of work and was never unhappy to be consulted. The Good Fellowship had sometimes been a helpful listening-post, and generally an innocent one. But this affair was coming too close to home.

'Yes possibly, Molly, quite possibly. Mr Morphew is in considerable trouble and I would not like to see him or his business harmed. Even if he's found to be blameless, they may mark him down as a troublemaker and make things difficult.'

Tom spoke up: 'In our conversation this morning he struck me as a practical and kind man – though I think he could drive a hard bargain. He's far from being a fool.'

'None of that would protect him, Mr Bristowe, especially in these times. But perhaps we should see what we can find out. I intend to make some discreet enquiries about this *Bufo*, and it would be useful to know more about John Emmet, and why he has involved himself in this with such relish.

'I think I might be able to help you there, Mr Cobb. My friend Will Lundy may know something. He visited the publisher's shop in connection with a legal case – that's how Mr Morphew was put in touch with me.'

'Did he meet Emmet there?'

'Yes, in fact he said the pressman had been encouraging. I don't know more than that – Will was being very secretive about it all – the reason for his visit, I mean. I've not pushed him into telling me.'

'More curious still! Then you could try to find out more. I suspect Emmet wants to compromise his employer for some reason, personal or political – it might be helpful to discover which.'

'As it happens, I'm calling on Will tomorrow. We're to dine together.'

'Excellent. Then see what you can find out. But be exceedingly careful.'

'I would trust Will with my life, Mr Cobb.'

'That's well said. But unguarded talk can be dangerous. You must impress upon Mr Lundy the necessity to keep matters between the two of you.'

'You're right, constable, given my thoughtless tattle earlier this evening. I promise I've learned my lesson. But Will knows how to keep a secret – even from me!'

Widow Trotter was warming to the idea of an investigation and did not wish to be left out:

'And I shall consult my friends in the Garden – with the utmost *discretion* of course. There may be something being whispered around the market stalls or down the alleys.'

'Ah yes, your *friends in the Garden*. Where would we be without them, Molly? They have certainly proved useful in the past.'

'But I'm also thinking of Mr Bristowe. He has been dealt a severe blow tonight. His expectations had been raised so high.'

She turned directly to Tom and spoke to him as if the two of them were alone in the room.

'This isn't the end of your hopes, Mr Bristowe. Indeed, it may be just the opportunity you need. Joseph Addison himself has read your poem, and who knows what that might lead to? By all accounts he's the most discerning of critics. And for him to have seen your verses...'

A glowing coal settled itself in the grate, and a spurt of flame hissed into life. Tom's mood lifted a little, and there was the trace of a smile.

'Yes, Mrs T, I must remember that. Perhaps I don't need to visit Will's after all!'

The three of them drank what remained of their coffees in a slightly more cheerful spirit. Altogether it had been an eventful day, with highs and lows, discoveries and complications. Each of them was beginning to sense that these local happenings were reaching out more widely. Perhaps it would not be possible for the Good Fellowship and its people to remain untouched by big national events outside. Perhaps they might even play a part in them? This was a thought that sent them on their separate ways with a feeling of uneasy anticipation, wondering what further discoveries might be in store.

Friday

30 January 1708

Chapter Seven

THE CLOCK WAS striking eleven when Will Lundy hurried into the courtyard in front of Temple Church. He had not intended to be absolutely precise as to time, but had been delayed by taking a walk in the gardens by the Thames. The weather was calm and the sky a brilliant icy blue, and days like this were rare in the smoky city. His normal Friday routine would have seen him joining the crush of students at the Stairs waiting for a Westminster boat, but today was a holiday, and a leisurely stroll through Temple Garden seemed just the thing. He had planned on being a little early, but it now appeared he had kept Tom waiting. A sizeable crowd was assembled outside the church, and people were gradually making their way past the huddle of shops that pressed against the ancient building. The place was struggling to assert its old dignities behind the commercial façade, and its lofty gothic windows rose defiantly above some ramshackle lean-tos. He scanned the busy scene to see if Tom was there, but couldn't catch sight of him.

This was a solemn feast day, which meant that devotion and display were equally in order, and the courtyard was full of spruced-up Templars of every kind – not the heroic crusading knights of five centuries earlier whose crumbling effigies still occupied the church, but the rather more polished Members of the Honourable Societies of the Inner and Middle Temples, whose chapel this now was. A goodly number of them were gathered here on this 30th of January to ask God's forgiveness and to expiate the nation's sins.

Some of the law students were chattering animatedly as they walked towards the western porch, while others moved more hesitantly, unsure whether the occasion was a social gathering or a spiritual exercise. The barristers and gownsmen were soberly garbed and their matronly wives and modest daughters well covered from the cold. This was not a brilliant assembly; but under their cloaks could be glimpsed the occasional flash of primrose yellow, pale blue, or iridescent green, a concealed silken plumage that was awaiting its moment to shine. The magisterial senior judges and benchers of the Temple were beginning to separate themselves from the throng so as to form a procession, and precedence was being diplomatically negotiated, with enough turning and bowing for a court ball.

On this day of all days, it was fitting that order and propriety should be observed. Amongst these figures Will recognised his own father, who even at a distance seemed to have an inquisitorial look on his face. While everyone fussed and shuffled, Judge Lundy maintained the stillness of an alert hawk. He was looking with particular coldness at the figure who was being ushered into pride of place in the company – an imposing, smooth-faced body who sported the largest and most powdered wig of anyone present. The man's starched bands and pudding sleeves marked him out as an ecclesiastical *rara avis*, and the one who was destined to take centre stage in the day's ceremony.

As he left the courtyard Will finally picked out Tom standing alongside one of the buttresses. He was motionless and solitary, his hat over his eyes, looking intently ahead as others moved around him. For a brief instant Will saw a figure of simple dignity, but he decided this must be the effect of his friend's suit of clothes which was dark enough to give *gravitas* to anyone. He was relieved to see there was no sign of the slightly lop-sided wig that usually sat on him like a sleeping cat. At that moment Tom turned and recognised him, and they greeted each other warmly, though there was little time to say much before they had to make their way into the church. Will sensed a degree of uneasiness in his friend's manner, but put it down to the occasion.

'This is a fine gloomy performance, is it not? But we'll set things right at dinner – I've ordered some special wine for us.'

'I've a great deal to tell you – and it's not good news.'

Will stopped in his tracks.

'What's this? But we're looking to toast your success!'

'Alas, Will, the case is altered – *the various turns of chance below!*'

'I don't understand. Has Morphew sent word already?'

'Hush! I can't speak of it here – there are too many ears.'

They were now inside the circular nave of the church where every sound echoed, and as Will drew Tom aside he almost stumbled over one of the sleeping stone bodies that littered the floor.

'But why the secrecy?' he whispered.

'You'll discover soon enough. I've not entirely lost hope, but things have become thoroughly tangled. It will be a relief to talk it over. I need your help and advice.'

'A dark enigma! I shan't be able to attend to the sermon.'

'Well, let it be a Christian discipline for you.'

They paused and looked up at the nave's circular roof, its ring of pointed arches rising above them like mitred heads in conclave. But the procession of black gowns was now making its way in and they realised they had to move quickly. Will guided Tom by the arm as they strode into the more spacious chancel where the congregation was assembled.

'Over there, look!' said Tom, and headed hastily for a bench by the north wall, where, if its occupants would only adjust their backsides a little, two young men could find room. The manoeuvre was accomplished with a combination of polite glances and determined shoves. The Temple dignitaries negotiated themselves into their places near the altar, and the main business got underway. Silence settled, and the weight of the occasion made itself felt. The ceremony of contrition and repentance began to unfold: *Deliver us from blood-guiltiness, O God…*

The Feast of the Blessed King Charles the Martyr was the day when the Nation atoned for its guilt – or rather when devout Anglicans asked God to forgive the Presbyterians. Fifty-nine years earlier, on a cold late January day, the King's head had rolled across the scaffold, the severed trunk pumping blood, and at one clean stroke the rule of the Stuarts had ended. But now, after the monarchy's glorious restoration, the Queen's grandfather was venerated as a Martyr of the Church, a Christ-like sacrifice to murderous rebels and traitors. On this red-letter day the Nation confessed its crying sins, and Church and State reminded the people that any challenge to their authority was a violation of the Natural Order. On this day, all were commanded to obey their governors: *Submit yourself to every ordinance of man for the Lord's sake.*

As the words of the epistle sounded forth through the chancel, Will began to register a slightly fusty smell rising over the place as a hundred damp old gowns rubbed together. In a seat nearby he could hear satin rustling, and as he looked at the faces around him he detected in their tiny movements a wide range of responses. He saw a nostril twitch, a brow become furrowed, a jaw being firmly set, a sigh suppressed, a slight tear dissolve an eye, knuckles clenched round a cane. There was tension and emotion mounting.

The centrepiece of the occasion arrived with the sermon, and the Reverend Dr Kettlewell, one of Her Majesty's chaplains, mounted the finely-carved pulpit with considerable *éclat*. His reputation preceded him – as a man of devout eloquence, or an exceedingly smooth performer. Opinions were divided, and on this day neither party would be disappointed.

'A fine old bird, isn't he!' whispered Will as the Doctor settled himself into his prescribed theme. By way of a twenty-minute preamble he offered his captive audience a more than adequate extract from the old *Homily against Disobedience and Wilful Rebellion*, where it was made clear that obedience to authority extended itself through all society... *Besides the obedience due unto Her Majesty, God ordained that in families and households the wife should be obedient unto her husband, the children unto their parents, the servants unto their masters...*

This was a tricky topic, not least for Dr Kettlewell. Nearly twenty years earlier he had refused the oath of allegiance to King William, and had in consequence cast himself into the wilderness as a *non-juror*. But on Anne's succession he found himself able, with an easy conscience, to declare full loyalty to the House of Stuart. Now the Doctor's star was rising. And at this moment in Temple Church his voice was rising too. He warmed to the homily's theme: the sacred duty of respect. The good Doctor was making it clear that to offer *a disparaging opinion* of men in authority was to undermine the very fabric of society.

By vilifying such men... he went on... *and by seeking to disparage their office, a man defies the duty which God has given us of respecting our public governors. Smart jests may draw an easy smile, but they are an encouragement to discontent and sedition.*

'So much for satire!' Tom muttered to himself.

There followed more in the same vein. But gradually, as the minutes crept by, there emerged out of the dark matter of the day a plea for human kindness and generosity. It was a remarkable turn, and after a further thirty-five minutes Dr Kettlewell's listeners found they had moved from a world of pain and guilt towards one of peace and love. One kind of bond had been replaced by another. The preacher ended with a rousing panegyric on the Majesty of the Law, upon whose pillars, he said, the State itself rested. The Law bound the monarch to her people; it was a divine sanction that held the nation together in equity and righteousness; it was the guarantor of liberties as well as an assurance of order and peace; it brought the authority of God into the world of men…

After the final prayer beseeching that the world might be *peaceably ordered*, the dutiful congregation rose and began to disperse amid much creaking and coughing. People were in varying degrees, and according to their individual prejudices, chastened, reassured, enthused, or disgusted. Some were confident that the Law was taking its rightful place in this vision of national regeneration; others – not all of them members of the student body – directed their steps towards a nearby alehouse.

Tom and Will stretched themselves, relieved to be moving again.

'A benevolent gentleman, is he not?'

'Ah, *the bond of love* – it's a winning idea. But alas for human nature!'

'You must learn to trust it more, Tom! Perhaps we do need to keep the peace with ourselves. And be less hard on others.'

'But the wicked will continue to prosper. They always play harder and move quicker. The good can't afford to be complacent – they need their own weapons.'

The two of them filed out of the chancel together, back into the round echoing space of the nave which many centuries ago – on the 10th of February 1185 to be precise – had been rendered sacred by Heraclius, Patriarch of Jerusalem, in the presence of King Henry himself. As they passed one of the recumbent effigies, Will looked down at the figure holding his sword and shield close to his stone body, both hands gripping his weapon as if ready to be called to action again.

'You're a modern crusader, Tom. Is this your ideal? Wise politician, smooth courtier, and fearsome warrior?'

'Perhaps the world has changed less than we think. Order is precarious. We can lose peace and prosperity in an instant.'

As he spoke, to his amusement he caught sight of Laurence Bagnall, no less, in earnest conversation with one of the Temple wives.

'Now there's a man who still thinks wise counsel can achieve something. Let us hope Mr Harley will take note.'

'But at this moment our friend is playing the smooth courtier, don't you think? Let's not interrupt him!'

They emerged from the porch laughing, and hesitated as to direction. Will took the initiative.

'We have a good while before dinner, and you have a story to tell me. I'm eager to hear everything. Shall we take a turn around Fountain Court? At this time of year you can be sure there are no flowers to overhear us.'

'You can be heard quite well enough here, young fellow!'

Will turned round to see Mr Justice Oliver Lundy at his shoulder, his piercing eyes looking straight into his.

'Father! Good afternoon! What did you think of the rousing sermon? A fine speech was it not?'

'The man is a courtly popinjay! The whole thing was a popish pantomime!'

He spat the words out with contempt. In response Tom broke in gently and provocatively.

'I take it you don't pay your devotions to the Blessed Martyr, Sir?'

'My devotions, Mr Bristowe, as you well know, are to punishing *real* evil-doers. A man's guilt is his own, not the nation's. What canting stuff that was!'

'The whole hour and a half must have been painful for you.'

'Yes, but I know my *duty*. On a day like this, the Law needs to be seen and respected. And, of course, I have the benchers' dinner to look forward to.'

'You are drawn here by the roast beef then?' said Will, smiling.

'No Sir, that is for you plebeians! Today we benchers are having *carp*. It was decided that a solemn feast occurring on a Friday was justification enough. Your tables will have to make do with the usual succulent beef, while I shall be picking bones from my teeth.'

'But live in hope, father. The pear tart may redeem all.'

'We all need redemption, William. Not least yourself. Good day to you both!'

Will's father re-joined one of his fellow benchers who had been hovering close by, and they walked off in a huddle.

The two friends followed slowly at some distance, heading back across the court in the direction of the Middle Temple. Will had been patient long enough, and so, as they walked, Tom at last began telling him of the events of yesterday, pieced together from Elias Cobb's report: how John Morphew had been taken into custody when he left the coffee house and had been questioned at the Cockpit; he told Will about the Ministry's fears over the elusive Bufo, their suspicions of Morphew, and how he himself was being implicated thanks to the angry verses he'd found in the coffee-room. Particularly he gave an account of Emmet's visit, and what he now saw was his interrogation.

As he spoke, Tom began to realise that Will was remaining silent, apart from an occasional grunt and half-groan. He was expecting to be interrupted and cross-examined, but Will kept his counsel. And so, as they paced on slowly, Tom found himself running through the whole story. He wondered if Will had learned this in his legal studies – allowing the witness to reveal all, before questioning him?

'... So, when Emmet called last night I thought he had brought me good news. Instead, he led me on and made me a fool. And now Hopkins thinks the Good Fellowship is a hotbed of sedition, and that *I* may be *Bufo!* Thankfully no-one paid me a visit during the night – I took Elias Cobb's advice and didn't attempt to hide. I hope that means they've found another tree to sniff around.'

There was a further silence. Will was hesitating, and seemed to be embarrassed. At last he spoke.

'So you think this Emmet is one of Sunderland's spies?'

'Yes – it seems he's been informing on Morphew.... You met him when you visited his shop near Stationers' Hall last week...'

Tom suddenly stopped in his tracks.

'... Will?... why are you saying nothing? Is it because your visit to Morphew had some connection with this affair? You told me you couldn't speak of it. Is this the reason why? You *must* tell me what happened.'

'Ah Tom, I'm sorry! I should have been open with you from the beginning. I'm afraid my good intentions have put you in danger. There's a great deal to say... Perhaps if I set my story alongside yours, then we can piece something together. I ought to have told you before, but it was such a sensitive business. In fact I swore – and Mr Morphew swore likewise – that we would forget the incident ever happened and never speak of it again... Let's find a quiet spot.'

The two friends knew there were strict confidences on both sides, but that it was high time everything was laid out between them. They had reached the paved court just beyond Middle Temple Hall, where an impressive fountain was playing in the early afternoon sun. They took a seat in a corner by the far railings where there were no inquisitive presences to overhear, and, so far as they knew, no spies in the thicket of wintry shrubs behind them.

'I know your visit to Morphew's shop was confidential,' said Tom. 'You told me it was in connection with work for your barrister-friend, Richard Sumner.'

'That much is true.'

'And when you said you'd agreed to meet with the publisher on the barrister's behalf, I assumed it was in connection with a law case.'

'No, Tom – that was what I wished you to believe. In fact it was a private commission, and a sensitive one. In the past few months, as you know, I've followed several of Mr Sumner's cases at Westminster Hall, and he has begun to share some details with me and allow me to attend interviews with his clients. Over these weeks he's come to trust me – chiefly because he knows I can keep a confidence with anything sensitive…'

'That's why I haven't pressed you to talk.'

'So, when a personal matter suddenly arose, and he didn't know where to turn, he confided in me, and I offered to help him.'

'Yes, you did seem pleased with yourself, and you made dark hints about how secret it all was. I think you enjoyed imagining yourself as Sumner's confidential secretary.'

'Well, I suppose that's what I was. And the thing *was* extremely sensitive.'

'Will you stop telling me how *sensitive* it was!'

'Sorry! Sorry!'

A promenading couple glanced over in their direction. Will immediately dropped his voice and spoke low, adopting a more casual air.

'Mr Sumner's sister is Lady Norreys – she's married to a baronet, Sir Charles Norreys, who seems to do nothing, except mix in high circles.'

'The name means nothing to me.'

'Perhaps because it's extremely respectable. Lady Norreys is an elegant lady, and in spite of living in St James's and enjoying quadrille she has succeeded in keeping her reputation – at least until now.'

'Aha! I have the whiff of a blackmail?'

'Yes, Tom, the wind blows from that quarter – or at least it did.'

'So it's *you* who are the knight of romance!'

'I hardly think so. Nowadays such things are conducted in a more practical way. But I must say Morphew behaved very honourably.'

'Tell me what happened.'

'Lady Norreys lost her pocket-book – dropped in a sedan chair, or in the street, she didn't know. It's not clear who found it, but within a few days the thing made its way to John Emmet.'

'I don't believe this!'

'Yes. Evidently among the booksellers he's rumoured to have an interest in handling private papers. Mostly he buys them legitimately, but they're sometimes gathered, shall we say, more *informally*. In the past Morphew has found him useful in negotiating for memoirs and letters – the kind of titillating stuff that hints at scandal and can be reworked as "fiction." It has a devoted readership and usually makes a small profit. But when Lady Norreys's pocket-book came into his hands Emmet thought he'd struck gold. He took out an advertisement in the *Courant* announcing that the book had been recovered and could be collected from Morphew's shop – for an unspecified reward. You know how these things are done. It was my job to be the intermediary. Richard Sumner naturally couldn't bring himself to go in person. He gave me thirty pounds to settle for him.'

Tom whistled at the amount. 'But that advertisement was a foolish move, was it not?'

'It was a veiled threat. I think Emmet intended to imply that some of the contents might find their way into print. It must have contained more than everyday jottings – probably an intimate diary, I don't know. Thirty pounds is a huge sum for a mere lost-and-found… Well, Morphew saw this notice and was evidently furious with Emmet. He told me it had made him appear little better than a blackmailer.'

'I'm glad he was disgusted by it.'

'Yes. I suspect that previously he'd turned a blind eye to some of Emmet's dealings; but this one crossed the line. Morphew is regarding himself as a more respectable printer now, and Emmet's actions angered him. Anyway, my mission couldn't have proved easier. When I arrived at the shop, Morphew handed me the pocket-book neatly tied with a scarlet ribbon and apologised for having appeared to demand money. For my own part, I asked him to accept a couple of sovereigns as Richard Sumner's thanks for his honesty – I understand it's the decorum of these things. In any case, I reckoned such generosity would be wise, given how *sensitive* the matter was.'

'Will!…'

'I fell into conversation with Morphew, and we talked a little about the publishing business. So of course I took the opportunity of telling him about my *talented friend* who'd just completed an important poem that he was looking to have printed. Well, you know the rest, and what arrangements we made… But during our walk to the Good Fellowship yesterday morning he told me that Emmet had paid five pounds for the pocket-book, and had asked the publisher to reimburse him. I'm afraid Morphew wasn't in the mood to be generous and gave Emmet another tongue-lashing.'

'Well, well,' said Tom, 'what a story! So Emmet is out of pocket, paying for the pocket-book *and* for the notice in the paper!'

'Happy he was not! But the story isn't quite finished. While I was talking with Morphew about you, Emmet walked into the shop and joined us. His eyes lit up when he heard what we were discussing. He's a sharp, enthusiastic fellow, and I must confess I was just a bit charmed by the eagerness with which he pressed your case. He seemed to think a Juvenalian satire would hit the taste of the Town right now. I really thought he was an ally! He said nothing at all about the pocket-book – but of course he must have been resentful and brooding on his ill treatment. I wonder if he saw your poem as a means of entangling Morphew in some dangerous business? Emmet would know the Ministry would be interested in hearing about a new satire.'

'So you think my poem may have prompted them to bring Morphew in for questioning?'

'It must have added to the Ministry's suspicions. I fear I must take some of the blame.'

'No, Will, we're both innocent – or at least too trusting. The blame lies elsewhere.... But tell me, how did Richard Sumner react when you returned the pocket-book to him?'

'With all the relief you'd expect – but it seemed more than that. He made a point of gripping my hand and saying *you can't know how important this is*. I know he's very solicitous for his sister's reputation, but this made me wonder if more is involved. He was extremely anxious that nothing should be revealed. I assured him Morphew had sworn to secrecy – and I swore likewise. I did mention Emmet briefly, but I told him the man was only a go-between and he shouldn't worry.'

'Ah, Emmet again! Everything seems to lead to him.'

'Yes – and the affair may not be closed. Morphew told me he himself hadn't looked into the pocket-book, and I think I believe him. But of course Emmet knows what it contains. Although he no longer has the book he could make trouble with its contents. From what you say, he's in Lord Sunderland's pay, which darkens the picture considerably...' He put his hand on Tom's shoulder. 'I'm sorry I held back from telling you of this. I wasn't to know... To think that all along I've been congratulating myself on my double success: the retrieval of the pocket-book *and* Morphew's interest in your poem.'

'You meant – and *acted* – well, but...'

'But things have unravelled in my hands... I'm worried, Tom! You and Morphew are being drawn into something dangerous – a State matter, no less. But all these suspicions are so fanciful – I think our political masters have drunk a magic potion.'

'Perhaps the rumours are true, and the Government is in turmoil? We can only imagine what plots and counter-plots are being spun at this very moment.'

'And our Bufo is playing his part – with relish.'

'It's a dangerous game, Will. Satire can expose evil, but it can also spread the nastiness around. Is Bufo working to cure the disease, or is he a symptom of it?'

'Perhaps satire always has to dirty its hands? After all, if you're cleaning the stables you'll get filthy yourself. I've been thinking about those verses you found. I wish I could have seen them. You can't explain how they came into the Good Fellowship?'

'No, I can't. The paper was squeezed tightly into the pamphlet, and it may have been inside when the pamphlet came into the coffee-room.'

'Surely it was deliberately inserted – to give the reader a shock? It was a Ministry pamphlet, you say?'

'Yes, a smug piece of hack-work, full of varnished phrases.'

'So the poem may have been designed as a satire on anyone reading the pamphlet?'

'Almost a private joke.'

'But it would be a clever way of putting such things into circulation. To hide seditious material inside another text, like a cuckoo's egg in a pipit's nest. And if deposited in different coffee houses such pieces could be copied and spread very rapidly.'

'It would be a kind of publication, far safer than leaving the paper lying around.'

'And much safer than printing... You say Elias Cobb is convinced Emmet is involved in this?'

'He must be,' said Tom. 'Remember the Bufo lampoon on the Duchess of Marlborough – Emmet told Morphew he'd found it outside their shop...'

'Yes, that does seem much too neat.'

'Well, it seems Emmet took the thing to Hopkins at the Cockpit – where I suspect he spun a different story.'

'Do you mean he incriminated Morphew with it?'

'Yes. It's likely he had the piece from one of those contacts of his... unless Emmet had run it off himself? As chief pressman he has a key to the printing-house, so it's a possibility.'

'Yes, I suppose such squibs can be printed quickly?'

'Certainly. It was only a single-sided thing. Emmet would be taking a risk; but if he knew when the printing-house was empty he could manage it. I've been wondering if he's a deep-dyed villain and is deliberately undermining Morphew's business.'

Will looked a little sceptical.

'To take it over himself, do you mean? It's a possibility. But that's the stuff of stage plotting, isn't it?'

'A true Machiavel, perhaps? From what you say about Lady Norreys, I think he may be exactly that – a man who has no scruples and is happy to make trouble for the people around him...'

They were suddenly interrupted by the sound of a distant horn. This was the ancient summons that drew the honourable members of the Middle Temple to their dinner. Although quiet, it reached across Fountain Court as far as the corner bench, and with it came the reassuring thought of food and sociability. The idea gave some comfort. They stood up together and headed purposefully towards the hall. The pair were not in celebratory mood, and both were brooding on their conversation. Having heard each other's stories and placed them together, they knew the fuller picture was a dark and complex one.

But Will was also thinking about Tom's future.

'I'm sorry your poetic hopes were raised so high, Tom.'

'Yes. Emmet let me glimpse a glorious vision before the fancy melted away. *Yea, even like as a dream, when one awaketh.*'

'But Morphew hasn't rejected your poem.'

'No, but under such threats he isn't likely to risk printing a satire that makes power uncomfortable. At least not at this time.'

'Perhaps you do him an injustice?'

'I would like to think so, but *Justice* is not to be relied on.'

They mounted the steps to the hall's antechamber where the smell of roasted beef began to fill their nostrils. The dark oak panelling seemed to be radiating it. The effect was not unpleasant. Tom sniffed.

'Well, the fatted calf has evidently been sacrificed.'

Both of them suddenly recalled what day it was. It was Will who spoke.

'Perhaps our new nation really does need to seek forgiveness?'

Tom nodded soberly. 'And perhaps we all need to love and trust each other more?'

The pair stepped into the sublime loftiness of the old Tudor hall, and instinctively their eyes were drawn upward. They stood and held their breath, as if not wishing to disturb the brooding spirit of the place. The massive hammer-beam timbers soared above their heads, and the curved braces were leaping across the space, transforming the heavy oak beams into an expression of lightness and joy. At once, Tom's features brightened.

'Oh, I meant to tell you, Will... Joseph Addison has read my poem.'

'*Addison?*'

'Yes, at the Cockpit. He read my manuscript – looking to see if it was seditious! But he did evidently give it his close attention.'

Sometimes Will found his friend completely and utterly perplexing.

'But that's wonderful, Tom!... Perhaps we might now risk having a *modest* celebration?'

Chapter Eight

'I'LL NOT HAVE it said... !'

'But, alas, Mr Grice, I've just *said* it,' replied Tom.

'Confound you, Sir, so you have! But I shall not have it thought...'

'But, Mr Grice, I am certainly *thinking* it,' said Will.

'Are you now, Sir? Well, upon my word you are *a pair of rogues.*'

'*Three* rogues, Harry,' added another young man, 'for I not only think it, but have remarked on it myself on several occasions.'

'Tush!... I say again, *tush!*'

Harry Grice gave the monosyllable its full weight of feeling so that it carried a rich cluster of ideas: annoyance, frustration, and defiance. But there was also a dash of amusement as he saw the three faces smiling at each other and began to appreciate the ludicrousness of his situation.

Tom and Will were enjoying their convivial dinner in Middle Temple hall. The wine did not disappoint, and their beef gained an added savour each time they looked toward the benchers' table where a gigantic, unappetisingly pallid carp was under serious negotiation. At their own table, flesh and spirit were nicely attuned and thoughts were flowing free. For their neighbours they had Will's fellow law student, Ned Rokeby, who had also contributed a festive bottle, and Ned's friend, Harry Grice, both of whom had arrived for dinner well primed with tavern ale. By the time the four of them had done justice to the pear tart Harry was regaling the others on the state of the nation.

'I maintain you do us a disservice,' he complained. 'You would tar us all with the one stick... And feathers too. Now, Mr Harley...'

'Harley has his own gang, and they make as much mischief as any of the others,' said Ned.

'It's all roguery, Mr Grice,' said Tom. 'All of them!'

Harry Grice leaned back slightly and adjusted his cravat, making room for more air to enter.

'You have me at a disadvantage, Sirs, in the matter of putting Mr Harley's case. My pistol is cocked, but my hand is a little unsteady.'

Like a kindly judge, Will took the opportunity to help the witness gather his thoughts. For a moment he imagined himself speaking from the bench in another famously lofty hall.

'Dear Mr Grice, I'm sure you are not so befuddled that you cannot give an account of *why* you believe your master is exempt from our general accusation. I am willing to give you allowance of speech – however slurred it may be – and my friends will attempt to listen with the minimum of interruption.'

'Will speaks for himself,' put in Tom. 'For my part, I reserve the right to add my shilling-worth whenever I think fit.'

'And my penny is on the bar too, Harry,' said Ned Rokeby, who was well used to ribbing his friend on this subject.

'Perhaps we may all examine the witness,' concluded Will, relishing his magisterial role, 'but first he needs to bring in his evidence.'

'But it's you three must make the case. I'm sure I can answer all charges.'

'Very well,' said Will. 'Let me begin with Mr Harley's conduct as one of Her Majesty's Secretaries of State...'

'Of course I'm not so pickled as to miss the joke,' persisted Harry, '– I mean, the joke of hearing lawyers complain of corruption. You all feed happily on it... Now, if I was to say...'

'The point is out of order!' declared Tom with mock solemnity. He was about to hammer on the table with his spoon, but glanced at the benchers' table where the great Lord Somers, formerly Lord Chancellor Somers, the legal genius of the Whig Junto, was presiding. Suddenly into his mind the stinging line came unbidden... *Foul Wharton's cully, mighty Somers' pimp...* his hand hovered in the air. Perhaps under the circumstances... He recollected himself and allowed Will to proceed.

'You will confine your remarks, Mr Grice, to the subject of Mr Harley.'

'... Mr Harley, and the handling of the nation's affairs,' put in Ned.

The impromptu court was pronounced to be in session and poor Harry Grice found himself in the witness-box. As a clerk in Robert Harley's office at the Cockpit he worked on the Secretary's correspondence, handling some of the department's less official material, which included extra-diplomatic communications, confidential reports, and intercepted letters. It was an ill-defined role that made him ineluctably part of the system, and he tended not to ask questions about it. But from his small desk he could glimpse the intricate mechanisms of power and the subtle manoeuvrings of influence – and appreciate the difference between them. And he was a part of all this himself. Harry's small cog was helping to turn the great machine of State.

The hall was starting to empty. He decided that a pipe of good Virginia tobacco would sharpen his wits, and began tamping down the combustible material in the little black bowl he held between his fingers. The others took this manoeuvre as a sign of desperation and watched him patiently. The moment he had kindled the flame and set a crackle going William Lundy put the charge to him. Under such a magnificent gothic roof it was easy to imagine himself at the bar of the Queen's Bench in Westminster Hall.

'I put it to you, Mr Grice, that Mr Harley is working to undermine the Government. Do we not hear that he is forever going behind the back of Lord Treasurer Godolphin to have private audience with the Queen? He is turning her against the Treasurer and His Grace the Duke. What has happened to the old *Triumvirate?* Harley, Godolphin, and Marlborough were on everyone's lips as the nation's own Grand Alliance. And now Harley is unsettling all.'

'This is hearsay only,' said Harry. 'It's all whispers.'

'But is it not true? Is he not "Robin the Trickster," the "*backstairs* minister"?'

'That's because he is – has always been – the Queen's man. Mr Harley understands her wishes, and Her Majesty trusts him more than anyone.'

'But that makes his fellow Secretary's position impossible.'

'Lord Sunderland was foisted on her by the Whigs,' Harry replied somewhat indiscreetly. 'His Lordship thinks only of *party*. The Junto requires blind obedience, and it acts as one man. If they were allowed any more power the Whigs would dictate to the Queen. She hates the tyranny of party, with each group seizing power in its turn – just think! – Every three years, with each election, we would have a revolution in our affairs! It is unimaginable!'

'But surely Mr Harley has his party too? He is in league with the Tories. Indeed he *is* a Tory in all but name.'

'No, no, I'll not have that! He knows Her Majesty detests party. Mr Harley wishes to bring the Queen's friends together from all directions, Whig and Tory.'

'So he *does* have a grand plan, Mr Grice?' put in Tom, and looked at the others triumphantly, 'the rumours are correct?'

'He and the Queen would wish to see a coalition of right-minded men. There is no secret in that.'

'But being *right-minded* – is that not simply being of the *Queen's* mind? What about the mind of the people?'

The judicial Mr Lundy cut in immediately (he enjoyed this privilege of being both barrister and judge):

'The mind of the *people*? Hush, Mr Bristowe! We shall have no treasonable talk in this court! I ask you to remember Dryden's fear – *that Kingly power, thus ebbing out, might be / Drawn to the dregs of a Democracy*.'

'A terrifying prospect!' said Ned with ironic indignation.

'But to return to Mr Harley,' said Will. 'Do you deny that he looks to rebuild the old Court Party?'

'... to set Court *against* Country,' Tom added, helpfully.

Harry Grice cut the air with his hand.

'But it is *party* that drives a wedge between Court and Country – which seeks to divide us into factions. A monarch who is no tyrant, and who rules through ministers, will always help to unify the nation. Witness our recent Union. It is but nine months old, and yet the two parliaments have come amicably together – it is Mr Harley's grand achievement!'

'But I hear there's discontent stirring, and the Scottish lords resent the power they have lost?'

'There are always such manoeuvrings. They are part of the political firmament. The scene will settle. You would have everything perfect at once.'

'I speak not for myself, Sir,' said Will, 'but am simply putting the case to you. You are insisting that Mr Harley is merely the servant of his monarch. But does he not seek to control her? Turn her to his wishes?'

Harry blew a cloud of tobacco smoke across the table, and scowled.

'You present him as a Marlborough and Prince Eugene

combined! There's no such great strategy. But you are alluding to Mrs Masham I think?'

'You have introduced her name, Mr Grice,' said Will, 'so I am happy to respond. Yes, with his cousin Abigail now the Queen's favourite, is Mr Harley not exceptionally well placed to direct events himself? A Lady of the Bedchamber has more power than any Minister.'

'But monarchs have always had favourites,' said Harry. 'It's because Mrs Masham is a woman – an influential woman! – that men like you are indignant. Were she the usual flouncing, whispering courtier you would think far less of it.'

'So, you deny that Harley is using her to influence the Queen?'

'Her Majesty is not so naïve, Mr Lundy. Of course she wants people around her who can serve and advise her, and she has the right to choose whom she wishes. You think everything is settled backstairs and in the bedchamber. That's not so. You should not be so suspicious.'

'I would not be so, Mr Grice, if Mr Harley were not obsessed with secrecy himself. Can you deny that he has the most universal system of spies and informers this country has ever known? Nothing of this scale was ever in place before, even when Walsingham ran his secret service for Elizabeth.'

'Ah, the peerless Gloriana! That's a heartening comparison – and a very just one. But I don't know where you draw all this from.'

'It's the talk of the Temple, I assure you.'

'The Temple Tavern, possibly! I can believe that.'

'But are there not informers everywhere?' persisted Will. 'It is said he has many agents, and they in turn have their deputies and assistants – that everything feeds back to Mr Harley, and that he hears not only what is happening, and is about to happen, but what is being thought – even what is about to be thought.'

'*Aegri somnia!* You must awake from your troubling dream, Mr Lundy! Government requires a constant supply of informations from every quarter, and it is any minister's duty to gather what he can. Lord Sunderland has his sources too. Throughout the land, people are happy to act as the Government's eyes and ears. They see it as their patriotic duty. But this is without purchase or pay, I assure you. The Ministry welcomes people's vigilance.'

'Vigilance is one name for it,' interjected Tom. 'Perhaps spying and double-dealing are others?'

'I'm not talking of the Government, Mr Grice,' added Will, 'but of Mr Harley's own secret service. The two are surely not the same?'

'Now we are entering a murky world, gentlemen. I really think this interrogation has gone far enough! It has been a useful exercise, and for my part I think the fragrant American weed has stimulated my faculties nicely, don't you? I see where this hackney is leading. Permit me to alight here!'

'Dear Harry. You're a charmer,' said Ned, 'and the most honest, patient, and well intentioned of men. We've been baiting you without mercy, and yet you've taken it in good grace. You know that we ask all these questions because we envy your place in the administration.'

'My "place" is a very modest one – a mere mechanical clerk.'

'But to work in the Cockpit is to be at the centre of things,' said Tom. 'And Mr Harley's office is the hub of the great wheel of public affairs.'

'I second what Mr Rokeby said,' concluded Will. 'You have taken all in good part.'

There was a pause. The sound of clearing pots and glasses and the scraping of plates was beginning to be heard in the now empty hall. They were about to rise, but Will pre-empted them and spoke again, more quietly.

'... But, without offence, Mr Grice, are you able to tell us about the unfortunate *Mr Greg?* I appreciate your need to be discreet – but the affair is now in the public domain.'

Harry Grice suddenly looked unsettled.

'I don't think I can speak of it,' he said quietly, almost mumbling. 'It is in my own office, after all – such a shocking business. As you will appreciate, I am restrained from discussing it – not forbidden, but rightly and properly *inhibited.* It is a terrible thing.'

Tom felt his chest tighten, and said nothing. The four of them had reached a highly emotive topic, and the one on which Robert Harley was at that moment most vulnerable. They had kept away from the appalling subject because it would have thrown a gloom over everything. They had tiptoed around this thing so carefully that it now seemed to be taking shape in their very silence.

Four weeks earlier, on the 31st of December 1707, one of Harry Grice's fellow clerks had been arrested for copying some items of confidential correspondence in Harley's office and passing them to the French. William Greg had been quickly tried for treason, and promptly sentenced to death. He maintained unwaveringly that Harley had not known of his treachery, nor been in any way complicit. But of course, rumour was saying otherwise, and the Whig lords were determined to persuade Greg to implicate his minister. The clerk's execution was being delayed from day to day while pressure was placed on him. A pardon and a large sum of money were being offered, but he was continuing resolute. This same afternoon, while these four young men were flexing their debating skills over dinner, William Greg was penning a letter to Mr Harley from Newgate gaol. He was not pleading for his wife and children, or seeking to have his sentence commuted, but was asking the Minister if through his great influence he might have his fetters removed. They were, he said, making it very painful to kneel.

This could be seen as the sincerest tribute to Harley's probity and the devotion of his staff. But Mr Secretary's position was becoming more than uncomfortable. Even if he hadn't colluded with the traitor or turned a blind eye to his doings, he was at least guilty of negligence. Robert Harley's enemies were circling. The Junto Lords, and especially Charles Spencer, Third Earl of Sunderland, were beginning to believe that the thorn which had tugged into their flesh for so long might finally be plucked out.

In Middle Temple hall, the servants were hovering and appeared impatient to clear the table. It was time for the four young men to leave. They knew the conversation should go no further. Silently acknowledging this, Will Lundy, Tom Bristowe, Ned Rokeby, and Harry Grice walked out into Fountain Court and looked about them. It was very still. The January dusk was falling and gave the empty court a palpable melancholy. Frost-work was beginning to form on the flagstones, and the fountain was no longer playing. Hidden from view, an alarmed blackbird was piping furiously at an intruding presence. But the men's after-dinner mood resisted the gloom, and their thoughts naturally turned to further activity. Where better, it was finally decided, than Covent Garden to supply fresh entertainment and lift the spirits.

'I suggest, gentlemen,' said Ned, 'that an early evening stroll in the piazza will enliven us. We can assess the produce newly arrived in the market – and perhaps see what fresh little doxies are on display.'

'And there is one young thing in particular whom Ned would very much like to encounter again,' said Harry.

'Ah yes, the delightful Jenny Trip!' said Ned. 'I would willingly take more snuff from her hand...'

Tom was taken aback. The others laughed at his change of expression.

'... Will told me of your new coffee-house idol, Mr Bristowe, and I paid a surreptitious visit there yesterday. She is an enchanting young lady. Such eyes!...'

'And such *wit*,' added Harry, pointedly. 'I hear that Ned met his match in repartee!'

'In that case,' said Tom, recovering his poise, 'I shall insist on being your host at the Good Fellowship. I know my landlady, Mrs Trotter, will be more than delighted to welcome you there.'

It was unanimously agreed, and the four of them began to walk in that direction. The precinct was eerily quiet and their shoes rang out on the cobblestones. Their laughter echoed around the crouching old houses, and from a distance came the shouts of the city and a gradually increasing rumble of early evening traffic. By night-time the Temple would become rowdy as students staggered home and gangs of lowlife from the nearby Whitefriars prowled its streets; but just now the enclave seemed a refuge from the busy world. At the top of Middle Temple Lane the great gates were closed, so they let themselves out through the small wicket doorway and emerged into the hubbub of Fleet Street. They turned left and passed under one of the narrow side-arches of Temple Bar, leaving the City of London behind them and heading westward in the direction of the Town. Ahead of them the long curve of the Strand led off towards St James's and Westminster, but they held to the right into Butcher Row, which would draw them up into Drury Lane and the delights of Covent Garden.

Chapter Nine

THE FOUR YOUNG men tumbled into the Good Fellowship in a flurry of mufflers and hats, and in an instant the coffee-room lost its quietness. The hum of subdued conversation was pierced by their voices which a few minutes earlier had been echoing round the Covent Garden colonnade. Several pairs of eyes were raised, a neck turned, and a paper lowered. Even the fire seemed to give a responsive spurt as the door banged shut behind them. The group settled down at a table and gratefully unlayered themselves. Tom walked over and placed a sixpence on the bar, where Jenny Trip was preparing for the evening crowd. She was presiding under the oak canopy with its carved finials and niches, and it struck Tom disconcertingly that the thing was rather like the ornate frame of a four-poster bed.

'I see my young gentleman is here again!' said Jenny, noticing Ned Rokeby in the party. 'I didn't know he was your acquaintance, Mr Bristowe?'

'Not until today, Jenny! We've all been dining at the Temple and have just made a tour of the piazza.' Tom leaned over the bar and gave her a confidential grin: 'Indeed I think you'll shortly be receiving a small memento of our marketing.'

'Well, I'm very partial to cabbage.'

'I think I'd better say no more!' He pushed the sixpence towards her. 'But now we've decided we're a little giddy and need a good dose of the dark liquor. As for me, my head is demanding a generous pinch of snuff. I think I have a cold coming.'

Jenny obligingly reached for the hinged wooden box.

'I hope this Spanish will serve,' she said. 'Mrs Trotter says we'll soon have a stock of *Orangerie*, and some *Imperial Golden* no less – and that's known to cure *everything!*'

Tom took the box from her before she could gallantly offer him some from the back of her hand, and gave her an inquiring look. She spoke confidentially:

'The mistress has been telling us her plans, and it seems we're all to become polite!'

'For you, Jenny, that will be no effort. But I suspect in Jeremy's case...'

'Oh, that campaign is already in hand. All afternoon Jem's been muttering about *elegance,* and he's put his body into training. Peter has been showing him how to carry himself – though the journey has been uphill so far.'

'I warrant our young Peter will be the polite host himself one day.'

'Yes, he's much taken with the idea. What a smart young fellow he is!'

Jenny's lappets of pale blue silk swung gently as she glanced over at the coffee-boy, who was attending to the new visitors. She fixed Tom with her bright eyes.

'... And so, Mr Bristowe, we're to be the *Bay-Tree Chocolate House!*'

'It's decided, then? What do you think of our intended reformation?'

'I think it's time we had a fresh wind in our sails. For myself, I'll be expecting some new muslin at the least... And we're to have a *mirror!*'

'That should attract the swords and ruffles. But I doubt it will improve the conversation.'

'On the contrary, a fine gentleman will be able to pass the time of day with himself quite happily.'

'And not fear contradiction,' said Tom. 'It's an agreeable idea.'

While he took his snuff, Tom looked around at the walls of the coffee-room. Along from the tall clock there were a few posters and notices, some Flemish prints, and the engraved head of a leering debauchee, described as Charles the Second.

'Did Mrs Trotter tell you she's planning to purchase some pictures?'

'In that case, Mr Bristowe, if we're going to be polite, then we must choose wisely.'

'Perhaps you have some ideas?'

Jenny leaned on one elbow. 'Well, speaking for myself, I'd like to see a romantic landscape, or a really handsome portrait – something to please the eye. None of your drunken Dutchmen smoking in a tavern. And I would not wish to be looking at a cow's arse all day.'

'You have a pretty good taste, Jenny – nothing common or low!'

'We find enough of that down Drury Lane. But it will be good to make this place a little more genteel. If we can't have ladies in here, we might perhaps have a picture of some.'

'Now that really would be a revolution!'

He turned toward the table where the others were settled. Will and Harry were in conversation, and Ned was looking questioningly in his direction. Tom beckoned him over and watched as the student negotiated his journey to the bar with some care. The young man was clutching what had once been a posy of snowdrops but was now a rather bedraggled bundle. Ned looked down at his sad offering from the market and consoled himself with the thought that it might strike just the right note of pathos.

After an amused glance at the floral tribute, Tom allowed Ned the field and went to re-join the others at the far side of the room where Peter had just poured the last dish of coffee. He saw that Laurence Bagnall was also at the table, and another man he did not recognise. There was a brief burst of laughter as he sat down.

'Hey, Tom! Listen to this.' Will was holding a sheet of paper in his hand. 'Jeremy found the thing in the upstairs chamber. It's from the Mutton-Chop dinner on Wednesday – an epigram I think you'll appreciate. It has a splendid title: *On Lighting our Tobacco Pipes with one of the Laureate's Odes.*'

'It seems they're good for something, then,' said Tom sharply.

'You anticipate, Tom!'

Will lifted the sheet as if it were a royal proclamation, and read aloud:

'*The Laureate's lofty Ode in* Anna's *praise*
From pipe to pipe the living flame *conveys;*
Critics, who long have scorned, must now admire
To see TATE's *verses kindling* genuine fire!'

'Very neat, Will, and read with proper dignity!'

Laurence Bagnall sighed audibly. 'A sad reflection – but alas, how just! Mr Tate's New Year offering was an exceedingly limp effort. As I recall, it had some banter about *smiling Union's golden wings.*'

'Perhaps you prefer his metrical Psalms, Sir?' Tom asked.

'No. I fear they prove that Piety is no substitute for Poetry. They are enough to drain the blood from any Christian heart.' He paused and took a critical sip of coffee. '... I relish more his poem in celebration of tea-drinking: *the warm nectar's pleasing force!* He calls it *Apollo's liquor,* and rightly. Now, *there's* a poet who is truly inspired by his subject! Why invoke the Springs of Helicon when you have the Chinese leaf?'

'But I see you are drinking coffee today, Sir? Is your own inspiration at a stand?'

'Ha! Today I am *revising*. My poem is largely finished and I am now subjecting it to harsher Judgment.'

The author of the forthcoming *Epistle to Robert Harley* was clearly in a genial mood, and Will gave him a fresh prompt.

'You must be delighted at the prospect of writing your poetry in the *Bay-Tree*, Mr Bagnall? Do you approve the new appellation?'

'I certainly do. It will become the home of the laurel, and I hope to see the house properly consecrated.'

'Perhaps Widow Trotter could ask Mr Nahum Tate himself to preside over the ceremony?'

At this remark Laurence Bagnall's jaw visibly tightened, giving the young men the distinct impression that he was hoping to fulfil that function himself.

Will came to the rescue.

'I understand our landlady intends to have a bay laurel bush in the doorway. So perhaps, Sir, Her Majesty's Poet Laureate might be invited to crown one of our own fellowship as his *deputy?*'

Mr Bagnall beamed, and nodded in approval at the idea.

'Young man, I commend you. You have the understanding of a lawyer and the genius of a poet!'

Tom leaned forward and spoke.

'Your poem to Mr Harley, Sir, is nearly completed?'

'It is in its final stage, Mr Bristowe; but I must *strike a second heat* upon the Muse's anvil. Then it will be ready.'

'Does Mr Harley expect this tribute? Mr Grice here is one of his secretaries at the Cockpit. I dare say he can be sworn to secrecy.'

Laurence Bagnall betrayed a flicker of uneasiness, but replied genially enough:

'Is he indeed? Though my poem is no *tribute*, as you term it. That's a servile word. I rather offer Mr Harley my thoughts on public probity, and on the role that private and domestic virtues play in the life of the nation. I trust he will be pleased to be associated with those sentiments, Mr Grice...'

Harry attempted a slightly awkward smile.

'... especially at this time?'

'Certainly, Sir,' said Harry, 'I'm sure Mr Harley will be gratified by the address. This is indeed a difficult time for him.'

'I was considering making an allusion to the traitor *Mr Greg* in my peroration – a veiled one, you understand. But it has been removed during revision. Although I am sure there was no collusion, there has been an unfortunate laxness in his office by all accounts.'

Harry was feeling embarrassed at the direction the conversation was taking. He was unsure whether this called for some acknowledgement on his part, or a defence of his minister. But in this he was pre-empted by Will.

'At dinner today Mr Grice spoke very warmly of Mr Harley, Sir, and exempted him from any universal charge of political corruption.'

'Such loyalty is commendable,' said Bagnall. 'But it is hard, nay impossible, to be a paragon. Perhaps in these times we expect our statesmen to be well practised in the darker arts? They do need to be apprised of them...' He paused and took another deliberative sip of coffee. His listeners, who had gauged the rhythms of his performance, stayed expectantly quiet. '... *Public life*, gentlemen, is like the spleen... It draws the ill humours of the Body Politic to itself. A man will eventually succumb. But happily, we can *purge* him whenever he threatens the State!'

Mr Bagnall sat back in his chair to emphasise the conclusiveness of his remark, and reached for his snuff-box.

'Do you not think the State is in danger *at this very moment?*'

The words came from the gentleman who had been sitting silently to Bagnall's right. At this unexpected intervention everyone's eyes turned back to the poet, expecting him to reply, but there was no move to do so. It was not clear the two men were known to each other. The stranger had a long-drawn face and slightly pursed lips. Distaste was written into every feature. But if Mr Bagnall had been contemplating a response, the man pre-empted him.

'... There is a tide of insurrection mounting. Everywhere I look I see our Constitution undermined and our nation's achievements scorned. The great Marlborough is belittled, and the Queen has fallen into the hands of those who would return us to tyranny. A treasonable spirit is let loose, and I fear its violence will undo us!'

His eyes were beginning to blaze with righteous anger, and as he spoke he drew from his pocket a thin sheet of paper. Tom strained to see, and from a distance it looked to contain several lines of writing in black ink.

'I have found this unedifying piece lurking inside this very room! It is an epigram, and is subscribed "Bufo." But this is not our beloved Laureate's work!'

Tom and Will stared at each other in helpless alarm. Neither felt able to say anything.

'Listen to this, Sirs!'

The man drew himself up stiffly, and read:

'A Whig, *a* Nettle, *and a* Toad,
They shit, *and* sting, *and* spit *their load;*
When ground and mix'd by Spencer's *hand*
The poison spreads throughout the land.'

The man seemed to shiver slightly as he pronounced each phrase. Yet there was a detectable relish in the delivery, as if his distaste was seasoning the words.

Tom and Will remained silent.

'A potent squib indeed,' said Bagnall. 'Worthy of Martial!'

'No Sir. This has none of the classic virtues. It is merely indecent – and treasonous. I found it on this very table. But it was not left openly and honestly. Oh no! It was cringing inside a pamphlet as if it dared not show its face. This is how faction works – by stealth and deceit.'

Will boldly intervened.

'But such things could never be said openly. The pillory – or worse – awaits anyone who would put his name to those verses.'

The man responded angrily.

'And rightly so! *Bufo* – the *toad* – is a venomous creature. The author declares himself to be one. He is boasting of his poison!'

Tom could not hold back.

'But does not the toad by tradition, Sir, also carry the antidote? He *wears yet a precious jewel in his head*.'

'In ancient Rome, young man, women squeezed toads to poison their husbands. No thought of any antidote there!'

'But to heal a poison you first have to recognise it.'

'All the more reason to deplore such secrecy. A secret poison is merely destructive.'

'But are you not building too much on this? Such little lampoons are common enough.'

'Not like this. This is certainly a libel on Lord Sunderland.'

'It is as well he does not see it,' said Bagnall.

'It is scurrilous. Perhaps he *should* see it. There is somebody in this place who wishes to cause harm, although he thinks he is being exceedingly witty. I shall show it to our hostess… Hey, young man!…'

He beckoned over Jeremy, who had been conscientiously tending the fire nearby.

'... Is Mrs Trotter in this place?'

'Yes, Sir, she was in the parlour.'

'Then will you fetch her at once!'

Jeremy looked at the others, as if uncertain how to respond. No guidance was forthcoming so he simply shrugged his shoulders and headed somewhat inelegantly for the kitchen.

Jenny Trip was looking at them from the bar. She whispered to Ned Rokeby and gestured him to return to his friends. There was a sudden disappointment in his eyes, but then they met hers for a moment and he found himself willingly obeying her silent command. He turned to face the room, steadied himself, and took the first heroic step. The place seemed full of anxious activity and the conversation had quite broken down. He approached the table and smiled innocently at everyone. Tom seized the moment.

'Well, Ned, was your gift gratefully received?...'

He seemed a little distracted.

'... The snowdrops?'

'Oh, yes indeed. She said their heads were drooping even more than mine. She undertook to raise them both. She is going to put them in water.'

'Well, that will do the trick I'm sure – and perhaps revive the flowers too!'

There was a ripple of relieved laughter. Widow Trotter appeared, wiping her hands on an apron, and beamed to see such a convivial gathering.

'Good evening, gentlemen. I'm glad to see you here. I trust you're finding everything to your liking?'

'We are finding more than we expected, certainly. But *not* to our pleasure!' said the stranger loudly.

Widow Trotter was taken aback and glanced quickly round the room to reassure herself that everything was in order. The man half rose out of his seat and thrust the piece of paper at her with a look of disgust, like a preacher denouncing from the pulpit. She feared the worst, and it was confirmed when she saw the lines of verse.

'I might expect to find such trash in a house of ease. Can you explain its presence here? It would seem that one of your regulars is proud of his bog-house wit.'

She took the paper and read it swiftly. 'I have no inkling about this, Sir, and I shall dispose of it at once – where it belongs.'

'But that is not enough! This is a seditious insult on the Secretary of State. Were it scratched onto a dirty wall it might be dismissed more easily. But this is a treasonable slander.'

'I'm grateful to you for handing it to me. You need say no more. I assure you I shall look into the matter *urgently*.'

And with a quick turn of the wrist Widow Trotter folded the paper and tucked it deep into her bodice, where it nestled under the pleated cotton shift. From this place of safety only the most impolite man would request its return. This particular man was no bold adventurer, and out of a mixture of nervousness and propriety he felt duty bound to let the matter – or at least the manuscript – rest there. He was silent, but she thought his eye flickered momentarily to the sword he wore by his side.

At once, Will intervened to lead their thoughts back to higher things.

'Did you know, Mrs T, that Mr Bagnall has completed his long poem? He is now adding just the final touches.'

'That's something to be proud of, Mr Bagnall. I like to think this room has helped inspire you!'

'I consider *inspiration* a very dubious notion, Mrs Trotter. But I'm bound to agree that the Good Fellowship has guided my poem on its way, and has provided several illustrative digressions. And of course, whenever I was at a stand I always had your *Hippocrene* to lift my spirits.'

'Now, there's an excellent idea!' said Tom. 'I think all *six* of us might benefit from Jenny's delicious composition – if Mr Bagnall will consent. Can you arrange it, Mrs T? I'll happily treat the company.'

'What an appropriate thought! I'll set about it immediately.'

Laurence Bagnall beamed with an almost childlike delight, while the stranger looked nonplussed at the goings-on around him. He was distinctly uncomfortable at the tide of jollity that seemed to be sweeping in. It was with palpable relief that Widow Trotter took Jenny's place at the bar and sent her off to prepare the *Hippocrene*. This exclusive concoction, named in honour of the Muses' fountain, was Mr Bagnall's personal restorative, invented when the poet was much indisposed with a cold. Mr Bagnall found that this warm egg custard whipped with brandy, sugar, lemon, and nutmeg, had a remarkable power to stimulate the animal spirits.

But by the time Jenny appeared with her tray containing six handsome glasses deliciously filled with the creamy substance, each with a little grated walnut sprinkled on the top, there were only five in the party to appreciate them. Without giving his name, the stranger had thought it best to slip quietly away. It was clear to him that the Good Fellowship was itself an odd combination of the warm, the smooth, and the acerbic. It was a dangerous mixture, and the stranger did not exactly know how he would report on his mission when he returned to the office.

Chapter Ten

IT WAS WITH mixed feelings that Widow Trotter watched the stranger depart. She was thankful to note him, slightly bowed and furtive-looking as he slipped out through the door, but was worried about the use he might make of the Bufo epigram. He seemed determined to broadcast it. While she was relieved to have the manuscript tucked away, it was unsettling to know it had been found in her coffee-room. There had been a hope that the first poem was an accident – but not any longer. As she busied herself at the bar she became increasingly uneasy. Who could the stranger be? Whose poem was it? And who had concealed it? The thoughts grated on her mind. No less annoyingly, her bosom had begun to respond to the ticklish paper which now seemed to be circulating surreptitiously. Given these mental and physical irritants, she could hardly wait to sit down with Tom and Will, pull the thing out, and talk matters over with them.

But at the table, Mr Bagnall and his four satellites were still deep in conversation. In the stranger's absence, and under the influence of the Hippocrene, creative conjecture was being given free rein about the man and his inflammatory poem. Tom and Will longed to share their thoughts with each other, but they kept heroically quiet. To no-one's surprise, Harry Grice was dismissive of the 'naughty squib' as he called it, and maintained that it should be laughed off as 'a mere frolic.'

Mr Bagnall, however, thought frolicsomeness could be satirically effective. 'But in this case I feel the lines have as much of the *frolic* as the Tyburn cart.'

But before the topic could advance further, all speculation was brought to an end in dramatic fashion when the door of the Good Fellowship burst open, and the assembled company heard an urgent cry.

'News! boys, news!'

It was Jack Tapsell, red in the face and breathing heavily, who had arrived hot-foot from the City. His words were directed particularly at Sam Cust and Barnabas Smith who were sitting at the table by the fire with a couple of other merchanting friends. As traders, they were men for whom the word *news*, especially when shouted across a busy room, could mean ruin or riches, a danger or an opportunity – sometimes both – and so they hung on every word as Jack unburdened himself.

'Two *French spies* are taken up!'

He was still half-shouting, and by now had the attention of the whole room.

'Smugglers – from Dover – and under *Harley's protection!* This will surely finish him!'

Jack's greatcoat was hanging off his shoulder and half-trailing on the floor, but in his eagerness he seemed not to notice.

'They are arrested and questioned… *papist agents*, running the whole contraband traffic off the coast. It's just as we suspected – they've been informing on our convoys!… And can you guess who they are?'

'Steady as she goes, Jack,' said Barnabas Smith. 'Take your time, and let's hear the full story – in order if you can.'

Coffee was called for, and in a few moments Jack was cradling the hot dish in his hands and gathering himself together.

Everyone was silent in anticipation, including Tom, Will and the others. Not surprisingly, they were wondering how Harry would react to the news.

'Well, my friends,' said a slightly more composed Jack, 'at last our complaints have been allowed. What we feared is all too true. *Valière and Bara are agents of the French!* It's been a double deception! To think that Harley has always protected them. We thought it was a sham, and so it's proved! He insisted they brought good information from Calais, but we knew it could only be common news – the stuff of the Paris gazettes and nothing more. No, all along it's been *our* intelligence they were feeding to their French masters.'

Barnabas Smith visibly winced and shook his head; Harry Grice reached for his pipe; and Laurence Bagnall began to confront the prospect of some major poetical revision.

'Aye, that's smugglers for you!' said Barnabas. 'They make money on both sides, and we honest traders are the ones to suffer. They have flouted every prohibition and made a fortune with Harley's connivance. The French got boatloads of our English wool for their weavers, and we got their detestable brandy – both illegal. What a bargain!'

'And to add to the shame,' said Jack, 'word has it the two of them were regularly wined and dined in Calais – at free cost – while they compiled their letters for Paris!'

'How many ships have been taken?' asked Sam Cust.

'That's to discover. The villains are to be examined minutely, along with their hired boatmen. Who knows what revelations there'll be? I wouldn't stake a farthing on Harley's reputation now – first the traitor Greg, and now this!'

'Valière and Bara! – that pair always had an insolence about them,' added Barnabas. 'They were always boasting of their power and credit. They thought no-one could touch them.'

'Well, they've been fingered now.'

While all this was being said, Tom and Will could not forbear glancing in Harry Grice's direction. They were hoping he would not be tempted into a public defence of his minister. It was clear that Jack Tapsell and his Whiggish friends were in no mood for any plea on Harley's behalf. An embarrassing silence descended.

Jack Tapsell's provocation, when it came, was delivered with a grim half-laugh.

'So, what do *you* think, Mr Bagnall? Perhaps your poetical *epistle* to Mr Harley should now be re-cast as an *epitaph?...*'

He turned round to his friends: '... That might at least make the thing *shorter!*'

Bagnall looked distinctly uncomfortable, but attempted to remain composed amid the laughter. Thoughtfulness came to his rescue.

'Perhaps I shall introduce a digression – on how loyalty is scarce to be expected nowadays, and how trust is easily imposed on.'

'Harley's *Papist* spies were indeed loyal, were they not? – to their own kind!'

'I share your unease, Mr Tapsell. One of the hazards of public life is reputation. It is always in hostage to events. But an honest man must pledge it, at whatever cost. A fleck is oftenest seen on the fairest skin.'

Jack gave a low whistle.

'You're a poet, Mr Bagnall, I grant you. It makes a fine image.'

'For that, I'm grateful to *you*, Mr Tapsell! It will certainly find a place in my poem, I assure you...'

He gestured with a generously open hand toward his opponent.

'... Provocation can often prove the better inspiration.'

On that graceful note, the two men sheathed their verbal swords with honour satisfied, and a general buzz of conversation resumed. Jack's friends shared a joke with him, and Peter was signalled to replenish their coffee. Ned made his way unsteadily back to the bar where Jenny was in occupation. At their table, Laurence Bagnall turned directly to Harry Grice.

'How will this news be received at the Cockpit, do you think?'

'The matter is already in hand, Sir, I assure you. Mr Harley does indeed have a very trusting nature – you are right in that. May I say that I, for one, shall be glad to read your poem.'

Bagnall stood up slowly and smiled at the three young men beside him. For a moment he was tempted to see himself as a combination of Dryden and Socrates. But the picture was immediately dismissed. Pride, it occurred to him, never raised a man, but merely bloated him... The neatness of the thought brought a sudden sparkle to his eye, and he knew he had to make haste.

'Will you excuse me, gentlemen?' He nodded to them all. 'I must return home and take my manuscript from its drawer. I have more work to do!'

Without further hesitation, Laurence Bagnall swept out of the room with a long and purposeful stride. Even the door seemed to open for him with fluent ease.

'Well, well,' said Tom, 'I do think Mr Bagnall aims to be the Addison of the Bay-Tree. I've not heard him speak with such natural authority.'

'He seemed to enjoy having an audience,' said Will. 'Perhaps his poem will do the business?'

'I'm ready to be impressed. The man may speak ill of inspiration, but I did detect a touch of the *furor poeticus*.'

Harry Grice was pensive and looked round at the coffee-room clock.

'A quarter after nine! I fear I must break up the party, Sirs. My apologies, but my duty lies at the Cockpit. This matter of the spies is sure to cause a stir, and I think I should be there. Mr Harley often comes late to the office, especially on post-nights. I think my presence may be required.'

'It's been a pleasure to make your acquaintance, Mr Grice,' said Will, 'and I hope we'll see you in here again.'

'You will indeed. It's been a useful and entertaining day for me... Mr Lundy... Mr Bristowe!'

Harry Grice got to his feet, nodding briskly to Will and Tom. But then he paused.

'I have to say I found the *poetry* especially noteworthy. It's a powerful currency, is it not? And like money, it can persuade, or corrupt – even when it seems to be frolicking!'

'Yes,' said Tom, 'and it can be spent well, or ill.'

'I'll be interested to learn more about this *Bufo*. His little jibe caused such consternation to our anonymous friend. It happens that yesterday I had wind of something of his. I overheard two of my colleagues at the Cockpit talking about "Bufo." At the time I did not mind it, but I think they were referring to a pamphlet... Do you know anything of this?'

Harry's question was an impromptu one, but direct and hard to evade. He suddenly sounded like a practised diplomat, a master of casual curiosity. It was Will who replied.

'Whoever he is, he would be well advised to remain anonymous... Do you think he may be known to Mr Harley? His sympathies are evidently not with the Whigs.'

Now it was Harry Grice's turn to think quickly. He met Will's entirely innocent smile with an even more radiantly innocent one of his own.

'Perhaps I shall find out tonight!'

With that, Harry walked over to the bar where a disconsolate Ned was watching Jenny intently as she stirred a little sugar into another gentleman's dish of tea. The attention was clearly being appreciated, and it convinced the young student that he ought to think of leaving for home. There were many alehouses along his route, he said as he declined Harry's offer of a hackney, and he still had five shillings in his pocket. After all, the night was not far advanced... But then he hesitated.

'Do you think I might ask Jenny to douse me now?' he said, with a wavering turn back toward the bar.

Harry took hold of him firmly.

'I think I need to kidnap you, Ned, and carry you back to your plantation in the wilds of Smithfield! Then I shall turn *westwards*. Good night gentlemen!'

Theirs was certainly a polite leave-taking, but was rather let down by a clumsy exit during which the coffee-room door and Ned's right foot seemed to have minds of their own. Tom and Will watched their dance-steps with amusement and offered appreciative applause as the door finally closed.

They were restive and glanced round the room. A movement at the far side of the bar caught their eye – it was Widow Trotter discreetly beckoning to them. The pair responded with a mixture of eagerness and apprehension, and at once followed their hostess out into the kitchen, where a delicious savoury mist was billowing around Mrs Dawes. It was tempting to linger, but the determined little procession held its course into the parlour beyond, a more dimly lit place where stillness at last descended.

Now in her wainscoted sanctuary, Widow Trotter sat down, and with considerable relief was able to divest herself of the troublesome manuscript. She smoothed it out on the table in front of them, grateful to see that the ink did not appear to have run, and placed a pair of lit candles alongside it.

'I thought this curious thing should be kept safe,' she said.

'That was a masterstroke,' said Tom. 'I certainly think he would have carried it away.'

'You should be relieved he didn't carry you off with it, Mrs T,' added Will. 'Thank Heaven we live in more civilised times!'

She looked intently at the paper, which appeared so small on the polished table-top.

'I must say I was shocked to see this. It means the previous poem was no accident. I take it the handwriting is the same, Mr Bristowe?'

Tom turned the sheet round. The thing was just four lines, but they confidently occupied the centre of the paper. It was the same deep black ink, and the same jagged, urgent hand, only here the writing was larger. But that was understandable given the space available.

'This is the same hand, Mrs T.'

'It looks as if it was written in anger,' said Will. 'The writing is heavy, with firm downstrokes. Perhaps this tells us something of Bufo's character? He's bold and impetuous. It's a loud voice I think...'

'But he's keeping a hold on it,' she said. 'These are verses, after all.'

'Exactly so,' said Tom. 'It's all part of the performance. The thing was not designed for general circulation. It was intended to be seen like this, taken out of its quiet hiding place and causing a little explosion to the eye. But look how the epigram is carefully set in the centre of the page so as to have its full effect. It has clearly been copied out. And the verses are correct and precisely punctuated. It's an odd match – a nicely formed epigram seemingly written in a scratched and furious manner, but displayed with care. Had it been meant for a printer or for open display it would be written out with more deliberation. So it's not an angry scrap, nor a clean copy. No. This is meant to perform for us.'

'Perhaps it tells us that Bufo's usual hand may be very different?' said Widow Trotter.

'Exactly!' said Tom. 'And the intense black ink – I can't help thinking it's part of the display. There may be little point trying to identify the hand. In the other poem too, although it was much longer, the lines were carefully spaced so that the poem filled exactly the two sides. It's as if the writer is conscious of the style of his *publication* – that he's aware of how a poem looks on the page and has even designed his own font.'

'I wish law-books could be so eloquent!' said Will.

'I think that takes us a step forward,' said Widow Trotter. 'But how was the paper conveyed?'

'The man said he found it inside a pamphlet – just as Tom found his.'

'Pamphlets are brought in here all the time, without formality – dropped in with the papers or simply left – and during the day we hardly take notice of them.'

'In a busy coffee-room it would be easy for someone to do that, or to slip something into a pamphlet without being observed,' said Tom, taking up the paper and weighing it in his hand, 'especially a small, folded sheet like this.'

'I'll ask my people if they've observed anything. The bar gives you a good view of the whole room, and Jeremy and Peter are constantly moving around the tables.'

Tom looked thoughtful and furrowed his brow.

'Perhaps I'm being mistrustful, Mrs T, but might the man have been *lying?*'

'About finding the paper, do you mean? In that case he's a fine actor: such convincing anger and distaste! His face was a picture.'

'If that were true,' said Will, 'then the man brought it here with the intention of causing trouble.'

'Well, it does seem a coincidence that he's the one who should discover it. Did he say which pamphlet he was reading?'

'None of us thought to ask him. He looked alarmed when you appropriated it – as though he had lost a trick.'

'Yes, I noted that,' said Tom. 'He didn't like to see our heroine play the watchman with the document and clap it into gaol.'

'And what a gaol! A lock-up where no visiting is allowed...'

'And the key is thrown away...'

Widow Trotter shook her head at them benignly.

'Thank you gentlemen! I'm pleased you think I did well. I wonder if there may be something in your suspicion. It was as if the very name *Bufo* was prompting the man's anger – as if he had encountered him before. By rights he should have been glad I took a severe line about it. I think I managed my indignation well.'

'Commandingly, Mrs T!' said Tom.

'– And we're told Mrs Bracegirdle has quitted the stage!' added Will, appreciatively.

But Widow Trotter remained pensive.

'All this watching and deceitfulness worries me. I thought I was the hostess of a coffee house, but now I feel like a criminal harbouring a nest of traitors... What is happening, Tom?'

He tried to be reassuring. It was the first time she had used his Christian name.

'Perhaps we should keep still for the time being,' he replied, 'and not push this any further? The clouds may blow over in a few days.'

'I'm not sure what we *can* do,' said Will, 'except wait on events – whatever they may be.'

'I expect Mr Cobb will call round if he has any news,' said Mrs Trotter. 'He's a busy man, but he promised to keep us informed.'

The three of them sat around the table for a while, conjecturing uneasily. They seemed to be slipping into a world where thoughts were becoming dangerous. Perhaps doing nothing would be best?... But then they remembered John Morphew. The printer was in real danger, and surely they owed it to him to remain vigilant? The little manuscript resting in front of them seemed only to emphasise the strangeness. How could a few neatly-turned verses arouse such anger?

But if they were expecting news, they did not have long to wait. There was a commotion outside the parlour door, and they heard a man's voice exclaiming loudly, followed by a laugh, a loud clatter, and an unidentifiable oath. Elias Cobb – who was not designed for surreptitious employment – poked a cheerful face round the door. He was holding half a hot venison pasty in one hand and was delving into his greatcoat pocket with the other.

'Things are busy in the coffee-room, Mrs T, and Jenny would like your help... But I told her it could not be for a few more minutes.'

A little incautiously he swallowed a lump of venison.

'I come with news from the Cockpit – *piping hot*... Aaah!...'

With a cry, his hand emerged rapidly from his coat and began fanning his open mouth.

'... Much like your excellent pasty... !'

'Mr Cobb! Settle yourself down. The coffee-room will have to expect me for a while longer. We also have news for *you*. I hope you can spare us ten minutes?'

Curiosity was aroused on both sides, but it was the pasty and the manuscript that decided the matter. While the constable was consuming his quickly-snatched rations Widow Trotter held up the epigram for him to read, and gave an account of the document's discovery and the dark picaresque adventure it had since undergone.

'So you see, Mr Cobb, the gentleman slipped away before we could find out his name. I haven't seen him in here before.'

'The more I think about it,' added Tom, 'the more he reminds me of Emmet – not physically of course, but looking like he'd come here for a purpose, either to find things out or stir things up.'

'If that's so, then he can't have learned much,' said Will. 'There was some discussion of Mr Harley and Greg the traitor, but nothing seditious. And Mrs T snatched the paper away before it could be examined.'

'So our anonymous visitor had the evidence taken from him?'

Widow Trotter looked at the constable.

'Do you think he intended to show the paper around and use it as evidence against this place?'

'Well, I've not had wind of any move against the Good Fellowship – you would know immediately! – and my men report all they hear...'

Elias stopped in the middle of the thought and drew himself up.

'But... I must tell you my own news, which I had intended to announce with a grand flourish. I hope it will please you... I'm assured that your publisher friend, Mr Morphew, is to be *released* – tonight!'

'He hasn't been charged?' asked Tom at once.

'No, I've had word that he is being allowed to go. I don't know the details, except that he was locked up overnight and was questioned again this afternoon – but this time I wasn't present.'

'That's good news,' said Will, beaming with pleasure, 'and hopeful for you, Tom!'

'What a relief,' said Mrs Trotter, who felt a sense of release herself.

'... But I heard that he became very angry,' Elias continued. 'He was told more about his pressman's doings. It seems Mr Emmet had been a one-man gazette. And some highly sensitive *private matters* were revealed also – though I don't know what they were...'

A look of apprehension passed over Will's face, and he glanced at Tom.

'But why are they still holding him?'

'I think there are other discussions taking place. It seems Mr Morphew is an important fellow, and the Ministry want to keep the pressure on him. He must be finding the whole charade exasperating.'

Widow Trotter stood up and crossed to the sideboard, where she reached for the decanter of claret.

'Well, I think this calls for a glass, Mr Cobb?'

'By all means,' said the constable. 'I've had a busy, dry evening...'

He waited for her to begin pouring, and then purposefully added: '... though I have something more to put before you all – something even more to the purpose...'

Wiping his hands, he reached back down into his greatcoat pocket and carefully drew something out.

'... It is only briefly in my possession, and you must not ask how I obtained it – but I know it will interest you. It tells us more about Bufo, and exactly why the Ministry are fluttering around like frightened chickens.'

And with those words he placed on the table a modest-looking octavo pamphlet of a dozen pages. The thing was inelegantly printed and appeared to be unsewn. And the title was boldly, though unevenly, displayed:

Bufo's Magic Glass:
A Vision of the Great World.

At the foot of the title-page it stated simply *Printed for the Author*, and it carried a motto in small italic type:

Whatever Foe *had wrought, or* Friend *had feign'd,*
Therein discover'd was, ne ought might passe,
Ne ought in secret from the same remain'd.

'Lord bless us!' said Widow Trotter. Is that Bufo's pamphlet?'

'Indeed it is. This is his satiric mirror on our political masters.'

Tom reached for it, and at once gave a look of recognition.

'The quotation is from Spenser – *The Faerie Queene* – it's Merlin's glass, in which Britomartis sees a vision of Britain's future.'

'Well, this is *Bufo*'s vision,' said Elias, '– or rather *accusation*... It's clearly high-flying Tory stuff. Mr Harley is glanced at, but not severely. No, all the venom – and what venom it is! – is poured on the Whigs, and especially the Junto lords. Somers, Wharton, and Sunderland are all roughly handled, and there's some highly-seasoned language. The thing has a strong whiff of treason! Bufo accuses them of plotting to frustrate the Queen and undermine Royal authority. Marlborough is praised – but only as a soldier, not as a man. He appears as a cowardly husband who is frightened of his shrewish wife and would rather storm about Europe than return and face her.

Tom was leafing through the pamphlet eagerly.

'I see it!' he declared, and read aloud:

'... *Happier by far when facing* War's *alarms*
Than risking life and limb in Sarah's *arms.*
Our glorious General *triumphs in the field,*
But to his peevish Spouse *will always yield.*

Will gave a low whistle.

'If that doesn't outrage the Duchess... I can hear her furious cry from here!'

'She may not have seen this,' said Elias, 'or at least not yet. All I can say is that Mr Hopkins and Mr Addison have read it, and they are both alluded to – libellously...'

He paused and his face suddenly looked solemn.

'... Mr Addison especially must be deeply shocked by what it says of him. The passage is worse than insulting.'

The constable took the pamphlet out of Tom's hands and found the page.

'Listen to this. Bufo is speaking of the Kit Kat Club and their Whig plots. Here's what it says of Mr Addison:

Caballing with the Kit-Kats *at their ease,*
His every motion straining how to please;
His person most genteel and most polite,
The model of a Whig H-----------e.

Elias stopped before the final word. Tom seized the pamphlet from him.

'Oh my good Lord – it can be nothing else. That's shocking!'

He passed it to Will, who was less reticent.

'*Hermaphrodite!*'

Widow Trotter immediately put down the two glasses she was holding.

'Poor Mr Addison,' she said. 'That's simply scurrilous.'

'I saw his face yesterday,' said Elias, 'and he looked as though the talk about Bufo's verses disgusted him. Reading this, I can understand why… And Thomas Hopkins too – there's also a passage attacking him.'

'Show me,' said Tom impatiently. 'I wonder… ?'

He looked at the page and went silent for a moment.

'Yes, there it is! It seems those verses I read here in the coffee-room are part of this poem.'

'Has the pamphlet been circulated, Mr Cobb?' asked Will. 'You told us yesterday that some copies had been seized from a Fleet Street hawker?'

The constable looked uneasy.

'All I can say is, there *may* be one or two copies going around – it's hard to say. But at the moment there's no general hubbub about it. The Ministry are watchful and anxious, as you might expect. I've managed to borrow this copy to show you – I won't say how – and I must take it away with me, you understand? So, you will no doubt want to read it at once. This is the satire that Hopkins thinks Mr Morphew is responsible for printing...'

'... And which *I* may have written!' said Tom.

The weight of the implication suddenly came home to him, and he felt a cold touch at his throat. Time was short, and Widow Trotter immediately took charge of the situation. She jumped up, put her head round the door, and called into the kitchen.

'Mrs Dawes!'

At the far end of the room a woman's face peeped round an open cupboard, and there emerged a figure in a long white apron. It was surprisingly trim for someone who had such an appreciation for rich flavours and good crusts.

'... Please make sure we're not disturbed – on any account! But first we need a pot of the best *Pekoe* – and four generous portions of your chicken pie. As quickly as you can!'

The cook looked intrigued, and set about it at once.

Back in the parlour, it was decided that the only thing to do was for *Bufo's Magic Glass* to be read aloud, and Tom was the obvious choice. Once Mrs Dawes had brought their sustenance and the door was closed again, he drew one of the candles near, settled himself, and began in a solemn voice to deliver Bufo's poem.

'Before a cave there sat a speckled toad
Who'd ventur'd from his damp and dark abode...'

The words unfolded the vision. Widow Trotter, Will, and the constable were held spellbound in the flickering candlelight as Tom's voice intoned Bufo's satiric verses. The poet was setting the scene for the revelation to come:

'... As Bufo's eyes gazed in the crystal clear
A dark and troubling vision did appear...'

That night, over in the City, John Morphew had made good progress along the Strand and Fleet Street, and was striding up Ludgate Hill approaching the mighty Cathedral of St Paul. On the way he had called at his rooms in Salisbury Court to wash and change his clothes. But he was anxious to see his shop, and particularly to check the printing-house and ensure all was well. He walked purposefully and with a grim expression, his eyes focused on the pavement ahead but his mind running over the extraordinary events of the past two days. The concentration was such that he took no notice of the scene around him. The massive new cathedral, which in daylight rose above the street as a gleaming white palace already greying in the city's smoke, was on this winter night a towering dark presence blocking out the stars.

As a matter of routine he turned left into the narrow alley that led to Stationers' Yard, an enclosed courtyard at the very heart of London's book trade. The hall of the Honourable Company of Stationers occupied the far corner, proudly upholding the ancient dignity of the nation's authors and printers; and facing it on the right, squeezed somewhat awkwardly toward the opposite corner where it jostled with two or three other bookshops, was John Morphew's domain. The windowed shop, which in the daytime was decorated with title-pages and small illustrative prints, was firmly shuttered; but rather than enter there, he turned into the narrow side-passage on the right. From here a door led directly into the printing-room, which occupied more spacious premises at the rear of the building. A lamp further along the passage was almost spent, so there was practically no light, and he had to rely on physical memory to locate the lock on the door.

But as he touched it, the door gave to the pressure and opened slightly. It was evidently unlocked – and yet the place was in total darkness. This meant that neither Emmet nor his assistant James Feeny was there. John Morphew tried not to be alarmed at what this could mean, but pushed the door firmly and entered the blacked-out printing-room. He knew where the candles were kept, and he had a tinder-box in his greatcoat pocket. He also knew the layout of the place, and so he made his way forward into the dark with some confidence. But suddenly his stride caught something large and solid on the ground. His balance gone, he reached out blindly for one of the presses as support, but his hand found only air and he fell heavily to the timber floor. His other flailing hand landed on something heavy and soft. As he moved his fingers, he touched woven wool, and what was without doubt a button. His other hand now felt damp and sticky. His chest was thudding alarmingly and his breathing was short and rapid, but he tried to remain calm. It took all his self-control to locate his tinderbox, take the flint firmly in his hand, and strike it against the steel. Twice nothing happened. On the third attempt there was the briefest spark – but it was enough to reveal the horror...

Chapter Eleven

'… The vision filled him with immense dismay
To see his country sink into decay.
"On me," said Bufo, *"let th'opprobrium fall;*
Wrongs, guilt, and infamy – I take them all!"
With that, the toad devoured the horrid crimes,
The nation's sins, the evils of the times.
Swol'n with misdeeds and scandal, stuffed with lies,
Bufo *dilated to a monstrous size,*
Then stretched his throat and sadly rolled his eyes.
Thus filled with poison, having done his worst,
This bag of foul corruption sighed – and burst.'

TOM ENDED HIS reading with a shudder, and his audience sat in stunned silence for several moments.

Widow Trotter was the first to speak.

'That's a dark and poisonous piece!'

'Yes,' said Will, 'it's a monstrous vision. Bufo is like the scapegoat of Leviticus – taking all the nation's sins on himself.'

'Or feeding on them?' said Tom. 'Such a poetical sacrifice is easily made. But it's artful. I was expecting a final curse, but instead he becomes a self-destroyer who draws all the fetid matter into himself. This really is like Will's scapegoat.'

'Politically speaking, it's clever,' said Will. 'It claims to go beyond party, and yet it has its own motives. He says the nation won't recover till all parties and placemen are swept away – but it's the Whigs who are singled out.'

'It's a Temple of Ill Fame,' said Tom. 'But did you notice how the Queen and the Church are free of the contagion? It's the men in and around parliament who are his *plague of rats*. What was the phrase? – *the restless, scurrying vermin of the State*.'

'Yes – a vision of a malign secular power! He seems to long for some kind of sacramental State.'

'But what a voice!' said Tom. 'He's a fiery pulpiteer with the terrible certainty of Good denouncing Evil. There's more than a touch of self-righteousness about it – and his final sacrifice is highly presumptuous!'

'That's true,' said Will. 'Didn't we hear the original yesterday? – He *taketh away the sins of the world?*'

'Presumption indeed!' exclaimed Widow Trotter. 'I don't think I would put my trust in *him*. I suspect the man has failed in his ambitions: there's a special bitterness in disappointed hopes.'

'But it's a powerful piece of invective,' said Tom. 'The Ministry's fears are understandable.'

'Well, gentlemen – and *my Lady!*' said Elias Cobb, taking a deep breath and getting to his feet, 'I must make my apologies. I have to hurry off and take this thing along with me. It must be back tonight, or its loss will be discovered...'

He gave Widow Trotter a meaningful look.

'... Until it is safely returned I shall guard it like my virtue.'

The look was returned.

'I trust you'll be more vigilant than that, Mr Cobb!'

'Do you think the thing has gone about the Town?' asked Will, 'Or are we its only readers outside the Cockpit?'

'I can say no more... But this may be only the beginning of the story.'

He pocketed the pamphlet and reached for a last morsel of chicken. There was a good deal of it left untouched.

'I'm thankful your Mr Morphew would seem to be exonerated. I doubt this is the kind of thing an established printer like him would take a risk with.'

'But it could be something in his pressman's line?' suggested Will.

'Ah, Emmet! Now there you're on surer ground. He has shadowy Grub-Street connections – knows the *dark alleys* of the trade. That's where the Ministry should be looking... Well, I bid you good day gentlemen – and *Lady!*'

With that flourish, Elias Cobb made his exit and left the three of them to contemplate the situation. Any optimism seemed to have drained away. Tom's reading had been a difficult experience. It was as if Bufo had been sharing their table and drawing them into his vision. The element of ventriloquism – dark tones rising from within another's body – was chilling. Tom looked drained and a bit shaken, and Bufo's words still seemed to be echoing around. Will spoke what was in each of their minds.

'Do you think Mr Cobb knows more than he's telling us?'

'I do,' said Widow Trotter. 'He was unwilling to talk freely. I know my friend Elias well, and he's rarely short of news and ideas. But just now there was little information, and no *conjecture*. He appears to be leaving that to us, don't you think? Not discouraging us from it?'

'Almost *encouraging* us,' added Will.

'But much of what we know is thanks to him. After all, he told us about the interview in the Cockpit, and he brought us the pamphlet – at some risk to himself. You must remember that the constable's position is an awkward one. He needs to be discreet, and he often has to move in a serpentine way.'

Tom roused himself.

'Oh, Mrs T!... Toads, rats, goats, and now serpents! They are such innocent animals. How easily we load our crimes and vices onto them!'

'Alas, you're right, Mr Bristowe. We're unwilling to allow that our vices are entirely human ones... But let's not sink into despair. The situation may be resolving itself – Mr Morphew appears to be safe!'

'Unless some price has been demanded of him?' said Will. The idea was an uncomfortable one.

During these exchanges Tom had been turning a thought round in his head.

'Mrs T, do you think I should call on John Morphew tomorrow? Or might that be intrusive? I feel I need to apologise to him, and assure him we've been concerned about his welfare.'

'Yes, I think that would be the right thing. But don't ask him directly about your poem. Mentioning your verses will be awkward, and he may show some annoyance – but you'll have to accept it with good grace.'

'He may of course be *defiant*,' Will interjected, 'and seize on Tom's poem as a way of showing it. Juvenal could have his say after all!'

'Well, I'll find out tomorrow,' said Tom without enthusiasm. 'If he does want to wash his hands of the poem, then I need to retrieve my manuscript. The only copy I have is in my desk upstairs.'

At that moment Will attempted to ease his friend's mind, but succeeded only in adding another unsettling thought:

'And of course there's a chance you may see Emmet – though I very much doubt it. After what has happened he'll surely be given his marching orders!'

'Or has skulked away already,' said Tom. 'I don't expect anything else. How can the man continue in his employ? He's behaved unforgivably. Emmet will surely be anathema?'

'I think Tom is right,' said Widow Trotter. 'You'll not encounter Emmet!'

Several dreadful minutes passed before John Morphew was finally able to light a candle. Each successive frustrating spark showed the blood on his hands, which were cold and shaking and seemed not to belong to him. But at last the tinder took, and suddenly a flickering beam transformed the enveloping blackness into an illuminated space. It was a theatrical light, and the human corpse, from which a pool of dark liquid had spread, appeared to be restless, almost twitching in the candle flame. He knew at once that it was John Emmet, splayed out face down on the floor, his twisted right leg almost touching his own. Dead, beyond any doubt. The kneeling publisher forced himself to lift the candle nearer, and as it moved he saw that the skull was decisively broken apart. The pressman's cropped hair allowed the wound to be clearly seen. His head was turned to the side and his eyes were fixed in a stare. And there, alongside the body, only a few inches away, he recognised his own silver-headed walking cane. The sight made him retch involuntarily. Its finely moulded spaniel's head, warmed and rubbed over the years by the palm of his hand, was now clotted with dark blood. He could almost feel it. It was as if he himself had done the deed, and his own anger had become a real act.

The thought was sickening. He was alone in the dark with Emmet's dead body by his side, and it was plain that the matter had finally been settled between them – by someone else. There would never be the confrontation he had planned, and no chance to clear the air. Instead there was this shocking closure. His feelings of resentment were suddenly repugnant, and a shudder of self-disgust ran through him.

He moved the candle further and saw the left arm stretched out along the floor. The hand was twisted and clenched into a fist – and there was a piece of paper crushed in it. He hardly dared investigate, but the candle seemed to have a curiosity of its own and he found himself reaching across the corpse towards it. He didn't need to touch the thing in order to see that some writing in heavy black ink was readable above the thumb. The words were unmistakeable and chilling… *Bufo's Curse*.

The publisher almost leapt to his feet, staggering slightly as he tried to keep the candle upright. He had to do something – find someone – report what he had found – tell somebody about this. But first he must wash his hands. He made his way beyond the partition to the far end of the room and put the candle down beside the type case. There was yet some soapy water in the rinsing-trough in the corner, and he began to perform the ceremony uneasily and with a conscious twinge of guilt as if he were washing away a crime. The water was discoloured by ink, and as he wiped his hands on a towel he saw that his cuff was steeped in blood. He needed more candles, but the thought of flooding the room with light made him afraid. The deed deserved to be shrouded in darkness and he didn't want to see more. His thoughts continued to tumble over each other. He must not stay here, but do something – find someone quickly – he had nothing to hide. But he remained rooted to the spot unable to move, like an actor in one of the old tragedies uncertain of his part. And to his horror he knew what that part was: he was the assassin with all his props scattered around him.

A minute later John Morphew was outside in the narrow alleyway. It was some time after eleven, and although the nearby buildings were firmly shuttered there was the sound of life in the streets. He determined to find a watchman and began to walk, trying to direct his feet calmly and not appear agitated. It was tempting to seize on the first person he saw, but he knew that would be dangerous: he must report the crime officially, and at once. But as he walked he couldn't help feeling suspect and furtive, and each figure he passed seemed to glance warily at him. His thoughts continued to run ahead: how had this happened? Who? Why? That was for later, he told himself. He must concentrate on the task in hand.

When the watchman's lantern swung towards him he was taken by surprise, and he grasped hold of the man's coat with relief as he stood in his path.

'You must come to my shop. I've found a body. Please follow me!'

The watch looked him up and down, without moving, and passed the lantern in front of his face.

'You look distraught, Sir.'

'Yes, yes, I am! There's been a murder – in my shop – please come at once!'

The watchman was not a man known to him, and he wondered how far he had walked. The return took longer than he expected, and it was a while later when the watchman, holding his lantern before them, led him along the side alley to the printing-house. The door was slightly open, and the room was now bright with light. Inside, two familiar faces were bent over Emmet's body: one was Joe Buller, the local City constable, and alongside him was Walter, the porter from Stationers' Hall across the court. At that moment the porter was carefully extracting the piece of paper from the clenched hand.

'Mr Morphew!'

It was good to hear his name being called out. Somehow he needed to be reassured of his identity, to come back into himself. The scene was an alienating one, but this was his place, and that corpse had been his friend... and it was his cane that Joe Buller was holding and carefully turning as he scrutinised its head.

'This is your cane, Mr Morphew, isn't it?'

'Yes, I found it by the body.'

'How long ago was this?'

'About ten minutes ago…'

The constable carefully placed the walking-cane on a table, resting it on a small wooden block so that the head was clear of the dusty surface. With a slight shock the printer realised that the ritual of gathering evidence had already begun. Things were happening very quickly before he had been able to explain and introduce these men to the scene he had discovered. The pair of them were already in possession of it, and he was playing the part of an intruder who had to explain himself.

'Can I see your hands, Mr Morphew?'

Although it was politely said, there was a menacing implication, and as he held out his hands as if ready to be shackled, the bloody cuff was shockingly visible. How long would it be before he was shackled indeed? He followed the constable's downward glance and saw that his coat was also tainted, and his left knee had a dark patch on it. He felt like ripping off his clothes and fleeing.

He needed to gather himself and take control of things.

'Let me explain what has happened…' he began, only to be interrupted by the watchman standing behind him:

'It's all too clear what has happened.'

'I came into the room and stumbled over the body. It was dark, and the door was open…'

He found himself talking hurriedly, anxious to put everything on record and tell his story. He knew he must establish his position while he could, before events moved on further. He had to make it clear that he was not the cause of this, but the first witness of what had obviously been an extremely violent attack. As he looked again at the crushed head he saw that the force of the blows – and there must have been more than one – had been furious and merciless. He was urgently reading the scene himself, trying to register everything before he was led away. John Morphew was astute enough to know that by midnight he would be standing before a magistrate. These men could do nothing else. As the discoverer of the body, the householder, the employer of the victim, and the owner of the murder weapon, he must be officially questioned. While all this was running through his head he continued to talk, though he knew that what he was saying was less clear, less careful and deliberated than it should have been. Things were pressing on him from all sides, and as the three men stared at him, what he saw in their eyes was an uncomfortable mixture of sympathy and disbelief. They were looking more than they were listening.

The scene was not prolonged unnecessarily. Over the next few minutes some further questions were asked about his actions, to which he gave truthful replies and offered as much detail as he could. He tried to be co-operative and began to sense that he was slowly reclaiming his mind and beginning to set out the facts more coherently. At the far end of the room the rinsing trough was examined, and also the towel on which some inky blood was found. What he had not noticed earlier was a line of partial footprints where his bloody heel had marked his track. He was naively comforted by the fact that they appeared to corroborate his account of his movements.

And so it was that John Morphew, printer and publisher, consciously holding himself erect, found himself standing at one end of the City magistrate's basement kitchen where the settling embers of the oven provided some warmth. The old gentleman, dressed in a nightgown and seated in a large oak chair, had been hauled out of bed to perform his civic duty, and as the midnight chimes rang out from St Paul's he began a further line of questioning, first inviting the constable, the watchman, and the porter to give their respective accounts of that night's harrowing events.

Constable Buller told how on his rounds he had noticed a dim light coming from the printing-house and found the door on the latch. He went in to investigate, and having seen the body he had run across the court to fetch his friend Walter from the lodge of Stationers' Hall. The two of them had lit more candles and were examining the body when Mr Morphew and the watchman entered. Yes, the publisher had been nervous and less than coherent in his account of what had happened, although in the circumstances it was perhaps to be expected… The constable related how Mr Morphew had claimed to have stumbled over the body, bloodying his hands and clothes, and had said that although the silver-headed cane with the dog's head did indeed belong to him, he had left it behind in his shop two days earlier. The watchman described how he had seen the agitated gentleman walking oddly along the street and stepped out to question him. The man had reached up to him and seized the lapels of his coat, attempting to pull him along the pavement. In the glare of his lantern he had noted the bloody clothes, and he thought the man sounded somewhat distracted.

At this, old Mr Dignum leaned forward in his chair as if peering through a shop window, and brought his eyes to focus on Morphew's stained coat. There was an uneasy silence while the magistrate scrutinised him. Suddenly the publisher became conscious of a coldness in his hands, and he fumblingly tried to hide them in his pockets. As he made the furtive gesture, he realised he was back at school, head bowed, shamefacedly awaiting the birch.

The magistrate's lips began to move.

'Tell me, Mr Morphew… exactly *why* have you been absent from your premises for the past two days? I understand from Constable Buller that you have been visiting *Whitehall*? Not the accustomed resort of a Fleet-Street printer!'

The glimmer of an ironic smile somehow turned the observation into an accusation.

There was clearly to be no escape. The question was a direct one, and so, in a halting voice that betrayed his discomfort, John Morphew was forced to reveal that he had been detained overnight by the Under-Secretaries of State in Westminster, where he had been questioned about certain printed items of a seditious nature – the treasonable libels of 'Bufo' – of which, he declared, he knew *absolutely nothing*. The protest sounded feeble, and as the whole embarrassing story of his earlier arrest unfolded, the events shaped themselves into a single narrative – of someone suspected, accused and angry, who had finally taken his revenge on the man who had informed against him. Emmet's brutal death appeared to be the climactic episode. With a sinking feeling in his heart, the publisher knew the magistrate would connect it all up; and indeed, from the moment he heard himself pronounce the fateful word 'Bufo' there was to be no way back. The paper with *Bufo's Curse* inscribed, crumpled by the fist of the dead pressman, was held out to him…

Throughout the interrogation, everything was done properly and by the book. The publisher was invited to state his case and explain matters. But the more he told the truth, and the more details he offered, the more the picture was filling out in all its macabre clarity. Whatever the larger fact, the incriminating fiction was convincing, and at the end of the proceedings the magistrate could do nothing else but order John Morphew to be dispatched to Newgate on a charge of murder. The wheels of justice were turning remorselessly and rapidly, and the trial would come on at the Old Bailey at the next sessions in a week's time.

Saturday

31 January 1708

Chapter Twelve

IN THE COURSE of his morning walk into the City, Tom's spirits rose considerably. As he emerged from Red Lion Court and turned southward into Drury Lane his steps were hesitant. Every side-alley offered an escape route. But he pressed on determinedly. He knew he owed John Morphew an explanation, although to call on the man so soon might look like pestering. With the obvious exception of John Emmet, the budding poet Bristowe was probably the last person Morphew would want to see – that clever young satirist who had caused such trouble and whose manuscript he couldn't bring himself to read.

Already the streets were busy and the shops saluted their customers with tempting wares set out before them. Above Tom's head dozens of brightly-coloured signs waved in the breeze and competed for attention like a line of eager children. It was a fine display. There were carved and painted images of everything from golden crowns and silver boxes to tin buckets and wooden tobacco jars, and he found himself looking up as he walked. Today there was a milder touch to the air and the sun was bright. Some of the signs boasted ornate ironwork and were hung so precariously low that tall hats and lofty wigs were in danger. Each picture told a story. He passed beneath a flying horse, a saracen's head, a three-masted sailing-ship, a needle and thimble, a harpsichord, a straw bonnet, a green man, ribbons, buckles, bonnets, garters… He almost became dizzy. It didn't take long for the freshness of the urban scene this Saturday morning to work its effect. Even the raucous street cries seemed to slip into a lively rhythm and echo one another in counterpoint. The city was wonderful!

Business was brisk, and being a Saturday the weekly routine of cleaning and sprucing was well underway. Servants, shop-girls, apprentices, and the occasional fussy proprietor were busy smartening their properties, polishing their wares, cleaning the sash windows and scrubbing their little patch of pavement. Several times Tom had to avoid a mop that was being wielded over-zealously, or step aside as a brush swept rubbish into the kennel. By the end of the day everything would be neat and presentable for the Sabbath – or at least that was the hope. But in some cases the dirt was merely being redistributed. As he walked by an open doorway a bucket rattled and a sluice of dirty water shot across the pavement in front of him. He tried to dodge it, but in doing so stepped off the paving into a muddy puddle that sucked his feet into it. In only a few seconds his smartly clicking walk had become a heavy tread.

A few steps later he heard a young voice addressing him.

'Clean yer honour's shoes?'

Bob the shoe-boy was sitting on a wooden box, a selection of cloths and brushes resting on a bag at his feet and a little iron tripod in front of him. There was a smile on his face. Had Tom been a suspicious sort he might have detected a touch of cheekiness; but at that moment it seemed an opportune encounter. When he greeted Morphew he needed to look less like a muddied drover, so his halfpenny would be well spent. He watched in admiration as the lad wiped the shoes in turn, picked up an earthenware pot and dribbled a thick black liquid over the leather, so deftly than none of it was spilt. The young craftsman let the mixture of soot and whale oil settle across the surface, and expertly worked it in until Tom's two shoes were gleaming, their newly lacquered surface bright as a japanned table-top. Tom beamed at him and gave him a full penny. As his steps resumed their percussive confidence he thought how paradoxical it was that such dirty materials could produce a pristine cleanness.

He suspected something might be wrong the moment he emerged into the court by Stationers' Hall and saw that Morphew's premises were still shuttered. He had to walk up close to read the small note on the shop door announcing that the place was closed for the day *on account of personal circumstances.* It was a roughly-written piece of paper – a scribbled message more appropriate for a butcher's stall. It was only to be expected that in Morphew's absence his people would find the situation difficult, but surely things should be returning to normal now?

The place was worryingly silent. There was an alley running alongside the shop to the right, and a little way down it Tom found the separate entrance to the printing-house. Here the heavy door was bolted and there was no response to his knock. Further along was a large window set high in the wall, and standing on tiptoe he eventually managed to catch a glimpse of some movement inside. With relief he knocked again smartly and loudly. After a lengthy pause the door was laboriously unbolted, but all he was permitted to see was a face with furrowed brow and wary eyes. The man was unwilling to move the door more than a few inches. Tom raised his cocked hat and politely asked if John Morphew was in the building.

'Who is asking?'

He introduced himself, but met with no response other than a slight lifting of the head and narrowing of the eyes. The man looked defensive, as if he was guarding something. Tom knew that in a few seconds the door would be shut on him. He must seize the moment. He had to appear friendly and arouse the man's curiosity while not posing a threat. So, in an earnest and innocent voice he told a glorious fib, blushing slightly as he did so.

'I had arranged to meet Mr Morphew here this morning. I know he has been in some trouble and am worried about him. I understand he wants to speak with me.'

There was another pause, until with painful slowness the door opened further to allow a more generous view of a balding man with bare arms and an apron who was continuing to eye him suspiciously. Suddenly the man shifted his attention and peered round Tom's shoulder into the alleyway before urgently beckoning him inside. All this was done in silence, and the effect was distinctly conspiratorial. Tom feared the worst and spoke without prompting.

'You look worried, Sir. I hope nothing is wrong?'

'Things are very wrong... You speak like a friend of Mr Morphew, and do not wish him ill?'

'Quite the contrary, Sir. He's been a generous friend to me and I'm becoming concerned about his welfare. Please tell me what has happened. Why is the place shut up?...'

Tom wasn't sure he had struck the right note. The man gave him a penetrating look, but replied trustingly:

'We heard Mr Morphew was in some kind of trouble over in Westminster. Do you have wind of this? His friends need to know what has been going on.'

Tom seized the chance to give a brief account of Morphew's arrest and questioning, and his suspected involvement in seditious writings.

'But the word, Sir, is that he has now been released – that's why I expected him to be here...'

But rather than look cheered, the man was downcast, as if his fears were confirmed. Tom broke the silence with another question.

'... So I take it you've not seen Mr Morphew? Do you know where he is?'

At this, the man was suddenly close to tears, and the response was genuine – he could not disguise it. Tom didn't know what to say:

'My dear Sir...'

For the first time, he noticed that the man was shuddering slightly, possibly with the cold for the room was unheated, but it seemed to be more than that – as though he had suffered a shock.

But again Tom's words went without a response, and so he filled the hiatus by asking to whom he was speaking. The man gave his name as 'James Feeny, pressman,' but then he hesitated.

'... Well, *second* pressman to be precise... although *now*...'

And he trailed off into a confused silence.

Tom was longing to speak but held back. The whole scene was becoming uncomfortable. He knew he must wait for matters to unfold at Mr Feeny's pace. Still in silence, but in preparation for a conversation, he was offered a tall stool, and the pressman drew up another for himself before asking what was clearly an important question.

'Are you also a friend of *John Emmet?*'

This was not what Tom had expected, and he replied hurriedly.

'I met Mr Emmet for the first time on Thursday – at the Good Fellowship Coffee House. We had a long conversation about my work – I write poetry. This is my connection with Mr Morphew – he's considering a manuscript of mine.'

This sounded naïve, and Tom began to feel awkward. He wondered what the pressman was thinking of him. But he didn't have long to wait before these adolescent embarrassments were put in perspective. James Feeny spoke firmly, with absolute deliberation.

'I have very bad news, Mr Bristowe. As a friend of Mr Morphew and Mr Emmet, it will dismay you to know that fate has brought them together in a terrible way... John Emmet's body lies in the next room, and Mr Morphew is in Newgate charged with his murder.'

After all the hesitations and silences, the sheer directness of this was brutal. Tom reeled with the shock, and the implications crowded in. But there was no time to think about them. As if a dam had broken, Feeny began telling his story. He was glad to tell someone, and needed little encouragement to unburden himself.

Feeny explained that he had arrived at the shop shortly before seven that morning, in the company of Paul Barnard their compositor, whom he had collected on the way. He himself had a key to the printing-house. Normally this wouldn't be needed because the apprentice would sleep in there with the door bolted; but the boy's mother had been ill, and Morphew ('he's a very considerate man') had sent the lad home for a few days. And so all this week they had needed the key. That morning when he and Mr Barnard had let themselves in they found Constable Buller there, standing guard over Emmet's body.

'He was lying on the floor, Mr Bristowe, just there!'

Tom hardly needed to be told: the outline of a large stain was still discernible, though the blood had been mopped up.

'It looked a ghastly sight – his head all crushed and bloodied! I nearly fainted. He had been viciously beaten – and with Mr Morphew's own walking-cane!'

This was another revelation, and Tom was speechless.

Feeny told what details he and the compositor had learned from Constable Buller about the body's discovery and the gathering of evidence, and in particular about the paper that Emmet had been holding.

'It was a poetical curse – a strange, ranting thing. I read it over, and it was a nasty bit of work. Mr Emmet was grasping it in his hand. *Bufo's Curse* it was called…'

Tom fought to keep calm.

'… But, would you believe, it seems Mr Emmet was about printing the thing. This morning they found a composing-stick with most of the curse set in type – he must have been killed while he was doing it.'

'You say the stick was found today?'

'Yes, it hadn't been noticed last night. It was over by the type-case in the composing room – we call it a room – beyond the partition there. The stick is small and would be easily missed amongst the clutter – you can see how much stuff is strewn around here. It was discovered by the gentleman who arrived this morning to take charge. Paul Barnard, who knows something of these matters, looked at it and said it was a queer thing altogether. The gentleman and the constable took it to the magistrate an hour ago – to be put with the other evidence. It will be needed for the trial.'

'So the body was also moved this morning?'

'Yes. We've laid Mr Emmet out in the warehouse at the back. The gentleman was anxious that it should be done and everything put right. He wanted the blood cleaned up too. He said they had found all they needed.'

'This "gentleman" – do you know who he was?'

'No. Mr Barnard and I had been here only a few minutes when the man arrived and started giving orders. He was a formal cove in a large wig. He insisted we close the shop for the day. And we were happy to do that, of course.'

'Had someone sent for him?'

'I believe he came from the magistrate, old Mr Dignum, who's less mobile than he used to be. Mr Buller knows the man.'

'He may be the magistrate's deputy perhaps,' said Tom.

'Well, he and Mr Buller set about examining the scene. Paul Barnard and I went into the warehouse to be out of their way and did a few jobs. Then we were asked to help move the body. We found a sheet and wrapped poor Mr Emmet in it with as much dignity as we could.'

'So by that time, in addition to the body, there were four of you – yourself, Paul Barnard, Constable Buller, and this nameless gentleman?'

'Yes. As I said, he and the constable left here an hour ago.'

'And where is Mr Barnard now?'

'He left at the same time to see what he could do in the way of arranging Mr Emmet's obsequies. There's no family, though I know he had a connection in Covent Garden – but he said little about that. We thought something should be done for him. Mr Barnard was very distressed.'

'So you've been alone here?'

'Yes. It's been a long hour.'

The pressman spoke it like a sigh. Tom shifted on the uncomfortable stool. His eyes were being drawn to the damp stain on the timbered floor and to the heavy printing press that stood beyond. The big beating heart of oak and iron was now entirely calm and holding its secrets. He looked at it wonderingly. Across the years, what a torrent of words that innocent machine must have turned out – what fleeting emotions it had captured – what conflicting causes it had served!

He recalled himself and tried to remain practical. There must be more questions he should ask.

'How did they make the place secure last night, Mr Feeny? Was there a key in the door?'

'No, they used Mr Morphew's key. They found Mr Emmet's still in his pocket, and they took that away too.'

'So, last night at the time the body was found, the printing-house door was unlocked and the key in Emmet's pocket…'

'Yes, that must be so.'

'And when you and the compositor arrived at seven this morning, the constable had already let himself in?'

'Yes, he wanted to be here before anyone else arrived. It was thoughtful of him. Otherwise Mr Barnard and I...'

Feeny broke off, flinching at the thought.

'And shortly afterwards,' Tom continued, 'the nameless gentleman called, and he organised the moving of the body and the cleaning up of the blood; and at this point the composing-stick was found.'

'Yes.'

'It was all very punctilious, but I hardly think a proper way of proceeding.'

'I was uneasy about it, Mr Bristowe... I'm afraid I was gruff with you earlier, but I can be forgiven for being suspicious. As they left, the constable and the gentleman told me to make sure no-one entered the place until some people arrived to carry out a full examination of the premises – including the shop.'

A *full examination* – this was yet another disturbing development. It occurred to Tom that he had better not linger, and yet there was much he wanted to see and to ask.

'So you're expecting the whole place to be searched?'

Feeny paused, grim-faced.

'I think that's what it amounts to, yes. Is this connected with the political business? Perhaps they'll be looking for something seditious?...'

He regarded Tom intently.

'... I've told you all I know, Mr Bristowe. I've not kept anything back. And I've done this because you seem an honest fellow who has Mr Morphew's interests at heart. I've known the man for twenty years, and the thought of him committing such a brutal murder is absolutely impossible. He sometimes has a sharp temper, but he has never raised a finger – even at Mark our apprentice. He's a sensitive man and always prefers to talk matters through. That he hammered John Emmet to death with such fury is out of the question.'

'In that we both agree,' said Tom.

'But can anything be done? You seem to be a gentleman who might know how to proceed. We understand the trial comes on very soon.'

'I intend to give everything to this, Mr Feeny, and I'll have others to assist me. I have a particular friend who knows Mr Morphew and has a sharp legal mind, and there are others who can make enquiries. I assure you there'll be no rest until we've done all we can. If you need to send me a message, I lodge at the Good Fellowship Coffee House in Red Lion Court, between Drury Lane and Bow Street. If any further news comes your way, please let us know at once.'

'I'm more than grateful to you, Mr Bristowe. You've given us a glimmer of hope.'

'It may only be a glimmer, but we must always hope! But right now, Mr Feeny, there are two important things I have to do. First of all, may I have a look over this room, particularly near where the body lay? Blood must have been spattered around. Can you show me where it reached?'

Feeny indicated the printing-press on one side, and an oak workbench on the other.

'These were both splashed. In fact, you can see where Mr Barnard and I cleaned.'

And indeed, Tom noticed the darker patches where a cloth had soaked into the wooden surface. It must have been a revolting task. He tried to examine the area carefully, but was conscious of time pressing. He stood silently for a moment, taking in the scene. He was readying himself and feeling apprehensive.

'You said there was another important thing, Mr Bristowe.'

'Yes, but I hesitate to ask... Do you think I could see the body?'

James Feeny had no qualms.

'Yes of course, I'd be grateful if you would take a look at it.'

Tom knew he had no choice. He had to view the corpse before it was taken away. Indeed, he was lucky to have the opportunity. This was what he told himself as he pulled back the sheet, which was surprisingly clean given the service demanded of it. He was braced for the shock of the skull, and a shock it was. But he tried to examine the wound like a physician, clearing his mind of the thought that only a few hours ago this was a living human being. He looked intently and forced himself to read what he saw. He then pulled the sheet further back to examine the rest of the body.

John Emmet had been laid out in a dignified way and his coat was neatly arranged. Blood had soaked into the dark woollen material, but otherwise he looked almost smart, though there was a button missing, and some of the stitching was loose on the left pocket. A fob was attached to his waistcoat pocket, and Tom felt the presence of a watch – this had not been a robbery. Then he turned to the hands. He didn't touch them, knowing they would be cold and stiff, but he brought his face as close to the fingers as he could without feeling sick. It was a frightful business and he was concentrating intensely. But much to his surprise, as the moments passed he began to realise that something of the priest was stirring in him and responding to the calm, intense scrutiny he was giving Emmet's body. He felt it as a kind of ritual – it was as close as he could come to bringing comfort.

He knew he should leave – he had to avoid being there when the men arrived to search the premises. But indignation was swelling inside him and made him want to confront the gang. He could picture what a violation it would be. At the same time, in his mind's eye he saw Will and Mrs Trotter furiously shaking their heads and telling him not to be such a fool – now was not the moment to risk being arrested himself! And of course they were right. He must return to the Good Fellowship and unpack what he had learned.

So Tom left the printing-house without any further delay, reassuring Feeny that he would keep him informed. The pressman was a forlorn figure as he stood at the door, a hand raised in farewell. He was understandably apprehensive. But Tom was feeling determined and buoyed up with the challenge. First he had to find Will or leave him a message. Together they needed to make sense of the events and decide what to do. He was sure Mrs Trotter would insist on helping too – and harnessed together, what a team they could be! They would reconnoitre secretly, inquire systematically, use precise logic, deploy instinct and intuition, follow the evidence scrupulously, but perhaps also make a leap in the dark – whatever it took. As he strode on his way to the Temple, for almost ten minutes – but certainly no more than that – he was confident something might be done to save John Morphew from the noose.

Chapter Thirteen

SEATED AT THE dining-table in the warm parlour, Widow Trotter and her two young friends had all the appearance of being a snug party. The fire glowed in the grate; their glasses were charged with liquid gold in the form of a refreshing orangeade; and spread before them was a fine example of Mrs Dawes's culinary invention. The spiced beef flavoured with cinnamon and apricots should have been a pleasurable indulgence, but they could feel the shadow of the scaffold hovering over the bright china and polished cutlery. The sociable atmosphere only heightened their thoughts of John Morphew alone in his Newgate cell, sniffing the despair of the place and beginning to feel the rope fold round his neck.

Will had been out when Tom called at his lodgings, and it was not until the afternoon that he returned to find the note wedged in his door. He read the words 'urgent conference,' and stopping only to fling his law books on the bed he hurried over to Covent Garden. By the time he arrived at the Good Fellowship various troubling possibilities had run through his mind. Even so, when Widow Trotter and Tom told him the news of Emmet's murder he knew the gods had devised a scene even darker than his imagination.

And now the three of them were seated at dinner as if taking their ease after the morning's labours. Mrs Trotter had insisted that John Morphew's prospects wouldn't be improved by grumbling stomachs and a chilly atmosphere. No, what was needed was a pause for reflection, with reason's eye trained on the matter in hand – *looking before and after* was Will's phrase. A conversation over a late dinner would encourage orderly speaking and alert listening, and these disciplines were needed if they were to find a path through the labyrinth.

They all felt partly responsible for Morphew's plight: Tom and Will had helped entangle him in the Ministry's suspicions, and Widow Trotter hated the thought that the Good Fellowship had witnessed his arrest. For each of them, doing nothing was not a possibility, and when they took their seats at the oval table (not quite a round one) they were ready to pledge themselves to the cause. If Morphew was trapped in some dark plot, then a benign conspiracy might be needed to counter it. No-one voiced it openly, but the impulse was partly curiosity as well as a zeal for justice.

First, the facts – or what appeared to be facts – had to be set out, and so Tom gave them an account of his visit to the printing-house and his conversation with James Feeny. Widow Trotter had heard only a hasty summary, so she was glad to have a more ordered version. Alongside her, Will leaned on one elbow and listened intently as if he were sitting in Richard Sumner's chambers. When the story was told, he sat back in his chair and shook his head slowly.

'Poor Morphew! I have to say things are not encouraging. I fear the picture is firmly in place and the "facts" knit together convincingly... What we have is *The Tale of the Angry Printer*. He has good cause to be furious with his pressman for involving him in sedition and blackmail: the man has spied on him and caused him to be questioned by the Ministry; he feels humiliated and thinks he is losing both his business and his reputation; so, when he's released he hurries back to his shop to confront the rogue, and what does he find? At that very moment the fellow is engaged in printing more of the seditious material; the printer is angry and strikes him over the head with his cane; it is done in seconds and is quite out of character. Suddenly faced with a dead body and the horror of his action, he tries to make it appear that he had merely stumbled on the corpse, but his reactions and his garbled account only heighten the suspicion...'

Will took a deep breath. For the others, it felt like Morphew's trial was already underway.

'... It is a story that hangs together in every part, and it makes sense of the killing. For anyone hearing it, no other explanation seems credible. Motive, passion, opportunity, weapon, behaviour – everything is consistent. And yet... '

He paused again, as if a jury were hanging on his every word.

'... we must assume that each link in this chain is wrong – or at least can be brought into question.'

His audience of two sat silent, awestruck – at least, they felt as much awe as anyone could while sitting in front of a good dinner.

'Well, that's our task,' said Widow Trotter, sensing the challenge ahead. 'You've given us the dramatic scene we must re-write. We need to keep it in our minds because it's the picture the jury will surely be given.'

This uncomfortable reminder helped concentrate their thoughts.

Will was first to speak:

'Yes, we need to think about Tom's visit to the printing-house. You said you examined the scene?'

'It was lucky you arrived when you did,' said Mrs Trotter. 'The room was being secured so no-one could view it before the body was taken away. Without Mr Feeny's account we'd have nothing to work on.'

'And of course anyone searching a place can always find exactly what they want to find – and if not, they can supply it themselves.'

The implications of Will's remark were chilling, but they had to face the likelihood that the printer was being systematically incriminated. His next comment was equally unsettling.

'What we *must* be clear about is Morphew's innocence. As yet, we have no proof of it.'

Will was casting a cold eye, and Tom and Mrs Trotter were momentarily startled. But they knew a lawyer's perspective was important.

'That's a sobering thought,' said a reflective Mrs Trotter, carefully setting down her glass of orangeade. 'Following our hearts can mislead us. We have to work from the evidence.'

'But I'm happy to do that,' said Tom, 'and from what I saw this morning I believe it's clear that Morphew did *not* kill Emmet.'

'Let's hear the case, then!' said Will encouragingly. There was a pregnant pause as Tom mentally gathered his papers together.

'First of all,' he said, 'we know what we're *meant* to think happened in that room. But what is the probability of it? Setting aside the chance that Emmet was there alone when Morphew arrived, there's the greater coincidence that at the moment he was struck he had *Bufo's Curse* clenched in his hand. And in the adjoining room was the most damning evidence – some lines from the poem in a composing-stick. The very neatness of it is suspicious. The compositor seemed to think there was something not quite *right* – it was a remark Feeny made, which we need to follow up – I wish I'd done so this morning! I should go back to the printing-house on Monday to meet Paul Barnard and ask him what he saw. He helped move the body, and apparently he and Emmet were friends. I'm sure Feeny will introduce me.'

'That's a good plan,' said Widow Trotter. 'We must note down what else you can ask while you're there. He and Mr Feeny are bound to know things about Emmet that might be helpful.'

'But we're still in the realm of probability rather than proof,' said Will. 'Perhaps this Mr Barnard will come up with some detail we can use? Do you think I might come too? Or would that look intimidating?'

Tom weighed the matter for a moment.

'I really think I ought to go alone. Mr Feeny opened his heart to me because he was anxious and needed someone to talk to. On Monday he may be more guarded, and a stranger – even a close friend of mine – might unsettle him.'

'I'm sure we can find a Monday task for you, Will,' said Mrs Trotter. 'Time is short, so it would be better to gather evidence separately. We can then begin putting it together.'

'Agreed!' said Will, and he turned to Tom. 'But we need to talk about the scene and what you found there. Did you examine the body? How much blood was there?'

'The main evidence had been removed. There was no piece of paper and no walking-cane. But I did look closely at the body. It needed a strong stomach, I can tell you!'

Tom glanced down at his half-full dinner-plate and pushed it away from him. He swallowed hard.

'Feeny and Barnard had made a brave attempt at cleaning up the blood, but the stain on the floor was still evident. As you would expect from the blows – and there must have been more than one – some blood had been spattered around: across to a printing-press on one side and a work-bench on the other. Cloths had been used to wipe them clean, and the damp marks were visible. But I was surprised by the bench. There were some wooden blocks and tools on the top, and it was dusty – it had clearly not been wiped. Now, Emmet wasn't a tall man, but a heavy blow that split his head open would surely have sprayed some blood across the bench. Instead, it was the *side* of the bench that had been cleaned – and only toward the floor.'

'Ah, so you're saying that the deadly blow was struck when Emmet was lying on the ground?'

'Yes, that's what it looked like to me.'

'Did you ask Feeny about it?' said Will.

'No, I didn't press him. Rightly or wrongly, I kept my thoughts to myself. I didn't want to seem suspicious. But I could observe it clearly enough.'

'You also looked at the body?'

'Yes – as close as I could bring myself to it. I've never been so sickened in my life… but I tried to see with the eye of judgment.'

Tom shut his eyes as if attempting to recall the visual details. His hands began shaping the air in front of him.

'The skull had been split, and one edge seemed to me more like a cut or a sharp indentation. The other side of the wound had been hammered on. I've thought about this, and the best explanation is that his head was split by something sharper than the knob of a cane. But the cane had been used afterwards…'

Widow Trotter looked at him.

'So, the implication is that he wasn't killed by the cane… but you say it has a dog's head – in silver. Couldn't that have been sharp enough?'

'I was wondering – but the side of the wound looked like something had almost sliced into it.'

At this point of the conversation, all three abandoned dinner-plates were huddling for company in the centre of the table. There was a real danger that Mrs Dawes would become discouraged.

'I also took a close look at his hands,' Tom continued, '– at the fingers especially…'

'Of course!' exclaimed Will. 'I think I know what you're going to say – or what I *hope* you're going to say…'

Tom smiled at his eager friend and paused to stretch out the suspense. He felt like a skilled card-player.

'Yes, I examined the fingers as minutely as I could, and there was no sign of ink. They were remarkably clean. It's not conclusive, but it suggests that Emmet had not been composing type. I don't know, but surely the fingers ought to have been tainted, especially if he was interrupted in his work?'

'You must ask about that on Monday,' said Will. 'I suppose it depends on how thoroughly the old type is washed.'

'I can see there's a lot more to be found out, and I think Paul Barnard could be informative.'

'You've already told us a lot,' said Widow Trotter. 'But I'm not sure we've reached proof yet, have we?'

'No, not strictly,' said Will. 'But it's enough to give us confidence that there's another story waiting to be uncovered. If we can only piece it together...'

'Do you think there's a *plot* behind this?' she asked, warming to the idea.

'There must be,' said Will, '*if* Morphew is innocent. It's clear the evidence is designed to point directly at him. The scene in the printing-room was contrived, and the set was worthy of the Theatre Royal. Morphew was meant to play his part, and he did so brilliantly. The stage had been carefully prepared to show him as the killer, and the poor man simply stumbled onto it.'

'But they can't have known he would find the body himself,' said Tom.

'No, but it was a possibility. They would know he was likely to go to his shop that evening. But the bloodied hands and clothes were a boon – and he even performed distraction and guilt! The paper and the walking-cane must have been placed there to incriminate Morphew and no-one else. Even if the body had been found by Mr Feeny the next morning, there was already enough evidence to damn him. And the motive for the crime was neatly in place. But perhaps the timing is the key. The performance would not have worked with the chief actor still in custody. It had to synchronise. This surely means the Ministry...'

'... Someone at the Cockpit at least, or someone run from there...'

'... Killed Emmet, and set up the scene to establish Morphew's guilt...'

'... Yes, everything points that way...'

'... So why did someone in the Ministry want Emmet dead?'

'... And why not have him killed anonymously, without all this contrivance?'

'... So someone seems to have wanted both Emmet *and* Morphew dead? Can we believe that?'

Widow Trotter was seated between the two of them, and during this antiphonal exchange her neck began to feel the strain. But she was also pursuing her thoughts.

'It seems to me, gentlemen, that we need to extend our sights. Trying to prove Mr Morphew's innocence is only part of the task. In court, all our details may have little weight and a jury might simply brush them away.'

'You're right, Mrs T,' said Will. 'Juries can be impatient of detail. What they like is a good story, and so long as they're given a compelling tale – one that makes sense and has convincing characters and motive – then they'll follow that. They don't want to assemble a case logically out of doubts and quibbles.'

'So we need to widen our inquiries,' said Tom. 'If we cannot prove Morphew's innocence, then we have to prove someone else's guilt.'

'And that *someone* has connections in high places,' said Will.

'It would seem so. The killing must have been *organised* – contracted and managed by someone in power.'

Tom and Will paused for breath. It was as if they had been riding hard with fields and hedges rushing by them. Their rapid reasoning had not been free of several assumptions, but the place to which it had brought them was uncomfortably real. They were contemplating a ruthless and painstaking murder; and whoever was behind it was perhaps at that very moment sitting back and smiling in satisfaction, no doubt feeling safely distanced from the crime.

During the pause, Widow Trotter took the opportunity to ask the inevitable question.

'And what is Bufo's role in this, do you think? Is he the key, or simply a distraction?'

Tom frowned slightly at having to contemplate that poisonous figure yet again.

'Perhaps the composing-stick and the manuscript of the *Curse* were there as properties merely... But who can say? This is something we need to find out. Discovering the identity of Bufo might unlock the whole plot.'

'We keep coming back to the idea of a plot, don't we,' said Widow Trotter, not without a degree of pleasurable anticipation. 'Perhaps this should guide what we do?'

'Yes,' said Will. 'We need to plan our course of action. Activity simply for the sake of doing something has to be avoided.'

'There's such a tangle of possibilities,' she said. 'We must *follow the threads* and see where each of them leads.'

Within a few seconds all three of them had lapsed into silent thought. Will lifted his head toward the ceiling and half-closed his eyes; Tom took a sip of his orangeade and stared down into the glass; and Widow Trotter scrutinised the remnants of cold ragout beginning to coagulate on the plates, as if searching for a pattern.

What was the true story? They would not save John Morphew unless they could discover it. They had to find the clew through the labyrinth and follow it – and hope things would soon become clearer.

It was Widow Trotter who broke the contemplative calm.

'I think I need to consult my friends in the Garden!...'

Tom and Will bestirred themselves and looked at her.

'... I must sniff out any dirty gossip concerning our Mr Emmet – the *enigmatic Emmet!* If he did have a Covent Garden connection, then we need to know it. And on Monday, Tom, you can find out more from Mr Barnard the punctilious compositor. I can't help but think the more we know of Emmet the closer we'll come to the centre of the maze. And you, Will... Perhaps you should try and discover the secrets of the virtuous Lady Norreys and her precious pocket-book? That will be an exceptionally sensitive task, given what it may contain – if the thing indeed still exists. Your friend Mr Sumner, playing the anxious and protective brother, might be pushed to reveal a little more? We know Emmet was involved in furtive dealings, and my nose tickles when I think about what that pocket-book might hold. Emmet knew its secrets, and your Mr Sumner *knew* that he knew. From what you've said about the book, a lady's honour may be the least of it. But whatever the contents, could it be enough for someone to have had Emmet *killed?*'

Mary Trotter paused, suddenly aware that Tom and Will were gazing at her in silent wonderment. At least that was how she chose to interpret it. She hadn't meant to take charge in such a masterful way, but after watching Elias these many years she had slipped naturally into the role of a constable instructing the Watch. The idea gave her a vivid mental image of Tom and Will all muffled up in heavy greatcoats with large hats pressed down over their eyes, and their legs squat and heavily booted – perhaps she should buy each of them a lantern and staff?... She smiled to herself.

The eager twosome, however, were viewing themselves more heroically.

'You are the Marlborough of Covent Garden, Mrs T!'

Tom saluted her in military style, and Will followed suit: 'Colonel Bristowe and Colonel Lundy at your command!'

'Oh dear, I've been issuing orders, haven't I!'

'No apology needed, Mrs T. We're both agreed that you will make the ideal Field Commander. And I'm sure you'll deploy your battalions to brilliant effect.'

Mrs Trotter was relieved to know that in spite of their heart-sinking situation the mood could still be one of hope and good humour. Their conference had offered a dark picture of human nature and brought a sickening scene into view. Sweetness and light seemed a long way off; but they were surely out there somewhere, and she was determined that her chocolate house under its new symbol of the bay-tree would do its bit to enlighten and civilise. This train of thought was the work of a moment. Within seconds she had recalled herself to the matter in hand.

'I'm conscious, gentlemen, that much of this has to wait until Monday; but time is pressing and I know you're both impatient for action – as I am too!... Given the urgency, I'm wondering if we can make our first moves *tomorrow?...*'

There was a sparkle in her eyes as she spoke.

'... With the Good Fellowship closed, I'll be free to call on my more talkative friends. They know what's blowing in the wind and will chatter away happily – especially on a Sunday when there's little else anyone *can* do! We have a nice arrangement: I hand over my small change of gossip and receive theirs, and an hour later we're all in profit.'

For a moment Will looked alarmed.

'Be careful, Mrs T – don't hand over too much!'

'I swear to spend prudently – I have a good supply, I assure you... But I also think we have to extend our range. My net can't reach the drawing-rooms of St James's, and something tells me that we'll need to peer into *high places...*'

She was now looking directly at Tom.

'... This isn't a back-street crime. It touches people of power and influence – the Ministry, even the Court. We must be prepared to follow where the trail leads us.'

She saw that Tom was responding with a slow nod.

'I've been considering, Mrs T, and wondered if I should make some use of my *connections?…*'

He tried to give the word an ironic emphasis, but this only made him sound more precious. He glanced at Will.

'… As it happens, I've arranged to give the wig an airing in Pall Mall tomorrow. The plan is to accompany my aunt and uncle to church in the morning and pass the day with them. I thought it high time I mingled again with the illustrious Pophams! I've not seen Uncle Jack for weeks, and he may be happy to retail some fresh Court gossip. Who knows but I may catch a whiff of Bufo? It would be useful to know what's stirring.'

'Your aunt and uncle will surely go to St James's Church in Piccadilly?' asked Mrs Trotter.

Tom took a deep breath.

'I think the plan tomorrow is for the *Royal Chapel*, and then a turn in Hyde Park – if the weather is amenable.'

Widow Trotter felt a flush beginning to rise.

'*Royalty* and the *Ring?* You'll be quite the thing, Mr Bristowe – and in a coronet coach! Will you have an *equipage?*'

'It will certainly be a coach. Cousin Lavinia will be of the party, so we'll be four.'

'Ah, the glittering tribe of the *beau monde!*' said Will. 'It has its charms, but I can see my father scowling at the very notion. For myself, I've always considered parading in the park to be a harmless show. Where would the satirists be without it? Perhaps Tom's *wig* will be satire enough?'

Tom was looking a little grave.

'I think my mind will be on other things. I'll not forget what I need to do.'

'I have a thought!' said Will. 'As you're venturing over into St James's… Sir Charles and Lady Norreys have a house in Charles Street, just off the square, hardly a minute's walk from the Pophams. Do you think the families may be known to each other?'

'That's distinctly possible,' said Tom. 'I'll try to find a way of mentioning her name, and see what the response is.'

'This is falling into place nicely,' said Mrs Trotter. 'A Sunday of religious observance, polite leisure, and family intimacy is exactly what's called for.'

'But what about you, Will?' said Tom. 'I'm sorry you can't easily be included. If I'd known when I arranged this...'

'No, no, you have an important job to do, and it's best you go alone. I think my time will be profitably spent if I pay a family visit of my own. The old man will be up in Hackney, and it will be worth the walk. I have a standing invitation. I'll have to humour my dull aunts and sit through a long sermon at the meeting-house, but afterwards there's usually a generous roast and a good fire. He is punctilious about the spirit, but tends to treat the body with more indulgence. Don't you think I might bide my time till the mood is *mellow*, and – delicately of course – introduce the topic of Morphew... ?'

'The Old Bailey!'

Widow Trotter and Tom understood the import. News of such a sensational slaying might travel fast, and if Will could gauge something of how the Emmet murder was being spoken of... ? It had already occurred to each of them that when John Morphew's case came to trial at the Bailey, Mr Justice Lundy was likely to be on the bench.

Although they had done less than justice to Mrs Dawes's repast, their dinner-table conference had been productive. They now had a clearer view of things, and plans were in place for the morrow. It seemed their day of rest was going to be an extremely busy one: Widow Trotter would scour around the Garden and gather what she could from her friends; Tom would mingle in high life and be alert for any chit-chat and scandal about the

Court; and Will would adopt the sober garb of the dissenting brethren and probe the rigours of the Law. They finally agreed to meet together for Sunday supper at nine o'clock – unless of course something very special detained any of them – and they hoped that by then they might all have something to report.

As she opened the parlour door, Widow Trotter paused and looked solemn. This was not in character, but she felt the situation demanded it.

'We know we're about something very serious, gentlemen, and that a man's life may depend on how we conduct ourselves in the coming days – on our resourcefulness, tact and vigilance – perhaps on our boldness and impertinence too! But I would not have us sink into gloom. That would dampen our spirits and dull our minds. On the contrary, we must preserve *good humour* above all. If we relish our task we shall perform it better!'

The widow's injunction struck home. No general ever roused his troops to better effect. Tom and Will smiled on her reassuringly – and Tom gave an impudent wink. It was clear she need have no fear. All that remained was to issue their marching orders for the morrow:

'Into battle, gentlemen!... And *follow the threads!*'

Sunday

1 February 1708

Chapter Fourteen

THAT SUNDAY MORNING at St James's Palace the chapel sermon was short and unmemorable, partly because everyone was anxious for the main business to begin. They had reached the point in the service when the Queen would *receive the sacrament*. This brought a lot of awkward shuffling while visitors were ushered out so that the remaining courtiers could settle themselves and perhaps find better seats facing into the central aisle. The scale of the place was cramped as if to discourage ecclesiastical display. There was no decorative plasterwork or lavish carving, and there was a marked absence of flying cherubs. It was just a rather plain, serviceable room. Given its name, the Chapel Royal ought to have been a place of regal magnificence, but in reality it appeared small and dowdy. When, however, the disappointed eyes turned upward they found a coffered ceiling covered in royal coats of arms, which hung overhead like a sumptuous Tudor cloak. The interlocking patterns allowed the mind to wander across its intricacies and notice how contrasting shapes might fit neatly together. Holbein's panels were unshowy: they offered no transcendent monarchs greeting the gods as old friends, no blowzy queens riding nonchalantly on golden clouds, but only a repeated pattern of armorial escutcheons, 'honours' not won in battle but achieved through dynastic marriage.

At ground level, all the finery was provided by the people – or rather by their clothing. Here were glowing ochres and ambers, satins embossed with filigree-work, fine silks and scatterings of exquisite lace. The dowdiness of the room only heightened the interest of the assembled courtiers in each other. But for all the wealth on display the scene still had an English sobriety. It was no birth-night ball, and so the brightness was tempered by elegant understatement. Instead of garish colours, the tones were darker, and effects were achieved through nicely placed detail. Here a fine ring or watch-ribbon caught the eye, and there a little fox-skin muff, or a delicate ruffle offsetting plum-coloured velvet. The women were equally fine.

Viscount Melksham's party was comfortably settled. The four of them had their backs to the dark wainscoting, and their raised seats gave them a good view of everything. Uncle Jack sat slightly forward and looked around, his hands resting on his cane which he tapped gently. It was not an impatient gesture but something closer to a Sunday contentment, a response to the quieter pulse of things. Beneath the lively curls of an ample dress wig his face wore a benign expression, which lightened further when a chamber organ began to sound, joined by a theorbo-lute, and then two voices, alto and bass, in harmony. His fingers slipped naturally into the rhythm. 'Praise the Lord, O my Soul!'

At his side, a youthful Lady Melksham sat more upright, held by the tight stays which encouraged her to remain composed and erect while her eyes darted about eagerly. As she observed the people seated opposite, her cheeks showed the hint of a smile. The effect was enlivened by a tiny black patch carefully placed beneath her left temple, which lifted slightly and gave her a quizzical expression. It could have been critical scrutiny or sheer delight, but in Sophia Popham's case it was a mixture of both.

She turned her head and whispered to a tall girl seated next to her who seemed to be finding the spectacle less riveting.

'Don't droop, Lavinia! Hold your head up. Quick eyes, quick mind! You should be taking everything in.'

In response, Lavinia Popham stirred herself slightly, but despite the occasion she had no desire to take *anything* in. She would rather things stayed where they were. But her step-mother would not be discouraged.

'Look what an elegant political huddle we have over there! Quite a miniature cabinet! This is clearly the place to be. Which of them wins the prize for the biggest wig, would you say?...'

Somehow Lavinia's mind couldn't engage with such niceties, and again she said nothing.

'... I think Mr St John's coiffure is the tallest – he's the one sitting with Mr Harley, in the claret-coloured coat. What a fine sight the two of them make! I wonder what stratagems they're devising?'

Lady Melksham began to feel she was talking to herself – as indeed she was – and so she went quiet. This allowed a little more space for the music, which was beginning to fill the small chapel. With the alto voice soaring above, the words of the Psalm continued to weave between the two performers, high and low in turn: 'Thou art become exceeding glorious; thou art clothèd with majesty and honour...' The musicians were hidden and the effect was other-worldly. As the moments passed, Lavinia Popham felt an increasing appreciation for those simple unhurried melodies that seemed to have a dimension of their own. She was able to live in the music for a while.

Seated to Lavinia's right, the fourth member of the party was absorbed in the display, but unlike his restless Aunt Sophia, Tom Bristowe was silent and thoughtful. After all, for him the event had more genuine novelty. The Pophams moved routinely in this courtly world, but he could still feel its strangeness and fascination, *clothèd with majesty*. His own clothes were smart and correct as befitted the royal occasion, but rather than wearing them, he somehow felt they were wearing him. He had to live up to their pretensions and present them to best advantage. His coat in a deep powder blue gave a good effect, and open to the sixth button it allowed the cream steenkirk cravat to tumble gracefully down over the ivory waistcoat. The black silk stockings were especially sleek and comfortable. That was all very satisfactory. However, he was at the mercy of his accoutrements. The full black wig appeared to be behaving itself, though it made his left ear itch annoyingly, which discouraged further head movement. The thing was a bit out of curl but he had done his best and had powdered it with dried ink, and now the sooty smell seemed to be irritating his nose and making him suppress a sneeze. He knew that would be disastrous and upset the wig's precarious equilibrium, so he held it in. His silver-hilted sword scraped the floor whenever he shifted in his seat; and he didn't quite know what to do with his calfskin gloves. Otherwise, he was enjoying the show and was taking the opportunity to scrutinise the congregation.

Tom overheard his Aunt Sophia's last remark and his curiosity was aroused. He glanced across at Mr Harley and Mr St John, who were seated further along the chapel near the altar, and even at that distance he could feel their magnetism. In stature Harley cut an unprepossessing figure, but there was something in his look, perhaps the half-amused curl of the lower lip, that brought his face to life. He was motionless but intensely watchful, and seemed ready to break into lively talk at any moment. Beside him was the contrasting presence of Henry St John, the Secretary-at-War, a handsome, well-built young man with a bold, imperious countenance, who mastered the Commons with his rhetoric as much as Harley did with his manoeuvrings behind the scenes. Together they were a formidable team.

Suddenly Tom was disconcerted to realise that Mr St John was looking over in their direction – indeed staring directly at them. It was unmistakable, and it was a look of sustained interest that was evidently meant to be seen. But before he could puzzle this out, a small commotion to his right indicated that the royal party was rising to its feet and readying itself. The sacramental climax of the service had finally come.

Her Majesty rose, and all eyes were turned on her as she began to approach the altar. In this confined space the pageantry lost some of its effect; but a degree of dignity was still possible and it was curious to see a royal occasion – usually such a distant thing – from close at hand. He could hear the creaking shoes and even caught the various perfumes as the retinue wafted by. It was a brief procession with the symbolic regalia of monarchy leading the way: the sword of State first, followed by four crowned sceptres, each being held by a favoured courtier. And then, as something of a shock, came the physical Anne herself. The ample body was swathed in velvet, and it hobbled down the aisle with painful slowness, each step a concentrated effort. Tom could sense an iron will driving this woman on. Her face was fleshy and the dark eyes had a melancholy far-away look, but also a touch of the sensual that recalled her Uncle Charles. She gazed straight ahead at the altar, undeviating.

In her train were the maids of honour, whose glances were less fixed, except for one who walked almost alongside the Queen, discreetly steadying her on her arm. This was Abigail Masham, and although no look was exchanged, Anne's reliance on her was plain. It seemed an entirely natural gesture and one that was more human than ceremonial. The consecrated monarch was not immune from crippling rheumatism, especially on a damp morning at the beginning of February. However, from the other end of the chapel the two harmonious voices blew these mundane thought away, and the anthem came to a close with a remarkably buoyant vision: '... He maketh the clouds his chariot, and walketh upon the wings of the wind.'

With considerable difficulty the Queen was helped to kneel on a velvet cushion placed on the chancel step, and as her knee sank into it she looked down at the marble floor, seeming unconscious of anything around her. There was a pause, and all went still. It may have been a moment of reflective spiritual calm, or sheer exhaustion, or perhaps she was remembering that the heart of Bloody Mary was in its final resting-place directly beneath her...

After the ceremony, outside the chapel Tom and the Pophams gathered themselves under the colonnade, standing silently with all the others as the Queen and her women made their way towards the private rooms of the palace. Bows and curtsies rippled gradually along the row of people as if wanting to propel Her Majesty achingly forwards. She paused to have a word with Robert Harley who bowed very low and touched the ground with his hat, and then, eventually, after a few minutes, they were no longer in the royal presence.

At once the hubbub began. Now they were all like children released from school, relishing their freedom. Lively conversation happily resumed and very soon everyone was being warmed by gossip – the combustible fuel of court life – exchanging comments, interpreting looks and gestures, encouraging conjecture to grow, picking up news, assessing, disparaging. The Court always seemed to be more fun when the royal family wasn't there. The fringes were the place to be. The Pophams contributed their share and touched on a good range of topics: Lord Melksham was concerned that the absent Prince must again be ailing; Sophia thought the Queen looked a little homely and lacked grace; Lavinia felt bold enough to venture an opinion about the beauty of Dr Croft's music; and Tom wondered aloud whether Mr St John and Mr Harley might be at St James's that morning for a reason.

No sooner had he made the remark than he heard a loud, confident voice behind his shoulder.

'Well, Melksham! what news is stirring in Wiltshire? Stands Monkton where it did?'

Tom turned to see Henry St John himself beaming at them, and quickly took a step aside to make room. Sophia brightened, and Lavinia looked uneasy. Uncle Jack smiled in response.

'Indeed, Mr St John, the place is crumbling away nicely – although my wife is seldom there these days. You must come and inspect it this summer. Or will something bring you down to Wiltshire before the election?'

'No, but I'll be at Lydiard in June, and the good citizenry of Wootton Bassett will certainly glimpse me at some point – I always enjoy election dinners. It's good to show my face and reassure them their *member* is still in working order!'

It was spoken with a knowing emphasis. His expression didn't alter, but Tom caught a wickedness in his eyes and sensed a slight frisson run through the group. He noted that Lavinia began to blush. The St John family borough needed to be kept *warm*, and the folk at the Crown Inn at Wootton always enjoyed their MP's conviviality and ribald wit. Charming as ever, St John pressed briskly on.

'What news of Frank? Is he returned from the Tour?'

'Very nearly, indeed. We expect to have news of him at any moment. He should embark for Harwich on Wednesday, and the winds appear favourable.'

St John responded with a warm smile and continued to rush ahead. There was something of a force of Nature in him.

'Excellent! Does he still have thoughts of a seat? As you know, we're looking for a second member, and Wootton would be a secure base for him – until the Whigs finally take over the kingdom – and unless of course Frank has turned Whig himself?'

There was a serious intent behind St John's half-question. For the past eighteen months Tom's cousin Frank had been away on the Grand Tour – not the leisurely southern adventure across the Alps to Italy, but the more Protestant and potentially Whiggish version which took in the courts of Berlin and Vienna, and returned through Holland. The northern tour was the better preparation for a diplomatic or political career, and there was less danger of an impressionable youth succumbing to the Circean charms of carnival, courtesans, Catholicism, or the Italian opera. Especially with regard to the last of these, travelling across a European war zone was considered the safer alternative. In the Honourable Francis Popham's case (to judge by the accounts he sent home in increasingly assured German) the young man had survived the experience unscathed and was ready to launch himself into public life. In this, Henry St John would be an extremely valuable ally. The Wiltshire estates of the Pophams and the St Johns were only eight miles apart and combining their interests made excellent sense. Both men knew this, and so the Secretary-at-War and the Deputy Keeper of the Privy Purse found it appropriate to step aside at this point and discuss some matters of consequence. Sunday may have been a day of rest, but in St James's, politics and devotion were often entangled, and opportunity had to be seized.

Lady Melksham and Lavinia were by now whispering together – a little sharply it appeared – and so Tom hung back and had a few minutes to himself while they worked their way to an understanding. What a busy, negotiable world this was, in which large and petty matters sat side by side, and accident and design took turns to shape people's lives. He felt he was being drawn into it more than he might have wished, and perhaps it would finally claim him? Court manners were gracious and easy, but also artful. He looked around at the assembled company and saw figures with elegant outlines turning and gesturing to each other, conscious of their expression, address, bearing. But a few yards away he noticed an elegant couple set a little apart from the others. They stood completely still and observant, and he suddenly heard them exchange words in French. He caught the phrase *Ces gens-là!* and smiled to himself in sympathy. Yes, were these really *his* people? At that instant he thought of John Morphew and Mrs Trotter, and Will, his closest friend, and he imagined them standing with him now, looking askance at all the pride and pomp of the occasion, its carefully managed ritual, and its powerful frivolities. The satirist in him surged forwards and he scratched his ear in annoyance. His wig shifted slightly, but he didn't give it any thought. He had to remember the business in hand and not let this fascinating occasion become a distraction.

An hour earlier he had been eagerly anticipating the ride in Hyde Park – if nothing else, it would, as Will said, feed the satiric muse. But now his enthusiasm was waning, especially if his aunt and cousin were to be at loggerheads. He hated bickering even more than prattle about fashion, and there would probably be a good deal of both. He was already becoming impatient for dinner-time when he might be able to dig for useful information. Most importantly, he needed to be alone with his uncle; but Sophia and Lavinia might have some piquant gossip about Lady Norreys. The more he thought about the coterie of St James's the less unlikely it became. He looked at the two Popham ladies and saw with relief that all was now smiles between them. He took a step forwards, and they turned happily to him. His aunt spoke.

'I'm sorry Tom – we have been neglecting you terribly. You must forgive us! There was a little matter to be decided about our jaunt in the park, and that is now resolved. Lavinia will be more than happy to join us, won't you my child? And she has just heard that I shall be arranging singing lessons for her. Such an important accomplishment!'

Given their argument, Tom instantly wondered which of these had been the bribe and which the threat. He thought he knew, but decided to be cautious.

'You have such a sweet voice, cousin, and I'm sure art can only enhance it! I'm delighted we'll be a full party for the park – Lavinia and I are looking forward to commenting on the passing show. It will be amusing.'

Tom was pleased with himself. His friend Will couldn't have done better.

But before he could gauge his success, Mr St John and his uncle rejoined them, and they were smiling too. Diplomacy had evidently triumphed on both fronts. St John threw a sparkish look at Tom's bashful cousin.

'And how is Lavinia – she's becoming quite a beauty, is she not!...'

The conversation at once became polite. Compliments were given, graceful enquiries made, and at the appropriate moment Tom was formally introduced to the Secretary-at-War, who warmed even further when poetry was mentioned.

'That's excellent, Mr Bristowe! – I'll look for your name on a title-page before too long. I've been known to whistle "Celadon's Plea" – but that's a mere trinket. I'm sure you are capable of something much more substantial!'

Tom blushed to find Celadon the centre of attention, and hardly knew whether to take St John's remark as a compliment – though it seemed to have been intended so. He glanced at his uncle, who was listening closely, and was relieved not to see a scowl of displeasure.

'I'll take that as the strongest encouragement, Sir,' he replied, with as much grace as he could muster.

'You know, *pastorals* are the coming thing, would you believe! Young Mr Pope has produced a wonder in that line, and Will's is humming with admiration – Tonson is about printing them in his miscellany. And that satirical rogue Swift says he's going to write some *urban* pastorals – I wonder what those will be? It's a typically wicked idea! Anyway, I wish you luck, Mr Bristowe – I really do. Poetry is no mean profession – and much less precarious than politics!'

St John held out his hand, and Tom had to stop himself from clutching it in both of his. He said nothing, but was conscious of his uncle taking note. His heart was beating almost audibly. Suddenly a lively jaunt in the Ring appeared a glorious thing, and he was more than ready for it. There would be a lot to observe and store away!

The Pophams now seemed to be at the hub of things, for at that moment the great Robert Harley joined them. The Secretary of State was clearly troubled about something and betrayed a nervous busyness that suggested he wished to be elsewhere. But he did his best to offer the expected pleasantries, and there were a few rapid exchanges. Harley's words tumbled over each other, interspersed with nods and thoughtful glances. Then, as soon as was possible without awkwardness, he made to depart and gestured his colleague to go with him. He touched St John on the sleeve while giving a turn with his other hand.

'If you'll excuse us, Lady Melksham, I'm afraid Mr St John and I have to be elsewhere as a matter of urgency. I hope we'll be able to meet again soon under less pressing circumstances.'

He bowed, as did St John, clearly a little nonplussed. But in the end both ministers of the Crown were able to take a prompt yet polite leave. The Pophams stood silent, to some extent flattered but also intrigued by what had just happened. Tom looked his uncle squarely in the face.

'Well, uncle, it seems a statesman is never off duty, even on the sabbath!'

'No Tom. That's why I usually try to keep clear of politics. But as you have seen just now, sometimes the nettle has to be grasped!'

Tom was about to reply when he saw his uncle's attention had been caught. He turned round and noticed that Mr Harley and Mr St John were being ushered by a footman into a door that led to the royal apartments. Perhaps the two of them were to take a genial coffee with Her Majesty – or was there more far-reaching business in train? Tom and his uncle exchanged a knowing glance. This was something else that he would enjoy talking about after dinner.

Chapter Fifteen

WHILE TOM WAS in St James's experiencing the formalities of court life, Mary Trotter was in a more relaxed mode in Covent Garden, being entertained with a glass of ratafia and a generous helping of local news. For Garden gossip, her old friend Mrs Ménage was a dependable source – 'dependable' in the sense of 'always flowing': the reliability tended to vary according to the beverage that flowed with it. Late on this Sunday morning, her special brandy, which she infused *à la française* with grape juice, lemon balm and hyssop, was encouraging lively and fluent speech – in herself and her visitor.

Adèle Ménage had once seen good times, and in the eighties her Covent Garden bagnio had attracted the finest gentlemen. But gradually the place had sunk to a bathhouse brothel and everything had remorselessly decayed: the fabric, the furnishings, the clients, and the trade. One or two of her girls were still in business, scattered around the Garden, and after she gave up the premises and moved to nearby Katherine Street she was still around to help them or offer refuge. But now she was reduced to a couple of rooms. This one was high-ceilinged and reasonably large, but cluttered with too much furniture. Thick rugs hung over the chairs and an elaborately carved sofa was squeezed up against an oak table covered in boxes. A delftware William and

Mary huddled together on top of a painted harpsichord, and beside it a bullfinch trilled insistently from its cage. Things may have become faded, but there was still a substantial quality to it all and a rich sense of style. It was only the space that had shrunk.

Mrs Trotter had to admit that her morning had been disappointing. She had mingled with the congregation at the church on the piazza – the other St Paul's – but her gleanings had been thin. It seemed the local apprentices had been creating mayhem with their football, as several windows in the square bore witness; one of the market stallholders had won a prize in the lottery and was giving away all his goods; there was some titillating conjecture about the parish curate's *amours* (a continuing story of several months' standing); and one of Lord Gameson's footmen had absconded overnight with most of the silver cutlery. It was all entertaining but very light fare. Whenever she casually inquired if they knew of a Mr Emmet who had called in at the Good Fellowship and had 'dropped something valuable from his pocket' there was no response. But here in Katherine Street, talking freely in this comfortable dusty room, she had hopes of something more substantial. If John Emmet did have a 'connection' in Covent Garden – and if it meant what she hoped it meant, then who better than Adèle Ménage to have wind of him?

But Widow Trotter bided her time, encouraging the flow of talk and contributing generously to it. She offered tit-bits on the transformation of the Good Fellowship into the Bay-Tree Chocolate House, and what new treats were in store. Mrs Ménage listened to her friend's plans with delight. Her eyes, grey and slightly hooded, sparkled with interest, and her wrinkles began rippling joyously round her face. '*Superb*,' she said with a lingering French intonation, 'it will be *superb*.'

For her, it was good to hear of somewhere that was rising in its ambitions and to learn about the new décor and Mrs

Dawes's ideas for the menu. Taking things further, Mrs Trotter risked describing the incident of Thursday's arrest and how the Watch had taken away the publisher for questioning. Word of the murder had evidently not spread here as yet, so on that she remained silent. Mrs Ménage was concerned.

'Ah, *Marie!* Is that another good gentleman for the pillory? I deplore it – such a waste of fruit and vegetables. Alas for our speech! There is so much we cannot say, and now we have only our thoughts that are our own... Indeed I begin to be fearful myself. *Zut!* I shall soon be able to insult no-one – sedition lurks round every corner!... Can I not call a lord a *nincompoop* – though he be the biggest fool in the world? And can a minister not be a *blockhead?* And in parliament... ah, parliament! Stop my mouth!... is it decreed there are to be no *sots* and *dolts* – no *dunderheads,* or even *ninnyhammers?*' Mrs Ménage flung out the words with obvious relish. 'I tell you what you must do, Marie... if your friend is put in the pillory you must take him one of your Mrs Dawes's exquisite dishes and feed it to him – and with a glass of your best claret also! Place a lace *serviette* around the gentleman's neck, and let him dine like a king! How the people will laugh!'

The image was an appealing one; but even as Mrs Trotter nodded and smiled broadly she was picturing a darker scene, and one not featuring a serviette. At the thought of John Morphew in his cell, the smile began to weigh heavy on her cheeks. At the same moment she saw her friend's looks lose their gaiety.

'Something is in the air, Marie. I feel it... It is as if the walls are watching us... Treason we speak!'

Mrs Ménage shuddered slightly and reached for her glass. There was an element of the performer about her, and for the briefest second Mrs Trotter imagined a flicker of limelight on her face.

'... You know poor simple Mortimer, who cries his wares at the end of this street, against Drury Lane?... Yesterday two young ruffians beat him, and took away the little pamphlet he was hawking. Ah! They broke his arm and belaboured the creature about the head – but it was the paper they desired… it was a strange thing – a *prognostication*…'

Mrs Ménage sipped her ratafia conspiratorially and lowered her voice as though there was a spy hiding in the tall armoire behind her chair.

'… It was a furious prophecy, written against the Whigs and consigning them as a body to *Hell!* What a terrible idea, Marie! I did not see it, but they say that is what he was crying. The poor soul had hardly taken his station but he was attacked.'

Widow Trotter tried to remain calm. This must surely be *Bufo's Magic Glass?* Once again it was the poor hawker who was the victim. It was evidently not a spontaneous assault. Was the attack a public warning? Whatever the case, it confirmed that the Whigs were determined to silence Bufo in whatever way they could.

Mrs Ménage saw her friend's interest was aroused.

'How strange it is, Marie! You know, when I left my beloved France I was fleeing from tyranny – the tyrant Louis! In that place I was an *hérétique*, and England was the place of liberty. But now I worry that things are changing. Here indeed we have no more the tyranny of government – but in its place I begin to see a tyranny of faction, the violence of *party*. It is certainly a paradox: what assures our freedom also brings us conflict.'

'Alas, Adèle, you may be right. We have liberty to speak, but only anonymously. We must be careful what we put our name to. Our masters may have given up the old licensing, but now they police the press *after* printing!'

'And it is the parties who do the policing! We know that what delights the Tories is treason for the Whigs, and what cheers the Whigs makes the Tories shake with fury! None can agree on what your *sedition* is!'

'Unless of course you quote Mr Locke and speak about *the rights of the people*. Then you're beyond the bounds. Look at the fate of poor Mr Tutchin – beaten to death in gaol...'

While her friend shivered in sympathy, Widow Trotter pressed on and carried the point further in her intended direction.

'... And now of course there's such a trade in private papers – stolen, lost, or sold. Even our thoughts may be taken from us and broadcast across the land. There are people who traffic in such things. They have contacts with the printers, and the more sensational the secret the better they like it. I'm sure Covent Garden is not without its brokers in letters and diaries.'

Mrs Ménage gave her a confiding look.

'You speak truer than you know, Marie. You can imagine what a price my own *memoirs* would command! I do not say I may not be tempted: times are hard, and I have had offers, and attractive ones...'

Adèle Ménage suddenly assumed the mantle of a fashionable Parisian courtesan, and turned her head elegantly toward the cupboard. Mrs Trotter wondered whether it was to acknowledge the location of her *cache* of papers or simply to emphasise her still striking profile.

'Do you mean you have begun writing your memoirs? They could make your fortune, Adèle!'

'True enough. But alas – if I wrote down what I know, they would also drive me into exile again. No, no! I dare not commit my history to the page... But I do have letters. And you know how prized such things are today.'

'You say you have had an offer for them?'

Mrs Ménage hesitated slightly, torn between pride and discretion.

'Yes, for one correspondence in particular – which, believe me, I keep well hidden! Someone I cannot name – even to you, Marie.'

Mrs Trotter felt she was on the brink. Now was the moment.

'This offer… was it perhaps from a Mr *Emmet?*'

It was a daring card to play. There was an awkward pause. Mrs Ménage had been holding her hand close to her chest. But now the lead had been given, and she accepted the invitation with good grace.

'I see you have encountered him. A busy, wheedling little fellow! Though not without charm, I have to say.'

'Yes, he came into the coffee house last week. I'd not met the man before. How did you encounter him?'

'Through the daughter of one of my old girls. Do you remember Betsy Primrose? What a name! She was always an innocent and never made the best of herself. And her daughter Kate is the same. I try to look out for the poor lamb, and she survives somehow. She works in Vinegar Yard under the name of *Clarissa* – that shows some ambition at least! It is a well-located *bower,* though her clientèle is fairly low. But perhaps things are about to change for her. Believe it or believe it not – she is very *taken* with our Mr Emmet, and he with her!…'

Widow Trotter felt a stab of sadness, but kept silent. Her friend at this moment needed no prompting.

'… This Mr Emmet – do you know? – is a printer, and he has high connections in the trade. He is a member of the Stationers' Company, and can talk with authors and publishers as an equal. He does work for the Ministry also…'

Clearly poor John Emmet had presented himself impressively.

'… Well, he is looking to purchase letters and memoirs, which can be politely disguised as romance. They sell well, and he thinks such things will become wildly popular. Have you seen *The Lady's Pacquet of Letters?* This is a book he was concerned with, and it took the Town last year… I must be careful what I say, but I think Mr Emmet is planning something new in that kind. I know he would love to see what I have!…'

Mrs Ménage drew her shawl more tightly around her as if conscious that she still had something that men might want.

'... Young Kate suggested that he should come and see me. But I fear I was able to give him no encouragement. The *consideration* was not what I had hoped. He told me he would see if a more generous offer might be made, and that is how we have left the business.'

Mary Trotter took another sip of her brandy, which was piquant to the tongue, and a vivid picture began to form in her mind. It appeared that Emmet had more than dipped into the manuscript trade, and she wondered how far John Morphew had encouraged his dealings. It had led him into a dangerous area. Such materials gave people a hold over others and could involve matters of reputation, exposure, accusation and threat. And when politics were added to the mix... John Emmet had been playing with fire.

'You say Mr Emmet did some work for the Ministry, and...'

'He does still!' interjected Mrs Ménage. 'Indeed I receive the impression that our Mr Emmet is busy in that way. I suspect he is on the trail of something! I know he wished to confide in me, but he became secretive and I could get no more from him. Nobody must follow his track – he is *Monsieur le Fourmi* indeed!'

She gave a warm, throaty laugh at her ingenious joke, and Mrs Trotter saw its import: the busy, ant-like Emmet had delighted in rumours and winding trails. She wondered how much he had confided in his *Clarissa* and what he might have entrusted to her. Perhaps Kate had come to share his hopes and ambitions? At that moment Widow Trotter knew she had to pay a visit to Vinegar Yard. It would be a difficult and troubling interview, and she would be the bearer of the worst news. Compunction pricked her, and she hesitated. Did she have the right to play that role? But poor Kate Primrose must learn the truth very soon – or she may perhaps know it already...

She realised Mrs Ménage was looking at her inquisitively.

'You are pensive, Marie! Let me give you some more *ratafie*. It is especially good, is it not? Will you stay for a little dinner? I want to hear more about your wonderful Bay-Tree. And before you go I have an exquisite *digestif* for you – it is the latest news about our curate!'

It was almost dusk when Mary Trotter finally left Katherine Street after what turned out to be a perfect 'little dinner.' Her host still relished good taste, and the spiced pumpkin soup followed by a roast pheasant with some sweet carrots was simple and delicious. Even the promised *digestif* did not disappoint. Adèle Ménage's tale of the curate's adventures was embroidered with the finest comic detail and indisputably took gossip into the realm of art.

There was a distinct pungency to Vinegar Yard, which told Widow Trotter that she was in a poorly-lit alley accessible to anyone walking home from Drury Lane Theatre. The elegant crowds either passed it by or paid it only the briefest visit. The place could hardly avoid being sordid and depressing with its leaning tenements that had survived the Great Fire almost touching at roof-level. The air seemed to have been squeezed out of it, and the humans were compressed also, mostly into single rooms – if they were lucky. In a city that was often troubled with heavy smoke, Vinegar Yard collected the soot. It was closed in on itself, and the doorways seemed to crouch inwards too as if shunning visitors.

And yet, as she peered around she saw that some efforts had been made to spruce the place up a little. Mr Filkins's tallow-chandler's shop made a presentable appearance, and a small tub of laurel stood by a painted door further along on the right. She couldn't help smiling at the picture. A defiant individual with a little flair had anticipated her, and she wondered if it was an omen for the Bay-Tree? It made her more determined than ever to carry her plans through. But at this moment she could not fend off the smell – dank and fusty – which hung over Vinegar Yard like an old blanket.

After several inquiries she was directed to a narrow entry at the far end of the court, and she peered inside. It was dark, but along the wall, where flimsy laths showed through the peeling plaster, she could make out several little wooden signs nailed up alongside a few more temporary pieces of paper. As her eyes adjusted to the gloom she was able to decipher the word 'Clarissa' painted in an elaborate hand on one of the signs, directing the visitor to the fourth floor. Widow Trotter suddenly felt her mouth go dry, but she paused only for a moment before stepping determinedly in. She would not turn back and took a deep, unpleasant breath as she trod carefully along the passage to the stairs.

The steps were uneven and steep, and random noises seemed to emerge through the walls of the place. After the second floor the staircase narrowed further, but now progress was made easier by a thick rope strung in loops along the wall. She felt her way upwards. It was like being on shipboard, and the structure began to sway and creak as she mounted higher. She could not help thinking of John Emmet making his way up these benighted stairs to Kate Primrose's refuge, his heart beating loudly just like hers.

It had been pitch dark, but she now began to detect a slight glimmering that showed from above like an eery will-o-the-wisp drawing her on. And as she turned to make the final ascent she was jolted to see a human hand holding a candle. There was silence only for a moment, before a harsh voice broke the peace.

'What do you want!'

It was a simple question, but had the force of a threat.

'I have come to see Kate.'

'Who sends you? What do you want of her?'

Widow Trotter paused on the stairs. A male figure was blocking her path, standing on the edge of the top step and looking down at her. A narrow-brimmed hat was pulled over his brows, which gave him an almost comical appearance, but the bulging cloth bag that dangled from his other hand lent a sinister touch.

'She is no longer here! Clarissa has left. You've had a wasted journey.'

The man remained stock-still in his commanding position. He was clearly expecting her to turn round and begin making her way back down the stairs, but with that figure hovering behind her it was not a manoeuvre she wanted to make. Better stand her ground, she thought. And she had to think quickly.

'I've just come from her friend Mrs Ménage. She is worried about Kate and has asked me to call on her. I hope she's not unwell?'

The question was politely framed in the hope that looks were deceptive and this man might not be the thief he gave every appearance of being. There was an unsettling pause while the candlestick began waving to and fro over her head. He was examining her features and clothes.

'So, you are a friend of Adèle Ménage?'

The candle lit up the man's face for an instant, enough to give a glimpse of a grinning mouth. It was only the briefest flicker, so it was hard to tell if this was a friendly look or a menacing one.

'Let us go down to my room, shall we?...'

Widow Trotter felt a surge of relief.

'... I am two floors down. Here, take my candle.'

A few minutes later she was seated in an unsteady armchair in a small but comfortable room lit by two pairs of smoking tallow candles. The man had introduced himself as Joseph Quinlan, a clerk at the Excise Office; and though there was a lingering disquiet in his manner and a nervous look in his eyes, he no longer appeared threatening. And at the mention of Kate Primrose he seemed almost relieved to speak.

'Yes, poor Kate's in a lot of trouble… but I can't say *what* precisely. Something bad has happened, and she ran from here not two hours ago – the only things she took were a canvas bag and her heavy coat. She told me she wasn't *ever* coming back – very distressed she was. I asked her where she was going, but she said it was best I didn't know… It was bad what that ruffian did to her – I didn't hear her cry out at the time, but I found her sobbing on the stairs. I've just been up to her room to see what I can salvage – in case she decides to return, you understand, and to keep her things safe… But she has precious little. She's been entangled in something. I blame that sneaking friend of hers. The little man was always popping up here and he spoilt her trade. But she thought he was a real gent, and I know he made her promises. But he struck me as a slippery fellow…'

The clerk was running on at speed, offering brief jottings rather than a connected account. It took Mrs Trotter a few minutes to settle him down and extract a coherent story from him.

Earlier that afternoon Kate Primrose had received a visitor who had threatened her and searched her room looking for some papers.

'He burnt her on the hand – branded her! But she told him she knew nothing. She put him on a false trail, and finally he left in a wild state. Poor Kate was lucky he didn't murder her. But she knew he'd be back once the scent ran cold, and so she didn't dare stay a moment longer. She told me she'd hidden the papers in a place they could never find, and would make sure they never would!'

'Do you think she might have taken them with her?'

'She was clutching a bag. If she took the papers away they would have been inside it. Otherwise, they are still in her room.'

Widow Trotter tried to see the larger picture. If they were such incendiary documents then she doubted Kate would leave them behind. She suspected Joseph Quinlan had himself been making a search, and this gave her an excuse to ask if she might help him look for the secret hiding-place, if there was one. The clerk was obviously uneasy at the suggestion; but knowing that she had caught him removing Kate's possessions he thought it prudent to agree.

The result was that Widow Trotter and the clerk soon found themselves in the attic room, tapping at the walls and examining floorboards. It was not dignified – indeed it was a kind of violation, and Mrs Trotter felt embarrassed at the pathetic furnishings of Clarissa's bower. The bed occupied much of the room, and there was a flimsy elbow-chair, a three-legged stool, and a small side-table bearing a few cups and plates. Alongside the rusty grate were a green chamber-pot, a single horse-shoe, and a toasting-fork with some half-toasted bread on the floor. While the clerk gave his attention to the floorboards, she examined the exposed bricks around the chimney and prodded the plasterwork, in the process scattering even more dust. A deal cupboard had already been wrenched away from the wall and was lying on its side. On a shelf by the table she noted an empty bottle of *Rosa Solis* and two mismatched glasses; and alongside them was another smaller bottle, also empty, which had held a cordial of a very different kind. She picked it up and read the label: *The Golden Unction* – 'a sovereign and infallible remedy which gives immediate ease to the most insufferable and tormenting pains, carries off any hard or malignant swellings, and is a wondrous cure for sore breasts and other distempers that affect the joints.' Her heart sank as she pictured Clarissa carefully anointing herself with the oil, and in that ritual perhaps seeking a balm for the pains of the spirit too.

After investigating every nook and cranny, Mrs Trotter and Mr Quinlan looked resignedly at each other. Nothing was to be found – at least by them. He professed to have no idea where Kate might have gone, and she assured him she would let him know of any news. She had gained the impression that he did have some concern for the girl's welfare. But now there was nothing further to be done or said. The clerk graciously offered to make her a pot of coffee, but she didn't wish to stay any longer. She was tired, and the thought of her warm and comfortable home was suddenly irresistible. She took her leave as quickly as she could and began the walk back to Red Lion Court.

Her investigations around the Garden had turned out to be surprisingly fruitful. It was clear that John Emmet had antagonised some important people. He had been prying into highly delicate areas and arousing suspicion, and thanks to him the unfortunate Kate was now in considerable danger. Once settled in the comfort of her parlour she needed to think about how they might trace her and those papers, whatever they were.

She was longing to know how Tom and Will had been managing their inquiries. Will's day with his family in Hackney was unlikely to reveal much, perhaps, although his agile legal mind might return with something. But she was quietly hopeful that the Pophams in St James's would provide Tom with a few hints about Lady Norreys. Widow Trotter could see a way forward. Indeed, she was eager for nine o'clock to arrive when the three of them would share their discoveries. But until then she would sink into her comfortable chair and give it all some proper thought.

At the coffee-room door she reached into her pocket for the key and yawned widely. Suddenly a strange mental image flitted into her head – of Kate Primrose and Lady Norreys side by side, holding hands. An incongruous couple! She was becoming sleepy and the world of dreams was creeping up on her… But as she let herself in through the door it occurred to her that the key to the mystery could indeed be held by two women of the most contrasting fortunes. Perhaps the answer might lie in bringing their very different worlds together?

Chapter Sixteen

MEANWHILE, THE POPHAMS' jaunt out west to Hyde Park was deemed to have been a success. The delights of seeing had been nicely balanced with the joy of being seen. Afterwards over dinner it was agreed that for a chilly winter morning the Ring had acquitted itself well. At the beginning of February the liveries may not have glittered in late spring sunshine or glowed in the warmth of a summer afternoon; nevertheless there had been a great deal of elegance on display, and in terms of fashion the abundance of furs had compensated for the paucity of feathers.

After their earlier devotions at the Chapel Royal (paying a morning visit to their Stuart neighbours) another choreographed ritual had followed. The family strolled home along Pall Mall, and little more than an hour later on that cloudy Sunday, along with dozens of others, the Popham carriage with its four occupants was in the park, making its leisurely way around the clump of trees fenced off in the centre of the circle, passing and repassing the various coaches, chaises and caleches that were being guided at a stately pace in the counter direction. In the procession at the Ring everyone must keep moving. Hats were lifted, smiles and compliments exchanged, inquiries made, invitations offered – but the replies needed to be brief. This was a challenge to the wits, given that any repartee had to be delivered sharply before the vehicles had crossed. Sometimes several circuits were needed until a conversation could reach its point.

The slowly turning circles, inner and outer, moved past each other, generating a palpable electric charge. Every movement attracted notice as glances converged and gloved hands eloquently unfurled. A few brisk young gallants rode on horseback, where they could manoeuvre as they wished, weaving between the favoured carriages and trotting alongside any selected for special attention. Whenever one of the men leaned over to take a sidelong look he shifted slightly in his creaking saddle, conscious of his velvet riding-breeches and handsome French boots; and a rider showed his mettle by the deft handling of the reins as he curbed his spirited horse and made its graceful strength his own.

Although he was in a convivial family group, Tom had felt uncomfortable and longed to walk and talk more freely. He had therefore happily volunteered to bring them all cheesecakes from the Mince-Pie House, a custom that was part of any Hyde Park occasion. Nevertheless, the pageant of the Ring had fulfilled his expectations. The satirist in him was intrigued by the conscious observance of *etiquette* but also by the informal details of the scene. He had glimpsed Dr Swift gleefully devouring a syllabub; caught an apple-seller slipping a billet-doux into the hand of a lady as she bought some fruit; and – wonder of wonders – he had viewed the dazzling beauty of Lady Mary Pierrepont whose coach was escorted by admiring outriders and preceded by trotting footmen in coloured silks.

The attention of the company had been particularly caught by three ladies attired in stylish buttoned suits and heavy skirts, each mounted on a fine gelding with its tail and mane colourfully plaited. Glossy-coated and bright-eyed, and with their heads carried elegantly, the women were quite the match of their horses, and all eyes were drawn to them. Tom had noticed that one of them raised a whip in greeting as she passed, but the face was not familiar. There had been so much to see and so many names and faces to register, each prompting a comment or conjecture. What untold stories were lurking there – and what soon-to-be-told ones! But undoubtedly the star of the event had been Anne Bracegirdle, being carried in Lord Halifax's superb coach and six, leaning out of the window and smiling at the cries of greeting and the doffed hats of her admirers as if she were taking a bow as Shakespeare's Desdemona or Congreve's Millamant. In retirement she had simply found a larger stage. Tom could not help thinking of Widow Trotter and how amused she would be when he delivered his account to her.

At nearly three in the afternoon, dinner in the Pophams' townhouse in Pall Mall gave them all a chance to assess that morning's events. Lady Melksham especially had absorbed the whole scene. She was practised in reading the nuances of look and gesture, and it had been clear to her who was receiving notice and of what kind. A slight dipping of a Duchess's head might represent a precious acknowledgement, and a withdrawing of the eyes a deadly snub. A lordly countenance could be lit up or frozen as required, and attention bestowed or withheld. This made the whole thing a great strain for many of the participants, not least Lady Melksham herself whose snail-horn sensitivity to slights and confidences was a burden to her. She tried not to mind, and part of her relished this world where honour and reputation could fluctuate like the swishing of a fan. Yet Sophia Popham, *née* Doggett, could never sink into relaxed enjoyment, never be entirely pleased with who she was and what she had. Reassurance was regularly needed, and at dinner she gave evidence of this almost pathological alertness.

'I do think Lord Tring was looking very fine – how that young man has blossomed since the Tour! He has filled out really quite comfortably. He was such a spindly youth. I used to think him an absolute *rake* – in the agricultural sense... Well, he certainly gave you his attentions, Lavinia! He's now something of a bold-looking gentleman, and an assured horseman too. He presented himself extremely well, do you not think, Lavinia?'

'He was thoughtful indeed, and very *assured* altogether. But he has no chin – and I don't like the way his eyes measure you: it's as if he's a tailor and you've just walked into his shop.'

'No chin? What will the future Earl of Welwyn want with a chin? And I know of no tailor with eight thousand a year!'

'I know that an heir deserves some respect, mamma; but in public life a profile is not to be despised. Lord Tring is a worthy man, though his smile does distort his face so. I can only think that *Italy* has left its mark.'

Tom could not quite muffle a laugh, and he noticed his uncle smiling too. His cousin was shaping up to be a satirist herself.

'I don't know what you can mean, Lavinia – though I applaud your powers of observation. You'll have the chance to scrutinise him more closely later on.'

'Mamma! What do you mean?'

'Lord Tring has promised to look in for supper at around nine. So, chin or no chin, you'll be able to observe him mastering Mrs Briggs's ham and pickle – elegantly I trust. Please be courteous to him.'

Lavinia's face registered mixed emotions, and underneath the apprehension Tom detected a glint in the eye, enough to suggest that his cousin was promising herself more amusement at Lord Tring's expense. Part of him felt sorry for the young man, although he was relieved his own supper engagement was likely to be more engrossing.

The conversation continued, and Tom's attention began to wander. He was becoming impatient for when he could sit alone with his uncle and learn something useful. Meanwhile Aunt Sophia was in her element, and he had nothing at all to add or to ask. He only half-heard the names as she ran through their encounters at the Ring and the little incidents she had witnessed. The beautiful Lady Mary Pierrepont was in the roll-call of course, as was the slightly questionable Lady Rastell, who had evidently been encouraging the competing attentions of Mr Digby and the Honourable Mr Sturgis... Tom yawned rather too obviously – this really was becoming penitential... Sir Hector Plum (what an odd name – did he hear it right?)... Alderman Brocklehurst... Miss Arundel... Lady Norreys...

Tom was suddenly jolted back to consciousness, though he caught little more than the name. He listened hard.

'... her friends of course. And there's something rather dashing about a female *chevalier*, don't you think? Might I not ride the Ring myself, John? It does not attract the disapproval it once did. I would so love Sheba to show her paces...'

'Was Lady Norreys one of the three horsewomen, aunt?' Tom asked, more abruptly than he had intended. It gave the conversation an awkward turn, and Lady Melksham was put out of her stride.

'Why do you ask, Tom? Do you know something of her?'

He realised what he had done and sensed a blush rising. The simple truth was now his only recourse. He tried to sound casual.

'I ask because she's a friend of Will's – or rather, she's the sister of Mr Sumner, his patron at the Temple.'

'Sumner?... I didn't know of the connection. Is he a bencher?'

'A senior barrister, of the Middle Temple. He lets Will help him with his cases.'

'Lady Norreys has a sharp mind too. I think she would make a shrewd lawyer herself – quite a Portia!'

Tom's uncle looked quizzically at his wife.

'I didn't know you were on such terms, Sophia. Do you visit her?'

'I have had tea in Charles Street. Julia Norreys is in my circle.'

'Ah, your *circle* – of course! What with the Ring and the Circle I'm surprised you don't all grow giddy. What a sociable whirl it all is. What do you ladies talk about?'

'Very little, John, you can be reassured about that – we are *women* after all. We shun all affairs of state and matters of business. No, we're a quiet little group. We simply drink tea, exchange recipes, and recommend milliners to each other.'

Lord Melksham knew when he was being teased, so thought it best to step aside gracefully.

'Lady Norreys is a good horsewoman, I admit,' he conceded. 'She certainly has the whip-hand of poor Sir Charles.'

'Her husband is a dolt, John, as you know well.'

Lord Melksham knew very well, and was happy not to argue the point.

'You put it unkindly Sophia, but I have to concede. Sir Charles is one of those men who would be much improved by having a profession – it would give him something to *do*. Not that he isn't an ornament to society: he handles his snuff-box with style; he tells a good story; he knows the right people; he has a discreet mistress; and his credit is good at White's... What more can such a man want?'

'No wonder Lady Norreys prefers her horse,' said his wife. 'The conversation is probably better...'

More than an hour passed before Tom and his uncle finally settled down together in his closet. The term 'library' would be an exaggeration – that particular room was one of the treasures of Monkton – though here in town there were several shelves of well-thumbed books between the painted panels. The two armchairs by the fire were comfortable, and a bottle of brandy kept them company on a small table between them. A Dutch genre picture of the scene would have been entitled 'A Winter Evening.' They had not talked like this for over a month, and so there was a good deal of family news, particularly about Frank and his journey through Holland, and from Tom about his father and the affairs at Winchester, which as so often centred on the latest escapades of young Wilmot Popham. Tom gave an account of his new lodgings over the coffee house, stressing that he had his own private entrance at the side of the building and so could keep himself a little apart from the distractions of the coffee-room. He of course broke the news about the literary pretensions for the Bay-Tree Chocolate House and didn't dispel the impression that his own arrival had partly prompted them. After his uncle's remark on the virtue of having 'a profession,' Tom had been apprehensive. But it was clear both of them were keeping to the distinctly un-Faustian bargain about his future on which they had shaken hands. He didn't mention the doubtful fate of *Crime and Punishment* but simply told his uncle that a 'substantial piece' was nearing completion and he had begun thinking about a publisher.

All these topics had to be negotiated before Tom felt he could turn the conversation toward the world of public affairs. By now the wigs had been dispensed with, and the Queen's Deputy Treasurer was very much the relaxed, affable Uncle Jack. It was as if those were two different people, and in the after-dinner glow of the closet the one was ready to talk freely, and perhaps indiscreetly, about the other.

It was evident that his uncle was finding Court life a strain.

'It's becoming intolerable, Tom! Kensington, Whitehall and St James's are a theatre of war. There's little of the hand-to-hand stuff as yet, but all the preparations are there – such a deal of caballing, manoeuvring and forging of alliances. You'd think the

Thames was the Meuse! Everyone is building up intelligence, dispatching spies and gathering reports. We're waiting for the cannon-fire to begin.'

'Word in the coffee house is that Mr Harley surely can't survive, and the French spies will be the breaking of him?'

'Yes, his back is to the wall all right. And William Greg's fate hangs over him more than ever. The Whigs are doing all they can to press down on the traitor. They've now offered Greg his life *and* a pension – can you believe? – and still he says Harley knew nothing. They're using bribery like the rack, increasing its force bit by bit. It's the man's wife and children I pity – he is determined to go to the gallows alone.'

'I met one of Greg's fellow-clerks on Friday, and he said that over in the Cockpit they are sure it was nothing more than carelessness.'

'In Harley's division, perhaps, but certainly not in Sunderland's. What an uneasy place the Cockpit must be – spies and whisperers everywhere – like the Turkish court!...'

He took a generous sip of brandy.

'... But never underestimate Harley, Tom – He's the wiliest plotter of them all. And he still has many friends. St John of course sticks by him – that's a real brotherly allegiance. And, as ever, the Queen is his staunchest ally. I think she'd stand with him in face of any assault – even one led by Marlborough himself!'

'Wasn't she having a private audience this morning – and with Mr St John there too?'

'Yes, and I thought Harley had the look of a man who expected bad news. He can often be deliberately vague, but this morning his mind was clearly elsewhere. I think there's another plot stirring...'

Tom raised an eyebrow.

'A Tory plot, or a Whig plot?'

'Aha!... Both, I warrant. Each side is trying to out-plot the other. And I'm wondering if the Queen is encouraging it. She's sorely tried, but that stubbornness of hers is worse than ever. The Whigs have become the enemy, and she sees Lord Sunderland as a mine they have laid underneath her. So everyone is apprehensive. Poor Marlborough is being doubly harried – by his Queen on his left flank and his wife on the right – and that's dangerous terrain even for a great general! At this moment he probably thinks the war has followed him here to St James's.'

'How *are* things in the Royal household, uncle? Are they easier than they were?'

This was the crucial question. Lord Melksham sighed and slowly got to his feet, freeing the last two buttons of his coat as he did so.

'That, Tom, is matter to be contemplated over a pipe...'

He walked across to his desk and retrieved a tobacco-jar and two pipes. This was an encouraging sign. Tom wasn't fond of smoking, but he knew that when Uncle Jack offered to share a pipe with you, then something was about to be unfolded, or a curtain lifted... The ritual began, and in anticipation Tom had a shot of emboldening brandy, and made a move.

'Rumour has it that Mrs Masham is well ensconced now. Has the Duchess been entirely displaced?'

'No, Tom, not entirely, nor is like to be at present. Matters of state don't allow it. But of course your aunt is already making plans. Sophia would like nothing better than for me to supplant the Duchess... "Keeper of the Privy Purse" does have a good ring to it.'

'Yes, it sounds much better without the *Deputy!*'

'Exactly so. As you can imagine, that's a word Sophia chokes on.'

Tom was lighting up his pipe and drew in some smoke. To his embarrassment he gave an involuntary cough.

'Now now, Tom! This is none of your coffee-house mundungus! You get only the best Virginian in this place.'

'I'm sorry uncle. I think my taste needs to be educated...'

He had to pick up the thread again. Meanwhile his uncle was pouring more brandy for both of them.

'... I was just thinking how uncomfortable things must be for you. I take it Mrs Masham has no ambitions to be the Queen's Treasurer herself?'

'Heavens, no! That would cause a terrific explosion. Her Majesty is happy to allow her generous funds, and I'm sure Abigail doesn't want the responsibility. I don't think she has any grand ambitions for herself. The Duchess on the other hand...'

'She must feel her power slipping away?'

'The Duchess is a fighter, Tom. She's the most tenacious woman I've ever known. But again, it's not ambition that's driving her but sheer self-will. She insists that the Queen – for her own good, mind you! – has to see things as *she* sees them. Over the years the Duchess has come to think for her, and she can't bear the thought that what she wills for the Queen is not what the Queen wills... Do you follow me? I'm trying to be enigmatic!...'

Tom smiled. His uncle might have made a successful politician.

'... You have to understand, their love and hate are entwined. There's no way back – though the final severing may be a good way off... But the outbursts are becoming worse. There was the most terrible confrontation the other day at Kensington. Rumour has it the struggle went beyond words – the Queen's pearl necklace was broken!'

The idea took Tom's fancy, and for a moment he could visualise the scene. He gave an involuntary whistle.

'Now *there's* something for a satirist to get hold of – if he dare! But that would surely be crossing the line?'

'If there *is* a line any more, Tom... And who is to draw it? Words nowadays are not owned but simply set free. So much is authorless. Verses are fathered anonymously and abandoned to their fate – *foundling* verses!'

His uncle looked down, his face reddening slightly as if he was recollecting something. Tom seized the moment.

'Yes, mere scraps of paper are hard to police. On Friday in the Good Fellowship an obscene epigram was left on one of the tables. It was a libel on Lord Sunderland – anonymous of course, though it was subscribed "Bufo." And a nice piece of poison it was too! Mrs Trotter confiscated it. It's not the kind of thing she wants to encourage.'

Tom paused and watched for his uncle's reaction. He was not to be disappointed.

'Hah! *Bufo*, eh? Well, well!'

'You've encountered the name, uncle?'

'Yes, Tom, I have, and only yesterday. The man has suddenly emerged out of the shadows, and his satirical voice is beginning to cause concern in Court circles...'

He immediately stopped in his tracks.

'... No, no, I really must speak less like a politician! To put it bluntly, this Bufo has *struck fear* into Sunderland and the Duchess. They're both angry of course, but they think his voice is a sign of something about to happen. It's spreading rapidly...'

'What is, uncle?'

Lord Melksham glanced quickly round the room and leaned forward in his chair, as if they might be overheard: it was the instinctive movement of a wary courtier.

'There is a rumour, Tom. It's being whispered around the Court that something is stirring and Harley is about to make his move... to form a government with the Tories! And so, libellous pieces against the Whigs – the most vicious of them carrying the name of *Bufo* – are being circulated through the coffee houses, perhaps to unsettle the enemy's position, like artillery before the charge.'

The larger picture was at last beginning to form. A revolution in the Ministry! Tom could hardly bear to keep silent but waited while his uncle attended to his uncooperative pipe. He didn't want to break the spell.

'... This will interest you, Tom... There's a verse pamphlet bearing that name – a substantial thing, not just a squib – which is being hawked at this moment. It's causing outrage and the hunt is on for the perpetrator. I wouldn't give a penny for his ears if they find him! The pamphlet is being kept off the streets but there are copies circulating in St James's. *Bufo's Magic Glass*, it's called. It's an angry denunciation of the Whigs – the strongest stuff you can imagine. Not the usual sloppy syllable-counting either, but more stylish – and all the more powerful for it. I warrant it comes from Harley's *scriptorium*, though they couldn't possibly own such a thing. The Duchess is glowing with rage. She figures in it. The thing goes beyond personal libel... No-one dares allude to toads in her presence – or even frogs.'

His uncle began tapping out his pipe in good avuncular style and looked sidelong at him with a wary eye.

'I hope you're not sinking to low satire, Tom? It's not the highest calling.'

'I take it you exclude Dryden, uncle?'

'Of course. I said *low* satire – there's no reason why a satirist shouldn't keep his dignity. Now *Horace* is a man you can trust...'

Tom leapt in before the talk could compromise him. He also needed to keep his uncle on track. He knew there was more to be revealed.

'But surely, uncle, there's 'low' stuff coming from Lord Sunderland's office too? It's said that his hacks and informers are almost the match of Mr Harley's.'

'Yes, I'm sure Sunderland's Whig writers are scribbling away while we speak. But right now I'm more concerned about what his mother-in-law is doing in that line.'

'The Duchess? What do you mean uncle?'

Tom was astonished at what was being implied, but tried to sound merely curious. His uncle paused and took a mouthful of the brandy.

'I shouldn't be telling you this, Tom. But God knows, I can't tell anyone else. I know you'll be discreet...'

Tom composed his features.

'... Have you encountered Arthur Maynwaring?'

'I know *of* him. Isn't he one of the Kit-Kats – a friend of Mr Addison's?'

'Yes, the Member of Parliament. He's a political busy-body. In distant days the man was a Tory, but now he's loud for the Whigs. He'll happily turn his hand to a pamphlet when wanted, or hire a hack if need be...'

'There are men like that on both sides, uncle.'

'Yes, but Maynwaring is a great worker behind the scenes. And he has fixed himself on the Duchess. He began as her agent, but now he seems to have become the driving-force. She's so taken with him, and so reliant on him – yet she still thinks he is *her* instrument. For a woman of her strength and determination it's hard to believe. And now I've discovered that Maynwaring even drafts her letters to the Queen! Can you believe it? He's making the Duchess a wedge between the Duke and Harley; he's prompting Lord Godolphin's suspicions, and arousing the Queen's fears. This should, of course, be none of my business, but when the Royal finances are in question...'

Lord Melksham paused. It was all pouring out of him, like the tiny beads of sweat glistening on his brow. He suddenly looked nervous.

'... Promise me, Tom, you'll say nothing of this – to anyone. You can understand why I ask it. I've said too much... Of course, there's nothing I can do. The Privy Purse is Her Majesty's to disburse as she wishes, with no interference from Parliament. But when funds find their way to a man like Maynwaring, and serve his dubious ends...'

'Are you saying he's drawing money from the Privy Purse to organise against Harley?'

'Not directly, but they're filtering through to him...'

His uncle closed his eyes for a moment and shook his head.

'... I can prove nothing of course, because it comes through the Duchess. Her Majesty still allows Her Grace the necessary *facilities*. There is an unspoken sanction, and payments to the great Duchess of Marlborough are not questioned. But this secret subsidy – behind the Queen's back and against her interest – troubles me.'

He drained the last of the brandy and set his glass down decisively on the table.

'So you see, it's not only Sunderland running spies and informers. His mother-in-law is weaving her own network too. And I warrant our "Bufo" is about to get a rejoinder from that direction – something equally vituperative. Maynwaring will see to it. I doubt we'll wait long.'

'It's an uncomfortable situation...'

'I said the terrain was dangerous, Tom. And the manoeuvrings... ah well!...'

He slapped the arms of the chair with his two hands and made to rise.

'... But it's time we set off for the drawing-room. Some tea will be waiting, and that will be very welcome. I think we both need refreshment!'

As they reached the door of the closet, Tom paused and turned.

'Thank you for telling me these things, uncle. I take it as a trust. You've been very open. I have to say that I also have a trust which I cannot break – at least not yet. I'd like nothing more than to open my heart to you – but others close to me are involved.'

His uncle looked taken aback.

'You sound worried, Tom. What's this about? Are you in trouble?'

'Not directly, uncle, at least not yet. But please... I promise to tell you everything as soon as I can. It may be only a matter of days. I'm sorry to sound so secretive.'

'My goodness, but you do indeed. And I thought *I* was the one with the surprises!'

He put an arm round his nephew.

'I respect your silence of course – on a matter of trust I would expect nothing less. But if you *are* in any trouble, then I want to know at once, do you hear?'

'I do, uncle. And I promise you shall.'

'Then let's say no more for this evening. We have to brighten up our countenances for Sophia and Lavinia. I hope we don't reek too much of tobacco!'

It was long after eight when Tom took his leave of the Pophams. He had been given a lot to think about and was intending to use the walk back to Covent Garden to take stock. On an unremarkable Sunday of routines and formalities, what revelations there had been! His family visit had exceeded all hopes. But while he walked along Pall Mall he was not alone: his young cousin Lavinia was tripping cheerily by his side. While he hesitated on the steps to say his goodbyes she had volunteered to walk with him a little of the way. 'What with the pews, and the coach, and the couch... my legs crave the exercise!' she had declared. All protests and fears for her safety that cold winter night were brushed aside. She would do it! It was only two hundred yards to the corner of the Haymarket, and the elegant thoroughfare was well lit. She promised she would go no further... And now, as if relishing this tiny moment of freedom, his cousin had a noticeable spring in her step. She was giving him a searching look and her voice was sprightly, even teasing:

'I wanted to have a moment's chat with you, Tom!... I was watching you at dinner, and I saw your interest in Lady Norreys... *and* I caught the blush rising while you asked about her... Is there something you'd like to tell me?'

Tom stopped dead in his tracks. This was not what he expected. He began to make answer, but in a slightly flustered way, and what was worse, he felt a tell-tale blush returning. He stuck out his chin boldly and gave a protesting laugh – he'd never met the lady! But his cousin's face was lit up with amusement.

'I don't know what Will Lundy may have said to you, but Julia Norreys is an exceptional woman, Tom. She has a bright and well-informed mind, and an extremely stupid husband. She's not one to talk much, however.'

'Except amongst the ladies, it would seem,' said Tom. 'How have you met her?'

'Mamma took me to Charles Street one afternoon for tea, and the two of them talked a little about their *cabal*. Mamma has joined the group once or twice. They are all women, of course – not a man in sight! Lady Norreys said they were glad to be free of the gentlemen's nice compliments and gracious enquiries – since they always stifle good conversation...'

The Honourable Lavinia Popham was sounding remarkably decided for a seventeen-year-old.

'... But don't believe what your aunt says, Tom. It's not a circle of fluttering females, all chinz and china. Women do have ideas, and Arachne's Web helps supply them.'

'Arachne's Web?'

'That's mamma's name for them. You mustn't say a word! They're a small band, only half a dozen, who like to talk about what women aren't supposed to talk about – politics and public affairs. In male company they would be laughed at, or even worse – smiled upon.'

'But that's wonderful, Lavinia. It's a pity they have to be so secretive.'

'I would love to meet them, but that's out of the question. Mamma is becoming doubtful of the proprieties herself, and I don't think she'll return. Mrs Manley is one of their number – I'm sure you know something of her reputation. That would explain the scruples!'

'The notorious Mrs Manley? How very scandalous! I suspect that in *her* circle news and gossip go hand in hand – as do truth and fiction.'

'Now, Tom, don't disappoint me. You sound like a disapproving father. I had thought better of you... I know mamma likes Julia Norreys a lot, and if you are *certain* you've never encountered her, then you must ask your aunt to introduce you! Lady Norreys is bored and beautiful... And you with your dark curls... ?'

And with that, the precocious Lavina Popham gave him a wicked smile, turned on her heels, and began heading briskly homeward. Tom was still motionless on the pavement, running things rapidly through his mind. For several seconds he was uncertain where he was. This had happened so very quickly.

'Goodbye Tom!' he heard her call from a distance. 'Don't forget Arachne!'

Chapter Seventeen

FOR WILL LUNDY, it felt good to be out of London and breathing the rural air, even on a bleak morning like this. He took long, purposeful strides, partly to warm himself but also to bring some life to the scene. It was not the easiest of walks, and his boots fought with the ruts of frozen mud that veered from side to side where the carriage-wheels had swerved. He made his way northbound from Bethnal along the country lane to Hackney, passing bedraggled market gardens and orchards that were still stark and bare. There were a few pockets of snow huddling under the hedges. Here outside the city, he felt keenly how everything was still locked up in winter. It would be several weeks before the greys and browns would turn bright green and everything burst into new growth. On this Sabbath day there was little human activity. To his right, the usually busy brickfield was deserted, and there were no stooping figures dotted across the turnip fields that stretched to the horizon. There were a few carts on the road, but at this early hour he passed only one or two fellow-pedestrians. Everything was eerily quiet, except for the lapwings that flapped and swirled noisily in the distance. The air was fresh, and he felt he could breathe freely. He quickened his step to get his lungs working.

Once the lane began transforming itself into the main street of the village, the scene became animated. The picket fences of Hackney were brightly painted, the hedges neatly trimmed, and behind iron gates were substantial residences set back from the road, edged by well-tended shrubbery and with white sash windows under handsome roofs. Here on Mare Street one or two smart carriages pulled out, carrying the citizens to their religious observances. Well-dressed couples were strolling together in the same direction, and a procession of young ladies walking two-by-two and holding hands was winding out of one of the village boarding-schools.

Hackney was the retreat for prosperous merchants, grocers and brewers, lawyers and professional city men, all seeking a rural idyll. There was money here – or at least its outlay: its serious making happened just a few miles southward in the City. This Middlesex village, in spite of its sprawling character, managed to look tidy and cared for, and so did the people, some of whom were heading over the bridge across the stream to St John's church for their Anglican worship. But others, Will included, were directing their feet towards a building that stood on Mare Street itself and was home to Hackney's dissenting congregation. Once again Will found he was later than intended, but he knew his father and his two aunts would already be stationed inside.

The Mare Street meeting-house had been formed by the conversion of a mismatched pair of dwellings. Its shape was irregular but the interior was surprisingly elegant and its galleries on three sides gave it a theatrical quality. It still had the feel of a house, and in this well-lit room everyone was close to everyone else. From his pulpit the preacher could almost reach out and touch his audience. The words came to you direct – nothing was hidden or mysterious. There was nowhere to hide or to be alone. When the room was close-packed as it was now, there was no echo: every sound was absorbed into a congregation soberly clad in good quality blacks and greys. Here, a pair of white gloves or a ruffle would cause eyes to narrow and set nostrils twitching. At this moment there was a subdued hum of conversation with everyone catching up on the business of the week.

Will made his way inside the meeting-house and looked around him. There were no private pews but only benches, and he knew that Mr Justice Lundy always liked to sit at the front of the central gallery from where he could encourage the preacher with his relentless gaze. Sometimes it made the minister feel he was in the dock rather than the pulpit. And his father was there now, looking down – rather frostily Will thought – and gesturing to him that there was an empty place in the row behind.

Will found a seat upstairs but had little time to collect himself before matters got started with the communal singing of a psalm. The performance was unaccompanied and was confidently led by the minister, a plain-looking, cheerful man with no pretentions to style or dignity. His baritone voice rang out above everyone else's as he led his wayward flock ever higher – if not in the spirit, then certainly in pitch. Will looked at the practical faces of the people around him, all suddenly caught up in the business of salvation. As they sang they seemed determined to free themselves from the earthbound world – but without poetry's help. The trite wording of Tate and Brady's psalms didn't seem very different, Will thought, from the grumbling language of the coffee house:

How num'rous, Lord, of late are grown
The troublers of my peace!
And as their factious numbers rise,
So does their rage increase…

'King David's message to the Stuart age!' he muttered to himself.

Whenever Will came to Hackney he was struck by the family atmosphere of the place – for good and ill. There was communal friendliness, but also a watchful concern for the congregation's inner health. Each individual was a soul to be saved, and the brethren took a proprietary interest in a person's character. The spiritual good of the whole society hung on it. As he listened to the sermon, which was an hour-long expounding of the twenty-sixth verse of the sixteenth chapter of Matthew's gospel – *For what is a man profited if he shall gain the whole world and lose his own soul?* – Will realised that the pastor knew his flock well. The practical emphases were unmistakable:

'... He that loses his soul, though it be to gain the world, makes a very *bad bargain* for himself! When he comes to *balance the account* and to compare *profit and loss*, he will find that, instead of the advantage he promised himself, he is to all intents and purposes, *ruined* – irreparably *broken*.'

At each phrase Will could sense the congregation flinch. The vivid picture of spiritual bankruptcy would strike home in Hackney. This was indeed 'plain and profitable' language!

Will's maiden aunts were stirred inwardly, and as the four of them walked home from the meeting-house Aunt Rebecca had some rare praise: 'I have an increasing faith in Mr Billio, brother – he is becoming *a burning and a shining light*.'

Dinah in particular had been shaken to the core, and declared that she would never in future 'pursue the world so eagerly as she had done.' Will looked at her and tried to imagine Aunt Dinah pursuing the world, but the thought was too unsettling.

That morning in the meeting-house the congregation may have battled against the world, the flesh and the devil; but in the afternoon the flesh had something of a resurgence round the dinner tables of the village. In the Lundy household the pork loin proved to be excellent. The crackling was especially crisp and ate very well, and Aunt Rebecca and Aunt Dinah duly sent their compliments to Mrs Pearson the cook.

For Will's part, he understood what was required of him on these family occasions and delivered a report on his progress in his Law studies. In Presbyterian Hackney Sunday was a day for rendering spiritual accounts, and so his father and aunts expected something of that order. Will told them about his mornings at Westminster Hall listening to the civil trials, where he could observe court procedure and pick up the language of pleading and cross-examination. He also mentioned his practical work with Richard Sumner, hoping to conceal how much he relished the human drama of the criminal bar, and how little enamoured he was with the intricacies of civil and chancery proceedings. At this point, his father's sudden question about what books he had been reading caught him off guard, but he was able to mutter something reasonably convincing about his progress with *Coke upon Lyttelton*. On the whole he felt he had come out of the session well enough to justify his father's continuing his allowance.

Late afternoon arrived, and the two Miss Lundys departed for another session at the meeting-house, eagerly anticipating what rigours might be in store. This meant that Mr Justice Lundy now had Will to himself. These could be uneasy encounters, and as darkness began to descend Will soon had cause to feel uncomfortable. The two of them were seated in high-backed oak chairs that had been carefully placed, one directly facing the other.

'*So*... you are as *impatient* as ever!'

It was a judicial summing-up. A less conclusive person might have added 'I see' or 'it seems', but his father's statement was terse and final: the evidence was clear and the only course was to find the accused guilty. Since childhood Will had always felt that no-one could imbue the little word *so*... with such a weight of implication as his father. After all, the man was used to having the last word. But on this occasion it challenged Will to show his mettle.

'I'm not impatient with difficulty, father, but with the endless quibbling and word-spinning. And all those dusty volumes! I thought I was taking after you in that... I know your own impatience with unnecessary details.'

'Ah! But you have to know the intricacies of the law first. Exact words are important. What is a *quibble* to you might prove to be a matter of life and death. You don't sweep the niceties away and set your own rules. We can't do that in religion, can we! The Bible doesn't let you pick and choose what you'll accept. The Law is built on precedent and statute – on those *dusty volumes*. You have to learn to speak its language and use its arguments. It's a living thing. Those volumes should never grow dusty. Sometimes I despair of you, William – you've always been over-hasty, always looking for a short cut.'

'But sometimes a compromise is necessary, father. The Law can loosen its grip, adjust itself to human situations.'

'The law does not ad*just* – it sets rules by which life should *be* adjusted. That is what *Justice* is.'

Will's father saw deep truths in etymology. But Will persisted.

Surely, the law recognises the force of particular circumstances, and special cases?...'

Will paused and took a deep breath.

'... *Occasional conformity*, for example.'

Will stiffened slightly as he spoke the infamous words, and at that moment he felt the cold air seeping from the large window to his right. His father gave him a piercing look.

'Ah, in that you strike home! *Occasional conformity*... What a slippery phrase that is – and what a license for hypocrisy! I try to avoid the subject with your aunts, but they know the devil's bargain I have to make. I'm afraid they regard me as something of a delinquent...'

He sipped his glass of elderflower cordial. Will nursed his own glass in his hands and looked at his father, who suddenly became reflective.

'... Yes, I am an occasionalist! And like all the others, I take – *on occasion* – the Anglican sacrament. And because I do that, the State forgives me my trespass against the Test. Every year the Law releases me from the Law. It is indeed paradoxical, isn't it – and you are right to use the point against me. But it is *the Law* all the same, and until occasional conformity is disallowed, I follow it, however much it sours my conscience to do so.'

'But if the Tories have their way...'

'Ah! If the high-flying Tories have their way, then my position becomes difficult. Our entire congregation will be pariahs once again. Many before me have shifted their ground. But I would find it hard, impossible.'

'I know you despise the 'High Church' mob, but so does Harley, and even the Queen is suspicious of them. You're in good company.'

His father gave a harsh, rueful laugh.

'In company with *them?* I think not! But when a man like me is made an enemy of the State, then there is something amiss with the Constitution – and what a creaking structure that is! We're overloaded with the splendour of Church and State – all that ceremonious flim-flam!...'

He paused, almost wondering to himself:

'... In truth, what does a man need other than his Bible and his conscience?'

There was a moment of pregnant silence.

'His law books?' put in Will cleverly.

'Ha! Yes indeed. Your Bible in one hand, your book of law in the other – and your conscience looking ahead to guide you.'

'But that didn't save my grandfather,' said Will, who was by now becoming reckless.

'Your grandfather took his punishment. The Law struck him down. It was a harsh law, but by 1662 it was the law of the land. Father paid the price for his conscience – and was willing to pay it.'

'But to be thrown out of his living, lose his house, his congregation, everything – and then not be allowed to come within five miles of the place... an outcast in deed! The Law was inhuman.'

'But it was the Law, William.'

'I really believe you think that unless a law is harsh, it is no law at all.'

'No, not at all – law can be a guide also.'

'But in the *criminal* law...'

'A criminal knows when he has done wrong – or should do! The matter is usually clear-cut. When I preside in court I am the voice of the Law. It is for others to invoke mercy, pity and forgiveness. That is not my province.'

Father and son were now settled into a dispute that had been rehearsed many times before and would, it seemed, never be resolved. Old sore points were touched on and familiar questions asked. Somehow they always managed to stay this side of real anger, and they soon began putting cases and testing principles. Will knew that if he was ever to make something of himself in the Law, then it would be thanks to these tenacious battles with his father.

At last, and at the right moment, a test case offered itself.

'Well, father, for the first time in my life I'm concerned in a murder case myself.'

Mr Justice Lundy looked sceptical.

'Murder? Surely Richard Sumner does not usually take such things? What case can that be?'

Will scrutinised his father closely. This topic needed the utmost care – and a more measured tone.

'I'm concerned father – not from the legal side for once, but because I happen to know both the accused and the victim.'

Will paused to gather his thoughts. But it was impossible to gloss over the sensational implications of this. His father's mouth opened, and his stare was equally wide.

'Are you talking about a current murder case? One in process now? What do you mean?'

'The killing occurred on Friday night, and as it happens, I...'

'The printer! Beat his pressman to death!' exclaimed his father somewhat injudiciously... It is *alleged*,' he immediately added.

'Then news of it has reached you?'

'Yesterday evening. Mr Dignum sent a message round. The Coroner's inquest is scheduled for tomorrow afternoon, and it will come to the Bailey at the end of the week – I may indeed be one of the trial judges. But what is your concern with these men? You can't surely be involved in any way?'

His father had begun to sound distant, as if speaking from the bench.

Treading with extreme care, Will told of his visit to John Morphew's shop. He didn't mention its main purpose but said he had called there about a pamphlet and decided to try and interest the publisher in Tom's poem. He had talked with both men.

'There's more I could add, father, but in the circumstances perhaps I'd better go no further.'

That was certainly the proper thing to say, and he paused before introducing a question about the rules of evidence in murder trials. Mr Justice Lundy, however, had no intention of moving on.

'Poets – printers – press-men! Why are you busying yourself in such pastimes? And negotiating with printers?... I've always liked Tom Bristowe – he's a serious-minded and thoughtful fellow – but now he's badly losing his way. He's moved from Grub Street to a Covent Garden coffee house, and I assume the Church is further than ever from his thoughts. If your friend wants to haggle in a print-shop, let him do it for himself! And a *pamphlet!* I shan't ask you what it was – I don't wish to embarrass myself. I doubt it concerned anything worth thinking about. How is it you've entangled yourself in this?...'

Will's father began weighing the situation. His parental concern and judicial interest were in equal measure aroused.

'... Does this mean you may be called as a witness?'

'No, no, not even as a character witness – I'm sure there are others who know John Morphew well.'

'I'm relieved to hear it.'

But Will began to wonder, and he started to feel uneasy. He was shocked at his own naivety. He had not fully considered what his involvement in the trial might mean. Perhaps he should indeed offer to be a witness? After all, he had been the go-between in the business of the pocket-book. It might be relevant to the possible motive for Emmet's murder. Will felt his neck sweating in spite of the chilly air, and as he talked his throat tightened and his voice went dry. Would he have to stand up in court as a material witness and – on oath – reveal the affair of Lady Norreys's pocket-book? It would mean dragging her name into a sensational murder trial. It was unthinkable... How would Richard Sumner respond to that? Will could see the nightmare taking shape. *Why* had he not thought this through? And to think he had ambitions to be a lawyer! He was still innocent and foolish.

Will tried to defend Tom and his poetry, but found himself hesitating. His words soon petered out, and he had ceased to think in an orderly way. He could see his father knew something was not right, that his son was visibly reddening. Judge Lundy was used to dealing with this kind of situation in court.

'William, what on earth is the matter with you?'

'I must say no more.'

'Yes, it would be improper for me to hear anything that could be used in evidence... But if you know something material to the case, you will need to make a statement.'

Will was now beginning to feel frightened. His pores were open and he felt vulnerable. A lawyer should be mastering a situation like this. He tried to hold firm and keep his counsel. He lowered his shoulders and breathed consciously. He even made himself smile.

'Well father, see what a lawyer I would make! I'll have to learn not to become too caught up in a case. But of course you're right. I must think matters through, and if there is any duty involved then I shall do it. But I've made it sound much too dramatic. I shouldn't have mentioned this to you today. Forgive me.'

'As I said, William, forgiveness is not my province...'

His father paused, his brows contracting, and he shifted uncomfortably in his chair. It was clear that judicial scruples were struggling with human curiosity. For a brief moment the latter won. He looked straight at his son.

'... Did the printer speak about his pressman to you?'

'Yes, he did, but...'

'In what terms?'

'Father – I don't think I should talk about this.'

'You are in some sort a witness, William – not of the crime itself, but of the printer's feelings, his anger perhaps? Is that why you are unwilling to say more? Are you agitated because you heard him say something violent?'

'No, father, nothing violent at all. He was vexed, merely... But please, you must not question me about this.'

Mr Justice Lundy recalled where he was, and drew himself back.

'You are right my boy, of course. I accept your point of order. I've often cross-examined you in the past, but on this occasion... If I am to have a role in the trial, then we must say no more. It would be prejudicial.'

Will felt relief, but he realised he had sowed suspicion in his father's mind. Part of him wanted to say more. At that instant he couldn't hold back.

'He didn't have his cane with him...'

'What do you say?'

'When we walked to the Good Fellowship – he had no cane. That's something you should know... But I'll say nothing more.'

His father raised his hand.

'Thank you, William. We have both said too much. We must let the matter rest there.'

And there it rested, at least for the time being. With their conversation uneasily suspended and neither of them relishing the prospect of making small talk, the pair soon found another way of engaging their minds. When the Lundy sisters returned from the meeting-house with their souls braced for the coming week they found the house quiet and only the clock making its presence heard. In the grate another log had been added to the fire and father and son were still in their chairs facing each other, but now across a chessboard. Given it was the Sabbath, the activity called forth a disapproving comment from Aunt Rebecca who considered it undoubtedly a *game*; but Aunt Dinah took a more conciliatory line, acknowledging that chess had a reflective and contemplative character and that any direct pleasure was minimal.

After only a few minutes Will was conveniently checkmated, and the activity, along with the accompanying theological debate, ceased. This allowed his aunts to propose the reading of a discourse *Concerning Meekness and Quietness of Spirit*, which would help to draw the evening to a close with some sobering thoughts. But at this point Will was able to make his apologies and offer to take his leave. His father also needed to arrange his son's transport. And so, sometime after eight o'clock Will was being swept along the dark country lanes in his father's coach, with Daniel the coachman driving the horses hard, a pistol tucked into his greatcoat pocket. Will's Sunday morning walk had been enjoyable, but at night the road between Hackney and Shoreditch was not to be negotiated on foot, and even coaches did not loiter. There were no patrols in these lonely suburbs, and the robbers made a good living.

At the same time over in Covent Garden, in the parlour of the Good Fellowship all was settled into a quiet Sunday evening. The fire had burnt low, and Widow Trotter was fast asleep, her slightly unkempt auburn hair thrown back in the chair. A guttural sound was coming from her throat, keeping a steady rhythm. A while earlier, a distant noise had left her undisturbed and she had slept contentedly on. In spite of the closed eyes, there was an expression of almost childlike wonder on her face, which flickered animatedly as the last candle guttered to its end.

In stark contrast, toward the rear of the coffee house Tom Bristowe's heart was racing as he ran up the steep staircase that led to his room. He had arrived back from St James's to find the street door in the alley had been forced, the lock broken and the hasp twisted open. He knew only too well what would await him, and his blood ran cold when he saw his door ajar. Once inside the room he glanced around. Nothing appeared to have been thrown about or broken, and there was nothing strewn on the floor. The place was just as comfortably untidy as he had left it. But against the far wall stood his small writing desk, and he noticed that its drawers were pulled open. He walked over to it, and his hand was shaking as he reached for the drawer where the manuscript of his poem had been kept. To his despair he saw that it was empty. His one remaining copy of *Crime and Punishment* had been taken. The first fair copy had been swallowed up into the Cockpit, and now the second had been stolen. The thing was gone – out of his hands – and perhaps gone for ever.

Tom suddenly felt bereft. In a moment of frenzy he flung his ridiculous overblown wig to the other side of the room as if blaming it for having distracted him, and his stupid sword followed it, clattering loudly against the wall. He saw that other papers were missing too – nothing finished, but working drafts of pieces that were yet to find their form. It had all gone – the little that he had achieved and some things that could have become worthwhile in time. As the full extent of his loss struck him, the last of his self-confidence drained away. He realised with a sobering shock that he was still only the harmless, melancholy *Celadon* – and nothing more. He was back where he started, sighing to the passing wind with that damned myrtle garland dangling from his hand. The pastoral image seemed to mock him. But perhaps it was in simple pastoral duties that his own future lay? Perhaps it was meant to be? At that moment, while he stood over the emptied desk, he saw himself in his mind's eye as an emblem. It was a vivid picture: the ambitious Tom Bristowe had turned into a simpering shepherd with a crook in his hand and flowers in his hair. Around him, however, were not sheep, but a flock of rustic villagers with their heads all turned toward him, mouths open, waiting to be fed.

Chapter Eighteen

'I BLAME MYSELF,' said Widow Trotter. 'I should have foreseen this.'

'We all should,' added Will gloomily.

'But I thought I was clear of suspicion,' said Tom half to himself. 'I'm the only one to blame. From the beginning I've never quite believed...'

His words petered out, and the threesome were left in stunned silence. Their nine o'clock gathering was to have been a convivial meeting when the adventurers would sit in the parlour over a light supper and hear each other's reports. It was meant to be a cool deliberation; but from the moment Tom's shouts had brought Widow Trotter back to consciousness, things flew off course. There had been some running about and searching, and when Will and then the watchman arrived shortly afterwards there was further inspection of the premises – though it told them nothing. They knew little could be done. But the correct procedures had been followed – the watchman had seen to that, happy to be out of the cold air and warmed by the house brandy.

Now the first flurry of anger and shock was over they knew they had to settle themselves and go through the day's events while they were still fresh. But thoughts kept returning to Tom's desk with its drawers open and empty...

It was Tom who broke the silence.

'Well, what's done is done... Please... I don't want this to distract us...'

He turned to Will and Mrs Trotter, and noticed their furrowed brows. He consciously relaxed his own, and spoke quietly.

'... We can do nothing more until we see the bigger picture. As for me, I've a lot to tell – high politics and low scandal! In fact I hardly know where to start.'

'And I've had an adventure,' said Mrs Trotter, recollecting herself, 'with another crime, and a missing person, to report.'

Will looked at the two of them a little enviously.

'And I've had a soul-improving day in Hackney. But I do have something pressing to tell you. It wasn't a fruitless expedition.'

Widow Trotter was leading them in the direction of the kitchen where some cold venison pasties, cheese and syllabubs could be found. Nothing was prepared, and the untended parlour fire was spent.

'Did your father know of the murder?' she asked Will.

'Oh yes – word had gone to Hackney *post haste*. He knew the circumstances. A sensational crime like this runs through the fraternity like wild-fire. It's already spoken of as the *printing-house murder*... The Coroner's jury meets tomorrow afternoon.'

'That's swift!' said Tom. 'How can all the facts be gathered before then?'

'The wheels turn rapidly with such things – two days is longer than usual. It's put down for two o'clock.'

'Dinner-time? But the jurors will be hungry!'

'It may take less than half an hour, and they'll dine well afterwards. They intend to view the body in the printing-house, and then adjourn to the King's Head Tavern for the depositions and verdict. This isn't a trial of the case, remember, but a determination of the facts – how Emmet died, and whether it was by accident, suicide, or unlawful killing. But it's hard to overturn what the Coroner rules, so I must be there, if only to observe and take notes. It will be like my Westminster Hall routine.'

'Should you say something?' asked Widow Trotter hesitatingly. 'Or can you only sit and listen?'

'It's very difficult, Mrs T. There *are* things to be said, but it may be wiser to keep them to ourselves till we have more facts.'

'But the Coroner's *facts* may prove to be fiction,' said Tom.

'Yes. That's the difficulty.'

'From what you say, his findings can only work against us?'

'They may do, simply by confirming a story – the *Angry Printer*...'

He turned to Tom.

'... Can you come with me? In something like this two heads are sure to be better than one – especially when one's mine.'

In the end it was agreed that both Tom and Will would attend the inquest and find out as much as possible.

And now, with the clock showing well past ten, the three investigators could at last settle themselves in front of the low-burning coffee-room fire and hear what each of them had discovered during the day. In the light of Will's news about the inquest, the urgency seemed greater than ever.

It was Widow Trotter who began, recounting with vivid detail her visit to Mrs Ménage and her unsettling experience in Vinegar Yard. The revelation of Kate Primrose's flight she left to the end, her voice rising with the climax.

'You can picture the scene, gentlemen: the poor girl frightened out of her wits, her hand burnt by a cruel ruffian, fleeing the place with only a small bag of her worldly possessions. Somewhere...' (she paused for dramatic effect) 'are those papers that her assailant sought, and which even now are putting her life in danger!'

An image of Cicero addressing his fellow-Romans from the Rostra flashed before Will's eyes. This woman would have nothing to learn about winning over a jury! He nodded thoughtfully:

'So, it's clear our Mr Emmet was developing a trade in intimate papers and was sniffing around for what he could find. Your friend Mrs Ménage is a shrewd negotiator and I suspect they would have agreed a price eventually?'

'Yes, I sensed she was relishing the thought of it.'

Will smiled:

'Any Covent Garden Madam will have tales to tell – the old story of courtiers and courtesans! An arrangement with Emmet would be profitable. How far do you think his business extended?'

'Well, he had contacts among the printers, and the possibilities for a blackmail are obvious,' added Tom.

'Yes, Lady Norreys's pocket-book – Morphew certainly thought he had over-stepped the mark there… I wonder how deeply Emmet was involved in Bufo's verses? We may have touched on only part of his activities. His political connections could be significant.'

'But can we assume his murder and the attack on Kate Primrose are connected?…' said Tom. He hesitated.

'… And what about this evening's theft?'

'If they *are* all connected,' said Will, 'then Bufo must surely be the link? We know there's alarm in the Ministry. So much is at stake: careers, reputations, the fate of the Government even. There could be a motive for murder hidden in there somewhere.'

Widow Trotter looked uncertain, and turned to him.

'But if Emmet was Bufo's agent, why not have him stabbed in a dark alley? Why risk setting up a murder in the printing-house so that Morphew takes the blame?'

'Well, if they think Emmet is the supplier and Morphew the printer, then I suppose it kills two birds with one stone.' Will pulled himself up. '– I'm sorry, that's an unfortunate image.'

'But what a risk they're running!' she replied, shaking her head. 'To murder two people – that's what it amounts to – merely for sedition?'

'*Merely?*...' said Tom, letting the word reverberate. '... Perhaps the three of us can have no idea how far this reaches.'

The tone was solemn. Widow Trotter cut through it briskly:

'We've found a trail, haven't we? The attack on Kate Primrose and the theft of Tom's papers – both within a few hours. Surely they must be the work of the same people, intent on silencing Bufo at any cost?'

Will was apprehensive:

'It's a trail alright. But it could be a trail of gunpowder.'

'It must take us back to Sunderland's office,' said Tom. 'It was they who arrested Morphew, and surely only they could have set up Emmet's killing, with its perfect timing and its carefully planted evidence...'

'But didn't those Whigs see Emmet as their man?' said Will. 'After all, they sent him to interrogate you. Wouldn't they want to protect him?'

'Yes, but what if they discovered he was not *their man* at all – but was creating the mischief by supplying the material?'

Will frowned.

'We keep meeting that problem, don't we – Emmet's scheming with both sides?'

'Yes,' said Tom. 'Perhaps we ought to think of him as a chameleon, forever changing his political colours?'

Now Widow Trotter was frowning too:

'I suspect the man had no principles and sold his services more profitably than poor Clarissa ever did!'

'Well, if we can find out who that gentleman was,' said Will, '– the one who had the body removed and found the composing-stick – then we'll be on surer ground.'

'I must ask the compositor tomorrow. We need to know about Emmet's activities in the printing-house, and this Mr Barnard seems to have been someone Emmet may have confided in.'

Widow Trotter sank back in her chair and looked into the distance. She remembered what Joseph Quinlan had said about young Kate Primrose and her pride in Emmet's literary connections, and what must have been her bright hopes for the future – *Clarissa* indeed! The poor girl!

She began thinking out loud.

'You know, I think Emmet began as a simple mischief-maker who sank in too deep... I wonder if this time he found something truly *dangerous?* A State secret perhaps? Something important enough for a person to torture a girl for – even to kill for.'

She bent down for the coffee-pot that stood next to her by the grate, and began refilling their dishes.

'... Emmet could have been using Vinegar Yard as his office. Whatever the intruder was looking for, it was well hidden. Somehow our brave Kate managed to deflect him and send him off elsewhere. She told Joseph Quinlan the papers were in a place they would never find. But she knew the man would be back.'

Tom filled his mouth with the hot, bitter liquid. To this point he had kept quiet about his own discoveries in St James's, not wishing to confuse their deliberations; but he knew he could offer a different perspective. He saw that in pouring the coffee Mrs Trotter was giving him the opportunity. After a short silence, he spoke.

'So far we've been thinking about the politics. But what about social disgrace? That could surely be a motive for murder too?'

'Yes,' said Will, 'politics is a dirty business – but if you add in a private scandal – the threat of public humiliation – it would make a poisonous brew!'

He glanced down at his dish of treacly coffee.

'This sounds like the prologue to your story, Tom,' said Widow Trotter. 'I must say you've been very patient. I've been giving you my little Dutch picture from Vinegar Yard, and now it's your turn to present us with the grand prospect from St James's. I'm bursting with curiosity! The world of the Pophams! You must promise to let me have all that nonsense tomorrow morning over breakfast. If you come down to the parlour I'll see you leave for Stationers' Yard well nourished.'

Tom grinned at her.

'It's a bargain, Mrs T – You'll hear about the Chapel Royal and the Ring, I swear. But there are things to report from my *tête à tête* with Uncle Jack – and a scandalous revelation from Cousin Lavinia that was even more informative.'

He had his audience gripped. Mrs Trotter and Will were agog, neither wishing to say anything that might delay matters.

Tom began by recalling his after-dinner conversation with his uncle about the situation at Court, the strife between Whigs and Tories, and the various plots and counter-plots. He was able to tell them that *Bufo's Magic Glass* was now circulating surreptitiously around St James's, so that the identity of Bufo was causing speculation, with one of Harley's hacks the most likely suspect.

'Uncle Jack says that people suspect this flurry of activity is a sign that Harley is about to make a bid for power – to form his own government.'

Will gave a long, low whistle.

'Gunpowder it is!'

'This was told me in the strictest confidence – and we mustn't talk of it beyond ourselves, you understand? I gave Uncle Jack my word.'

Widow Trotter was holding her eagerness in check:

'Say no more, Mr Bristowe – we'll keep mum. These are high politics! But you say Bufo has been causing a stir at Court?'

'Yes, and the ripples are spreading. His libels have begun appearing in some coffee houses – small printed half-sheets. And one of them is the *Caricatura* of the Duchess – you remember – the thing Emmet told Morphew he'd picked up outside his shop? Well, it seems the Duchess has been raving like one of the Furies, and vowing revenge on the perpetrator. The sky has been visibly darkening round her head!'

'That's no surprise,' said Will. 'Our friend Bufo is edging his way to treason...'

A dark look suddenly shadowed his face.

'... It certainly puts Morphew in danger. I'm afraid to say this – but do you think the Whigs might be staging his trial as part of their political game? If they can link Harley to Bufo's libels, the Queen will be disgusted, and without her support, he's finished.'

'As plots go,' said Tom, 'this is positively Machiavellian. With Emmet silenced, the Whigs have their scapegoat, and they can take revenge on Morphew too. That would certainly suit the Duchess.'

The three of them fell silent.

'Politics, politics!' Mrs Trotter muttered with a shake of the head. 'It's all a sport. These men are like apprentices with a football – kicking it to and fro.'

'The women too,' said Tom with a smile. 'Uncle Jack tells me the Duchess has her own crew of spies and hacks, organised by Arthur Maynwaring.'

Will looked surprised.

'Maynwaring the Kit-Cat?'

'Yes, he's very close to the Duchess – her right-hand man. He's the power behind the tiara!'

'Well, we know she utterly detests Harley and the Tories. And if Harley is about to make a deal with them, she'll do anything to stop it.'

'And Maynwaring will do anything to serve her. A middling Whig with high ambitions is a fearsome thing! My uncle thinks the Duchess is so angry that she'll demand Bufo is answered at once. Maynwaring may be setting about it right now.'

'I've never met the man,' said Will, 'but I've heard he has a venomous wit and can froth and spit with the best of them.'

'It should be quite a contest. Things are moving swiftly. I can only think our poor Mr Bagnall is being left behind by events – this is not the best time to be offering Mr Harley public advice!'

Widow Trotter shifted in her seat and her eyes peered into the darkness that shrouded their cosy fireside.

'You mean you think the finger is pointing at Lord Sunderland and the Whigs – even at his mother-in-law, the Duchess?'

Tom winced slightly and reached out for his dish of coffee.

'That's certainly the picture – a *political* murder. But still, I think there's another possibility – a different scene we should bear in mind.'

Widow Trotter smiled at him.

'Ah yes, scandal! You said your Cousin Lavinia had something important to say. I'm longing to hear!'

Will and Mrs Trotter both had an expectant look. Tom paused sufficiently to enjoy the moment. He set his dish of coffee down.

'I've seen Lady Norreys.'

'You've seen her!' Will's eyes lit up expectantly, 'and… ?'

'And I can conceive that her private pocket-book might indeed be something remarkable.'

'Tell us more!' said Widow Trotter.

And so Tom did. He told of the strikingly handsome horsewoman at the Ring with her two besuited companions, and how the three of them needed no brilliant equipage to turn people's heads; that Julia Norreys was evidently a woman of lively parts with her own coterie; and that she had a doltish husband who didn't seem to appreciate her.

'Aunt Sophia is a friend of hers and has attended some of their private meetings. *Arachne's Web* she calls them – not altogether affectionately. Lavinia told me their talk is unbridled – far beyond a school of gossips. I took the impression that they're not above talking politics!'

'And might they be *enfranchised* in other ways?' wondered Will.

'They sound to me a refreshing society,' said Widow Trotter. 'Perhaps not popular with their husbands; but they are clearly women with minds of their own.'

Will and Tom looked at each other. Tom felt her train of thought keenly.

'Ah, Mrs T! If only you lived in St James's and had a clear two thousand a year. What a life you might lead!'

'Yes, it's a glittering thought. But it would be a narrower existence than the one I have now. Here the widow sets the rules. I converse with whoever I please; I follow my own tastes; and if any man misbehaves I can show him the door. And I have no *reputation* to keep spotless...'

She gave Will a searching look.

'... Lady Norreys came close to being another of Emmet's victims, did she not? I wonder what hold he felt he had over her. What could be worth *thirty* pounds – a full year's good wage! – to keep secret?'

This was now the question at the front of their minds. Tom spoke again.

'We've been assuming the business was concluded with the return of the pocket-book. But I wonder – might Emmet have hinted that he knew the book's secrets, and threatened to reveal them?'

'Yes,' said Will. 'With the book's return Morphew must have thought he was drawing a line under the matter. But perhaps our Mr Emmet had other ideas?'

'He had certainly lost a lot of money by the business. It can only have built up his resentment.'

'And so he reported at the Cockpit,' said Will. 'He showed them Bufo's *Caricatura* of the Duchess, spun a tale about Morphew's involvement, and at the same time hinted that *you* might be Bufo? Elias Cobb seems to think so.'

There was a moment of silence. Tom raised his eyebrows.

'So many scenes! Which of them is the true one, do you think?...'

They had certainly been given food for thought. But at this point Widow Trotter called a halt. She raised her arms toward the two young men.

'Well, I think we've made some progress, gentlemen. We have at least a sketch of the possibilities. Tomorrow morning, Mr Bristowe, I hope you can talk with this Mr Barnard and find out what Emmet was up to in the printing-house. You'll then be on hand for the inquest at two. And what about you, Mr Lundy?'

'As it happens, I'm reporting early to Richard Sumner. We're heading off to Westminster Hall together. He has a case at the Common Pleas. It may be over quickly, which will leave us plenty of time to talk.'

'Excellent! That can just be managed. Whatever the embarrassment, Mr Lundy, you need to turn the conversation onto his sister's pocket-book, and what it contained...'

She noticed Will give a momentary shudder.

'... Do you think you could manage that?' She softened her voice: 'I realise it won't be easy for you.'

'But it has to be done, Mrs T. As it happens, I was thinking about it in the coach this evening. My father raised the possibility that I might be called as a witness at the trial. But the thought of having to stand up in court and explain about the affair of the pocket-book…'

'No!… Oh my…!' Widow Trotter was alarmed. 'Surely you're safe from that?'

'I would hope so – but perhaps I should confront Mr Sumner with the possibility that his sister's name might be mentioned at the trial. Hence the need for him to tell me – *in confidence* – anything that might be potentially embarrassing. I could then help avert the danger.'

Tom looked anxiously at his friend.

'But Will, that's dangerous. You would have to ensure he doesn't think you'll exploit it yourself.'

'That's why I'm shaking at the thought. But I know he trusts me, and I'm anxious to shield Lady Norreys. I hope he'll see that.'

'Well,' said Mrs Trotter, 'that's a Monday morning challenge for both of you! With Tom at the printing-house and you in Westminster Hall, we shall have two fishing-lines in the water.'

'Now that's a metaphor I like,' said Will. 'Tempting the wily trout! And what about you, Mrs T? You have a business to run, of course.'

'Yes indeed, and tomorrow morning I'll be busy in the coffee-room. I've arranged to view a sketch for our new Chocolate House sign – a bay-tree in all its splendour! I hope it looks something like. And I'm intending to send Jeremy over to the Exchange for the new china – a frightening risk, but one I have to take. But by the afternoon I may be able to slip out into the Garden. We all know what I need to do.'

It was Tom who hazarded an answer.

'Try and find Kate Primrose before her enemies do?'

'Yes, if she's still in London – perhaps taking refuge in a brothel-house where she can hide more easily? Discreet enquiries are needed. I must ask my friends. What Clarissa knows could be vital, if she can be persuaded to speak of it.'

'After her terrifying experience...' Tom began. But the sentence trailed off into silence. All three felt a touch of it themselves – it had been that kind of day. The very opposite of a day of rest.

But there was somebody else whose day of rest had been disrupted, and at that moment he made his presence known at the door of the coffee-room. An anxious Elias Cobb was ushered in, his face frowning, and he looked at Widow Trotter with concern.

'Joshua has told me what's happened. I had to come at once. He spoke something about poetry being stolen. I hope my fears are wrong?'

'You're not wrong, Elias. Poor Mr Bristowe here has lost all his papers.'

'All... ?'

He looked around angrily, as though the culprit ought to be there in the room to face his wrath.

'... But I knew nothing of this. I took it that you were out of danger, young man.'

Elias's voice showed real concern.

The tale was briefly told, a quick inspection of the scene made, and within ten minutes the four of them were back cradling their dishes containing a concoction that was by now so thick and harsh that it stretched the definition of coffee to breaking-point – Peter Simco would not have approved. It was getting late, and none wished to go into the details of their Sunday experiences yet again. The adventurers were all tired, and Will needed to make his way back to the Temple.

An hour later only Widow Trotter and Elias remained, sitting together by the low embers of the fire. Exhausted as she was, she was giving the constable a careful account of everything they had learned that day. In particular she told him about her discovery of Emmet's home-from-home in Vinegar Yard, and how Kate Primrose had been threatened by an intruder looking for Emmet's papers. Elias whistled, and expressed the view – not for the first time – that she was better equipped for the job of constable than he was. He promised to make enquiries.

'You must let me help in this,' he said quietly, 'I'll do what I can – ask questions and sniff the air. But take great care, Molly, and trust no-one – not until this affair is over. I needn't tell you how serious the matter is.'

Monday

2 February 1708

Chapter Nineteen

FINDING PAUL BARNARD was not easy, and Tom's frustrations returned when he found himself standing once again outside John Morphew's premises. The place remained shut up, with no sign of life either in the shop or the printing-house. Faced with a wasted journey, he turned round dejectedly and was trudging out of the yard, scraping the cobbles in annoyance, when he suddenly remembered Walter, the porter at Stationers' Hall who had come over to help Constable Buller inspect Emmet's body. Not only was there a good chance he would know the compositor's lodgings, but he must surely have his own account to give. Tom berated himself for his naivety. Why hadn't he thought of it before? What a green investigator he was!

And so, with new purpose he walked across to the imposing brick-built hall at the far end of the yard, and looked up at its elegant windows. He couldn't avoid calling to mind what the building represented. Stationers' Hall was the custom-house of the literary world, the place where the nation's books, from the bulkiest tome to the flimsiest leaves of verse, were recorded. For a few moments he indulged in the melancholy thought that after last night's theft no work of his would ever be entered in its hallowed registers alongside those of Shakespeare, Jonson, and Dryden.

But the pang was only a brief one, and he dismissed it with a heroic shrug. A nearer approach gave him a glimpse of the porter busying himself in his basement office. A quick descent of some stone steps and a tap on the window brought him inside to a comfortable seat and a coal fire. The man seemed glad of the distraction and introduced himself as Walter Treadwell, porter and watchman to Stationers' Hall. Tom's first instinct was to feign ignorance – inquire about the closure of John Morphew's shop, then gradually wheedle out some information. But in his present mood he was heartily sick of deception, and so he broached the subject directly. He looked into the man's warm-coloured face and bright eyes, and decided to trust him.

Tom told his own story first: how he had been invited into the printing-house by James Feeny, had viewed Emmet's corpse, and was concerned to hear that Morphew had been charged with his murder. He understood that the porter had been called over when the body was discovered and had helped gather evidence.

It was a bold move; but fortunately Walter Treadwell was interested in Tom's account and eager to respond with his own story. He told of the first horrifying sight of Emmet's body, the arrival of Morphew and the watchman, the collecting of evidence, and the final scene in the Magistrate's kitchen when a distracted Morphew was questioned about the crime. Tom gained the impression that the porter's tale had been polished over many retellings. It seemed to conform to what he had heard from Feeny, though there were some luridly embroidered details: the floor streaming with blood, the face of the victim, side-on, staring out in fear along the floor – those eyes! – they were something he would never forget (Tom's own inspection had shown an expression that was remarkably placid – probably Feeny and Barnard had composed his features and closed his eyes when they laid him out?).

Tom asked the porter how Constable Buller had seemed when he summoned him over to the printing-house.

'Mr Buller was breathless, Sir, and very brisk, as you might expect in the circumstances. There were hardly any words and we hurried over at once. When we walked into the room he made sure I saw the whole scene – the weapon by poor Mr Emmet's body, and the bit of paper in his hand. He told me to retrieve it but not touch anything else. He said I had to remember the details I'd seen – as if I could forget them! It was all done most properly. We lit more candles – though this only made the shock of seeing him worse. Poor Mr Emmet! He used to keep himself very close and I didn't know him well. But he was valued – Mr Morphew thought highly of him, and his friend Mr Barnard would put up with his little ways. A bit of a complaining sort sometimes is Mr Barnard, but I've never heard him say anything really bad about Mr Emmet, though we knew he'd been dabbling in what he shouldn't – scandalous letters and suchlike. They say Mr Morphew was furious with him – angrier than he'd ever been in his life! But to commit such a deed… It's most unlike him. He must have been sorely tried.'

As the porter spoke, Tom realised how imagination can play the dramatist, how the theatre of the mind can create scenes that might have been, or ought to have been. The killing clearly made terrible sense to Walter, as it no doubt would to a jury. Tom understood what a struggle lay ahead.

Suddenly there was a rap at the door and the porter got to his feet. It was the boy with the post.

'You must excuse me, Sir. I'm afraid my most pressing job of the day has arrived and I must about things. I'm glad to have talked. I'm sorry you also experienced that scene – we'll neither of us wipe it from our minds… Well, I've signed my sworn statement for the Grand Jury, so we can only wait and see what happens.'

Tom left Stationers' Hall with the murder scene imprinted even more vividly on his inner eye. He was glad to have met Walter Treadwell, although it was sobering to think that even a friendly acquaintance could find Morphew's guilt credible.

Now he must find Paul Barnard, the compositor. The address the porter had given him took him eastwards past St Paul's Cathedral and along Paternoster Row to a decent little paved court. This would have been a quiet spot but for the harsh noise of a knife-grinder going about his trade. The man was bent over his stone wheel, his foot working the treadle hard, a comforting pipe billowing smoke from his mouth. As he approached, the man paused and held up a pair of scissors, wiping them with a rag. Tom noticed the cuffs of his coat were shredded, and his leather apron too. He hailed the grinder and was about to ask directions, but the man didn't hear him, and the whining and scraping began again, echoing round the court with a noise that sliced through the nerves. The poor fellow must be deaf, Tom thought, and no wonder – but then he saw a kerchief tied round the man's temples keeping small pads in place over his ears.

Eventually Tom found the right door, and in response to his knock he was confronted by a harassed Mrs Barnard with a little girl tugging impatiently at her apron. It was not an opportune moment for a conversation, but over the sound of grinding metal she redirected him to a nearby chop-house in Queen's Head Passage. 'You'll find him there – *breakfasting!*' she half-shouted with the kind of intonation that suggested her husband's breakfast could be a prolonged affair that went beyond mere bread and cheese.

When Tom arrived at Dolly's, the main room was well filled and noisy, and the smell of frying meat overwhelmed everything. Tom managed to squeeze through the crush to inquire of one of the waiters, and eventually he tracked his man down to a corner table by the far wall. At that very moment Paul Barnard was rising from his seat and finishing his bottle of ale. Clearly his breakfast was over, though he didn't have the appearance of someone who indulged his appetites. He was rather slight and bent, and his spectacles gave him a wary look. But when Tom introduced himself he was happy enough to converse, and suggested they move into the next room where coffee was to be had. There was less noise here, and the two of them sat at a small table by the window.

Once again Tom decided that honesty was required. So after introducing himself, he spoke briefly about his experience at the printing-house and what he had learned from James Feeny.

It didn't take long for Paul Barnard's feelings to show themselves. When Emmet's name was mentioned, the compositor seemed a little embarrassed. His face was taut and suspicious, and the few words came out awkwardly. But Tom persisted gently and explained his own part in what had happened. He was expressing shock and offering his condolences when, without warning, the compositor plucked off his spectacles and touched his eyes lightly with a handkerchief. Tom noticed that the man's fingers were small and delicate, and the movement nimble and precise. It had not struck him before, but he realised the obvious fact that a bull-like, big-fisted man would be as out of place in front of a type-case as he would in a china-shop.

'Mr Feeny and I had to lay him out. We did the most decent job we could – tried to make him look composed. But of course he had stiffened by then, so it was not easy.'

It had clearly been a gruesome ritual, and Tom could feel the man's horror at it.

'You both did a fine job. When I saw Mr Emmet's body late that morning he did look peaceful – and *composed,* as you say. The eyes especially – closed as if in a calm sleep. That must have been a terrible task. Mr Treadwell spoke of the corpse's frightful stare.'

'Thankfully the eyes were closed already, Sir. The thought of him staring out at me – that would have been too much to bear!... But it was the blood that was the worst. The gentleman was very particular about cleaning up the blood.'

'Ah yes, the gentleman who took charge – Mr Feeny told me about him. Do you know who he was?'

'No, Sir, but I think the Magistrate, old Mr Dignum, must have sent him. He had a commanding voice and a sharp manner. But Mr Feeny and I were happy to follow orders and let someone else take the responsibility.'

'I can well understand it. The two of you did all that could be asked of you – much more indeed.'

'Mr Emmet had no family, Sir. I've been making what arrangements I can.'

Then there was silence, a natural pause while the two of them sat in contemplation, as if showing respect for the dead. Tom allowed the seconds to pass, sensing that a great tide was welling up inside the man and would surely demand release. In the end, a simple heartfelt comment of Tom's was enough.

'Poor Mr Emmet. He didn't deserve such a fate...'

The compositor looked at Tom. His eyes were full of angry grief.

'... I told him he was very, very foolish. I pleaded with him to come to his senses. But he insisted he would go through with it... John Emmet was a stubborn man, Sir, a tenacious man who wouldn't let a thing drop. He had such big ambitions – of being a printer himself and having his own shop – and it drove him on. He busied himself furiously. You could see it when he was pulling at the press. Such big hands for a small fellow! Working it with his shoulders – and the determination on his face...'

Mr Barnard's recollection of Emmet was vivid, and he continued talking rapidly and animatedly. It seemed as if a dam had broken and the man was pouring out his thoughts for the first time. Tom could only sit and listen.

'… For the rest of the time he was forever meddling and prying. John Emmet loved secrets, Sir, and he was convinced there was deception everywhere – that everyone knew something he didn't. Publication was his line, but it was the private that excited him – the things on paper that didn't find their way into print. He had his own business by way of dealing in manuscripts, and Mr Morphew was happy to make use of him, at least at first. It was quietly profitable all round, and Mr Emmet did well enough trading papers in the City and Covent Garden, and especially in St James's. It was the *beau monde* that fired him most. He loved nothing better than getting his hands on a few juicy letters or a diary… You'll recall *The Lady's Pacquet of Letters?* – those private letters that were taken when French pirates boarded a boat as it crossed over to Holland?…'

Indeed Tom did: it had caused quite a stir a few months previously.

'… Well, it was Mr Emmet who handled the transaction, and Mr Morphew negotiated to publish the remaining part of them. There is a pile for sale in his shop right now. The *Pacquet* seems to have encouraged the Town's taste for those things – for secret memoirs and such stuff. Well, *thereby hangs a tale,* as the good poet says…'

The compositor took a sip of his coffee.

'… But more and more he was keeping Mr Morphew in the dark. He soon realised he could make money – good money – dealing for himself. When Mr Morphew became uneasy about it, John took things out east to the presses there, where things can be run off quickly and no questions asked. He still worked here, but all this began to distract him, and Mr Morphew challenged him about it. Only last week there was a pocket-book he got hold of which excited him no end. He was gleeful and said it would make his fortune! Well, it turns out he took a step too far and tried taking payment for the thing – you see, it was stolen goods. When Mr Morphew found out, he was angry and insisted he send the book back to its owner – John told me she was a fine lady who would have paid richly. But he ended up taking a bad hit on it. Mr Morphew said he wouldn't allow his premises to be used for criminal dealing. I remember his very phrase: "Emmet," he said, "if you insist on striding off to the gallows, you shall *not* leave from here... !"'

Tom noticed Barnard shiver as the irony struck home. He looked at the man and wondered if he should ask some questions, but the impetus was already there and so he stayed silent for a while longer.

'... But he didn't leave off, Sir. He had to settle one last affair – and it was a big one. He said it would *shake the State* – those were his very words! He was determined to see it through and was full of confidence. And to my shame...'

Paul Barnard's throat tightened and his voice broke. He reached for the dish of coffee.

'... To my everlasting shame... *I helped him.*'

'Helped him how? As a go-between?'

'I helped with the printing, Sir. We did it during the night – the two of us. It was a rich commission. For one hard night's work – twenty pounds! We were to share the money.'

'Did something go wrong, Mr Barnard? What was it you were printing?'

'No, it didn't go wrong – in fact, between us we made a good fist of it – for something so very rushed as it was. Just fifty copies, mind – and the pages were simply folded. We could do no more in the time. It was all delivered as contracted. But in the end, *payment was refused!* They took the books but refused to pay him. At least that's what he told me. He was sweating with anger about it – said he'd been betrayed. He swore he'd do no such political dirty work again.'

'*They?*... Who was he working for, do you know?'

'He wouldn't say, and frankly I was happy not to be told. But it seemed plain enough – after all, the poem was an execration against the Whigs.'

'So it was a commission from the Tories? Perhaps from Mr Harley and his friends?'

'Well, I've heard there's a lot of money flows from them in one direction or another – for anyone who's prepared to sell himself... Yes, Mr Bristowe, I reckon this was a bag of *Tory* sovereigns – no doubt in my mind!'

'But what made you get involved?'

'Because I thought it would be the end of the matter – that it would draw the line and we could both go back to the job we loved doing. We were a good team, the three of us. I did all the important composing, and John Emmet and James Feeny handled the presses. We could turn over a decent-sized pamphlet in a day, and a solid enough book in a week. Mr Morphew called the printing-house "Vulcan's Smithy." He said that when we were swimming along, no one could beat us.'

At this point Tom hazarded an intervention.

'Then what do you think happened on Friday?'

'It's a difficult business, Sir, but Mr Emmet had begun dealing with political people – very secretive. I knew we were doing wrong. At first I said no, absolutely not. But he pleaded with me – said that he needed the money badly so he could get married and start his own little business. He said he didn't care a fig for the politics of the thing – that both Whigs and Tories could go hang! This was a commission he thought he could handle – but only with my help.'

Again the compositor halted, conscious of how his words were tugging at his conscience. Tom realised it was becoming a confessional. For the past few minutes he had felt his heartbeat quickening. Every step seemed to take him nearer the words he was hoping – or fearing – to hear.

'What was it the two of you were printing?'

'A scurrilous poem, Sir – a strange uncomfortable prophecy! *Bufo's Magic Glass* it was called – a fanciful title for a fanciful thing. I knew it was strong stuff as I set it up. You see, when we compose we try not to become involved in the words – they're simply arrangements of letters, and it can be distracting to follow their meaning. But these words struck home. It was as though the thing might explode in front of me – each line crackling and electric. Frankly, I was glad to be rid of it! It was like nothing I'd ever composed before... Well, we ran off the copies during the night. John had a strong pull on him. And I fed the press and folded – the kind of thing I can do when needed – it's what Mr Feeny would normally handle.'

'Did James Feeny know what the two of you were up to?'

'Oh no, Sir! We had to cover our tracks and make everything right again. Those were the worst moments – washing and distributing the type and re-organising the paper store. Mr Feeny would have been outraged – and so would I normally. But somehow I found myself dragged into it. I'm ashamed, Sir... And now John Emmet is dead! It seems Mr Morphew discovered what John had been doing and lost his temper with him. I can understand it – there's a rumour he had been selling secrets up at the Cockpit. He was a stupid fool altogether! I don't know exactly what he was up to, but he seemed mightily pleased with himself.'

'So, Mr Morphew knew nothing about this? Emmet had been using the printing-shop as his own?'

'That's the long and the short of it, yes. He said the pamphlet was intended to be sent for printing out east, but since Mark our apprentice was back home with his parents for the week our shop would be empty through the night, and so the thing could be managed.'

'But where did the manuscript come from? Do you know how he got hold of it?'

'No, Sir, he kept quiet on that. He didn't let me see the original.'

Tom checked himself. Had he heard right?

'The original?'

'Yes. The copy we were using was his own. He'd transcribed it all very neatly – John was a good penman. He said the actual manuscript was crabbed and badly written, and with some distinctly odd orthography! So he had prepared the copy himself.'

Tom's mind was racing. It was an absurd thought, but... could Emmet have been Bufo? – the idea wasn't ridiculous, though he had to admit that Emmet was probably concealing his source. That meant the originals might still be found somewhere. He wondered... Perhaps it was Bufo's papers that Kate Primrose was guarding?

But before he could pursue the idea, he became conscious that Paul Barnard had stopped speaking and was staring at him. The compositor appeared to have realised he was opening his heart to a stranger, though a genial one. The man looked guarded and seemed about to call a halt to their meeting.

Instinctively Tom uttered a loud sigh, as if he shared the unease of the occasion.

'Oh what a terrible situation, Mr Barnard! Do you really think John Morphew could have done such a deed? I must admit I find it hard to credit. I found him an open and generous-minded man.'

'Indeed he is,' said the compositor, relaxing a little and becoming pensive. 'He always was a thoughtful person. Not the kind to be violent at all. But none of us knows what will push us over the edge, do we?'

The philosophical tone was unwelcome, but not unexpected. Tom at once came in sharply.

'But we should both have faith in him! I considered Mr Morphew was a man I could trust – and I still think that.'

Paul Barnard's face lightened at the thought.

'You're right, Mr Bristowe. And perhaps I should trust myself more too – I mean, trust my own feelings, such as they are... But we shall know the truth very soon.'

Tom shook his head slightly and shifted in his chair.

'The truth? We must hope the trial will reveal it!'

'What do you mean?'

Now it was Tom's turn to be unguarded.

'I mean that what *appears* to be the case may not *be* the case. Neither of us has heard Mr Morphew's account of what happened. And I for one cannot subscribe to his guilt until I've heard him speak.'

'Does that mean you intend to be at the trial?'

'Yes certainly. I'm concerned in Mr Morphew's fate. Anything more you can tell me would be greatly valued – and may possibly help him.'

Tom looked at Mr Barnard and felt he had won him over – that he had struck a note in tune with the compositor's heart – had reminded him of what he truly felt and had perhaps forgotten.

'Well, Mr Bristowe, I would dearly love to help you. But I'm not sure what I can add.'

'It's been good of you to talk so freely, Mr Barnard. There is one particular question that I hope you may be able to answer...'

Tom had something stored in the back of his mind and pulled it forward.

'... I remember that Mr Feeny said you thought there was something strange about the composing-stick – that it was odd in some way?'

Tom was hoping the compositor would say he'd not seen that particular stick before, and that in some feature the composing didn't witness to Emmet's hand... But he was to be disappointed.

'No, it wasn't odd in itself, Sir. I don't really remember what I said – but I recall reading the lines. They were a *curse*. It was as if a witch was pointing her bony finger directly at me. They made me feel distinctly uncomfortable – queasy even.'

'I take it the composing was beyond question Mr Emmet's?'

'I don't know what you're implying, Mr Bristowe, but yes, it was John's handiwork. I could tell from the spacing. You might not believe this, but every compositor has his own style. John could be clumsy – composing wasn't his line... And it was his stick of course. We each like to use our own. Does that disappoint you?'

Tom's slight hope had slipped away. It seemed that Emmet had indeed been setting up *Bufo's Curse* for printing when he was interrupted.

'But... when I examined Mr Emmet I saw that his fingers were clean. Could he really have been setting type?'

'Like any printing-shop, Mr Bristowe, we pride ourselves on our clean type. It's all washed before it's distributed. Working with dirty type is slovenly, and it leads to bad, blotchy handiwork.'

He felt deflated, and it was clear that Mr Barnard knew it.

'We are clutching at straws, Mr Bristowe. I myself have been turning the matter over endlessly. I'm sorry I can't help you.'

But Tom pressed on with a further question.

'Is it the case, then, that Mr Emmet had printed one or two other small pieces involving this *Bufo*? I'm thinking of one attacking the Duchess of Marlborough.'

'Ah yes – the *Caricatura!* – that was its title. I remember it was subscribed *Bufo*. It was from the same manuscript. John read out the passage to me with great relish. He said he thought Bufo was a man after his own heart. He had run off a few copies of those lines on the Duchess the previous night, as a trial. He said he was tempted to circulate them – said he'd pay anything *to see that she-dragon breathe fire!* He'd kept them in the forme so we could re-use them.'

This fitted the account Morphew had given: how he had caught Emmet with a copy of the *Caricatura* and had challenged him. Emmet must have taken the paper to the Cockpit and told them it was from Morphew's presses. And the same, Tom realised, would be true for *Bufo's Magic Glass* – that it was Morphew's work.

Paul Barnard was now looking drained and disconsolate, and Tom shared the feeling. They had both been re-living a terrible experience. But he knew he had made the man think and perhaps had raised a nagging doubt in his mind. Their conversation had clearly unsettled him – he could see it from the compositor's hunched shoulders and drawn look. This was not how Tom wanted to leave things. Determined to clear the air, he rose to his feet and pointed to the door that led back into the chop-house.

'We've both had substantial breakfasts this morning, Mr Barnard, but I trust you'll let me buy you a glass of good Nantes brandy. I'm sure Dolly's can provide! It would be refreshing to talk a little about other things – the latest doings in the literary world, perhaps? Have you seen Mr Philips's *Cyder?*'

Tom led the compositor back into the busy distractions of the chop-room. He was grateful to Paul Barnard for his honesty and openness. As for himself, he'd discovered a lot. But the picture that was forming was not of Morphew's undoubted innocence: the facts were not making the pattern he wanted to see. Morphew was more enmeshed in Emmet's dealings than he had expected, and his hopes for the composing-stick and the clean fingers were unjustified. Far from proving that the evidence had been planted the following day, it now seemed certain that, when he was killed, Emmet was preparing to print the *Curse*.

After a genial hour of literary gossip Tom began making his way back in the direction of the printing-house, and his thoughts turned to Will in Westminster Hall. He hoped his friend's conversation with Richard Sumner was yielding something more solid and positive. As he walked, he cast his mind back over what Paul Barnard had told him and was more than a little disconcerted to find himself re-enacting in his imagination the dramatic scene of the Angry Printer.

Chapter Twenty

WILL ALWAYS HAD conflicted feelings when he walked into Westminster Hall. No-one could fail to be awe-struck by the ancient grandeur of the place, especially the huge timbers of the roof which stretched across the expanse. Towering over your head was the weight of the nation's history, the supportive structure of the State. The oak beams were delicately poised as if hung there by some mysterious force; and up in the echoing vault the twenty-six floating angels, thirteen on each side, were looking down impassively on the activities below, just as they had looked down on deposed kings and condemned traitors in centuries past. The massive impersonal load seemed temporarily suspended above you, ready to crush everyone beneath like beetles under a wheel. The imagined threat was hovering, and yet all was reassuringly regular and ordered – indeed beautiful. Thankfully, every piece of shaped wood and hewn stone was nicely balanced and in perfect alignment.

The same couldn't be said for the ramshackle confusion that confronted you at ground level. The nation's legal holy of holies also functioned as a busy market-place, with courts and shops all sharing the one large room; and on either side of the hall there were dozens of stalls selling goods of many kinds. It was a general meeting-place for idlers who enjoyed being part of the throng, casually browsing at the bookstalls or ogling the new millinery. Numbered among the strollers were lawyers and attorneys ready to have their gowns twitched with an offer of employment; and students from the Temple were there, hoping to squeeze into one of the law courts where they could observe and take notes.

On this Monday morning, the hum of conversation made Will think he was in a huge coffee house, and the smell of roasted beans was tempting enough for Richard Sumner to suggest they fortify themselves. As they began to make their way through the mêlée, Will could see that two of the courts were already in session at the raised upper end of the hall where stone steps led to a space reserved for the monarch's throne. The Queen's Bench occupied the left-hand side, and next to it, to the right, the Court of Chancery was hearing witnesses. Huddling behind their thin panels of wood, the two courts occupied cramped box-pews where barristers and witnesses had to make themselves heard above the general hubbub. Under conditions like these it helped to have a strong, ringing voice and commanding presence. Mumbling would never do. Secret whispering, however, was extremely effective.

The third court of law was their destination today. Half way down the hall on the right-hand side, squeezed into a temporary wooden structure that could be easily dismantled for state occasions, was the Court of Common Pleas, where shopkeepers, landlords, tenants, debtors and fractious neighbours were bringing actions against each other.

Will and Mr Sumner had discussed their case in the wherry that had brought them from Temple Stairs, and Will was all prepared to listen and take notes – the dispute would be an intriguing one. While the barrister went off to purchase the coffee, he held the brief in his hand and began to feel like a barrister himself. But his own 'case' made him apprehensive –

questioning Richard Sumner about the pocket-book would test him to the limit. Fortunately, he thought, he would be able to settle himself during the court proceedings and introduce the subject afterwards, once their business was over.

But these plans were to be frustrated. Before reaching the coffee-counter, Mr Sumner had talked with the Clerk of the Court and discovered that the two parties to the dispute were nowhere to be found. The truth was that the road from Braintree was impassable and so the matter of Wilkins versus Frodsham had been shelved. This unlooked-for stroke of Fate meant that Farmer Wilkins's Essex field would have to remain waterlogged for a while longer, while his neighbour Squire Frodsham's pond would have a temporary reprieve. It was a double blow. Will had mastered the technicalities of land-drainage and was a little disappointed that he would not be able to offer his thoughts. But this was as nothing to the alarm that shivered through him as he reached for his dish of coffee.

Richard Sumner suggested that, given these annoying circumstances, Will might profitably pass his morning attending the Queen's Bench – if he could squeeze into a seat. He himself would browse among the books for a while and then pay a visit to a local attorney before returning to the Temple.

This made things difficult. Will had to speak there and then. The result was sudden and awkward.

'I was hoping, Sir, to talk to you on another topic – the conduct of a Coroner's Inquest.'

This sounded naïve, and Will knew it – they were the words of an over-eager pupil determined to impress. The barrister's eyes registered surprise.

'Westminster Hall is hardly the place for that, Will. But it's something I'll be happy to discuss with you at an appropriate time – though of course I've had little experience of inquests myself. What makes you mention this now?'

Mr Sumner's nostrils twitched slightly and joined his eyes in expressing quizzical curiosity.

'I ask, Sir, because I shall be attending a Coroner's inquest this afternoon, and I very much need your guidance... I was hesitating about mentioning it, but felt I should, given that it touches, though only incidentally, on an affair I was concerned with on your behalf.'

What a fine sentence! Will took a much-needed breath.

Richard Sumner was now directly attentive.

'What? Has there been some accident or death? One of my clients?'

'No, Sir, I'm afraid it's a more sensitive matter. I'm embarrassed to raise it, but you'll come to hear very shortly if you are not aware of it now...'

'*Aware?* Is this something that may cause difficulties? You look hesitant, Will, as if you're unwilling to mention it...'

He stepped even closer and suddenly dropped his voice further.

'... What kind of embarrassment are you hinting at?'

'I wasn't going to tell you. I may be unnecessarily anxious, but I wouldn't want anything to emerge that might cause trouble.'

'Anxious? Trouble? What *is* this? You must tell me at once.'

'John Emmet.'

'Emmet? You mean that printer-fellow? The go-between with the pocket-book?'

'Yes, Morphew's pressman.'

'But you said everything had been cleared, and the business was concluded.'

His hushed voice was now edged with anxiety. Will tried to speak calmly and reasonably.

'I've never given you the full details of my meeting at the publisher's – after all, the important thing was to recover the book. But I'm afraid there was a sordid incidental matter that

I wanted to keep you clear of… It seems that Emmet had been hoping to extract more money from you, but Morphew overruled him.'

'I should have known! I deliberately didn't question you closely about it – I think I suspected as much. That's why I gave you such a large sum. You must have understood this yourself, Will.'

'Indeed I did, Sir. I realised it was a matter of extreme delicacy… But you need to know the upshot of it… Emmet is dead.'

For a brief second it seemed that Sumner's face relaxed in relief at the news. But a moment's thought brought another urgent question:

'You say *dead*. A Coroner's jury suggests it was suspicious.'

Will's whispered reply seemed to cut through all the noise of Westminster Hall.

'Yes. Murder.'

Richard Sumner swung his body to the side and almost dropped his dish of coffee – he wasn't attending to what his hand was doing. He looked up at the roof, as if seeking an answer to his next question.

'Does this close the affair, do you think? Or open it up afresh?'

'This is what I'm anxious to discover, Sir. I think I need to be there to hear what is said.'

'Yes, indeed you do. Thank you, Will. News of this hadn't reached me, so I'm somewhat alarmed, I have to say. I thought the matter was at an end.'

Will sympathised with the barrister and felt a twinge of mental pain himself. It was like a wound reopening.

'But as things stand, it is worse still… John Morphew has been arrested and is likely to be charged with the killing.'

Richard Sumner saw the full ominous picture.

'But that's terrible! It is sure to be a sensational trial. What can we do?... What might we *have* to do?'

'Nothing will touch you, I sincerely hope – or your sister. It seems Emmet was a dealer in private papers, and he had other irons in the fire. Nevertheless...'

'My sister?... Everything must be done to keep her name clear of this!'

'I understand completely. Nevertheless, there is a chance that mention might be made of the pocket-book when Morphew is questioned at the trial. He might argue that Emmet's behaviour was a provocation – that it aroused justifiable anger.'

'What did the printer *do?*' Sumner interjected. There was a whiff of contempt in his voice.

'Emmet was beaten to death, Sir. But it's entirely possible Mr Morphew was not Emmet's killer. I hold out the hope that his innocence might be proved.'

'But what have you to do with it? Why let yourself be involved?'

'Truth to tell, I'm involved further – but fortunately so, I think... While I was at the publisher's I got wind of another scandal – that Emmet was attempting to implicate Morphew in sedition. He had denounced him to the authorities. If there *is* extenuation, then it's surely to be found in that quarter, not in anything that would compromise your sister's honour.'

'Her *honour...* ?'

The barrister spoke sharply. Will was taken aback. He had not been expecting this.

'... My sister's honour?... I assure you, Will, that is not in question at all!'

Will realised he had been making an unjustified assumption about the pocket-book's contents.

'Mr Sumner, I... I deeply apologise. I wasn't for a moment suggesting that...'

Will broke off – because he had clearly been suggesting exactly that.

'No, no! It is not my *sister's* reputation that is at stake here. Not at all. There is a much higher honour involved…'

Mr Sumner checked himself. In court the barrister was accustomed to directing the questioning and drawing the truth from an unwilling witness. Somehow he felt things were the wrong way round.

'… It is fervently to be hoped that this Morphew doesn't stoop so low. You assured me he had not looked into the book.'

'That's true, Sir. It's what he told me. He assured me of it – and I believe him.'

'Nevertheless, the pressman had seen its contents, hadn't he? I'm sure he must have slavered over its pages. He sounds like an unscrupulous prying dog to me.'

Will saw that Mr Sumner had reached the point where he was looking for help and reassurance. He needed to seize the initiative.

'I assure you, Sir, I'll do everything I can… I shall be visiting Mr Morphew in Newgate tomorrow.'

'What! Are you sure you wish to put yourself into the thick of things like this? Why expose yourself to such horrors?'

'It's because I'm convinced that he didn't kill Emmet. You have several times told me – emphasised to me – that circumstances should always be questioned. That a nicely structured story may be a convenient fiction, and only when those neat pieces are rearranged do you see the untidy truth… I intend to prove his innocence!'

'But that's what he must do himself – when he's tested, *he* has to convince a jury.'

'But a man alone in prison is the last person able to hunt down the facts that might exonerate him.'

'Facts? If you really believe he is innocent, then you'll need your facts to be solid and incontrovertible. I speak here as a barrister, Will. In my experience facts are seldom allowed to stand in the way of a good verdict.'

'I take note, Sir. But to return to my point. If I'm able to talk with the publisher tomorrow, I might guide him away from mention of your sister's pocket-book. I swear I'll do all I can to steer his mind elsewhere...'

Will saw that Richard Sumner was uneasy and harassed, and that he would rather nothing more was said on the matter. Will's only chance was to keep pressing until the revelation came, and offer himself as a friend and ally.

'... The *truth*, Mr Sumner!... I beg you to tell me the truth. I swear to do everything I can to keep this quiet. I speak honestly when I say that I'm better able to do so if I know the full situation... I hope I've proved that you can trust me. The steersman needs to know where the dangerous rocks lie.'

They both stood in silence. Around them, the multifarious life of Westminster Hall went busily on. It was the usual mixture of solemn judgment, light-hearted wit, intense thought and frivolous pastime. The two men were standing at the centre of it all, yet they felt oddly private amidst the bustle. People brushed past them but didn't hover. It was a place where everyone seemed to have their own business to mind. Then, after a thoughtful pause, Richard Sumner spoke – in a rather formal manner, Will thought. Perhaps it was helping the barrister make sense of events.

'Lady Norreys's pocket-book is – was – a kind of commonplace-book, an account of conversations. I would wish to say *private* conversations, but I'm afraid they were not treated as such, and a record was taken. My sister, Will, is an independent and masterful woman, and she has formed around her a group of women of a similar disposition. They meet to gossip about everything you can imagine. From the account I've been given it seems to be a committee of censure on private and *public* life – the line is seldom drawn. It is a mere tea-table – there are no more than five or six of them. But they form a kind of female *cabinet* – and a regularly high-flying Tory one it is! And one of their number – though I'm assured she attended only once... is Mrs Masham...'

It was now Will's turn to be shocked.

'... I'm sure Abigail Masham is ordinarily a discreet woman. For someone so completely trusted by the Queen she would have to be. But I regret to say that on this occasion her tongue was loosened – I cannot tell how – not merely through tea I would assume – and indiscretions were voiced... No, more than that – disgraceful *intimacies* were discussed. It is shocking, but my sister – with what gleeful excitement I do not know – took the revelations down. She wrote down things that should never have been thought, let alone spoken. But alas, they were the subject of their chatter in the excitement of the moment. My sister, I have to say, attempts to make light of it. But it disgusts me – and if published it would involve *Her Majesty* in the deepest embarrassment. I can hardly bring myself to allude to it.'

Richard Sumner turned his head away as if wanting to breathe some purer air. Will seized the opportunity.

'I will spare you having to speak of it, Sir. You needn't continue. I take it that things were revealed about the close alliance between Her Majesty and Mrs Masham – close, perhaps, in ways it is hard for us to understand.'

Will's glorious euphemism soothed the moment, but also prolonged it. The barrister, with the precision of a practised interrogator, felt he needed to flesh out the implication, man to man.

'Yes, Will. You touch on it exactly... strong affections... physical details of the Queen's body that only an intimate – an extreme intimate – could know...'

Both men understood that the time had come to draw the curtain – having seen what lay behind it. Will assumed a formal tone himself, as if a solemn oath were being taken.

'You may leave this to me, Sir. I fully understand now, and I promise to exercise extreme care and vigilance on the matter. When I talk to Mr Morphew, I shall do my best to guide him elsewhere. As I said, I'm convinced he does not know the incendiary contents of the pocket-book.'

'Yes, we must pray he did not read it. If he is a man of honour he will not have done so.'

Will could see the picture clearly. It made sense of the barrister's anxieties and of his huge relief when the pocket-book was returned. But what about Emmet? The pressman knew the value of the book – its dirty 'value' for someone wishing to cause mischief, not only at Court but to the State itself. Surely, if Emmet thought he might have to surrender the book, would he not transcribe the hottest parts and keep them?... And did he offer his copy to an interested party? If so, who was it? Both Whig and Tory would pay a very high price: the one to procure it, the other to destroy it. And perhaps death was the price Emmet himself had been asked to pay? If so, then which side exacted it?

Will felt he had walked over the coals unscathed. It had been a difficult conversation, but he had achieved far more than he expected, and his relief was almost euphoric. But thoughts of the imminent Coroner's inquest brought him down to earth. In the end he parted on good terms with Richard Sumner, something which in itself was cause for gratitude. Master and pupil shook hands, both of them feeling the need to be alone and think about what they had just heard. The barrister wished Will luck with the inquest and slipped away to turn the pages of some old books.

For another few moments Will remained standing in the centre of Westminster Hall, and looked upwards. It was a room that over the centuries had witnessed countless revelations. Measured against these, his brief conversation with Richard Sumner had been nothing – a mere whispered echo of those momentous accusations that in years past had shaken the pillars of the State. The architectural image brought an ironic smile to his lips. This vast, seemingly unsupported canopy appeared Samson-proof! But he could not help wondering what hidden strains and weaknesses the old structure might conceal – and what could be eating away those beams in secret?

Chapter Twenty-One

An Inquisition &c taken at the King's Head Tavern in the Ward of Farringdon Within, London, the 2nd Day of February Anno Domini 1708 before George Rivers Coroner on view of the body of one John Emmet lying dead at the premises of John Morphew Printer at Stationers' Yard in the said ward, by the oaths of John Lingard, Richard Lapeley, John Hicks, Richard Hicks, Josiah Smith, Samuel Row, William Whitehand, David Wilford, John Walker, Stephen Lee, Henry Quantock, William Waddis, Thomas Motley, William Trickett, Nicholas Chapman, Robert Gill.

They find that the said John Morphew Late of London Printer on the 30th Day of January in the year aforesaid upon the said John Emmet feloniously and wilfully did make an assault and that the said John Morphew with a certain walking-cane of his own property did wilfully strike and knock down and did then and there give unto the said John Emmet on the rear of his skull several mortal wounds of which he instantly died at the premises aforesaid. They accuse the said John Morphew of murder.

Witness:
Joseph Buller constable
Walter Treadwell porter
Samuel Bennett watch

—⚬⚬⚬—

'NOTHING LESS THAN a farce! A puppet-show from beginning to end!'

Will's exasperation had been mounting during the inquest, which had passed chaotically and taken less than half an hour. Good order was not helped by the crush of onlookers, which made the close viewing of the body difficult for the sixteen jurors. At Morphew's premises they were swept into the warehouse by the crowd that had assembled, and although the Coroner had attempted to keep control and 'admit only those persons who had a direct involvement in the business,' the inspection was cursory. Constable Buller's commentary seemed to satisfy them, especially when he wielded the still-bloodied cane and demonstrated exactly how the blows had fallen on the dead man's skull. It was so convincing a performance that the audience gasped in horror as if they were watching Macbeth murder Duncan. By this time the Coroner had accepted that it was not to be a model exercise of his duties. It had been compromised from the beginning. He was only glad that the cause of death was clear for all to see – even for those who stood on tiptoe in the doorway, or the men at the back who were perched on bales of paper.

At the start of the performance Alderman Rivers had made it clear that he considered the whole exercise 'most irregular,' in that the body in question had been moved and the scene of death cleaned and tidied. To those around who could hear him, he announced that he was most unhappy with what had been done – although he appreciated that in such a workplace there would be a natural wish to remove the gore…

The Coroner was eager to adjourn to the nearby tavern where the depositions would be taken, and in the process there was so much chattering and pushing that any note-taking was out of the question. And any thoughts Tom might have had of offering his considered analysis of the nature of the wound and the pattern of bloodstains were soon dispelled.

The situation improved little in the upstairs room of the tavern, where the cause of death was agreed *nem. con.* The accounts given before the Magistrate were repeated, and Walter Treadwell was there in person to confirm his written evidence. The watchman, named as Sam Bennett, spoke eloquently about his fright at seeing the suspect wandering in the street, and his description of the night-scene came vividly alive. The suspect's disturbed and bloody appearance made him appear, he said, like one distracted – a being with some terrible thing on his conscience. At this point Tom and Will had noticed some of the jurors nodding in agreement: they knew that dark deeds will out, and how guilt shows itself.

Constable Buller had re-assumed his role of demonstrator. His account moved back and forth between the blood on the victim, the blood on the cane, and the blood on the suspect, until one large crimson stain seemed to spread over the terrible act of which Morphew had been a part. The composing-stick was shown, along with the small sheet of paper that had been clutched in the victim's hand. The jurors asked for it to be read aloud, and the Coroner, who was not without a degree of histrionic skill, obliged. Will and Tom were not the only ones to shiver as the words of *Bufo's Curse* rang through the room. The voice seemed to be delivering its own evidence and confirmed the sordid nature of the incident. It was agreed that in the printing-house the *Curse* had been in the process of being printed, and both Emmet and Morphew were tainted by the idea.

The Coroner reminded the jury that the inquiry's job was to decide on the manner and cause of death, and not to allow circumstantial matters to blur their findings. Nevertheless, it was accepted that there must have been an altercation between the two men, and the *Curse* appeared to have been its provoker. It was for the trial jury to decide, he said, if such provocation might be regarded as an extenuating circumstance and lead to a verdict of manslaughter, or if the suspect's wild behaviour might be taken as evidence of mental imbalance. It took very little conferring for the Grand Jury to agree on a charge of murder, without prejudice to the trial's fuller consideration of the evidence. On that basis, the Coroner announced, the suspect would be tried at the Old Bailey on that charge, the trial set for Thursday the fifth of February.

Tom and Will had gasped at the thought. Just two more days.

'That was not at all like Westminster Hall,' said Will ruefully as they walked together in the direction of Covent Garden. 'What a performance!'

Tom had been baffled by the pace of it all and by the inescapable feeling that the inquiry had operated merely mechanically. Nothing had cast doubt on the supposed facts, and their worst fears had been confirmed. It could only be hoped the criminal trial would have a fuller consideration of the evidence and allow doubts and questions to be raised.

'Is this the Law in operation, Will? If so, then Heaven help us.'

'Yes, we talk of the Majesty of Justice, but a farce like this brings the whole idea into contempt.'

'At least, at the trial John Morphew will be able to speak in his own defence, won't he? And he can question the witnesses?'

'Yes, but he'll make his speech when all the witness evidence has been given. And it's hard for an accused man to conduct his own questioning… And of course, Morphew is sure to face some embarrassing questions himself.'

The two of them walked on in thoughtful silence. The situation was grave. It appeared the legal trial was expected to be a formality. Were they the only people not prepared to accept the story of what happened? Did no-one else have doubts? But they had to keep going. Only two full days were left to discover the truth about John Emmet's killing. *Who* and *why*? That last question was the key to everything. They couldn't answer the first till they had discovered the second. Why had the pressman met such a violent end?

By the time Tom, Will and Mrs Trotter came together round the parlour-table they knew there was a great deal they needed to share, and that new scenes were opening up. Tom described his conversations with Walter Treadwell and Paul Barnard, and Will reported on his meeting with Richard Sumner in Westminster Hall. The porter, the compositor, and the barrister all had something to contribute. The information from Paul Barnard and Richard Sumner was especially important, albeit the two scenes were pointing them in different directions.

At the centre of the first was Bufo and his incendiary verses. From what the compositor had said, it was clear that Emmet had been involved up to his eyebrows, procuring, transcribing, and printing them – indeed there was still the possibility that he himself was 'Bufo.' True or not, the very suspicion could have led to his killing. Sunderland and the Whigs were determined to silence the poisonous voice; the Duchess of Marlborough was also incensed, and who knows what her unscrupulous agent Arthur Maynwaring might be capable of?

On the other hand, they couldn't afford to ignore Lady Norreys's pocket-book. What Richard Sumner had divulged meant that its contents, if made public, would expose the Queen to scandal and ridicule; and if Abigail Masham were shown to be the source, the revelation would put an end to Robert Harley's neatly-plotted scheme to form his own government.

What could have provoked the murder, then? Bufo's fulminations, or Mrs Masham's indiscretions? Which posed the greater threat? At this stage, Bufo appeared the likelier, but behind both of the scenes lay the power-struggle between Whigs and Tories, between the Junto's designs and Harley's ambitions. And there at the centre of it all was poor, meddling Emmet, a man with big ambitions of his own who seemed to have revelled in stirring up trouble and upsetting everyone.

'The more I think about this,' said Widow Trotter, 'the more I wonder which party had greater cause to want Emmet dead…'

'And Morphew put on trial,' added Tom.

Will looked doubtful:

'We've been assuming those motives are linked, haven't we? But we shouldn't discount the possibility that Morphew was simply being used to draw the fire. After all, that's exactly what has happened, isn't it? Morphew will take the blame, and the matter will be closed. Except that one side or the other will doubtless exploit the case, perhaps with a pamphlet – something like *A True Account* – or *Last Confessions*. The Whigs can present Emmet as Bufo's agent, a grubby Tory scandalmonger who got his deserts; and the Tories can paint him as a Whig informer who was exploited and then abandoned by them.

Tom beamed with admiration.

'What do you think, Mrs Trotter? Will this man be a successful lawyer?'

'Yes, there's something in this. It seems Emmet had his own plans and didn't regard himself as in the pay of either party.'

'And yet,' said Tom, 'Paul Barnard told me he turned violently against Harley's faction. He had risked everything to print *Bufo's Magic Glass* for them, only to find himself brushed away and the promised payment refused. It seems he'd served his purpose and could be dispensed with. It meant of course that Harley could disown the pamphlet if he needed to. Was the killing of Emmet their final move, I wonder?'

'On the other hand,' said Will, 'remember that the pamphlet was Emmet's work. Surely the Whigs could never see him as anything other than a troublemaker? They could never really trust him.'

Mrs Trotter turned to Tom.

'And perhaps there's more. Remember, Emmet was boasting that he knew of something big and far-reaching...'

'Yes, something that would *shake the State*. Paul Barnard told me those were his words.'

'... Exactly,' she continued. 'Could that be the contents of the pocket-book? If we're thinking about the *State*, perhaps there were more revelations?'

'I suppose it could be something we've not discovered yet?'

Tom spoke the words with a gloomy half-sigh, and looked around him. They were all conscious that only two days remained.

Widow Trotter sensed despondency looming. She leapt to her feet.

'We've given the matter plenty of sober deliberation, haven't we! Well, I think at this juncture we all need a glass of Madeira. It may encourage us to think more freely and creatively – *outside the room*, so to speak...'

She went over to the sideboard and became the hostess.

'... What might be a good idea is if we say in turn what questions are still puzzling us, however small. I suspect each of us has some niggling thought which we haven't yet voiced – I know I do! Perhaps a trivial detail or a little nagging doubt could be crucial... Shall we try this? Who wants to begin?... What about you, Will?'

Will's head was lowered and he seemed hesitant. He slowly brushed the hair away from his forehead and looked up at her.

'You may not like this, Mrs T, but I do have a nagging doubt. One I can't dislodge, however hard I try. And I think there's only one way to remove it.'

'Tell us... I think I can guess what it is.'

'John Morphew's innocence.'

Tom and Mrs Trotter exchanged uneasy glances. They knew they were trusting their convictions. Deep down, they longed to know – absolutely to know – that the publisher hadn't simply lost control and done the terrible deed.

'I've been thinking about that,' said Tom. 'Perhaps our lingering doubt is a tribute to John Morphew? The fact that we don't *know* makes our belief in him the greater.'

'I admire your faith, Tom,' said Widow Trotter. 'But you say there's one way of settling this, Will?'

'Yes. And it's something we have to do. We surely can't continue acting at such a remove from Morphew himself. We have to stop playing with conjectures and intervene directly. We must visit Morphew in Newgate... I think Tom and I should go there tomorrow. In fact, I told Richard Sumner this morning that I would do that. What do you say, Tom? The two of us... into the jaws of Hell?'

Tom gulped visibly.

'Yes, I'll come with you. It's something we have to do. We must talk to Morphew in person. After all, he'll know best how we can help him.'

Widow Trotter warmed to the idea.

'And I think you can help him with regard to the trial. The poor man must be utterly lost. There may be things you can tell him, Will? – advice about how he should act on Thursday? From what you said of the Coroner's inquest, there's a danger the right questions will never be asked, and the thing will be decided without Morphew being able to defend himself.'

'According to the Law, Mrs Trotter, his one defence *is* himself. There will be character witnesses of course. But I'm worried they will only be able to say how out of character that violent act is. Perhaps the best we can hope for is the "moment of madness" idea, which would allow a verdict of manslaughter.'

'But those repeated vicious blows to the head? It was more than a moment,' said Tom, 'and they'll prove that Morphew was angry when he left the Cockpit. He may even have made threats.'

'All the more reason for confronting him with this. He best knows what the prosecutor is going to argue against him.'

There was a moment's silence. They could feel the pulse of the situation, and by an odd rhythmic coincidence their arms lifted simultaneously and raised three glasses to their lips. Widow Trotter smiled at the symmetry. Perhaps they really were a team?

'And what about you, Tom? Is there any niggling question we ought to think about?'

'Hmmm... well yes, I suppose there is... It's just what you say, a small question, but it won't leave me alone.... *Who closed his eyes?*'

'Ah!' exclaimed Widow Trotter.

'From Walter Treadwell's account it appears that from the moment he and Constable Buller examined Emmet's body the correct procedure was followed. The constable was right to fetch someone who could act as another witness, and the porter did his job conscientiously. That's why I'm troubled by the detail of the eyes. Treadwell said that Emmet's eyes were staring widely. The constable told him not to touch anything, but only to remove the paper from Emmet's fist, which he did. Yet Paul Barnard, the compositor, insisted that early the next morning when he first saw the body, and before he and James Feeny did the laying-out, the eyes were closed.'

'But doesn't it simply mean that Constable Buller closed Emmet's eyes?' said Will hesitantly, aware that it was an obvious point.

'Yes of course. But when – and why? If he was so concerned that the porter shouldn't touch anything on the body, then why close the eyes?'

'I suppose,' said Widow Trotter, 'he wanted to let the poor man rest in peace?'

'Exactly,' said Tom. 'But Buller is the constable. He's concerned with gathering evidence. And he did that rigorously, as we know. Yet, when he gave his report at the inquest, he said nothing about the eyes...'

Now it was Will's turn to say 'Ah!'

'... Constable Buller treated the whole scene like a lurid drama, and he spared no effort in communicating it. And yet he was silent about Emmet's stare – the very thing that struck Walter Treadwell unforgettably... but the constable chose to ignore it. I wonder why? And yet, we agree he must have closed the eyes.'

Widow Trotter began to feel they were making progress.

'You've touched on something there, Tom. I think we need to know more about this Constable Buller. Elias Cobb is our man for that. He's calling round tonight and I'll make sure I ask him. It's a different jurisdiction, of course. But Mr Cobb has many contacts.'

'And remember, we suspected Mr Cobb must know more than he's saying. Perhaps after last night's theft he may be willing to speak? The loss of my papers clearly angered him – as if someone had gone too far.'

'Yes,' said Mrs Trotter, 'and he said that Emmet *knew the dark alleys*. Well, I can tell you this – my old friend Elias knows where some of those alleys lead, and who is behind the doors – very respectable doors!'

It occurred to Tom and Will that Widow Trotter and Elias Cobb formed something of a partnership. Both were wise old hands and knew their patch of ground thoroughly. And if the hints were to be believed, they had been collaborators in the past.

'And what about yourself, Mrs T?' said Will. 'Has anything been tapping away at your thoughts?'

Widow Trotter took a considered sip of her madeira.

'My mind keeps returning to Kate Primrose – to *Clarissa*. The more I think about the poor girl, the more I'm convinced she can unlock all this for us. If only we could identify the man who searched her room!'

'Yes, said Will. 'If we could find Clarissa...'

'But the tapping sound I hear – a distant one – keeps saying "Adèle Ménage."'

'Do you think she knows more also?' said Tom.

'Well, she knew of Kate and Emmet, and she knew something of Emmet's plans – I warrant the two of them had talked more than business! Adèle is protective of Kate and spoke about her almost as a daughter. If the girl has fled for her life then she'll surely be in communication. In the Garden there are many hiding-places for a Clarissa – if she's prepared to work. I suspect Adèle will soon know where she can be found. But I doubt she'll want to reveal it, especially if the girl is in danger.'

Tom looked at her earnestly.

'Perhaps you should call on Mrs Ménage again and tell her about Emmet's murder and Kate's flight? She may not know of either yet, and it might be easier for her to have the news from a friend. And if she *has* heard, I'm sure she'll value having somebody to talk to. I imagine she'll be alarmed.'

'You're right, Tom. I ought to call, if only to help reassure an old friend. Perhaps that whisper of mine was the voice of conscience? Anyway, I'll go and see her this evening. But I need to be in the coffee-room for a spell. I've been expecting Jeremy to arrive at any moment with the new Chinaware – although how it will arrive, and in what degree of fragmentation, I really don't know… then I'll go over to Katherine Street.'

From the slightly harassed expression on her face it was clear that Mrs Trotter wasn't relishing either prospect. At that moment both Tom and Will realised how much they were expecting from her – perhaps too much? They had to remember that Mary Trotter also had a business to run. The transformation of the Good Fellowship into the Bay-Tree Chocolate House wasn't going to happen by rubbing a magic lamp.

'We ask a lot of you, Mrs T,' said Tom. 'If there's something we can help you with – like unpacking valuable porcelain…'

'Or gluing it back together,' said Will.

'… Then you must set us to work at once. Our big task tomorrow is the journey into Newgate. But for the rest of this evening we are at your service!'

'Agreed,' said Will.

Widow Trotter looked at the two eager recruits, who leapt up ready for action. This was an opportunity not to be missed and she didn't want to look a gift horse in the mouth… It occurred to her what a strange expression that was, though she assented to the idea that if someone *gave* you a horse you should ride it, not check its teeth.

Back in the coffee-room they didn't have long to wait before a handcart arrived in Red Lion Court and a broadly smiling Jeremy appeared at the door. Widow Trotter was alarmed.

'A cart?… Was that wise, Jem? It's a long pull from the Exchange. And all those cobbles! Surely you didn't need a whole cart? I was expecting a carefully wrapped parcel…'

'Ah, but Mrs Trotter, I've saved you time! – I called at *both* exchanges. I thought with a cart I could also collect that big mirror of yours – the one they've been keeping for you at the glass warehouse over the New-Exchange. I knew you'd be pleased if it all came together. I called there on the way back and they loaded the mirror easily enough…'

'The looking-glass! And you've been all the way down the Strand as well…?' A terrible thought struck her.

'How have they loaded it? Not on top of the parcel I hope!'

Tom and Will noticed what a quick turn of foot Widow Trotter possessed when the need arose.

The looking-glass, which was fortunately there in one piece, proved to be a handsome thing, even when Barnabas Smith stood in front of it – though he declared that he for one would not feel the need always to be prinking and preening himself. The Monday evening customers, a mixed bunch as usual, were happy to advise on the mirror's location and assess its capacities. Much depended, it turned out, on how well it reflected the self-esteem of each of them. In the end, it was placed conveniently alongside the street door, next to the row of wooden pegs which had now made their appearance. Mrs Trotter saw that the mirror would provide anyone behind the bar with a slightly different angle on the room and a more complete survey of the tables.

Tom and Will had begun unwrapping the cups and bowls – China's finest exports – which in spite of Widow Trotter's fears had somehow managed to survive their hazardous journey from Cornhill – when the door opened and a tall, scarlet-liveried footman walked in. The powdered bob-wig on his head nodded slightly in the direction of Mrs Trotter before he handed a letter to Tom, to whom it was directed. Tom broke the seal, and as he cast his eyes over it he flushed a little. The whole room had gone silent with expectation, but his response was disappointingly brief.

'Thank you Arthur. No written reply. But you can say the answer is *yes*.'

The footman gave another nod and made his dignified exit, his eyes taking in the full length of the mirror as he did so.

Widow Trotter exercised her seigneurial rights and asked to know the contents of the message. Tom blew out his cheeks and held up a handwritten invitation card, which was accompanied by a letter.

'Read it, Mrs Trotter… I'm going to be especially busy tomorrow. This could be a perfect opportunity to take our investigation further!'

Mrs Trotter beckoned Will over to the bar, and together they read the note in silence.

Dear Tom

Are you sitting down? Well, I hope you'll be pleased. A ridotto! Don't ask me exactly what it is, but Lord Tring was telling me he went to some of these in Venice, where they are quite the rage. (I think it's different from a risotto – which is also promised – it's edible apparently.) He has persuaded his mother to host one tomorrow night. I warrant it will be just an assembly with lots of drinking, cards and chatter, but you must come in a mask (this is important) – and he says there's to be a delicious spread of delicacies – – – and some fine Italian food as well!! No dancing I think, so you needn't be nervous. I'm not sure that Lady Welwyn, with her St James's Square ways, quite appreciates what this may turn into. But the good Pophams will be there so there'll not be a revolution. They are determined to watch over their daughter, although with masks who knows? Lord Tring is an odd young man and an obliging, good-humoured sort, and I prevailed on him to send my Cousin Tom an invitation. So here you are! And I also prevailed on him (a lot of prevailing!) to deliver one to Lady Norreys… Yes, Tom! Would I not make a fine impresario (you see my Italian knows no bounds!). I'll say no more. I think the whole evening will be a scandal-feast. I rely on your being there.

Your obliging Cousin

Lavinia Popham

'Well, what an opportunity!' said Mrs Trotter, seeing the practical side of things. 'You must go, of course! Look upon it as your duty. You know what is required of you...'

Will grinned at his friend.

'And when duty calls, Tom, a man has to be ready! Lady Norreys, eh?... Is there something you're not telling us?'

'Lavinia has this idea...'

'And it's a very good idea,' said Will.

'I agree,' said Mrs Trotter. 'You'll be able to advance our inquiries.'

'Mask to mask!' said Will.

And so it was decided. Widow Trotter agreed to find Tom a vizard for tomorrow night, and he would try to be at the ridotto in St James's Square by nine. The invitation hinted it would be a late affair.

After the unlooked-for interruption the three of them went back to work, and an hour later the room was already assuming a different character. The new Chinaware had been cleaned and polished, and was on display at the bar for all to admire. (Peter Simco was especially delighted, though he understood the extra responsibility it gave him.) The place was undoubtedly taking shape as the Bay-Tree Chocolate House, and Widow Trotter ran the phrase over her tongue as she looked round the room.

On the far wall, King Charles the Second had undergone a martyrdom less bloody but equally final as that of his father, and had been ousted by a print of his niece Queen Anne displaying her full regalia. The pipe-smoking Dutchmen had been replaced by a composition of field and water-meadow which did feature several cows, but the artist had aligned them very discreetly. And now alongside them, pictured in all her glory, was Anne Bracegirdle as Aphra Behn's Indian Queen. Crowned with a plumed headdress, she was canopied by a large parasol and waved her feathered fan at the customers below, as if she couldn't bear to quit her adoring audience. Two Queen Annes! Mrs Trotter glowed with delight at the wit of the thing.

By the door, the tall looking-glass was declared to be a polite addition, and it attracted a lot of close scrutiny and many compliments. To Widow Trotter's relief, everyone seemed pleased with the improvements thus far. She made a final round of the tables, snatched a piece of toast and a slice of savoury jelly, and left for Katherine Street and Adèle Ménage. Tom and Will remained in the coffee-room for a while, talking over the day's events and thinking about the challenge that faced them in Newgate. They were solaced with the thought that tomorrow they might bring some hope to John Morphew and be of practical help to him. But they knew the experience would be a disturbing one. It would take them far from the congenial delights of chocolate house or *ridotto*.

Chapter Twenty-Two

'SO MUCH NEWS, Marie!... You must tell me what you know!'

Even as she opened the door, the expression on Mrs Ménage's face showed a woman torn between an eagerness to talk and a longing to hear. But while Widow Trotter made her way into the room and settled herself on the substantial couch, the talk swept everything aside. It was immediately clear that Adèle Ménage was troubled. Less than an hour earlier she had heard about Emmet's killing and knew that John Morphew – 'your printer, Marie!' – would be charged with his murder. She began busying herself with a fresh bottle of claret and finding another glass, her hands trembling slightly. Questions were being asked but with no pause for an answer, as if she wanted to know more but was apprehensive of what she might discover. Widow Trotter remained quiet while all this went on. Beneath her friend's excitement she was sure she could detect fear.

What Mrs Trotter soon began to realise was that Adèle Ménage did not yet know of Kate Primrose's flight. She thought it wise not to mention it at that moment.

'Your printer, Marie – the one Mr Cobb arrested at your Good Fellowship – I had not made the connection! It appears that my Mr Emmet – *our* Mr Emmet – worked for him! You told me he was taken up for sedition – do you think Mr Emmet involved himself in that? Did they quarrel, do you think? They must have! And I wonder what has happened to Mr Emmet's papers? He said he had a valuable *cache* and desired to add mine to it. Do you think another person killed him and stole them? Have they thought of that? Was there a robbery? Mr Emmet knew very important people – do you think he offended them? I know there are people who would wish to lay their hands on my own things...'

Mrs Trotter noticed her give a nervous half-glance toward the tall cupboard. It was the slightest flicker of the eye, but detectable. She knew she ought to intervene to calm her friend's worries, and yet she sensed that something unspoken might be about to reveal itself.

After a determined sip of claret Mrs Trotter knew she had to respond – ruthlessly.

'You are right, Adèle – we live in a dangerous world! There are spies around, and nothing is safe...'

She paused and lowered her voice just a little.

'... Only last night at the Good Fellowship, my poor lodger Mr Bristowe – the young poet I told you of – had all his papers stolen. Would you believe it? They broke in through the side stairs and emptied his desk. He's very distraught... Imagine, Adèle, losing all your work!'

Mrs Ménage was imagining it only too vividly. An elegant *frisson* ran through her entire body.

'Ah, none of us is secure, Marie! Nothing in this world is safe! But what are the Watch doing? What does your good Mr Cobb say of this?'

'He thinks a plot is afoot – and that John Emmet was implicated in it.'

'I knew it! *Monsieur le Fourmi!* His trail leads everywhere.'

'We think the printer has been wrongly charged, and that somebody else – some other people – killed him. As you have said, Adèle, Emmet knew too many intimate secrets. There must be *others* who wished him dead – who are perhaps watching and plotting even now. This whole business is far from over, you can be certain of that…'

Widow Trotter was being shamelessly dramatic. This was not the reassurance her friend had been looking for. Mrs Ménage began wondering how many of these *others* there might be and where they could be hiding.

'… In fact, it is to be doubted Mr Morphew was the man who killed him. I know I can confide in you, Adèle…'

By now Mrs Ménage was finding the role of *confidante* increasingly unsettling. Mrs Trotter pressed unrelentingly on.

'… if this thieving and killing is to stop, it is important we know all we can about Mr Emmet's affairs, and what he may have been planning… I know he opened himself to you, Adèle. Did he seem frightened? Did he speak to you of anyone, perhaps? Was there someone of whom he was afraid?'

'No, no – he said very little. To me, he was the man of business – no more than that.'

'He told you nothing that might help us?'

'It is Kate Primrose you must ask… Poor Kate! The girl will be very distressed to hear the news. I wonder if I should go to her…'

Mrs Trotter doubted a climb up to Clarissa's bower was really in contemplation – this was not an ungenerous thought, just a shrewd one – so she let the phrase lie. At that moment, as if sensing the tension, Mrs Ménage's caged bullfinch began an insistent piping. The bird's slow arpeggios seemed to emphasise the melancholy silence that had suddenly settled on the room.

'Ah, Kate Primrose! You haven't heard?'

'What should I hear, Marie?'

'That she has fled from Vinegar Yard – it would appear for good.'

The effect of this news was as she expected. More questions and conjectures tumbled over one another; but this time Mrs Trotter intervened, and while her friend was replenishing their glasses she began a full account of her visit to Kate Primrose's lodgings, her conversation with Joseph Quinlan the excise clerk, and the fruitless search of Kate's room that followed.

'Just think, Adèle, the man burned her on the hand with her toasting-fork, demanding to know where those papers were, but the brave girl was able to send him on a false trail. And now she has vanished. Do you have any idea where she could be? This may be of great importance. A man's life is at stake.'

Mrs Ménage's eyes sank deeper under her brows as she tried to recollect.

'Kate has a sister, I know. The woman lives out at Colchester – or is it Chelmsford? An honest woman, not in the trade... But Kate would not travel there. Is she not more likely to seek hospitality in a whore-house? There she could disappear with ease and keep herself private... She has not called on me, I can assure you of that. You know I would tell you if she had.'

Widow Trotter felt her friend's direct, hard look. Adèle Ménage was far from naïve, and she must remember it.

'Of course,' said Widow Trotter, shifting the topic slightly, 'she may not have heard about Emmet's fate. We don't know what that ruffian said to her. Might she even try to get in touch with Emmet? That's a worrying thought...'

She pulled herself up short. This was going too far.

'... I'm sorry, Adèle – I'm being insensitive. Forgive me. All this must have come as a shock to you, and you must be a little worried.'

'Ah, Marie, I'm not an *ingénue*. I have seen much. But sometimes a thing will happen that touches us close. I fear I have betrayed my anxieties. You think them excessive, I know...'

Mrs Trotter was about to deny this, but her friend raised a hand and stopped her.

'... But I see you have your anxieties too, Marie. You are anxious about the papers, are you not? These are important to you.'

Mrs Trotter checked herself. The bullfinch's simple notes now seemed to have taken on a slightly mocking tone.

'Yes, you are right, Adèle. To put it plainly: we want to save Morphew from the gallows. But we lack the evidence. We need to know who was bargaining with Emmet, and who wanted to silence him. Something among his papers could unlock the mystery. We thought you might be able to help us. That's why I have come.'

'I understand Marie. I knew that – but it is good to hear you say it. You want my help.'

'Badly – if there's any help you can give.'

'You said that Kate had hidden her papers very well, and she told the clerk that no-one would find them?'

'That was how Mr Quinlan put it to me. He wondered if they were in the bag she was carrying when she fled.'

'That is possible. But perhaps they were not so bulky? You said that the man searched the place... '

Mrs Ménage paused and took a generous sip of her claret.

'... I know that Mr Emmet asked Kate to hide some of his papers – she revealed as much to me. There were things he did not wish to store at his own lodgings – for good reason, it now appears... But there was one item that Mr Emmet thought of particular importance – a paper which our Clarissa had to guard especially closely...'

Mrs Trotter was listening intently. This was the critical moment. Perhaps they would at last home in on Bufo's documents?

Mrs Ménage stood up.

'... Kate entrusted it to me and stressed that it was to be kept close – you see how I am confided in! I was not to mention it to a soul, and I swore to guard it for her. Mr Emmet had told her it was something of national importance. To me it looks a small thing. But its significance may be far-reaching. Perhaps you need to see it...'

She turned round for a moment.

'... Do you understand what I am doing, Marie?... How much I must trust you in my turn?'

Widow Trotter felt slightly abashed. She had not been entirely open with her friend, and she watched almost hypnotised as Mrs Ménage stepped towards the armoire. The tall cupboard had a secretive character, and she realised that the marquetry on its doors suggested a vaguely human double-profile. It was a piece of furniture that might feature in a French romance...

But Mrs Ménage walked past the cupboard. When she reached out her arm, it was to the birdcage, a domed creation of twisted wires that had at its base a broad metal band housing a removable tray – or so it seemed. But part of the tray didn't open until she took a tiny key from a purse at her waist and reached behind the cage. The bullfinch became instantly playful and pushed its curved beak through the wires as her hand delved into the secret compartment. Widow Trotter looked away, somehow feeling it was a private moment she should not observe.

A minute later the two women were seated side by side on the couch, and in front of them was a letter with its glowing red wax still firmly attached, carrying the imprint of a small head – obviously a seal made from a sixpenny piece. Mrs Trotter was puzzled. If the letter had not been opened, how could its importance be known?

'Kate Primrose entrusted this to me. It was Emmet's greatest prize, she said. But she has now fled, and her life may be in danger. So I think we should examine its contents, should we not, Marie?'

With that she turned the letter round. There was no envelope – it was simply a tightly-folded sheet of paper sealed with red wax. A brief direction was written in a fairly small, sprawling hand. It read: 'The Honble. Mr St John. By hand.'

Widow Trotter was not a person to be silently thoughtful at such a moment.

'Mr *Secretary* St John? This I did not expect!'

Mrs Ménage's fingers went to the seal, but Widow Trotter stopped her. She touched the wax lightly. She realised she had stopped breathing.

'Look Adèle – do you see? The seal has been re-attached. It has been done with great care, but do you discern a tiny stain at the side? The alignment is almost perfect. But you can just see where the wax has been pressed down a second time. This is John Emmet's work, surely?'

'You are right, Marie. Our Mr Emmet wanted it to appear unopened. Perhaps its value would thus be greater?'

'But who would pay to reclaim it – the writer? or the recipient? Who would be more embarrassed? Our Secretary-at-War could raise a large sum… but perhaps the highest price of all would be paid by a third party?'

'Let us see, shall we?' said Mrs Ménage, lifting the seal with a crack and beginning to unfold the crisp sheet of paper.

The letter was written in a careful, slightly ungainly hand. It was neat enough, but not the fluent hand of a hurried man of affairs. They both saw at once that it carried a woman's signature.

To Mr Henry St John, Esq.

My dear Sir

I write to you as my last and final Hope. I have no right to approach you – but out of despair I think of you as the only person who might help my husband at this latest hour. William Greg is no practised traitor Sir, you must believe me. He has ever loved his country and wished to serve it. His devotion to Mr Harley remains unshaken, and he has always regarded Mr H. as a man of principle whose many repeated kindnesses to him have made him feel nothing but gratitude and admiration. He will say nothing against Mr H., and indeed is prepared to die in order to preserve him from his enemies.

You must know Sir, and I swear to you, that my husband saw and confessed his error, and Mr Harley was indeed prepared to cancel the score – he told my husband that his crime had shone a light on his own careless oversight of his office – that too much had been left open and unattended, and there was not that regulation and good order that there should have been. He said there was nothing of special import and reassured my husband that as he had sworn never to err again he was prepared to wink at it (those were his very words Sir). I know that William sank to his knees and thanked him, and indeed swore profusely he would never do such a foolish and evil thing again. And that is how it was left.

But you know too well the turn of events, Sir. That Mr Harley's circling enemies have seen their chance, and are determined to bring him down. My husband must be made a sacrifice. And believe me when I tell you William is prepared to go to his death in silence, he understands that in spite of Mr H.'s generous forbearance the crime of treason has become known and now there is nothing Mr H. can do. My husband must go to his death.

William understands how very very foolish he has been. But he refuses to say one word against his good Mr H. He believes that would be the greater treason. Indeed, at our last meeting he told me that his own death would be nothing near so ignominious as would a life prolonged in such a way, and he would not save it by prostituting his conscience.

Alas, Sir, I have no such scruples. I have only a wife's love, and a mother's conscience. I beg of you, Sir, that you might do whatever lies in your power. I know Mr H. can do nothing – but you are his great and trusted friend, and you understand these things – and you may perhaps find a way to help my husband.

Finally Sir, I beg you not to reveal my hand in this. William indeed knows nothing of it – I ask you to burn this letter after it has come into your hands. I would have you believe, Sir, that I write under the severest apprehension and with a sense of your great goodness and kindness in the past to my husband. If there is anything you are able to do, you will have the undying gratitude of me and my poor family.

I am Sir, yours
Most Sincerely,
Elizabeth Greg

The two women looked at each other in shocked silence for a moment. Widow Trotter was the first to speak.

'So, it is plain. Mr Harley knew of Greg's treachery – and was prepared to turn the blind eye – to *wink at it*... This will bring him down!'

'More than that, Marie – it will lay him open to a charge of treason himself. It could be a death sentence.'

'*Shake the State*...' The insistent phrase was again echoing deep in Widow Trotter's head. She could almost feel the tremor as she glanced down at the innocent writing-paper scratched over with ink. How slight in itself, yet how vast its reach could be! She wondered how far the thing had already reached – but perhaps no further than Emmet?

'... What shall we do?'

Her question was quiet and wondering rather than urgent. Mrs Ménage's reply was also quiet, but firm.

'We shall do nothing, Marie. I opened this letter in the hope that we might be able to help Kate Primrose. But it brings us no nearer her. Until we know of Kate's situation we should leave this thing in the safe keeping of little Bully here. Let it remain a prisoner of the birdcage! It may have its moment – or it may not. I think it is not for us to decide. And so I must ask you to promise me your silence.'

'I give you my promise, Adêle. You may be right: this astonishing document could distract us. If Emmet was holding onto it for future use, then its time has not yet come... But, do you feel safe having it here, now you know its contents?'

'Ah, Marie, I do have anxieties, but they are not for myself. I have passed many dangers in my life. I believe I can hide a little scrap of paper fearlessly, don't you?'

She lifted her glass, and Mrs Trotter joined her. She looked at her wise old friend and began to suspect that all along it had been her own fears that had been palpable during their conversation. Mrs Ménage remained thoughtful.

'I do want to help you, Marie – you and your printer Morphew. Do you wish me to ask after Clarissa? I can do it with discretion. She may not have moved far from here. Our Covent Garden is such a labyrinth, and a young girl may disappear so easily... I promise to do what I can.'

'Thank you, Adèle, your help would be invaluable. The trial is on Thursday, so you see how pressed we are! My lodger Tom and his friend Will are helping me. We are a sturdy team, well harnessed together.'

'And I trust our Constable Cobb is able to assist you?'

'Yes, Elias has assisted us in many ways, and – as I now remember – he's to bring me further news this evening. It had quite slipped my mind!'

'Then you had better go at once, Marie. I understand. Each minute is costly for you. If I hear something to the purpose I shall send a note round to the Good Fellowship immediately – or are you now the 'Bay-Tree'?

'I already think of us as the Bay-Tree Chocolate House, but we have our formal opening celebration in a week's time. I know the rules, but on that occasion at least, it would give me real delight to welcome you there if you were able to come. As you know, my plans for the place have set aside an upper room for the ladies...'

Mrs Ménage smiled conspiratorially.

'Take care, Marie. There are some *ladies* who would exploit your generosity.'

'From you, I take that to be less a warning than a promise! Good night, Adèle!'

Widow Trotter turned at the door.

'You are right, of course. Your letter must stay here in this room, and so must our secret. I sense that poor Kate Primrose may be somewhere near – perhaps in some wretched attic with even fewer things to call her own. She does not deserve this.'

'All the more cause to find her, Marie. I am – how do you say it? – putting my shoulder to the plough. You must now picture me as one of your team!'

Chapter Twenty-Three

WIDOW TROTTER ARRIVED back later than intended to find that Tom and Will had already departed for the Temple. The pair had left a message with Jenny Trip at the bar to say they needed time together to prepare for their Newgate visit. There were things to discuss and ideas to be thought through – and perhaps one or two law-books to consult. Tom would stay the night and the two of them would walk over to the gaol in the morning. She was not to worry, they had said.

Her brow furrowed immediately. It was prudent of them, although she wished she'd been able to mutter a few words of encouragement. But the task had to be left in their hands. She smiled inwardly and delivered a little homily to herself about not attempting to control people. After all, Will was astute and had some experience of the law, and Tom was a persuasive young man blessed with the human touch. Together they would surely be able to help John Morphew and perhaps discover something material to Thursday's trial. But merely to think about that terrible place was chilling her. She could smell it in her imagination. Every breath taken in that disease-ridden hole might be dangerous. Widow Trotter was not religiously inclined, nevertheless at that moment she offered up a silent hope – hardly to be called a prayer – that they wouldn't find the experience too harrowing.

After this brief contemplation she recalled herself to the here and now. Elias Cobb was already in the coffee-room, and she recognised her old friend from behind, his heavy coat trailing on the floor and his hat on the bench beside him (he would have to be trained to use the new pegs). He was hunched over the table, leaning on one elbow with his pipe billowing thoughtful curls of smoke, through which she could make out the shape of Captain Roebuck talking animatedly. The Captain was hugging his trusty campaign wallet, strung, as ever, round his waist. This signalled that matters of principle were in question. In response, the constable appeared to be nodding encouragingly – or perhaps he was simply acknowledging the folly of life in general? The Captain really was fully engaged! As she came nearer she caught the words 'disgrace!' and 'infamous libel!' She wondered whether to mount a swift rescue, or make a tactical withdrawal and allow the skirmish to play itself out.

There was no second thought. Mrs Trotter knew the constable's time was precious, so she moved in boldly.

'Settling the affairs of the nation, Captain? You sound in good spirits!... and Mr Cobb, good evening! If you've a moment I'd like to bend your ear myself – if the Captain will release you.'

'Ah! Mrs Trotter! Just the very person...'

The old soldier was ready for a fresh hand-to-hand encounter; but the constable reached out and called a halt, giving him the kind of look that would make a troublesome wasp fall from the sky.

'The matter is in hand, Captain! The hostess and I have business to discuss.'

And so it was that a few minutes later a grateful Elias Cobb was seated in the parlour with a fresh dish of coffee before him. However, 'Mr Cobb's pipe,' as it was known, was confined by hallowed tradition to the coffee-room. He was now in Widow Trotter's own space; and while the tobacco-smoke added to the rich taste of the public room, in the parlour she preferred the fragrances that seeped in from the adjacent kitchen.

Elias Cobb was obviously concerned.

'Our friend *Bufo* is causing a stir again. I'm afraid Captain Roebuck is mightily offended. He has found a copy of the *Caricatura*.'

There was something in the way the Constable looked at her as he spoke.

'Not… ?'

'Yes, in the coffee-room here, not half an hour ago.'

Mrs Trotter sank into a chair. Her voice sounded tired and close to despair.

'Will this never end, Elias?… Why is it *us*? What is happening?'

'Come now, Molly, you should take heart. It seems you don't hold the copyright any longer. Bufo's pieces are out in the open, and since yesterday they've been fluttering into a good few taverns and coffee houses. I understand one of them was read aloud this morning in the Cocoa-Tree, where it was received with great acclaim.'

'The Cocoa-Tree? No wonder! That's a red-blooded Tory house. No Whig would ever set foot in the place – unless he wanted his head in a Jacobite punchbowl.'

'My spies tell me some of the poem's choicest lines were cheered to the echo.'

Widow Trotter sighed.

'Well there's no warmer audience than the believer, is there?'

'They say copies are being made as we speak – and more copies from those. The thing has caught the mood of the hour. It's rousing the Tories and provoking the Whigs, just as you would expect.'

'Yes, how predictable it all is! I'm worried we shall find poor Captain Roebuck enlisting with the Duke again. The *Caricatura* handles his hero pretty roughly, doesn't it?'

'Yes, but not nearly so violently as the Duchess.'

'This will make Her Grace even angrier – if that's possible – and her agent Maynwaring more desperate. This public ridicule is sure to infuriate him… Oh, Elias. What is happening to us all?'

It was an unanswerable question, and the constable let the exclamation reverberate in the silence. For a moment, both of them were locked in thought.

Instinctively, Widow Trotter reached for a plate of sweetmeats and set it down on the table in front of them. She was worried – not just about Morphew's case, but more widely. The political scene was becoming frantic and desperate. Destructive passions were being stirred up everywhere – challenges delivered, insults hurled, claims fabricated, accusations mounted – and the seething cauldron was being fed by both sides. The rage of party had taken over. Everybody had an opinion and everybody wanted to be heard, but no-one was prepared to listen. Even in that quiet room she sensed the catastrophe coming. It may not be now, but it would surely come. And unless people could hear and respect each other – and above all smile and laugh together – she didn't hold out any hope…

Here endeth the lesson, she thought. Enough of that! She mustn't become self-righteous. She also realised that Elias was scrutinising her closely.

'I'm sorry, Elias. You caught me playing the philosopher to myself.'

'Would that be the laughing philosopher, or the weeping one?' he asked, grinning from ear to ear.

'Not the first, alas – but perhaps things will change. We must set our minds to the matter in hand. I do have a great deal to tell you…'

She sat up in her chair and looked as if she meant business.

'… You need to know about this afternoon's inquest, which was evidently something of a farce; but Tom had a productive morning with Paul Barnard the compositor, and he met the porter at Stationers' Hall who was at the murder-scene.'

'Excellent. I want to hear all you can tell me – and I have something for you from the Cockpit. But we shall need to be brisk. I may have to depart hastily. I'm expecting one of my men back from Rose Street. It appears a girl's body may have been found in one of the tenements. It hasn't been officially reported but I fear it's another young harlot dead by her own hand. It's all too likely, those poor creatures!… I shall need to hurry over there if the story is true.'

Widow Trotter felt a hint of unease but cast it from her mind and gave the constable a sketch of the inquest and what they had learned during the day. She knew it would only be a partial picture. Will's discovery about the pocket-book couldn't be shared, even with Elias, and the revelation of Mrs Greg's letter had to remain locked in Bully's cage. Not even Tom or Will must know of it. Perhaps the thing would not prove material – the picture wasn't yet clear.

But there was much else to relate. She told him of Will and Tom's plans to visit Newgate, and about Tom's meetings with the porter and the compositor. He took the news about Emmet's printing of *Bufo's Magic Glass* in his stride, and confessed that it tallied with what he had heard in the Cockpit.

'Yes, everything changed at that second interrogation, when Morphew became angry. It seems Emmet had told them the pamphlet was printed on Morphew's presses, and with his knowledge. When it was put to him, Morphew laughed at the idea, but then he was shown the thing and saw that it used one of his own distinctive ornaments – no doubt about it! You can imagine his outrage.'

'I'm sure Hopkins delighted in proving it to him.'

'Yes, Morphew said it was impossible, or he would have known of it. But the proof was there in front of him. And another revelation angered him even more…'

'Another?'

'They made it clear they knew the contents of Lady Norreys's pocket-book...'

Widow Trotter's hand closed on a chocolate sweetmeat and crushed it. She continued looking at him, open-mouthed.

'... It seems Emmet had the more vivid entries by heart and rejoiced in recalling them. Rumour has it there were revelations about Mrs Masham and Her Majesty, very compromising to both of them. Can you believe it? Emmet was obviously determined to impress his Whig masters. How Hopkins's eyes must have lit up! He was aching to view the original and was annoyed to hear the book had been returned to Lady Norreys. That was another black mark for our publisher!'

'But how horrified Morphew must have been. Do you think it was a deliberate plan to wind him up like a clockwork soldier and then release him?'

'You may be right. By the time Morphew stormed out of the Cockpit he was ready to confront Emmet and vent his anger.'

'Oh dear, it's what I feared. The interrogation will be played out in court, no doubt.'

'No doubt at all. He had every motive for striking Emmet, and cudgelling him pretty hard too!...'

There spoke the experienced Covent Garden constable. His blunt words made Mrs Trotter even more uneasy. She began licking the chocolate from her hand.

'... I'm sorry, Molly, that was not what you wanted to hear.'

'It's best we know. I expect Tom and Will are going to have the story from Morphew in the morning.'

Widow Trotter got up to wipe her hand more decorously on a cloth, and she began replenishing their two coffees.

'There's something else that's worrying me. It was your mention of that dead girl in Rose Street...'

The constable looked surprised.

'... You remember on Sunday night I told you about Kate Primrose – Emmet's *Clarissa* – and how she was attacked and had fled Vinegar Yard...'

'Oh – are you thinking it might be her?'

'I suppose it's possible. She was expecting her attacker to return. That was why she fled.'

'But this one is rumoured to be a suicide. The girl has hanged herself... and it may be a false report in any case – we must hope so. But let's see what Mudge has to say when he returns. He's a good observant fellow – well trained! I know he'll be taking a close look at the scene.'

Widow Trotter reached for her dish of coffee. The conversation had found its way neatly to her hoped-for subject.

'What you say puts me in mind of the constable over at Stationers' Yard who found Emmet's body – Constable Buller. He apparently handled everything very scrupulously.'

She was half-expecting a nod and a smile from one of the brotherhood of constables, but instead Elias looked directly at her, unable to conceal a flicker of disgust.

'Ah! *Buller*, did you say?'

'So you've encountered him? I wasn't sure your paths would have crossed, given he's in the City's jurisdiction.'

'I do know of him, but by reputation only, so what I've heard may be unfair. We men of the law do talk with each other... We're quite a club, so we get to hear of things.'

'Elias, you sound like a gossipy courtier!'

He realised his hesitation was becoming more eloquent than any speech.

'Well... a City of London constable is a special breed, of course. They're appointed for a year, and they tend to be men in business or trade who have City friends, so they come to the job with *interests*, you might say. Like many a City constable, Joe Buller isn't a working officer of long experience. He doesn't set his hand to things.'

'Unlike *you*, Elias,' said Widow Trotter without irony. He ignored her and pressed on.

'The constable polices his City ward – his own small precinct – and this works well on the whole. But Joe Buller seems to have concerns that extend well beyond his patch of ground.'

Widow Trotter was intrigued.

'*Concerns, interests* – Do you mean *corruption?* Is Buller in someone's pay?'

'Let me say, he's known at the Cockpit – at least in Lord Sunderland's division. I've heard his name mentioned, but he never comes himself... My own role there is an open one – they know I'm not in anyone's pocket. That's why they find me useful sometimes. The Cockpit doesn't hire me, though my expenses are more than covered.'

It was a nice distinction, Widow Trotter thought.

'But Constable Buller... ?'

'Constable Buller is an *operator*. To tell the truth, I suspect there's a fraternity, and he is part of it. He's at home with schemes and plots. This is before his appointment as constable. But I know nothing at first hand – it's just the way he's spoken of. If it's important to you, I can find out more?'

'Yes please. It sounds as if he's more than just a constable.'

'Well, let's say he can call upon *wider resources*.'

'Or be called upon by them, perhaps? There was a remark Tom made earlier this evening. It made us think that Constable Buller's precision and efficiency at the scene, and his performance at the inquest, was that of someone in control, as if he were organising the event himself.'

'Split me! That's a serious accusation to make of a constable.'

'I don't mean committed the murder – Heaven forbid! – but that he was determined to present the death exactly as *he* saw it – to make sure everyone accepted his version.'

'Was he not just being officious?'

'Yes, no doubt. But what you've said about his links to Sunderland at the Cockpit...'

'And to the Earl's mother-in-law too I think...'

'The Duchess?'

'Yes, I heard his name mentioned in connection with her Secretary, Mr Maynwaring. I know Buller has court connections. Joseph Buller is a man who can make himself useful in all sorts of ways.'

'Like *you*, Elias,' said Widow Trotter, this time with irony. And this time he didn't ignore her.

'I do move in a murky world, Molly. But I hope I have allegiances...'

'I know you do, Elias. But I rely on you to help us further. We need to know more about Buller. We seem to be in the gloom – just glimmers here and there rather than any guiding light.'

'A will o'the wisp!' said Elias, finishing his coffee. 'You should be careful where it leads you, Molly. It's easy to have suspicions, but sometimes we can suspect too much, just as we can trust too much.'

'Those are wise words, Elias – the fruit of experience!'

He sat back in his chair and suddenly looked restless. He had remembered Mudge the watchman, whom he had dispatched to one of the insalubrious tenements in Rose Street. As so often, it struck him how much pain and misery there was all around – it was never out of reach. He only hoped this had been a false alarm and that Mudge would have found nothing sinister.

He was soon to find out. A few minutes later there was a noise in the kitchen, and the two of them heard Jeremy exclaiming loudly. There was a bang on the parlour door and it swung open. The voice of Mudge was heard as he attempted to squeeze past an indignant Jem. They were both strongly built young men, and Widow Trotter suspected the door-frame wouldn't hold out indefinitely.

'I tell you I'm expected!' Mudge was declaring.

'Indeed he is, Jem!' said Mrs Trotter. 'You must let him in. You've been a good doorkeeper. But this one has a warrant – he's no intruder.'

In a short time, the young watchman was settled in a chair and given a dish of coffee which he seized gratefully, risking a burnt throat as he tipped half the contents down it. From the look on his face the news was what they had feared.

'There's a body all right, Mr Cobb. A young woman – about eighteen I'd say, though she'd painted herself up like a forty-year-old. You'll need to come and take note of it. She's strangled with her own garter. Lying half off the bed and her face all twisted and her neck stretched out. She'd tied the garter round the bed-post... it's a strange bent shape she's in... it's horrible, Mr Cobb... And it's beginning to stink!'

The watchman paused and seized the dish of coffee again.

'Ah! So the body's been there a day or two, you think?'

'Without a doubt, Sir – I would say more. She'd not been seen since Wednesday.'

Mrs Trotter felt an uncharitable surge of relief. Whoever the girl was who had met this grisly end, it clearly wasn't Kate Primrose.

The watchman seemed to hesitate slightly before continuing with his report, not accustomed to being the centre of attention.

'I took the liberty, Sir, of talking with one of the ladies in the building, who said she was surprised the girl had taken her own life – that she'd been in good spirits last time they talked. Her trade was improving, she said, and things were looking up for her. There's a bit of a story to tell in fact... It seems the girl had confided in her...'

Mudge paused, wondering whether he should proceed or save it for the constable's ear alone. The looks on their faces should have left him in little doubt.

'Does the dead girl have a name?' asked Widow Trotter.

'I'm sorry. Yes – she was called Polly Gray.'

Mrs Trotter exchanged a questioning glance with the constable, who seemed not to have heard of her. The girl had a perfect name for a country ballad.

'*Polly Gray* – a simple rustic name. So innocent!'

The watchman frowned.

'Though not so innocent, if the story's true…'

The man looked at Elias, who motioned him to continue.

'… Well, this Polly had had something of a windfall, it seems. A client of hers, after his night's entertainment, found himself in considerable disarray – *paralytic* disarray, you might say. It appears the man left several deposits behind him – not only the contents of his stomach but also various items that had been in his pockets.'

Elias fought to suppress a smile. His young watchman had little to learn of the ways of the world. This was the familiar trap.

'The old story, Mudge, eh?'

'Yes Sir, though in his case what he carelessly entrusted to Miss Polly's keeping were two articles of note: a very superior gold watch, finely engraved, and something else that could be nothing, or might command a pretty penny. The woman said the girl had laughed at it and wondered who the fine gentleman was to have had such a thing! She told her she hadn't recognised the name but that it sounded like he was someone special.'

The watchman paused to finish off his coffee, prompting Elias to speak with as much benign patience as he could command.

'I know you've had an eventful evening, Mudge, but I'm afraid we've no time for riddles.'

'Of course, Mr Cobb, I'm sorry… It was a *letter*, and Polly obviously thought it suggested connections in high places. It might have been a lord's name on it. I asked the woman but she didn't know. I also asked her about the engraving on the watch – if there was a name – but Polly hadn't told her… I'm afraid my witness isn't much help, is she?'

Widow Trotter was attempting to contain her excitement and adopted a look of detached curiosity, allowing Elias to press on undeterred.

'What happened to the watch? Did she fence it?'

'Yes, and from what the woman said there'll be a notice in the paper. You know the form, Mr Cobb. It will find its way back to the gentleman – for a generous reward of course… The letter, though, she was also expecting something for, if it turned out to be important – something *significant*, you might say.'

'Significant it may well be. Where is the letter now?'

'It was passed on, Mr Cobb. This Polly had already found a buyer. I don't think our young miss was a country milkmaid! It's clear she understood the ways of the world… I'm sorry, I've chattered on…'

'No, no, that was a good presentation of evidence – and you've been thinking about what the watch and the letter could tell us.'

'That does make suicide unlikely, don't you think?' said Widow Trotter. 'Young Polly Gray doesn't appear to have been at her last shift.'

'No, you're right,' said Elias. 'It may indeed be a murder scene. And therefore I must off to Rose Street without delay. And it also means, Tobias Mudge, that you will have to return with me…'

He looked encouragingly at the young watchman.

'… But be cheered – you're learning your trade. And if the generous Mrs Trotter would allow us to kidnap one of Mrs Dawes's famed venison pasties, it would ease the weight of our task considerably.'

The request was a polite one, and the châtelaine gave her consent. She ushered the constable and the watchman out into the kitchen. Elias turned and whispered to her.

'The buyer of the letter – could it be Emmet, do you think?'

Mrs Trotter knew the answer all too well. But her own whisper was a brief and guarded one:

'He would certainly be in the market for it. What a trail the man has left!'

And the trail, she saw, now appeared to have reached no less a figure than Henry St John, the stellar orator of the Tories, and Harley's intimate ally. The young man's adventures with low-life whores were common knowledge, but this particular night of debauch had brought about a girl's death, and the whiff of treason hung around it, adding to the scent of corruption in her Rose Street tenement. It was not only Harley who was threatened by the discovery of that letter.

From the hubbub in the coffee-room it was clear that her attendance was urgently required, so there was no opportunity to say more. In any case, she needed time to consider what she had learned. Constable Buller's role at the murder scene was looking increasingly suspicious – as were his Whig paymasters, if that's what they were. But now they were faced with a second killing.

With poor Polly Gray an entirely new path was opening up just as they were beginning to find their way, and a third text had emerged from the shadows where John Emmet operated. Now they had Bufo's verses, Lady Norreys's memorandums, and Mrs Greg's letter. Three small pieces of writing, each of which touched the nerves of the political world. Each was a serious threat to somebody: to Sunderland and the Whigs, to the Marlboroughs, to Abigail Masham, to the Queen, to Robert Harley, and now it would seem to Henry St John. Widow Trotter was momentarily awestruck. Beyond any doubt, it was a roll call of all the most important people in the Kingdom. And every one was in danger of being embarrassed – or much worse. Whether or not John Emmet had intentionally set out to lay a mine under the foundations of the State, he had somehow succeeded in doing just that.

Tuesday

3 February 1708

Chapter Twenty-Four

A SKELETAL FEMALE hand suddenly twisted through the grated window and cupped itself against Will's shoulder.

'A *thrum*, a *thrum!* Yer beauty! Tip me *thrums* fer pity, Sir!'

Will's neck tensed with the shock and he flinched away instinctively, lifting his arm as if to ward off a blow. Behind the grate a shock of matted hair was visible, and a pair of staring eyes that looked less pitiable than accusing and dangerous. On his other side, Tom stopped in his tracks and turned toward the voice as the hand continued to grope in their direction. He began fumbling for his purse and a few pennies, but it was already too late. A well-directed shot of spittle struck Will by the corner of his mouth, and a torrent of oaths followed, interspersed with cackling laughter that echoed round the archway. They both caught a whiff of the foul prison air that was seeping out into the street, and which made more experienced pedestrians keep to the centre of the foot-passage. The place was exhaling its disease-ridden miasma, which still had power to bring people down like the infamous plague-breath of forty years back.

Above their heads loomed the spikes of the great portcullis that hung inside the stone arch. This forbidding approach gave the City of London the character of a castle guarded by fortified gates and an ancient wall. The well-named Old Bailey stood next door along the wall to the south. The gaol and the courtroom were convenient neighbours, so that chained bands of prisoners could be herded easily between the two – a traffic that did little for the charm of the place. This unwholesome entrance into the City was far from welcoming. Rather than opening itself out to the capital's more expansive north-west, the New Gate seemed to be holding back that world, a defensive gesture confirmed by the insalubrious ditch of the Fleet which they had crossed a few minutes earlier, a sluggish stream that carried the detritus of Smithfield down to the Thames, and which served as the stinking moat of the metropolis.

'Welcome to Newgate,' said Tom ruefully.

It was a little after nine o'clock, and the two of them had paused for a few seconds under the arch of Newgate Bar, as if they needed an ounce more resolution before entering the gaol. When they turned toward the prison lodge Will gripped his leather satchel tightly and pointed up to three elegant female forms who were gazing on the scene from their lofty niches. *Justice, Mercy,* and *Truth* were frozen in stone, their graceful gestures offering calm and certainty to all beneath.

'There they are,' said Will, 'the three guardians of the Law! Reassuring ladies, are they not?'

'In theory, perhaps,' said Tom. 'But they're unmoved by what passes below. They have hearts of stone!'

'Unlike my ill-humour'd friend behind the grate.'

'But they're uneasy sisters. If the three of them sat down together I'd expect some noisy disputes.'

'Yes indeed. I wonder who would have the last word?'

'It's that third lady who concerns me,' said Tom. 'She's often left out of account, isn't she?'

'That's because she's the most inscrutable...'

'And so often maligned and prostituted...'

'Well, I hope she'll be at the Sessions House on Thursday!'

The two friends knew their little allegorical fancy was only delaying the moment when they had to enter the all-too-real prison. After an exchange of grim glances they made their way into the lodge.

The place was remarkably busy. It was almost like the lobby of a theatre, with inmates and visitors all crowded into the same space. At her shop, Mrs Spurling was doing good business selling beer, wine and tobacco to the better-provided prisoners, and she was chatting with a group of debtors as if they were passing the time in Covent Garden market. Further along, after overnighting in the local roundhouse, a couple of hardened felons were having their ankles shackled. The look of weary resignation on their faces suggested they knew the routine. And over on the far side was the heavy oak door of the men's condemned hold. It was ajar, and before it stood a prisoner who would be joining Monday's procession to Tyburn, holding a woman in his arms. The young man's chain looped round her shoulders, and together they formed a silent picture of leave-taking. Not being allowed into the cell, she had handed over her eighteen pence for a snatched interview; but what should have been an affecting scene was made awkward by the noise of the hammering and the distracting bustle of the place. The pair didn't have even a corner to themselves.

Gathered around a large table were other visitors waiting for attention, holding parcels, bottles, and in one case an incongruous embroidered cushion. There was some lively negotiation going on. The atmosphere of the place was stale with human sweat, and a cold dampness rose from the stone floor. Somewhere out of sight was a fireplace, but this contributed only a bitter haze of smoking coal that pricked the eyes.

Ten minutes passed before Tom and Will were finally able to stand in front of the Deputy Keeper, a well-fed body with big hands who held a ledger open across one arm and clutched a quill in the other.

'Is this your first visit to our hostelry gentlemen?'

The language of the genial host was disconcerting. Perhaps he took them for curious travellers here to view one of the sights of London? After their inquiry he consulted his book, and the conversation was brisk and to the point.

'Will you take a couple of sweet bags, gentlemen? On the Common Side it's advised.'

'The *Common Side?...* '

Will was alarmed.

'... The *Master's* Side, surely? After all...'

'Alas, Sir, Newgate is about to burst. We're thronged. The Bailey sessions began yesterday and there's hardly room on the floor. All beds are taken, and I have near a dozen waiting to be moved to the Master's Side. In a day or two we'll be thinned out, of course.'

Tom reached for his purse, but the man shook his head.

'No, Sir, there's nothing we can do today – whatever the consideration. You must understand me. But Mr Morphew has now been moved up to the Middle Ward, where it is at least possible to breathe – and there's some light there.'

It was said coolly, without regret, though with no relish either. Tom was shaking and beginning to feel sick. Will's anger was rising.

'Do you mean to say our friend has passed three days on the Common Side?'

'We have done what we can in the circumstances, Sir. He was taken out of the Stone Hold on Sunday morning.'

'Lord Jesus!' said Will, red in the face. There was a sudden hush as the shocking oath broke from him. The *Stone Hold?* This is criminal, Sir!'

But nothing was going to be gained by anger. The man, who was well used to receiving curses, looked at them impassively as if not a word had been said. Nothing would disrupt the routine of his busy office. He delivered the practical information without emotion and in a firm voice.

'This morning, Sirs, I think you'll find him in High Hall, taking a walk and conversing with the other prisoners. Mr Morphew has been reading to some of them and offering advice and counsel.'

As the man pocketed the two shillings offered him, he did a little extra business of his own.

'As I said, Sirs, can I recommend you each take a bag with you?...'

He reached into a box and extracted a couple of small linen pouches containing crushed sprigs of rosemary.

'... These may allay the foulness.'

'Do you take us for delicate court ladies?' said Will indignantly, his eyes still blazing.

There was no reply. Tom took the two bags and handed over a sixpence.

'We can leave them with our friend perhaps?' he said. 'Come along, Will. Let's in and find him.'

A warder with rattling keys hanging from his waist showed them the way. After a few twists and turns a big oak door studded with nails was unlocked, and Tom and Will were left alone to trudge through the body of the prison.

At once the suffocating nastiness of the Common Side closed in on them like a fog. There were no windows in the passageway, and they knew they had sunk back into a world of eternal night. Every surface was wet and grimy; their eyes began to sting, and each breath was an invasion of the lungs. Somewhere just out of sight they detected sounds of scurrying and a scraping of chain against stone. Much closer there was an indistinct muttering and a pair of eyes silently watching them. A dark form shifted with a metallic clink. A dog barked insistently. Further off, echoes of an angry altercation merged with a burst of laughter and a sudden wild hooting. Perhaps a game of cards or dice was in progress, or a fight? Or was it merely some desperate drunken revelry? As they made their way past a series of dark doorways the smell of stale piss and vomit was choking, and came to them in waves. They pressed the herb-pouches to their noses; but the resulting mixture of sweet and savoury was nauseous, like a horrible witches' stew.

'How could anyone eat in this place?' said Tom with a shudder. 'I'm sure I could keep nothing down... Look there!'

They froze on the spot. Tom was gazing at a half-naked figure slumped on the floor by a door-post. He was clutching an empty wooden bowl, and an ominous gurgle was coming from his chest. They had seen many a drunk in the London streets, but there was something especially disturbing about this man. His eyes were fixed, and they could hear the viscous phlegm fighting to escape from its bodily prison. It was as if the man's immortal soul were pleading for release. It struck Tom that Newgate itself was a giant human body, and they were now working their way through its intestine depths.

A minute later the two of them were able to breathe more freely as they mounted the stone staircase to the next level, where the stench subsided a little. But then an unexpected spicy fragrance asserted itself when they passed Jack Ketch's kitchen. This was the room where traitors' heads, before their exhibition above the street, were boiled with bay and cumin to delay putrefaction and deter the birds.

With each step in this terrible place they felt they were dragging themselves up from the pit. Finally, after a further flight they reached the topmost floor which housed the prison chapel and a substantial, tall-ceilinged hall with dirty windows and a few benches. Here the prison swabber, who had been mopping the floor, was lounging across a stone slab that occupied the centre of the room like a sacrificial altar. The thing formed a pivot round which the prisoners walked, in a scene that reminded Tom uncomfortably of the Ring in Hyde Park. But this object had another practical purpose and was shunned by some of the prisoners who knew it was the anvil on which their chains would be ritually struck off as they made their way down from the chapel to the waiting Tyburn cart.

Tom and Will saw John Morphew at once. He was walking with his back to them, his small but dignified steps fighting against the shackles that fastened his legs. When he turned and saw them his face brightened in surprise, and he extended a hand as he approached, wincing with frustration at his painful slowness.

'Well well, my young friends, welcome to my lodgings – humble and sparsely furnished – but the rent is cheap...'

The tone was jaunty, but John Morphew was a changed man – they saw it at once. He was already visibly thinner, his shoulders slightly hunched, and his skin taut and eyes bloodshot as if he'd been keeping watch through the night and hardly dared to close them. The lack of sleep had left its mark, and his coat was smeared and creased through tossing on the prison floor. A few days of Newgate had transformed an easy man of business into this tense, edgy figure who was trying hard to be his confident self and appear relaxed among friends. The affability was obviously screening humiliation, and he was embarrassed to appear before them in that guise. They noticed that an attempt at shaving had been made, but the result was a nasty gash on the chin, which in this place boded ill.

Morphew beckoned them to a spot under one of the high windows where a bench had been vacated. He leant back against the dirty whitewashed wall with Tom and Will taking their places either side of him. This should have been a bright room, but the winter light was wan and grey, and many of the panes of glass were cracked and papered over, which drained the colour out of everything. It seemed to drain their resolution too. They had come ready for a searching interview; they had planned out points for clarification, and what practical matters needed to be discussed. But now, sitting in that soulless room with Morphew by their side, they felt totally lost. It was as if they had crossed the River Styx into a shadowy underworld where judgment and reason were powerless and they were in the grip of fatal forces. This was not a place for open minds and clear thoughts.

They eased their awkwardness with the gifts they had brought. But as they handed them over, every item seemed to be a comment on his plight: a bottle of brandy from the Good Fellowship; a jar of honey and a spoon; a couple of apples; woollen gloves and a pair of socks; a small parcel of Virginia tobacco with a pipe; an unauthorised edition of Prior's poems, and a copy of Congreve's *The Way of the World*. The publisher held the treasure together on his lap, and just for a moment he looked on the verge of tears; but with a defiant turn of the head he thanked them with breezy cheerfulness, remarking that it was not in fact his birthday for a whole fortnight.

Morphew felt very uncomfortable himself. The unexpected arrival of Tom and Will called to mind the whole ghastly drama of recent days; but like them, he held back from broaching the topic of Emmet's death and what had led to it. The scene would have to be faced – they all knew it – but for the first few minutes they broached the brandy instead. Morphew took a sip and passed it to Will and Tom in turn. His relief at sitting between two friendly faces was palpable, and he eagerly led the talk, which soon became a veering monologue.

'I'm exceedingly glad to see your faces, young Sirs – and to know that I've not been forgotten. One or two friends have called and I've had sympathy from them, and some thoughtful words as well. But very few have ventured in here. I did think my fellow Stationers would stand by me, but to a man all those revered gentlemen have kept well away. They must think I've disgraced their profession!... Thursday's trial will be upon me in the blinking of an eye, but I wouldn't wish it further off – the thing has to be confronted. And if the business goes against me... It's an odd thought, Sirs, but I've reckoned that I may have exactly one hundred thousand breaths left to take in the world. Would you believe that? It seems a mighty sum, doesn't it!... But I dare say they will pass very quick...

'It's a paradox, but I do believe this swift pace of things may save my life: another week and I must succumb to the fever – they say it carried off three souls only yesterday. That's why I spend my days up here when I can. The air is rather better and there is more of it... But equally, the fleas have more space to exercise!... I see you have Mr Chandler's bag of herbs? – a nice little trade he has there. It helps the visitor no doubt, but believe me, after a day of smelling those things the nausea of the Common Side is preferable. The sweet herb makes things worse... I swear I'll not have rosemary with my mutton ever again!'

Morphew smiled, but his eyes avoided theirs as he continued his stream of talk. Tom and Will were astonished by the publisher's equanimity and his continuing humour, as if he had driven from his mind all thoughts of what might face him on Monday morning, should Thursday's verdict go against him. Was this stoicism? Or foolish optimism? It was not quite what the two of them had been expecting, and in some ways it was harder to manage. But then he told them of the unspeakable horrors of the underground Stone Hold where he had spent his first night; and of his move to the Lower Ward, a dire precinct known as 'Old Nick's Backside,' with its stone paving covered in piles of excrement, and the lice so plentiful that they crackled beneath your feet. The Middle Ward, where he lodged now, at least had a wooden floor.

'Because I'm charged with a murder – and a sensational one too – I command a certain awe in here. They don't moderate their language or their sickening behaviour, but I'm thankfully left alone... and in this place, being *left alone* is no small thing, believe me...'

For the first time they could see fear in his eyes.

Although the talk was defiantly flowing, the voice itself didn't lie: they heard a nervous catch in it. They knew that its assurance was achieved through iron self-control, which once lost would bring collapse.

During this time Tom and Will had been glancing at one another, and it was Will who finally brought them to the practical matters. Morphew had spoken a great deal, but had said not a word about Emmet, or about the bloody scene in the printing-house – nothing at all to the purpose. If he was shutting out the nightmare, then he must do so no longer. Will looked squarely at him, and told him they had to direct their thoughts to the trial and confront the events of Friday night – and what the prosecutor might make of them in court.

Will reassured him they would both be present, and he himself would make what use he could of his legal experience – little enough though it was. But first, he said, they needed to hear an exact account of what had occurred on Friday night... The scene in the printing-house would hold the attention of everyone in the courtroom, and it would not be an easy audience: the place would be full to bursting and the hubbub would be considerable. Will told him about the chaotic Coroner's inquest and the warning it had given. The strain of the trial would be immense and the Bench might be set against him from the start – he had to be prepared for that. But *he must hold onto the truth*.

Will continued to look Morphew between the eyes. During the questioning, he said, the slightest hint that he was side-stepping the facts would be disastrous. The truth had to radiate from him like a beacon. Everything must be firm and clear. In the course of the trial he was sure to be provoked: lies would be told, or things said that cast his every action in a murderous light. But he must not be led into unguarded comments or show any annoyance. Will's voice was insistent. The details of the scene must be fixed in his mind. Other narratives would be offered and attempts made to paint an imagined scene. But he must remind the court that *he* was the first man to stumble on the body and had seen everything in all its horror. The shock had almost robbed him of his senses – had made him appear distracted. But that was the surest sign of his *innocence*. A man who had committed such a merciless attack would be determined and alert, not frantic and distraught. Human nature – every God-given human instinct – cried out against the act, and the sight was enough to threaten reason itself. The very thing the prosecutor presented as a sign of his guilt would in fact be a sign of his innocence....

Will had almost forgotten himself, and for a brief moment the dingy Upper Hall of Newgate gaol rang out with an eloquence that it can rarely have witnessed. Morphew was concentrating intently, and as he heard the speech unfold and the voice gaining in confidence he gazed into Will's eyes, and his face seemed to relax a little. He was hearing words he needed to hear. Locked inside this place and, what's more, locked inside himself, he had begun to lose his grip on the simple truth. Different scenes had swept before him – what others must have thought, and how others must have read the situation. But he knew Will was right. During these final hours he had to bend all his thoughts to what he himself had experienced, and keep that clear in his mind.

Tom was also stirred by what he was hearing, and he noticed Morphew give a gentle accepting nod, as if a sudden recognition had come to him. At that moment Tom and Will looked at each other. Nothing needed to be said. Here was a man who longed to embrace the truth, not someone who had done a murderous deed and was concerned to evade the facts. Morphew's fear was of others' fictions. His reaction to Will's speech told them all they needed to know. This man had seen that the truth was the only thing that could save him.

Morphew swallowed hard. For a few minutes he had been taken somewhere else, to a better and clearer place. But now he could taste Newgate again. There was a bitter sigh.

'If only I had someone who could present my case to the Court as you have done here!'

'Alas,' said Will. 'You are allowed no spokesman other than yourself. But all the more reason for you to speak from the heart – to show that you have nothing to fear from the facts.'

'But how can I *discover* those facts, Mr Lundy? I can speak from the heart, but will that be enough? The facts are so few! What really happened to poor Emmet? Who did that brutal thing? I've been pondering the question endlessly.'

Tom leaned forward.

'And so have we. During the past two days we have been making inquiries.'

'Ah yes,' said Morphew, 'I had a visit from James Feeny yesterday. He told me you had called at the shop and were generously concerned about my fate.'

'We are a team – Will and I – and our Mrs Trotter – and the good Elias Cobb…'

'Very good people, all!' echoed Will.

Morphew looked askance.

'Constable Cobb? But he was the man who arrested me!'

'Yes, but that was a task he had been charged with. Since then, he's been helpful to us. We've learned about your questioning at the Cockpit, about Emmet's accusations, and the printing of *Bufo's Magic Glass*… Just now he's busy on your case. We are all on Emmet's trail.'

'I fear it's an exceedingly devious one, Mr Bristowe. Emmet had connections in many places – some of them I did not know of, and didn't ask about. I'm greatly to blame in that. He had a lot of freedom to fish in waters that he chose. I should have asked more questions!'

'Well, that's what we are doing. We've uncovered some of his private ventures, and it's clear he knew of dangerous truths. He was becoming a threat to some important people.'

'We have facts to share with you,' said Will.

'And you with us, we hope,' Tom added.

Morphew raised his hand.

'Hold, gentlemen... This is truly heartening, and most unlooked for – the first glimmer of hope I've had. I long to hear about your efforts on my behalf... but please, before we begin I owe you a speech of my own. The trust you place in me is sobering, but I am shrewd enough to know you must have wondered if I was indeed the killer. You have spoken about truth, Mr Lundy, and so before we bring our facts together I must do as you suggested and give as full account as I can of the events of Friday night – the truth, exactly as I experienced it.'

Chapter Twenty-Five

Quietly, therefore, and with deliberation, John Morphew began telling his story: his night-time return to the printing-house; the unlocked door; his stepping forward blindly into the room; the stumble; the rough wool of the buttoned coat; the sticky pool of blood; the tinderbox shaking in his uncooperative hands; the sudden lightning spark when Emmet flashed into view; the gruesome corpse that seemed to be stirring in the uncertain candlelight; the horror at seeing his own cane covered in blood; the paper crushed into the stretched-out hand announcing Bufo's curse; his desperate panic…

Tom and Will were drawn into the scene as it unfolded and were left in no doubt that Morphew was re-living the experience: his eyes were a drama in themselves. As he spoke, they began to share his sense of being carried along in a trance and forced to assume an identity he didn't recognise. His account reached its climax in the magistrate's kitchen, with the three figures of watchman, porter, and constable becoming his ghostly accusers as they dangled the evidence of his guilt before him. Tom and Will could understand how he had begun to lose touch with the innocent John Morphew.

Finally, with relief, they left those events behind. The talk moved to the publisher's experiences at the Cockpit and the earlier ordeal of his questioning. It was during the Friday interview, he said, that the full picture of Emmet's deceptions became clear.

'On Thursday I had been questioned by Mr Addison and Mr Hopkins – roughly, but for a purpose. There were things they wanted to discover, suspicions they put to me – and in the end I could see the direction of their thoughts. But the next day it was different… now they were accusing me directly and goading me. They said they had the full picture before them. Now – would you believe it – they were telling me what *they* knew, and gloating at my discomfort as if they were laying bare my soul. And they soon made no secret of who their source had been.'

'This confirms what Elias Cobb had heard,' said Tom. 'He told us Emmet had been blabbing at the Cockpit. It was when you learned about *Bufo's Magic Glass*?'

'I learned of that, and much more. You'll be interested to know that they were indignant about the Good Fellowship and its seditious leanings – and indeed about the dangerous young satirist who lodged there and who might be the anonymous Bufo. And now, of course, they knew that *I was Bufo's printer*. I denied it, but they brandished the pamphlet, and the fact was there to see – my presses! But how could Emmet have done the job single-handed?'

'I'm afraid he didn't,' said Tom. 'On that occasion Paul Barnard helped him.'

'Ah, I see…' Morphew groaned to himself.

'He told me he now regrets it deeply. Emmet had begged him – as a friend.'

'I understand – John could be very persuasive. Certainly at the Cockpit he sold them a convincing bundle of fact and fiction – but to them it made complete sense.

'Do you think they were provoking you?' said Tom.

'What they were saying was meant to agitate me – I see that now. They wanted me to break and confess. They left me for several hours, and then returned to press me again, and then once more I was left alone. I think they were playing with my mind. It was clear they considered me a serious political enemy.'

'Did they openly accuse you?' said Will.

'Yes, and with relish! According to them, I am under Harley's spell – a ringleader of disaffection. I am driving forward a Tory plot to vilify the Whigs and blacken the reputations of the Junto lords. In our secret battle-plan (so they told me) satire is preparing the way, and Bufo is destined to become the Voice of the Nation. His apocalyptic revelations are meant to stir up disgust and fear, so that the people will demand the cleansing of public life and a return to the *old virtues*. The high-principled Mr Harley will then be welcomed as the man to protect the State and save the Queen from her enemies.'

'That sounds like a villainous plot!' said Will.

'Yes, and they see me as instrumental in it.'

'But surely,' said Tom, 'it is Harley whose reputation now hangs by a thread – the Greg affair, the French spies…'

'Yes,' said Morphew. 'All the more reason for him to fight back and use the weapons of satire to turn the battle around – to mount a charge into the heart of the Whig position. That's what they fear.'

'Toy soldiers!' said Will with a dismissive grunt.

'Perhaps so,' continued Morphew. 'But this is no table-top skirmish. The stakes are high. The nation is unsettled, and both sides are turning to violence.'

Tom was looking thoughtful.

'And so my own satire appeared to be a part of this?'

'Not only that, but thanks to Emmet's meddling, the Whigs have come to see the Good Fellowship as a nest of disaffection. You can understand their train of thought: I had called there to take delivery of a substantial new satire; Laurence Bagnall was writing a commendatory epistle to Mr Harley; the high-Tory Mutton-Chops were toasting the King over the Water; and I was collecting Bufo material from you…'

Up to this point, Tom's imagination had been absorbed in Morphew's plight, but now he was distinctly uneasy – the idea pressed too close. He thought of his own stolen papers and what might be construed from them… but this was no time to be intruding his own fears. His attention returned to Morphew, who was talking of his response to the interview:

'… So you can understand how angry I felt. Emmet – the man I had regarded as a friend and helper – was now accusing me to the Ministry, threatening to ruin my reputation and destroy my business.'

Will stepped in and spoke boldly, catching the emotional tide.

'And the matter of Lady Norreys's pocket-book must have angered you? I know how offended you were at Emmet's behaviour.'

'It was outrageous!' said Morphew at once. 'He was attempting to extract money from Lady Norreys's family – and when I intervened, he had the gall to suggest I was interfering in his business!'

Will continued urging the topic.

'Did you know the book's contents, Mr Morphew? You told me you had not looked into it.'

'That was an untruth, I fear – I can admit it now. I said as much because I wanted to avoid arousing your curiosity. I was wrong – but I had seen Emmet's game, and it made me determined to put a stop to it…'

His breathing was becoming quicker.

'… So, imagine my horror – when my questioners said they knew the book's secrets! He had told them every low detail –

and of Her Majesty! It was dishonourable – nothing less than *treason!*'

Will laid his hand on Morphew's arm, which had begun waving expressively.

'No, no, you must avoid that word. *Treason* is not to be spoken about! In court it will be picked up, and you will be accused of using it lightly. They will turn the word against you. Remember, their intention is to associate you with anger and violence. Emmet was your agent: he was procuring seditious material for you, and it was being printed on your presses.'

'But that was unauthorised!' said Morphew. 'Done behind my back in the most despicable way. I was furious at how he had behaved.'

'Yes, your outrage was natural, but you must be careful not to re-live it in court. I'm afraid I've been feeding your anger deliberately – but only to make this point to you. Listen to me! At the trial you must present your passion as righteous indignation, stern disapproval, concern, shock, embarrassment – *anything but anger*. There is a fine line to be drawn. The more you show your anger at Emmet's behaviour, the more you give them weapons to attack you.'

The publisher turned to him, narrowing his eyes, yet showing the hint of a smile.

'You will make a fine prosecutor some day, Mr Lundy. You pushed me over the edge… I shall try to heed your advice on Thursday, I promise you.'

'I think your questioners at the Cockpit were pushing you in just that way,' said Tom. 'They will be well practised in the art. And Mr Addison has a subtle intelligence – though I'm sad to think of him treating you so roughly.'

'But you are mistaken, Mr Bristowe – he was not one of my interrogators on that second occasion. I'm afraid I didn't make that clear… No, there were three of them. It was a stern tribunal!'

Tom and Will looked at each other.

'Do you know who they were?' said Will. 'Hopkins was surely one of them?'

'Yes, Hopkins was there again with his cold angry look – the man has ice in his veins!'

'And did you recognise the other two?'

'They didn't introduce themselves – but one of them I knew – Mr Maynwaring, the Member of Parliament. He's a Whig of the most determined character. I must say he gave no quarter! If Hopkins was as cold as a torpedo, Maynwaring waved his flaming sword. They were an ill-matched couple.'

Tom's pulse quickened. Will pressed further.

'And what about the third man?'

'His name is Voyce – I caught it at the end of the final spell of questioning. I know nothing of him except that he was clearly Mr Maynwaring's *factotum*. Smartly dressed though, and with a sour, disapproving look to him. He fawned a good deal and had little to say – and then only hesitatingly, as if he felt he needed Maynwaring's permission to intervene. He was taking notes... Of course I've since discovered that he's been pursuing a more active role.'

'What do you mean?' asked Tom.

'James Feeny told me. Before dawn on Saturday the man came to my shop unannounced, and took charge. He was giving orders to the constable and insisted that the body be moved and the blood mopped up. He treated Feeny and Barnard like servants – didn't do them the courtesy of giving his name, though Feeny has since learned it. The presumption!...'

Morphew paused.

'... You both look excited – does this help you?'

'It does indeed,' said Will. 'We've been puzzling ourselves about him.'

'We thought he had come from the Magistrate,' added Tom. 'But this makes sense. The man must have been dispatched from the Cockpit – and from what you say, quite possibly by Maynwaring himself.'

'And you tell us you've encountered Maynwaring before?' said Will.

'Yes, and it's not an episode I recall with pleasure – quite the contrary. It was before Christmas. A pamphlet was brought to me for printing at very short notice. His printer had failed him, and *could I oblige?*... But the thing was a rant, gentlemen, a clumsy attack on Mr Harley as a Jacobite plotter. Sad trash altogether – the usual name-calling. I told him so, and said I would have nothing to do with it. The man disclaimed the piece, but he took my words so badly it made me wonder if he had penned the thing himself. I'm afraid I was not very politic!'

Tom gave a half-smile at the publisher's candour. How Maynwaring must have winced!

'You know, of course, that he is the Duchess of Marlborough's Secretary?'

'No, I did not... so he interests himself in her affairs, does he?'

'Not only that,' said Will, 'but he loves making his voice heard – anonymously of course – and he assumes the public is at all times eager to hear it.'

'This explains why he became so angry at the interview. He challenged me about a wicked piece of invective against Her Grace...'

'The *Caricatura!*' exclaimed Tom.

'Yes, that was the title. I had found Emmet clutching a copy – very crudely printed – and asked him about it. He said he had picked it up in the street. But now I know he printed the squib himself – on my presses – part of his silly game! But Maynwaring became very heated and brooked no denial. I was producing trash fit for the gutter, he said, and the Duchess was enraged by it.'

'This is something we must pursue,' said Will. 'There is a line here, Tom, is there not? A chain of command – do you see it?'

'I think I do. The Duchess – the secretary – the factotum – and…'

'… And the constable,' concluded Will. 'It makes sense.'

'This Mr Voyce interests me,' said Tom. 'I wonder… Can you describe him more exactly? You said he looked *disapproving?*'

'Yes – he seemed to be sneering at me. But I think it was the turn of his mouth. He looked as if he'd been forced to swallow some unpleasant medicine.'

'Perhaps he had?' said Will. 'I think we may have seen that expression before, have we not, Tom?'

Recognition came at once.

'Yes of course! I can picture it now: a long, sour face – a slightly drooping eye…'

'That sounds very like,' said Morphew. 'Where did he cross your path?'

'In the Good Fellowship – on Friday evening too! He must have come there directly from the Cockpit after your questioning.'

'So… what was his purpose, I wonder?'

'I think we now know,' said Tom. 'The gentleman paid us a visit, and by some odd chance happened to light upon another example of Bufo's genius – a manuscript epigram attacking Lord Sunderland. It was very much in Bufo's vein, and he brandished it like a bailiff's warrant. We suspected he may have brought the paper with him. I'm afraid everyone closed ranks against the man, and he was forced to slip away.'

'That would make him scowl even more,' said Morphew. 'During our interview the very word "Bufo" made him flinch.'

Tom shifted involuntarily in his seat.

'That's our man, Will – do you not think? We're finally assembling our *dramatis personae.*'

'But of course, there is still one player who remains elusive...'

Will turned to Morphew.

'... Do you have any idea how Emmet procured the manuscript of *Bufo's Magic Glass?* We were even wondering if Emmet himself was Bufo... did he show any talent of that kind?'

'I wouldn't say so,' said Morphew. 'He had a nice critical eye, but no bent for writing poetry himself – at least I never had a hint of it. But he did have extensive connections – among City people and also at the smarter end of town. He could sniff out anything that was on the market. I have to admit John Emmet was very astute. It's odd to say, but he could inspire confidence and had winning ways when needed. Someone may have entrusted the poem to him without giving their name because they wanted it printed anonymously. It would cover their tracks and they could be sure Emmet would find a home for it... Oh dear, the truth seems as far off as ever!'

As Morphew pulled himself forward on the bench they realised how tense and fragile he was looking. The two of them were making a show of being confident, but they had to remember that Newgate was a place that closed in on you and drained hope away. The prisoner glanced round the hall as if recalling himself to the bleak realities of his situation.

'We are undoubtedly making progress,' said Tom as warmly as he could. 'What you've told us has been invaluable. We now have much more to think about.'

'Tom's right,' said Will. 'The picture is becoming clearer. And Widow Trotter and Constable Cobb are working in your interest too. We all have inquiries that we're pursuing... We'll not trouble you with them now, but we do have cause to be hopeful.'

Tom nodded.

'Don't lose heart – we're beginning to have some sense of what must have happened.'

They both looked at Morphew, who seemed to be struggling to lift his countenance and attune his mood to theirs. Perhaps he was thinking of what that night would bring?

'I hardly know what to say... You are both new friends, but you are the staunchest a man could wish for. You have given me good advice and much to ponder. Undoubtedly this counts as a good day. Be assured, I'm more anxious than ever to survive my ordeal... but, gentlemen, I fear my mind is tiring – and my body too... While I can still concentrate a little, could you inform me further, Mr Lundy? I have to bring my thoughts to bear on the trial – it is a scene I have been closing off. I do need to know something of the procedures. Thanks to James Feeny I have secured some character witnesses...'

And so the three of them turned to the matter of the murder trial. Tom and Will stayed by him for a further half hour, talking about practical things; and Will offered more advice, not only about responding to questions, but about what questions he might himself put to the prosecution's witnesses. No doubt Constable Buller would play a dramatic part in the proceedings, and the watchman and the porter would surely have their say. But there might be other witnesses called...

'The man is a hero!' declared Tom as they emerged from the filthy wards of the Common Side back into the prison lodge. 'Such courage and good humour – and thoughtfulness too. We *must* succeed, Will. We cannot let him go to his death! It's too terrible.'

'And what a death-in-life he's already enduring! How does he keep up his spirits? Before today, Newgate was just a grim idea to me – but the reality is insupportable.'

Both of them were taking deep breaths, as if they had just risen to the surface of some noxious pool.

'We brought him a little cheer I think,' said Will, 'and we've learned something important too.'

'Yes, the connection with Maynwaring is stronger. The links run from Buller to Voyce, to him…'

'And up to the Duchess,' said Will solemnly.

'And when you add Hopkins and Sunderland… Altogether it's a formidable Junto corporation, strong enough to crush anyone who gets in their way.'

The two of them stood and looked at each other. It was Will who posed the inevitable question:

'So, are we thinking it's a political murder? To put it simply… a Whig plot?…'

He said it tentatively, almost nervously.

'… Or a deed arranged by a devoted agent?'

'*Who will rid me of this turbulent priest?* said Tom. 'Yes, that's a possibility… Emmet and Morphew skewered on a single spear!… But are we really in that Machiavellian world?'

'Well, policy always rules in matters of State. Remember that somewhere, in this very prison…'

'Ah yes – William Greg of course! I had forgotten him.'

'Being kept alive in the condemned cell, only to face the hardest possible temptation; offered the gift of liberty, of a pension, his family, and his life – the greatest gift of all. A simple signature may be all that is required of him. It's a kind of torture… Now that's *policy* for you!'

A few minutes later a glass of Mrs Spurling's citron cordial was helping suppress the nausea of the place, and Will was taking the opportunity to chat with the Deputy Keeper about his most notorious prisoner. It appeared the traitor was being kept in a more secluded part of the gaol, away from the other prisoners.

'There's certainly comings and goings, I have to say. Everything is on hold with Mr Greg at the moment… but the matter is out of my hands. I simply act on the Keeper's directions.'

Will was informal and entirely at ease. He smiled and took a sip of the cordial.

'Could you tell us who has been visiting him?'

Mr Chandler looked at Will as if he were a schoolboy who had just asked after the headmaster's wife.

'That Sir, to put it as politely as I can, is none of your... business...'

The man made a pause before the final word – whether from hesitation or delicacy it was impossible to say.

'... It's a Ministry matter, and I know nothing of such things.'

'I ask no names, Sir,' said Will, who was now turning a florin deftly in his fingers, and playing with it nonchalantly. 'The merest hint...'

The man gave him a conspiratorial twinkle.

'He's being visited by both sides. That's all I know, and all I can say... It's a tug of war.'

'Mr Chandler – my compliments to you! You are a man of probity.'

He shook the man's hand warmly, pressing the silver into his palm. Tom was taken aback, but kept silent until they were out of the lodge.

'Well, what were you negotiating there, Will?'

'Just a little matter about William Greg. Our Deputy Keeper rightly kept his confidence. But I learned something of interest from him. It's not much, but it adds to the picture.'

'And what is that?' asked Tom, intrigued.

'Mr Greg is being visited by *both sides*. Evidently Whigs *and* Tories are finding their way to his cell. It's a tug of war, he says, and there's bidding and outbidding going on. How these politicians thrive!'

They walked back through Newgate arch – this time keeping to the centre of the passageway – and once again Will stopped and pointed upwards, now at the Holborn side of the tower.

'Look there! More emblems for you. This time we have *four* ladies to send us on our way – and what beauties they are! *Liberty, Peace, Plenty,* and *Concord.* In fact, everything a great nation needs!'

'Ah, *the mountain nymph, sweet Liberty!*' said Tom sadly. 'The words of hopeful youth! I must admit she has never seemed sweeter than now, after that suffocating place… I wonder if old Milton recalled his youthful words in his final darkness?'

'You're growing lyrical, Tom! But I think there's a satiric touch about it too… Did you notice what was curled at Liberty's feet?…'

Tom turned round again.

'… That's Dick Whittington's cat.'

'Well I never!' said Tom, looking up at the stone figure. 'Do you remember our adventure at that pot-house in Oxford, Whittington and his Cat?'

Will smiled at his friend.

'Ah yes – the true liberty of youth, Tom!'

Chapter Twenty-Six

NEVER HAD TOM felt less like an evening's entertainment. The experience of Newgate had overwhelmed him, and his imagination was stored with its horrible images as thoroughly as the fetid smells of the Common Side had seeped into his clothes. He could still hear the scraping of the chains. It was as if each man's crime were pulling him down – a foretaste of that final descent when the rope would tighten. Tom shuddered, and he felt the dead weight on his mind. He tried to tell himself that some distraction was exactly what he wanted just now, and a few hours of gossip, wit and laughter would be restorative. But part of him felt he ought to be doing penance and be turning his mind to more serious matters.

In the normal course of things he would have succumbed to a sudden indisposition; but Widow Trotter had stiffened his resolve and immediately packed him off to the Hummums for a prolonged soak, welcomed him back with some oranges in brandy syrup, expressed excessive admiration for his Popham suit (as he now thought of it), and made him try on her authentic Venetian mask, which made him look like a salacious cockerel. She had also reminded him that the *ridotto* would not be an indulgence but a mission – and one that might turn out to be as important as his Newgate journey. This had decided him, and so he had set out determined to make a sacrifice to pleasure.

Since then, he had undergone a thorough jolting in a sedan chair, with the two brawny Irish chairmen trotting at a furious pace, undaunted by the icy rain that was buffeting them. The wise Mrs Trotter had advised him to take a chair to St James's and not demean himself with a hackney:

'On a night like this, Tom, the square will be packed with fine coaches, and a poor hackney trying to squeeze its way in will have no chance. In a chair you can weave between them easily and be delivered to the door.'

The delivery was duly made amidst flapping umbrellas and wet capes, though not without difficulty. On the pavement in front of the mansion the link boys and footmen jostled with the ragamuffins and street sellers who crowded round the steps. Accompanied by banter and insults, pennies were thrown into caps, and for charity a few posies and sweetmeats were purchased. One enterprising woman was offering simple black face-masks to anyone who had come unprepared.

Once the formalities of arrival had been negotiated, Tom was able to join the swirl of fashion in Lady Welwyn's drawing-room. The mask constricted his sight a little, but it allowed him to scrutinise things in a slightly mysterious way, and he found himself scanning the spacious room for curiosities. The townhouse was no Venetian palace, but it had splendours of its own and was making quite a show. A vast allegorical ceiling may have been lacking, but there were gilt leather wall-hangings and decorative plasterwork with plump cherubs enacting all kinds of excesses. At the far end he could see a couple of card tables where he noticed his Aunt Sophia already ensconced; and in a shell-shaped alcove to the side was a small group of musicians in the throes of a flute concerto. The contest was being closely fought, but the flautist appeared to be winning narrowly. There was no sign of Uncle Jack and Lavinia, and he guessed they must be in the neighbouring dining-room where a spread of Venetian delicacies was promised.

The drawing-room was already well filled, and romantically lit by two mighty chandeliers which held enough flickering candles to light a house for a month. The beau monde of St James's saw this enchanting new *ridotto* as an opportunity to demonstrate how colour could add life to a canvas. Scarlets and crimsons, turquoise and lapis lazuli predominated, with touches of lemon yellow here and there. The tints were shifting like a restless silk curtain, with the music adding extra grace-notes to every turn of the head. Guests were conscious that an exotic spirit ought to preside and were doing their best to encourage it. But on this English February night no-one quite knew how Venetian they were meant to be. One group, however, had made a determined effort and seemed to have stepped off a gondola during the carnival: their bodies had arrived shrouded in impressive cloaks; one especially lavish mask sprouted a pair of golden wings; another doll-like face was ringed by orange feathers; and a third sported a dazzling papier-mâché creation featuring a giant nose that endangered anyone who came close. All this riot of colour was thrown into relief by a single male figure who was dressed completely in black except for the ghostly white mask that jutted out under his hat.

Tom was impressed, and stationed himself beside a large handsome fireplace where he could sip his sweet wine and survey the company. There was a hint of excitement in being incognito, and he began to look forward to sidling round the room before he could be recognised. But at that moment he became conscious of being scrutinised himself. He glanced round and saw a leering face close beside his shoulder. It was a marble Bacchus, cup in hand, ogling him through a bunch of grapes. He instinctively lifted his gaze, only to alight on a painting of an Arcadian shepherd and shepherdess who were bending to kiss while a bemused sheep looked on. He tasted the delicious wine, and without thinking set his cuffed wrist on his hip, feeling blessedly relaxed. It was warm, and around him the panelling glowed in the candlelight. A profusion of birds and fruits, exquisitely carved in limewood, fluttered and tumbled over each other.

Behind him there was a sudden ripple of laughter.

'Cugino mio!'

He turned, and there stood a real shepherdess – or was it a milkmaid? – her rustic bonnet and little apron offering a picture of coy innocence. The mask in delicate pink lace added a sophisticated touch, but did little to disguise a grinning Lavinia beneath it.

'I recognise that suit, Tom, but the mask is something new! You look like an escaped chicken. I shall have to shoo you back to the farmyard!... Where did you get that admirable object?'

'From a Drury Lane bagnio, I warrant – it smells of leather and orange peel. Mrs Trotter intended well, but I'm having doubts about the thing.'

'It has a Venetian air – I'm sure Lord Tring will be delighted. He's made such an effort to be *genuine*. Have you seen his wondrous Harlequin costume? He's frisking about from group to group and causing merriment wherever he goes. Such ease and cheerfulness! He wants me to bring you to him...'

His cousin leaned nearer and lowered her voice.

'... And, joy of joys! Lady Norreys is over there playing cards, with her back to us, do you see? She's wearing a gauze veil. I succeeded in settling her with your aunt for a game of whist. Wasn't that clever of me? So you can go over and greet Sophia quite freely – and she will have to introduce you!'

Lavinia gave him a sweet smile. It was clear that she had been reconnoitring the rooms and already had a tale to tell of what was stirring. She ran through one or two of the more whimsical costumes and their wearers, and conjectured a few identities. In particular she wondered about a pair of roguish-looking gentlemen who had positioned themselves by the alcove and appeared to be comparing notes on the field as if evaluating likely fillies at Newmarket.

'Look at those two, Tom. The one on the left I'm sure is Mr Sturgis – the *honourable* Mr Sturgis indeed! – though honour, I hear, is not something we are to expect from him. It's too much to assume a title-page will be true to the contents.'

'You're a shrewd reader, Lavinia. But as the *honourable* Lavinia I hope you'll admit at least one exception?'

'Of course... but I have to wonder about honest *Tom* – it's such a forthright name! Could any man live up to it? It's impossible to expect deception from a *Tom*.'

'Perhaps I've as much honesty as Aunt *Sophia* has of wisdom?'

Lavinia smiled, but then her attention suddenly shifted and her whole face lit up.

'And how *saintly*, I wonder, is Mr *St John*?... Perhaps we shall discover, since the man appears to be making his way towards us!'

Tom glanced round in anticipation, and certainly the supremely elegant figure heading in their direction could not be mistaken. Tom noticed the impeccably folded cravat, tied with a red ribbon, which flowed almost to the waist where it vied with the lace cuffs, before the eyes were drawn further down to a pair of shoe-buckles bright with diamonds and knotted with more ribbon. Under the rakishly angled hat a simple black mask covered his eyes, leaving the mouth free to smile in warm greeting. Lavinia instinctively raised her hand to meet his. He bowed gracefully and kissed it.

'Miss Popham! – what a vision of innocence! I trust your little lambs are all healthy?'

'You must know that in Arcadia, Mr St John, sheep are never ill.'

'I stand corrected... And of course the days are always warm and clear. – But alas! swains are not always *true*, are they?... And this... ?'

'This is my cousin, Thomas Bristowe...'

'Ah yes – of course, Mr Bristowe. We meet again. The *cock* deceived me – a fine thing it is indeed! For a moment I thought myself on the Rialto!'

Tom's blush was helpfully hidden. He caught a glint in Henry St John's eye that may have been playful collusion, or something colder – the mask made it hard to tell.

'... I hope your poetry is progressing, and that you've shaped some polished lines today? Does your cousin ever read his verses to you, Miss Popham?'

Lavinia was a little disappointed at the direction of the conversation, but let it take its course, and the topic of poetry duly took over. There were several minutes of lively discussion before she caught sight of a friend and promptly made good her escape. As she turned, she gave her cousin a sharp look and made a decisive nod toward the card tables. And so Tom was left alone with Henry St John, who, to his surprise, did not seem abashed at Lavinia's brisk departure and was happy for their talk to continue.

'Alas, Mr Bristowe, I had thought poetry would be a pleasing topic with your cousin, but I fear I was mistaken. Perhaps I too readily introduced the subject of *Paradise Lost*. Satan and Eve was not the wisest thing to choose! – I hope I said nothing to make her uneasy? I'm determined to make up for it later and inquire if her singing lessons have begun.'

He smiled quite affably, and Tom responded in similar vein.

'Lavinia is an enthusiast for Milton, Mr St John – but I think she esteems our first mother more highly than you do.'

The tone was amicable, and when St John enquired again about his poetic ambitions Tom responded sadly with the news of his stolen papers. He had no sooner mentioned the theft than it occurred to him that he should have been more circumspect. Had he opened the door too wide? The fate of his poem and his blasted hopes were now no secret. St John was shocked, and his words of concern were sympathetically urged. He pressed Tom further about what had happened, and what his publishing plans had been. Once the name of *Morphew* was mentioned the talk moved swiftly on to Thursday's trial and what was likely to ensue. St John was animated... How frightful the incident was, and what sacrilege too! The printing-house – that place which should be devoted to cultivating the mind and enlightening the spirit!

Tom felt he was being drawn out, however kindly, and wanted to take a step back. He knew he should say nothing about the case. That must be left hidden. Perhaps he had already revealed too much?

But St John was warming to the topic and was soon commenting on Emmet's fate – how there were rumours that he was a trader in secret memoirs and scandalous correspondence.

'What a devious trafficker the man seems to have been, Mr Bristowe – bringing the world of Grub Street into St James's!...'

By this time Tom was becoming distinctly uneasy and sensed footsteps coming nearer.

'... In your dealings with Morphew, Mr Bristowe, did you ever meet this Emmet fellow? He does appear to have been a bit of a rogue!'

Tom tried to be evasive, and his voice began to convey a hint of nervousness. He was unwilling to say he had met the murdered man, but found himself having to mention Emmet's visit to the Good Fellowship and their talk about poetry. St John was naturally curious about what Tom had made of him.

'Did he strike you as an honest sort? Or was there something sinister about him?...'

Tom hesitated. St John surged on.

'... But perhaps *poetry* was not the chief thing on his mind! I hear he was known to the Covent Garden ladies and picked up some of their talk... I fancy it was not the only thing he picked up!'

Tom fought to keep calm, and remarked that at their brief meeting Emmet had revealed little of himself.

'Our exchanges were cursory, Mr St John. Had I known what his fate was soon to be, I would have been more curious – a missed opportunity there, I think!'

Tom saw St John's mask shift slightly as his temples creased into a half-smile. Occasionally, he thought, a mask could be revealing. It gave the person a little too much confidence – and covering the face might expose the voice?

Thankfully the talk shifted at last, and they were both able to agree that poetry was a noble calling and had to fight its ground against the public's taste for scandalous romances and society gossip. It was a subject Tom was happy to seize on, and their conversation ended cordially with St John offering the hope that Tom's poem would soon be restored to him. It could surely not have been destroyed, he said – indeed perhaps the more likely danger was its printing – anonymously, or even under another's name?

'Poor Swift is being foisted with things not his own – and Matt Prior is finding himself published without his consent – greatly to his embarrassment.'

It was a flattering comparison, and the two of them parted, agreeing that in the modern world of letters there were few scruples about such things.

Tom's attention now turned to the card table, where Lady Norreys was still seated. She had her back to him, and he saw that her gauze veil was hanging to one side; but from where he stood he could not make out her features. He would just have to take a chance and grasp the moment. He waited until the hand had been played out, and then stepped confidently forwards, hoping he didn't look too threatening. Lavinia had set up the scene to perfection and everyone performed their part. Tom noted that Lady Norreys at once pinned up her veil, which now left only the neck exposed, before looking round and reaching out her hand. His formal bow was nicely managed, and Lady Norreys, much to his surprise, declared that she was tired of cards and needed to take a turn about the room. Would perhaps Mr Bristowe be so kind?

She rose, and Tom was taken aback by what was revealed: a pair of cream silk pantaloons girded round the waist with a bright red sash. A small jacket striped with silver thread completed the costume. He nodded to the other card players and handed this exotic lady in the direction of the fire. Young Aunt Sophia watched the manoeuvre closely, drawing her Columbine mask tightly to her face with the stick and scrutinising the pair as they walked away.

Before they could speak, the music ended with a flourish, and a scattering of applause ran round the room as the flute-player, red-faced but otherwise unscathed, took his bow. Lady Norreys appeared to be beaming under her veil.

'Ah, Scarlatti! What a sprightly piece – and how clever of Lord Tring! He brought two of his sonatas back from Italy – unpublished ones!'

'He does seem taken with all things Venetian – I've not seen his Harlequin costume yet.'

'When I saw him last he was flitting between the dining-room and the kitchen. He told me he's very anxious the food should be *a puntino!...*'

She pinched the air with her thumb and finger.

'... Among much else he's promising us a pair of delectable rice dishes, and everyone's curiosity is aroused. How delightful for a wet February night!'

One or two groups were now making their way out to explore what culinary offerings there were. Tom took the hint and gestured in that direction; but Lady Norreys demurred.

'No, Mr Bristowe, do you mind if we talked a little while?'

Tom began to realise that Lavinia's diplomacy had been carefully managed on both sides. He was wondering who was guiding whom. He took two more glasses of wine from a footman and gave one to Lady Norreys. She received it silently, and before anything further was said he found himself once again on the far side of the fireplace. Bacchus's expression now looked distinctly conspiratorial. Lady Norreys was of a height with Tom, and so his eyes were level with her veil, which shivered slightly in response to her breath. Tom's mask felt hot and uncomfortable.

'So, Lord Melksham is your uncle, Mr Bristowe? He is always well spoken of – which is quite a tribute in St James's.'

'Yes, Uncle Jack is an honest, genial soul, and a little out of place in the world of politics. He's not the smooth courtier.'

'Heaven forbid! There are too many of those. And a sad dearth of honesty! It must be hard for a man in his position to remain above the *mire!* Do you talk much with him about such things?'

'I hear a little about what goes on at Court...'

'And what *goings-on* there are, Mr Bristowe! I warrant he has to be discreet, given what his eyes must light upon.'

'The Queen's finances? Yes, he does have a trust to fulfil, and has to be very guarded.'

'Ha! How does he jog along with the *Duchess?*'

Lady Norreys, Tom decided, was a direct woman. She didn't attempt to prepare the ground, and once through the polite formalities she would be quick and bold. Her pocket-book would not be lacking in sharp observations and opinions.

'Her Grace does not consult my uncle very often. They have little to do with one another in the run of things.'

Tom knew his bland answer would not satisfy her, and it was met with a dismissive sniff.

'No, I would think not! The Duchess has her own *machinery* – and what a performance she makes of it!'

Lady Norreys had the knack of alighting on certain words as if they might be contagious, which made Tom wonder if her letters were full of underlinings. He was trying to think of a reply that would be simultaneously witty and non-committal... but she pre-empted him.

'... Mr Bristowe, I would like to talk to you on a ticklish matter – we need to sit down... Look! – they are leaving that *divan...*'

The unusual word promised oriental indulgence, but she strode towards the thing with purposive briskness and took occupation. Far from guiding her politely around the room, he had now been well and truly captured. The initiative was certainly hers. He had of course been hoping to raise a difficult subject himself – could it be the same one? Were they already on common ground? He was at once to discover.

'You are a close friend of Will Lundy's, I understand?'

'Yes, we were students together. My *fidus Achates!*'

'Then I shall not ask you if he can be trusted... But you must tell me, Mr Bristowe, has he spoken to you about a highly sensitive errand he recently carried out for my brother, Mr Sumner?'

There was a pause. This was his opportunity and he must seize it; but he must not profess to know of the book's contents...

'Yes, it is a secret between us – I didn't expect to speak of it with you. Will gave me to understand there were potential *difficulties* involved. I'm glad the matter was resolved without embarrassment.'

'You may say so, Mr Bristowe, but I can hardly agree. That is what I need to inquire of you.'

'Whatever it is, you can count on my being discreet...'

He tried to sound confidential yet open – but in his oppressive disguise he could not be both. His discomfort was mounting. How could he be open when he was trapped inside something so grotesque! He suddenly felt ludicrous. He reached behind his head and rapidly untied the beaked mask.

'Damn the thing! I apologise, Lady Norreys, but I can't be shut inside this suffocating mask. I must look absurd.'

Her gauze veil shuddered.

'There are many here who look worse, Mr Bristowe... But perhaps *this* will be more suitable for you.'

She reached in a rather unladylike way into the pocket of her trousers and produced a simple black eye-mask.

'I took the precaution of buying this at the door – so I should have something in reserve. I think you are the more in need of it. It allows a degree of mystery without distorting the face... Let me!'

Tom bowed his head, and Lady Norreys deftly tied the ribbon behind his neck. She gave the top of his head a little tap.

'There you are! Now we can be more at ease, can't we!...'

Tom wondered if she would choose that moment to unveil herself, but he was disappointed.

'... Now tell me, what has happened to the printer, this Mr Morphew? I was told he behaved very well over the pocket-book, and is indeed the person I have most to thank... But now he's charged with murder, with killing his pressman – that villain who tried to extort money from me. I'm fearful of what may be said at the trial. Can my book have been the quarrel between them? I pray not!'

Tom tried to be reassuring. With much care and circumspection he gave Lady Norreys an account of Morphew's plight, and of the visit he and Will had paid to Newgate only a few hours previously. They were convinced of his innocence, he said, and were doing what they could to discover the truth. Morphew was resolved not to mention the pocket-book in court, and had told them – in general terms – that the contents were incendiary and he would never voluntarily allude to them. Tom handled the topic scrupulously and was pleased he had found the appropriate words to calm her fears. But she still seemed anxious. He continued to reassure her.

'Believe me, your Ladyship, this Emmet had many irons in the fire, and he upset many people. Will and I shall both be at the trial, and we're confident the book's contents will not be mentioned.'

'Mr Bristowe – what you say is very thoughtful, and you've explained the situation fully. It appears this poor Morphew may be a victim too... If it will help you, I think you need to know more about the book's contents, which you say you are ignorant of. I shall be open with you...'

Lady Norreys withdrew the pin securing her veil, and the gauze swung away to expose her face. The dark, searching eyes made him feel exposed – they would not brook deception – and she was looking at him intently.

Quietly, and without hesitation, she told him about the memoranda touching on the Queen. She explained that she had noted down in ridiculous detail some intimate revelations about Her Majesty and Abigail Masham – told to her by Mrs Masham herself. Why she had done that foolish thing, she knew not, and she had repeatedly castigated herself for it! The material was merely disgusting to anyone who did not understand Her Majesty and the tragic difficulties of her life.

'I shall say no more on the subject, Mr Bristowe. The pocket-book was stolen from my closet by one of the servants, and I gather the hussy sold it to the scoundrel Emmet for five pounds – half a year's wages! No wonder she fled the house. This Emmet must have read the thing, and I suspect he did not keep it to himself. I shudder when I think of it...'

Lady Norreys looked down as if ashamed, but she remained thoughtful.

'... I don't know if that information will help your publisher. But it is the uncomfortable truth. You can appreciate why he does not wish to speak of it in court... Do you fear the worst for him?'

Tom confessed that he was extremely worried. Their one remaining hope lay in Emmet's political entanglements, especially his involvement in printing the verses of *Bufo* – a man whose invectives had burst on the scene in recent days and were threatening the great Whig lords – men with the power to silence a lone voice that was reducing them to ridicule.

'We are running out of time. But if we could identify this *Bufo* it would bring us nearer to discovering who killed Emmet.'

Lady Norreys remained silent. She was white-faced, as if she had donned another more ghostly mask. Tom saw that something was turning over in her mind, and he kept silent too. Then she appeared to reach a decision. The eyes were suddenly determined, and facing his. Tom drew back slightly. It was the look of a warrior about to draw his sword.

'So, you do not know about the poems?'

'The *poems?*'

Tom could feel his heart beating rapidly.

'In the pocket-book...'

'I don't understand – poems in the book?'

'Yes, Mr Bristowe, loose papers in the book's *pocket*... at the end. You will appreciate that I did not wish to say anything about this... but your printer's life is in danger, and if it may help to save him...'

She looked into the distance as if viewing a prospect and taking in all its parts.

'... The pocket was empty when the book was returned. I was more concerned about the loss of those verses, if truth were known. My brother knew nothing of them – I merely told him about the memorandums – and so he was full of joy when he handed the book to me. I tried to look relieved, but I knew it was hopeless – that the verses had been removed. It seems they had reached the one man who could do the worst with them... And now they have been *prostituted* in the most embarrassing way. The things are being handed around town – and a mish-mash of material has reached print. The thought horrifies me!'

Tom was stunned.

'Is it you, then?... Are you *Bufo?*'

'Ah no, Mr Bristowe – I cannot claim that distinction. The name must have been Emmet's idea – some of the pieces were about a toad. This morning I saw a copy of *Bufo's Magic Glass* – Emmet had set fragmentary portraits together and framed them as a prophecy. That Emmet was an ingenious man. He would have made a good editor.'

Lady Norreys spoke the words almost sadly, with a sense of their irony.

'Do you mean that Emmet re-worked your materials before he printed them?'

'They are not *mine,* Mr Bristowe – not really mine at all. And Emmet seems to have played fast and loose with them. I hear there are other printed fragments being circulated – stuck on walls and lamp-posts. They are spreading from street to street like the plague!'

She did not attempt to hide her indignation. A few yards away a couple of male masks swung round toward them, sensing the commotion. Lady Norreys at once gave a ringing laugh and leant over to whisper in Tom's ear. The two figures turned away, now gossip-fuelled. Tom was confused. He had to know more. He asked her quietly.

'You must tell me – whose poems are they?'

'I am but the secretary, Mr Bristowe – though some of the lines are mine… I think I owe you an explanation. We are a small club of ladies…'

'Arachne's Web!…'

Tom spoke without thinking. Lady Norreys was obviously puzzled and gave him a quizzical look.

'… I'm sorry… I've heard you called so. I'm afraid I've broken a confidence.'

Around the edge of Tom's mask a blush of embarrassment spread.

'Ah, I see! I detect the ring of Lavinia's voice – she is an incurable tattler – am I right in that?'

Tom was forced to nod meekly.

'… But it's an ingenious name – I think we might adopt it – I shall put it to our next meeting!… We have indeed been weaving a web, Mr Bristowe, and one not pleasing to the gods, it seems… We are a group of women who – strange to say – discuss the news and express opinions – remarkably not about fashion and gossip, but about ideas, and about public affairs. We interest ourselves in what passes in the political world – and we argue – and we laugh – and we make verses! The verses began as mere bagatelles, but we are now in earnest. We find release in them, and of course we find ourselves being satirical. What intelligent woman could not contemplate some of our *great men* and not find matter for satire? And some of our great women too! Her Grace the Duchess is one of our favourite topics, and her doings have supplied us with much mirth and outrage – in equal measure.'

Tom found himself beaming in wonder.

'Do you make verses spontaneously?'

'Yes, often. We rhyme, and we cap each other's lines. But we also bring along couplets or epigrams ourselves and read them to the company – for correction and improvement. Mrs Manley is the most prolific of us. She has a sharp wit, and much of our cleverest verses are thanks to her. But the thoughts and words of us all are in the mixture. We seem to have become a single voice.'

Lady Norreys closed her eyes, lifted her chin, and spoke from memory:

Collective bodies in close Union join'd
Remain invincible while so combin'd;
But when divided fall an easy prey:
The Whole *does in its weakened* Parts *decay!*

So you see, Mr Bristowe, we are a *collective body* – and all the stronger for it!'

'So what fell into Emmet's hands was a bundle of miscellaneous satirical portraits?'

'Largely, yes. I was acting as a scribe and keeping records. Much of the scribble was consigned to the flames of course, but it was my role to preserve the best. We were to assemble a larger poem out of the pieces, and were to discuss the possibilities soon. Mrs Manley was in favour of composing a miniature epic with a toad as the hero who goes off adventuring. She wrote a little of it, but there was much more to be done in that way and a lot more narrative to write. Alas, Emmet's editorial effort is clever, but crude and truncated – a series of squibs joined together.'

'So, in a way, Emmet took over your role?'

'That's an uncomfortable thought, Mr Bristowe. But you're right. And what a hellish outcome there has been! Emmet has died – and Mr Morphew may die too. And all for poetry.'

'But we don't know at whose hand Emmet died, and what the motive was…'

Tom hesitated. The big question had to be asked.

'... What shall I do – what *can* I do – with the facts you've told me? I don't want to cause trouble to you and your friends.'

'Truth should always out, Mr Bristowe. It is when we obstruct it that the worst can ensue. The great Aphra Behn is our patron-spirit, and our group meets under the sign of Astraea, Goddess of Justice. So how could we not wish your cause well?...'

Tom received a benign smile.

'... If any of this can help save an innocent man's life, then you must use it... but only as a last resort. There is strength in speaking through a mask: people listen more carefully, and the words often gain in scope and power. Our collective voice is important to us, Mr Bristowe – and we should like to preserve it.'

Tom felt the force of the sentiment.

'I promise you, only in our direst need... when all else has failed...'

He was now thinking quickly. The revelation about 'Bufo' fitted neatly into place: it explained how Emmet had procured the materials and made them his property by reworking them. He recalled what Paul Barnard had said about the fair copy of *Bufo's Magic Glass* – it must have been Emmet's own title. Clearly, he had become swept up in Bufo and made the angry voice his own... But there was something else that intrigued Tom. The mention of Delarivier Manley made him want to know more.

'You say that Mrs Manley is very active in your group?'

'Yes, she *spins* more busily and expertly than any of us – quite an inspiration! And she has the knack in her prose too. Have you read *The Lady's Pacquet of Letters?*'

'Is that Mrs Manley's work?'

'It certainly is – though of course she disclaims it. She has a lively interest in scandal, and it seems the public does too. After the popular uproar, she managed somehow to discover a further *pacquet*, and this time it was Emmet who negotiated it – and John Morphew who arranged the publication.'

'Yes, I've heard something of that, but I didn't know it was Mrs Manley's enterprise.'

'She is enterprising and daring, Mr Bristowe! You may not know this, but the Duchess regards Mrs Manley as her implacable enemy, and anyone who advances her cause is marked out. The grudge is a deep one. She has never forgotten the *Secret History*! Our friend Manley protests it was not hers, but the Duchess will have none of it. We like to picture her stamping her feet whenever the name of *Manley* is mentioned. Oh yes, we have had a deal of amusement at Her Grace's expense!'

Tom at once thought of the Duchess's latest fury at the *Caricatura*. He thought of Arthur Maynwaring, and of his henchman Voyce, and Constable Buller... More and more he was coming to understand what risks Emmet had been running, and what the consequences might have been. There was some serious thinking to be done...

... but no time in which to do it. A sudden *halloo* sounded forth, followed by a volley of idiomatic Italian, and the figure of Harlequin in a multi-coloured mask and chequered suit bounded towards them. In a few disconcerting moments their hands had been seized, and he and Lady Norreys were whisked off in the direction of the dining-room. The room had become crowded, and Tom thought himself plunged into a Commedia dell'Arte scene with carnivalesque faces smiling and scowling by turns, and bright silks and satins hissing around him. The musicians had struck up again, and he felt buoyant, caught up in the rhythm of celebration – but Lady Norreys had disappeared. He was hardly able to recollect himself before he was sampling the delights of the tables, which were being continually supplied by footmen holding aloft dishes and bowls that trailed delectable aromas. Harlequin's silken arm was resting on his shoulder, and his host's rippling laugh was ringing in his ear as together they savoured the delightful anchovies in little parcels of pasta, and a dish of creamy rice with garlic and mushrooms.

Wednesday

9 February 1708

Chapter Twenty-Seven

Tom lifted his head from the pillow with extreme care, stretched his legs, tousled his hair, and scratched behind his ears, marvelling at the suddenness with which the physical world could reassert itself. He blinked and wondered where he was. He thought the clink of china had woken him, and there was a tray at the bedside, but the human hands that had delivered it were nowhere to be seen. He certainly didn't recognise the room. Slowly he began to piece together a recollection of being assisted up some stairs and having his stockings removed. He remembered music, food, laughter, hugs, and grape-brandy – a lot of it – and a lot of bodies too, including his own, moving in a dance. With sudden alarm he looked across the bedroom and was relieved to see his clothes folded neatly over a chair, and his watch propped up beside the tray, on which stood a small teapot, a cup, and a china plate holding a slice of toast surmounted by a poached egg. The watch showed it was a little after ten. He gave thanks to Saint Anthony, guardian of misplaced things, that he hadn't come to consciousness on a Covent Garden bench or in some sordid brothel-house – though he shuddered to think how easily that might have been. No – the window of his room was tall and elegant, and the furnishings told him he was still in St James's.

Twenty minutes later Tom was sitting on the bed feeling cautiously optimistic. He had begun reassembling his identity, successfully attaching each item of clothing to the correct part of the body; he had negotiated the pouring of tea into the cup, and had found a way of transferring the eggy toast into his mouth. In a moment of inspiration he had also thought to look out of the window, where the view told him that he was in an unfamiliar room of his uncle's house in Pall Mall.

After a further ten minutes he was downstairs investigating whether anyone else in the place was alive. He popped his head round the dining-room door and discovered his uncle at the table confronting his own breakfast egg. The pair greeted one another like warriors who had survived a terrible battle. A dose of strong coffee brought them to a state of well-being, and in a short time they were able to talk fairly coherently about the previous night's events and make comparison of their headaches.

Lady Welwyn's Venetian masquerade had apparently been declared a wild success, and the charming word *ridotto* was on everyone's lips and beginning to circulate round the Town in questions and exclamations. Everyone agreed that on that stormy night Lord Tring had been an enchanter, infusing his guests with the festive spirit and drawing them, willing and unwilling alike, into tipsy dance and jollity.

Silence temporarily descended while Lord Melksham scanned the Gazette, and this gave Tom the chance to ponder. The midnight revelries remained blurred, but his memory of the earlier part of the evening was now returning, and he recalled with a shock his conversations with Henry St John and Lady Norreys. Both had been revealing, though in different ways. Why had Henry St John been so eager to discover what he knew about Emmet's activities? The man was a consummate politician and seemed to be probing him and observing his reactions. The concern about his stolen papers sounded sincere, but again there was an excess of curiosity. Why did Tom sense that St John was seeking confirmation of something he already knew?

And now he himself knew the identity – the identities! – of Bufo. That chilling oracle, so powerful in its vision and confident in its judgments, was not an individual voice at all, but a communal one. Its prophecies and curses had struck a chord with Emmet, so that he had become their instrument. Arachne's Web had little time for tea-table pleasantries: Mrs Manley and her friends were fired to talk and speak their minds – and High Tory minds, it would appear! Tom wondered if someone in Harley's office might be encouraging their association.

John Morphew's links with Delarivier Manley gave him food for thought. The Duchess hated her, and it would be easy for Maynwaring to point an accusing finger at Morphew's shop as the source of the poisonous libels. Something told him that Maynwaring's factotum Henry Voyce, with his disapproving mouth, must be concerned in Emmet's death. Could he have set up the scene in the printing-house, played the assassin's role, and then ensured, with Constable Buller's help, that the stage was cleared afterwards? Tom wondered what power Maynwaring had over Voyce – would he really use him to silence Emmet and Morphew forever? Tom shivered at the thought. Both sides were raising the stakes, and the political play was becoming deep and dangerous, with Sunderland's faction and Harley's faction determined to meet their enemy head-on.

These thoughts were running through Tom's mind when he became aware that his uncle had lowered his paper and was looking at him with interest.

'You're very pensive, Tom!... Are you ready to talk about Newgate?'

Tom jumped as if a nerve had been struck.

'What do you mean, Uncle?'

'I ask because last night when we were walking home, and Arthur was helping to carry you, you were mumbling about *Newgate*. You were clearly agitated. Sophia and Lavinia were striding ahead, but I caught something of it. I was befuddled myself but I know you mentioned the *gallows* and the *Common Side*, as if you were horrified by something. What has been going on, Tom? On Sunday you told me you were concerned in a matter you couldn't tell me about. What I heard last night was the voice of someone lost and frightened. If you're entangled in a criminal affair – God forbid! – then I must know. I can keep a confidence if need be.'

Tom looked at his Uncle Jack and was swept by a sudden sense of relief. Yes, now was the time to unburden himself – about what had been happening, and what he, Will, and Widow Trotter were trying to discover in preparation for tomorrow's trial. Tom expressed a willingness to speak, and Lord Melksham settled himself back in his chair while his nephew unfolded his story.

Tom began at the beginning and described how he had been implicated in Morphew's plight thanks to his Juvenalian satire – how the poem had aroused suspicions in Sunderland's office and had led to the theft of his papers. (His uncle's head, which had begun shaking at the mere mention of Juvenal, was now directed at the ceiling.) He then described the distressing visit to Newgate, and related everything he could about the case. But he kept silent about the pocket-book, and about Bufo's identity. His uncle's bafflement on the subject suggested that no-one at Court knew the truth. Finally, Tom brought the subject back to the Duchess and Arthur Maynwaring, a relationship about which he knew his uncle had worries of his own.

'I've kept your secret faithfully, uncle. But I must tell you, the more we inquire, the more we discover of Maynwaring's activities. He was one of John Morphew's interrogators, and we keep encountering his name. I daren't say what we're beginning to suspect...'

The look on Lord Melksham's face showed indignation and alarm in just about equal measure.

'It's what I thought! – Maynwaring is working his way into the Cockpit and meddling in Ministry affairs. Can nothing stop the man? And I suppose Lord Sunderland may be using him – no-one is better placed to run between him and his mother-in-law.'

'And our suspicions?'

His uncle's voice became almost a whisper, as if the words could hardly be spoken:

'You seem to be suggesting that Maynwaring may have contracted for the pressman's killing? That's a frightening thought, Tom. Perhaps nothing is impossible, alas! These are feverish days...'

His uncle looked puzzled.

'... But I don't understand. You say this Emmet had recently gone over to the Whigs and was sent by Sunderland's office to spy on you? Which side was the man on?'

'He foolishly thought he could serve *both* sides, and I think both parties were finding him increasingly embarrassing. The Whigs, especially the Duchess, were angry – after all, he had just printed the *Caricatura* against her. And he was known to be Mrs Manley's agent.'

'Oh dear, yes. Mrs Manley! The Duchess simply loathes the woman, and anyone connected with her. The *Secret History* infuriated her. It was the contempt shown for the Duke that angered her most, I think.'

Tom was thoughtful.

'Our problem is, Emmet was an elusive busybody with no allegiance to any party. That's why I need to ask you about Mr Harley's side of things. You're quite close to him...'

Tom's uncle looked slightly uneasy, as if the remark had been made accusingly.

'... We wonder what Mr Harley's faction has been doing. It's difficult because we know Mr Morphew is Harley's admirer and was quickly marked down by the Whigs as Bufo's printer.'

'Yes, Tom, I understand that. But remember, in the political game Robert Harley is a bigger and wilier player than anyone. And there's something of importance going forward, I'm sure of it. I'm not in the ministerial circle, but I know it is happening in corners and in corridors. Nods and glances. Wigs brushing close against wigs – I've seen it, Tom!'

'I've heard that Harley has a gang of informers who report to him daily. Is that true?'

'Not exactly. Our friend *Rumour* is an untrustworthy creature. That's not quite how it works...'

His uncle put down his paper and gestured over Tom's head with his right hand.

'... Think of an elegant mansion in St James's. The lord paces around his grand rooms, talking with friends, hearing reports, and making his wishes quietly known; messages are carried down the back stairs to the working rooms where orders are given, deliveries made, accounts settled. Down there, many little people, whom the great man does not know and will never see, are busy on his behalf, keeping the house functioning.'

'And somewhere, kept well out of sight, are the *necessaries*,' added Tom with a grim smile.

'Indeed yes. No modern house could function without them. And you can be sure that in the dead of night men come and remove what has to be removed.'

Tom finally hurried into the Good Fellowship well after eleven, ready to make his apologies before delivering his news. But the moment the door opened he saw that the coffee-room was already in the grip of a news-frenzy of its own.

Jack Tapsell – once again the loudest voice in the room – was standing with a printed sheet in his hand, declaiming its contents to the whole company, who were pressing around him, some with wide eyes and others with even wider grins. At the further tables, dishes of coffee were suspended in mid-air. From the flush on his cheeks it was clear that a lively performance was reaching its climax:

... The consequence of this was such,
Our good and gracious Queen,
Not knowing why she e'er went wrong,
Came quickly right again.

And taking then the wise advice
Of those who knew her well,
She Abigail *turn'd out of doors,*
And hang'd up Machiavell*!*

The ballad came to an end to a scattering of applause, a couple of *huzzas*, and a cry of 'Harley to the Tower!' One resilient soul shouted 'Now sing it, Jack!'

'No, he'll spare you the singing of it!' said Widow Trotter firmly, stepping forward and taking the paper in her hand. 'You and your friends can favour a tavern with it tonight, Mr Tapsell. But be careful which tavern you choose!... Meanwhile, as it was delivered to us, we shall hold it at the bar.'

Tom could see that her genial intervention was edged with annoyance – the place had become a fairground booth. She began encouraging the huddle to settle themselves, and as they began to move to their places Tom noticed Will sitting against the far wall beckoning him over. Mrs Trotter was preoccupied in restoring order and almost pushing the chattering men into their seats, so Tom thought it best to move there quickly and without fuss.

Will was about to speak, but Tom cut in at once.

'What the dickens was that, Will? I've missed quite a performance, haven't I!'

'That's not the only thing you've missed. Where on earth did you spend the night? We have been surmising – entirely to your credit, I'm bound to say.'

'At my uncle's – I've so much to tell you… but that ballad… I caught the very end of it. It's about Mrs Masham and Harley, is it not?'

Will frowned.

'Yes, Harley the *Machiavel*. How the Queen is sure to hang him – and send the sluttish Abigail packing. It ends prophetically, as you might imagine. *Honest Sunderland* is finally listened to, and Her Majesty at long last comes to her senses and embraces the Whigs! It's the Junto response we were expecting – but much worse.'

'But the thing is predictable, isn't it? Tit-for-tat?'

Will lowered his voice.

'Yes, but it begins with an *imputation* about the intimacy of the Queen and Abigail – the stuff of the pocket-book! It's anonymous, but I think Arthur Maynwaring has been busy scribbling again…

Whenas Queen Anne of great renown
Great Britain's *Sceptre sway'd,*
Besides the Church, she dearly lov'd
A dirty Chamber-Maid…'

'You remember it!'

'It's hard to forget… That's how the thing begins. And there's a memorable phrase about the two women's *dark deeds at night.*'

For a moment Tom was speechless. An oath stuck in his throat.

'About *the Queen?*… What does our hostess say?'

Will looked across the room and saw Widow Trotter signalling to them.

'I think we'll soon be finding out – it appears we're wanted in the parlour. Thank Heaven you're here, Tom! She was becoming concerned, you know – and not a little impatient.'

Widow Trotter herded them silently into her inner sanctum and at once made for the sideboard and the decanters that stood there. Her back was facing them, braced for what was to come.

'Well, Mr Bristowe, I trust you've returned from the high life with something we can use. Things are beginning to look dark, and the minutes are slipping away. I feel we're so near – yet still the truth eludes us.'

She seemed tired and disheartened. Tom could feel the worries working their way out of her, and without waiting for her to turn round he poured out his apologies. He confessed his over-indulgence at the ridotto and recalled the vague memory of being half-carried back to Pall Mall.

'But please don't despair, Mrs T! I may have ended the night in a sad pickle, but I've been scouting to good effect. I have a packet of news that any hawker would long for.'

And so, with the sparkling fruit cordial before them and their eyes also beginning to sparkle with fresh interest, Will and Widow Trotter listened while Tom gave an account of his conversation with Lady Norreys. He told them about her fears that her diary's secrets would be broadcast at the trial. (They agreed this new ballad was a chilling omen.) He told them what he had learned about the High Tory politics of Arachne's Web, and their contempt for the Duchess of Marlborough.

Finally, and with the satisfaction of a well-managed climax, Tom revealed the most sensational item of news... that the women's political discussions had resulted in a *poetic* collaboration, and that Emmet had purchased not only Lady Norreys's private diary, but also, in the diary's pocket, those devastating fragments of poetry that would become the voice of *Bufo*.

At this final revelation Will and Mrs Trotter looked at each other, their faces mirroring the flash of light that had struck them both.

'Halleluia!' declared Widow Trotter.

Will face brightened.

'So, the pocket-book memorandums and Bufo's verses are from the same source!'

'Yes,' said Tom, 'and I suspect Emmet was prepared to use them both – one against Harley, and the other against the Whigs. The two sides again! He removed the sheets of verse from the pocket-book and said nothing to Morphew about them.'

'They were his insurance, I suppose?' said Mrs Trotter.

'After a fashion, yes. When Morphew became angry and refused his expenses, Emmet must have seen these 'Bufo' fragments as recompense – and a very profitable one.'

'Profitable if he could interest Harley in them,' said Will.

'Ah yes – and we know what became of that hope!'

'Emmet's rage must have been worse than we thought,' said Widow Trotter. 'It was understandable, given the pains he'd taken with *Bufo's Magic Glass*. Perhaps he felt proud of the thing – after all, it was like his own foster-child.'

'Yes, his anger at Harley's refusal to pay is clear,' said Will. 'But where does that leave us? We're still faced with the same question...'

He paused, eyeing an imaginary jury.

'... *Which side had more to gain from Emmet's death?*'

A few heartbeats later, it was Tom who rose to the challenge:

'The picture of a Whig plot is certainly a tempting one – after all, Maynwaring and Voyce interrogated Morphew together, and it was Voyce who brought that epigram into the Good Fellowship – *and* tidied up the murder-scene. And now Maynwaring has produced an anonymous prophecy to counter Bufo's – all this strengthening his position with the Duchess...'

He had set his glass down and was beginning to crack a hazelnut. The clenching and release of his fist felt good – as if he was somehow getting to grips with the situation.

'... But at breakfast this morning Uncle Jack spoke about Harley's gang of informers, and it made me think we've underestimated their ruthlessness – and the extent of their reach...'

He passed the dish of filberts and the nutcracker to Will.

'... It's all very secretive of course, Harley's *system*. There are paid agents and hired sneaks who report to them. It's very extensive and no-one knows how far it reaches – not even Harley himself, I warrant.'

'Yes, he must have his equivalent of Maynwaring and Voyce,' said Will, 'the trusted lieutenants?'

'I asked him about Harley's people. Identities are carefully concealed, but he thinks Daniel Defoe is a spy. It's said he did important work in Scotland and kept Harley regularly informed, and he may still be active here, right now.'

'That doesn't surprise me. Defoe is tuned to Harley's every thought, and the *Review* is much indebted to his purse I've no doubt!'

'Yes, Harley has a very *large* purse... But I also pressed Uncle Jack about anyone who might be working secretly – a possible agent-for-hire who would be willing to use violence. He was a bit taken aback at this, but he did offer a name we might take note of: *George Deacon*. He's an elusive character, and Uncle Jack says there's something being hushed up concerning him – he's not sure what. The man is a dangerous rogue but seems to be under Harley's protection.'

'That's something we can ask Mr Cobb about,' said Widow Trotter. 'I hope he'll soon be calling in with news.'

The thought made her uneasy. At any moment Elias would be arriving with an account of the dead Polly Gray, and so she needed to inform them of it before he did. The girl's theft of the letter would have to be mentioned, and her sale of it to Emmet; but she knew she must keep silent about Henry St John and Mrs Greg. Concealing this from her friends was painful, but she had given her solemn word to Adèle Ménage... The letter's contents, and the far-reaching matters of State that hung on them, would continue to weigh on her like a guilty secret.

She eased her awkwardness by replenishing their glasses. The young men were struggling with the filberts whose shells were shooting off in random directions. She was just about to settle herself again and embark on her own story when Tom intervened with another enthusiastic revelation.

'Now! You must sit down, Mrs T, because I have something more to tell you about last night's adventure. It was another conversation I had with a *masked* figure, and it was enigmatic – worthy of the Venetian Council of Ten!'

Widow Trotter knew her moment had passed, but Tom was at a high pitch of eagerness. Will threw another nut into his mouth and mumbled that he was longing to hear more of Tom's surreptitious flirtations.

'But this wasn't a lady, Will... No, I had an entirely diplomatic, but very suggestive exchange with our Secretary-at-War, no less! And it convinced me that he might somehow be involved in this murky business...'

'*Henry St John?*' exclaimed Will, more loudly than he intended.

'Yes he!' said Tom. 'You won't believe me, but the man began questioning me about Emmet! I'm longing to know what you both make of it.'

He looked at Widow Trotter, hoping for a bright-eyed smile of anticipation. But instead he was met by a frozen expression of alarm.

Chapter Twenty-Eight

TOM'S ACCOUNT OF his masked encounter with Henry St John at Lady Welwyn's Ridotto could have been a scene from an Italian romance; but Mary Trotter understood the darker threat behind it: she knew the disturbing truth beneath the politician's vizard, and what fears were pricking him. Seated next to her, Will was also becoming increasingly unsettled as the implications of St John's questioning sank in.

'Well I never! A Government minister interesting himself in a disreputable scandal-monger and his Covent Garden haunts! I think you're right, Tom – he must surely know about Emmet's dirty trade. That wasn't simple curiosity, it was anxiety. I think he's concerned about something.'

'Yes, that's what I thought. I'm even beginning to wonder if St John might be directing Harley's *Office of Information* – if that's what we should call it?'

Will smiled.

'You mean, helping to *run his gang?* It's a possibility. He's certainly Harley's confidant and has the closest Tory allies – he's really three-quarters Tory himself!'

'And I suppose the arrangement would allow Harley to be impartial in any negotiations, and St John to do the dirty work?'

'These statesmen!' declared Mrs Trotter with a shake of the head as if they were schoolchildren pinching fruit in the market.

She was feeling distinctly uncomfortable as Tom and Will began piecing their evidence together. Having read Mrs Greg's letter she knew exactly why Henry St John was anxious to trace Kate Primrose. She tried not to squirm in her chair, and knew she had to tell them about the letter before things went much further…

But Tom wasn't finished.

'We know someone is on Kate Primrose's trail and is prepared to use violence to discover what she has. That man who searched her room and burnt her hand – we've been assuming Hopkins's people were behind it… But we now know that Emmet's digging around was upsetting both sides. I wonder if Harley's spies are also hunting for her?'

'But so are we!' announced Mrs Trotter, suddenly sitting bolt upright. It was a confident exclamation and was received in shocked silence. She knew her moment had come. The two young men were taken aback by the dramatic gesture.

'I think there's more you need to know, gentlemen… I can reveal something else that might possibly help us…'

'You're being enigmatic, Mrs T!' said Tom, lowering a dark eyebrow.

'Ah yes! A revelation is approaching,' said Will, employing his own version of the Lundy stare. 'What have you been doing, Mrs T?'

Widow Trotter looked around the parlour to remind herself that she was on home ground, and began telling them about the discovery of Polly Gray's body in the Rose Street tenement – how the girl had stolen a letter from one of her courtly clients and had sold it to some unknown dealer.

'Emmet!' said Tom. 'It must be, surely?'

Will looked apprehensive.

'You call her *Polly Gray*... it has the ring of an invented name to me. You don't think she and Kate Primrose could be one and the same?'

'Yes,' said Tom, 'are you sure this isn't our *Clarissa*, and that the man hasn't finally caught up with the poor girl?'

'To judge by the state of the body,' said Mrs Trotter, 'the girl died on Thursday or Friday. It's certainly not Kate, who fled from Vinegar Yard on Sunday afternoon.'

'But was the letter really something to interest Emmet?' said Will. 'I wonder what was in it?... If this Polly knew Kate, then it would explain why she offered it to him.'

'Yes,' said Tom, 'in that case, it can't be coincidence. Two girls attacked, and both had manuscripts in their possession... I wonder... perhaps we've been following the wrong trail all along.'

'What do you mean?'

'If Kate's attacker is the same man, then...'

'... he was searching for that letter!... He had killed Polly Gray, but she no longer had it. Then he tracked down Kate Primrose...'

'And again he was frustrated!' said Tom excitedly.

'But where is the letter now? And what does it contain?... What do you think, Mrs T?'

As they swung round to face her, Widow Trotter was reeling. She knew the answer to both questions and was feeling uncomfortably like a suspect herself. It was impressive how her friends were thinking as one. At this delicate moment she needed to sound a note of caution.

'Excellent, both of you! But are we not running ahead of ourselves? Remember your warning about stories, Will. Elias has yet to confirm that the girl was killed – though it does appear likely, given the circumstances.'

'Whatever the case,' said Tom, 'it's more urgent than ever that we find Kate Primrose. She's in the greatest danger. And if her attacker was the killer of Polly Gray, then isn't he likely to be Emmet's killer too?'

'That would be very neat – if she could identify him,' said Mrs Trotter.

'It's a slim chance,' said Tom, 'but it would be manna in the desert.'

'Manna? No, what we need are *camels!*' said Mrs Trotter with a sweep of her hand. 'We have to keep moving. You and Will must set about it, and there's no time to waste. Find people. Ask questions. I'll have to stay here until Elias calls. I'm expecting to learn more about Polly Gray, and about Constable Buller – and I need to ask him about this George Deacon who works for Mr Harley... And then – *then* – I shall call on Adèle Ménage again. She may have known Polly Gray, and she could tell me if there's a connection to our Clarissa...' She paused for breath. 'Oh dear, there's so much to do – and a busy coffee-room to attend to as well. I've been neglecting it shamefully!'

'You can't do everything!' said Tom with concern. Mary Trotter's eyes were restless, and she was obviously under strain. 'Can we not call on Mrs Ménage for you?'

'No, Tom, I think that would alarm her. Adèle is a very sensitive woman – she's wise and thoughtful, but she needs to be handled carefully – like porcelain. I'm able to share her confidences and draw things out of her...'

She paused for thought.

'... I know what you can best do this afternoon, but it won't be easy – and it may not be very pleasant.'

Tom and Will exchanged glances. Suddenly the sick odour of Newgate seemed to scent the air again.

'Don't look quite so fearful, gentlemen. I'm only asking you to call on some of the other ladies of Vinegar Yard. One of them may have an idea where Kate is. You must ask around – see if you can draw confidences...'

'*Confidences*, Mrs T?'

Tom was blushing. But also, she noticed, was Will – though not for entirely the same reason.

'Try to be discreet,' she added in a no-nonsense voice. 'And you will need to split up, or you'll draw attention to yourselves – it would look like an interrogation.'

Will looked at his friend, and then at her.

'Perhaps, Mrs T, can I suggest that Tom goes to one or two alehouses instead? Lots of things can be picked up there. Leave the Covent Garden ladies to me!'

A smile flickered across her face.

'Yes that sounds a wise plan, Mr Lundy... but, both of you... *please* take care! I would not ask you to do this if matters weren't so serious. It's a desperate last throw – but we must do all we can! Finding Kate Primrose is everything now.'

'But she will probably have changed her name,' said Tom.

'Undoubtedly!' said Mrs Trotter. 'That's one thing you need to discover – if you can find a friend she has confided in... And you could attempt to call on Joseph Quinlan who lives two floors below Clarissa's bower. If that man did return, then Mr Quinlan may have encountered him. His hours of work at the Custom House may be irregular – so there's a chance he will be at home.'

Once again, Tom and Will felt a little like the Night Watch receiving their charge. They were now readied for their mission, and after an emboldening dish of coffee they left the Good Fellowship and headed off, leaving Widow Trotter to turn things over in her mind.

It had been a trying hour, but she felt relieved that she had managed to steer the talk away from Henry St John. Her promise to Adèle could not be broken. She longed to involve Tom and Will completely, but for the moment they had to work in ignorance of the letter's treasonable contents. She hoped they would eventually understand...

To judge from Tom's account, the Government Minister must now be desperate. She began trying to think St John's thoughts, and they were chilling ones. His lost letter with its explosive revelation simply had to be found, and perhaps no price was too high? All of his political hopes, and those of Harley too – his friend's life even – depended on it. But his gold pocket-watch must also be at the forefront of his mind: to recover the watch might lead to the recovery of the letter. Yes, she thought, the man must be frantically scanning the newspapers for an advertisement: "Dropped outside a tenement in Rose Street... the owner describing the marks may have it again..." She had been searching in the papers herself and found nothing. It had occurred to her that if she hurried round to the particular shop or tavern as soon as the notice appeared, then...

Her musings were interrupted by a sharp knock, and Elias Cobb's head peeped round the parlour door.

'The coffee-room is humming, my lady – I've been left to make my own entrance! Jenny and the others are busy as bees. She tells me you've been having a conference with Will and Tom?'

'Yes, they left ten minutes ago. I wasn't sure when you would call. I've set them to hunt for Kate Primrose. Finding her is more urgent than ever – it's our only course left before the trial tomorrow. Have you brought news that can help us?'

'Not about Clarissa. But in other directions I've had some success. At least you may find the picture has cleared a little...'

Widow Trotter was not so hurried that she neglected the courtesies, and while he spoke she was standing at the sideboard pouring him a glass of his favourite claret.

'... It's pretty certain that Polly Gray was killed, as young Mudge suspected. Her body was distorted, and it didn't look natural – as if she had been forced to twist against her will. It was like a violent embrace gone wrong. But there's no clear proof, and in a case like this it's always assumed the girl did the deed herself, out of despair.'

'But in Polly's case...'

'I agree. I talked with one or two of her neighbours, but there's little to add to Mudge's account: she fenced the gold watch, and the letter was sold on quickly. Emmet is likely to have been the buyer: one girl said that Polly had taken it to *Drury Lane* and was hoping for a good price. But there's nothing further. And we don't know where the watch went from there; but it wasn't hidden in her room – we had it searched.'

Mrs Trotter tried to look innocently thoughtful.

'At least that points to Emmet as having the letter, does it not?... But you say you have something else for me – could it be about Constable Buller? You were going to do some burrowing.'

'Yes, and I hope I've burrowed well. Listen to this...'

He savoured the wine and the moment simultaneously.

'... I can't reveal my source... but it seems our Constable Buller was keeping watch on Morphew's shop *before* his arrest – and not in a desultory way either. He had been instructed to report on Morphew's movements. And it was Maynwaring who organised this.'

'Are you sure, Elias?'

'That's what my informant tells me.

'Maynwaring, eh? Well, we know the Duchess was angry with Morphew, but this means her secretary was acting on it – with or without her knowledge.'

'I thought that would give you something to chew on. You can tell Tom and Will when they return. But it's mere chit-chat, you understand – nothing more.'

'Have no fear, Elias. It drifted in on the wind... But if your little bird is speaking truth, then it brings us close to the night of the killing...'

She watched as Elias finished off his wine.

'... Does that mean Buller used someone – perhaps a street urchin – to keep an eye on the place? Perhaps they saw a figure entering the printing-room on Friday night?... And did Maynwaring *send* them?'

'There's much for you to ponder... Well, my good lady, I leave the information in your care. I knew it would delight you. But remember, I rely on your honour!'

Elias rose from his chair.

'Wait, Elias. There's another thing I need to ask you...'

He paused, and Mrs Trotter gave him a close stare.

'... *George Deacon.*'

She saw a flicker of unease cross his face.

'You're not troubled with him I hope.'

'Why Elias, what *trouble* does he bring?'

'Well, he's been known to frighten people out of town. A visit from George Deacon is not a comfortable thing, I assure you.'

Widow Trotter was taken aback.

'You mean he can be violent? Who is the man? Who does he work for?'

Elias was clearly unsettled by the battery of questions. He sat down again, on the edge of the chair.

'Merely a catchpole, Mrs T, a *bum-bailiff*. Not a sociable sort at all. But he has a sordid reputation.'

'Is he no more than that, Elias – just a collector of debts?'

There was a pause as Mr Cobb deliberated for a moment. Widow Trotter kept silent, intrigued by her friend's uneasiness. Seconds ticked by before he spoke again.

'This is difficult, Molly. Mr Deacon is *protected*. Nothing would seem to adhere to him – and yet he's known for a ruthless enforcer, a man who presses hard on anyone unfortunate enough to need persuading.'

This reticence on her friend's part was unlooked for, and she wondered if Elias was hamstrung in some way.

'You say "protected" – do you mean politically?'

'We're on dangerous ground Molly… But it's known that George Deacon is a convenient resource when awkward things need to be done – I've never inquired too closely. The Ministry finds him useful.'

'The Ministry? But which faction, Elias? The Ministry is divided against itself.'

'The man is nothing, Molly. He has no status, no place in the system, no gang of followers… But that's what makes him dangerous. You could think of him as a leech: he lives in the muddy water and can be made use of at any time. He does a job and slips away again…'

Widow Trotter thought it was an odd caricature, but Elias looked serious.

'… You might think nothing would be easier than to take him off, but he's too useful – and he knows too much.'

'Is he in Mr Harley's camp?'

It was a direct question. Once again she was looking at him closely. His reply was immediate and unguarded.

'Yes. He does dirty work for Harley and St John. But, as I say, he's not to be spoken of. My encounters with him have been brief. It is said he has done very bad things – but there's no point in bringing them to notice. Only grief and frustration would result.'

'I'm astonished, Elias… But don't look so worried. I haven't encountered him directly. It's just that his name has been mentioned as someone who might be concerned in our affair.'

'That would make things very difficult… I can say nothing further.'

'Perhaps you'd better not. I see it's unsettled you… I know we have to tread carefully.'

'You must keep me informed, Molly… I'm sorry not to be able to do more.'

And that was how things were left. Elias Cobb took his leave as suddenly as he had appeared, and Widow Trotter was left sitting back in her chair, gazing at the wall. Just when she thought the picture was clearing, new images – vivid ones – had interposed. On Friday night, at the very time of the murder, it seems Joe Buller was keeping a close eye on the printing-house – on the instructions of Arthur Maynwaring. He hadn't discovered the murder scene by accident.... And, who knows, somewhere in the background may have been Harley's enforcer, the menacing George Deacon? With Harley and St John facing disgrace, the business was serious enough for him to be playing a part. One fact was certain: *both* sides had dark shadows – or murky depths – she couldn't decide which.

Elias had been right. She was urgently needed in the coffee-room. It was humming nicely and there was hardly an empty seat. Peter Simco was darting about from table to table like a ballet-dancer, trying not to look flustered, and Jenny was out of the bar helping him. Even big Jeremy was busying himself by collecting plates and bowls and conveying orders to the kitchen. She thought worryingly of Kate Primrose and Mrs Ménage, but there was simply no time to go over to Katherine Street yet. Time was ticking away.

A good twenty minutes passed before the place began to settle into a manageable rhythm. It was still busy, but she might perhaps be spared for a while. But at that moment, as if some crazed stage-manager were working the machines at a pantomime, the coffee-room door opened and a tall, long-haired gentleman appeared, carrying a large painting. He was holding it at an angle, but an acute observer could make out a burgeoning expanse of green foliage, and the words 'Bay Tree' in bold capitals underneath it. The Good Fellowship's transformation was about to be completed. The newly-commissioned signboard had arrived. Standing behind the artist was a stout young man of more artisanal appearance who carried a bag of tools – a distinct indication of optimism on the painter's behalf.

In the coffee-room a commotion at once began, and a knot of interested connoisseurs formed around them. It was only with difficulty that Mrs Trotter was able to usher the pair of them through the kitchen door. She asked them to wait in the parlour while she wrote a hurried note.

Adèle, I am detained here or I would call in person. We are running out of time, and still have no news of Kate Primrose. Tom and Will are dispatched to Vinegar Yard, and are asking around the neighbourhood, but my hopes are not high. Has Kate contacted you? Events have begun to move quickly, and it's more than ever clear that the letter is of vital importance. May we discuss the matter further? Let me know if you have news. You are a good and reliable friend! I apologise for this hasty scrawl – I hope to be able to call round this evening.

Mary Trotter.

P.S. Do you know of a Polly Gray? She may have been a friend of Clarissa's. She has met a violent end in Rose Street. But more on this when I see you.

She folded the sheet tightly and wrote the direction boldly and clearly. Grabbing hold of Jeremy's coat as he walked past her, she pressed the paper firmly into his hand.

'It's important you wait for a reply, Jem – if there is one. Do you understand? I trust you.'

'Yes, Mrs Trotter.'

'Katherine Street. The apartment is above Mr Denniston's Toy-shop. There's a door at the side. Take it there now – no dawdling!'

Jeremy gave a little salute and set off on his mission. Widow Trotter braced herself and turned to face the two gentlemen, who were cradling the impressive picture between them, now the right way up.

'Well, it's certainly a flourishing specimen,' she said…

A few moments later Jeremy had turned the corner into Bow Street, when he paused and looked at the note he was carrying. It was not sealed – Mrs Trotter could be careless about such things – and so it took him no more than seconds to unfold it and read the contents. Jem was a surprisingly good reader, and this caused no problem. He also had a sharp memory, and by the time he had folded the paper once again he was master of its contents. There was someone nearby who would be eager to learn of them. He hurried on, determined and unsmiling.

Chapter Twenty-Nine

TOM AND WILL paused briefly outside the Good Fellowship, feeling a little like scouts on the eve of battle being dispatched behind enemy lines. It had been decided that Will would head down Drury Lane to Vinegar Yard, while Tom would cross the piazza towards Rose Street – the respective haunts of Kate Primrose and Polly Gray. As the moment came, they looked at each other and realised how strange it was. The two of them were more used to planning an adventure together, but this time there was to be a parting of the ways. A pleasurable jaunt was turning into a formal duty, and, what was worse, they found themselves almost standing to attention – which would never do.

'Well, Tom, I hope you're ready to play the ale-house tippler?'

'Almost. I'm confident I'll sink into the part, as you will rise to yours... Are you prepared for the delights of Vinegar Yard?'

'Not entirely...'

Will consulted his watch.

'... Don't you think we need to work into our roles a little? Perhaps a cheering beverage would set us up? It would be time well spent.'

'We can relax over a pint-pot and remind ourselves what we're trying to discover. We have to be easy and natural, remember.'

'Exactly. We mustn't draw attention to ourselves.'

'And we must be careful not to ask too many questions. Friendly chat is what will be productive – letting confidences develop.'

'And sometimes it's the trivial things that will suggest most.'

'Agreed. Good-natured tattlers are what we need!'

'And tattlers are what we *are*, Tom – at least for the next few hours.'

And so they considered and deliberated, and did their best to settle into a carefree manner. And an hour later, having attained just the right balance between confidence and caution, the two agents left on their mission. While Tom was settling himself in at the Angel Tavern in Rose Street, Will was treading gingerly up the dark staircase in Vinegar Yard.

It was past dinner-time, and as he half-groped his way towards the second floor, Will became aware of an unholy alliance of cheap tobacco, sweet rosy perfume, stale urine, and some distantly frying onions. No-one could breathe freely in a place like this, he thought, and his chest involuntarily tightened. But each time he expelled the sickly air, he ingested yet more of it, with every breath layering the stench onto his tongue.

He found Joseph Quinlan's door and gave a jaunty knock, but there was no response. He waited and knocked again, but the man was out. Will knew there was only one thing to do. So he continued up the narrowing stairs towards the top of the building, having to bow his head and twist his shoulders as he neared the garret. This unwholesome fire-trap had been poor Clarissa's refuge and her business premises. He almost felt pleased at the thought of the girl making her escape, though he knew it was probably for somewhere even worse.

At the head of the stairs he stopped in the dark, disconcerted because there was the unmistakeable sound of someone moving around inside the room. At that instant, under his right foot a loose floorboard creaked and the movement behind the door stopped. Whoever it was had instantly frozen, just as he had, and for several seconds there was a strangely intimate silence: two people, unknown to each other, listening, aware of the other's presence – and perhaps both more than a little apprehensive.

Will broke the silence with an unthreatening 'Hello?' and stepped up to the door, knocking gently. After a few seconds it opened wide, and the garret's occupant stood there facing him, radiating as much glory as the murky room would allow. She was a young woman with lavishly-worked curls, smiling, and pressing down her dress. There was a ribbon dangling from one hand, but no shoes on her stockinged feet. There was no hesitation now.

'Hello Sir. You've found me, I see!'

Her eyes shone, and she indicated with her hand that he was welcome – indeed, he almost thought, expected. There was a thin black velvet band around her arm and a loose bracelet at her wrist. She looked him up and down.

Will found it hard to respond with equal ease, and hesitated on the threshold.

'Clarissa, is it?'

There was a flicker of disappointment, he saw. But it was immediately thrown off, and she continued to smile as she spoke.

'Oh no, Sir. *Clarissa* is no more. She's gone. I've just taken occupation of the premises.'

It was an oddly formal phrase, as if she were proudly announcing ownership. Will took the final step under the lintel and unbent himself. He looked around. The room showed little sign of having been ransacked just three days before, though he noticed a bucket and brush by the fireplace and a well-filled sack on the floor next to the bed. The bed itself was piled with clothes, and a black cat, more suspicious than its mistress, was arching its back at him. He felt slightly embarrassed at his assumption that she was Clarissa's successor in the trade.

But the girl didn't allow his uneasiness to linger. She spoke briskly.

'Have you been sent by Mrs Purslowe?...'

Will was nonplussed and found himself humming hesitantly in response.

'... I've hardly settled in here, as you can see... You're not one of Clarissa's regular playfellows, are you, though you were thinking to see her?'

'I wasn't sure...'

'Well, she's fled. No notice given, and the room thoroughly wrecked. Mrs Purslowe is very angry, as you'd expect. There was three weeks' rent owing too. The *celestial* Clarissa vanished without a trace – flitted off to higher things, no doubt! Poor Mrs P has a business to run, and she's cast down by it. But I'm hoping things are going to improve... You'll be welcome here at any time, Sir...'

Will was being scrutinised once again, head to toe. There was near six feet of him, and the girl was beaming as she made the survey, as if she were admiring a lofty building.

'... We can settle between us just what you fancy – you'll find me accommodating for most things. Clarissa was over-nice, and I know her clients could sometimes feel the chill of it... You'll not find me so strait-laced.'

Will swallowed hard. Their conversation – a less than appropriate word under the circumstances – had already run out of control. But that was no bad thing. The girl was self-assured and at ease, and ready enough to chatter about anything. He was trying to seem assured himself, but was uncertain how to respond.

'I've intruded... your lodgings are clearly not yet ready. I see you're sprucing the room up... But I should ask your name...'

The girl composed herself, hand on hip, breathing in and lifting her neck.

'Corinna, Sir. I'm simply Corinna.'

'It's a lovely name – very graceful!'

'Indeed Sir, yes. Mrs Purslowe likes us to take a name that will charm and delight our gentlemen. *Clarissa* never lived up to hers, she says. But I'm determined that *Corinna* will be on men's lips and make them smile. I've moved here to the Garden from Holborn. I want to be among the theatre-folk you see, and especially the literary gentlemen. I have some books...'

Will saw a little library of a dozen or so volumes on a shelf by the right hand wall, and what looked like a few copies of plays, tied together.

'... I can read well enough, and have a fondness for poetry – and romances.'

'You're a creature from romance yourself, Corinna, I can see that... But can we sit and talk for a while? I'm a little thirsty. Do you have something?'

Will was settling in, and five minutes later he was sitting on a wooden chair holding a glass of brandy. Corinna had placed herself on a stool by the bed, one leg stretched out to expose a green silk garter. The scene was set, and it soon became clear that this young Corinna was guilefully innocent. They were able to talk freely, and their opening exchanges were frank and amusing. He let it emerge that he was acquainted with one of Clarissa's customers, a Mr Emmet, and had heard rumours that she was in trouble. The girl didn't know of the circumstances, and the name 'Emmet' meant nothing to her.

'So you thought you would come and cheer her, Sir – and make her more easy. You're a most thoughtful gentleman, I can tell that.'

It was said with a knowing smile.

'So you don't know where Kate Primrose is now?'

The moment the words had left his lips he knew he'd taken a false step. He could almost hear the floorboard squeak. Corinna's face fell.

'You disappoint me, Sir. Do you have a particular interest in finding *Clarissa?*' She deployed the name with emphasis. 'Or is she *Kate* to you?'

Will threw caution to the winds.

'She's Kate Primrose, I confess. There are fears for her safety… Do you know the name *George Deacon?*'

Will was shocked at himself. He had rapidly leapt over several fences, perhaps unwisely, but there seemed nothing to lose. As he spoke the name he saw an immediate response in her eyes.

'I don't know what you want, Sir, but what would *you* be doing acquainted with him?'

'So, you know the man, do you?'

'The bailiff? Only by reputation, mercifully… But I thought Clarissa had passed him on.'

'Passed him on?… I don't follow.'

'Sent him elsewhere, Sir.' She hesitated, '… where his *tastes* could be better catered for.'

This was unlooked for. Will had stumbled on something – he wasn't sure what.

'So he wasn't pressing her for a debt?'

'Oh no – though that's how he creeps up on some girls. He knows where debts can be called in, and he buys them up – for advantage… But please, Sir, I don't wish to speak of him. He's a man I never wish to encounter. Thankfully I've nothing to tell you more… But I had thought Clarissa was rid of him.'

Will noticed her glance at the door. He realised the girl must now be apprehensive, and he admonished himself. Why had he slipped into this interrogation? It was just what he'd meant to avoid… But the die was cast – though cast luckily, he had to admit.

'He sounds a terrible man, Corinna. I'm sorry for mentioning his name. But what you say confirms his reputation, and it makes me worry even more for Kate... Did George Deacon have some hold over her? You speak of *tastes*.'

'Yes, Sir. But you'll forgive me if I don't talk of him further.'

'Perhaps I can guess... he's known for a violent man...'

She remained silent, and looked away.

'... Did he beat her?'

'All I can say is... almost anything can be bought in the Garden. There's a market for most things. Flogging cullies, Sir, have their place – but what Mr Deacon demanded was not for the high-minded Clarissa. That's why she passed him on to Daphne.'

Daphne? Will was taken aback. This was nothing less than a mock-pastoral marketplace where nymphs could be wooed by simple shepherds or be assailed by rampant gods – Virgil or Ovid? The client could take his pick.

He watched Corinna, her head now leaning against a bed-post.

'Daphne... Is she perhaps another of Mrs Purslowe's girls?'

'Yes, Sir – or was. Daphne was less scrupulous than the rest of us, and it was a dangerous game she was playing... I promise myself never to sink to that. I hope to keep what self-respect I can.'

'Sink to what, Corinna?'

The girl sat up a little and rubbed her arm, as if she felt a cold draught.

'Daphne sometimes took advantage... she was known to offer an encouraging *cordial* – to enliven the proceedings. And some clients would find it disorienting.'

Will sensed a sudden chill in the air. He half-knew what would follow.

'Has this Daphne fled too, then?'

'No, Sir, She's dead. A few days ago. Over in Rose Street.'

After the encounter with Corinna, Will took refuge in a nearby pot-house where he sat contemplating his mug of ale and taking stock. That was a determined girl, he decided, and her business was in a fair way of succeeding. She had a definite charm about her and was nobody's fool – a prudent head on remarkably soft shoulders! She had certainly been open with him. It was now clear why Polly Gray had run to Kate with that letter, and what the link between them was: they were both Mrs Purslowe's girls. Poor *Daphne* – his heart sank at the sweet name – had met a nasty end just when she thought her fortunes were turning... He needed to talk with this Mrs Purslowe, who might have suspicions about Kate Primrose's whereabouts and would probably have something to say about George Deacon – and certainly about the comings and goings in Rose Street and Vinegar Yard.

He tried to gather his thoughts together. Was it Deacon, then? Had he killed Polly Gray during some violent game which had nothing to do with the letter? Clearly, the man already knew both 'Clarissa' and 'Daphne' intimately, and perhaps all this had no connection with Emmet's affairs? Will had two pictures of Deacon that he was struggling to fit together: the Covent Garden bailiff who harried the local prostitutes and took his violent pleasures with them; and the brutal government enforcer in Harley's pay, set on finding Kate Primrose's papers, which now included the dead Polly's letter. He wondered what could connect them. It seemed unlikely, but perhaps there was some direct link from the mighty Robert Harley and Henry St John to poor dead Polly Gray... Could there be?

He began thinking he should make his way over to the far side of the piazza and the warren of filthy alleys that hugged Rose Street. Tom would no doubt be gallantly imbibing and hearing tales about Polly from low-life gossips and street whores. The image made him suddenly uneasy, and he wondered if he should go at once and reassure himself that Tom was not face down in a gutter with a knife between his shoulder-blades. He shuddered at the thought. Corinna's talk about Deacon was troubling his imagination. But it was not very far to Maiden Lane, and if they wanted to find Clarissa before tonight... He pushed aside his drink and resolved to call and see if Mrs Purslowe was at home. And in any case, he and Tom had arranged to meet on the piazza under St Paul's portico at six. There was time to find Mrs Purslowe first. Will found himself warming to his investigation. He supposed it was the lawyer in him who enjoyed seeing lines of thought knitting together: case proved – job done.

But something misgave him. It was nothing specific, but at that moment it occurred to him that it was not unknown for the stalker to become the stalked. A trail could lead to a trap – he was enough of a countryman to understand that. He got to his feet and headed for the door, his mind working hard. In taking those few steps Will missed noticing a figure who had been sitting behind him at a distance, hardly looking at him but biding his time and watching to see if he spoke to anyone. The eyes were narrowed and untrusting, couched under dark brows. It was an intense face, mask-like, almost disengaged from the human. As Will left the place, the man at once finished his drink and without fuss slipped out after him, turning determinedly in the same direction.

Will continued down through Vinegar Yard towards Bridges Street, picking his way carefully over the cobbles. It was almost dark now, and the narrow, twisting alley, which never saw the sun even in mid-summer, was closing down above him. A single lamp high on the wall remained unlit, and the alley took a dog-leg turn to the left into a pool of darkness. A pair of muffled figures passed him in silence. But seconds later he became aware of a firm tread coming up behind him, outpacing his. At the very last moment it broke into a run. Will half turned, instinctively swinging his arm as he did so. There was a crash and he was thrown off-balance, feeling a sudden sharp pain beneath his shoulder. His legs collapsed from under him, and he gave a spontaneous cry and fell to the ground. As his head struck the cobbles and he sank into unconsciousness, he saw a pair of thick boots walking calmly away.

Thursday

5 February 1708

Chapter Thirty

EARLY NEXT MORNING the Good Fellowship was taking stock of the night's dramatic events. There had been much coming and going, and everything had been upset. In the parlour Widow Trotter was trying to hold things steady, while Tom had dragged himself away from Will's bedside. The patient himself was now heavily drowsed in an upstairs room. A surgeon had dressed the wound and pinned his arm to his side by a large bandage; and since then, the anodyne pills had done their work. Mr Proby had announced that by great good fortune the blade had missed the lungs and the main artery, and had merely sliced into a muscle. If infection could be avoided and the wound regularly re-dressed, then the patient might recover. But such wounds, he declared, required unceasing vigilance, and he would of course continue to make his expertise available. He was happy for everyone to know that he had achieved some remarkable successes in patients with duelling wounds of various descriptions...

Mr Proby's attentiveness could not be denied, but by the time his commentary had reached its end there were others besides Will who saw the attractions of sedation.

After his miserable sojourn over in Rose Street, Tom had decided to anticipate the rendezvous with Will and make his way to Vinegar Yard. Outside the Bunch of Grapes he saw the landlord in urgent consultation with Mudge the watchman, and from them heard the news of the recent 'assault.' A young gentleman had been stabbed, and the victim, evidently near to death, had been carried into the tavern. A local quack was in attendance and at that moment was pouring a generous shot of brandy over the wound. This was a sound precaution which restored the patient to immediate consciousness but did little for his sense of well-being. Loud blasphemies rang out through the window, unmistakeably in Will's voice.

Once Will had revived enough, he was carried along Bow Street to the Good Fellowship, where he could be properly looked after. Mr Proby was summoned, and advice and treatment given. The surgeon made it clear that on no account should the patient even consider attending the Old Bailey sessions. He had lost a lot of blood, and the air in the Sessions House was so tainted with the fever that a mortal infection would be sure to result. It was vital that he remain quiet and rest as much as possible. It was his opinion that for the next few days, food – particularly red meat and good quality claret – would make an excellent restorative. It would augment the blood and encourage the animal spirits to flow. They were the body's messengers, he said, and needed to exercise themselves, enabling the muscles to ebb and flow again.

Will had been indignant.

'So, I'm to lie here drunk on Bordeaux wine and crammed with roast beef while John Morphew is on trial for his life! How can I do that?'

But he was given no say in the matter, and since then the opiate had done its work.

Now the place was quiet, and Tom and Widow Trotter sat together in the parlour sharing breakfast while they thought of Will and of that day's trial. Neither of them had slept, and both were utterly cast down by the turn of events. It was clear that Tom would have to go to the Old Bailey alone.

Earlier, it was Will who had been the most composed of the three. He had insisted on delivering his report, wincing with pain as he told them about his visit to the ambitious young Corinna and what he had learned about Mrs Purslowe, Kate Primrose, Polly Gray, and George Deacon, figures who together formed a sordid Covent Garden miniature. They were the proprietress, the merchandise and the customer of a shabby little business tainted with deceit and violence.

'Do you think we have our murderer?' said Tom to Mrs Trotter, hardly daring to speak those words.

'In Deacon we have someone capable of it. But it's baffling. We have different scenes, and each is becoming more convincing – but they are incompatible...'

She paused and looked into the fire as if searching for something in its restless flames.

'... Everything seems to turn into a question. Was Emmet's murder personal or political? Was it *Harley*'s faction – Deacon or some other hired assassin – or was it the *Whigs*, set up by Maynwaring, Buller and Voyce? Was it, God forbid, on the Duchess's orders?'

'And now it's Will!' said Tom in a mixture of despair and anger. 'He was very nearly killed!'

He suddenly clenched his fist and brought it down hard. Knives and glasses rattled on the table. His voice was hoarse, almost choking.

'How could it *happen*? Someone followed him, Mrs T! – He must have been watched. Nothing was stolen from him – he was simply stabbed in the back and left in a gutter for any dog to piss on – his face in a puddle – the blood seeping through his clothes – left until some poor wretch tripped over him...'

Mrs Trotter noticed there were tears in Tom's eyes.

'... But *how*...? *How* could it happen? If only we'd stayed together! We could have helped each other. But there I was, half-seas-over in a stinking pot-house – I don't even recall the name – listening to endless gossip about whores and thieves! I could compile a whole directory of Covent Garden low-life! And what did I learn to the purpose… ?'

It was shaping up to be a rhetorical question. Widow Trotter was shuddering at Tom's rage, and thought it best to keep silent. But, as if he'd suddenly heard himself shouting, he pulled back and tried to compose his thoughts.

'… I'm sorry, but I learned so little. When I mentioned George Deacon there was an uneasy silence – and after what Will's told us I can understand why… And yes, poor Polly Gray – *Daphne* – was involved with him. From what I managed to pick up, she was known for a cheat. She'd been in trouble and was despised by some of the girls. I did find two of them who knew Kate Primrose, but neither had heard of her disappearance. One of the women spoke fondly of Adèle Ménage and suggested I should ask her! Eventually I resolved on walking over to Katherine Street myself; but after what you'd said, I decided I shouldn't… And so I just sat there, thinking dark thoughts.'

Widow Trotter sighed.

'Ah Adèle, yes. Things have been so busy that I've still not been able to call on her. I sent Jem round with a note yesterday afternoon, but there was only a verbal reply – to say she could say nothing! It was most unsatisfactory. I hope she doesn't feel I'm pestering her… I'll wait till later and then go myself. Adèle is very sensitive to slights.'

'I did notice Jeremy, as it happens,' said Tom, 'in the piazza.'

'The piazza? What time was this?'

'When I was heading over to Rose Street, about an hour after we left here… Will and I had a bit of dinner first before we went our separate ways.'

'But I told Jem to go *straight* to Katherine Street and come back at once. He knew it was urgent. What was he doing in the piazza? The creature's such an idler – I've never known the like! Left to his own devices the fellow would be dawdling all day to no purpose.'

'Well, he looked like he had a purpose yesterday – he was striding through the colonnade very determinedly, and at some speed.'

Tom at once noticed a change in Widow Trotter's whole body. Nothing was said for a moment, but it was as though a shock had run through her.

'What's the matter, Mrs T?'

'I've just had a terrible thought…'

She stood up and walked to the door, then hesitated, and turned, her mind working rapidly. To his astonishment Tom saw her face was flushing with anger – or was it fear?

'I can hardly credit it… Jem?… I need to speak to him.'

'What have I said, Mrs T?'

'You've raised a thought – a possibility – something that could change everything if it's true. But Jem?… I must see him as soon as he gets here…'

Tom was baffled and wanted to know more. But Mrs Trotter cut him short. She spoke firmly.

'Let's not be distracted. You have a lot to think about. Leave this with me. *You* must ready yourself for the Bailey. I doubt you can do anything at the sessions, but you must attend, if only to see what unfolds…'

She sat down again, and sank back into the chair.

'… I think we've failed, Tom.'

'Not yet. Mrs T… I know Will can't be there, but if there's anything I can do or say, I'll try my best.'

'That's all you *can* do. I sense the truth is very near – only just out of reach…'

She looked across the room as if watching for something to materialise.

'... But time has simply run out for us. It was always going to be difficult. So much has been happening so quickly.'

'But all is not lost, Mrs T. Don't forget that Will was able to coach Mr Morphew a little, and gave him some good advice. He'll not lack friends in court, and they'll surely speak up for him.'

'But what will the others say – the ones who are intent on destroying him?'

'We must wait and see. They'll have to *prove* their case. However dark it looks, it's all circumstance.'

'Do you think Will's father will be on the Bench?'

'It's more than likely,' said Tom. 'I take it you've had no message back from Hackney?'

'No, nor from the Temple – I sent to both, so he must know by now what's happened to his son.'

'And what a shock it must have been... but we can reassure him about the wound, thank God.'

Ten minutes later, and Tom had splashed cold water on his face, put a comb through his hair, and said a brief prayer; and after donning coat and muffler he was striding in the direction of Drury Lane and a Hackney coach. It struck him forcibly that it was exactly one week ago that John Morphew had taken this very path, only to be dragged into a nightmare. And only yesterday he and Will had set off along here with such determined hopes... Tom shivered at the thought of how precarious our lives are. How quickly things can change, and everything be lost.

Not long afterwards, as Jeremy Jopp shuffled into the Good Fellowship ready for his day's work, a solemn-faced Widow Trotter was blocking his path. When she ordered him directly into the parlour he knew it was serious. On previous occasions –

quite regular ones – he had been scolded by her, but behind the annoyance he had always glimpsed some affection, a feeling that he'd disappointed her hopes. Jeremy had worked in the coffee house for a full year now, hauled in by Henry Trotter for the most menial tasks – anything that required brute strength or dogged effort. But he had been grateful for it. Before then, his father had been Mr Trotter's inseparable drinking companion in the nearby Coach and Horses – until the day he had drunk himself under the table for the last time. There was undoubtedly a kindness in the Trotters' giving Jem refuge and a job, and since then there had been some kind of bond between them. He was not family, of course, but he did feel a kinship with the place, and with Mrs Trotter herself – for all her sternness.

But when he saw her glowering face he knew this would be different. His mind ran over the events of recent weeks, and his own role in them, and he feared the end had come.

'Do you have something to tell me, Jem... ? What has been going on?'

There was silence, and a shuffling.

'I don't understand, Mrs T.'

'That note you carried yesterday – which I left unsealed.'

Jeremy swallowed hard, and began making a sound. It was not words, but a kind of uncertain clearing of the throat. The direct question had unsettled him.

'I don't know, Mrs Trotter... I hope I've not disappointed you?'

Widow Trotter's eyes blazed.

'*Disappointed?* Is that all you think it is – *disappointment?* This is not your usual stupidity. This time I want an explanation – and I think you know what for...'

She paused, hoping he would speak, but he hesitated.

'... Well, I'll tell you my suspicions. You took a message yesterday – an urgent note – to Mrs Ménage in Katherine

Street. But you were seen half-running in the piazza when you should have been delivering it.'

'But I did deliver it, Mrs Trotter. And brought back a reply.'

'You did eventually. But what took you *that* way? Where did you go? Was it some other errand?... And don't tell me you wanted to buy flowers!'

There was no immediate response. Jem looked down, and again hesitated. His silence was confirming her fears.

'You know what happened last night to Mr Lundy, don't you? He was attacked and stabbed, and nearly died. Someone had been following him – someone determined to do him harm, to prevent him from being at the trial today. Can you think how that came about? Do you understand what you may have done?'

'I . . I . . never thought, Mrs Trotter...'

'Ah! Yes you did, Jem! You thought about *yourself*. And that was *all* you thought! You had no mind for your friends here, your obligations. Tell me exactly what you did. You read that letter, didn't you! And you showed it to someone!'

Jeremy suddenly gave a wordless wail, like a wounded animal. He slumped into the nearest chair, burying his face in his hands to hide from her.

'Mrs T.... . I don't think you'll *ever* forgive me... Yes, I did read it – and I told someone of it... I've been very bad.'

'You must tell me everything, Jem. A lot hangs on it. Indeed, someone's *life* may hang on it.'

'But I'm afraid, Mrs T... I've been drawn in, and I don't know how to get out... And after what they did to Mortimer...'

'Mortimer the street-seller? What connection do you have with him?'

'We're both entangled with them, Mrs T.'

'*Them?*'

Jeremy lifted his head to her, mouth open, and his eyes like two frightened creatures cowering inside a forest of dishevelled hair.

'It began a while ago. Mortimer has always accepted things from anyone – leaflets, pamphlets, lampoons, drawings – sad trash some of it! He buys things, but mostly people thrust them at him with a few coins, and he hawks them for a penny. You know how it works, Mrs T – sometimes he finds himself in trouble, but he makes a living... But at Christmas the Ministry threatened him. He was told to report on what was given him – anything *unofficial*, that is. He was made to run and *inform* – give *names*...'

He spoke each dangerous word slowly.

'... But he didn't like it. It made him suspected – hampered his trade and put him in danger. It was difficult enough standing on the street doing what he did – but this made things worse... and look what happened! He was beaten badly. His arm will never heal properly.'

'Yes, I heard about it. He was selling a pamphlet attacking the Whigs.'

'No, no, Mrs T! You don't understand... he *refused* to sell it. He told them he'd had enough of being an informer, and wanted nothing to do with such things. He even told them he'd sell nothing but tracts and sermons from now on! And that's why they beat him. They told him to hawk them, *or else*... and when he said no, they began hitting him cruelly.'

'You mean, the people who attacked him were the ones who wanted to circulate the pamphlet?'

'Yes, Mrs T... but Mortimer defied them. They left him on the ground with the papers scattered over him.'

'So it looked like the Whigs had attacked him.'

'Yes... yes, I suppose so. I hadn't thought of that... But Mortimer said both sides were as bad – each one thought he was their enemy. Now he's decided to leave political trash alone for good, and sell *soul-improving* things.'

Widow Trotter was herself sitting down now, and thinking hard. It was a disturbing picture, but it didn't surprise her.

Things had become so heated in recent weeks. Poor Mortimer had found himself exposed. But how had Jeremy become caught up in this? He seemed frightened, and so she tried to sound less accusing.

'And what about you, Jem? What drew you into this?'

'It began last autumn, Mrs T... I was asked about the Mutton-Chops. I had these verses – the sweepings I usually threw away when I cleaned up. I was told there was a *market* for such scraps and I'd be paid for anything of interest to the Ministry. We know it's often Popish stuff – and when the gentlemen are near to finishing their bowl the pieces can be pretty stinking – not the kind of thing you like to see in the coffee-room.'

Widow Trotter knew this was the case, and it had embarrassed her. But she thought Jeremy threw the trash away.

'Was that all, Jem?'

'Oh no, Mrs T. They began wanting to know what I was *hearing* when I waited on them. Who was saying what, and whether any treason was being spoken. I had to listen and report to them. They told me I was being patriotic, and that these kind of people are wanting to bring over the French, and drive out the Queen!'

Widow Trotter felt solemn and hopeless. She hardly dared ask anything more.

'Is that where it ended, Jem?'

'No, Mrs T. They began to be curious about what I could pick up in the coffee-room – anything that smacked of scandal or treason. In the last weeks they've been pressing me hard.'

'You talk of *they*, but who do you mean, Jem? Who were you reporting to? You must tell me. I insist you tell me! I shall try and protect you.'

Jeremy was shaking slightly. For such a big fellow the effect was almost like a satirical print. She waited.

'I've been threatened, Mrs T, if I speak of any of this...'

'Who are *they*, Jem?... Listen to me. You mustn't sink in any deeper – then your life would certainly be in danger. Now you're only a petty sneak – but if you let this go on, they'll put more and more on you, and make you take greater risks, believe me... Who are *they*?'

Jeremy held his breath for a moment.

'His name is Deacon... Mr Deacon. But I don't report direct – it's done through a shop in the piazza.'

Widow Trotter took it all in. She cast her mind back over events and could see Jem in the coffee-room always hanging around the tables, his mind never entirely on the job. She also saw him in the parlour. By now her mouth was dry, and the words didn't come easily.

'There's something I have to ask you... Were you reporting on us as well? On what you might have overheard – even our discussions in here? You have to tell me. What did you pass on?'

Jeremy looked down at the floor.

'I heard you and Mr Cobb talking about that printer, Mrs T, and how he'd been arrested... and his man Mr Emmet – the one who's been murdered... You said that he'd come from the Cockpit... he'd been in the coffee-room talking with Mr Bristol.'

'I don't believe it! How did you know all this? Our private conversations... and you ran off to report on us?...'

There was silence. The big question formed itself in her mind.

'... And did you bring anything *into* the coffee-room? Were you given any papers?... Be truthful, now!'

'No, Mrs T, I swear I wasn't.'

'No pamphlets to leave in the coffee-room, perhaps?'

'No... Well, only once, Mrs T – about a week ago. Mortimer gave me a pamphlet. They had given him two or three to get rid of – to leave in the coffee houses – so I took one off him. Just leave it on the tables, he said.'

Now it was Widow Trotter's turn to sink her head into her hands. Her mind ran over the scene. The hawker must have been given a handful of pamphlets with Bufo's secret messages hidden in them. And poor simple Jem had brought the thing in... But then it struck her. *Simple?*

'Jem, you're not as slow and confused as you like to seem, are you?'

'I try not to be, Mrs T, it's just...'

'I know. You've been distracted. Your mind has always been on something else, never the job in hand!...'

Jeremy nodded silently.

'... Well my lad... from now on things are going to be very different! There'll be no more slouching around the tables. I'm going to keep you busier than you've ever been in your life. And once a task is done, there'll be another *two* waiting for you. *Do you hear me?...*'

His face lit up, but he couldn't speak.

'... You've been a fool – a sneak – a traitor. But now you're on *our* side. You take orders from no-one but me. And if anyone tries to play games with you, you come to me at once. Do you hear?'

'Oh yes, Mrs T! Yes, yes!...'

He jumped up.

'... Thank you! I'll work hard, I promise you.'

'Well, let it end there. I must tell Mr Bristowe and Mr Lundy – and I'll have a quiet word with Constable Cobb when he returns here – he needs to know what has been happening. But I shall not broadcast your stupidity to anyone else. You must put all that behind you.'

Jeremy left the parlour chastened, but he was light of heart and bursting with relief, determined that things would be different from now on. He hurried to check the coffee-room fire, top up the cauldron, make sure the tables were well scrubbed, sort the papers, wash anything left in the kitchen, clean the bar, make ready the little procession of coffee-pots for the day's duty...

Back in the parlour, Widow Trotter also felt chastened. She went into the kitchen and began heating some soup. Perhaps she should have known? Now it was easier to understand the events of the past week and why her coffee house had become a place of suspicion – how the malevolence of the political world had found a way in. Lots of images began hurrying through her mind; but they came to rest on Tom and Will. Those bright, innocent young friends who had been full of hope for the future were now having to face disturbing challenges and great risks – even to their lives. And yet they were doing so uncomplainingly. Both were determined that right and truth must prevail. But her heart sank when she thought of what the coming day might have in store.

She sighed out loud, and, soup-bowl in hand, began making her way upstairs to see if Will had emerged from his deep sleep.

Chapter Thirty-One

As soon as he alighted from the coach and saw the bustle of people crowding the gate of the Old Bailey Sessions House, Tom knew he was missing the company. This was Will's busy world, and his friend's last hurried advice was echoing in his mind.

'Take some shillings with you,' he had said, 'they will get you inside – perhaps even a seat – but don't be afraid to mingle and circulate... you might expect solemnity and order, but the Bailey is closer to a theatre or a cattle market – perhaps a bit of both. There are pens and noisy spectators, and much weighing and assessing: the beasts are paraded, the price decided on, and the hammer falls! Everyone takes a view. But remember, it's the ones that are whispering who are the important people – look out for them. Look for anyone in the room involved in our case. Ask the order and find when it's to be heard. See who is to prosecute, and observe him, and take note of anyone he talks to. Find Feeny, and Barnard – they're sure to be witnesses.... and Walter the porter too... and watch Buller and Voyce... they'll no doubt be there... And my father...' He took a rapid breath. 'He should be on the bench – see if you can speak to him – he'll be concerned, so tell him I'm likely to live – tell him where I am...'

Will's rapid words had flowed with anxious desperation before Tom had been made to step aside and allow the medicine to do its work.

And now, here he was with everything spinning round in his head. How could he possibly do all of that? He realised that unlike his friend he could never feel at home here. This courtroom was a place where the most private pains became public, where secrets and fears were opened up and every question became an accusation. Tom worried that the trial would have an unstoppable momentum as it moved to a predetermined end. In this place it needed skill, knowledge and experience – and ruthlessness – to survive... Luck also, he suspected.

But such negative thoughts would never do. He had to think himself into Will's mind and draw on his energy and astuteness... Yes, he must talk to people, set about the business, be observant and show some initiative... But first of all – he realised to his embarrassment – he had to find the way in.

Beyond the heavily-spiked boundary-wall, the inner courtyard was becoming busy. As Tom made his way forwards he could see over people's heads directly into the Sessions House, of which the whole of that side was open to the elements. Facing him, beyond the tall Doric columns, was the judges' bench, raised high. It was clear that Their Honours not only had a vantage-point in the courtroom, but were able to look into the yard and weigh the shifting mood of the spectators as they engaged with the event, much like the groundlings in the old London playhouses. Here, your life might depend on how you performed. It was the character you presented that was on trial.

Eventually, a couple of shillings got him through the press and into the courtroom proper. There were public seats ranged on either side, and the best views were to be had from the galleries; but Tom decided he would position himself at ground level near the action. He walked around trying to take everything in, consulting his watch and surveying the court in a slightly stern and impatient way, as if his time were being wasted. This lent him the appearance of someone who was to play a part in the proceedings. He smiled knowingly at a bewigged attorney who was making his way to the table beneath the judges' bench. Opposite was the raised witness-box, and facing it the dock where Morphew would stand. Both commanded the room. It was evident that the lawyers and clerks had to look up at the defendant and the witnesses. Unlike the elevated preacher, here the silver-tongued barrister must speak from below. Tom wondered if this demanded a more subtle rhetoric? Well, he would soon find out.

He did what he could by way of preparation. *Regina v. Morphew* would come after a dozen cases of theft, which he was assured would take less than an hour and a half. 'Hemp' Lundy was indeed to preside at the murder trial. And the prosecutor was to be Mr Roger Nugent – a gentleman, he was told, 'of vast experience, with a tenaciousness in the art of cross examination that would do a bloodhound proud.' He managed to offer a few words of encouragement to James Feeny, whom he found looking up in dread at the witness-box, contemplating his ordeal to come. The poor man seemed sadly tongue-tied and could only reassure Tom that he would speak about his employer as warmly as he could.

By now the room was filling up, and the officers were beginning to take their places at the table. Tom handed a note to the Clerk of the Court to be conveyed immediately to Will's father, giving the latest reassuring news about his son. Widow Trotter had suggested this in the hope that such a personal reminder of the fragility of human life might help soften the Justice's heart for the required few hours. Around the room Tom counted half a dozen dishevelled men with pikes who were there to maintain order, but he saw no sign yet of Paul Barnard or the other likely players in the drama to come. He was certain of one thing: that somewhere outside, in the bail-dock, John Morphew was penned in with the thieves, sharpers and pickpockets, awaiting his time of trial.

He continued to scan the room, and for a brief moment thought he had seen Henry Voyce over at the far side, near the door. The figure was hidden behind a knot of people in animated discussion. Tom stepped a little to the side. Yes, it was indeed Voyce – and he was whispering. Tom craned his neck in order to make out the other figure. He caught a glimpse, but the man was a stranger, and a few seconds later the pair of them had disappeared through the door. So Henry Voyce was in the building – and it appeared he was working behind the scenes. It was a worrying sign.

The minutes ticked by, and the hour of ten was approaching, when Tom noticed Walter Treadwell squeezing his way in from the yard. There was time for a brief exchange, and so he made his way over. The porter had been detained by business at Stationers' Hall and had just arrived. Tom was able to tell him that their case was not due for some time, and they began to talk. Walter was flustered, and Tom saw from his restless glance that this was not just the hurry of his arrival, but a more uneasy apprehension. The man in fact looked haunted.

'What is it, Mr Treadwell?' he asked. 'You appear to be searching for someone?'

'No, Mr Bristowe, no, I assure you. I was merely wondering if Constable Buller was here...'

He broke off nervously. Tom sensed that the man was not looking for the constable, but on the contrary was fearful of finding him. What could have happened to unsettle Buller's co-witness to the murder scene? Tom was suddenly alert and knew something significant was there to be grasped – perhaps this was a moment for boldness? He quickly told the porter the news of Will's stabbing, and his suspicion that it was connected with the case – after all, he and Will had been asking questions about the murder, and perhaps that had alerted someone important?

Walter Treadwell was struck at once. Tom now had his whole attention, and the eyes showed how the news had startled him. At the same instant there was a stirring in the courtroom, as if Tom's words had activated a sense of alarm in the place. The porter drew Tom close to himself and spoke with quiet urgency.

'You must tell Mr Morphew to ask about the *key*... ask the watchman about the key – in Mr Emmet's pocket.'

There was a flurry of people around them.

'What precisely, Sir? What should he ask?'

The porter's voice was low and urgent, and his mouth was at Tom's ear.

'Why did the key have *blood* on it?... Sam Bennett the watchman – the one who found Mr Morphew in the street – he took the key from the body – out of the pocket. He told me he thought there was some blood on it – merely a smudge, but enough to leave a mark on his hand. How can that be, Mr Bristowe? I've been puzzling about it. I asked Joe Buller, but he laughed it off – said the very idea was nonsense.'

The porter's eyes began their uneasy search again.

'What is it, Mr Treadwell? What has the constable said to you?'

'I must say nothing more, Sir... I've told you nothing!'

Tom pressed his arm, and then smiled broadly:

'Nothing at all, Sir. I'll leave you to yourself... Look, what a busy concourse this place has suddenly become!'

Tom gave a light-hearted gesture around the room with his hand, as if he was exchanging relaxed pleasantries with a friend. But this was not lightness of heart. The truth was, he had just glimpsed Constable Buller at the far side of the room, looking in their direction. They must not appear conspiratorial. He nodded at Walter, turned away, and hurried to his seat.

Only seconds later the Court rose to its feet, and the several judges filed in with some formality. The Lord Mayor, a rubicund city gentleman with a rolling gait, led the way, his heavy chain bouncing on his chest; and then came the tall, impressive figure of Mr Justice Lundy, his black robes edged with fur, a black girdle round his waist, and a full white wig tumbling over his shoulders. Hemp's kestrel-like eyes were sweeping the room, and Tom found himself singled out as if he were a vole in a ditch. He had enough self-possession to respond with a look of hopeful concern nicely calculated to keep fatherly feelings ticking away. Tom found himself observing minutely in his turn, fascinated by the little gestures with which the bench negotiated their precedence and asserted their authority. Eventually, with a creaking and swishing clearly heard above the hush of the room, the Majesty of the Law became seated.

The respectful silence had been only temporary. With the arrival of the first prisoner – a frightened girl of about seventeen dressed in a cotton shift who was charged with stealing a handkerchief – the hubbub got under way with the crowd by the far wall beginning their running commentary on proceedings. The girl pickpocket was only the first in a procession of unfortunates. The indictments of petty larceny were read out, and one by one the cases hurried to their conclusion. Every incident and foolish mishap was re-lived. One after another the accused came into the dock to confront their crimes, which seemed to involve a comic miscellany of portable objects – the small and the even smaller. As well as the usual stolen snuff boxes and lengths of cloth, there were buttons and buckles, a pair of tongs, a hand-mirror, kettles and saucepans, and even a box of rhubarb. The felons had trusted to their sharp wits and light fingers, and had expected to disappear up the street or melt into the crowd. But each act of pilfering met its nemesis. Tom's interest was especially caught by an older woman, Annie

Martin, charged with stealing a pair of pink silk gloves 'to the value of fifteen shillings' from a haberdasher's shop. They must have looked exquisite as she slid them onto her tiny hands, and the woman had succumbed to the temptation.

Tom longed to be lifted out of the oppressive place, closing his eyes and willing himself elsewhere. But it had to be admitted that the scene was never less than lively, and the crowd kept the tragi-comic entertainment moving along with ribald jokes, shouts of disapproval and mounting waves of muttering. This created such a din that words were sometimes lost and the witness or prisoner drawn into the banter. The hammer was repeatedly struck on the bench, only for the sound to sweep in again. Will had been right. Inside this place, human life lost all dignity, becoming a succession of sad little scenes played before an excited audience, each one a cameo of stupidity and hopelessness.

Finally the jury shuffled out of the room. They were gone for only ten minutes before the succession of verdicts came. The effect was almost burlesque: 'Jennifer Hart, indicted for stealing a cambric handkerchief, value ten pence. Guilty. *Branding*... John Wood, indicted for stealing a pair of shoes, value two shillings. Guilty. *Transportation*... Richard Gash, indicted for stealing nine pairs of women's stockings of value one guinea. Guilty. *Death*... Charles Lodge, indicted for feloniously stealing a box, value six shillings, and four pound of rhubarb, value twenty shillings, from the shop of Joseph Pargiter. Guilty. *Death*... And finally, as Tom looked on anxiously, Annie Martin, indicted for carrying away a pair of silk gloves, value fifteen shillings, from the shop of Thomas Fowkes. Guilty. *Death*.' The irony was painful. It was well known that many a St James's lady sported much finer gloves on an account that would never be settled by her husband.

A brazier was brought in, and the brandings carried out there and then in open court. The young pickpocket had one hand shackled while the other was firmly held and the iron reached for. The girl turned her head away and let out a terrified scream, only to discover that the 'cold iron' had been used on her – the nearest step to clemency. The drama was intense. Tom found himself gasping audibly. The image of the cattle market was only too real. There was a ruthless routine about the whole operation. How cheaply bought were these lives, he thought – just a handful of shillings. Each one a bargain.

The brazier was removed, but the bitter smell of the coals still lingered in the air when John Morphew, Publisher, of Stationers' Court, finally climbed into the dock. He resisted the attempt of one of the pikemen to push him up the steps, and Tom noticed thankfully that he was unshackled. Rather than cowering, he was straightening his shoulders and surveying the courtroom with the air of a man who had nothing to hide. Mr Justice Lundy, as High Court judge, now took the chair, and with almost no pause the charge was read out, and the defendant's plea of 'Not Guilty' delivered in a voice that was quiet but firm. The prosecuting counsel was up on his feet beginning to relate the events of Friday the Thirtieth of January.

The Court was reminded of the verdict of the Coroner's Jury, and the case against the accused started to take shape. Moment by moment, with chilling inevitability, the Tale of the Angry Printer began to impress itself on the expectant audience. The motive for murder was built up with remorseless clarity: Morphew's shop being used to print the vile libels of *Bufo*; the publisher questioned on suspicion of sedition; his fury at being accused; the intense resentment voiced against his pressman; his storming out of the Cockpit in a mood of angry vengeance. If anything, Mr Nugent's skilful narrative intensified the emotion of the story. He gave it the satisfying sweep of a well-plotted drama where every episode fitted neatly into the next.

With the events that led to the murder established, the hitherto quiet audience became utterly silent as the curtain rose on the night scene in the printing-house. The shocking violence of the killing was described, and the bloody walking-cane took on a grotesque character. The prosecutor held the object aloft for all to see. The spaniel's head caked in gore spoke eloquently of the deadly outrage. 'If only,' Mr Nugent averred, '*if only* this small animal could speak, what dreadful horrors would it tell!' And with a deft turn, while everyone in the room was reeling to the blows that rained down on Emmet's head, he instantly shifted the picture to John Morphew's bloodied clothes. They were, he said, 'the badge – *the crimson livery* – of his guilt.' The man's voice rose to a climax. '... And so the deed was done! The accused stood over the corpse, surveying his handiwork, his dreadful vengeance complete!'

Tom was aware of the jurors, seated six and six on both sides of the dock, all turning their eyes onto the accused. Morphew flinched slightly, as if brushed by an invisible hand, and tried to keep his own gaze fixed and dignified. Mr Nugent, swinging round to embrace his rapt audience, *assured* the Court that the prosecution would press for the full charge of murder – not manslaughter or accidental killing. The case would be made, he said, that this act was premeditated, and the degree of violence went far beyond that of a haphazard blow or a sudden passion.

The histrionic performance was much as Will had predicted, and as Tom listened to the eloquent sentences, which unfolded in all their certainty, he fought to dispel the vivid mental picture they offered. The scene had been set, and a succession of witnesses would now be called to tell the story over again, step by step. Tom knew he must act about the key. He took from his pocket a small sheet of paper and a pencil – he'd come prepared – and wrote a note to the prisoner, making it as brief and clear as possible, and adding: '... Bennett could prove your friend, also

Treadwell. I think both have been coerced by *Buller.*' Tom was folding the sheet when he paused, reflected for a moment with furrowed brow, then unfolded it again. '... I'll take the stand if you wish,' he added, '– call me to witness to your reputation – I can speak about the body?'

He beckoned the court messenger over, and the note was duly delivered into Morphew's hand. The publisher saw him and gave a scarcely detectable nod of acknowledgment. But it was enough. The whole court instantly seemed to turn their attention to the dark-haired young man with a pencil in his hand and a high colour creeping up his face.

The witnesses were now called in turn to give their accounts of the fateful events. The first was Henry Voyce, who took the stand as if mounting a pulpit. Tom was a little surprised, having thought such a behind-the-scenes operator wouldn't wish to appear publicly. But it turned out he had a lot to say. His face seemed to ooze distaste as he spoke, and his solemnity set an uncomfortable tone. The man looked around apprehensively and clearly felt he was sojourning among the heathen. There was a ripple of laughter in the crowd. Tom's spirits lifted. 'An oily *Reverend*, isn't he!' rang out from somewhere, and there was more laughter. The Court was called to order, but the atmosphere had changed. Mr Nugent pressed on, encouraging Voyce to describe the shocking nature of the 'Bufo' verses, printed by the accused.

Morphew interrupted in protest.

'I knew nothing of it! The printing was done without my knowledge!'

The prosecutor rounded on him.

'Well, well, we hear from the accused! An intervention! Let me then seize the opportunity, Mr Morphew, and suggest that you allowed yourself to be dragged into the gutter, and your presses to be put to seditious use.'

'It was done behind my back!'

'Really, Mr Morphew? Are you asking the Court to believe that something so substantial, which came – as you accept – from your own presses, took you by *surprise?...*'

The word was emphasised, and delivered with an exaggerated lift. There was sniggering somewhere in the crowd. Mr Nugent frowned and became terse.

'... Do you allow your employees to print whatever they want? Are you telling us that you lost control of your business – just as you lost control of your *temper?*'

Tom found himself gripping his knee with his hand. This was heading in the wrong direction. Morphew consciously paused and looked straight at his questioner, brow clear, and voice under control.

'Perhaps I have been too trusting, Sir, I admit. Mr Emmet had worked for me for several years, and as my business grew I had come to respect and rely on him. I discovered – much to my disappointment...'

'Your disappointment, Mr Morphew? Or your *anger?*'

'I have never found anger to be helpful, Sir. Indignation sometimes, yes – when warranted. But anger is usually a sign of weakness.'

'But he had betrayed your trust, had he not? Betrayed *you?* Is this not what you are saying?'

'*Betrayal* is a strong word – it is not one that I would use.'

The prosecutor was becoming unsettled.

'And what word *would* you use, Sir?'

'I was *disgusted,* Mr Nugent. The pieces were too vituperative for my taste.'

Mr Justice Lundy leaned forward and addressed the prosecutor sharply.

'From your opening remarks, Mr Nugent, I take it you will be showing that the accused stormed out of his interview at the Ministry in a state of anger at the deceased?'

'Indeed, Sir, yes. My witness, Mr Voyce, is about to come to that.'

'In that case, Mr Nugent, you must direct your questions to *him*. I don't like this confusion! I'm sure the jury wish to hear from Mr Voyce... From the look of him, I suspect the gentleman does not wish to be detained in this place longer than is necessary.'

Tom detected a glint of humour in the Justice's eyes. Could it be?

The prosecutor gathered himself and turned once again to the witness. There followed more on the interrogation at the Cockpit, and Voyce's account emphasised Morphew's mounting rage at what Emmet had told them. The angry printer had declared, he said, that his pressman 'needed to be taught a lesson,' and his hearers were left in no doubt that it would be a *harsh one*. Here Voyce's tone darkened and gave the idea a dramatic edge. The members of the jury were intent and still.

'In my judgment,' he continued, 'Morphew was angry not because of the surreptitious printing, but because Emmet had revealed the secret...'

He looked around the court before adding darkly:

'... We suspect that Emmet had been a *Tory spy* helping to circulate these same libels.'

At this remark a courtroom murmur began, thickening the atmosphere like distant thunder. Voyce looked pleased with himself.

Finally, for a rhetorical climax, he was invited to offer the Court his views on Morphew's reputation as a publisher. This he did with relish, singling out for particular scorn the *Secret Memoirs* and *The Lady's Pacquet of Letters*, and more generally what he termed 'the *promiscuous* nature of the materials that have issued from the accused's shop.' Voyce's pursed lips gave the very idea a dubious cast: there was, he implied, something intrinsically corrupting in the *miscellaneous*. These tendencies, he said, had come to a head with *Bufo's Magic Glass*, a treasonable piece so repugnant that even Morphew now wanted to disclaim it – 'although,' Voyce added enigmatically, 'the publisher had previously given his blessing to *this thing of darkness*.'

'The poem is a vile thing indeed,' interjected the Lord Mayor. 'I have seen it – it is an outrageous libel!'

Mr Justice Lundy took up the questioning.

'For information, Mr Voyce – do we know anything of this malign toad, this *Bufo*?'... Can you advise the Court?'

Voyce at once assumed an officious manner, which came easily to him.

'His identity remains a mystery, Your Honour. The Ministry has exerted itself greatly to track him down – so far without success. Mr Emmet maintained that the materials were supplied covertly and anonymously. The truth of the matter is difficult to ascertain.'

'You have no clue that will lead you to his identity?'

'Inquiries are being made, and suspicions canvassed. But nothing has yet been determined. They are rantings, Your Honour! Bufo's accusations lack all respect and decency, and they are directed against men of honour and public service...'

Voyce paused for effect, then added:'... We believe Bufo is being used to spread disaffection and unrest. He is clearly some *Jacobite* trouble-maker who seeks to unsettle the Constitution. In whose pay he is, we know not... but there is a *Popish* taint to all he says!'

The imputation caused an immediate stir, and the courtroom murmur was becoming a hum of suppressed anger. The judge nodded in acknowledgment, and after a signal from the prosecutor, Voyce turned away and was stepping down.

'Just a moment, Mr Voyce. I have a question to ask you.'

The prisoner's hand was raised.

'The accused may do so, of course,' said Mr Justice Lundy obligingly.

Voyce had to settle himself again. Morphew was now levelling his gaze at the witness, and suddenly he had the room's attention.

'You speak about my questioning at the Cockpit, Mr Voyce, and you offer an opinion on my reputation – both of which I find a gross distortion from the truth. However, I understand your concern. If I have done anything to *unsettle the Ministry*, then I must apologise to the Court...'

This greatly amused the popular audience.

'... The probity and wisdom of our great men should not be brought into question – I understand that – but the normal punishment for this misdemeanour is surely not to be arraigned on a false charge of murder! This is not a regular proceeding.'

At this there was more hilarity and a scattering of applause. The judicial hammer came down hard on the bench.

'No statements, Mr Morphew! – I will not have statements made – especially gratuitous and inflammatory ones. It is *I* who decide what is regular in this place. You must confine yourself to questioning the witness. Do you have anything material to ask?'

'Yes I do, Your Honour,' said Morphew with the utmost deference, 'I wish to pose a question that Mr Nugent has unaccountably omitted to ask.'

'*Indeed?* And what question might that be, Mr Morphew?' asked the Justice, his patience becoming stretched. 'Please enlighten us!'

'Mr Voyce, I want to ask you if you could describe the scene of the crime for us? The body in the printing-house.'

Voyce was taken aback. He looked round the room as if searching for advice from somewhere. The judge intervened.

'That is not a question, Mr Morphew...'

He paused meaningfully. '... At least not in the strictest sense... But perhaps it could be re-phrased?'

'Thank you, Your Honour,' said Morphew, risking more deference (he didn't want to sound too obsequious). 'Then can

I ask you, Mr Voyce, where was the body positioned? And what was the extent of the blood?'

There was an awkward hesitation.

'Constable Buller will shortly be speaking about that,' said Voyce, who could not avoid sounding out of his guard.

'Yes of course, I expect so. You clearly know the trial arrangements, and I wouldn't like to alter your schedule… But given that you had the advantage of viewing the scene *before you had the body moved and the blood mopped up*, I thought the jury would wish to hear about so significant a thing.'

Voyce became momentarily tongue-tied. He looked at the judge, but received no assistance from that quarter – quite the contrary. The Lundy brow was lowered.

'Yes, Mr Voyce, I understand from the Coroner that you asked for Mr Emmet's body to be moved before the Grand Jury had viewed it? That was irregular, I have to say. You had no authority to do that.'

Voyce now looked embarrassed and was struggling to recover his poise. Over the next few minutes, however, he managed to stumble out enough to satisfy his hearers, and he continued to maintain that the Constable and the Watchman had examined all the evidence closely on Friday night. Tom could not help but admire Morphew's clever tactics. Voyce's interference had now been established, and this might be useful later. Will would certainly have approved.

The trial continued its course, and Joe Buller took the stand. There was a swagger in the constable's manner that spoke of self-confidence and experience, and the Court was treated to a detailed account of his discovery of the body in the printing-house, and of Morphew's dramatic entrance. The publisher's bloodstained clothes were again described, and his distracted demeanour stressed. Buller recalled the questions put to the accused, and his unsatisfactory answers. There duly followed the constable's examination of the corpse and the bloody murder weapon on the ground beside it. By now Buller's enactment was well rehearsed and had its due effect. Once again the prop was brandished – though in that regard Mr Nugent had stolen his thunder.

And then Nugent turned to the piece of paper that was found clutched in Emmet's hand, containing some satiric verses with the title *Bufo's Curse*. This paper was, he informed the Court, important for the prosecution's case – a point that Constable Buller wholeheartedly endorsed. It was clear, he said, that when Morphew entered the premises he had found Emmet in the act of setting the poem in type with a view to running off copies for distribution the next morning. The composing-stick had been discovered, and this showed that Emmet had been interrupted in his work. The satiric leaflet was to be the latest eruption of Bufo's poison. Buller underlined the point that after his interrogation at the Ministry, this discovery must have fanned Morphew's anger into flames.

The prosecutor drove the point home remorselessly.

'*If* we are to accept the prisoner's assertion that Mr Emmet deceived him, then this paper must have raised his anger to the highest pitch. Mr Morphew entered his premises vowing vengeance on the deceased, and found his pressman with the incriminating poem in his hand... The outcome must have been a violent one!'

Mr Justice Lundy intervened.

'The paper is here for us to see, I hope?'

'Yes, Your Honour,' said Nugent, arcing his hand slowly into his waistcoat pocket as if to draw out nothing less than a signed confession. 'I produce it here.'

It was a *coup de théâtre*, and the packed galleries leaned forward to view this scrap of paper. Othello's handkerchief had never drawn more attention.

Mr Justice Lundy beckoned with his fingers, and the paper was handed up to him. He scanned the few lines, and the expression of pained disgust that crossed his face left no-one in doubt of what he thought.

A shout came from amongst the standing crowd.

'Let it be read!'

'Aye, we'll hear it! Read it!' became the universal cry. There was even an audible murmur of agreement coming from the more polite gallery.

'Mr Nugent, perhaps you could let the Jury hear what this furious ranter has to say? I don't wish the thing to be passed around from hand to hand. You had better deliver it to us generally.'

Mr Nugent was hardly able to contain the smile of satisfaction that was straining his face muscles, and he couldn't resist giving the accused a hint of it. The room fell silent. The prosecutor knew he held everyone in thrall.

'*Bufo's Curse!*' he announced in chilling tones, and began declaiming the lines:

Curse on the authors of our present woes,
Through whom the Nation's *desperate ills arose!*
Whether in private or in public great,
Shelter'd in Church, *or honour'd by the* State;
Whether a mighty legion, or a few,
A blind, mistaken, or a wilful crew;
Whether Whig, Jacobite, High Church or Low,
Threaten'd by Spencer, *mis-led by* Defoe;
Suborn'd by St John, *or by* Harley *brib'd,*
Or swept along on Churchill's *stinking tide;*
Caught in the Junto's *dark and treacherous schemes,*
Or in the Tories' *plots behind the scenes –*
Curse on 'em all, who lend a helping hand
To ruin and despoil our Native Land!
Living or dead, may none escape their due!

I point the finger – you! *– and* you! *– and* you!
All restless – for the crying wrongs you've done –
May your souls wander when your sands are run;
And your vile dust by wicked hands be torn
From its tall urn, and made the people's scorn!

The effect was electric. The thing seemed to be hitting out at everyone, and everyone in the room was stirred by it – and physically roused too – '*you!* – and *you!* – and *you!*' The whole place was one animated conversation, a mixture of glee and outrage. There was relish for some phrases, revulsion at others. None could agree, and all were unsettled. The hammering on the bench went for nothing. Tom had already heard these words at the inquest, but in this feverish amphitheatre they had their full dramatic effect. He shuddered. They were the authentic tones of Bufo. It was a voice of universal disillusionment – an attack on the very Constitution of the Nation. He looked around at the seething audience. If only these people could know the source of those words and what a truly promiscuous text it was! – a communal authorship among whom Emmet must surely be counted. Tom thought he could detect a colouring added by its frustrated and angry editor, a man who at the end saw himself exploited by both sides of the political divide.

It took many seconds more of hammering, and the waving of pikes in the air, before the crowd was quietened. The atmosphere had become unruly. Mr Justice Lundy rose to his feet and raised his hand. He announced solemnly that any further disturbance would force him to suspend the sitting, and even call for a military presence. He would have no such *anarchy*, he declared. At that moment Tom caught Morphew's eye and saw that it was anxious, even lost. The face seemed to be asking a question of him – and one he could not answer. As he returned the look, Tom knew there was more than a printer on trial here.

Chapter Thirty-Two

After the disturbance in his court, Mr Justice Lundy was anxious to move the business on. He spoke briskly to Constable Buller in the witness-box.

'This *Curse* – You are certain that it is genuine?'

'Yes, Your Honour. Mr Voyce assured us it was.'

The constable looked beyond the seats toward Henry Voyce who was by now observing events from the far corner of the room. Voyce shifted uneasily, not expecting to be the centre of attention once more. The judge addressed him.

'Can you vouch for the piece?... You are still under oath.'

'Yes, Your Honour. The handwriting is his, and it is in character.'

The judge was thoughtful. He turned back to the witness.

'You are right to note its importance, Constable. The verse blusters a good deal, but the invective is vicious. Undoubtedly the thing issues from a sordid and disaffected mind. It casts a pall over this whole case. The response we have just witnessed bears out its explosive capacity...'

He frowned at the crowd.

'... Such a treasonable document might well arouse anger and violence. You carry your point on that, Constable. The disturbance has brought it home to us.'

Tom detected one or two nods around him, and his spirits sank. He sensed that the mood in the court had changed. The reading of *Bufo's Curse* had turned things against them. Earlier Morphew had skilfully disavowed anger, but now everyone in the room had experienced how natural his anger must have been. Tom wondered about the jury: had they felt the motive for the killing on their own pulses?

Perhaps unadvisedly, Joe Buller was beaming at the judicial bench with some satisfaction, confident that his contribution to the trial had reached its effective climax. His Honour Mr Justice Lundy continued to look grave.

'Does the defendant wish to ask a question of the witness?'

Tom noticed that Morphew was leaning for support on the bar of the dock, and his hand was trembling slightly. The strain of the occasion was beginning to weigh on him. But he managed to keep his voice clear and firm.

'Yes, Your Honour, I do.'

'Then may I remind you to use the *interrogative?*'

Morphew offered a humble nod.

'You have described, Constable – very vividly – seeing the door of the printing-house ajar and entering the premises to find Mr Emmet's body. You had of course the advantage of a lit candle – the room was illuminated – but would you agree that the body was so positioned that anyone entering in complete darkness would have stumbled over it?'

Buller was now frowning slightly, annoyed that his evidence was being revisited.

'A stranger might, who did not know where to find a candle!'

It was a neat reply, and a look of satisfaction suffused the constable's face. Morphew hesitated, wrong-footed... He had of course stridden confidently in the darkness. He knew every inch of the room...

He began to respond, but the judge cut him short.

'You do not have the luxury of arguing the matter out, Mr Morphew! This is not a debate. Do you have any further enquiries of the constable?'

Tom was leaning forward in his seat watching the sparring, He was feeling nervous, and his palms were sweating. The rules were such that this could never be a fair encounter. Morphew continued the best he could.

'Would it be possible, Constable, that on that evening Mr Emmet had let someone into the printing-house – a person who had commissioned *Bufo's Curse* and was hoping to collect it? Would it be possible that Emmet was working late to fulfil an order from someone who was intending to use the *Curse* for political purposes? Might it be that...'

He was interrupted by the judge's impatient hammer.

'Mr Morphew. These are all conjectural propositions! They are questions the constable can hardly be expected to answer. This *someone* is entirely hypothetical.'

'With respect, Your Honour, this someone is *not* hypothetical – far from it – he is the *murderer!*'

There was an intake of breath around the courtroom. Morphew had realised that if he could not make statements or answer the witness, then he could certainly answer the judge. Tom noticed Voyce by the far wall. A thunderous look had taken hold of him – it was clear that things were not proceeding as smoothly as planned. But the judge's patience was wearing thin.

'This is yet more conjecture, Mr Morphew!'

'I sincerely apologise, Your Honour... the procedures of the Court are unfamiliar to me. I do not mean to breach its decorums...'

In urging his innocence, Morphew was prepared to risk a little naivety. He pushed ahead while he could.

'... Might I ask the constable whether – except for *Bufo's Curse* of course – anything else was removed from Mr Emmet's body on Friday night?'

Buller appeared nonplussed and looked at the judge. His Honour returned the look politely.

'The question is a simple one, Mr Buller. Are you able to answer it?'

Once more Tom felt a satiric undertone in the judge's words. The constable's reply when it came sounded grudging, as if it had been wrung from him.

'Well, the deceased did have the key to the printing-room in his pocket... It was thought best to remove it when the place was secured for the night. I took it into my care.

'And you made use of it the next morning, did you not?' said Morphew, who was beginning to feel his way into the barrister's role. 'When you returned very early to the scene of the crime?'

'Yes, I returned there shortly before seven. I wanted to be on hand when the pressmen arrived – otherwise they might have stumbled on the body...'

At once the judge's eyes – and Morphew's eyes – and Tom's eyes – all widened at his choice of phrase.

'... I mean to say, I did not wish them to be alarmed when they discovered it. I wanted to be there to reassure them that all was in hand.'

Tom fought back a smile, and glanced over to see how Voyce was taking this – but all he saw was the back of the man's head as he slipped out of the door. There was murmuring in the courtroom. Morphew said nothing more, thinking it best to let those final words hang in the air. Mr Justice Lundy took the initiative.

'You may step down, Constable. Your evidence has been most enlightening.'

Joe Buller left the witness-box a little unwillingly, as if he had a great deal more to say about the matter. The walk back across the courtroom was not the triumphal progress he had hoped for.

Sam Bennett the watchman was the next witness. With a nice rhetorical touch, Mr Nugent introduced him as the man who, late that same night, had encountered the accused *wandering* the streets, and had *apprehended* him. The words were smuggled in cleverly, as if the printer were then already under suspicion. Morphew wanted to protest, but something held him back. He felt it might be wiser to bide his time and not appear too aggressive.

The watchman was in a co-operative mood, and in response to the prosecutor's promptings he spoke to fine effect about his disquieting experience. He stressed the defendant's wild eyes, his bloody garments, and his suspicious appearance generally – it was irregular, he added, to be *wandering the streets* at that time of night 'when honest folk are a-bed,' and the man had seized him by the collar in a threatening manner.

Mr Justice Lundy leaned forward.

'Mr Bennett, the court appreciates that the accused must have appeared to you an alarming figure – but can we assume that in the course of your duties you encounter many more dangerous situations?'

'Perhaps, Your Honour... but I'm paid to be *watchful* and take close note of things... I only want to tell you how Mr Morphew appeared to me on that occasion. He did look like a guilty thing!'

The watchman cast his eyes up at the gallery, as if seeking out his audience.

'He may well have done, Mr Bennett. But his guilt – or otherwise – is what *we* are here to decide on.'

Morphew seized the moment.

'Your Honour, can I ask the witness – did I not at once *report the murder* to him, and beg him to follow me?'

Judge Lundy looked at the witness and awaited his reply.

'Yes – you said you had found a body, and you wanted me to come and see it... But I had already stepped in front of you so as to prevent any escape.'

Mr Nugent coughed slightly and reminded the court of his presence. He took up the questioning again.

'What you are telling us, Mr Bennett, is that you stopped the accused – he didn't stop you?'

'Yes Mr Nugent – that's exactly how it happened.'

The prosecutor moved swiftly on to the next stage of the drama when Morphew and the watchman made their entrance into the murder scene. The members of the jury already had the picture imprinted on their minds, and yet again the grisly pageant was rehearsed with Nugent's help. The same details were noted, the disposition of everything confirmed, and the bloody weapon duly described. By now it seemed as if a magic lantern were projecting a spectral image of the scene onto the courtroom wall for all to see.

But there was a further detail they needed to register, and Morphew was eager to elicit it. He intervened.

'Can I ask the witness, Your Honour, about the key that Constable Buller mentioned earlier – Mr Emmet's own key to the printing-house, which was in the pocket of his coat?'

'And what do you want to know about it?' said the judge, genuinely curious.

'I want to ask you, Mr Bennett… Who removed the key from the pocket… ?'

The watchman suddenly looked nervous, and hesitated.

'… On oath, Mr Bennett!' Morphew added pointedly. At this presumption the judge scowled but said nothing.

'Why, *I* did, Sir. But I didn't think it of consequence to mention it. I then gave it to Constable Buller.'

'Was there anything about the key that you noticed – anything that might be of interest to the Court?'

Tom waited with baited breath. He saw the watchman glance desperately across to the far wall where Henry Voyce had been standing. The eyes searched, but no guidance was to be had from that quarter.

'What do you mean? It was quite a small key, for such a heavy door...'

'You are no doubt right, Mr Bennett. But was there anything *on* it? Did you find it was marked in any way?... Dirtied?'

'Well...'

This was like extracting juice from a lump of coal. Morphew lost patience, and spoke loudly.

'Did you see any *blood* on it?'

The temperature of the crowded room was palpably rising, and the watchman's face was glistening slightly.

'Well, I did wonder if there might have been... I saw my finger was a little smudged.'

The prosecutor cut in sharply.

'But was there not a great deal of blood around the place, Mr Bennett? Might it not have come from anywhere? From the accused, indeed, when you apprehended him?'

'Yes, Sir, that's quite possible,' said the watchman with obvious relief. 'I can't be certain – though blood it was.'

The opportunity had passed, and the watchman left the witness-box. As for the key – the idea had been raised, but little more. Morphew looked downcast, not knowing what was left for him to say or do. Tom saw he was tiring visibly.

Hope rose a little when Walter Treadwell took the oath, but the man appeared to be even more unsettled than before. The prosecutor led him along the well-worn path to confirm the narrative that was now established. Yes, he said, Constable Buller had brought him from the porter's lodge to view the body. Yes, Morphew did have a frantic look. Yes, the manuscript of *Bufo's Curse* was clutched in the dead man's fist. Yes, he could confirm that the walking-cane did belong to the accused, and he was rarely to be seen without it.

'The cane was almost part of himself,' said the porter sadly. 'Morphew and his spaniel were well known. He would hold it up sometimes and ask it questions – ask its opinion! It was his way of thinking a matter through – discussing it with himself.'

Walter Treadwell broke off, his voice wavering. It was an intimate and endearing picture, and one that the prosecutor took note of with a slight smile. The questioning continued, and the answers were predictable, like the ticking of a clock. Tom's frustrations were mounting.

But suddenly the rhythm was broken. The porter swung round to take in the whole Court and at once found a stronger voice.

'I have to say this to everyone! John Morphew is an honourable man! – A kindly, thoughtful man! I've known him for many years and *cannot* believe he could act with such violence!'

Walter Treadwell was almost shouting.

The prosecutor was indignant. The judge's hammer struck the bench.

'Mr Treadwell! You must not be so agitated. The court can accept your evidence as to the character of the accused. But there must be order! You have made yourself a hostile witness. I will allow your statement, but must warn you, you are here to answer questions. We are now establishing the primary evidence, do you understand?'

The porter was abashed, but was satisfied he had made his point. John Morphew's gratitude showed in his face and prompted him to ask an immediate question that might ride the wave of sympathy in the room.

'Mr Treadwell, judging from the head wound, would you not agree that the person who killed our mutual friend John Emmet, attacked him ferociously and with repeated blows?'

'Certainly yes,' the porter readily agreed. 'It must have been done without mercy. No friend, however provoked, could ever have done it!'

When Walter Treadwell's testimony was finished there was a slight break in the proceedings. Tom saw Mr Justice Lundy and the Lord Mayor put their heads together in earnest consultation. After about a minute the Justice spoke.

'Mr Nugent, the prosecution case would seem to rest here. But there is something I want to point out to you. It concerns the murder weapon – the walking-cane with the spaniel's head, which it has been shown belongs to the defendant, and was regularly used by him...'

Judge Lundy paused, and Tom thought he had at that moment caught his eye.

'... I am duty bound to point out that no evidence has been submitted which proves that Mr Morphew was using the cane that day... in fact, I have here a written deposition from Mr Cobb, the Covent Garden constable who attended the defendant's questioning at the Ministry. It would appear that when he was apprehended on Thursday Mr Morphew did *not* have the cane with him. This seems to me material to the charge, and is something you may wish to consider.'

Mr Nugent, who was an old hand at managing the unforeseen, looked remarkably unperturbed and simply asked if he could 'take advice for a moment.'

Tom saw that Voyce was back in the room, and he watched in amazement as the prosecutor made his way over to him. There followed a whispered discussion, heads together, and faces solemn.

'While Mr Nugent is taking advice, Mr Morphew, let me ask you myself. Did you have the cane with you that day?'

'No, Your Honour,' said the much-relieved defendant, his face suddenly brighter. 'I certainly did not. I was going to make that very point in my statement to the Court. The previous evening I left the walking-cane in the printing-room, leaning against the wall by the door. I had some books to carry and didn't want to be encumbered.'

'Thank you, Mr Morphew. It may be useful to have that on record.'

The judge turned an enquiring look on the prosecutor, who had finished his consultation and was back at the table.

'Thank you, Your Honour,' he said, gathering himself. 'I ought to point out that I was awaiting the accused's statement in his defence, and intended to ask him to confirm that on his way to his shop on Friday night he called at his lodgings in Salisbury Court, where he changed his clothes. Perhaps the accused could now agree that is what happened?'

'Yes I did, but, as I've told the judge, the cane was in the printing-house. I had left it there the previous day.'

'We have only your word for that,' said Nugent sharply. 'Your Honour – might I have a brief word?'

The prosecutor made yet another excursion, this time around the table to the judges' bench, where he conducted a hushed exchange with both the Justice and the Lord Mayor, before returning to his place. He spoke enigmatically.

'Thank you, Your Honour – and Your Worship... then I shall proceed on that basis.'

Mr Justice Lundy and the Lord Mayor both nodded. All this was puzzling. Something was being plotted, Tom suspected. He didn't like the whisperings and odd movements. Matters were now so finely poised, with the mood of the Court hesitant and uncertain. He prayed there was no surprise looming.

The routine of the trial at once resumed with the defendant's calling of his character witnesses. Here the court was treated to some warm tributes to Morphew's humanity, his kindly treatment of his apprentice, his wisdom... though it was conceded that he could on occasion be a demanding taskmaster and was impatient with incompetence and slapdash work. Tom felt this could hardly count against him.

But one thing disrupted the process. Morphew addressed the bench.

'I'm afraid I cannot produce my final witness, Your Honour. My chief compositor, Mr Paul Barnard, is absent from the Court. I had expected that Mr Nugent would in fact call him, given that Mr Barnard had helped Emmet to print *Bufo's Magic Glass* – that scurrilous pamphlet. I was hoping to question him, as I was expecting it would advance my cause.'

'Well I'm afraid it can't. It seems neither you nor Mr Nugent is able to produce him. So any such evidence must remain unheard.'

Morphew was unsettled, but turned slightly in the dock, gripping the bar tightly as he did so. He was still managing to hold up, but was clearly physically weak.

'In his place, if I may Your Honour, I would like to call Mr Thomas Bristowe.'

This was Tom's moment. His heart was thudding hard as he mounted the witness-box and took the oath. The sensation of being raised up in the middle of that crowded room, with so many pairs of eyes trained on him from every direction, was extremely uncomfortable. It was not an audience but a crowd, and the place was less like a theatre than an arena. He tried to put gladiators from his mind and set his thoughts in order. In response to Morphew's invitation, he spoke briefly about their conversation in the Good Fellowship on the previous Thursday morning. He emphasised the man's good humour, his relaxed state of mind, not least his optimistic plans for the future of his business. He appeared, said Tom, to be very much at ease…

'I called on Mr Morphew again at his shop on Saturday morning – only to find that he was under charge. I was able to talk with Mr Feeny, and he spoke to me in just such warm terms as we have heard, saying he regarded his employer as a friend, and someone he could trust utterly.'

Thank you, Mr Bristowe,' said Will's father, almost benignly. 'That was when I was able to examine the body...'

The statement brought a sudden jolt to the proceedings. The judge's brow was raised.

'Are you telling us, Mr Bristowe, that you saw the body yourself on Saturday morning – two days before the inquest?'

'Yes, Your Honour – but I didn't merely see it – I examined it carefully – and the room too. I thought it might prove important. Mr Feeny had been ordered not to allow anyone on the premises, but he permitted me to come in and talk with him.'

The prosecutor was on his feet.

'Your Honour, this is most irregular. This gentleman is a character witness only. We have already heard from those who saw the body.'

'Yes, Mr Nugent, I understand that,' replied the judge, '– but he has been properly called by the defendant, and the Court is duty bound to hear from any witness who may have something material to contribute. This may be significant evidence, and so we need to hear it. I shall therefore invite Mr Bristowe – under solemn oath – to relate his findings. *Concisely*, if you would, Mr Bristowe!'

Tom swallowed hard, and to the best of his ability gave an account of the head wound and the distribution of the blood, as far as he could explain it. He described the layout of the press-room.

'... From my examination I noticed that there was no blood on the top of the bench, where we might expect it, but only at the bottom, near the floor...'

The Court appeared attentive, and he did his best to put his points clearly. The details were uncomfortable, but necessary.

'... And furthermore, it seemed to me that the head had been cut open by something sharper than the head of a cane – that there had been both a splitting and hammering...'

While he offered this considered interpretation, Mr Justice Lundy's face was growing ever darker; and when he came to the matter of the blows, he was stopped in his tracks.

'Mr Bristowe! – The Court has been very understanding in allowing you to give this report, and patient in listening to it. But I have to say that all this *analysis* is speculative only. You are sinking into the most minute – I may say *microscopic* – details, which can have no place in establishing the true and complete picture of the killing. That is what we are concerned with. The members of the jury have heard what you have to say, but I expect they would agree with me in wanting to avoid so much subjective *intricacy*. Thank you, Mr Bristowe!'

There was nothing for it but for Tom to leave the witness-box. He gave Morphew a rueful glance and received a look of thanks in return. 'Hemp' Lundy had said his piece, but of course the jury were not obliged to accept his direction. Tom was clinging onto that thought when His Honour announced that before the final stage of the trial when the defendant would offer his speech of defence, he was calling a further witness for the prosecution, who would have something very material to say about the now infamous walking-cane.

Morphew appeared alarmed and puzzled. He turned again to Tom, his face full of apprehension. All Tom could do was raise his shoulders in bafflement. Neither of them knew what this mystery witness held in store.

Chapter Thirty-Three

THE MAN WHO was called to the witness-box under these exceptional circumstances was, Tom thought, a slightly odd-looking gentleman. He was quite tall and fashionably dressed, but his clothes hung from him a little awkwardly and he moved uncomfortably in them, almost as if his wiry body were filling a dead man's suit. The furtive look on his face confirmed the impression of someone who had not expected to be there, and who felt ill-at-ease. He was carrying a cane, though when he took the stand he was not sure what to do with it, and the thing remained gripped in his hand as he swore the oath. He had been announced as *John Wise*, and as Tom searched his face an ingratiating expression suffused it, the eyes flicking rapidly from place to place. He felt a cold hand gripping his heart. This man did not bode well.

Mr Nugent offered a grateful smile and thanked the gentleman on behalf of the Court for having returned to London at short notice in order to present his evidence. The prosecution, he said, had given up thoughts of his being able to attend, considering the state of the Essex roads. But the Romford coach had struggled boldly through, and there he was, ready to play his part in the proceedings.

At this point his audience seemed unaccountably to be

withholding their gratitude. There was some whispering and a few sidelong looks in the gallery.

'Could you tell the Court, Mr Wise, where you were on the evening of Friday the Thirtieth of January, and of your encounter with the defendant – which I think will be seen to have an undoubted bearing on this case?'

Mr Nugent's phrases constituted a polite invitation, and Mr Wise did not disappoint. He related that some little time after ten o'clock – though he couldn't be absolutely precise as to time – he was making his way towards Fleet Street and the Strand, having unadvisedly taken a *short cut* from Paternoster Row, where he had enjoyed a light supper with a few City friends – he was interested in books and had had a fancy to take a look at Stationers' Hall on his walk...

Judge Lundy intervened.

'Mr Wise, we do not require you to give us a detailed itinerary. Can you simply tell us where you were when you had this *encounter?*'

'*Cock Alley*, Your Honour.'

As a factual statement this left little to be desired; but the man's answer brought a sudden fluttering of fans in the gallery, and not a little sniggering. 'Know it well!' shouted a joker in the crowd below. 'Aye! A short cut – and a short *thrust* too, I warrant!' another wit replied. There were unbidden smiles from every part of the courtroom.

But not from Mr Justice Lundy, who shot the coldest of stares toward the crowd, which was in danger of becoming boisterous again.

'Describe to us exactly what *happened*, Mr Wise,' he said firmly, and with ill-concealed impatience.

The gentleman told how he had been making his way with care along the alley, and just as he was passing an oil lamp high up on the wall, he met the accused hurrying in the opposite direction – in the direction of Stationers' Court.

'I saw his face in the lamplight. He looked very angry,' said the witness. 'Indeed he almost knocked me over. I heard him shout "Out of my way!" and as he bumped into me, he lifted his arm and threatened me with his cane.'

'His *cane*, Mr Wise?' asked the judge. 'You are prepared to swear upon oath that you saw the defendant with his cane? Can you describe it?'

'Yes, Your Honour. It's the one that has been shown in court – over there on the table – with the dog's head. It looked a fearsome thing, and I thought he was going to beat me.'

John Morphew was transfixed. He cried out in protest.

'This is a lie! An entire fabrication! I protest! I have never seen this man in my life before!'

Mr Nugent turned to him, as if to offer help.

'Well, Mr Morphew, according to this witness you were at that moment in no fit state to see *anything* clearly, but were intent on some business of your own.'

'Exactly, Sir,' added Wise. 'That's as it was. The gentleman had a distracted air. His eyes were wild and staring.'

'But this is caricature!' shouted Morphew. 'How dare you spin this grotesque fiction! How dare you invent such wicked lies! Who is your *paymaster*?'

The judge stopped him.

'Mr Morphew! We shall be hearing your own statement very shortly, when you will be able to respond to Mr Wise's evidence. Until then you must show some restraint! I'll not have a shouting-match in my Court! Your case will not be helped by this angry response.'

The printer was silenced, but his eyes were on fire and his anger fully on show. Tom sat horrified at the spectacle playing out in front of everyone. But who wouldn't have been furious at what was clearly an invented story, a big lie from start to finish? He had heard Will speak of 'Knights of the Post' – gentlemen who would give evidence to order – and surely, this shifty makeweight of a man must be exactly that, hauled in by Voyce to deliver the missing keystone of the prosecution's evidence, to fill neatly and securely the gaping void at the centre of their case. Tom felt physically sick. What was there left? What could Morphew say to win the jury round?

It was the death blow. There was no way back. When his time came, John Morphew delivered his speech to the Court with eloquence and sincerity – it shone through every word. But the killing evidence had registered with the jury, as had the outburst of Morphew's anger – his righteous indignation at what he knew to be a public lie delivered on oath. The defendant's eyes had been seen to blaze, his arm to rise up in spontaneous outrage. For one intense moment they were granted a magic-lantern show of the Angry Printer come to life. The threatening vision of Cock Alley was in the room – Morphew and his spaniel. However much the members of the jury may have wondered otherwise, they could visualise the scene; and nothing Morphew said thereafter in his defence – no mitigation or explanation – could dispel it. He spoke bravely and well, and after those ten minutes there were few among the crowd who were not impressed by his account. But the twelve good men – responsible and respectable citizens of London – looked thoughtfully on from their boxes, pondering the matter. They understood what they had to do.

Mr Justice Lundy summed up the evidence fairly, but he stressed that the jury had to set aside the insignificant details that confused the picture, and bring themselves to focus their thoughts on what had been placed on sworn record: the sordid background situation of Bufo and his libels; the more immediate build-up of Morphew's anger and vengeance; the rushing figure in the alley wielding the cane; the disturbed, wild figure wandering the streets after the deed was done; the bloodied garments; the confused account given to the constable; the volatile character of the accused evident in Court...

Then there was a pregnant pause. The room was absolutely still. Mr Justice Lundy's eyes shone out.

'Speaking for a moment as a man and a *person*,' he said – it was a surprising turn – 'I find myself to some degree sympathetic to the experience of the defendant. Emmet's paddling in dirt and scandal was disgusting, his behaviour treacherous, and his end – it must be confessed – little to be lamented. Emmet was indeed no saint! But the defendant was his employer and carried some responsibility for him and his behaviour. He had allowed his presses to be used to undermine the State. We have heard how, for eighteen months previous to the killing, he had encouraged Emmet to scrounge for papers on his behalf. Emmet was the defendant's night-soil man, dealing in dirt and sedition. With respect to the crime, the evidence of the material witnesses is all in place... But the defendant has not admitted the deed. He has in consequence not invoked *necessity* or *accident*; we have heard no plea of *imminent peril*, or of *temporary insanity*. The prosecution has demonstrated *evil intent*, and nothing has arisen to counter this. No circumstances of extenuation have been claimed. The defendant's powerful speech – one of the most eloquent I can recall – contained no word of acknowledgment or regret – merely self-justification. The accused wishes to go *scot-free!* Well, that is his choice.

'Members of the jury, in that case you may feel that he must face the charge of murder squarely. Intention is the key. His anger, it transpires, was not sudden and brief, but implacable and intense. We have heard that he set off on that fateful journey with but one thing on his mind, and he gripped his cane as if it were a sword of vengeance – however righteous! He almost knocked over Mr Wise as he approached the printing-house, carrying the weapon that was to shatter his pressman's head like china-ware.

The blows, as Constable Buller has shown, were heavy and many. Whatever his anger – however understandable it was – the crime was *murder*, and it is on that charge that you must decide.'

The twelve City householders made their way out of the courtroom, already talking together. Tom did not dare to listen, and sat for a moment with his head cradled in his hands. Then he looked up to see two pikemen stepping into the dock to mount guard on the accused while the jury deliberated. John Morphew appeared limp and lost, and Tom couldn't even catch his eye. The man seemed to be staring blankly ahead, as if stunned. No-one else was moving. The judicial bench had not been vacated. The Justice and the Lord Mayor were conferring quietly. It struck Tom that nobody in the place expected to be kept waiting for more than a few minutes. Whatever debate there might be among the jurymen, the verdict would not be long delayed.

Tom thought of Will, bandaged up and lying in bed at the Good Fellowship, and never before had he wanted so much to be with him. He could not help thinking that somehow, had Will been there, more might have been done – some expedient found, or argument suggested. He cast his mind back over the events of the trial with its alternations of hope and despair. He wanted to think he had done his best, and he could hear Widow Trotter's voice consoling him in just those words. But it had not been enough. The forces organised against Morphew had proved too strong, too utterly ruthless. Tom had hoped that the truth would emerge into the light – that the pieces would be carefully put together and rationally weighed, and the fantasy of the Angry Printer seen for the fiction it was. Instead, the Old Bailey really did prove to be a theatre – and less a space for human actors than a makeshift stage for wooden puppets moved by unseen hands.

Tom knew it was a desperate situation. But perhaps he was thinking too much on the dark side? Those twelve men, after all, were human beings, and they must have been moved by the defendant's words to them. Tom had been struck by how heartfelt Morphew's speech of defence had been. He had begged them to confront any niggling doubts they had, and above all to discount the outrageous fiction of this 'Mr Wise' who had suddenly been produced by the prosecution, as if to order. Tom was sure he would have been won over; but when he scanned the faces of the jurymen he knew they would be hard to persuade. They were downright characters who disliked awkward questions. They wanted answers, not doubts. What's more, during the trial the jurors were not gathered in a single body, but seated at a distance on either side of the dock, so that Morphew had been forever turning from one group to the other, twisting his back round in the urgency of his message. It had made Tom feel slightly giddy... He stopped himself. This wouldn't do. He had to keep hope alive, if only for a few minutes more... *Dum spiro spero!*

And after those few aching minutes there was a stir in the room. The twelve men were walking back to their places, now silently, and avoiding Morphew's eyes.

The remaining minutes of *Regina versus Morphew* passed routinely. The Sessions House had witnessed the ritual many hundreds of times, and would no doubt do so for decades to come. The judgment of 'guilty' was delivered, with the foreman announcing it almost with regret. And Mr Justice Lundy reached for what appeared to be a little black handkerchief and set it atop his wig. It should have been an absurd gesture; but at that moment it had the force of absolute finality. In a voice of impressive dignity and weight, Her Majesty's Justice pronounced sentence of death by hanging. To be carried out on Monday next. And *God have mercy on your soul*. The guilty man was at once held, and taken down, and his arms shackled behind his back. The next stage of the terrible Newgate ritual was about to begin. Morphew, in an almost insensible state, was gazing at the floor, his legs trailing as he was carried away.

Chapter Thirty-Four

'IS IT ALL over?'

Widow Trotter's question hung in the air, and the silence answered it. Tom was standing in the doorway of the parlour, and she could tell from his face that the very worst had happened. For a moment neither of them knew what to say.

He sank his head and sat down, unbidden.

'It's death. He is to be hanged on Monday.'

'Not even manslaughter, then? – I had hoped...'

'No, there was no mitigation... The trial was remorseless, Mrs T – like a machine. Once the wheels began to turn there was no escape. There was an evil mind driving it all. Henry Voyce gave evidence, and he seemed to be haunting the place, whispering and consulting – I'm sure he or Maynwaring laid the whole scheme... The prosecutor was well briefed – he was a sly performer and he gave no quarter... Oh, Mrs T, it was terrible – the way our hopes were raised and then dashed. Poor Morphew at the end was a broken man.'

'And what about the judge? Was it Will's father?'

Tom nodded.

'*Judicious* – as I expected. He was firm and punctilious. By his own lights he was even-handed, and all was done by the book... But he was so impatient. The minutiae seemed to annoy him. He only wanted to see the general picture. For him, the truth was bold and clear… I've so much to tell you…'

He broke off.

'… But I have to see Will – is he all right? If only he could have been there! This will be a grave blow to him.'

'I went up ten minutes ago, and he was sleeping like a child. It's best we leave him for the time being. The medicine he was given seems very strong. He was conscious for a short spell this morning, but nothing he said made any sense.'

They both sat in silence for a while. Tom's face was suffused with melancholy.

'Is it over for us, Mrs T?'

She straightened herself in her chair.

'No, Tom, it's not over – far from it. We now have to work even harder and make best use of the time we still have. The trial simply came on us too soon. We're not going to give up now.'

'Well, I'm ready to do everything I can. Should I go and see Uncle Jack at once? – There may be a way he can help us. I have to talk with him!'

'That's good, yes… But we must share our stock of news first. We mustn't let things run away with us.'

Tom's frustration had been mounting all day, and he was thirsting for action.

'I'm sorry, Mrs T… I just feel I have to be doing!'

'Of course, and you will. But first, there's something you need to see, and something you need to hear… Since you left this morning there have been developments…'

Tom's attention was caught.

'… And you must also tell me more about the trial. I don't expect a full report, but I want to know what was said, and what sleight of hand there was – you've been hinting there was some trickery. It may suggest a line of enquiry…'

Tom noticed a gleam in her eye. In spite of the verdict, he could see that her old enthusiasm was bubbling up again.

'... But you also need to *eat* something, Tom – It's now almost five, and I doubt you've even thought of dinner.'

He frowned as if the very idea was a distraction, but his empty stomach said 'yes, please.'

'I'll delve in the kitchen for something savoury. But first of all, you must read this – it's come for you...'

Mrs Trotter reached over to the sideboard and took up a letter from a pewter tray.

'... It was delivered by hand an hour ago – look at that crest! I've been longing to break the seal, but have been practising heroic self-control. Something tells me its contents may be important.'

Tom took the letter and turned it over. The paper was gilt-edged, and impressed into the black wax was a handsome crest. It appeared to be a chevron with three birds – crows perhaps? It was not his uncle's seal. He hesitated. A thought was beginning to form.

'Open it, Tom!'

He broke the seal and unfolded the paper. Rather than being a full letter, it was a short note:

Mr Bristowe –

I have news for you – The poems have been returned to me! The package was brought this morning by a frightened girl – I talked with her and tried to learn something before she fled – She did not ask for money –

If you wish to call, I shall be able to reveal more –

I hope you will also bring news of the trial – I am anxious to hear what occurred –

Julia Norreys

'Read this, Mrs T! – it's from Lady Norreys...'

Widow Trotter's hand grasped the note. Tom heard her breathe out heavily while she read.

'... The *frightened girl* – don't you think it must be Kate Primrose? Who else could it be?'

Her face lit up.

'Yes, it means she's alive and hasn't run far. Do you think Lady Norreys has her address?'

'I must call on her and find out. Can you believe it? It seems they talked together!'

Just then, an unbidden image flashed through Mrs Trotter's mind – of Lady Norreys and Kate Primrose standing hand-in-hand. The unlikely pathos of it struck her – what tricks the mind played!

'The poor girl – she wanted to restore the papers. She wasn't asking for payment.'

'I think she's settling Emmet's affairs, Mrs T – disentangling herself... I now see what I have to do. I'll call first on Lady Norreys in Charles Street, and then look in at my uncle's. That's my mission.'

'But first...?'

'But first, I need sustenance. *Bring me some pie!*... And while I eat, you must tell me your other news, and I'll tell you how the trial unfolded. There's so much we have to share.'

After Widow Trotter's news about Jeremy, Tom's early-evening walk to St James's passed in something of a trance. Down Long Acre the crowds were bustling around the shops and filling the pavement, but he hardly noticed them. By the time he crossed the open space of Leicester Fields his steps had settled into a rhythm, and his thoughts kept returning to the revelation of

Jeremy's treachery. Granted the fellow had acted naively, but the damage could never be repaired. In passing on the contents of Widow Trotter's note he had put Will's life in danger. Deacon, or one of his ruffians, must have got wind of Will's visit to Vinegar Yard and followed him.

Jem was evidently not as doltish as he appeared, and his stupid dawdling had been far from innocent. The discovery of his spying made sense and explained why the Good Fellowship had come under Ministry observation. What with Emmet telling tales about the place to Hopkins and Maynwaring, and Jeremy reporting to Harley's people, the coffee-room had become the centre of a political tug-of-war.

And yet, all these suspicions had sprouted from just a few tiny seeds: a trashy pamphlet that Jem had brought into the coffee-room, Will's involvement in retrieving Lady Norreys's pocket-book, some scraps of drunken versifying around the Mutton-Chops' punchbowl, and his own lost poem too. The fiction became real, and a plot had taken shape in people's minds, just as it had at the trial. That's how suspicion works, Tom thought: it encourages things to grow and supplies its own food. As he strode on, he turned recent events over in his mind, and by the time he stood waiting to cross the busy Haymarket he was meditating gloomily on the State of the Nation.

He realised that during the last few days he had lost some of his innocence. He had begun to see how sociableness – the very thing that should help us find good in each other – was bringing mistrust and opposition. What had gone wrong? Community was breeding faction. Little groups with their own interests were setting themselves against others. It was party warring against party. Perhaps *Bufo's Curse* was not a rant after all? He was beginning to think those verses were properly indignant. Yes, he thought, the finger is pointing at all of us.

Caught up in these reflections, he recalled just in time that he was heading for Charles Street, not Pall Mall, and he found himself sooner than expected at the door of the Norreys' elegant townhouse, reaching for the knocker.

Alexander the footman showed him into a smallish room off the entrance hall, where a newly-lit wood fire was crackling. Its walls were decorated in what looked like Chinese silk, and Tom's eyes followed the twisting branches of cherry blossom amongst which brightly-coloured birds were playing, peering from behind leaves or hanging from gnarled twigs. He was in danger of sinking into reverie when the door opened and Lady Norreys walked briskly in. She was clothed in silk herself – a green silk robe – and her hair was only half-dressed. A slightly flustered Tom rose to greet her.

'Mr Bristowe! Forgive the *dishabille* – you catch me preparing to launch myself on an evening party – the basset-table is beckoning! But I'm glad you've been able to call here so soon.'

'Yes, I was given your note when I arrived back from the trial. I apologise...'

'No, please don't! Let me sit down. You must tell me the verdict first of all. From your face, I fear the worst for your friend.'

'He was found guilty of murder, and will hang on Monday.'

She frowned with distaste.

'Was the sport bloody? These trials are like bear-baiting. You must be cast down by it?'

'Yes, it was unrelenting, and organised... but we are determined to fight on...'

Tom saw that a further question was forming on her lips, but he anticipated her.

'... I can tell you, Lady Norreys, that your pocket-book was not mentioned. No allusion was made to it.'

Her hands sank into her lap and she visibly relaxed.

'Thank you, Mr Bristowe – that's a great relief. But I trust that in not raising the matter...'

'No – it would have made no difference. The prosecution knew their ground and they never left it. They were remarkably well-managed – ruthlessly so.'

'And Bufo? I warrant that name was heard more than once!'

'It was – and in the most dramatic of circumstances.'

Tom began telling her about the reading – or rather performance – of *Bufo's Curse*, which had held the courtroom spellbound. Tom tried to remember some of it – he had written down a few of the lines. Lady Norreys smiled. She was amused at the title, and told him she recognised the verses from which it had been re-worked.

'Ah yes, that's our clever Mr Emmet again. What a waste! The man could wield the satirist's sword!'

Tom was looking for an ironic turn, but the praise seemed genuine. He went on to tell her briefly about his own evidence, and about the surprise witness who had lied on oath – that in the end Morphew's conviction had been inevitable.

'I'm shocked, Mr Bristowe. I've heard of such things – and when the charge is a capital one, giving false evidence amounts to murder.'

'Yes – it was outrageous, and it made Mr Morphew angry. I'm afraid that told against him. The jury didn't like it.'

Lady Norreys now had a picture of the day's ordeal, and how it must have played out as a gruesome mixture of tragedy and farce.

'I'm glad you are continuing to search for the truth, Mr Bristowe. But your time is very short. That's why I wanted you to know at once about the visit I had this morning – that strange girl who returned my papers to me...'

Tom was going to respond, but Lady Norreys was happy to speak without prompting.

'... The manuscripts were not all mine – there were a few transcriptions also, and one or two other things, I assume in Emmet's hand – I've not examined them fully yet. I need to go through them carefully tomorrow. Meanwhile they are well hidden from my husband's prying eyes, though he has been out of the house all day... and last night also,' she added.

Tom's urgency sounded impatient.

'Lady Norreys, this could be of the greatest importance... did you discover where the girl is living now?'

'No, she was very wary and unsettled – you see, my footman imprisoned her! The girl called at the basement kitchen and thrust a parcel into his hands. She told him it was for his mistress – that she was returning something I had lost. She was about to hurry away, but Alexander locked the door and sent for me. He suspected a theft or some other dubious dealing... Well, as soon as I saw her I knew what she was about.

'I sat her down and made it clear that I was grateful, and she became a bit easier – a glass of brandy helped... She told me about Mr Emmet and what had befallen him. This was when the poor girl became a little tearful. It seems the man had made promises to her and was full of ambitions to set himself up. But his activities had introduced him to some dangerous people and drawn him into matters of State. He had used her lodgings to store his papers, and this had put himself – and her – under suspicion. Last week she fled for her life and took the material with her. Emmet's death has terrified her, and she longs to free herself of the whole business. She insists she had always discouraged him. And now she's determined to set things right. Returning the papers to me was her way of cancelling his debts – wiping the slate clean. Rose wants to start afresh.'

'*Rose?*'

'I pressed her, and she told me her name was Rose Carter – I suspect it's invented. Or perhaps it's her new name? A sign of her life to come.'

Tom nodded.

'Ah yes. And so Kate Primrose becomes Rose Carter… the promise of spring becomes the glory of summer.'

'We all live on hopes, Mr Bristowe – that's a charming thought.'

'So you were given no hint of where she is now? We desperately want to find her.'

'I know how concerned you are – that's why I asked her for an address. I promised it would be kept close, but she shrank at the thought, and I can understand why. At this moment the girl needs to feel safe. She's now settled elsewhere, with a new name, and with none of those papers that brought such trouble. Once the storm has blown over I'm sure she'll be easy again… but of course, that's too late for you, isn't it?…'

Lady Norreys inspected Tom's furrowed brow.

'… With that in mind…'

She paused, as if approaching a delicate matter.

'… I took the liberty of telling her about you and Mr Lundy, and about the terrible trouble that has come to John Morphew. She knew of the murder, of course, but hadn't realised it was a false charge – that he was being made to take the blame for what was probably a political killing. This frightened her even more. But I watched her and could see her finding some determination beneath her fear. She's quite a strong young girl I think – she's had to be! And returning my papers was a brave thing to do.'

'Yes it was. You say she didn't ask for money?'

'No – and when I offered her something, she refused. It's clear she shuns the idea – too much like Emmet.'

'But does that mean she wants nothing more to do with the case?'

'I don't think so. As I said, I saw some steel in her.'

'Do I take it, then, that you gave her my address? I do hope so!'

'I took that liberty, Mr Bristowe. I thought it was the only thing to do... She may get in touch with you when she has thought matters over. I did stress how urgent it is, and gave a glowing account of your virtues – I told her you were sweet-natured, and a man of the highest principle – that indeed you were considering becoming a clergyman by profession.'

Tom grinned and reddened. No doubt the mischievous Lavinia had been telling tales.

'That's a desperate throw! I trust it won't deter her.'

'The thought should have occurred to me – but it didn't.'

'Will and I have been trying to find her...' Tom suddenly checked himself. 'Of course, you won't have heard what has happened to Will...'

Lady Norreys looked concerned. She caught the worry on Tom's face, and her own blanched.

'What? Is it something serious?'

He found himself telling her about the previous day's events, and how Will had been attacked and seemingly left for dead. As he spoke, all his fears surged up to the surface, and when he described seeing his friend stretched out on the alehouse table, he was visibly shaking.

'... But he's now in good hands, and it looks likely he will recover – although a wound so deep is always dangerous.'

Lady Norreys was shocked and looked at him intently.

'That makes your efforts at the trial even braver, Mr Bristowe. I can't tell you how earnestly I want you to succeed. You have a great cause to fight – and not just on Mr Morphew's behalf. A larger principle is at stake...'

There was a sudden fervour in her speech. Tom thought it would be a fine thing to watch her debating with Mrs Manley and the others. At that moment a thought struck her, and she leant forward sharply, touching him on the knee.

'You must go and see your uncle. He is a man of some influence. There may be something he can do?'

'As it happens, Lady Norreys, my plan is to go from here directly to Pall Mall. I hope to find him at home. As you say, there's not a moment to lose. Monday will be here before we know it.'

'In that case, Mr Bristowe, you must be gone at once...'

She sprang to her feet.

'... I mustn't detain you any longer. But you have to forgive me – I've offered you the most miserable entertainment... But I hope to put that right soon. Meanwhile I insist you keep me informed. I shall be thinking about you and Mr Lundy tonight – indeed, I suspect I'll be so distracted that my skill at cards will utterly desert me. But I shall bear the financial loss stoically.'

They were now at the door, and paused. For a brief moment Julia Norreys caught sight of her own image in the decorative wall mirror. Its oval frame was a riot of acanthus leaves and roses all covered in gold leaf, and it transformed her into a living portrait, bright-eyed and slightly dishevelled, as if a painter had tricked her off in rapid brush-strokes. She turned back to the earnest young man.

'How stupid our pastimes are, Mr Bristowe! How we allow our time to pass in such mindless pleasures. Yet just around the corner is a dangerous and cruel world which we choose to ignore. It's a sobering thought, isn't it?'

Chapter Thirty-Five

As Tom walked into the coffee-room he saw that Jenny Trip was presiding behind the bar. She caught his eye and turned aside from the two young men who were engaging her in conversation.

'You've missed the judge, Mr Bristowe – he's not two minutes gone!'

'Has Will's father been here?'

'Yes, and he had a dismal face on him. I think it's the look he carries around with him – the Law is a heavy matter! Your Mr Lundy, though, is wide awake and anxious to see you. Mrs Trotter says he's been running on at a gallop since he awoke, full of questions and hardly pausing for breath.'

'Is Mrs T with him?'

'No, she slipped out a while ago. She's over at Katherine Street visiting her friend. I don't expect she'll be long. But Mr Lundy will be glad to see you.'

And Tom was very glad to see Will. He was sitting up in bed with a thick woollen muffler over his shoulders, looking remarkably alert and eager to talk. Papers of different kinds borrowed from the coffee-room were scattered round him as if he was determined to make up for the missing day. His whole constitution seemed excited, and it was clear that his father's visit had not left him easier in his mind. Tom began to wonder if the coffee-pot he had brought with him was altogether a good idea.

A few moments later Will cradled the hot dish in his left hand and sipped the coffee hungrily. In fact this seemed to settle him a little, and they were soon able to talk more calmly about the trial.

'Mrs Trotter tells me you performed heroically, Tom. I doubt there was anything more *I* could have done.'

'But it wasn't enough. My carefully rehearsed argument went for nothing. The fine particulars were too minute, and my deductions nothing but speculation – it was as if I was interrupting the proceedings. I remember your words about the impatience of juries – how right you were! *Justice* isn't a wise matron holding her scales in balance – she's a lazy old woman who turns a deaf ear when it suits her.'

'I'm afraid I've just tangled with His Honour the Judge on that very subject. In fact it turned into a blazing quarrel. "Hemp" is unshakeable sometimes – like a dog at a butcher's heels – won't give an inch! I put the case to him directly, but he insisted that in Court the sworn statement is all. The only truths are those witnessed on oath, and the rest is conjecture, which is slippery and not to be trusted.'

'That's well and good. It might work in a God-fearing Commonwealth.'

'Exactly, Tom. It's his religion – he thinks every witness is a soul standing before God. It says much for his integrity, but the way of the world is different.'

'Did you ask him about the Knight of the Post?'

'Ah! Mr *Wise!* – do you think the name was Voyce's little joke? – Yes, I pressed him hard on it – and on much more. Now the case is no longer *sub judice* I could tell him everything. And I spoke my mind, believe me. He didn't like it, and the more I told him of our investigations the more uneasy he became. By the time I reached our visit to Newgate he was exceedingly grim. He was having to face the thought that his beloved courtroom is a place of lies and deception. I refused to give up until he swore he would inquire about the mock-gentleman from Romford. I think he is genuinely shocked.'

'But a man of his experience, surely... ?'

Tom's question brought no answer, and they both drank their coffee. He noticed that Will became tense with pain when he moved.

'... But of course, at the trial it was John Morphew who was the true hero. He remembered your advice and acquitted himself bravely. You would have been proud of him. He certainly unsettled Voyce and Buller – his questioning was tenacious – he's something of a bulldog himself.'

And so, Tom went on to give Will a full account of the trial's dramatic course. He could see that his friend was growing increasingly restless. By the end, instead of being cast down, he was animated and thirsting for action.

'But what are we going to do *now*, Tom? I've been insensible all day – and that busy surgeon threatens to return tonight and dose me again. I hate to be lying here chewing the lotus – is there nothing I can help with? I want to be active!'

He shifted his position slightly and winced with the discomfort.

'No, you've got to lie still and be patient. You've already done something important: you've sown the seed of doubt in your father's mind, and he's not a man to let doubts linger. We may yet see something come of this.'

Will's mind was obviously racing.

'I never did speak with Mrs Purslowe. Did I tell you about Mrs Purslowe?'

'Yes, Will, you told me yesterday – before you slipped away on your golden cloud.'

'She's sure to know something – Kate Primrose was one of her girls, and so was Polly Gray – Kate and Polly – *Clarissa* and *Daphne!* The nymphs of romance! And I told you about the enchanting *Corinna* did I not? She's now in Clarissa's place. We have to go and see Mrs Purslowe. She must know something...'

Tom looked with concern at his friend.

'This is all in hand, Will. I'll go there tomorrow morning and do what I can. Right now you have to calm yourself. Your father excited you, and now I've been running on about the trial and making you restless, just when you need to have quiet.'

'But I don't want quiet, Tom... I'm sorry, I just keep thinking how much we need to know. It's all crowding into my mind: Maynwaring – Voyce – Buller – the Duchess – Hopkins – Sunderland – Addison – Harley – St John – Deacon – If only we could capture them all, lock them in a room together, and make them tell us the truth – tell us what has been going on! It's there, Tom, isn't it?'

Tom nodded. He understood. This wasn't mania, but rather a pent-up vexation at all that had been going on. And he shared something of it himself. Will continued trying, not very successfully, to control his thoughts:

'You must stop me from talking wildly... It's just that I feel I've lost a whole day when every hour is vital – every second. I've been thinking, Tom. Tomorrow is the Queen's Birthday, is it not?'

'Yes, the day of days! – there'll be fireworks exploding everywhere, and bonfires and illuminations wherever you look.'

'And the *Birth-night Ball* at the palace tomorrow night... You told me you'd been invited to join your uncle's party.'

Tom laughed at the absurdity of the thought.

'Whatever made you recall that? It's unthinkable after the horrors of this morning. The very thought of mingling with all that finery – the glitter, the fashions, the formality of the whole performance. I certainly shan't go.'

'But you *must* go! In my imagination I can see you there. I feel something is going on – and that's where it's going to happen!'

'Your imagination has been too restless altogether, Will.'

'But I'm serious. You've told your uncle about the trial, haven't you?'

'No, not yet. I called round this evening, but he's out until late. I'm going to call again tomorrow for an early dinner, when I've had my meeting with Mrs Purslowe.'

'But don't you see, Tom, right now we need to be in the thick of things. That is where they'll be – *everybody* will be at the Royal ball! Your uncle is very busy and you may miss him again. You must send over a note telling him you'll accompany them to the palace. You have to go with them!'

Tom looked at his friend.

'What on earth can I learn at the ball? I doubt I would discover anything to our purposes. And besides, I ought to stay here in case there's a message from Kate Primrose.'

Will was startled.

'*What?* Now it's you with the frenzied imagination. I know you think I'm not making sense, but…'

'I was intending to tell you, but I've been hanging back. You've had so much news all at once, I wondered if I should leave you in peace.'

'Tell me! What is this about Kate Primrose? I have to know.'

'Well, it's hopeful news – as hopeful as anything we have at present…'

With a degree of reluctance Tom told Will about his visit to Lady Norreys, and about Kate's return of her missing 'Bufo' papers.

'… So, there's a chance that Kate might – only *might* – wish to see me. But I hardly dare to hope…'

'I don't believe this, Tom! You tell me all the disheartening news, but the one thing that could cheer me you leave unsaid.

This could be our lifeline! I know I've been raving a little, but *good* news isn't going to tip me into Bedlam.'

Tom looked shamefaced. Will was right of course – his logic was impeccable.

'I'm sorry, Will. I think I'm the one who is confused. It's just that I've been so concerned about you. The surgeon said you shouldn't be excited. All the time I've been thinking I should let you rest.'

'No, Tom, it's rest which has made me anxious. I want to be active – at least in mind. The more news the better. That will calm me down. It's a paradox – but like most paradoxes it's *doubly* true.'

Tom was heartened to hear his friend's wit returning. He saw the force of what Will had said and allowed himself to relax; and so for a while they talked things over quietly as if they were sitting in a tavern together.

But this was to be a night of further revelations. They had not long settled into their conversation when there was a noise on the stairs and Widow Trotter made a dramatic appearance in the doorway. She stood there hesitating, like a messenger on the stage bringing news of a battle, but who had forgotten her lines. She looked at Tom and Will with widened eyes, torn between delivering ill tidings and announcing an important discovery. She was bringing both, and so was a little perplexed.

'What is it, Mrs T?' said Will. 'Has something happened?'

Mrs Trotter strode into the room and sat down heavily on a chest at the foot of the bed.

'It's Poor Adèle!…'

She threw her cloak open and took a deep breath.

'… Where will it end? Another victim! This business of ours is far from over – first Kate Primrose, then Tom, and now Adèle!'

'Do you mean she's had *visitors?*' said Tom, who at once saw the drift.

'Yes, and not invited ones – her apartment has been thoroughly tumbled. They've carried off her precious papers – almost all of what she had – her bundles of letters... I've been trying to comfort her, but the poor woman is inconsolable. She was out at the time or I dread to think what would have happened. She's quite frail, and this has shaken her...'

Widow Trotter looked shaken herself.

'... She has lost her past – *and* her future.'

Tom and Will looked at each other. It was Tom who spoke.

'But, Mrs T, why have they taken her papers?...'

He was looking thoughtful, and his mind was working quickly.

'... Is there a connection here?... I suppose Emmet is the link?'

'Yes, Tom. There's a very strong connection. I hardly know where to begin... This could be a helpful turn of events. It sounds heartless, but at long last we may have found our *clue*, and yet I can only feel uncomfortable about it... Poor Adèle!... You see, I'm the one to blame.'

She was beginning to sound despairing.

'*You*, Mrs T? How can that be?'

'It was the scribbled note I sent round to Adèle yesterday and stupidly left unsealed – the note that Jeremy read. I mentioned a shared secret. It was a dangerous matter not to be spoken of, and yet I alluded to it in the note... I mentioned the valuable *letter* that she was guarding.'

She awarded the word its proper emphasis. Will spoke first, his mind hurrying.

'*Letter?* What letter?..... You can't mean the one that Polly Gray stole and sold to Emmet?'

There was an electric silence. Mrs Trotter nodded.

'Of course!' said Tom, 'Kate Primrose must have taken it to Mrs Ménage for safe keeping.'

She was reddening by this point. It was partly embarrassment at her earlier silence, but also a glow of relief at being able to lay her burden down at last and tell her friends the truth.

She told them how during her visit to Katherine Street Mrs Ménage had brought the sealed letter from its hiding-place and showed it to her in the strictest confidence – and that it bore the direction *To the Right Honourable Mr St John*.

The revelation hit home.

'Henry St John!' Tom cried out.

'Did you read it?'

'What did it contain?'

Widow Trotter had expected a note of resentment – after all, she had been keeping this news from them. But they were simply excited. They hung on every word as she described how she and Adèle had sat down, had broken the seal and read the letter together. She emphasised that she had sworn not to speak a word of its contents to anyone – and that this had been a binding promise.

Will was leaning forward eagerly, his face registering a physical pain that his mind was ignoring.

'Yes, but what did it *say*? Who was the letter from?'

'Why are you telling us now, Mrs T?' said Tom, more quizzically.

'I can tell you now because Adèle is *angry*. She is indignant at the theft of her papers, and at the trial verdict. She wants us to pursue the matter and use the letter if need be. I had told her about your loss, Tom, and she sees you as a fellow victim… But we must keep the secret between us still – not for the sake of it, but because of what the letter contains. It concerns something which, if known, will *shake the State*.'

She pronounced the portentous words with a due sense of their effect. Will was clearly unhappy:

'But now the letter has been stolen, Mrs T – this *secret* – whatever it is – will be secret no more!'

'Ah, Will!... fortunately my old friend Adèle is a wise old bird, and she chose another wise old bird to guard the letter... The document was kept separate from her own papers, concealed in a secret drawer in a birdcage. Her cupboards were searched and her wardrobe dashed to the ground and its contents taken. They rampaged about in frustration! The birdcage was pushed over and the old bullfinch escaped. But they didn't think to examine the cage carefully... and so the letter was still in its hiding-place. When I was there just now the bird was perched on the cornice, singing its commentary on the adventure and telling the world how it had heroically survived.'

Tom and Will began smiling. It was as if a page had turned.

'But the contents, Mrs T,' said Will quietly but insistently. 'What did the letter contain?'

So, at last, Widow Trotter could tell them of Elizabeth Greg's letter in which she begged Henry St John to help save her husband's life; and how the document revealed that Robert Harley had concealed Greg's treason and had offered to turn a blind eye to it. The import of this news struck Tom and Will forcibly. It was a document to arouse fierce political passions and make men do anything to possess it – both those who longed to use it, and those who needed to destroy it.

'That's motive for murder indeed!' said Will. 'I can see why Harley and St John might kill to recover that letter. And Sunderland too of course – it would give him enormous power over them. Think how he could exploit it!'

Tom turned to Mrs Trotter.

'You said Emmet had re-attached the seal – so he clearly knew the letter's contents and the fortune it could command. Given his ambitions he would surely offer it to both parties?'

'Yes, a foolish, deadly game! And now, thanks to him, Kate Primrose and Adèle are in danger of their lives.'

'And we have to be careful too,' said Will, 'because we're all dispensable. We're insignificant characters in the drama, and easily brushed away. But now perhaps we can cause a stir? We've achieved a lot on our own, but at this point we need help from *on high* – and I don't mean the saints in Heaven!'

'What *do* you mean?' said Tom.

'It's in the Great World that fates are decreed – in Westminster and St James's – and that's where Morphew's fate will be decided. Isn't this our opportunity? We know the whereabouts of the letter, and we know what it contains – and this gives us power. Surely we have to take the initiative now and raise the stakes... confront Henry St John himself!'

Will was fired up and spoke as if he were rousing a street mob. His two hearers shrank back a little. Their hearts assented, though they remained in their seats.

'You mean, confront him with the killings of Polly Gray – and Emmet?' said Widow Trotter tentatively, hardly believing she was speaking those words.

'Well, with what he may have done directly, or indirectly through a proxy. After all... we do have friends in high places.'

Will looked meaningfully at Tom, who shifted in his seat.

'Is that why you want me to go to the ball tomorrow? That's a fearful mission!'

Widow Trotter's antennae shivered.

'The *ball?*... Do you mean the *Birth-night Ball?* At the palace?'

'Yes, Mrs T. I'm to go with the Pophams... but after today's happenings I decided I just couldn't face the idea.'

'But Tom,' persisted Will, 'we badly need the help of your uncle. You have to talk with him and ask his advice. Open your heart to him and explain the situation. He's intimate with St John, and to have him on our side...'

'Are you suggesting Tom tells Lord Melksham about the letter?' said Mrs Trotter doubtfully.

Will paused. He understood what taking that step might mean.

'Only Tom can judge that, Mrs T... but if events warrant it...'

'Uncle Jack is trustworthy,' said Tom, 'and he trusts me too. He tells me things in confidence sometimes – bits of gossip that it does him good to talk about. If I reverse the play, I'm sure he'll understand.'

'Does that mean you'll do it?' said Will. 'You'll go?'

'But I could do that tomorrow when I pay my call in Pall Mall.'

'No, Tom, if this is to be carried through, you must be in the same room as Henry St John. He will surely be at the ball. It's your only chance!'

Tom felt queasy and looked to Widow Trotter for support. But a glance in her direction told him it was a vain hope. He felt ambushed.

'But what should I do? Do you expect me to accuse St John? To whisper in his ear? Appeal to his sense of honour?... Threaten him with a blackmail?'

'Listen, Tom – this letter implicates not only Harley, but St John too. The men's fates are bound up together in Greg's treason. If the contents become public, then St John's career will be ruined. During the past few days he must have been sweating with worry, wondering if the letter would be brandished in court. Surely he'll embrace anyone who brings reassurance? You can discover what he really thinks of Morphew, and what his own role has been. In a way, it's continuing your conversation at the ridotto.'

'But, Will, *he* may be our murderer! After all, it's his pocket-watch and his letter – and you've admitted he might kill to recover it.'

'In that case, your position is all the stronger – though I admit more dangerous...'

Tom was beginning to wonder if this whole conversation had been a whirling fantasy. Will was clearly tuned to a high pitch; his talk was wild and the whole scheme reckless... but there was a grain of sense – just a single grain – in what he was saying. Morphew's life was hanging by a thread, and perhaps this was the moment for a bold enterprise? Tom smiled to himself when he thought that the great Marlborough might regard such a skirmish as a thrilling challenge.

'I'll go to the ball,' he said.

Friday

6 February 1708

Chapter Thirty-Six

HALF WAY ALONG Rose Street, Mr Gallini's shop was easy enough to find. The apothecary advertised himself by a giant pestle and mortar in wrought iron, which dangled precariously over the doorway. Widow Trotter had seen the notice in the newspaper half an hour earlier: *Found in Rose Street, a handsome gold watch, with crest finely engrav'd. The owner describing the marks may have it again for a consideration...* At once she had jumped up and determined to pay a visit. If the timepiece was still unclaimed she might be able to inspect it – not to claim it herself, but on the pretext of offering Mr Gallini a purse of guineas for it in a week's time, should the owner not come forward...

She opened the door apprehensively, hoping she would be early enough to have a sight of the precious object. A bell tinkled by her ear as she negotiated the step down into a room that had something of the character of a necromancer's grotto. Bunches of herbs hung from the arched ceiling, and the alcoves on three sides were shelved with row upon row of bottles in all shapes and colours. She had expected an unsettling odour to hang about the place, and was pleasantly surprised by the warm herbal smell and the hints of liquorice and garlic that seemed to predominate. After a few seconds, a figure appeared who was hugging a large moulded vessel to his stomach. It was no alchemist but a well-rounded gentleman with a shock of grey frizzled hair. He put the exotic object down on the counter with care.

'Ah! Mr Gallini, is it?'

'Madam, it is!'

Widow Trotter made her inquiry with a polite directness and an encouraging smile, assuring him that she simply wished to register her interest in the watch as an object of *virtù*.

Signor Gallini's reply was equally gracious.

'Alas, madam, I am sorry to disappoint you, but the watch has this morning found its way back to its owner. A happy outcome for him – though not, I fear, for you!'

Widow Trotter expressed her disappointment, but continued her inquiry. If she couldn't view the object itself she would try to learn what she could about it. The apothecary was most obliging. No, the watch had no initials engraved, but was distinctive as it carried on the outer case a handsome family crest of a boar with a crown above it, finely chased in silver. 'It was an exquisite item indeed – I was sorry to part with it!'

Widow Trotter thanked Signor Gallini warmly for his trouble, and ventured to inquire who had collected the item… it was clearly a rare piece and she was curious to know…

The apothecary continued to sustain a polite countenance. The person who collected it was not a gentleman, but a well-dressed young lady. Her brother had unaccountably lost it while walking along Rose Street a week ago… She gave no name, but was able to identify the distinguishing features of the watch – and was delighted to recover it.

'Yes, and how fortunate that an honest man found it, Mr Gallini! – I take it the thing was dropped outside your shop? You must have looked down at it in astonishment.'

The apothecary rode the lively question with ease.

'It was a passer-by, madam – an honest citizen indeed! There was a small consideration, which I shall certainly pass on to him...'

As she made her way back towards the piazza, Mrs Trotter felt she had accomplished something, though her reception was not at all as she had expected. What a polite apothecary that was – unlike her surly old gentleman in the Colonnade! But the man evidently had a nice little extension to his business and could perhaps afford to be cheerful. She noted the shop and quickened her step homewards, thinking about the engraved crest and its aristocratic signification.

It was well into the afternoon when Tom returned from his own visits, ready to change into formal attire for the ball. Mrs Trotter was bursting with curiosity and anxious to reveal her own news. And so, within half an hour she had settled things in the coffee-room and convened a conference around Will's bed – an arrangement that appeared to give him the role of presiding chairman.

Tom was much relieved to see him.

'I'm glad you're wide awake, Will – in spite of the surgeon's best efforts, I suspect?'

'I'm afraid I've behaved very badly. When his back was turned I tipped the soporific into the piss-pot and gave a fine performance of swallowing air.'

'The prognosis remains good,' said Mrs Trotter. 'The wound is clean, and Mr Proby re-bandaged him. I only heard him cry out once!'

'And that was in protest at his endless anecdotes. I've had to live through some horrific cases. He must find me humdrum in comparison.'

'Good! I hope you continue to disappoint him,' said Tom.

'You'll be glad to know that our field-general has something to report. She's been keeping me in suspense until you arrived.'

'In that case, Will, you must call us both to order, and let her have the floor.'

And so Widow Trotter began describing her visit to the apothecary in Rose Street, and what she had learned about the watch.

'... It's a fine thing by his account – solid gold, with a grand crest – a boar surmounted by a crown, embossed in silver. A good thirty pounds' worth, I would think...' Tom whistled.

'... But the man didn't collect it in person. It was a woman.'

'St John's face is well known,' said Will, 'so he wouldn't call there himself. Surely it must be him?... The crown points to a distinguished family.'

'It looks almost certain,' said Tom. 'But I'll ask my uncle this evening. He'll know Henry St John's coat of arms and can confirm it. Oh dear, this makes my mission even more delicate. If I mention his watch, he'll think I've been prying into his activities.'

'Well, he'd be right,' said Mrs Trotter helpfully. 'So you must tread carefully and take things one step at a time... We're loading a lot onto you!'

Will was restless.

'But what's your own news, Tom? Did you come face to face with the redoubtable Mrs Purslowe? I've been picturing her as a virago.'

'Well, she's a woman of business certainly. She has a string of girls who cater for most tastes and all pockets. But it would be unwise to cross her. When I mentioned Clarissa she exploded in annoyance. I told her that Kate had been physically attacked, but that made no difference. "Well, she should have come to me!" she said, and I suppose she has a point.'

'I take it she doesn't know Kate's whereabouts?' said Mrs Trotter.

'No, certainly not. I suspect our Clarissa is hiding from her as much as from her attacker!'

'And what about Polly Gray?'

'Now in that, Mrs Purslowe gave evidence of humanity. She's been startled by the killing – and she's certain Polly *was* killed. She's had suspicions from the beginning, but what convinces her is a visitor she had only yesterday. The woman is nobody's fool, and now she realises there must be a link between Polly's killing and Kate's flight. She told me in some annoyance that *I* wasn't the first to come inquiring...'

Widow Trotter looked away, hardly daring to ask.

'... She's received a visit from George Deacon.'

'That man is haunting us!'

'What was he after?' said Will. 'He wouldn't be inquiring about Polly, would he?'

'No,' said Tom. 'It was Kate Primrose he was looking for. I tried not to appear embarrassed, but Mrs Purslowe could sense my awkwardness – "I suppose you're after her *papers* too, are you?" she said. "I don't know what the girl was up to, but what value any papers of hers could have defeats me!" She gave me such a contemptuous look. "I'll tell you exactly what I told him," she said. "If I get wind of that Clarissa, she'll have *nothing* to call her own – not even the clothes she stands up in!"'

Widow Trotter was living the drama.

'That confirms what we suspected. Deacon must surely be searching for the letter, and the trail has led him from Polly Gray, to Kate... and to Adèle...'

'Yes,' said Will, 'he's been hired by Harley's men to find the letter at all costs. That's what we have to assume... but something is making me uneasy... In all of this, are we not forgetting Mr Morphew? He has been the victim of Maynwaring and Voyce, and their Whig paymasters. But now we're taken up with the opposing gang – with Harley, St John, and their man Deacon. Is this distracting us? We're tangled in *two* spider's webs! We have to think how they might be connected.'

'I'm sure they are, said Tom. That was part of the conversation I had with Uncle Jack when I left Mrs Purslowe's.'

'Good – so your talk with Lord Melksham yielded something?' asked Mrs Trotter.

'On both sides. We had a good half hour's conversation... I told him I would accompany them to the palace.'

'Excellent!' said Will. 'Did you broach the subject of the Greg letter?'

'Not its contents – I thought I should keep that card in my hand. But I did tell him we suspect Henry St John is using Deacon to track down a stolen letter, and that a girl may have been murdered because of it.'

'What did your uncle say to that?'

'He shook his head in dismay, but wasn't entirely surprised. He says it's political manoeuvring, with each party digging furiously in the dirt. But he was shocked at St John's involvement. I told him I hoped to confront him tonight – if I can keep my courage up.'

'Did he mention Harley?' asked Will.

'Yes, and he's convinced Harley and St John are acting in close partnership – holding secret meetings and backstairs discussions. Something is afoot, and he thinks the storm will break soon.'

'Well, that may be the wider picture,' said Mrs Trotter, 'but how does it help *us*? The only picture I can see is poor Mr Morphew in the condemned cell – the horror of it! And on Monday he is to be strung up at Tyburn – if he survives until then. He's lying there at this very moment, counting off the hours, lost and terrified...'

The blood drained from her face as she spoke.

'... I'm sorry, gentlemen. I know we're doing everything we can, but I frankly despair of these great men and their *manoeuvrings*. We discuss them endlessly and watch the pieces changing position on the board... But can we not do something to shake the pieces up? Can't we intervene? With your uncle on our side, Tom, we have a chance.'

This was fighting talk, and both Tom and Will shared her restlessness. Tom nodded in agreement.

'Yes – perhaps we have to confront them. We know things about both sides – enough, perhaps, to pin these men in their corners. Can we somehow make use of their enmities?'

'What do you mean?' said Mrs Trotter.

'Well, once we have our facts to hand, we can choose our place to strike – set one against the other. Both Secretaries of State – Harley and Sunderland – have it in their power to release Morphew without appeal to the Queen, and that could work for us. The threat of having their plotting exposed and reaching Her Majesty's ear – might persuade one of them to settle the matter?'

Will was impressed.

'That's bold enough, Tom! You mean, we must challenge the two parties directly?'

'Yes, we need a lever to prise them apart – make their antagonisms work for us.'

'I think the two of *you* are politicians,' said Widow Trotter, not altogether admiringly. 'You certainly seem to have read the same manual!'

'To catch a fox, you have to think like a fox,' said Will.

Widow Trotter gave him the kind of smile that age bestows on youth.

'That brings us to tonight,' said Tom. 'Will tells me he's had a premonition that the Birth-night Ball will bring the crisis. If so, we must await the *dire event*, whatever it is.'

'That sounds fanciful to me,' said Mrs Trotter, 'but he may be right. Perhaps narcotic dreams can be prophetic?'

She spoke; and as if someone were answering her words, a distant bang was felt and the room gave a slight shudder. There was an ominous sound on the stairs, and for a few seconds the three of them thought they were hearing the irresistible tread of Fate. When the door finally opened and a red-faced Elias Cobb appeared, they were only partly reassured: his entrances in recent days had boded ill, and so they feared the worst.

'I think you should see this,' he said, 'I've just given a penny for it in Drury Lane.'

He held out a printed broadside, its text in closely-set type beneath a crude illustration. Widow Trotter took it from him, studied it for a moment, then looked sadly into his eyes.

The sheet of paper featured a woodcut in which, alongside a poorly-drawn printing-press, a man with a crazed expression on his face was hitting another over the head with a walking-cane. The text was obviously the narrative of Emmet's killing as described in yesterday's trial. Its title was eloquent enough. It read:

> *The Curser Curs'd! A True Account of the Frightful Murder in the Printing-house. With the genuine Curse of Bufo.*

'Oh, Elias!' she said. 'Already the vultures are gathering!'

Chapter Thirty-Seven

'... And so, Mr Cobb, you see where we stand!'

Will paused, and looked at Tom and Mrs Trotter in turn.

The constable's large frame was perched on a stool by the foot of the bed and he felt distinctly uncomfortable. The three friends had been telling him of their latest discoveries, and now their attention had turned to himself.

'What we require from you, Mr Cobb,' said Tom, 'is the entire truth. We've been trying to see patterns and motives, but now the conjecture has to end. Things have to be pushed to their crisis.'

'There are great dangers,' said the grim-faced constable. 'I don't want to see any of you come to harm.'

Will raised a hand.

'Then look at *me*, Mr Cobb, and tell me what you see! I might have come to less harm had I known more...'

Elias looked at the young man bandaged and propped up in bed, and kept silent.

'... The man who attacked me knew my movements. I'll never forget the last thing I saw just as everything went black: the man walking off nonchalantly as if taking a stroll in the park. He was so sure of himself, Mr Cobb! He knew about

Tom and me – where we would be and what we were looking for. And he knew because of Jeremy's spying. When Jem took the contents of that note to George Deacon's secret office – if that's what it is – we were all put in danger. But *we* knew nothing of it!'

'Ignorance is more dangerous than knowledge,' added Tom philosophically. 'I lost my precious papers because of it. The thief knew exactly what he wanted and where it would be found.'

'But I've been as shocked as any of you at what has happened – and especially by Jeremy.'

'Shocked, Elias, perhaps,' said Mrs Trotter, 'but not truly *surprised*. You've known about Deacon's activities – more than a little. You hinted as much to me on Wednesday.'

Tom added to the battery.

'We should have been told about Deacon and his connections to Harley's gang. We've left him out of the picture for too long – and look what has happened!'

Mrs Trotter became effusive.

'Elias, my old friend – you have to help us! Mr Morphew is to die on Monday, and we're determined to do all we can to stop it. We need you on our side.'

The constable was taken aback by the comment.

'I'm *entirely* on your side, Molly! How could you doubt it? But in my line of work I have to keep in the shadows. I'm forced to be a little devious and glean what I can. Believe me, I'm still pursuing your cause... but it worries me to hear you're going to break cover. It sounds desperate.'

'And desperate action is needed, Elias! The powerful have to be confronted with their crimes. We finally have some power ourselves, and we must use it.'

The constable knew when he'd met his match.

'I surrender! But please don't think I've been misleading you. The forces you are facing are organised against each other.

And just like Emmet, you've been caught in between, raising the suspicions of both parties. I've told you a great deal...'

Elias shuffled on his uncomfortable stool and undid the remaining buttons of his coat.

'... Your surmise about Henry St John is all too plausible. The young man has a reputation for whoring, and he often boasts of his frolics. I'm not surprised Polly Gray cozened him. And you're right about his role in Mr Harley's faction: he cultivates links among Harley's friends, including Defoe and the whole set of hacks-for-hire; and he and Harley run ranks of informers and tattlers. It's clear that Jem has been one of those. They all feed into the system. George Deacon is securely placed within it, but from what you say he seems to have overstepped the mark. Until now the man has been confident of protection – but this could leave him exposed. He may have become an embarrassment.'

'But his activities must be known,' said Tom. 'Does no-one have authority to move against him? It seems innocent people can be snatched off the street, while a violent rogue like him is given full licence.'

Elias shook his head.

'There would need to be a serious charge. The "powers that be" will handle him carefully, given all the dirty corners he's been in.'

'He may have been putting another ruffian to work on his behalf,' said Widow Trotter ruefully. 'These people are like fleas on rats!'

'Ah, said Tom. That rings a bell... *In Spencer's service like a rat serves fleas, / Sign of our body politick's disease.*'

'Bufo again!' said Will. 'Little did we know how far the disease would spread...'

His brow furrowed.

'... But is there more you can tell us about the other gang, Mr Cobb? – about Buller, Voyce, and the scheming

Arthur Maynwaring?... And where does Hopkins fit into the picture?'

'Very uneasily at present, Mr Lundy. A power struggle is rattling the doors at the Cockpit. It's only a tremor as yet, but Mr Addison and Mr Hopkins are finding your schemer Maynwaring is getting above himself...'

Elias leant forward, elbow on knee, suddenly more intense.

'... One thing I *have* heard – only today – is that Mr Morphew was released last Friday night on the orders of Mr Hopkins and Mr Addison – much to Maynwaring's annoyance! He and the Duchess had been pressing for a prosecution. Maynwaring was furious that they over-ruled him and allowed Morphew to slip away!'

'That would explain why he and Voyce took over the second interview,' said Will.

'Word has it that knives are out in the Cockpit,' said Elias. 'That's the sum of all I know...'

He paused and looked at Mrs Trotter.

'... Just crumbs of gossip – little things let fall... You mustn't think I'm holding anything back.'

She returned a smile. Her friend was managing to bear up under his rough treatment, and she offered a helping hand:

'I have to say, gentlemen, Elias has been doing what he can. The Watch have been patrolling around Katherine Street in case Deacon or one of his gang thinks of paying a return visit. We tried to reassure Adèle, but she's naturally fearful. Mr Denniston – he of the toy-shop – is accommodating her downstairs in his apartment while her own is set right.'

'That's good,' said Tom. 'But perhaps the Watch should pay a visit to that shop in the Colonnade – Jeremy's reporting station? Let *them* feel threatened – enough to shift their operations elsewhere!'

'Yes,' said Will. 'And we ought to be looking after Jeremy too.

After his revelations, he must be fearful of retribution – I know I would be.'

'You're right,' said Elias. 'These are not people to provoke. Your Mr Barnard the compositor, for example...'

'What of him?' said Tom. 'He was nowhere to be seen at the trial, and never gave his evidence... Are you saying he was frightened?'

'He was warned not to appear as a witness. I had a note to that effect from a friend who was observing the proceedings for me...'

'You had someone attending the trial?' said Mrs Trotter.

'Indeed I did,' said Elias with a knowing smile. 'After all, I had a direct interest in the case, and I wanted to make sure my own evidence was on record... Incidentally, he spoke highly of your contribution, Mr Bristowe...'

Tom and Will looked at each other, both amazed at the constable's capacity to seize the initiative. It was clear he had his own office of intelligence – where did it all end?

'... It seems that Paul Barnard was persuaded not to show himself. Mere mention was made of his dear wife and child... and that was enough. The prosecution thought he might reveal too much and not be in tune with the evidence of Voyce and Buller. They wanted things to be tidy.'

Tom shook his head in despair at how predictable this was.

'And so, Justice is suborned,' said Will solemnly. The whole fabric of the Law is torn to shreds. What a profession awaits me!... perhaps it's not for me after all.'

'On the contrary!' said Tom vehemently. 'Every part of the Law needs reformation – from the Law of the Land to the law of the streets. You can't wash your hands of it. And from what you told me, I warrant your father is coming to see it more and more.'

'I've done my best with him. He has always been suspicious of power, and he detests the endless political warfare. And as for the Court and its luxuries, nothing sets him *growling* more! It stirs the Cromwellian spirit of his grandfather. The fearsome Colonel Lundy fought the tyrant Charles at Marston Moor, and I think Hemp sometimes wishes he had a troop of horse himself!'

Mrs Trotter gestured toward Tom with a graceful sweep of her hand:

'In that case, I'm glad he can't see this young gentleman in all his finery – it would annoy him so!'

Throughout their conversation Tom had been conscious of his St James's clothes. He had already changed into what was a relatively plain version of Court dress – his Popham suit. It fell far short of the lavishly embroidered birthday suits that would be gliding around the ballroom as if by their own impetus. But he understood what was hidden beneath all that courtesy and decorum. The whole occasion would be an elegant dance in which delicate manners and crude power partnered each other.

Tom said his goodbyes with a wave of his hat, and after a few mock-bows from his friends he began negotiating the steep stairs in his buckled court shoes, leaving Widow Trotter, Constable Cobb and Will to continue talking among themselves. Some minutes later, while Tom was climbing into a Hackney coach in Long Acre, upstairs in the attic sickroom the three of them continued to deplore the corruptions of the Law, the childish political battles, the lack of trust in society, the vicious backbiting, the violence and intolerance that were everywhere... The bill of complaint grew longer as the minutes passed, and there was a great deal of nodding and shaking of heads.

And at that same moment, down at the southern end of Covent Garden, Adèle Ménage was leaving Mr Denniston's shop in

Katherine Street. She was apprehensive and looked around warily, drawing a heavily-cloaked girl closer to her side. Kate Primrose had a determined expression, but couldn't avoid being conscious of the silk pocket beneath her petticoat in which something of inestimable value nestled, a thing that needed to be well guarded. Night had drawn in, and the link-boy, with a cheeky look on his face, raised his sputtering torch high and strode briskly ahead. Mrs Ménage and Kate followed close, almost wishing they could go even faster. It was not a long walk to the Good Fellowship, but in the circumstances they were more than a little anxious.

And with justification, for walking some way behind, and keeping pace with them, was a figure that moved with long, nonchalant strides. It was not gaining on them, but was biding its time – the lower part of Bridges Street was more than usually busy. At the corner of the alley where Will had been attacked, and where some of his blood still marked the darkened cobbles, the man was about to make his move; but suddenly four boisterous apprentices emerged, hallooing loudly, and he held back. The two women were alarmed and urged the link-boy on towards Russell Street. They crossed the thoroughfare that led to the piazza, and headed rapidly up Bow Street, the unseen figure still tracking them.

It was when they reached the turn into Red Lion Court that the man surged forward at them. With a fierce cry of 'Off with you, boy!' he sent the link-boy packing – or thought he had. The young lad momentarily held his ground and waved the torch boldly in the man's face. Kate and Adèle saw in a second that his look boded very ill, and the knife in his hand boded even worse. Mrs Ménage's reaction was instantaneous – they were not far away from the coffee house now. She shouted to Kate: '*I have the letter!* Run for your life! *I'll give it to him!*' In an instant Kate had thrown off her cloak and was running into the quiet court. The man hesitated for a moment, looked at Adèle, cursed her, and then ran after the fleeing Kate, each stride double hers. She was light on her feet, but her rapid steps were no match for his long booted strides. Some ten yards short of the Good Fellowship he caught hold of her. The knife was held at her throat.

'I'll take that!' he said, and snatched the small cloth bag that dangled from her left hand. 'I know what you're carrying!'

His voice was edged with desperation.

Kate let out a loud scream. The man saw Adèle Ménage coming nearer with Kate's cloak bundled under her arm, and he hesitated again. He was losing control, and the two women were both looking at him. Which of them had the letter? A sash was raised in the coffee house, and a face showed itself. At the same instant, the coffee-room door opened. Kate screamed again. The man, now furious and frustrated, saw someone hurrying towards him from the doorway with a knife – a small one – in his outstretched hand. At this, the would-be assassin shouted a furious curse, spun on his heels, and ran up the court towards Drury Lane, his knife in one hand and Kate's bag in the other. Just before the arch he was met by a large figure with tousled hair, who spread his brawny arms wide and stood his ground as the man, and the knife, approached.

'Out of my way!' the man shouted. But suddenly an expression of puzzlement crossed his face, and he checked himself momentarily.

'Move aside, Jem!' he cried, just as he realised that the solid figure who blocked his path intended no such thing. The knife lunged forward, but Jeremy met it with a flailing sweep of his left arm, just as his right delivered a direct punch. The big fist didn't pause at the man's chin, but followed through as if the face had not been there. The man reeled back, jarred and dazed, but still conscious. Jeremy seized the moment and pushed him to the ground, flinging himself on top of him. The man's knife had cut into his arm, but Jem was able to grasp the wrist with his other hand and hold it in a vice, beating it against the cobbles. Now a second figure was bending beside them, holding a small, well-polished blade against the man's carotid artery. The villainous eyes blazed with fury; but the hand that held the blade against his neck did not shake. It remained firmly pressed to the man's skin until the knife was surrendered by the would-be killer's hand.

A few seconds later, a group from the Good Fellowship had gathered around them, horrified, but awe-struck at the sight. The figure in black was laid out on his back, with sixteen stone of Jeremy straddling his chest, while a bright-eyed Captain Roebuck crouched beside them, making expert use of the blade that had served him well in Marlborough's Flanders campaign.

And there too was Constable Cobb, standing above the prostrate figure. With a determined look he knelt down. The villain's mask-like face was staring in silent anger.

'Well, well – Mr Deacon!' said Elias, 'So you are attacking defenceless women! A cruel sport, but I reckon it's all finished now...'

Elias reached down into his coat pocket.

'Turn him over!'

Hands seized Deacon from all sides and swung him onto his stomach. The constable secured the handcuffs behind his back, and the job was done. By this time, Widow Trotter was in the group. On hearing the screams she had run downstairs after Elias. But now, while others gazed at the handcuffed assailant being pulled roughly to his feet, she was looking with concern at Jeremy. The young man was pressing a hand against his bleeding arm, and alongside him was Captain Roebuck delving into his old campaign wallet. He extracted from it a large linen handkerchief and a metal bar – always useful things on a battlefield, though rarely needed in a coffee house – and, with Jeremy gazing in silent wonderment, he began applying a tourniquet.

Mrs Trotter was rarely speechless, but for a few moments as the drama unfolded in front of her coffee house, she was rooted to the spot and could only stand and stare. There was so much to take in. It was as if all her friends had been called to arms. Her heart was beating heavily, and with mounting excitement she saw that after their earnest talk about pushing things to a crisis, 'things' had decisively pushed themselves – because there, hanging back on the far side of the little crowd, was Adèle Ménage with her arm protectively round a girl. That must surely be Kate Primrose! The whole scene was shocking, but Mrs Trotter could only give thanks.

And then, as if the spectacle were not already vivid enough, she turned and saw a tall young man in a nightshirt walking gingerly towards her. An unsupervised Will Lundy had decided he could no longer bear to be laid low.

At that moment Elias manhandled Deacon towards them, a look of complacent pride lighting up his face.

'Look after Mrs Ménage and the girl, Mrs T. Take them into the parlour and settle them down in the warmth. I shall be back with you as soon as I can – once I've given this gentleman a place for the night. He's a violent one, and has now felt the lash himself!'

But Will remained motionless in front of them, blocking their path. Like a ghost he stood transfixed, gazing at Deacon's boots.

'There, Mrs T! Look there!'

His hand was pointing downwards.

'Come along, Deacon!' said Elias impatiently. 'You have a charge to face!'

Will's response was firm and decisive.

'Indeed he does, Mr Cobb. I would know those boots anywhere – and that ripped seam hanging from the hem of his coat… They were inches from my face when I lost consciousness. I'll never forget them!… This was the man who stabbed me!'

Chapter Thirty-Eight

THE FIRST THING Tom noticed was how hushed the state room was. It was crowded, but could not be said to be bustling; there was brilliance all around, but little gaiety. The people moved with deliberation – there was certainly no swirling and laughing. Her Majesty the Queen was occupying a large oak chair slightly raised on a dais, and her presence meant that formality was regulating everything. Her Birth-night of February the sixth was the most sumptuous occasion of the Court year, and the state apartments of St James's Palace set a lavish style, challenging the humans to shine in their turn. The mimicry was intense. A gentleman's well-turned calf had to compete in beauty with the table leg against which it rested; handsome mirrors returned their respects to anyone who inquired of them; and the candle sconces were helping to animate the scene by imitating the glitter of diamonds. Against the walls, Delftware vases full of roses and tulips defied the winter season, their blooms exquisitely executed in silk, which complemented the magnificent dresses on display.

But there was no hiding the stiffness of the living figures, who were formed into little muttering groups making polite observations about the brilliance of the occasion, the brilliance of the company, the brilliance of the jewels. The conversation, however, as Tom had experienced it, was merely paste. Perhaps the wine, borne about by liveried footmen, would soon allow the courtly regimen to loosen.

But he had never seen clothes like these before. The looms of Spitalfields and Lyons must have been busy for months creating the fabrics. No-one could miss the Duchess of Marlborough in a mantua of emerald green damask, which was pulled back to reveal a golden petticoat woven with ferns and nosegays, the whole effect culminating in a pinnacle of finely dressed fair hair sprinkled with jewels. A good five yards away, the Queen's undulating waves of indigo velvet were offset with pearls, and a head-dress of yet more pearls and silver lace. In style, they were an ill-matched pair. Across the room, people's eyes were flicking back and forth from one woman to the other, noting the coldness between them and how their necks were elegantly inclined away from each other like a pair of haughty swans. There was an almost audible crackle of embarrassment in the space between.

Amidst this dazzling finery, Tom was doing his best. Before the Popham party had left for the palace, Lavinia and Aunt Sophia had taken him in hand and equipped him with more suitable birthday gear. This included a pair of gold buckles for his shoes, a tasselled sword-knot in blue and gold, a respectably flowing chestnut wig, and an extremely decorative brocaded waistcoat – very *à la mode*. Aunt Sophia had assured him that on this gaudy night the male ball-goers would be vying with each other, and that modern courtiers jousted not with lances but with waistcoats. Tom had accepted the inevitable. Not for the first time he glanced down at the gorgeous silk creation that was hugging him thanks to some last-minute sewing. He had always liked cornflowers, but the intermingled ears of golden wheat made him look like a field ready for harvesting. As he walked slowly round the edge of the room he was relieved to see another waistcoat sporting vibrant red poppies, but took care not to stand in its vicinity.

There was some stately music coming from the adjacent ballroom, but no sign yet of the ball proper having begun – if it was to begin at all. It was clear that Her Majesty's lameness would prevent her dancing. The illness of Prince George dampened her enthusiasm and she found it hard to walk unsupported, so that the chair she sat in had become a throne and the large reception room an awkward presence chamber. When they had to, the figures glided warily, as if too much locomotion might be thought impolite.

But there was clearly something going on. The action may have been subdued, but a sharp observer could read the stage-directions. The Duke of Marlborough and First Minister Godolphin were whispering together, both glancing in the Queen's direction; and the Duchess in her turn was glaring at her husband. A statuesque Earl of Sunderland occupied the no man's land between, eyeing with suspicion a specimen in a fine amber wig who hovered behind the Marlboroughs – Arthur Maynwaring, MP, no less! Tom could glimpse the pageant beyond the shoulders of other courtiers as they moved. The whole room resembled a large orrery with heavenly bodies of different magnitudes sedately circling the sun. He himself was in the further reaches of the system, but could catch hints of the drama that was playing out.

Tom saw the Queen suddenly beckon with her hand, and felt the *frisson* that ran through everyone when Robert Harley emerged and promptly bent beside her. As if making a gesture to her whole court, Anne spoke quietly into her minister's ear and touched him on his sleeve. There was some complacent smiling and nodding from Harley himself, and for a moment the two of them seemed caught up entirely in each other's company. At this, the Duchess in her green damask stared poisonously at the makeshift throne. She once more glowered at her husband, who had ceased to whisper with Godolphin and was now watching the little intimate audience. Sunderland appeared disgusted with the whole business, and Marlborough's brow was furrowed. Tom found the scene gripping, and imagined how it might be scripted by a skilful dramatist.

Since his arrival he had been looking out for Henry St John, but the Secretary-at-War was conspicuously absent. He began to worry that their plans would be frustrated and the evening be an anti-climax. He glanced yet again at the doorway, but there was nothing stirring. He badly needed to talk with his uncle, who had left for the palace hours earlier to busy himself with financial matters. As each minute passed Tom was feeling more awkward and out of place. The female Pophams had gone to inspect the decorations in the ballroom and he was wondering whether to join them. But suddenly to his relief, there was Lord Melksham heading in his direction with a slightly malicious twinkle lighting up his face as he took in the full effect of the Bristowe costume.

'Well, Tom, I have to say you've brushed up well – though your waistcoat is very *ancienne mode*… I distinctly remember wearing it last year…'

He spoke quietly in Tom's ear.

'… Have you been watching the show over there? It's as good as being in a stage-box – more gripping than anything at Drury Lane!'

'What's going on, uncle? The Queen is cherishing Harley in front of the whole court, as if she's determined to make a point.'

'Yes, I've been half expecting a sword to be produced and him to be dubbed an Earl on the spot! But of course she needs him in the Commons.'

'But where is Henry St John? I don't see him anywhere.'

Without replying, Lord Melksham gave Tom a slight nudge and indicated that they should move away. The two of them walked slowly, and eventually stationed themselves in a corner alongside a console table that was all twisted gold and inlaid malachite. His uncle rested his hand on the surface, and Tom put down his glass.

'It's what I thought, Tom – things are happening. I've picked up more than rumour, but it's not quite as I imagined it… That whispering between the Queen and Harley just now – her intimate confidences before everyone… it's not a sign of Harley's strength, but of his weakness – the danger he's in. The Whigs have wind of his move, and they've anticipated him.'

'How do you know, Uncle?'

'I was about to speak to the Duchess – a mere courtesy, you understand. She had her back to me and didn't know I was so near. It was a whisper through gritted teeth to her secretary Maynwaring, but I caught it distinctly… she said: "We've got him!"'

'*We've got him?*'

'That must be Harley – it can be no-one else. She said it with triumph, as if she longed to shout it aloud. Maynwaring saw me and looked embarrassed.'

Tom shivered as he heard this.

'But what can it mean?'

'Now, there I have to rely on my source – close to the Queen, and not to be divulged!… I hear that the Duke of Marlborough has written a strong letter to Her Majesty – *this very day*.'

'On her Birthday? That makes a point in itself, does it not?'

'Yes, a decisive one. It's as if they want the crisis to come at once.'

'But what does it involve?'

'It's what a lawyer might call an *ultimatum*. Godolphin and Marlborough are both resigning – the Queen's First Minister and the field commander whose services she cannot afford to lose at any cost!'

'Marlborough? Would he desert her?'

'It seems he has been prevailed upon. Something has happened to set both men irrevocably against Harley.'

'But are there no conditions, Uncle?'

'Yes – just one… that Harley must go. And at once. She has to dismiss him!'

Tom looked around and gave a low whistle.

'In that case, she has just given her answer, hasn't she – in the most public way? Does that mean Marlborough will resign his commission? The consequences for the war…'

'Not just for the war, Tom, but for our international alliances – the French will be exultant… If this is true – *if* – then I really don't think Her Majesty has any choice but to hold on to him.'

'To the Duke? And let Harley go?'

'Yes – Harley and St John, and their friends. I can't believe they would continue to serve if Harley were forced out. It will be a huge triumph for the Whigs! This is profoundly secret, and in confidence – it's not general rumour, and my informant is determined it shan't be! I was inclined to disbelieve it, but what I've just seen makes sense of every particular. Each glance was eloquent, and the Duchess's whisper too. No wonder she looked furious when the Queen made so much of Harley. But I watched him while they spoke, and he was all ease and confidence… I think he can't yet know about Marlborough's letter – if my informant is right.'

Tom's mind was racing. At that moment he was thinking of another letter, and the convulsion it would cause if it were known… He now saw the possibility that a rumour of Mrs Greg's letter had reached the Marlboroughs – not the paper itself, but word of what it contained. If Emmet had indeed revealed the contents to Maynwaring, the news would be with the Duchess in a trice, and she would triumph in telling her husband. So Maynwaring must have bided his time in hope of retrieving the manuscript, but had at last decided to wait no longer. The evidence of Harley's complicity in treason would be enough to turn the Duke and Godolphin against him and break the old triple alliance for good. But without the documented proof it would rest only on Emmet's word – a dead man's word! That would probably be sufficient to convince Marlborough, but not to bring in an indictment against Harley. There could be no trial, no impeachment, no formal charge of treason... But *with* the actual letter, then all would change! Not for the first time, Tom saw the full magnitude of the document these men were searching for. He felt suddenly restless – that he really ought to be at the Good Fellowship in case Kate Primrose was seeking him out. If only he could divide himself in two!

All this was the thought of a few seconds. His uncle meanwhile was savouring his wine and casting his eyes toward the dumb-show at the far side of the room. And there, at last, Tom saw Henry St John. He had slipped into the room quietly, and like an expert chess-player was taking in the disposition of the important pieces. His uncle saw him at the same time.

'There's your man, Tom. Are you sure you want to engage with him? And are you certain about that letter of yours? I'm uncomfortable with the whole idea. I can't believe he's troubled by a whore's threats. The St John I know sails through such waters with ease – *pleased with the danger when the waves run high!*'

'But you know why I have to do this, uncle...'

'Yes, your publisher-fellow of course. But promise me you'll not make St John angry – especially at this moment. He might brush you away like a troublesome fly... If you talk to him, you must be extremely careful. He's not a man to antagonise.'

Tom understood. It worried him too. And at that moment he wished he was anywhere other than in that stifling public place. But he knew he had to be brave. What bait would draw St John in? Should he begin with the trial, as Will had suggested? He could present Morphew as the victim of Whig plotters – that might win him… or he could be bolder and mention Kate Primrose, and watch for a response… and then there was the explosive topic of the letter itself, *To the Right Honourable Mr St John*, which Polly Gray had stolen and sold on, along with the engraved gold watch. With this in mind, and almost holding his breath, he turned to his uncle.

'I need to ask you about a little thing. It may seem odd, but I don't ask without reason.'

Lord Melksham uttered a small *aha!* and gave his nephew his full attention: he knew this was going to be something important.

'What is that, my boy?'

'The St Johns – your neighbours – can you describe their family arms?'

'You mean the coat of arms? Not in detail – but I would certainly recognise it.'

'No, I really mean the crest. There will be a St John crest, surely?'

'Yes – he seals his letters with it. It's a pair of mullets.'

Tom was taken aback.

'*Mullets?* What… *fish?*'

'No, Tom, *stars* in heraldry – *gold* stars in his case! Five-pointed. What makes you ask?'

'I was thinking it would be a wild boar – with a crown over it.'

'A boar? You're thinking of Richard the Third. No, it's certainly golden stars – *two mullets or*…'

Tom was nonplussed.

'… What's the import of this? Is this the seal on your letter? If so, it wouldn't be addressed to St John *and* sealed by him…'

'No, of course, Uncle. It's just that the girl who stole the letter stole the man's watch as well. I didn't tell you this… and the watch was engraved with a heraldic boar – and a crown.'

'A crown? Well that suggests royalty. It may not have been St John after all – perhaps you've misjudged him! I'm afraid I don't know very much about heraldry – though Sophia thinks I should. You'll need to go to the College of Arms.'

Tom knew he had to think hard. He wondered if he should finally be open with his uncle and tell him about the letter's contents. But he hesitated and decided to hang back, at least for now. And so, after a few more minutes of genial gossip, Lord Melksham headed off towards the ballroom where there seemed to be some musical stirrings. He could hear violins and an oboe beginning to combine in a sprightly way. Tom was left looking over at Henry St John and wondering what to do. He suddenly felt very confused. The Greg letter was their lifeline, the one way they could reach out to Harley and St John. He had to engage with Henry St John and find out what the man knew, and what he thought. But now, rather than confirming things, the gold watch had complicated them.

Tom's mind was working furiously. And at that moment, as he looked across the room again, he realised he was gazing directly into the man's eyes. St John was looking straight at him. For several seconds, both of them stared and hesitated, wondering who should take the first step. Tom felt flushed and unsteady, but he knew he must make the move.

But at that instant a liveried footman came to a halt by St John's side, bowed and handed him a note. It was read, and even from that distance Tom saw that its contents were a shock. The usually easy St John was suddenly tense, and his face became thunderous. He stepped out at once – though not in Tom's direction. As he followed the footman towards the door he turned to give Tom a final brief glance. There was no mistaking its message. It said that he would be back.

Chapter Thirty-Nine

KATE PRIMROSE REACHED into her silk pocket and drew out the letter. She held it toward Will, her small hand shaking slightly, and he took it gently from her.

'So this is the incendiary letter? It looks innocent enough, doesn't it!'

He began unfolding the paper with trepidation.

'I think you should read it out, Mr Lundy,' said Widow Trotter.

In the parlour of the Good Fellowship the scene was a deceptively domestic one. Seated by the fire and cradling their glasses of madeira, Kate Primrose, Mrs Ménage, and an obstinate Will (who ought to have been in bed) were warming themselves inside and out, and Widow Trotter had finally been able to join them. The coffee-room was abuzz, but things were now organised there and at last she could settle down with Kate and the others. After all their anxiety and urgent searching, she could hardly believe that the elusive Clarissa was here beside her hearth and ready – she hoped – to tell her story.

Earlier, with the ferment at its height, Mrs Trotter had guided Will and the two women into the sanctuary of the parlour before taking charge of things in the coffee-room. So much had to be looked to – not least a surgeon for Jem. But he had protested that it was merely a flesh wound and he wanted to sit with Captain Roebuck and share the heroic honours. A punch-bowl had been supplied, and the two comrades-in-arms were being thoroughly toasted. They didn't want for pasties and syllabubs either.

Widow Trotter took a sober view. She knew the violence of Red Lion Court was not going to be the final scene – far from it. George Deacon was in custody and ready to receive his just deserts – if justice could be expected. But there was still drama to come, and the piece of paper in Will's hand was a guarantee of it. Other people were not going to let matters rest there.

Will began reading the letter aloud. It was not traditional fireside fare, and the snug setting made it even more unsettling. Elizabeth Greg's passionate appeal to Henry St John affected each of them, not least because they sensed that her *last and final Hope* was a futile one. Will's expressive voice added to the poignancy. When he reached the words *he was prepared to wink at it,* he glanced up at the others, and the lawyer in him flashed a look of alarm. Only seven words, but they put Harley's whole world in danger. Pausing slightly at the phrase *I have only a wife's love, and a mother's conscience,* Will took in the full sadness of its eloquence. By the time he reached the close he could imagine himself in court listening to the last plea of the condemned.

'The poor woman,' said Widow Trotter. 'Hearing it again, I'm struck by her husband's devotion to Mr Harley – and by Harley's forbearance...'

'Forbearance? – or *folly?*' said Will.

'Perhaps, yes, but it says something for both men as human beings. We can only imagine what passed between Mrs Greg and her husband – how she must have begged him! And the children...'

'It's a scene out of classical tragedy,' said Will, turning to Mrs Ménage. 'I wonder what Monsieur Racine would have made of it?'

Mrs Ménage nodded in acknowledgment.

'It would not have ended well, *Mr Lundi*.'

During the reading of the letter Kate Primrose had sat with her mouth slightly open, almost forgetting to breathe, but now she tugged on a lock of wispy blond hair that hung over her shoulder.

'What words!...'

She looked at Will, and sighed.

'... You read them so well. I could hear her speaking!'

Will and Widow Trotter were longing to question her, but they held back. Young Clarissa had been through a succession of frightening experiences: the branding by her attacker, her flight from home, John Emmet's death, the threat of being hunted down – and now Deacon's knife at her throat. It was enough to make anybody fearful and tongue-tied, especially a girl of her age with no protectors. They knew they had no right to press her...

But Kate Primrose did not wish to be a victim, and she knew it was time her own voice was heard. A disconcertingly bold look seized her features as she swung round and faced them both.

'I expect you want to question me, and I'm ready to tell you everything. I don't give a fig for myself, so you mustn't worry... Adèle and me, we're both angry, and want to help.'

Mrs Ménage smiled at her young companion and nodded in agreement:

'Kate and I have little left to lose, Marie. And with you and your friends we may help to punish those who have hurt us – and perhaps save your Mr Morphew? That cruel man *Deacon*... we were the *bait*, were we not? We drew him to you! And thanks to Constable Cobb and the brave Captain – and to your stout Jeremy (God bless the boy!) – the villain will meet his fate, we trust!...'

She turned to Will.

'... Just think – he thought to *murder* you, Mr Lundi! That man has caused such pain – to Kate also...'

She looked at Kate, who gave a shiver of abhorrence.

'... She does not wish to talk of him and of what he tried to do to her. Thank God he moved on elsewhere – but not before he had given her marks that will stay with her...'

Will and Mrs Trotter were silent but aghast.

'... It was poor Margaret Graham – Polly Gray, she called herself – who met her end, thanks to him.'

'Are you saying that it was Deacon who killed her?'

'Yes, Marie, her last cry was heard, and he was seen... But those people in the tenement are so terrified that they refuse to speak. They know what he can do!'

Widow Trotter almost jumped from her seat.

'But now that he's in custody, perhaps they might reveal what they know?'

'We would wish so,' said Mrs Ménage. 'For too long that beast has hid himself – but, thank God, we have brought him out of the shadows!'

Kate Primrose's face gave assent, and she set her glass down. She was a slight figure, though her pink cotton dress sat well on her, and a coral necklace hung down almost to her lap. But what could have been a simple effect was marred by the assortment of bangles and rings that clung to her, and there was a clutter of brooches too, half-hidden by the ruffle at her shoulder. It looked like the tasteless excess of a Drury Lane nymph; but it struck Mrs Trotter that the fugitive girl must be wearing what little jewellery she possessed. She didn't have the luxury of a toilette table covered in boxes and jars.

Kate blushed slightly at being the centre of attention and began speaking in an unwavering voice.

'Madame Ménage has told me about you, Mrs Trotter – how you and your friends have been searching for me – I've caused you all such trouble!... Mr Lundy has told me of the trial, and about Mr Bristowe and his papers, and the visit to Newgate... But he warned me I had to keep my own story till you were here with us... He said that if we didn't wait for you, you'd never forgive him and would chase him all the way to Charing Cross.'

'Quite right,' said Mrs Trotter. 'And I would have caught him too – and thrown him into the Thames.'

The tension eased a little. There was a moment's silence, and still no urgent questioning. Whatever she had to say must unfold in her own time.

'Madame Ménage has told me what you're trying to find out. You'll want to know about me and John, and about what he was up to *at the end...*'

She paused on the chilling phrase, but seemed unafraid of it. Settled into a chair too big for her, Kate Primrose may have looked frail and vulnerable, but they saw determination in her.

Kate's next words were welcome ones.

'... I *know* Mr Morphew is innocent, Mrs Trotter. He trusted John, and John liked him. They worked together well... But then John began to take advantage and do business for himself. He was always a step ahead of people, you see – they made things easy for him with their greed and stupidity...'

There was a touch of scorn in her voice; but when she began speaking of Emmet it was with affection and respect – and exasperation too. They were struck by her assurance.

'... He began to think he could turn lead into gold. He had such pretensions! You see, he had a vision of having his own printing business... And he loved the excitement of reading private letters and papers. He saw it could bring him money – bring *us* money, he said. At the end, I tried to stop him – he was sinking in deeper and meeting with dangerous men... That was when he began keeping things in my room.'

Will stirred himself.

'Did he show you that pocket book, Kate? The one with the poems in it?'

'I saw the poems – not my thing at all! He said they were strong political stuff, and something could be made of them... And then he read the diary and was very secretive about it. All I know is, the book had been stolen from Lady Norreys, and there were things in it to embarrass her. I returned the poems to her yesterday. She's such a strong lady, and she told me it was good to stand up for what's right. She said I'd shown myself to be strong too. That was when I heard about you all, and poor Mr Morphew being accused. She said I must find you and do something to help!'

'You're a brave girl, Kate,' said Mrs Trotter, 'and you've brought us fresh hope.'

'I told Lady Norreys I was sorry for what John had done – trying to get money from her – and I was ashamed for him. Mr Morphew had seen what he was doing and put a stop to it. John was so resentful, he kept the poems for himself and brought them to me. He said the pieces were a jumble. He sat poring over them and began copying them out and patching bits together. I would hear him whoop with joy sometimes – and he read some of them to me.

'He had contacts with Mr Harley's people and saw his chance to make money by printing them. He didn't tell me much, but I think he was printing things at night and hawking them by day. I don't know how far it went... But he returned furiously angry. He said they had refused to pay him. He stamped and raved and said he would *show them!*'

'Did he encounter Deacon in all this, do you know?'

'I think he must have done, Mrs Trotter. There was an agent he saw. John had an agreement – not written down of course! He kept a lot of that secret. He would work on the papers, and then disappear... . He said Ministers were *taking notice*. It thrilled him, but it worried me. There was a gleam in his eye which I didn't like. Mr Lundy says he thinks John must have been accusing Mr Morphew to them, and inventing tales about Mr Bristowe too… I swear I knew nothing of that. If I'd known he was telling such lies…'

Her words trailed. Will and Mrs Trotter glanced at each other. It struck them that it was not just they who were learning new things.

'… And then there was this letter…'

She reached out and took the document from Will.

'… This was going to change our lives, John said… He said it would make our fortune…'

Kate's knuckles were whitening while she spoke. The inoffensive paper began to crease and fold into itself as her small hand tightened its grip.

'… When I think what this letter has done! I wish it had never come to us!'

Mrs Ménage leaned over and put her hand on Kate's knee. Widow Trotter's curiosity surged.

'Did Polly Gray bring the letter to you?'

'Yes, she called on me. And she also had a *gold watch* with her, which belonged to the same gentleman…' Kate paused. '… I think you know how she came to have them?'

'Yes,' said Will, 'we've heard how Daphne enhanced her clients' pleasures…'

'She drugged and robbed them,' said Widow Trotter, frowning.

Kate was unabashed and nodded to herself.

'Polly was ruthless, Mrs Trotter. She took risks that others would tremble at, and she never listened to advice.'

'Did Mrs Purslowe know about her dealings?'

'Yes, and she expected a share of the profits too. But Polly was resolved she wouldn't get to hear of this transaction…'

A thorough woman of business, Widow Trotter thought.

'... The watch Polly showed me was a fine thing – very heavy and all gold, but with a bit of silver decoration. She was taking it to a fence and thought she could get five guineas for it! But it was the letter she wanted John to look at. She knew John traded in papers and thought he could say if it was special – something that might have a price... Well, I showed it to John that evening, and he opened it – very delicately so as not to damage the seal...'

'You mean the letter had not been read?'

'No, it was sealed. And very important it looked to us...'

Kate Primrose sat back slightly and took a breath.

'... I watched his face as he read it over to himself, and he was like a child gazing at the fireworks... he didn't tell me the contents, and his voice was back in his throat, as if it could only be whispered. Madame Ménage has told me it's a dangerous letter, but it's just a poor woman begging for her husband's life, isn't it?'

'Yes, Kate, that's exactly what it is... But you have to understand, it means much more – a great deal more rests on it – men's lives and reputations.'

'Mr Greg's life, I know... Can't you show it to Mr St John? If he could only read her words he might do something to help her?'

She looked at Will and Mrs Trotter, her eyes pleading on Mrs Greg's behalf. The two of them felt uneasy. It was Kate who had put her finger on the pain of the thing. But how could they explain the bigger picture?

It was Will who responded.

'So, it was certainly Mr St John who had been robbed? Polly recognised him, did she?'

'Well, she spoke of him by that name – but it may have been because of the letter. He wasn't a regular client of course – she wouldn't have robbed one of her regular gentlemen. All

I know is, she told me he was a smartly dressed young man, and well spoken – very much as you would expect… but she did say he was befuddled and over-eager when he arrived. None of the niceties, you might say. Down to business at once! The entertainment came later… .'

She suddenly held herself back, aware of her audience.

'… That's all I had from her. She was smiling when she spoke of him, as if he'd taken her fancy… and yet she did *that* to him! Filched his watch and his letter, and packed him off in a stupor. He must have been in a very bad way… Does that help you, Mr Lundy? I've told you all I can.'

'You've given us a vivid picture, Kate,' said Widow Trotter. She rose from her seat and began replenishing their glasses as generously as she could. Will took matters to the next stage.

'What you've said has been very helpful, Kate, I promise you… But, if you're able, can you tell us what happened to the letter – before you took it to Mrs Ménage? Did you hide it in your room? It's important that you tell us about the man who attacked you. He was looking for the letter, wasn't he?'

'We had thought the man was Deacon,' said Mrs Trotter. 'But this was a stranger, was it? Did he try to torture you?'

'So many questions!' said Kate. 'I've tried not to recall… The man was hot and trembling – not like Deacon at all! I can't describe him, but I'd know his voice. You see, he was masked – like a stage highwayman, with his hat pulled down – and he had a pistol in his belt which he waved at me… But I know real highwaymen don't wave their pistols, they point and cock them! I tried to be calm. I told him I used to have John's papers, but now he'd taken them away to his own place.'

'So he asked about *papers*, not a letter?'

'Well, he asked about papers *first* – but when I said he was at liberty to search but wouldn't find any papers, he called out for a *letter*. He said he knew I had it, and wouldn't take no for an answer.

He began to ransack my room – the shelves and cupboards – and the bed too. He threw aside the mattress. He emptied things and flung them about. Then he asked me if I had it on my person.'

'Was that when he branded you?' said Will.

'He was desperate, and the pistol was all for show – discharging it would bring a crowd running! He saw the toasting fork – I'd propped it in the fire when he burst in on me... it was terrifying because he began pointing it at me. I fell over a stool and tried to protect myself, but he stood over me and brought it down on my wrist.'

She lifted her sleeve a little way to reveal an angry red scar.

'He pushed the thing at me and kept asking me where the letter was – I told him John had it – but he cursed and said the *scheming bastard* had nothing – *not any more, he hadn't!...*'

Kate stopped in her tracks.

'... Of course, he meant John was dead – but I didn't know it then. I screamed, and he became frightened and rushed to the door. He must have been afraid of being caught... but he did say something before he ran off... He said, "If we don't find it, you'll have another visit – be sure of that!"'

'*We?*' said Widow Trotter.

'Yes, not *I* ,... *we*.'

'So the man can call on other forces.'

'That's why I had to leave the place. I knew someone else would come next time – someone more ruthless.'

'That's curious,' said Will. 'He doesn't sound like a hired ruffian at all.'

'A polite bully!' said Mrs Ménage. 'Our Covent Garden is full of them!'

Mrs Trotter was pensive. They had learned a lot, but still nothing to take them beyond suspicion and conjecture.

'But can you think of anything else, Kate? Any detail that might help identify him?'

'I've said all I can about the man. He was stupid and thoughtless. He looked everywhere – except in the most obvious place! There was a cloth bag full of pegs hanging from the top of the bedpost – at the far side – dangling there in full sight… but he never touched it. He stamped on the floorboards and overturned the table… I couldn't believe it. He was unbelievably stupid!…'

Kate took a sip of her madeira.

The girl has a lively tongue, thought Will.

Men sometimes see only what they want to see, thought Mrs Trotter.

'… But I need to tell you about John's business with the letter… You see, he was making moves. He had an assignation…'

Kate took another sip and settled herself further into the armchair, which cradled her. The fire was warm, and she was with people who wished to protect her. For the first time in days she felt secure and able to speak.

'Take your time, Kate,' said Mrs Trotter. 'We are longing to hear.'

'Well, it was last Friday evening – the day he died – John arrived in a strange mood. He was grim-looking and distant. When I made to welcome him he brushed me off and said he had something important to do first – business matters with the letter. He had some fine paper with him, and he set out his ink and pens and began copying – very carefully and precisely. I was sewing and watched him. He was very skilful in that way.'

'Copying, Kate? Do you mean copying the letter?'

'Only the *direction* of it, Mr Lundy – the name – *to Mr St John*, as it says. He hushed me and wouldn't say anything until he'd finished it. His eyes were concentrating and he took real pains. Then he prepared the wax, and sealed the paper with a sixpence.'

'Ah yes, of course, Mrs Greg's seal.'

'Then he brightened, and said *that would do it*. So then I opened a bottle of wine, and we started talking about his plans for us. He even laughed...'

Kate's words caught in her throat, and she stopped, her eyes glistening. The three of them realised it had been their final meeting. Widow Trotter was about to speak, but Kate's hesitation was only brief, and she pressed on, determined to have it all said while she was able.

'... As I say, he'd arranged to meet someone... John didn't usually tell me details of his affairs, but I knew this was going to be different. Making that empty letter was a strange thing to do, and I asked him about it. I didn't expect he would tell me, but this time he spoke, and there was a look of malice in his eyes, as if he was ready for a plot and was feeling pleased with himself...

'Well, he said he'd met the gentleman that Daphne had cozened out of his letter, and was going to see him again that very night – that the man had been wild and fidgety at their first meeting. John told him the letter was hidden away and still unopened, so its secret was safe. He said the gentleman looked mighty relieved, and swore he would give a lot for the thing to be handed over with the seal unbroken. John of course knew what it contained. He'd managed to reattach the seal so as you'd never know it had been touched.' Widow Trotter could not keep her peace, and interrupted.

'This man,' she said, '... was it Mr St John?'

'I don't know... but he was certainly the man Daphne robbed.'

'How could he be sure?' said Will.

'The man said so – he had lost his gold watch as well, he said, and wanted to know if John had wind of it. He said the gentleman tried to look nonchalant, but there was a frantic look in his eyes, and he was clearly anxious to have the letter back. John knew the paper was something special and how very important it was. He told the man he would bring the letter for him – but only for a huge price. He named *one hundred guineas.*'

Widow Trotter gave an involuntary gasp.

'A fortune indeed!'

'The gentleman was thunderstruck and began to be suspicious. He cavilled at the price and said it was outrageous. But finally he said he would do his best to raise what sum he could – that he needed a day to organise it. John said the man looked nervous and very uncomfortable.'

'I can understand it!' said Will. 'So, you're saying this was the man Mr Emmet went off to meet on Friday night? And that he was planning to hand him an empty paper – not the real letter at all!'

Kate looked a little embarrassed.

'Yes, but it wasn't strictly a cheat – John said he wouldn't take the true letter with him, as it would be too dangerous – he couldn't take the risk. You see, he thought he might be set upon… I don't think he was intending to hand the thing over, but simply to see if the money was ready or not. He thought the man might bring a friend and they would pounce on him!'

Will whistled to himself:

'This is all very devious – but perhaps he thought he couldn't trust anyone anymore?'

'That day he was damning both sides,' said Kate, 'and when he left, he took another piece of verse with him and said he was going to print it. It was a *curse*, he said, wishing a plague on both parties.'

'Yes, *Bufo's Curse*, he called it…' said Widow Trotter. She was going to say more, but broke off – Kate didn't need to know that the dead Emmet was found clutching it in his hand.

She glanced at Will, who took the hint and at once drew their thoughts back to Mrs Greg's letter. He had been pondering.

'… I wonder, Mrs T… The letter was sealed when it was

taken from the man's pocket... What if it wasn't Mr St John that Polly Gray robbed, but a gentleman who was carrying the letter *to* him? He lost his precious watch, but also lost the letter entrusted to his care. Since then, he's been frantically trying to retrieve it – our incompetent highwayman!'

'But did Mr Emmet give no hint of who the man was?' said Mrs Trotter. 'Did he say he was important – a public figure?'

Mrs Trotter was grasping at a straw. Kate shook her head.

'I'm sorry I can't help you more,'

'Dear Kate,' said Will firmly. 'You have helped us more than you know... I'm hesitating to say it, but what you are telling us is that John Emmet was heading off to meet this man the night he died?'

'Yes, Mr Lundy. John was to meet him at 10 o'clock that night – in the printing-house.'

Will involuntarily stretched out a hand to Mrs Trotter, who seized it.

'You see what this means, Mrs T!' he said. 'There's no other conclusion to be drawn. John Emmet had an angry confrontation with this man in the printing-house. Something happened – perhaps the man paid the money over and opened the letter only to find it was blank?'

'Or the man told Emmet he didn't have the money – we know he's a violent character – and he saw the cane and hammered Emmet over the head, and took the letter from the body...'

'Yes, and only later did he discover the trick.'

Mrs Ménage gazed at the pair of them, hand in hand like entranced Shakespearean twins.

'Whatever the case,' said Will, 'we surely have to conclude that the man who killed Emmet is the man who owns that watch – that unique gold watch with his crest on it – *a boar surmounted by a crown*.'

Widow Trotter was beaming.

'That identifies him, Will… And, as you say, it's possible it may not be Henry St John. But if not, then who could it be? Poor Mr Bristowe is at the Birth-night Ball about to confront a Minister of the Crown and implicate him in a murder… but if St John never received that letter, he may know nothing of the business. I wouldn't like to be in Tom's shoes!'

'But, Mrs T, we can identify our killer tonight – we can do it – *I* can do it! I know where to go – the College of Arms. It's just off Thames Street, by St Paul's.'

'Oh no, no, no! You must go nowhere – that would be complete folly! You can't be trailing off in your present state. Let it wait till tomorrow, and we can send a message over.'

'But in our emergency, Mrs T, every minute is precious. Think of Mr Morphew. We can't afford to leave this for another night to pass. If we do identify the man, we still have only slight evidence – a fragile chain of association. We have to convince others. We're not there yet… I have to go to the College.'

'But it will surely be shut at this time?'

Will was breathing quickly.

'I know the place, Mrs T – I went there to research for Mr Sumner – It was an inheritance case and I had to find a family tree… I know the porter – he's sure to remember me – it was only a month ago – the porter will be there. I can take a chair, and insist they handle me *gently* – I wouldn't entrust my body to a Hackney… I swear I'll be careful, Mrs T! But, don't you see? – in two hours' time we might know who killed John Emmet!'

Will's eyes were animated, and his hair shook as he spoke. The hair alone wouldn't take no for an answer. And Widow Trotter knew her curiosity was simply bursting to get loose. Will's mission was foolhardy, but… this last bold adventure could win them the prize?

'You must eat something, Will, and wrap up very warm!'

Less than half an hour later, a thoroughly swaddled Will was being carried in the direction of the College of Arms. He had negotiated for the vehicle to proceed at a dignified pace, but the two stout chairmen still had a pronounced roll as they swung him over the cobbles. He began to sense the discomfort and the madness of his journey – but inside he was glowing with anticipation, and part of him even wished the men would hurry themselves a little more.

Chapter Forty

IN THE BALLROOM of St James's Palace the dancing was at last to begin. The opening *minuet* had been called, and the select performers displayed themselves along the room in elegant pairs. They were led by the Queen's cousin, the Duke of Richmond, and his more diminutive Duchess. His Grace was still a youngish man, but the face was already becoming jowly, and the dark eyes glowed beneath thick eyebrows. He's very much his father's son, thought Tom, and indeed the King Charles of thirty years before seemed to be in the room. The music sounded and the dancers were set in motion, creating stately patterns across the gleaming *parquet*. Each step was dainty and precise, and the figures glided to right and to left, forwards and backwards, making small quarter-turns, approaching and retreating, alternately searching for and evading their partner, the couples now side by side, now in confrontation, then gliding coolly past each other. Every manoeuvre was nicely choreographed, with each pair finding a part in this intricate ritual. It was like a subtle courtship: coy and playful, but at the same time majestic and assured. Tom watched transfixed and could not but think of the dance of State, with its graceful moves and careful weavings.

An impatient Lavinia was standing alongside him, watching the performance. In her cream and blue brocaded silk she looked very much the young woman, though there was still something girlish in the twitching of her fan and the jaunty turns of her head. Her eyes were bright and restless. Tom whispered to her.

'I hope your feet are ready for tonight, Lavinia?'

'They've been in training for weeks, Tom – and Mr Isaacs is very flattering about my right ankle. I'm pleased to say I have his new dance pat – I only hope Lord Tring is going to play his part.'

'Ah yes, *The Union!* With a name like that the moves are bound to be intricate ones – you'll both have to keep in step! Is he a good dancer?'

'He handles his horse well enough, so I expect we'll trot along happily. Mamma is eager to see us in action.'

'Aunt Sophia is certainly sparkling tonight!'

'Well, I should think so. She spent most of yesterday rehearsing her clothes and jewels.'

Tom looked round the room with its mobile human décor. Powdered gentlemen continued to strut slowly, guiding their dress-swords with care, and the more veteran ladies tottered under the weight of their silver lace. But his mind was on other things. In Henry St John's absence he had been pondering and had determined to tell his uncle the facts about the Greg letter. Tom knew that at some point he might need his help and advice.

He wished Cousin Lavinia luck with Mr Isaacs' much-anticipated exhibition dance, and set off in search of his uncle. He eventually found him in a reception room paying his compliments to a Dowager Duchess who was holding court by the far wall. His uncle caught his eye, and with some relief extracted himself from the group and came over.

Henry St John was mentioned, and in response his uncle suggested they find a place where they could talk privately. An obliging footman indicated a closet where the musicians had deposited their gear. It was a little cluttered but there was space for them to perch on a couple of chairs.

'You look unsettled, Tom. I wish you would tell me what's troubling you. You said Will was on the mend, so I hope things are still favourable in that quarter?'

'Yes, he's in expert hands and is impatient to be active again.'

'Excellent! That's a good sign. I know your friend the publisher is facing a terrible end, and that must be preying on your minds… But you say you want to talk about Mr St John. I'm not clear why you concern yourself with him – I thought our friend Maynwaring was shaping up to be the villain! I'm still puzzling over what you told me this morning – that St John could have contracted for the pressman's murder because of a compromising letter. I find that such a wild idea. It doesn't fit my picture of him at all!'

Tom knew he owed his uncle the truth, and he was ready to pay the debt in full. While they sat in the small room crowded with spare music stands and instrument-cases, Lord Melksham was spared no detail and no suspicion. When Tom had finished, his uncle saw that Mrs Greg's letter was indeed compromising in the most far-reaching way – that it threatened the reputation, even the life, of the Secretary of State. And Harley's fall would bring down St John too.

'So you see why we think the letter may have led to Emmet's death? It seems Polly Gray was killed for it, Kate Primrose was attacked for it, and my papers and Mrs Ménage's were stolen in a search for it.'

'But this is momentous, Tom! I see the picture now… And you think word of this letter may have reached the Marlboroughs and prompted the Duke into making his move today?'

'Yes, it may have – but State politics I can happily set aside. What concerns me is poor John Morphew. An innocent man is to hang on Monday morning. We can't let that happen, uncle! Henry St John *must* know something about Emmet's death – whether he's responsible or not – and I'm determined to challenge him about it!'

'You are putting lives at risk with this, Tom, you understand?'

'One life is already at risk, uncle – an entirely innocent one!'

Lord Melksham looked intently at his nephew, who was beginning to blaze. He knew of old that when Tom's passion was roused there was usually something important at stake – and no hiding from it.

'Tom, Tom! Let's talk this through for a moment… I think I see what you are trying to do. But have a care! Your challenge is shaping up to be an *accusation*…'

Tom was about to interject, but his uncle raised his hand.

'… Mr St John will think you are using the letter against him – that there is some threat on your part to publicise it unless he and Harley secure Morphew's release… Is that what you are hoping for?'

Tom heard his uncle's words and was shocked. Perhaps he *was* hoping Harley would pardon Morphew in return for the letter – that was the unspoken logic of his intentions. It was a blatant blackmail of course, and the sheer daring of the idea had suppressed the thought. He shuddered – this would make him no better than a criminal himself. However fine the motive, he mustn't sink to that.

Tom felt sobered and drew back from the edge. For several minutes more, and more calmly, the two of them talked. He told his uncle that Kate Primrose remained elusive in spite of their efforts, and that they knew George Deacon was also searching for her. As the discussion continued Lord Melksham saw how desperate his nephew was and what danger it placed him in. Speaking quietly and solemnly, he promised that if evidence were found to exonerate John Morphew, then he would personally intervene and press Mr Harley to use his pardon. But it had to be done according to the proper form. They must not sink to threats and tricks.

'And – if there's no other course – I might even bring myself to confront the appalling Arthur Maynwaring… But I would be eternally grateful if that were spared me.'

Tom felt relieved. The situation was no less dark, but their conversation had reassured him and clarified his thoughts. The two of them headed back in the direction of the ballroom, and Tom wondered if he should simply allow the delights of the dancing to have their way. He smiled at his uncle and thanked him for his words of guidance.

'I must think a little further about whether to press myself so determinedly on Mr St John!'

Lord Melksham nodded approvingly and went to seek diversion in the supper-room. Tom was left pondering. He remembered the look that the Secretary-at-War had given him, and feeling suddenly unsettled he cast his eyes around to see if St John had returned. With some relief he did not see him.

But what he did see all too clearly was a bob-wigged footman approaching with a silver salver. The man halted, bowed, and with a practised sweep of the arm held the tray out toward the bright cornfield of Tom's waistcoat. A folded piece of paper was poised at the centre.

Before Tom reached out he knew what it must be. It was indeed a note from Henry St John, and it requested Mr Bristowe's company down below in the park. The royal fireworks were to begin, it said, and Mr St John thought it would provide them with an opportunity to talk.

Meanwhile, Will was realising that the Queen's Birthday was not a night to enjoy a quiet ride through the London streets. The capital was thronged with revellers. Fire-crackers were exploding everywhere and coloured sparks flew through the air. Milling around on the pavement and into the road, groups of patriotic citizens were viewing the illuminations that flickered in many windows and doorways: images of Her Majesty, of

Britannia, the Union Flag, Marlborough on horseback – not to mention entwined roses and thistles and other symbols of the new nation. Other folk, with less of patriotism on their minds, were there to relieve the citizens of their purses and snuff boxes. Mingling with the crowds were pickpockets, wig-snatchers, and coney-catchers of all kinds, and the night was now at that stage when celebration was beginning to tip over into disorder. Everywhere in the metropolis the Watch was at full stretch, and the local roundhouses were filling rapidly with drunks and petty thieves, left till morning to contemplate their crimes or simply return to consciousness.

On such a night a slow-moving sedan chair was part of the entertainment, and had it not been for his two stout chairmen Will's vehicle would have been overturned more than once. It was set down on one occasion while the pair saw off a gang of apprentices with their fists. Will was struck by the no-nonsense heroism of the men, who guarded their heavily-bandaged charge as if he were a treasure to be defended from marauding pirates. They grumbled and growled, and swore and shouted, and somehow managed to bring the chair to its destination intact.

An immensely relieved Will was delivered into the open quadrangle of the College of Arms. It should have been a quiet spot, but even here the sounds of distant revelry echoed round the walls. He gave the two men a half-crown each and promised them a warm welcome at the Good Fellowship if they could wait and see him safely back there. The journey had shaken him up and the wound was nagging him.

But at least he didn't need to find the porter, because the man found him. A black-coated figure ran out to investigate an arrival at such an odd hour, and to explain that the place was closed, and had been so since noon in honour of the Royal Birthday. There followed a vigorous exchange – less an altercation than a clash of priorities. Mr Barson was finally persuaded that he could indeed recall Will's previous visit, although it took a couple of florins to lodge the memory firmly in his mind. Will was not ashamed to swear that someone's life was at stake, and his eloquence and the shiny coins finally won the day.

'I can't leave you in the building alone, of course,' the man said, '– and even allowing you entrance out of hours is most irregular… but I think you are in luck on this occasion…'

The porter reached for his keys and straightened his back.

'… *Rouge Dragon* is in the court room!'

The very words had the force of a heraldic blazon – it was the voice of romance. Will's spirits rose. One of the heralds was still in the building! It was a stroke of good fortune, and he began to think that his foolish mission might even succeed – something he had begun to doubt during the journey. With no more ado he followed the porter across the courtyard and up the steps of the pedimented central block, leaving the two chairmen in the yard to light their pipes and take flasks of brandy out of their pockets.

Mr Dudley Downs, Rouge Dragon Pursuivant, was no Spenserian knight, but a perfectly friendly individual with a scholarly brow, neat spectacles, and a reassuring stoop. Somehow he seemed a little out of place in the elegantly ornamented court room where claims of inheritance and precedence were tried. Here a tall balustrade kept the petitioners at bay while aristocratic faces glared at them from the panelled walls. Thankfully, Mr Downs was far from formidable, and on being told of Will's mission he beamed warmly at the thought that their records could save a man from the gallows. Will didn't go into details, but Mr Downs liked nothing more than delving into the armorial archives, especially the lavishly coloured scrolls of vellum on which lines of inheritance were painted.

'Let us see what our *library* can tell us, Mr Lundy!' he said with a scholar's thrill, and led the way to an adjacent galleried room where the heraldic records were held. This was a different, much older world, and Rouge Dragon purred with pleasure. Will gazed on the hundreds of hallowed volumes, many of them thick folios that might take two to lift, and at once he began to feel the truth coming within arm's length. His mind was so excited that his throbbing shoulder was hardly noticeable.

On hearing the details of what they were to search for, Mr Downs shook his head.

'No, there's nothing royal about the crown – it finds its way onto many a crest!... but the boar... well, our infamous King Richard sported it of course – but so have other families not of royal extraction. One that comes to mind at once is De Vere. Does that chime with your researches Mr Lundy?'

'No, Sir, I'm afraid not.'

'Well, let us see – There is a manuscript index we keep for an eventuality such as this. It is not exhaustive, you understand – not by any means – but it is the place to start. I shall bring it down for us.'

Rouge Dragon made his way up a spiral staircase to the gallery, and a little way along the shelves he pulled out a substantial hide-bound volume. Will was tense with excitement as the book was manoeuvred down the stairs and laid on the desk in front of him. *Index Armorialis* was incised into its spine. The pages crackled between the herald's fingers as he began turning them with scholarly deliberation.

'Yes, Mr Lundy, here we are – the wild boar!'

He angled the page toward Will, showing a beautifully painted animal with black spiky coat and fearsome tusks. A dangerous creature, eh!... Now let us see... Campbell is a possibility?'

He looked at Will, who shook his head in disappointment but nevertheless pencilled the name into his notebook.

'De Vere, of course, as I said... but the boar *surmounted with a crown?* – no – in spite of the De Vere pretensions!'

He smiled, then turned back to the book, humming slightly to himself. After a few seconds there was a sudden exclamation.

'Aha! Mr Lundy – I think we may have it! What do you make of this?'

Mr Downs turned the book round again, and there Will saw the image – a wild boar, surmounted by a *crown*. He froze, and a cry burst from him, which echoed round the tall room.

'Le Grice!'

'Does that make sense to you, Mr Lundy? Yes, I should have known – Le Grice, or simply 'Grice' – a family with a distinguished history...'

The herald began his scholarly disquisition, but Will was elsewhere, his thoughts racing... Of course, it made perfect sense. Harry Grice worked in Harley's own office – and in an unofficial capacity. *Unofficial* indeed! Will could see a chilling picture of a young man he had remembered as warm and open... But who better placed to be dispatched on an urgent mission – someone self-assured, genial, ingratiating... The images succeeded each other rapidly: Harry Grice holding a toasting-fork, Harry Grice confronting Emmet... stealing Tom's poetry manuscripts!... Will's throat was tight and dry. He stood up quickly, euphoric, but also alarmed at the implications. As he did so, his body gave a shudder; the room became darkened, and the shelves began to sag and swing around him. The throbbing in his head became louder.

'Mr Lundy! Are you feeling unwell? – You are white as a sheet!'

Will collapsed onto his knees, his head sunk against Rouge Dragon's gaitered leg. The herald looked down anxiously and saw warm gules spreading across the white bandage around the young man's shoulder.

Chapter Forty-One

THERE WAS A loud crash, and the night sky above St James's Park was suddenly illuminated by an explosion of light. A brilliant shower of golden rain began cascading to earth, and in the glow of it Tom immediately saw Henry St John standing beside the palace wall further along the carriage-drive. He had been in shadow, but as Tom approached he stepped forward and indicated that they should walk a few yards further into the park itself. There were armed soldiers stationed around the perimeter of the palace, and as the two of them turned the corner they could see through the wintry trees that the Mall was crowded with spectators all looking over at the canal, where the firework display was being conducted.

Every eye was caught by the spectacle as the darkness flashed and colourful starbursts reflected in the expanse of water. St John stopped. There was another shuddering bang followed by a ghostly flicker of blue. Tom thought it was hardly the place for a quiet conversation, but this was no occasion for drawing-room whispering. They would not be overheard, and perhaps the tumult in the skies would license them to be more direct. Tom may have thought he could put St John at his ease and quietly elicit his thoughts, but it was looking set to be a frank encounter.

The spot where they halted was relatively secluded but no less noisy, and St John took advantage of the charged atmosphere around them.

'Mr Bristowe! I trust there will be no unnecessary delicacy between us – no evasiveness under the guise of scruples. I intend to be candid, and I hope you will be too. It is time the two of us talked honestly.'

'I would welcome it, Mr St John. You are an extremely busy man, and I know you wouldn't seek this meeting were there not something momentous at stake. I think we both know what form it takes. You will be well acquainted with uncomfortable documents – slight papers on which weighty matters depend.'

The Secretary-at-War looked amused at Tom's assured manner. The young man was meeting him face to face. Each needed to know what the other man knew – and what he wanted. St John repaid him in kind.

'Yes, I think we understand one another...'

There was a slight pause, and a sudden determination.

'... The *letter*...'

He paused again, as if his hand were on a chess piece but was hesitating where to place it. He was hoping Tom would guide him. Tom knew this was an opportunity to be reassuring. His tone was guileless.

'You are anxious, Sir, I can understand that... And I don't wish to add to your fears or make the situation difficult for you. Quite the contrary. It is a fraught time for the Ministry – and for Mr Harley especially...'

At that moment, somewhere along the canal a huge mortar was ignited, and from its mouth a stream of rockets soared noisily into the sky. There was crackling and squealing, and a meteor-shower of glittering sparks spread out above the trees. Both men were stunned for a moment, conscious of the theatrical effects that seemed to be turning their meeting into a dramatic scene – one with heavenly portents worthy of Caesar's Rome. The irony wasn't lost on them.

'… I haven't seen the letter itself, Mr St John, but I know of its contents – as I think you must do too…'

St John nodded slowly.

'… I know that in it Mrs Greg begs you to intervene and save her husband's life – and in making her plea she reveals that Mr Harley knew about the treason and was prepared to overlook it.'

The minister winced at the blunt summary.

'Did you learn this from that damned Emmet? The letter was *stolen*, Mr Bristowe, and when the troublemaker got hold of it he determined to cause the greatest damage he could – and make his fortune from others' destruction… Well, he has met his fate! I would like to say it was undeserved – but I cannot.'

'So he was demanding money, was he? That's no surprise.'

St John looked at him.

'How much do you know, Mr Bristowe?… I suspect you would ask the same of me, eh? We are both *in the dark*.'

There was a disarming directness to his words, and Tom realised it was an invitation, and perhaps an offer too. He formally took the lead.

'You are right, Sir. On your part, you wish to know the whereabouts of the letter and how you can retrieve it… whereas I am concerned about the innocent man who is to be hanged on Monday. I need to ask if you know who killed Emmet – and if you can point me and my friends toward him.'

'You state the matter succinctly, Mr Bristowe. We both have something to gain from this interview…'

They became aware of a hissing sound that was growing louder. In the distance, along some timber ramparts, a pair of giant wheels began turning, driven by jets of fire and spinning ever more quickly. In the middle, flaming candles spelled out the name ANNA-R in capitals twenty feet high. St John found himself almost shouting.

'... Tell me then, Mr Bristowe, do you know where the letter is? And how I can retrieve it?... There! You have my *plea* to you! I am not ashamed to call it such. You know how much hangs on this.'

'Mrs Greg's document is in safe keeping, Mr St John, and is being kept from both sides. We know that Lord Sunderland and his Whig friends would kill to lay their hands on it. Perhaps they have already done so...'

'And you believe the same of us, no doubt? Of Mr Harley and myself?'

'To be candid, Sir... We understand George Deacon is in your pay, and we know his reputation. We know he is on the letter's trail – and we assume you have set him on...'

Tom stopped himself – he had said more than enough. St John did not hesitate in his reply.

'Yes, Deacon has made himself useful to us, and has been in quest of the letter... But you will not be aware of what has happened this evening in Covent Garden...'

Tom was alarmed. There was something coy about St John's manner that he didn't like.

'... As you witnessed, Mr Bristowe, I was called away from the ball just now and given the news... It seems Mr Deacon has been arrested – outside the Good Fellowship of all places! And my informant tells me that he attacked Kate Primrose... You will know the name?...'

Tom was lost for words. St John bent towards him and managed a loud whisper.

'... I think, don't you, that our plot is reaching its crisis?'

Tom could hardly believe what he was hearing.

'*Kate Primrose?* – outside the Good Fellowship?'

Tom knew he should have been there! His imagination was painting the scene vividly. Kate must have come to find him –

and there was the vicious Deacon lying in wait. Tom couldn't hide his alarm.

'... Kate?... Is she hurt, Mr St John? What did he do to her?'

'I understand she is unscathed – that he merely threatened the girl. And now it seems Mr Deacon is arrested. I have no more details yet, except that he has been bundled off to the local roundhouse to await charges in the morning...'

St John's face grew taut.

'... Where is the letter now, Mr Bristowe? We have searched for it, but to no avail. It is a private letter, addressed to me – and as such it is properly mine to read. I'm sure you appreciate that.'

'Does that mean it was stolen from you, Mr St John? Was it taken from your pocket?'

Tom knew that was the crucial question.

'No – it never reached me – though I have since been told of its contents. The letter was stolen before it could be delivered... If Kate Primrose has the letter, Mr Bristowe, does she want *money?* She could name her price – there would be no difficulty, I assure you!'

He spoke with urgency. His words were accompanied by the distant sound of screaming as exploding squibs danced around youthful legs. The two men were attempting to remain reasonable and controlled.

'Mr St John... it is indeed your letter. But I happen to know the circumstances of its theft. They are embarrassing ones, and it would be understandable for you to distance yourself from them.'

'On that matter, Mr Bristowe, I am no liar. You must accept my word as a gentleman – and I trust you will!... *I never received the letter.*'

Tom realised he had stepped onto dangerous ground. His eyes glanced at St John's right hand, which rested on the hilt of his sword.

'You have my assurance on that, Sir. I would never doubt your word. But I hope you will understand why I needed to ask the question.'

St John nodded gravely. He raised the hand to his waistcoat pocket and drew out a superlative enamelled snuff box. In silence he handed it to Tom and watched intently as the Bristowe fingers and thumb did their best, the wrist making an elegant turn up to the nostrils, ending with a clean double-sniff. Tom snapped the box shut and returned it gracefully to St John, who began performing the ritual himself with nonchalant ease.

'Mr St John… You must stop protecting Deacon!…'

Tom was surprised at his own boldness. He looked anxiously at the Minister, who paused, the pinch of snuff held to his nose. Tom pressed on.

'… You know the man is a vicious criminal!'

The Minister completed the manoeuvre coolly, and the box found its way back to his pocket.

'He is a rogue, Mr Bristowe, no doubt about that! And now it seems he is a blundering and ineffective one. You are seeking the truth, so let me give it you… The man disgusts me! In the past he has proved a convenient tool for us – but like many tools, he can be replaced. I have to say that in this affair he was at first acting under my direct orders, not at the command of Mr Harley… In fact, I should tell you that I have kept Mr Secretary entirely ignorant of Mrs Greg's letter and what it reveals…'

Tom raised an eyebrow.

'… You find that surprising, but it is true. Mr Harley has plots enough forming against him, and I am wanting to spare him this – though it will not be for much longer I fear. His enemies are circling… But I tell you frankly, Mr Bristowe, George Deacon appears to have been pleasing himself in this business – *exceeding his brief*, a lawyer might say.'

'Did he kill Polly Gray?'

St John flinched as the question came.

'Yes, alas, he did... it seems the man already knew the girl as a client, and – I don't know what happened – he pushed her too far. What Deacon did was stupid, and led nowhere. He was reprimanded severely for it – *dismissed* in fact. I sent him packing! But he found his discharge hard to accept... And from that moment, finding the letter has become his personal mission. He is no longer working for me, but *against* me, do you understand? He wants to give himself power over me.'

Tom was disconcerted, but St John's words had the ring of truth. Tom began to wonder how far Deacon's angry zeal had reached.

'My friend Will Lundy was stabbed on Wednesday evening...'

'Yes, word came to me of that attack. I hope the young man survives it... I assume it was Deacon's doing... It was not at my behest, Mr Bristowe. I am sorry for it.'

'You have been following the case closely?'

'I had news of the trial, certainly. I feared mention might be made of the letter, but I gather Arthur Maynwaring's gang never looked beyond those *Bufo* verses, thank God. They were determined to blacken Mr Morphew's reputation, weren't they! And they sadly succeeded. I've always thought he was an unlikely murderer...'

St John's voice was forced to rise again as a noisy rocket exploded into white fire above them.

'... If you are searching for the man who killed John Emmet, then I suggest you look in that direction – to Maynwaring and that fellow Voyce... I assure you, neither I nor Mr Harley had any hand in it. In fact, Morphew has been something of an ally to our cause. He is of independent mind, and that makes his co-operation all the more valuable.'

It suddenly struck Tom that he had told St John very little, while on his part he had learned much that could be helpful...

but the big question was still unanswered. He was beginning to feel frustrated. George Deacon's fall – if that's what it was – was heartening news, and he wanted to be back at the Good Fellowship as soon as possible. But there was still no link from Deacon to Emmet's murder. Tom began to wonder what more he could do at this moment.

But Henry St John wasn't finished.

'I remain worried, Mr Bristowe, and have heard nothing to reassure me. You say that the letter is safe – and yet Deacon attacked Kate Primrose this evening... I have to ask myself: did he snatch the letter from her before he was arrested? This is my biggest concern. Might the letter no longer be private? What can you say to me about this?'

St John was continuing to press him. Tom began to wonder if he would ever be allowed to leave the park before he had given a satisfactory answer. Perhaps a more positive turn was needed.

'What I can say to reassure you, Sir, is that to my latest knowledge, Kate Primrose passed the letter on. She is most unlikely to have had it on her person when she was attacked.'

'Do you know where it is right now?'

'I cannot say, Mr St John, especially given your news about Deacon. The situation may be changing rapidly.

'So you won't tell me?'

Tom was beginning to feel like a hunted hare. At every twist and turn the hounds were getting closer.

'No, I cannot tell you.'

'You *will* not tell me?'

'I *cannot*, Sir.'

St John turned away, almost like a piqued lover. He gazed up at the night sky, which was suddenly quiet, and dark enough for the moon to be visible. Then he turned round again.

'Why will you not tell me? I shall pay generously. No violence will be done.'

'Mr Morphew…'

'Is that your answer, then? – Morphew?'

Tom's mind was racing. He had been standing his ground, but was conscious of sounding evasive. It was clear that Henry St John was looking to strike a bargain… but what sort of bargain? Tom was becoming nervous. If only he had Will's negotiating skills!

'Mr St John… I feel we are in a blind alley… If the letter is indeed of such inestimable importance to you – as I think it is – there may be a way out. If Mr Morphew were to be pardoned…'

Tom was not allowed to complete what would have been a long and hypothetical sentence.

'I can offer no such thing, Mr Bristowe – as well you know! I don't like the smell of it. Justice has taken its course – albeit brutally – and until a new case is made, Mr Harley cannot stoop to that. You must find fresh evidence!'

'I understand Lord Sunderland also has it in his power to give a pardon…'

'What are you implying?'

Tom was beginning to sweat, and wished he had not stepped in that direction.

'Could we not make an appeal to him? He may be less scrupulous than Mr Harley…'

The Secretary-at-War was now giving Tom a look that was a mixture of astonishment and contempt. Tom swallowed and felt a blush coming on.

'I see all too clearly where this is heading, Mr Bristowe – and I warn you not to go there. If you say more, I shall take it as a threat and shall respond as such. Why should I not have you arrested immediately? Pressing a blackmail on a Government Minister is a most serious thing…'

Tom was feeling light-headed. St John was right, of course. And Lord Melksham had been right too. Why had he not kept his uncle's words in mind?… But perhaps St John had stopped him just in time, before the hint had become an accusation? He felt humiliated and a little childish, and longed to be elsewhere. His look must have reflected the rueful turn of his thoughts, because St John noted his discomfort.

'… But rest assured, Mr Bristowe, I take what you say as hypothetical only – in the way of putting a case, as it were. And I see the force of your reasoning. You and your friends are desperate to save Morphew, and indeed Mr Harley and I also have an interest… I shall see what I can do… You have the letter in safe keeping, I trust?'

The same question had sprung back again.

'It is very safe, Mr St John. Your people have tried to unearth it – from Polly Gray, from Kate Primrose – and from poor Adèle Ménage…'

'And from you too, Mr Bristowe… Yes, I'm afraid Mr Deacon searched your room.'

So, it was Deacon who had paid him a visit on Sunday! Tom felt suddenly queasy at the thought of that man rifling through his things… And where were his papers now? He shuddered at the picture of Deacon poring over his poems.

'… You have much to ponder, I see. I shall leave you to your thoughts…'

St John was turning to leave when another loud detonation sounded in the distance. On the ramparts beyond the canal a huge golden pyramid flared into life, with rockets criss-crossing the night sky behind it; and at the apex a magnificent shimmering crown began to form in red, white, and blue. Cheers and applause rang out, interspersed with a wild youthful whooping. St John stood his ground for a moment.

'Neither of us should be proud of our conversation tonight, Mr Bristowe – and of what we have revealed of ourselves. I understand the strength of your feelings – your wish to save your friend... but you must never sink to the level of your enemies. It is a principle necessary in politics, especially at this time. I detect something of a political head on you – though I doubt you'll ever admit it... It's a pity you have no ambitions in that direction – unlike your Cousin Frank! Frank Popham has definite ambitions, and I am hoping to be able to assist them...'

St John's words sounded casual, but his face remained intent and serious.

'... I have great respect for your uncle – though I have to say that the thought of you consorting with the Whigs in this business fills me with distaste – especially as it is they who have pressed Morphew almost to death. To think of you trading secrets with the Junto would make me flinch from the whole affair...'

So, that was where the Minister wished to end it! He was being given a clear warning. Frank's political career, for which the young man had been groomed since his schooldays, was in jeopardy.

'... I think we must leave the matter there, Mr Bristowe – at least for now.'

St John took a few steps back towards the palace – there was no gesture inviting Tom's company. But then he stopped and swung round again.

'I want my letter back, Mr Bristowe! It is addressed to me and is a private communication. To withhold it is theft – and to trade it with the Whigs is tantamount to *treason*. I would advise you to inform whoever possesses it of that fact. Goodnight to you!'

As St John walked away, Tom found himself shaking, and not merely with the coldness of the air. It had been an uncomfortable interview; and although he had learned much, it scarcely brought them nearer Emmet's killer.

But Deacon was becoming the most likely suspect. If he was acting for himself it made him even more dangerous – if

St John was speaking the truth. But could such an enigmatic politician be trusted? Or was his whole purpose to deflect suspicion onto the Whigs? Tom thought for a moment. The Minister's fear that Deacon would lay his hands on the letter did seem genuine, as did his wish to keep Harley ignorant of its contents… But he cursed himself. Why, oh why, had he hinted a threat? He had meant to reassure St John but had succeeded only in antagonising him. Had he thrown the chance away? But then a handful of words echoed in his mind: *I shall see what I can do* – could they build any hope on that? Or was the return of the letter being made a condition before St John would exert himself? One thing was clear: they needed sure evidence of Morphew's innocence. No pardon could be contemplated until they had found the killer…

Tom realised he had been standing musing to himself for some time. The firework display had come to an end, and the large crowd was dispersing, some choosing to stroll back under the avenues of trees or along the vast canal, while others made their way home to Pall Mall and St James's. A few were lingering with the intention of enjoying the park's nocturnal delights. Tom suddenly longed to be with friends, and he began walking back towards the palace. He felt drained by the conversation with St John. The man was certainly wrong about one thing – politics was not his line – not at all! His mind couldn't be endlessly on the stretch like that. It was exhausting.

'Mr Bristowe! Well met, Sir!'

The jaunty greeting came from a smart-looking figure approaching him by the palace wall. Tom's face brightened.

'Well, well! Mr Grice! How good to see you. What did you make of the fireworks? Was it not a wondrous display?'

'Enough to gladden the hearts of the nation! And I was pleased there were no *unforeseen* explosions! All the bangs and bursts seemed to run without a hitch – and what colours!'

The two men fell into conversation, and Tom was at last able to relax. There was laughter and a little ribaldry, and when Harry suggested they take a stroll, Tom was happy to accept. He knew he ought to be back at the ball, but he needed to unwind first, and Harry Grice's genial company was just what he needed.

Chapter Forty-Two

THE MESSENGER BOY gave Widow Trotter a wide grin and reached over the coffee-room bar with his folded piece of paper. It was a page torn from a notebook. The young lad was breathing heavily, which spoke of urgency, and she unfolded it with some apprehension.

> *We have our man! It's HARRY GRICE – from Harley's office – his crest on the watch! Send word to Tom – I am detained here and must rest. Please take care! Will.*

The pencilled words were a little shaky, but their import was clear and the capital letters spelled out the answer they'd been searching for. Widow Trotter read the note several times as if making sure of it… Harry Grice! It gave her a jolt. She wanted to rejoice but her imagination troubled her: *I am detained here and must rest…* she could see Will lying on the floor of Heralds' College with his bandages shaken loose, bleeding and in pain. She tried to banish the grim picture (which was in fact remarkably accurate) and tell herself that he was being rightly cautious and would return in his own good time. But now the call to arms had come. There was a lot to do, and wheels to be set in motion.

So... it wasn't Henry St John who had been carrying the letter! She had been having doubts and now they were confirmed. She remembered Harry Grice quite clearly as the self-assured young man with the polite manners and winning smile, bantering with Tom and the others at the corner table, all of them fuddled and merry – although Harry Grice, as she recalled, seemed somehow more alert. But perhaps that was only in retrospect? It had been last Friday night, exactly a week ago to the very hour, and – she realised with a shock – the night of Emmet's death. She called to mind her last view of Harry guiding a fearfully drunk Ned Rokeby out of the door. He had left the party abruptly, anxious to report at the Cockpit, he said – and yet he headed *east*. She remembered distinctly. He had made a display of insisting he would deliver Ned to his lodgings in Smithfield and then turn westward. But he can have done no such thing. He must have gone on to Stationers' Yard... and kept his ten o'clock rendezvous with the angry Emmet.

Mrs Trotter was thinking quickly... Yes, Will was right, Tom had to know of this at once. At the palace he was in the thick of things and could talk with his uncle, and – if it wasn't too late – he needed to be careful with Henry St John. She recalled Tom's parting words: knowledge might be dangerous, but ignorance is worse. Perhaps something could be done tonight?... Well, it had to be tried!

She hurried into the parlour where Elias was planted. Half an hour earlier the constable had returned to the Good Fellowship and had taken a bite to eat with Kate Primrose and Mrs Ménage, mortified that he had missed Kate's revelations and anxious to receive his own report. Taking Deacon into custody had been no easy task: the Birthday Night was wild and a lot was happening. In the end he had secured Deacon in the makeshift cell beneath his own office, well shackled too. He didn't want to risk piling him in with the unruly crowd that was packed into the round-house.

Within five minutes Widow Trotter had decided the matter, and she eagerly set out her plan to Elias. She herself would go to St James's Palace and send a note up to Tom. She *must* talk with him in person! And there were Kate's revelations to be given him too. It was such an important thing, and Tom might have news of his own which she needed to hear... and of course, she added, to be outside the palace on the Birth-night might bring its own surprises...

Constable Cobb beheld her indulgently, wondering how to discourage the adventure; but that look of hers, which he knew of old, could not be countermanded. And perhaps they should tell Tom the news at once. His reply was courteous and practical.

'You have my approval, Mrs Trotter. And *I* shall come with you! On a night like this the streets are unruly for a fair lady, and there may be no hackney to be had – if not, then I can claim one as an emergency. I'll not have you wandering about at this hour. What's more, my presence may be useful if there's anything urgent to be done. What do you say?'

Widow Trotter was secretly delighted. But she thought once again of Will. Something told her all was not as it should be. She wrote a hurried note telling him of their plan and added an exhortation to rest, and send for a surgeon if need be. The messenger boy had been waiting, happily munching on a slice of toast, so she sent him off again with tuppence and watched him run up the court towards Drury Lane. Mrs Ménage and Kate, who had done enough adventuring for one evening, were content to stay in the warm parlour, sink down in their chairs, and wait for sleep to claim them.

And so, with little prospect of sleep themselves, Widow Trotter and the Constable sallied forth to the palace, not quite knowing what they would find there but certain that Tom must be told. In truth it was hardly a plan at all, but it drew them into action. And after the frustrations of the past week it was heartening to have the target in view, however distant. In their heart of hearts they suspected that all was not yet easy.

In the park, Harry Grice was in an affable mood. The embers of his pipe were glowing in the dark and the warming smoke curled around him in the frosty air. The two young men were pacing slowly along the path while Tom gave a witty sketch of the ballroom scene he'd left behind: the courtly men like strutting peacocks, their wigs wafting powder at every nod; and the women glaring through their paint and paste, sinking under swags of silver. And everywhere so much expensive swishing and clinking! The glitter of it all! – And yet the uncomfortable stiffness too, with the Queen's presence casting a solemn formality over everything.

'But I have to say, your Mr Harley brightened her. She made a point of smiling on him in front of the whole Court – singled him out for her conversation – talking intimately and even touching his arm. There were a few jealous looks being cast, I can tell you! It was quite a display. The Marlboroughs were scowling and Godolphin looked as if he'd chewed on a worm-eaten apple!'

Harry laughed.

'You say the Queen was showing Harley public favour? That's good. There's such a deal of Whig plotting going on – they're determined to bring him down. But she knows her man – how loyal he is… The Junto are relentless, Mr Bristowe! They'll stop at nothing – there's no trick they won't try.'

Tom had been intending to set politics aside, but this was drawing him in. Perhaps a little exploration might tell him something?

'How is the mood in the Cockpit, Mr Grice? The last time I saw you, you were hurrying over there – we'd had news of the French spies if you remember. And with the Greg business still unresolved… you must feel under siege? I trust you're fighting back!'

The remark was made lightly, but it hit home more strongly than he'd intended. Harry Grice stopped in his tracks. They were standing by a lamp, and Tom saw the eyes looking at him intently.

'I wasn't going to mention it, Mr Bristowe – after all, this is a night for celebration – but I want to say how sorry I am to hear about your friend Morphew, the printer. It must be weighing on you. I understand yesterday's trial was a relentless affair – and shocking too.'

'You've had a report of it, have you, Mr Grice?'

'Yes, we had a man there observing – given our concern with those *Bufo* verses. They have angered the Whigs mightily, and the Duchess has evidently been calling for blood! It seems your Mr Morphew has been another victim of the Junto. They're well organised and can call on considerable forces… But perhaps I shouldn't have raised this. I don't want to sound like a wheedling politician. We ought to talk of lighter things.'

'Don't apologise, Mr Grice. I appreciate what you say. The prosecution were intent on dangling Bufo round Morphew's neck. Yet the poor man knew nothing of the printing. Emmet did it secretly behind his back.'

'You are convinced of the man's innocence, then, Mr Bristowe?'

'Utterly! He was well and truly *staged* – made to play his part in a scene. He innocently stumbled into it.'

Tom paused, conscious of letting his feelings show. Harry Grice looked sympathy and spoke with understanding.

'It was an ordeal for you, I can see. And from what I've heard, you spoke bravely in Mr Morphew's defence – with considerable detail about the scene of the crime. But your evidence was discounted?'

'It appeared to be. My carefully argued case fell to the ground. No-one wanted to listen. I know I can *prove* the killing was done by another – I just need someone to hear me out. I think it was someone embarrassed by Emmet's papers – and threatened by what they might reveal.'

Tom knew he could say no more. Harry had his own reasons for not wanting to pursue the point, and shook his head.

'What a waste of a life! I've heard good things of Mr Morphew – that he's a man of probity – not common in his trade. What a terrible quicksand he stepped into – and it's swallowed him up.'

'We're still keeping our hopes alive, Mr Grice. The waters haven't closed over his head just yet.'

Harry had begun beating out his pipe on the lamp-post in practised fashion, striking it with short, precise strokes while directing his attention to Tom and continuing to move the political talk forward.

'I understand Arthur Maynwaring was conducting things from afar? – By the by, have you seen that loathsome ballad on Mrs Masham being handed round? Treasonous if ever a thing was! It's obviously Maynwaring's brain-child. And what a perverted brain it is! The man has planted himself in the Whig camp and is ready for any dirty job. He must have been running Morphew's trial too, don't you think?'

Tom was trying to bring his thoughts into focus and see where their talk was heading.

'Yes, I suspect so. But in the Sessions House it was his henchman Henry Voyce who was managing the show. He was accusing Emmet of being a Papist spy in the pay of the Tories. And he produced a Knight of the Post at the last moment to seal Morphew's fate. It was shocking!'

'The thing sounds so like a Whig plot, Mr Bristowe. If Morphew is innocent – and I believe you – then someone among them knows the truth. Have you pursued that? I can picture them over in Sunderland's office rubbing their hands with satisfaction. Where did Emmet get those poems from? Do you know who *Bufo* is? Might that not be the key for you?'

'We have been pursuing it I assure you. Emmet had quite a collection of papers. The man was a dealer in scandal and nasty secrets – a slippery character altogether.'

'A *toad*, you might say! Perhaps he himself was Bufo? What do you think?'

Something held Tom back. The conversation, congenial though it was, was slipping along too easily. He had to be careful.

'Perhaps it may remain a mystery – for ever!'

'But there must be a *cache* somewhere, don't you think? And perhaps there's more poems to come? That's what we've been asking ourselves in the Cockpit.'

'I doubt it – but who can say, Mr Grice... but your Mr Harley must be pleased with the effect the satires have had? Sunderland and the Marlboroughs come in for rough handling.'

'But the latest Bufo piece was read out in court, I gather – a curse that lashed out in all directions? I hear that this time Mr Harley was hitched into the rhymes too! Perhaps no-one is safe?... But you think we shall hear no more from Bufo?... How can you be certain?'

Tom swallowed and tried a smile.

'I'm not, Mr Grice. Indeed, there may be more to follow. We must be on the lookout.'

'But seriously, Mr Bristowe, have you been looking for Emmet's papers? If you could track them down you may find the evidence to exonerate Morphew? Rumour has it that Emmet had a whore in Covent Garden and would store all his things there? If you could only find *her*...'

In spite of the cold, Tom was feeling flushed and uneasy. Harry Grice may have been enthusiastically trying to help, but the questions were beginning to grate. Why did he always encounter people who seemed to be probing him – trying to find out what he knew? Even Harry was doing it. Of course, working in Harley's office would make him concerned about all this. The man was certainly a bundle of curiosity. And how near he was coming to the heart of the matter!

By this time they had begun strolling further into the park, away from the regular path and towards the wilderness where bushes and more mature trees grew in clumps. The talk was still stubbornly political, and they canvassed the question of Emmet's papers until Tom became restive. Harry persisted.

'And what does Will Lundy say of all this? I'm surprised he wasn't with you at the trial. He must have been angry at how it went – and his father on the bench too!'

This sounded provocative, and Tom had to remind himself that Harry was speaking out of naïve enthusiasm. He suddenly became conscious of being in the dark. They had wandered further than he thought.

'Let us turn back, Mr Grice, while I tell you the news – you clearly haven't heard. I have to tell you that Will was attacked on Wednesday night – he was stabbed.'

'Stabbed? In the street?'

'Yes, down in Vinegar Yard – a gloomy court off Drury Lane.'

Harry Grice continued to walk slowly beside Tom, betraying no hint of the shiver of recognition that the words *Vinegar Yard* had given him. His own nightmarish adventure down there was still vivid in his mind.

'That's shocking to hear – poor Will! Was it a street robbery? Is it serious?'

Harry's concern was intense.

'No, not serious, we *think*. He was stabbed in the shoulder. He lost a lot of blood and has to rest completely. Thankfully he's been given refuge at the Good Fellowship, so he can be watched over and cossetted. Mrs Trotter will see to that.'

Harry's innocent questions continued.

'Vinegar Yard? What would he be doing down that way? Was it after the theatre? I warrant the scoundrels were lying in wait. What did they take?'

Tom was beginning to find Harry's urgency wearing and intrusive. He was longing to be back at the ball, a glass of wine in his hand, watching Lavinia tripping it with Lord Tring. It would be much warmer in there too.

'It was no robbery, Mr Grice... but I'd rather not talk about it. We've been very worried about him.'

'Poor Will – but no robbery, you say? You don't think...'

There was a moment's respite as Harry paused and thought.

'... I'm sorry... I shouldn't say more... but you don't think it might be to do with the Bufo business, do you?... Vinegar Yard? I'm trying to recall... didn't Emmet have his whore there?'

Tom was now alarmed. This had to be stopped. Thankfully they were now under a lamp once more. Tom stood his ground.

'Mr Grice, I must apologise. Can we say nothing more of Bufo and all he has led to? The very topic is an uncomfortable one. It's good of you to interest yourself like this, and what you say of Mr Morphew is encouraging. But the affair is far from simple.'

Tom's mind was working. Harry Grice knew about Vinegar Yard! He may have thought he was doing the probing, but that was the true revelation. Tom longed to be off, but he also longed to know more. He wondered if this might be the moment to turn matters round on Harry. He must have encountered Deacon, by report at least, and might know more about his work for Henry

St John – dealing directly with Emmet, perhaps? And was Deacon indeed now acting on his own? This was an opportunity he had to seize.

'We are wondering if *George Deacon* might have been involved in the attack on Will. Do you know anything of the man? He would seem to be an evil creature always ready to sell his services – that's what we've heard.'

The remark clearly went home, and Harry Grice couldn't hide his discomfort. Now it was his turn to be wary, and Tom could see it in his eyes. They were standing under the lamp, and Tom noticed his face taking on a furtive look. All the genial bravado had ebbed away. What was happening? Tom was beginning to feel unsettled in his company, even a little anxious. Perhaps he shouldn't have played that card.

'George Deacon? – Yes, Mr Bristowe. An unpleasant character. Although it's well beyond my sphere. I think he's one of those unscrupulous agents who bargain with both sides – a bit like our Mr Emmet!'

It was an unguarded remark. Tom went cold. Emmet bargaining with both sides? What was the man saying? He appeared to know more than a little about Emmet's activities. *Out of his sphere*, he had said, but for a mere understrapper in Harley's office he knew more than he should. Tom wondered what Will would do at this point. Would he draw back, or press on? Tom hardly paused.

'So, are you saying this Deacon has been doing service for Mr Harley? The man clearly is without scruple…'

'What do you mean? Mr Harley?'

'No, I meant, if Deacon is serving both sides… that would make it uncomfortable for him if he visited the Cockpit!'

Tom was trying to make light of it. But Harry Grice was looking increasingly ill at ease.

'I really don't know about this, Mr Bristowe – I've only

heard the man's name mentioned... but are you saying you think *he* stabbed Mr Lundy?'

Tom swallowed. What were they doing? It was as if they were testing one another, each man needing to know, and yet afraid of revealing...

'As I said, it was no robbery. Perhaps it was someone determined that Will shouldn't attend the trial? I don't know... but George Deacon is clearly on the trail of something. It would help us to know what.'

There was no response – just an eloquent silence. Tom sensed that Deacon was a source of embarrassment not just to Henry St John, but to Harry Grice as well. Remembering St John's words, he began to wonder if Harry also knew more than Robert Harley did – was he in St John's confidence? Might he even be working for him?... And was it merely a coincidence that Harry Grice had been in his path tonight? The alternative possibility was unnerving.

It was at that moment, with an electric feeling unsettling them both, that Harry Grice decided it was time to go – Tom's suspicions were evidently veering in his direction, and he was feeling awkward. Unthinkingly, Harry took out his watch and consulted it.

'Well, it's later than I thought, Mr Bristowe, I think I have to head home!'

The night was still, and the air was becoming frosty. The lamplight from above was icy sharp. The gold of the handsome pocket-watch glowed in Harry Grice's hand as he consulted the dial. Then, with an elegant snap he closed the lid, and Tom saw, brilliantly etched in silver, the outline of a wild boar, and above it a crown.

He was transfixed. All the threads of discomfort and suspicion converged in his brain. There it was! The gold watch stolen by Polly Gray in Rose Street. Before him was standing the man whose pockets had been emptied that fateful night – the man carrying the letter for Henry St John. He recalled Mr Secretary's words – that the letter had never reached him. Of course it hadn't… Harry Grice was meant to deliver it, but he'd been diverted on his mission and succumbed to Daphne's sorcery. He had reeled off into the night in a stupor, leaving both letter and watch behind. Had he then tried to retrieve the letter from Kate Primrose – muffling himself up and making his own unwise journey to Vinegar Yard? – taking along a gun he didn't intend to use?… So much was beginning to make sense – at last.

Seconds passed in silence. Harry Grice saw Tom staring intently at the watch, and at that moment he too realised that a curtain between them had dropped away. Both of them were exposed – each sensing real danger from the other. Harry was now looking at him.

'So, Mr Bristowe – you *know!* I see I've been unguarded. You recognise this watch, do you?'

Tom's look was enough.

'And I have been unguarded too, Mr Grice. What have we been doing?'

'We have been playing a game, the two of us…'

Tom saw him touching his sword. The fingers were curling round its hilt.

'… You know about my humiliating nocturnal adventure.'

It wasn't a question, it was an accusation. With a sudden swishing sound the sword blade was out of its sheath.

'What are you doing, Mr Grice?'

'I'm continuing the play. This must be settled between us, don't you agree? I see no other course.'

Harry Grice's voice was surprisingly determined, and cold as the frosted breath that came with it.

'You're mad! This is absurd.'

'We may not have spelled it out, Mr Bristowe, but we have both delivered insults to each other – in thought at least. We must do the gentlemanly thing. I ask you to draw. I'm only sorry that your pathetic dress-sword looks hardly adequate for the task – and I doubt you were in the smart set at Oxford. No swords allowed in the library!'

It was said with disdain – a verbal thrust. Tom knew that the thrust of his sword would follow. He saw its naked point being held toward his chest, and began to shake. His absurd waistcoat was taunting him, and his dress wig even more so. What a fop he must look! One moment lounging in the royal ballroom, and the next out in St James's Park at night, with a half-crazed swordsman about to charge at him.

'Draw! Or I'll run you through for a coward!'

These were taunts he could take. What he mustn't do was draw himself – that would simply bring his opponent on... it would also license him to be killed – the victim of a sordid duel!

He determined to do nothing, and took a step back. That corner of the park was now horribly quiet – and the place had been so busy! Tom shouted loudly through the trees.

'Sheathe your sword! This is *murder!*'

His cry rang out – but as soon as he had made it, Harry thrust at him without waiting for him to draw. He would kill him all the same.

Another step back – and another thrust, this time only inches from the silken cornfield. Thrust again! Tom drew his sword – simply to keep him back – but it was swept aside. Yet another thrust came, which he managed to twist away from. He tried to remember how to adopt a defensive position, but it was hopeless. There was nothing he could do. There was a malevolent look on Harry Grice's face as he leapt forward and made a vicious sweep. Somehow Tom parried it – he didn't know how – he was trying not to retreat but to hold his ground – that had to be safer. But he knew he was seconds away from being skewered on Harry's blade. Another swift thrust, and their swords clashed. Another thrust. At that moment Tom's pompous wig shifted on his head and hung across one eye. With a shout of frustrated anger he grabbed at it with his free hand and threw it straight at Harry Grice. The wig caught on the end of Harry's sword, quite pierced through and looking like a slice of toast. He was distracted for a moment, and Tom frantically made a thrust himself, which caught his opponent on the arm. There was a cry of disbelief. Tom shouted out again, and was suddenly aware of three men running towards them. Soldiers! One of them threw himself on Harry, and the other grabbed Tom's sword and flung it to the ground. The patrolling footguards must have heard the commotion. A great wave of relief surged over Tom, but he saw that Harry was clutching his arm.

'This man attacked me! I had to defend myself! Look! He has injured me!'

The third soldier grabbed Harry's hand roughly.

'A scratch, by the look of it – serves you right enough! Well, what do we think, boys? A pair of silk-button duellists, are they not? This wig has had its death blow!'

The other soldiers laughed. He held up Tom's full-dress wig under the lamp like a decapitated trophy.

'A truly aristocratical headpiece, gentlemen!'

He struck it with his hand and the powder flew over his tunic.

'Well, what shall we do with these fine fellows, do you think?'

Tom and Will were bent over, facing each other, the two soldiers pinioning their arms behind them.

'Let's cool them off in the canal!' said one of them.

The sergeant smiled, obviously tempted by the idea. But he demurred. They were both gentlemen, after all, and might have connections… a less violent humiliation was perhaps in order.

'No, Corporal – I think the round-house is their lot. They are offenders against Her Majesty's peace – not that there's been much of that tonight! We must do things by the book.'

But on that night of rowdy celebration, the *book* had to be set aside. Tom Bristowe and Harry Grice were marched off to the first watchman they saw, only to be told that the round-house was completely full and the local magistrate was on business somewhere. It was a chaotic night!

And so, the two duellists were taken to the guards' barracks nearby, where a suitable lock-up was found down in the cellars – suitable only in the sense of being cold, bare, and smelling of horse – and well away from everything.

The guardsmen made their delivery, and the heavy door was shut on the two of them.

'But he'll try to kill me!' shouted Harry Grice in protest.

The corporal grinned:

'Then you'll have to settle it like men – with your fists! Good night gentlemen! The watch will call on you in the morning. For both your sakes, I hope the fight doesn't last too many rounds – thirty should be enough, I think!'

There was more hilarity, and the three guardsmen went on their way. And suddenly there was silence.

Inside the cell was a pile of stinking horse-blankets, a stool, and a low oak bench set against the wall. Nothing more. And the place was entirely dark, save for the uncertain light that a small window gave from the illuminated parade ground above, where a few torches flickered bravely. Tom and Harry were saying nothing, but each was thinking hard. It was going to be a terrible night. If things were to be settled between them, would it be by fists or by talk?

Tom knew which he preferred – but what more was there to say? Did the full truth have to come out – on both sides? And what would that mean for each of them? Tom looked at the crouching figure who was occupying the stool and had his head in his hands. He knew that, whatever was going to happen, sleep – dangerous, vulnerable sleep – was not an option.

Chapter Forty-Three

WIDOW TROTTER AND Elias found themselves having to walk the last furlong to the palace. Pall Mall was seething like a beehive. Sedan chairs packed the pavement, and lines of extravagant coaches were ranked along the street. It was an exhibition gallery of equipages, each newly furbished for the occasion. The horses glistened and the lounging grooms wore their new liveries with pride, sporting gold braid on their jackets and coronets on their breeches. But on this Birthday Night Mrs Trotter strode past the modish display without pause. Her mind was on practical things, and Elias too was thinking hard about how they might convey the note to Tom. It was no simple matter. The billet had been written, addressed to 'Mr Bristowe (with Viscount Melksham's party)' and sealed, and it looked suitably important; but beyond the crush of gawping onlookers they still had to penetrate the cordon of guards at the gate beneath the tower. Here female charms proved less effective than the no-nonsense persistence of a constable, and the note was finally taken by a liveried footman stationed inside the arch for that purpose. He looked at the direction.

'The young gentleman is in demand tonight!'

It was a muttered observation, but audible enough for Elias to detain the man by the arm and ask the meaning. The footman was disconcerted at the spontaneous arrest, but kept his dignity.

'Not an hour ago, Sir, a note was sent up – by Mr Secretary St John, no less!'

Widow Trotter overheard the name and was all ears with alarm.

'And what was its import, may I ask?' Elias prompted.

The footman began shaking his head, and the constable's grip tightened. The man pointed out that he had no way of knowing the contents – but the young gentleman had left the palace – he could only think it was a summons. Mrs Trotter stepped forward and explained that their note had reference to the same matter, so they would be grateful if it could be delivered quickly. It was when a worried looking Lord Melksham appeared some ten minutes later that they knew something was wrong. He hadn't seen his nephew for almost an hour, and had just heard from the footman about the earlier note.

'Henry St John is upstairs in the state rooms,' he said, 'and has been there for some time... but I can't find Tom!'

At this point they needed privacy, so Lord Melksham led them both into the quieter colonnade where they could talk without being overheard. Even so, he glanced around him, leaned on his cane, and spoke quietly.

'I can tell you that tonight my nephew has given me a full account of everything, and how things stand with your investigations. In particular he's told me about Mrs Greg's letter and what it contains. I assure you I'm sworn to secrecy! An hour ago Tom was all for charging Mr St John with it, but I urged caution and tried to dissuade him. But it now seems that St John himself has sought a meeting – out in the park!'

Mrs Trotter gave him an anxious look.

'But you say Mr Bristowe hasn't returned?'

'It would seem not. I thought he would be with his aunt and cousin in the ballroom, but no. And they haven't seen him either... I must return at once and ask St John what is going on.'

Lord Melksham looked crestfallen. This was exactly the confrontation he was hoping to avoid – and now he was in danger of bringing it about himself.

He settled them on a bench in the colonnade and made his way back to the state rooms. After a quarter of an hour he returned from the interview looking a little less grim-faced. He told them that according to St John, he and Tom had strolled in the park: they had watched the fireworks together and discussed various matters, particularly Morphew's trial and how it had been conducted, and Tom had inquired if St John might intervene with Mr Harley to have Morphew pardoned.

'And of course,' said Lord Melksham, 'St John told him he could do nothing of the sort. Not unless new evidence was found.'

'And so, Mrs Greg's letter wasn't talked of?'

'Mr Secretary didn't mention it – and I thought it wise not to do so either... but it seems Tom did make a strong plea on Morphew's behalf – rather too strong, St John says. But they parted reasonably amicably – he tells me they were able to *clear the air*. He left Tom in the park – looking *contemplative*, he says.'

'Poor Mr Bristowe,' said Mrs Trotter. 'The interview must have cast him down. But I'm glad nothing was said about the letter.'

But now it was her turn to give Lord Melksham the evening's news. He seated himself beside them and heard with mounting amazement about events at the Good Fellowship: Deacon's arrest – the reading of Mrs Greg's letter – Kate Primrose's story – and finally Will's note from the College of Arms.

'So you see, My Lord, the pieces all fit together. We now know that Mr Grice met with Emmet in the printing-house that night, desperate for the return of his stolen letter. But Emmet had brought only a blank, and was asking a hundred guineas! And it was at ten o'clock – the very hour of the killing… This is our new evidence – evidence of Mr Morphew's innocence!'

'And of Mr Grice's guilt, you say?' said Lord Melksham. 'It is certainly a very different scene from the one painted at the trial.'

'Yes, My Lord,' said Elias. 'Not the Angry Printer at all – rather the angry victim of a blackmail!'

Tom's uncle was looking thoughtful.

'It would seem so. The evidence is quite precise… This Mr Grice needs to be questioned at once…'

Another furrow was added to Lord Melksham's brow.

'… But what has happened to Tom? Could he have returned to the Good Fellowship, Mrs Trotter?… He would surely not have done so without telling me – it's most unlike him.'

'Well, he never came back from the park,' she said in darkened tones. 'There are mischief-makers abroad on a night like this.'

Elias immediately got to his feet.

'I must walk round there. Soldiers will be patrolling. And I must talk to the Watch. We'll soon know if there has been a robbery, or some such thing… You must stay here, Molly.'

'No, Elias, I can't sit on my backside feeling anxious. We must go together. Something is tapping at me. Tom is in trouble… Remember what happened to Will! Tom knows more than he should – as do we all!'

Lord Melksham also stood up, a resolute expression on his face.

'You mustn't alarm yourself, Mrs Trotter. I know everything now, and intend to do something about it… With our wits and determination we can expose the truth of this sordid affair. If Tom has been hurt in any way I shall never forgive myself!… Mr Cobb – Mrs Trotter – I'm glad to have met you both at last. Tom is blessed to have such friends…'

With an endearing, almost naïve formality Lord Melksham shook their hands.

'... This has been a curious night altogether, and I warrant it holds more surprises yet. *You* must both to the park – and *I* have to confront Mr St John again. This question of the letter has to be settled, and I shall challenge him about it – and about Mr Grice as well. I suspect the young man was acting as St John's agent in the business... but we shall see – You must leave that side of things to me. Let us meet here again in half an hour – and please to wait if I've not returned. Her Majesty has very thoughtfully gathered all our leading actors together for the occasion. There are some *big-wigs* in the palace tonight who need to be shaken out of their complacency. A big tiara also!'

And so the three of them set about their respective tasks, unaware that only a few hundred yards away two wigless young actors were playing out a scene that would determine the matter decisively, for good or ill.

In their makeshift dungeon, Tom was looking at Harry Grice and wondering what the man was going to do. He was still cradling his head in his hands, but whether through despair or regret, in calculation or mounting anger, Tom couldn't be sure. The figure hadn't stirred for a full minute. His breathing was audible and regular, which suggested concentration. Tom was seated on the bench opposite, his mind restless. He couldn't help but picture John Morphew at that moment sitting just like him, head back against the wall of his condemned cell and brooding on what was to come. Tom felt very close to him.

And what might he himself have to face before morning? He knew his predicament was serious; but there was also something faintly absurd about it – the stuff of picaresque comedy – and he couldn't help seeing it as a travesty of Morphew's plight. Here he was, caught up in a schoolboy duel, arrested by laughing soldiers, thrown into their smelly lock-up, falsely accused by a nervous suspect – and perhaps facing death at his hands. He was thirsty, and his lips were dry... Was he, as he suspected, shut in a cell with John Emmet's killer? The thought made him watch his antagonist closely. It was pitch dark, but the occasional glimmer of the distant torchlight gave moments of eery animation. The man's breathing continued firm and easy, and was beginning to sound worryingly determined.

Suddenly the figure stirred into movement. Harry Grice lifted his head and spoke the first words – and they were indeed determined ones, directed to himself as much as to Tom.

'I really think I must kill you here. I can see no other way...'

Tom stopped breathing. It seemed his own life was already discounted. He wondered whether to fling himself at Harry in heroic desperation and bring the death struggle on. But he waited. He sensed that something else was being planned, and his curiosity made him hold back. The next words Tom heard were less dramatic, as if spoken by another person.

'... Mr St John has told me you know about the stolen letter – that you know where it is and won't return it. This is simple theft. The letter is *stolen* – it is not yours to keep! How stupid you are, Mr Bristowe! You could have handed the letter over, and all would have been forgotten.'

In replying Tom evaded the accusation.

'So it was you who brought the news of Deacon's arrest tonight?... You work for St John!'

'Yes, and have been proud to do so.'

'Do you also do his dirty work?'

'The dirt is not on *our* hands, Mr Bristowe... He said you even tried to bargain with him over the letter and went so far as to accuse him of being prepared to kill to have it back. How dare you threaten him like that!'

Tom could scarcely believe what he was hearing.

'This is hypocrisy, Mr Grice! The man will happily use you to kill for him. What dirtier dealing can there be?'

'You think you know a lot, Mr Bristowe – but how I long to disillusion you! I long so much that I'm prepared to stay your execution until I see the truth dawn in your eyes... Then I shall kill you.'

The voice was chillingly routine. Tom knew he now had no choice.

'You reckon without my strength, Mr Grice! A man fighting for his life!'

'In that case, you should rush at me now... Or are you curious to have the mystery solved? The choice is yours... If you wish, you can die knowing nothing further.'

The question was a confident one. Tom was silent, and Harry's assurance grew.

'Of course, Mr Bristowe, because I play the villain, I don't play fair...'

He reached down into the lining of his waistcoat.

'... I fear I have another weapon.'

Out came a knife. It was small, but would certainly do the business. Tom almost choked at the neatness of it all, moment by moment. It was as if every move he had made that evening – every word he had spoken – had brought him nearer the trap, and it was finally about to close on him.

Harry Grice remained nonchalant. He held the knife loosely in his palm and adjusted himself on the stool.

'Mr St John told me he gave you good advice – he encouraged you to discover a Whig plot to kill Emmet – but instead you seemed intent on implicating him. You really should have confined your suspicions to the Junto. Much safer!

After all, it was they who wanted Emmet dead – as well you know.'

'So it was you who murdered Emmet! And you think that to kill me will lift the accusation from you… I can picture the scene. On Friday night you went to the printing-house to retrieve your letter, but perhaps Emmet laughed at you, did he? Or demanded too high a price?… Is that what happened, Mr Grice?…'

There was silence; but through the gloom Tom detected the hint of a smile on Harry's face.

'… And now poor Morphew will die on Monday, and then all will be settled – or so you hope. The events will be remembered as the famous incident of the Angry Printer. And that trashy broadside – from one of your hacks I've no doubt – will be the official record. Am I right…?'

Again there was silence.

'… You must have been delighted to see the Whigs muddying the waters – not only assembling the case against Morphew, but writing the script for it. How good of them to distract us as they did! We were convinced the Junto had planned the killing – it bore the stamp of their ruthless logic – and yet it seems Emmet's death had nothing to do with Bufo… I think I see how you arranged it…'

At every sentence Tom spoke, Harry Grice's smile grew wider, almost admiringly, as if he were hearing a child reciting.

'You have mystical powers, Mr Bristowe!'

'But I fail to see how killing me will help you. It will surely raise suspicions and shine a light on your affairs. You forget, I'm not alone in knowing the truth about you.'

There was a sudden outburst.

'The *Truth!* Ah, what confidence! You know the truth, do you? I think not!… well, let me tell you how life goes on in this world… All is over with me! I am beyond making sense of things… I have been disowned, Mr Bristowe, and sent packing!

Mr St John says his patience is at an end, and he now washes his hands of me. He told me so tonight – and his anger was intense. I must shift for myself, he says, and find a living where I may. I've lost everything, Mr Bristowe! – all my hopes and plans – and I cannot but think it's because of *you* – I can only see it that way... And so, if I kill you, it's not only to silence you, but to vent my anger. It will be a *catharsis* – I'm sure you know how powerfully that works...'

'And did it work with Emmet, Mr Grice? Did that ease your resentment at his blackmail?'

'You have everything so neat, Mr Bristowe – I admire your tidy mind. But nothing is ever neat in this world – it's confused, illogical, the stuff of accidents! Have you not seen that? That night in Rose Street I was damnably drunk, a bloody fool! And since then every step I've taken to recover myself has made it worse – has pulled me in further... And now I have nothing to lose!'

Tom noticed a wildness about Harry's eyes, which were catching what little light there was. He realised – what he should have seen before – that the man had been drinking heavily. Until this moment Harry had shown icy self-command – the disciplined sobriety of the confirmed sot – but now his passion was betraying him. Tom was witnessing the agitation of a man who could take his drink but couldn't take the troubling thoughts the drink unlocked. Those were now escaping, and they were breaking down his defences.

Tom was thinking fast, and suddenly understood: Harry Grice was longing to tell his story. It would no doubt be a confession... and if that could bring the catharsis that Harry longed for, there was a chance his own death might not figure – that it would cease to be the answer. And so Tom spoke to his cellmate with deliberate calm and reassurance. The darkness helped.

'I think you should tell me everything, Mr Grice. I guess that you have not yet done so to anyone – least of all to yourself. I am here to listen to you.'

The voice came out of the gloom:

'I'm done for, Mr Bristowe!'

'Well, that makes two of us, Harry! We have plenty of time – so tell me your story. I'll not judge you – but I badly want to understand.'

And so the story began to unfold.

Greatly to Tom's relief Harry Grice began at the beginning and seemed to be settling into what would be a rambling tale. Tom hoped he might be able to prolong it with questions. The more Harry talked, he decided, the calmer he might become – so long as the anger could be channelled. And so Tom listened intently – not only to Harry's words but also for any human presence that might be stirring within earshot of their cellar. But all seemed shut down for the night. Only an occasional distant shout from the parade-ground reminded him what day this was.

Harry began with his life as a humble clerk in Harley's office, routinely copying correspondence and extracting from agents' reports – until the Greg affair had given him his opportunity. When the scandal broke, Harley's enemies had seen their chance to bring him down, and had begun visiting William Greg in gaol, pressing him to incriminate his minister.

Tom interrupted to express his disgust at the Whigs' tactics, and their cruel bribery – for that's what it was – of Greg and his family.

'Yes, his family!' said Harry. 'That's where I've been trying to help. William Greg is my friend. We began working in Harley's office the very same week, and we became close. Since his trial, both sides have been visiting him in Newgate – the Whigs to bribe him, and Mr Harley's friends to stiffen his resolve.'

'Yes,' said Tom, 'I've heard about that – it must be a kind of torture – his poor wife!'

'Elizabeth Greg has been very brave. At first she begged her husband to consider her and the children – but William's devotion to Mr Harley has proved unshakeable, and so she agreed to say nothing more. But she's somewhat stubborn herself. The Whigs continue to assail her, but the more they have pressed, the more she has come to hate them. She boasted to me that, like the Queen, she was resisting the blandishments of the Junto – and Her Majesty was no bad example!'

'And so, you visited her?'

'Yes. Being a lowly clerk meant I wouldn't be noticed. I was given authority, by Mr St John himself, to offer her reassurances that she and the children would be looked after – that a pension would be arranged for her. You may say this is bribery too – but I answer that it is charity, not persuasion. She needed to know that she would not be left destitute.'

'And Greg was no doubt informed of what was being arranged?'

'Yes indeed. Mr Harley could not offer him his life, but at least he could mitigate the torture a little.'

'But Mrs Greg's letter, Harry – did you oversee its writing?'

'No, certainly not! I had visited her at home one or two times – to sit with her and ease her thoughts. About ten days ago, as I rose to leave, she pressed the letter into my hand. I saw the direction and asked its contents – but she simply said: "Give it to Mr St John – it is a private message from myself. He is Mr Harley's close friend, is he not? You may guess what I ask of him. I have no hopes of it, but it is a plea I must attempt!" Well, I accepted the letter – I could not refuse her – and took it to be her final appeal. I was right, of course… but there was something else said in the letter that I never guessed at. You know to what I refer. If I had known it then, I would have burned the thing immediately.'

'How did you discover its contents? Did you open it?'

'No! I have opened the letters of spies and traitors more than once – but not here. How could I hand it to Mr St John already opened? I would never have been trusted more! No, it was when I realised the letter had been taken. I called on her at once and explained what had happened, and that was when she told me of its contents. She was alarmed that she had revealed a secret her husband had solemnly entrusted to her. Indeed, she wept in front of me. She confessed her weakness and her desperation. What irony! Mr Harley's goodness in overlooking William's treason had kept her silent – but now in gratitude she had revealed it!... The letter was to be destroyed on reading, she said, but alas... you know the outcome!'

Harry Grice's stool suddenly grated on the floor – but he wasn't rising, only settling himself again. Tom urgently needed him to continue the story.

'So this brings us to Rose Street, Harry... what took you there that night?'

It was a naïve question, but Tom reckoned a hint of innocence wouldn't be amiss and might draw out the tale a little.

'*What took me there?* Lust, Mr Bristowe! The pricking in the loins! What else? On my walk home I called at a tavern and was full of spirits. A gang of clubbable Tories was gathered round a punchbowl, and I was invited to drink a toast to Her Majesty – to the True Church – to the downfall of the Whigs – to Prince George and the British navy – to the repeal of the land-tax – to our mistresses – to Mrs Bracegirdle – to the Martyr Charles – so many toasts! At the end I think I proposed a toast to the tom-cat under our table... And so I left them in a mood of high adventure. I found myself in Rose Street and remembered how George Deacon had boasted of his remarkable girl, Daphne, who was so obliging and who would say *no* to *nothing!*... The devil was in me, and I hauled myself up there... I think you know the rest...'

There was a pause. Tom felt his heart beating harder as the succession of events unfolded. Perhaps Harry was right – what a chain of accident and coincidence shapes our lives!

'… Well, after my little Covent Garden adventure I came to consciousness the next morning in St Paul's churchyard, would you believe? What disgrace! But at least it was consecrated ground. My pockets had been emptied, and my beautiful watch had been taken – it was my grandfather's, such a precious heirloom! – and the letter was also missing. But it was the watch that concerned me, and I gave little thought to the letter. Indeed I had no clear memory for the rest of that day, and only at evening did I begin to recall the details of my visit to Daphne…'

Tom heard him give a grunt of revulsion.

'… The taste in my mouth was frightful – it was the taste of abject humiliation – the savour of disgust. When I saw Mrs Greg again and heard about the letter's contents I called on Mr St John at once. I was frantic and hardly knew where to turn. I confessed all, and he was furious at my stupidity – as I was myself. I offered to return to Rose Street, but he said that George Deacon was the man for that task – after all, Daphne was his whore. Deacon could sort it out well enough. But…'

Harry made a sudden pause. Tom waited a few seconds – he sensed that Harry was beginning to find it hard re-living the scene.

'… But… that vicious fool Deacon! I don't know what happened – but poor Polly Gray met her end. She had wasted no time in fencing the watch and selling the letter – it seems she was a practised cozener – and Deacon must have been enraged. Perhaps he decided to punish her by taking his pleasure violently… We can only guess!'

'That's shocking,' said Tom quietly.

'And so, yet again Mr St John had cause to be angry. Things were beyond his control. He dismissed Deacon from his service and ordered me to make contact with Emmet myself. Oh God! What a train of disasters!'

Suddenly Harry rose from his stool and stood to his full height. He strode a couple of paces and leant his head against the door.

'What wouldn't I give for a pipe of tobacco? The bastards took them from me!'

Tom could hear Harry striking his forehead against solid oak. If only the man could settle himself with a pipe! A frantic anxiety wasn't helpful. Tom did his best to speak words of sympathy and seized the chance to draw Harry back to their own arrest. The guardsmen's mockery was something they could re-live together, and for a moment it brought them onto the same side.

But it was not long before the story picked up again.

'And so, we come to John Emmet... I knew the man would be trouble the first time I met him. He admitted to possessing the letter, but refused to reveal its hiding-place – and there was something about his manner – it was as if he were playing with me. I felt like a trout on a hook. He made me admit the importance of the letter's contents while professing to be ignorant himself. There was a confidence about him that suggested he knew what was hidden under the seal... I reminded him that the letter was stolen and he was behaving like a criminal – but instead of laughter I received a smile of collusion – as if we both had dirty hands. The man was beginning to sicken me!... So, imagine my horror when he named a *hundred guineas* as his price! I could not believe it. But the look he gave me told all. He knew exactly its worth – a price that would secure his future. For him it was a fortune. "I'm sure Mr St John will see the wisdom of the bargain!" he said, twinkling with his eyes in that annoying way. I could have hit him!...'

For an instant Tom warmed to Harry Grice. It was a disconcerting moment.

'... Well, I agreed to attempt raising something like the sum. But as I was leaving he added words that struck a chill through me: "I'm sure Mr Maynwaring will prove able to match the amount..." *Will prove!* He spoke as if for him the bargaining was just beginning!...'

Tom spontaneously gave a low whistle. Emmet had taken a mighty gamble. It was the deep play of a practised gamester.

'... And so it proved. When I arrived at the printing-house on Friday night I simply stepped into his trap. I walked hopefully into the place, but I met a man determined to frustrate and rile me. I had not dared ask Mr St John for the money – that would have provoked him beyond measure. Instead I hit on the expedient of raising it in the City. There are lenders with whom the Cockpit deals, and a political loan can be expedited. Our credit is good, and I thought the account would be gratefully settled once the bargain was done...'

Tom understood very well. He was beginning to learn something of how the system operated.

'... I managed to raise sixty pounds – a small enough sum to the banker, but it was without collateral – and added twenty of my own. I thought the amount of eighty pounds would prove enough and Emmet would seize at it... But instead I met with derision. He dangled the words *hundred guineas* at me, like a shopkeeper addressing a street urchin... and then I received a tirade against *Mr Harley and all his works*. I discovered that the Bufo pamphlet Emmet had printed – *The Magic Glass* – had been repudiated. I know Mr Harley was displeased with it, especially for its libel against Mr Addison whom he respects, and had refused to sanction payment. So Emmet had been left bearing the expense himself. His resentment was extreme, and within a few minutes he was telling me that if I offered *five hundred* guineas he would not give me the letter! He told me he was printing off that very night another invective from Bufo in which Mr Harley would receive a warning shot – and there would be more to follow!... As for Mrs Greg's letter, he said he would let Arthur Maynwaring have it – someone who would be able to make the very best use of it...'

Tom caught his breath and exhaled loudly.

'... And then I saw the letter itself – or what I thought was the letter. It certainly looked like it – the same seal and direction. He took it out of his wallet as if to taunt me. He said he had been betrayed by Harley, and wanted me to carry a message to him – that *Nemesis* was at hand. The man was crazed! He was determined to cause the most trouble he could...'

Harry was breathing quickly as he re-lived the experience. The enveloping darkness must have released his imagination.

'... Emmet put the letter in his pocket and told me to leave. But I was desperate – I sprang at him and reached for the thing. He fought me off, but I managed to seize hold of it. This incensed him even more, and there was a wild struggle. That was when I landed the blow on him – a punch that lifted his chin and sent him reeling backwards.... . His skull came down hard on something sharp projecting from one of the printing presses. It seemed to skewer him. His eyes blazed and he twitched for a few seconds before becoming still. Dead still! Something had been severed, and he was lifeless in a moment, stock still, and staring out. I knew at once... I lifted him down to the floor...'

Harry was by now catching his breath as he recalled the scene.

'... I was lost! I took hold of the letter and pocketed it. When I stood up and saw him lying there with the blood seeping from his brain, I knew I had to do something. I was frantic and my mind was hurrying on. I wanted to run off, but told myself I had to think. I saw the manuscript of the curse which he'd dropped on the floor, and I thrust it into his hand and closed the fist. I'm ashamed to say I thought it might deflect suspicion onto someone else. I didn't know that Mr Morphew had been released that night and would soon be blundering onto the scene. I simply thought the paper would implicate Emmet in the printing of *Bufo* – and would distance his death from me, and from the letter.'

'And what about the key, Harry? Tell me about that.'

'Ah, the key! Yes, there I thought I was being clever. Emmet had locked the door on us, so I had to reach into his pocket for it... but as I left, it occurred to me that I should return it there. I thought it would suggest the door was unlocked when his attacker entered – that it was a stranger who had fought with him, not someone he had let in. The Whigs' outrage at *Bufo* made me think the scene would cast suspicion on them...

'And that was how I left it... But when I reached home, I decided to break the seal. I knew I could say Emmet had broken it... You can imagine my horror when I saw that it was a mere blank. I looked at it more closely and the paper was slightly different – a little heavier. I knew at once what he'd done... that the genuine letter was still being kept somewhere, and that what he'd dangled before me had been an empty sheet!.... And that was when attention turned to Kate Primrose – to *Clarissa*...'

Tom was astounded by what he was hearing. Something was not right. He was thinking about the walking-cane, the supposed murder weapon. He was wondering how to raise the matter.

'Harry!... So you didn't kill Emmet deliberately – you didn't *murder* him. You fought with him and he broke his head open on the press! It was manslaughter at most!'

'Yes, but how could I confess? Who would believe the truth of what happened?... You see, by the time the "murder" was discovered, the body had been tampered with – and the cane used on him with incredible violence. The printing-house had become a *murder scene*... Shortly after I left, someone entered that room and rearranged the picture to tell a different story!'

Chapter Forty-Four

STAIRCASES CAN BE private places. In a drawing-room or ballroom a man is in a polite space and available for social chit-chat and easy conversation; but two men close conferring on a staircase with their wigs turned to the wall are not to be interrupted. The Secretary-at-War and the Deputy Keeper of the Privy Purse were in conference, and other passing ball-goers were schooled enough in social forms as to let them be. The men's voices were in hushed negotiation – as intense as any between envoys concluding a treaty.

Lord Melksham had had little difficulty in persuading Henry St John that it was time the unfortunate business of Mrs Greg's letter was settled. The two Wiltshire neighbours were long acquainted, and their families far longer, and co-operation had served them well in the past. At first St John was alarmed that his friend knew all the details, but he soon saw that finding the truth of the Emmet affair would advantage both of them. Each set out what he knew, and together they began to contemplate what lay before them. St John was speaking gravely.

'... Yes, alas, the hapless Mr Grice has left victims in his wake! – And now it seems John Morphew must be added to the list. You're right to have suspicions. It's quite possible the young man did kill Emmet at that meeting... But are you sure this Clarissa is telling the truth?'

'I cannot see she has cause to lie,' said Lord Melksham. 'We know that her man Emmet had a rendezvous in the printing-house that night with Mr Grice, and brought along a forged document for which he was intending to ask a hundred guineas. It was a serious blackmail – as serious as could be imagined.'

Henry St John leaned forward and his voice sank to a whisper.

'Yes, Mr Grice was acting on my behalf, but I swear I knew nothing of that meeting in the printing-house, nor about the money. It was his own arrangement – he must have hoped to set right the chaos he'd created. He did seem shocked at the news of Emmet's killing. He said that at their first encounter Emmet had refused to hand over my letter and was threatening to transact with Maynwaring and the Whigs instead. So much Grice told me – and I didn't enquire further. He knew I must remain ignorant. He did not own to any violence – but then, why should he? That second meeting in the printing-house was a dangerous thing to attempt, and I can well understand why he said nothing of it... Do you think he must be your killer?'

'The evidence is circumstantial, but seems strong to me – and the motive is stronger still. Is Mr Grice quick-tempered?'

'He has been known to pick a quarrel, especially when in drink – though in that regard he's no worse than many a man. But with this business over the letter he has compounded one stupidity with another. He has left a trail of damaged lives behind him – and all because of that wild night with Daphne!... I'm ashamed to say it's the only act of his that I can understand! When he told me of his adventure he was frantic. He castigated himself like a Spanish penitent.'

'But you knew of his visit to Kate Primrose on Sunday?'

'That I knew about, I confess. He said he'd discovered that Emmet had kept his papers over in Vinegar Yard. But I didn't know how he would handle it. I had sent Deacon packing – and never thought Grice might use similar methods.'

'They didn't have your sanction?'

St John looked into his friend's eyes and couldn't disguise a slight flicker in his own.

'People are eager to serve their political masters, and they know men of power may often will the end while wishing to remain innocent of the means.'

'And so, the guilt can be assumed by another – it's a dirty trade, Henry!'

'We are driven by ambition and fear – two sides of a single coin.'

Lord Melksham had nothing to add. Those bleak words brought home to him what risks Tom and the others were taking in letting themselves be drawn into that ruthless world. He recalled himself to his chief anxiety.

'But this sermonising doesn't help us with Tom. I'm worried about him. Why has he not returned from the park? You said your interview had been largely amicable?'

To Lord Melksham it seemed that Henry St John suddenly blanched as if he had read the omens of death. What came out of him was almost stuttering, and he was looking askance.

'I regret to say... having heard your news... that I may have been instrumental in running your nephew into danger. I was not a little annoyed at the course our exchanges took, especially at Mr Bristowe's suggestion that I might trade my letter for Morphew's life. So I left him a little brusquely – to think matters over, as it were... And on my walk back I saw Harry Grice still lingering after our stormy interview. I fear I encouraged him to engage Mr Bristowe in conversation, in case he might be more successful and persuade him to hand over the letter. I gave the wretch a final chance to redeem himself.'

Lord Melksham was horrified.

'You mean Harry Grice and Tom were thrown together by you – a meeting from which Tom has not returned?… By God, if anything has happened to him!… Had you no suspicions of Grice? Did you not question him closely about his interview with Emmet?'

St John looked abashed.

'No, I didn't wish to press him. I admit as much! Perhaps in my heart of hearts I was afraid of what he might reveal. The fiction he told me – if that's what it was – sat easier in my mind. I didn't want to believe that the dealings over my letter were instrumental in Emmet's killing – let alone that my own agent may have done the deed…'

St John took out a handkerchief and mopped his brow.

'… I'm sorry Jack. This was unlooked for. What can I do?'

It was said almost despairingly, and it was an invitation that Lord Melksham was determined not to forego.

'I'll tell you. This must be settled tonight. Tom's friends – Mrs Trotter and Constable Cobb – are in the park now…'

He hesitated, hardly daring to continue the sentence.

'… They are looking to question the Watch and the soldiers to discover if anything untoward has happened. It's most unlike Tom to run off, but if he picked up a scent he may have acted precipitously. I confess to being very fearful… We must work together, Henry…'

Lord Melksham brought his head even closer.

'… I am resolved the letter *must* be delivered to you as intended – to destroy it if you wish. It is stolen property and has brought nothing but death and violence. It is best it were consigned to the flames!… But first we must do two things: we have to find Tom, and confront Harry Grice. On that score, in ten minutes I may know the worst. I've arranged to meet the constable down in the colonnade, and he will possibly have news. I would be grateful if you would accompany me. I trust to God these fears will prove to have been foolish…'

In response, St John put out a hand to the wall as if to steady himself. Lord Melksham did not relent.

'... Who knows but that Mr Grice has done something reckless. You sent him packing this evening, and he may be desperate. I doubt he was in a forgiving mood when he confronted Tom.'

Henry St John felt the force of this, and he wasn't free of anxiety himself. It occurred to him that a resentful and angry Harry Grice would not feel bound to serve his interest any longer – quite the contrary. He shuddered to think that between them both Deacon and Grice could do him serious damage.

'You say the letter is in safe hands?' he asked.

'To my knowledge, yes. It has been kept from both sides.'

Lord Melksham was right, although what he didn't know was that the dangerous document was much closer than he thought. In fact, it was at that moment attached to the person of Elias Cobb. With Mrs Ménage and Kate Primrose being left behind at the Good Fellowship, it had been thought advisable that the letter should be placed in the guardianship of the Law – not in its majesty, but in its reliable bulk.

And at that very moment Elias himself, along with Widow Trotter, was struggling to enter the palace precincts again. They had worrying news to tell, which made their frustration all the greater. Without Birth-night finery it was hard for them to distinguish themselves from the milling crowd. But eventually the friendly footman recognised them, and his faith was justified when he saw not only Lord Melksham but also Her Majesty's Secretary-at-War striding in their direction.

Meanwhile, in the underground cell of the barracks, Harry Grice paused after his dramatic account of the killing. He was breathing hard, and Tom could see that the recital of it had cleared some of the mist from his mind and had made him confront the events – terrible though they were. This could be no bad thing, he thought.

'I killed him, Mr Bristowe! – but I didn't beat his head in without mercy. I couldn't ever do that… Someone must have arrived after me and seen the cane by the door.'

'*The cane?* You remember seeing the walking-cane?'

Tom was suddenly ridiculously hopeful. The idea made him forget his situation for an instant.

'Yes – a fine thing. I recall noticing it by the door, propped against the wall. The silver hound was looking at me. I thought it was rather dapper, and took it to be Emmet's.'

Tom recalled himself, his mind racing. He could glimpse a path opening up and knew he had to make for it.

'But Harry, you say you could *never* use such violence – and yet, when you called on Kate Primrose you didn't hesitate to brand her with a hot toasting-fork. How could you do that to an innocent girl? Doesn't it make your compunction about Emmet seem unlikely? You terrified her!'

'I was desperate for the letter and hardly knew what I did. I thought only to play the highwayman. It was humiliating. I thought she would simply hand the thing over, but she raised a squall and became agitated… But this is absurd. Why are you interrogating me like this? Are you charging me?'

'No, I ask for good reason – because a lawyer would seize on this point at once. You would have no defence!'

Harry Grice was taken aback.

'My *defence?* What are you saying Mr Bristowe? Are you picturing me on trial? You are very sly, Sir – or a dreamer!'

'No, Harry, I'm thinking of when I accompany you to a magistrate and listen while you tell him the full story of these events – the *truth* of what happened in the printing-house…

When I will stand beside you and vouch for everything you have just told me.'

'You *vouch?* How can that be evidence? This is ludicrous! You must turn your mind to yourself, and what awaits you!'

'But can you not see, Harry? There are others who know what I know – and who will leave you no escape – they know of your meeting with Emmet, and its purpose. But I am the only one who understands what truly happened. I believe every word you've just said, and will swear on the Bible to your honesty – it's plain to see! You have told me your tale before you kill me, and that means there can be no deceit in what you've said – it's the surest evidence of your innocence... But it also sets us on the trail of the man who finished the job – the vile creature who hammered Emmet's head in and placed the cane by the body to incriminate John Morphew. That is the man we now have to find! And *when* we do – don't you see? – we shall be able to release Morphew – and *exonerate you!*'

The die had been cast. It had been Tom's final throw. Everything hung on how Harry Grice responded. Tom looked in his direction, and through the gloom could make out the knife, still in the palm of his hand, turning and turning as he caressed it thoughtfully.

'That's all well enough...'

A terrifying silence followed.

'If you kill me, Harry, you kill the one person who can save you...'

Again there was no response, just the slow turning of the knife. Tom heard a distant rumble, as if a storm were brewing, and some drunken cries.

'We have the letter – and we shall give it back to Mr St John to destroy. My uncle will see to it. And his friend St John will be incredibly grateful... it could be the making of you. Your nightmare will be over.'

There was another cry, and a door banged. The sound was coming nearer.

'What's that?' shouted Harry in alarm. 'Someone is coming!'

He stood up. Tom froze. The spell had been broken. Harry was in a panic again.

'Stay still. Harry... Hide the knife! Let us say nothing. Keep calm!'

By some miracle Harry began fumbling in his waistcoat. His mind must be like a feather, Tom thought. They waited a few seconds more. There was a burst of laughter and a couple of torches brought an eery glimmer to the place. The shouts were now only yards away; but then there was a hushing and a sudden stillness. Tom could make out some words.

'It's damnably quiet!' – 'D'ye think they've done for each other?' – 'I'll give *five* that one of 'em's lifeless.'

'Done, a crown for a shilling!'

'Let's take a look!'

The men were near now. There was a jangling of keys, and their cell door opened to reveal six drunken guardsmen looking for an adventure. There was silence, then a cry of disappointment when they saw the two prisoners.

'Look'ye Jerry! They're sitting like children in school!'

'You disappoint us, gentlemen. We thought you'd box it out like men!'

'We came to bind your wounds.'

'And mop up the blood!'

'This is a sad sight... but we'll not be robb'd of our sport, will we?'

'Let's match 'em with Jerry – each in turn – we're sure to need a mop then!'

The largest specimen of martial manhood stepped forward, a grin spreading over his scarified face, which was criss-crossed like a Good Friday bun.

But he was to be disappointed.

'That would be bloody entertainment!... But there'll be no odds with such one-sided sport. No – we've a pair of prize-fighting gladiators right here! Let's have the bout now!'

There was a shout of agreement.

Tom didn't know whether to feel relief or even greater alarm. For a moment he had thought rescue was at hand, but the footguards had returned with their drunken mates ready to watch a bare-knuckle fight. It was a frightening thought. Tom had gradually won Harry Grice's confidence, and just minutes ago he could glimpse the possibility of a confession, and an absolution – and perhaps a chance to begin again.... But now they were being set at enmity once more, and in the crudest way possible. Was it to be a fight to the death after all?

The two prisoners were hauled out of their cell. The flares were affixed to the walls, and the place became a ghastly dungeon with leaping shadows. There was a lot of laughing as Tom and Harry were stripped to the waist, and their shoes removed.

'Well, what have we here?...'

One of the soldiers picked up Harry's knife, which had clattered to the floor.

'... So, one of you was not going to play fair, I see!...'

He looked at the two boxers, their arms securely held – there was to be no escape.

'Well, gentlemen, we'd better have a lively bout – or one of you will find *this* at his throat!'

The soldier took a step towards Tom and brought the knife up to his chin. He smiled menacingly.

'We want to see a bold encounter, gentlemen!... And now the odds! What will you give me?'

The place was full of raucous amusement. The Birth-day Night was to end in sport. And bets were about to be laid.

Chapter Forty-Five

MEANWHILE, IN THE state rooms of St James's Palace the Birth-night Ball was in full splendour. Upstairs in the ballroom the dancing was giving universal satisfaction: the band was tuneful and keeping time with the dancers' motions, and the extravagant fashions – male and female – were being displayed to best advantage. Mr Isaacs' *Union* had been performed to enthusiastic acclaim, though a group of stern-faced Whigs muttered against the intricate political choreography that had inspired it. Lord Tring's feet behaved well, and after it Lavinia Popham was able to continue walking without difficulty. Everything shone and glittered as it should.

By contrast, down in the wintry courtyard a less elegant scene was playing out. Across it, two mismatched couples were converging hurriedly. One pair was decked out in extravagant Birth-night finery, while the other two looked homespun and practical. All were apprehensive about what their next steps would be, but it didn't take long for the quartet to find a common purpose. There was no time for introductions.

'Any news of Tom?'

Lord Melksham's anxious question was half-shouted across the colonnade, and from that distance the expressions of Widow Trotter and Elias did not bode well. As they drew close, the constable tried to give a reassuring reply, but he was breathing heavily and couldn't avoid sounding troubled.

'It's not the worst, My Lord... But pretty bad nonetheless... Your nephew has been in a duel! The sword-fight was stopped before the outcome could be fatal.'

'He's been arrested, my Lord – but we've yet to discover where he's been taken – he and the other gentleman...'

'*Other* gentleman? Good God, St John!...'

He turned to Mr Secretary, who was hanging back sheepishly. Lord Melksham saw all his fears being realised. He continued, a little breathless himself:

'... It must be Harry Grice! He and Tom were conversing in the park. Mr St John here has told me of Mr Grice's activities. It must have ended in violence!'

'Mr Grice was *here?*'

Widow Trotter was astonished, and found herself looking at an embarrassed St John, who was by now heartily regretting his nocturnal adventure.

'What *activities* are these?' said Elias, asking a question to which he thought he knew the answer. His hand moved spontaneously to the side of his coat.

Mr Secretary's discomfort was complete. There was no escape, and he felt duty-bound to explain Harry Grice's doings as sparingly as he could. For Elias and Mrs Trotter the picture became clearer and more worrying. It seemed that Tom had encountered an angry and hunted man who might be close to desperation.

'But what of Tom?' said Lord Melksham. 'Are they in the round-house, or before a magistrate?'

'Neither, My Lord,' said Elias. 'We understand the round-house is chock-full tonight. Our duellists were hauled off by some soldiers – we've yet to discover where... The procedure, shall we say, was informal.'

'We found an officer,' said Mrs Trotter, 'a Major Gearey. He was very helpful and has promised to find out what has gone on. The men were footguards who'd been on palace duty. He's none too happy, as you can imagine...'

She paused before adding a further detail.

'... We're told, My Lord, that one of the duellists is injured – but we think not seriously.'

Lord Melksham gave a groan and demanded as much detail as she could give. But there was little to add.

'You've done well, Mrs Trotter. Thank God someone was there to put a stop to the fight... We must make our way to the gate. Let us hope this can be resolved quickly.'

The four of them began walking towards the crowded entrance, and after further questions and answers – none of which was reassuring – the party found itself on the pavement outside, with Elias and Mrs Trotter looking for their unhappy Major who had promised to return. Several chairmen began making polite enquiries of them, and further along two hackney coachmen were coming to blows. By this time Henry St John was ill at ease and attracting notice. Widow Trotter's eyes were scanning the crowd. Confusion reigned. Lord Melksham turned to his friend.

'Well, this is a Birth-night to remember, is it not?'

He spoke it with a smile, but St John remained silent, answering only with a look of rueful discomfort. Lord Melksham was uneasy himself. If they were going to confront Harry Grice, then he needed his ministerial friend to hand. The crisis was coming, and he was now impatient for it. He was thinking of Tom and what might be happening to him. How could the boy have let himself be drawn into a fight? There must have been a confrontation. He began picturing the scene, but it made him flinch.

Henry St John was also creating a mental picture, which featured a vengeful Harry Grice ready to do anything, or say anything...

Suddenly, to their relief, Mrs Trotter gave a cry.

'It's Major Gearey!'

A tall, red-coated officer came into view. He was frowning, and stepping as briskly as he could across the cobbled street. The man looked like he had a purpose and was not about to waste time in polite small-talk.

When he saw the two extravagant Birthday-suits, he halted smartly and appeared taken aback – and with good reason, for inside one of them was somebody he would rather not have encountered at that moment. But the Major recovered himself and gave an impeccable salute.

'Mr St John, Sir!'

The Secretary-at-War acknowledged him with a nod, sensing the slight awkwardness, but ready to move things forward.

'Major Gearey! What news do you have for us?'

The officer acknowledged Mrs Trotter and the others before replying.

'The two young men are evidently back at the barracks, Sir, under lock and key.'

Constable Cobb, who knew about these things, looked concerned.

'Are they in a cell together, Major? Are they being watched? The two of them have just been fighting to the death!'

The officer tried to sound easy but knew his answer would not be joyfully received.

'My information is that they are down in the cellars, Sir. Locked up together. I have come to take you over there. We can walk it in ten minutes.'

In the subterranean vaults of the barracks, the night's sport was beginning. Bets were being laid, and Tom and Harry were made ready, like a pair of fighting-dogs about to perform for a holiday crowd. It was reckoned 'evens' at this stage – but the odds would shift once the blows started to land. Tom was holding off panic. He tried to think of it as a gruesome ritual that must be gone through; and indeed the place reminded him of a damp crypt, a place for unholy rites and the piling up of bones. The guardsmen were deaf to all entreaties, and their laughter echoed around the cavernous arches. The stone flags beneath were wet and slippery, and laid like gravestones. There was a bitter smell in the air, which could have been blood, and might indeed soon be.

The battle-scarred Jerry announced that there were to be no rules, with nothing disallowed – except scratching or hair-pulling.

'We'll not have you brawling like a pair of Wapping fish-wives!'

The six guardsmen sat on benches ready for their entertainment. A bottle was being passed around, and the mood was almost genial as the match began.

The two boxers were tentative at first, feeling less like opponents than fellow victims about to come under heavy bombardment. Each took up a well-balanced position, left foot forward, neck drawn in, fists tightly clenched and held out from the face. The style was impeccable, and many seconds went by as they advanced and retreated, taking a step or two, forward and back, each of them checking the eyes of the other for any likely move. More long seconds passed, and they circled slowly. The guardsmen were restive and began shouting encouraging obscenities.

Stung into action, Harry gave a grunt and lunged forward. Their fists collided painfully. Tom pushed him away and jabbed twice, but Harry was just out of reach. They closed again, with Harry prodding and Tom holding him off with his forearms. It was all quite polite, but nothing to the purpose. Their audience made their derision known.

'Have you ever seen such delicacy? They're fly-flapping each other like a pair of pastry-cooks!'

Jerry leapt to his feet and grabbed the fighters by the nape of their necks.

'Come! Let's have some blood!' he shouted, and struck their faces together with an audible crack.

A cheer broke out as the two of them reeled backwards. Tom saw his chance and dug hard with his right fist under Harry's rib-cage – then the same with his left. His opponent winced and began hammering away rapidly, without much design. One or two blows found their mark, but Tom aimed at Harry's stomach and winded him. There was another cry, and the blows came thicker and faster. A sudden cheering rang out from the benches. Tom heard his odds shortening. But in that second of distraction Harry's bare fist thundered between Tom's eyes. His head shivered, and for a moment he could see nothing. But he held himself in position and fended off more blows, managing to trade some himself. He jabbed hard and full on Harry's right ear, and there was a cry of pain.

What was he doing? They were worse than animals thirsting after blood! Tom's thoughts revolted. How could they have been forced into this barbarous spectacle?

Each was now trying for the knock-down blow. At least it might end the thing quickly. Tom wondered if he should let himself be felled... But at that moment he looked at the furious Harry with his jaw set and eyes blazing, and something made him resist. He told himself to stop thinking and start being angry.

The taste of blood was in Tom's mouth, and he realised that blood was also seeping from his right ear. He clenched his teeth. He'd been protecting his face, and had held back from smashing his fist at Harry's nose. Why was he so fastidious? Again he was distracted for an instant, and suddenly realised that Harry had taken his chance and grabbed him by the waist. He felt himself being lifted in the air, and swung round over Harry's left hip. He somehow managed to protect his head as he clattered onto the stone floor.

There was delirious delight, and the spectators cheered. Cries of 'A fall!' and 'Ha-rry! Ha-rry!' went up. Harry responded and came in for the kill. But Tom spun to the side and grabbed his opponent by the leg, twisting it hard. Harry almost slipped on the greasy stone and his defences were down. Tom lashed out with his fists again. At this, Harry pushed forward with both arms and clutched him tightly, making punching difficult. Both of them were now out of breath and gasping. They reeled for a moment, then stopped moving and embraced one another like a pair of Roman wrestlers, their sore cheeks wedged together. There was hooting and stamping from the guardsmen. Suddenly Tom realised that Harry was whispering in his ear.

'Let's do for Jerry, Tom! – when he's close – you punch him in the bollocks! – I'll go for his chin – a second only – then run for the door – run like the wind! – *Right?*'

They were both wheezing, and continued to lean over each other's shoulder.

Jerry and his friends were becoming impatient.

'Break, the two of you!'

'No resting! You've only just begun!'

A bench scraped against the floor, and the mighty Jerry got to his feet. He strode forward and once again reached out, this time to separate them...

With a cry of 'NOW!' the corporal got a painful surprise. With every ounce of his remaining strength Tom struck him in the groin, and the moment he doubled over, Harry delivered a mighty punch to his face. The hulk reeled. Tom and Harry were already running barefoot on the stone slabs, and were past the guards before they could rise. The door was a good twenty yards off but they made it in seconds, not daring to look behind. It opened with a creak of protest, and the two young men, naked to the waist and spattered with blood, rushed through it.

There was a cry of alarm. Widow Trotter somehow managed to stay on her feet as Tom and Harry ran into her. Henry St John jumped backwards in astonishment. Constable Cobb raised a hand to halt them and turned his attention to the two pursuing guardsmen who burst through the door. Major Gearey was blazing with rage and screamed out an order. Jerry and the other soldier froze, mouths open like fishes on a mudbank. Tom's uncle simply stood and watched, a feeling of relief mingled with puzzlement.

For a moment everyone was in shock. Then four more drunken soldiers stumbled through the door to join the party, and found themselves huddling with the others like naughty apprentices while the officer lambasted them with his tongue. Her Majesty's Secretary-at-War was shocked by the scene, but also impressed at how the Major asserted his authority. This was a barracks on a Birth-night, not Blenheim, yet there was a lesson here: regimental discipline was restored without the need of a dog-whip or a rope's end.

But an explanation for the fracas was a priority. It was tempting to postpone an inquiry, but Major Gearey, with St John's consent, set about things at once. A surgeon was sent for; the six soldiers were placed under guard; the two combatants' clothes were gathered up; Harry received the close attentions of the constable; while Tom was almost weeping with relief as Mrs Trotter and his uncle sat him down on a stool.

'What have you been doing, Tom? Thank God you're all right! How did…'

The Major interrupted her.

'Let us leave the explanations for a few minutes more – if you please ma'am. It's important that everyone hears everything together… And to that end, I would ask you all to move, if you will, to my office…'

He glanced at St John, who nodded his assent.

'… A surgeon will be brought there, and also a bottle of the best red port.'

And so, with torches held aloft, the motley procession of the brilliant and the bedraggled, of uniforms and naked flesh, made its way out of the cellar. Everyone was anxious to hear the two men's story, but as they followed the briskly walking Major they were shocked into silence. All of them knew there was much more that needed to be asked and answered, but they wouldn't have long to wait. Curiosity – perhaps the primal human passion – was eager to be satisfied.

Chapter Forty-Six

SEATED IN THE Major's office, Tom Bristowe and Harry Grice eyed each other cautiously. Of the two, Harry appeared the more suspicious, but that was partly a frown of pain as the army surgeon dabbed and poked him. The doctor had seen much worse on the field of battle, and his fine-toothed handsaw thankfully stayed in its bag. The young men were reeling from the two duels they had fought that night, and were now trying to read each other's mind. This was not easy, given that they were finding it hard enough to read their own. Harry was wondering if Tom was going to be the accuser or defender; and Tom was working his way to the conclusion that Harry no longer wanted to kill him.

Major Gearey began the formal questioning, curious to know how the sword-fight had begun and how his men had become involved. This was difficult terrain, and they were both aware of the Major's presence constraining what they could say. Harry looked nervous while Tom began explaining that they were friends, and it had been a stupid quarrel over a pocket-watch... Harry added that he believed Tom had been speaking ill of him to Mr St John and had lost him his position.

'I was inflamed and resentful, Sir – and not a little drunk.'

'But both of us were to blame for letting the thing flare up so badly,' said Tom.

Major Gearey was intrigued and raised an inquiring eyebrow at Henry St John.

'Well, Mr Secretary, what are we to make of this?'

St John had not been expecting the amicable *rapprochement*, but didn't allow his surprise to show. He knew Tom must have discovered something. So he took a calming breath, and explained to the Major that some *confidential official business* had reached its crisis that evening – a difficult matter he hoped would soon be resolved – and that Mr Bristowe had certainly not spoken against Mr Grice – although he could see how the unfortunate suspicion had arisen.

Tom nodded in agreement.

'I'm pleased to hear what Mr St John says. During our captivity Mr Grice and I thrashed the matter out.'

'Indeed you did!' said the Major, smiling at the two bloodied faces. 'Perhaps your little *thrashing* has sobered you both? I trust you've learned a lesson tonight!'

While these extraordinary exchanges were taking place, Constable Cobb and Widow Trotter looked at each other, and Lord Melksham looked at both of them. They were witnessing an almost clubbable geniality and could scarcely believe what they were hearing. Tom and Harry were behaving like firm friends, their words as emollient as the balm that the surgeon was applying to their wounds (Lord Melksham began to wonder what was in it). But Tom and Harry were not finished yet.

'Your men acted promptly, Major,' said Tom, 'and undoubtedly saved a life – mine most probably!'

'And they saved *me* from becoming a killer!' said Harry.

He realised he had just set his foot in a gin-trap and went cold with alarm. But nothing happened. Major Gearey pressed on, and asked for an explanation of the boxing match. Once again the pair of them made light of it.

'We were naturally fearful,' said Harry,

'– and didn't consent,' added Tom. 'But your men were determined to have some sport on the Birthday-night, and decided that we could provide it!'

'They had prevented a fatal duel, Major, and I reckon they felt they had a right to see some action...'

'... and they thought we could settle our scores without lethal weapons.'

Major Gearey looked thoughtful.

'But they're drunk – more than half seas over!'

'Celebrations, Major – after all...'

'All right, gentlemen! All right! I see your drift – I do indeed...'

The Major looked at Tom and Harry, and then at the other four, who had been maintaining an interested silence throughout. He sniffed out something – he wasn't sure what – but it was clear that this particular jury was for acquittal. His officer's nose told him there was something not quite right... Nevertheless, such a company... perhaps they knew what was best. They certainly knew something he didn't. He stood up.

'Thank you gentlemen. What you've told me has been very helpful. I shall leave you for a short while, as I need to question my men. Be assured I shall tell them what you have said. I shall also tell them they have behaved disgracefully tonight – and that, were it left to me... However, I shall confine my *lashing* to the tongue!...'

The others appeared relieved, but they all remained silent. The Major began to feel unwanted.

'... I sense, gentlemen – and lady – that the six of you have things you wish to discuss – things more easily aired without my presence… I shall return here in half an hour – which I hope will be sufficient for you?'

'You have handled this judiciously, Major Gearey,' said the Secretary-at-War, smiling generously. 'And I shall remember it… I'm sure we can leave you to settle the whole affair.'

And with those persuasive words ringing in his ears, the Major – still more than a little unhappy – went off to *settle the affair*, taking the surgeon with him. The other six were left to hold their own inquest. The door had hardly closed before it began.

'Well, gentlemen!' said Lord Melksham, 'I think we're owed an explanation!'

'It was like sitting at a new play and trying to follow the plot,' said Widow Trotter.

'It's clear that matters between you have advanced somewhat,' said St John, 'and I for one am relieved to see it.'

'You mentioned the watch, Mr Bristowe… I take it there was some revelation concerning it?'

'You are unerring, Mr Cobb…' said Tom, impressed with the constable's powers of detection.

He glanced at Harry, who was looking apprehensive.

'… I have a lot to say – but Mr Grice here has some explaining to do, and I think it is he who should speak. While we were shut up together in that cell, he told me the truth about how Emmet died. I have no doubt it *is* the truth – an *unvarnished tale!* And if he will recount the same facts to you now, then I'll vouch for what he says. In the cell it was delivered to me by way of a confession – a *last* confession.'

Lord Melksham was taken aback.

'What exactly are you saying, Tom?'

'I am saying, Uncle, that it was intended to be *my* last hour… But when Mr Grice had finished, I think he felt a load had been lifted from him and saw that his best course from that moment would be to trust to the truth…'

Tom delivered his announcement solemnly.

'... Mr Grice is prepared to swear that John Morphew had nothing whatever to do with Emmet's death, and is completely innocent...'

Widow Trotter slapped the arm of her chair and lifted her head to the ceiling with a suppressed cry.

'Swear before a magistrate?' asked Elias, who looked hard at Harry, almost frowning. There was a pause before Harry replied.

'Yes, constable – swear on oath. You see, I was there. I saw what happened – and I alone was responsible... I killed him.'

The three words were the simplest possible and echoed in each person's mind. Widow Trotter looked intently at the young man as he spoke, and felt a surge of relief. But something whispered to her that it was not the final answer. The expression on Harry's face told her that what they were about to hear would not dispel the mystery, but lead them into the heart of it.

It was Henry St John who gave the necessary prompting.

'We are ready to hear your story, Mr Grice. You owe it to us, and to yourself. Please do not be inhibited. This is no court of Law – though you will understand that for us you speak on oath.

'Indeed I do, Sir – most solemnly.'

And so, for the next twenty minutes Harry's story unfolded. Tom heard it over again with barely suppressed excitement. The change in Harry was quite remarkable; and it occurred to him that the events of the past week must have left their mark. His encounters with Polly Gray, with Emmet, and with Kate Primrose, and the bruising confrontations with Henry St John, must have been a waking nightmare – though entirely of his own making. It was a tale of stupidity, weakness and cruelty; and when he described his visit to Kate Primrose in Vinegar Yard all three were combined. However penitent he was, that scene could not be decently veiled.

When Harry came to the struggle in the printing-house, his audience was spellbound. It made for a dramatic climax and yet it brought the opposite of a conclusion. It appeared that someone else had come upon the body and made it tell a different story. Emmet's death may have been explained, but not the plot against Morphew.

Lord Melksham was weighing what he'd heard. 'So, you are telling us that the man fell and broke his head open – but, rather than leave things as they were and report the accident, you stayed to arrange the body and place the paper in his hand... and then you returned the key to his pocket... Those were deliberate actions – not those of a man who was frantic.'

'They appear so now, My Lord, but it was very strange at the time... The panic made my mind race, and in the horror of the moment everything seemed clear. I knew if I reported the accident I would have to account for our quarrel... explain the letter... and that of course was unthinkable.'

'But why didn't you simply run from the scene?' asked Elias.

'I come from the world of spies and informers, Mr Cobb... All I could think of was how to deflect suspicion. But it's curious. When I look back I seem to be watching someone else do those things.'

'That is to evade responsibility, Mr Grice! It was you who did *those things* – not some ghost...'

Elias was frowning.

'... How do we know you didn't also seize the walking-cane and finish the job?'

This was the vital question, and Harry knew it.

'I swear to you – on oath – that when I left the room, that cane with the dog's head was resting against the wall, a few inches to the right of the door. You must believe me... *I saw the cane.*'

He suddenly looked shamefaced. Lord Melksham shook his head.

'You are a confused creature, Mr Grice. A man prepared to use violence, yet almost embarrassed at doing so – and doing so very incompetently!'

'I'm not proud of what I've done, My Lord, or what I am. But now I want to help you save Mr Morphew's life. I know he is innocent, and I lay myself open to your judgment – and the Law's... I deny nothing I have done. You must not charge me with more.'

The others looked at each other. No-one spoke, but each of them sensed that Harry Grice's story appeared genuine. He was not evading the unpleasant truth about himself. Much had been explained; yet there remained one last big unanswered question, not least for Harry himself. Until they could prove that someone else had wielded the cane, he was likely to be charged with murder.

Henry St John was far from settled in his mind, and broke the silence.

'I think I believe the story. The man who beat Emmet with the cane is a far more ruthless and decisive character than Mr Grice here...'

St John paused. They all looked at Harry, who felt uncomfortably like a courtroom exhibit – which is more or less what he was.

'... Someone like George Deacon.'

'Yes,' said Mrs Trotter, 'the man had already killed Polly Gray, and Emmet now had the letter.'

'I dismissed Deacon and threatened to fling him to the wolves if he didn't disappear for good... but that gave him a new grudge against me. He still wanted the letter – but now for himself – remember what he has attempted this evening! The man wants to destroy Mr Harley and me.'

Tom was looking doubtful.

'Yes Sir, Deacon could have killed Emmet without compunction, and the motive is a strong one. We can all picture him doing it… but Mr Grice's account changes things. This wasn't murder, and whoever wielded the cane wasn't thinking about the letter. It was surely someone who wanted to incriminate Morphew… And we know who those people are.'

'Ah the *letter!*' said St John, with an almost despairing sigh. 'Damn that letter! What damage it has done. It was written to me – and yet I seem to be just about the only person who hasn't read it!'

Exactly on cue, Widow Trotter turned to Elias and gave him an encouraging look. The moment had finally come. But in the Major's tidy office there was to be no *deus ex machina* descending gracefully from a cloud-capped ceiling, only Elias Cobb fumbling in his coat and pulling out a crumpled sheet of paper.

'You may read it now, Sir. In this room it is yours to do what you wish with it.'

Henry St John saw the light, and reached towards it. The surprise had shaken him.

'Well, I shall do it the courtesy of reading it – for poor Mrs Greg's sake.'

There was silence while he did so. His lips moved slightly with every phrase.

'It was written in such innocence,' said Mrs Trotter, 'and is so well intentioned. But it has done nothing but harm…'

'It was written in pain, too,' said St John, holding it carefully in his hand. 'Poor woman… but there is nothing I can do. Greg has been found guilty of treason and received his sentence. Mr Harley's hands are tied. He cannot possibly pardon the man – he's too closely involved in the case. And the Whigs' suspicions about his conduct would then be confirmed.'

'They are more than *suspicions* – as the letter reveals,' said Widow Trotter firmly.

St John felt uneasy, conscious of becoming the politician – not a congenial role in such company. He looked squarely at the young man who had caused him so much fear and embarrassment, and saw someone who might still be of use.

'Mrs Greg and the children will be well looked after – I intend that Mr Grice here will see to that. It will be his responsibility. I'm sure he will negotiate the matter skilfully for us.'

Harry heard the words with astonishment. He hardly dared think that he had any future at all – but clearly St John thought he had. The others were struck by the ease with which power may be exercised, and how a mere turn in a conversation could alter the trajectory of a life.

The minister was not finished. He still held the letter in his hand and looked at Lord Melksham.

'Well, Melksham, after what we've heard from Mr Grice, it's clear what you and the others have to do. A pardon for Mr Morphew is a possibility, and I shall be happy to convey to Mr Harley the facts I've heard just now. Mr Grice's confession has been brave but perilous. You need to pursue the question of who wielded the cane. In my conversation with Mr Bristowe earlier this evening I urged him to confront the Whigs. I'm sure they cannot be blameless…'

Like a practised parliamentarian, St John looked solemn and gave his next words their due weight.

'… There is a Junto plot behind this, I'm certain – and they chose Morphew as their victim. If you can discover it – and find out who beat Emmet's head in – then I'm confident Mr Harley will have every cause to be grateful, and will be happy to see Morphew pardoned. It is a grave injustice that we all want to see righted.'

As with many a politician, there was astute calculation beneath the generosity. A deal was on offer, a *quid pro quo,* and they all knew it. As if to solemnise the sealing of the bargain, Henry St John lifted up Mrs Greg's letter and held it out before them.

'I'm sincerely grateful to you all for delivering this to me. What adventures it – and we – have had! But I am not sorry to bid it goodbye.'

And with that, he swung his hand elegantly to the candle, and they all watched intently as the paper was enveloped in flame.

Chapter Forty-Seven

MAJOR GEAREY'S RETURN was perfectly timed, as if he had planned his entrance; but it was also disconcerting. As he walked into his office the diverse group was sitting in silence, all eyes trained on a little mound of grey ash in the middle of his table. A smell of burning was in the air. The Major was astute enough to ignore this evidence of pagan sacrifice – his evening was complicated enough already – and he acknowledged his guests politely, with as much cheerfulness as he could muster after the forthright discussion he had just been having with his guardsmen.

'I have retrieved as much as I can of your things, gentlemen,' he said thoughtfully, and laid down a heap of assorted belongings, which included two swords, a silk waistcoat featuring a distinctly storm-ravaged cornfield, a twisted mass of human hair, and a pristine gold watch that glistened on top of the pile.

The company was grateful, and the Major was warmly thanked for his hospitality and his capable handling of the drama. Her Majesty's Secretary-at-War took him by the hand and assured him that he would remember the Major's professional abilities – which would no doubt be tested further in the coming campaign. His battalion was to leave for Brussels in a few weeks' time.

The little platoon that made its way from the barracks was tired but beginning to feel more hopeful. A bargain had been struck with Henry St John – not the one they might have chosen, but one that offered hope, and needed to be seized on.

'It has to be done tonight,' insisted Lord Melksham as he led his party in the direction of the palace, 'while the cast is assembled. I have barely an hour – but I'll see what I can do amongst the Whigs. It will not be easy.'

It had been decided that people would go their separate ways. Widow Trotter insisted on taking Tom back to the Good Fellowship to nurse his bruises: he was aching and exhausted, and was also anxious for news of Will. Constable Cobb would keep Harry Grice under guard until morning, when he could join the queue of miscreants appearing before the Covent Garden magistrate. And Lord Melksham and Henry St John, decked in their courtly finery, would return to the ball. In the barracks they had been feeling uncomfortable – like a pair of Duchesses in the sixpenny gallery.

It was now nearing midnight, and the last flourish of the birthday celebrations was approaching. In the street outside the palace, chariots, chairs and carriages were circling, and one or two elegant figures departing from the ball were hailing them.

Suddenly Mrs Trotter gave a cry.

'Elias, Look! – Over there, in that coach! Can it be?'

The constable narrowed his eyes. People and chairs were milling around and his view was obscured; but then he saw, on the far side of the street, a figure leaning out of the window of his coach and casting his eyes over the crowd.

'Well I'll be… if it's not the Justice himself!'

Widow Trotter turned to Lord Melksham.

'It's Mr Lundy, my Lord – Will's father! Can he be looking for us? Has he heard about Will, do you think?'

Mrs Trotter waved at the coach and began making her way towards it as fast as she could, weaving around several chairs that blocked her way – so much seemed to be happening at once. 'Hemp' Lundy saw her and flung open the coach door. A firework exploded nearby and the horses were startled, their harness jingling. The coach swayed alarmingly and gave a sudden jerk as he was stepping down, so that he found himself falling into her arms. It was not a judicial entrance, but at this moment dignity wasn't on his mind. He was on a mission, he said, and was the bearer of important news.

The party found a quieter spot by the palace railing where they could confer – it was far from ideal, but the judge was anxious to have his say, and the group gathering round was impatient to hear him.

'I had almost given up hope of finding you,' he said, tugging at his cloak and loosening it from his neck. 'It's such a throng; but I decided to take the chance, and Will was insistent. I know each minute is important – and you will want to take action immediately.'

He began explaining that he had come directly from his son, who was now safely back at the Good Fellowship with *two* surgeons fussing and squabbling over him.

'Oh, thank the Lord!' said Widow Trotter spontaneously.

'We've been very alarmed about him,' said Tom. 'What happened, Sir?'

'Will has had an adventure – and, I may say, so have I! He insisted you should know my news without delay.'

Judge Lundy told them that a few hours earlier an urgent note to his rooms in the Temple had called him over to the College of Arms, where he found Will had fainted away. His wound had opened up afresh and he was in the college library being tended by a local surgeon. While the man worked, Will had told him of his discovery about Harry Grice and the crest on the pocket-watch – the substance of his note to Mrs Trotter.

'It raises material new evidence,' said the judge. 'But after my inquiries this afternoon I can add considerably more – things pertinent to the trial verdict – or rather the *mis-trial*, as I now see it.'

It was an extraordinary admission, and the look on 'Hemp' Lundy's face showed he felt it painfully. He recalled the encounter with his son the previous afternoon, when Will had spared nothing in saying what he thought of the trial, especially the evidence about the walking-cane. His son's indignation had made him determined to discover the truth about 'Mr Wise' whose testimony had been so deadly.

The judge had instructed the Clerk of the Court to look into the matter urgently, and within hours he had the full picture: 'Mr Wise' was in reality a Mr Brown, a character who was more familiar with Cheapside than with the wilds of Romford.

'I discovered – exactly what Will had suspected – that this "Wise" was a mere chancer who was prepared to play any part asked of him… And so, I demanded an interview with Henry Voyce, the man who appeared to be organising the prosecution.'

'You've talked with Voyce?' said Tom excitedly.

'I thought I should, given the revelation about Mr Brown. Mr Voyce's role was unusual and it made me suspect some political manoeuvring. And how right I was!… Well, I confronted the smooth-talking Mr Voyce, and he began to droop and wither under my questioning. It was a distressing spectacle. The man soon lost his composure, and could only stutter and protest! And when I hung the threat of perjury over his head he became distinctly squeamish; then he grovelled, and in the end he threw the blame onto someone else… onto Mr Buller, his tame constable.'

'Ah! We've always assumed Buller was his tool,' said Tom.

'But what Mr Voyce finally admitted was that Constable Buller had *tampered with the body*. Those were his words. I asked him to explain, and it's clear he meant more than simply the moving of it. But then he went quiet and refused to say more, except that Buller was responsible. He ended by saying that the authority for it did not come from him.'

'*Authority?*' said Tom. 'That means Voyce is pointing upwards, does it not? – to someone whose name can't be mentioned. Buller clearly thought he was serving the wishes of his political masters. This fits what we've heard of him – that the constable was happy to do their bidding if it brought a reward.'

'Well, I certainly intend to pursue this. My son's intuitions are persuasive. Our politicians have been up to their tricks again...'

At this, Henry St John shifted uneasily. He was excited by the revelations of Whiggish malpractice and was itching to intervene; but he held back, content for the moving finger to move where it would. He was not disappointed.

'... I assume the smooth-talking courtier Maynwaring has been dirtying his hands in the business. But this isn't my province...'

The judge looked directly at Lord Melksham.

'... But you, Sir, may be able to pursue it?... I believe both Voyce and Buller have been involved in a plot against Mr Morphew. This is the only inference I can draw from what Voyce told me.'

Lord Melksham glanced at his nephew, who was hanging on every word.

'Your Honour, this is exactly what Tom and the others have been suspecting – a plot to destroy Mr Morphew and avenge themselves on *Bufo*.'

'Well, I cannot believe Voyce would act independently. I suspect the puppet-master must be Her Grace's secretary.

I strongly suggest you look in Maynwaring's direction... Meanwhile, I have requested an interview tomorrow with the Lord Chief Justice.'

'Hemp' Lundy's audience were stunned. This was the voice of The Law – which for once went beyond simple legal judgment. It was carrying the Law into a new area – pursuing justice through investigation. This was not his province, as he had said, but he seemed remarkably open to it.

Time was pressing, and they knew that more action was needed that very night to bring matters to a conclusion. This had to be done at the ball. The others would make their way back to Covent Garden. Judge Lundy would return to the Good Fellowship with Tom and Widow Trotter as grateful passengers in the coach.

'Yes, I want to go home, now,' said Tom. Widow Trotter was delighted to hear him use those words and she began thinking practically: Mrs Ménage and Kate Primrose would no doubt still be there, along with Will, and she would organise a little late nourishment. It had been an extraordinary day of repeated shocks and revelations – more than her mind could take in – so it would be good to settle in the parlour and have an easy hour – albeit a late one.

But there was no relaxation in prospect for the others. Elias commandeered a hackney and directed the coachman to his office where Harry Grice could be kept safely for the morrow. And the two harassed ball-goers readied themselves for the state rooms, where their absence had been raising questions. Lord Melksham was determined to seek out Arthur Maynwaring, and he hoped against hope that the man was still there dancing attendance on his Duchess. Strangely, he was beginning to relish the thought of a confrontation that a couple of hours ago had made his heart sink in dismay. He promised to bring any news to the Good Fellowship early the following morning.

'You must not wait up tonight, Mrs Trotter. I have two difficult confrontations ahead – Mr Maynwaring is a slippery customer, and I must press him hard...'

He lifted his collar and took a deep breath.

'... and before bed I must also negotiate a peace with my beloved family... After my truancy tonight I think the confrontation with Sophia and Lavinia may be the more ticklish of the two.'

Arthur Maynwaring, M.P. was in the full flow of his wit when Lord Melksham found him. He had a little audience – of three – and was addressing them in a mellow, almost melodic voice. His head was framed by a sculpted niche, which added to the elegance of the effect; but behind him a marble bust of the Emperor Caracalla appeared to be frowning at this over-dressed interloper who was spoiling his view. The Duchess's secretary made a classical figure himself with his Roman nose and arched eyebrows, roofed by a luxurious golden wig, which seemed to caress his shoulders as he turned from one to the other of his auditors. His words poured forth:

'... To my mind, Sir, the lady is less an *agreeable* than an *awful* beauty: her love is a sudden flame rather than a glowing fire – it singes but does not warm... I confess she *gazes* skilfully, and has a devastating *glance* – surely no mean skill for a woman of the Town!... but you must seize your moment. I particularly advise you, if you wish to prosper, to look for the *second* twinkle in her eye. That is your infallible ticket to a night's entertainment – but you should not hope for more...'

There was a ripple of knowing smiles among the company. Lord Melksham joined them and received a welcoming nod and the flicker of a cuff in his direction.

The entertainment continued in a similar vein for a minute or two before the group began to disperse and Maynwaring reached for a glass of champagne from a passing footman. Lord Melksham did likewise, and the pair stood together.

'This is positively my final *lubrication*, my Lord. I shall need it before I venture into the desert of Soho Square. My coachman will toss me about like a tennis-ball, so I shall need to be just a little insensible – I am aiming for a moderate pliableness rather than utter dissolution!'

When Arthur Maynwaring was in a mood like this it was hard to find some purchase on his mind, or anything to command his attention. Lord Melksham was aware that the conversation would run away if he didn't rein the man in.

'I'm afraid I must jostle you myself, Mr Maynwaring. It's an urgent business, and I need a little of your time before you depart. I have an important matter to raise, and it is in your interest to hear it... I know a place where we can be alone and have it out.'

'*Have it out?* My goodness! Are you challenging me to a duel?'

Maynwaring smiled a little nervously. He was uncertain where the dialogue was leading, but hoped to keep it this side of serious. Lord Melksham at once disabused him. He made it quite clear what their topic would be, and that the fates of several people hung on the outcome – 'not least your own, Mr Maynwaring!' he added, pointedly.

By the time they were settled in the closet where Lord Melksham and his nephew had conversed only a few hours earlier, Maynwaring was extremely uncomfortable. This confrontation was not something he had anticipated. The situation was awkward, the tone was decidedly wrong, and he felt suddenly vulnerable. The wooden violin-cases scattered around him looked like miniature coffins.

Lord Melksham had decided to take the direct approach.

'There is a lot you need to know, Mr Maynwaring, and I shall keep nothing from you – just as you, I trust, will withhold nothing from me. In this room we can speak the truth, and I would advise you not to evade it. To this end – and to set an example – I propose telling you everything that I know about your activities over recent days.'

Maynwaring was dumbstruck, partly at the presumption, but also at the thought of what Viscount Melksham – a man familiar with details of the Privy Purse – might actually *know*... He realised he was not being invited to respond, so kept an apprehensive silence.

'Let me begin with what I've learned within the past hour. I take it you are apprised of the dramatic events at John Morphew's trial yesterday morning...'

As Maynwaring listened, he soon became aware that His Lordship knew a great deal – rather more than he himself did. The trial had been a risky venture, and he began to think how he could distance himself from what had occurred. It had been cleverly improvised and brought the desired result; but he saw that Voyce's zeal for the cause had left them both dangerously exposed.

While Lord Melksham spoke he was watching Maynwaring's mobile features and trying to gauge the man's responses. He noted signs of unease and embarrassment, and a moment of sudden interest when the man was evidently hearing something new. It was as if the leaves of a book were turning before him. Within a few minutes he was convinced that here was Henry Voyce's employer.

'... This trial, Sir, was no casual affair. A man's life was at stake, and the crucial evidence, which swung the verdict, was procured by Mr Voyce – and it was an entire fiction. I must tell you that not half an hour ago I talked with His Honour Judge

Lundy who presided, and he is outraged at what went on in his courtroom. In fact, he is to take the matter up with the Lord Chief Justice tomorrow. A serious miscarriage of justice has occurred, and he holds your Mr Voyce responsible.'

'*My* Mr Voyce? My Lord, I...'

'He told me of his suspicion that the authority for this disgraceful proceeding came from yourself...'

'My Lord, I must protest! A Member of Parliament needs assistance, and Mr Voyce is useful in all sorts of practical ways – acting as my amanuensis and conducting researches. But he is not *mine*. He has interests of his own and pursues them as he thinks fit. I know nothing about this "Mr Brown" you mention. Such things are beneath my notice.'

Maynwaring was becoming unsettled, and his protests lapsed into indignant bluster. Lord Melksham was happy to let him run on. He listened while Maynwaring displayed the full extent of his probity, innocence and righteousness – and then chose his moment to close him down. In a few brief seconds all Arthur Maynwaring's virtues were drawn tight around him until he couldn't move. He was swathed in hypocrisy.

'Mr Maynwaring, my position in Her Majesty's household gives me access to the details of the Privy Purse. Indeed as Deputy Keeper – not an honorary position – I am responsible for ensuring that everything is above board with the Royal finances. Of course, Her Grace the Duchess continues to have privileges, and the Queen is content to allow her funds for certain uses – I cannot say more. But over recent months I have become concerned that certain disbursements were being authorised that were more dubious in nature. I shall not go into details, but... if I told you that they had reference to yourself...'

'My Lord, I must protest, I am Her Grace's secretary...'

'Yes, of course... but I had cause to follow up several payments from the Queen's account, and they coincide at every point with identical payments into your account with the Goldsmiths.'

Maynwaring jumped to his feet.

'This is a monstrous intrusion! You have no right...'

'Please sit down, Mr Maynwaring and calm yourself. You must not assume that I am about to reveal any of this. Indeed, I'm sure you will give me no cause to. I have no desire to embarrass the *Duchess*...'

The talismanic word startled Maynwaring. He opened his mouth to speak, thought better of it, and sat down again with as much silent dignity as he could muster.

'... My position gives me contacts with the Goldsmiths, and it is clear that you have been using funds from the Privy Purse to conduct some of your own business – I've no doubt with the Duchess's sanction. I don't wish to pry any further, but I suspect they concern activities over which Mr Voyce – the valuable and ingenious Mr Voyce – has control...'

Maynwaring (a man of wily intelligence who understood the game) knew he was trapped, but that his escape route was about to be shown him. He listened carefully.

'... I said I wanted us both to be truthful. You will allow that I have been so – perhaps overmuch – and I'm sorry it has unsettled you. I don't require you to incriminate yourself, but I need you to tell me about the events of last Friday night when John Emmet met his death. Earlier in the day, you and Mr Voyce helped interrogate Mr Morphew, and you taunted and riled him, so that when he was released – I understand against your wishes – he was in an angry state. Mr Voyce made much of this at the trial...

'But what immediately concerns me is what occurred in the printing-house that night – not at the moment of Emmet's death, but in the hour following. If you can inform us fully about that, then I'm sure we can put this terrible incident behind us. To put it bluntly, Mr Maynwaring, I want to know about Constable Buller, the man who found the body. We have reason to believe that he took a more active part in events. Can you enlighten us?'

Maynwaring thought quickly, and his eyes narrowed.

'I'm not clear how you come to know of all this, my Lord, but I am in your hands. I shall tell you what I can. Constable Buller was indeed active that night. As the local constable he had been keeping watch on the premises, but he exceeded his authority. Mr Voyce was concerned about what Buller had done, and he insisted that I talk to the man myself.'

'You interviewed Constable Buller?'

'Indeed I did, my Lord, and I asked him for a full account of what occurred. With some prompting – and less than willingly – he complied. I promise to do my best to recall the details for you, but I must stress that what Buller did was neither arranged nor sanctioned by me. Mr Voyce was severely embarrassed by it, and concerned that he might be blamed for what happened.'

It was the old, ageless story, Lord Melksham thought: authority and sanction, responsibility and blame, the policy and the deed – the whole slippery system of power! The thing worked so beautifully because it held ideals aloft while keeping the dirty deeds down below. Power allowed you virtue – gave you the means of disclaiming evil and protecting yourself. The ones who laid the design would always win, while those that did the work would often lose. After all, any tool could be thrown away. Whatever the party or cause it served, the system would always survive. It was altogether too convenient.

Lord Melksham admonished himself for his cynical thoughts. He sat back and listened carefully while Maynwaring fulfilled his promise.

Chapter Forty-Eight

'I'M SURPRISED YOU know about Constable Buller, my Lord. I shan't ask how, but you clearly know he's a man with a violent nature. You will also know that he has been useful to us in reporting on John Morphew's activities. I make no secret of the fact...'

Like many a wit, Arthur Maynwaring delighted in hints and insinuations. But in his case there was the additional element of the pamphleteer who could leave subtlety behind when it suited him. He knew the unburnished truth was required, and so he adopted the honest approach.

'My Lord, I regret the awkwardness that has arisen between us. I suspect you consider me a fawning time-server who wears his principles *à-la-mode* and is ambitious only for himself...'

He made a little pause for Lord Melksham to demur – but the polite gesture was withheld and he was forced to continue.

'... In recent months I have become close to the Duchess, and she has come to rely on me for advice and support. Her Grace has allowed me to see how vulnerable she is. She has quick and delicate feelings, and is easily wounded by unkindness. Her bond with the Queen remains close, and she has been greatly hurt by the rift between them. In recent days that poisonous libeller *Bufo* has caused her exquisite pain. Perhaps her anger has been excessive – I know it has – but she is not alone in that. Morphew's scurrilous productions have scandalised many and have prompted angry words in their turn. We can all see how the political debate has become coarse and bitter.'

This was disingenuous in the extreme. Lord Melksham couldn't keep silent.

'I agree, Sir. Indeed, the most recent contribution takes the prize for crudeness. That nasty ballad on Mrs Masham belongs in the gutter with the rest…'

He detected a quiver of Maynwaring's nostrils and sensed a discomfort. So he pushed the stiletto further.

'… At least Bufo has style and wit! The author of those sing-song verses is wise to remain anonymous – I've rarely seen such lumbering stuff!'

Maynwaring flushed visibly, his jaw tensed, and Lord Melksham knew he had his man. It was a delightful moment. But he spared his victim and said nothing, allowing the practised politician to move on unruffled, as he thought.

'But my Lord, it is the seditious intent of Bufo that sets him apart. His *Magic Glass* is no mere jocular ballad, but an assault on the constitution of the State. Lord Sunderland suffers vile mockery, and Mr Hopkins and Mr Addison – the virtuous and honourable Mr Addison – are traduced in shocking terms. It was surely not unreasonable, when suspicion lighted on Morphew, for us to begin observing him closely. I do not apologise for making use of Constable Buller to report on his affairs, and Henry Voyce, as you know, has concerned himself with this. I left the practical details to him – I have to confess ignorance of what precisely went on…'

Lord Melksham frowned, and Maynwaring sensed a slight touch on the tiller was needed.

'… In this I was remiss – I confess it! I should have taken a firmer hold on things. It was when I questioned Mr Buller that I saw how enthusiastically he had committed himself to the cause – and with what excessive ingenuity!'

'You must tell me all, Sir. I have my suspicions, but it will be good to know the truth from you.'

'I shall give it you my Lord.'

With a deliberation that seemed out of character, Maynwaring began to relate how Joe Buller had been keeping an eye on Morphew's premises for some time. And while the printer was detained for questioning in the Cockpit there were suspicions that Emmet would use the opportunity to pursue his clandestine enterprise.

'We realised that Emmet was a double-dealer, brazenly informing on others while driving the business himself. He was continuing to dirty his hands with seditious material, and we suspected that Morphew, in spite of his protests, was in collusion – that he was allowing unregulated printing to take place. We had to take action…

'Well, I have to say Buller relished the task. Bufo's verses had outraged him and he was determined to put a stop to Morphew's activities. He hated to think it was happening in his ward! The constable, my Lord, is a man of stern principle who detests Grubstreet trash. The mockery of the Duchess angered him most. As a patriot, he couldn't allow a great lady to be insulted so cruelly. I'm afraid that on one occasion Mr Voyce had to restrain him from having Morphew set upon!…

'According to his own account, on that Friday evening he was expecting Morphew might return to his premises, and so he went periodically to observe if there was anything stirring. Towards eleven that night he noticed a candle flickering in the printing-house and the door was on the latch. When he stepped inside he discovered Emmet's body lying on the floor, with yet another outburst from Bufo – that terrible curse – clenched in his hand. Buller told me he assumed there had been an altercation – that Morphew had returned and the two villains had fought. Blood on one of the presses showed that during the struggle Emmet had fallen and struck his head. It was obvious that Morphew had fled…

'Well, for good or ill, Constable Buller decided to take matters into his own hands. His detestation was so great that when he recognised the walking-cane he decided to lend a more lively idea to the scene. If Morphew had caused Emmet's death, then he…'

'But this is extraordinary!' said Lord Melksham in disbelief. 'What could he gain?'

'It's hard to say. Perhaps the satisfaction of bringing retribution to someone he hated? Joe Buller is an officious constable – punctilious to a degree. Of course I questioned him closely on the matter. He confessed there was something random and careless about the death that he didn't like. It was 'untidy,' he said, and the story it told was an unsatisfactory one. He said he wanted more demonstrable evidence. In truth, I think he longed to have an honest, downright murder. I don't pretend to understand what ran through his mind, my Lord… There was the cane, and there was the body…'

'You speak of him as a mad dramatist.'

Maynwaring gave a rueful sigh:

'Yes, and perhaps an aspiring actor too. I think Buller longed for a plot in which he could play a leading role – and with the hated Morphew as the villain it had a special relish!… Yes, it was fiction, but for him it told the real story – and he saw that to present it as murder would rid us not only of Emmet but of the man who had employed him. It was so *neat,* he said.'

Lord Melksham sighed at the terrifying logic of the thought.

'When he confessed this to you, was he feeling repentant? In which case why did he give such a tremendous performance in court? My nephew said that at the inquest he also enacted the killing with gusto.'

'Perhaps he was *steep'd in blood so far* and simply had to follow it through? I gather his performance brought the killing to life! It's clear that he enjoyed re-enacting what he had done.'

'That's a terrible indictment, Mr Maynwaring. I'm surprised Buller confessed to it. There is something coldly vindictive about what he did – albeit on a corpse. And with respect to Morphew it was tantamount to murder. This is a serious matter, and he must face the consequences.'

Maynwaring gave a resigned half-shrug.

'Well, so be it! I agree with you that we cannot allow such meddling with evidence…'

Lord Melksham was struck by the ease with which Maynwaring was conceding the ground to him, and wondered if this would continue.

'Did you ask Constable Buller about what happened next? There was drama to come, wasn't there?'

'He told me he wiped the blood off the printing-press before he left. Not surprisingly, he had caught some of it and needed to change his coat. When he returned to 'discover' the crime he saw that Morphew was there! He crouched in the shadows, and when Morphew left he hurried across to Stationers' Hall. You know how events unfolded after that.'

'The whole thing reads like a bloody farce,' said Lord Melksham, shaking his head. 'So many entrances and exits! I can hardly credit it.'

'A tragic farce – if there be such a thing.'

'But how did Buller seem while telling you all of this? It's a remarkable story in every way, and I doubt he could relate it without emotion.'

'The constable is a *precise* man, my Lord – a man of fact and calculation. We may find this distressing in the extreme, but he is proficient in what he does, and isn't easily distracted.'

To this point Lord Melksham's curiosity had been well and truly satisfied. There was more he wanted to ask, but he was conscious of time passing, and he knew he needed to learn about someone else's role. He wondered if Maynwaring would be equally co-operative when Henry Voyce's activities were brought into question. He was determined to find out.

'But I have to ask you about Mr Voyce – *your* Mr Voyce – who was remarkably active in this affair. We know he arrived at the printing-house the next morning and took charge. Indeed, he was reprimanded by the Coroner and by Judge Lundy for disturbing the body. He must have had a purpose in this. What was he doing there?'

'I'm afraid that was something of a misjudgement on his part – as he now acknowledges. When Buller reported to him, he was dismayed at the violence with which the constable had acted, and how the scene of death was already compromised.'

'So you are saying Buller admitted what he had done?'

'It was less an admission, my Lord, than an expression of pride in the ingenuity he had shown.'

'*Ingenuity?* I've not heard perverting justice called that before.'

'Just so, my Lord. Mr Voyce felt he had to take a hand. He arranged to meet the constable at the printing-house at six the next morning to take his own survey of the place; but he was delayed, and when he arrived he found the pressman and the compositor were already there. He had hoped to see if anything had been missed.'

'That was most thoughtful of him,' said Lord Melksham with unaccustomed sarcasm. 'And that of course was when he discovered the composing-stick in the further room?'

'Yes – an important piece of evidence as it turned out.'

There was a glint of satisfaction in Maynwaring's eyes. Lord Melksham was quick to dispel it.

'And entirely *misleading* evidence it was too! The presumption in Mr Voyce's actions is astonishing. And it was all done in the absence of the Coroner! Nothing gave him the right to busy himself in that interfering way.'

'Alas, my Lord, things were not handled well. Perhaps he should not have shifted the corpse – but he felt it looked so indecent in its pool of blood, and so out of place in that room.'

Maynwaring was sounding a note of pathos and doing it well. There was an awkward pause. Lord Melksham was feeling increasingly uncomfortable – and not just physically. Both men were aware of the embarrassments of playing and replaying the little drama of Emmet's corpse. From the instant of his death, John Emmet had become a stage property decked out by others to tell their own tale. It was a thoroughly unpleasant business, but at least its demeaning intricacies were becoming clear.

Maynwaring's face began to compose itself to a judicial *gravitas*, and he broke the silence:

'Of course, this means that Morphew will be exonerated and have his sentence lifted – and I think we can all be satisfied. I shall be happy to help secure that outcome... As you have said, my Lord, if we can put this matter behind us and not cause further distress to Her Grace, then we shall both be content. I am confident of persuading her that during these past days Morphew has been taught enough of a lesson!'

Lord Melksham gave Arthur Maynwaring a long, cool look. The man had somehow managed to recover his equanimity and thought himself back in control. Telling Buller's tale had come as a relief and now he was smiling almost benignly. But this subtle creature mustn't be allowed to slide off into the undergrowth. His Lordship spoke bluntly.

'At this moment, Sir, I'm not concerned with the Duchess's finer feelings, but with practical things – what *you* can do to ensure that Morphew is pardoned. It is within your power to act on this immediately, and I must see that it is done!'

Lord Melksham was in haste to make their contract secure. It was not the noblest of treaties, and its terms were not edifying. But time was pressing, and for that reason he forbore supplying Maynwaring with Harry Grice's story – that would have to wait a while longer. At this moment the man must continue to believe that Morphew was the one Emmet had fought with in the printing-room. He made Maynwaring agree that they would both set the new facts before Henry St John, who was lingering at the ball to hear the result of their conference. He himself would send an urgent message to Judge Lundy, who would then have a full brief to lay before the Lord Chief Justice. Lord Melksham knew that was their insurance, and he hoped, their guarantee. He was struck by the irony of the outcome. Rather than a conflicted system working against them, its jarring parts were being ingeniously adjusted to each other so as to help their cause.

Lord Melksham couldn't suppress a flicker of satisfaction at bringing the opposing parties together in this way. He was almost looking forward to witnessing Maynwaring and St John in temporary alliance – the two politicians, Whig and Tory, manoeuvring elegantly to salvage their reputations, each hiding his embarrassment from the other. It was a sordid affair altogether. But he knew that out of it, for once, something good would come – and some kind of belated justice. How rarely could that be said! The corrupt Constable Buller would face his punishment; Morphew would be exonerated and released; and Deacon would, he trusted, go to the gallows. What would happen to Harry Grice was still uncertain and was largely in Kate Primrose's hands. Not all of this was satisfactory, and he had to admit that the nice resolution of the plot was perhaps more pleasing than its morality. Such was the way of the world.

At this juncture neither man wanted to linger. But matters were decided for them when the closet door opened and a sharp-nosed face peered round it. They saw the man was carrying a bassoon under his arm, and behind him was an oboe, followed by a procession of violins… The music had evidently ended, and it was time for the instruments to be put away. In the quiet aftermath the ball-goers would be performing their polite leave-takings, or lingering just a little longer with friends and acquaintances.

Saturday

7 February 1708

Chapter Forty-Nine

Lord Melksham cradled the precious bottle with one hand and opened the door of the coffee-room with the other. The warm, spicy air patted his face and brought a radiant smile. He saw Widow Trotter behind the bar look up expectantly.

'The treaty is concluded!' he called out, doffing his hat and striding up to her. 'The parties have come to an agreement. Morphew's pardon is in train, and he is likely to be released tonight!'

Widow Trotter was speechless for a moment and could only beam with joy. With slightly glistening eyes she gave thanks, and breathed out a reply:

'So he'll be spared the Tyburn sermon. Thank God for that!'

'You've done it, Mrs Trotter – the three of you! Such forces were ranged against you – such a labyrinth of plots and lies, and threats, and violence... I'm astonished at what you've achieved. We must celebrate!'

She noticed the bottle and smiled back at him.

'I warrant this will be a Saturday morning like no other. We must tell Tom and Will at once – they are together up in Will's room. You've a tale to unfold, I'm sure.'

'A scene you could only imagine, Mrs Trotter. I'm bursting to tell you.'

'We could not have managed this without you, my Lord. Our efforts carried us only so far. Without your connections and your persistence we should have failed at the last. The system would have defeated us.'

'Yes. It *is* a system, is it not? The machine of power! But it was you three who outfaced it – and with what courage! In the end we were able to use its turning wheels to our advantage.'

'Did you work on people's fears and suspicions? Or something nobler?'

'A mixture as always. There was a grain of hope too – and I think a little remorse of conscience. Vices and virtues can be equally productive.'

Widow Trotter seized some glasses, and together they climbed the stairs to the upper room, where Tom and Will were talking quietly. Will was in bed sporting a fresh bandage, and Tom occupied a chair. Not to be outdone, he boasted two bandages: one binding his hand and the other pinning down his left ear and forming a nice symmetry with the black eye on his right.

As the door opened, Lord Melksham took in the scene and shook his head in admiration.

'Upon my word, gentlemen, this is a hospital for heroes!'

The next few minutes were all delight and relief. Lord Melksham, too excited to sit down, gave a fairly breathless summary of his news. The two invalids forgot the pains of the moment and reached out to shake his hand strongly. He in turn, more delicately, seized Mrs Trotter's. Had the room not been a bit cramped there would probably have been dancing as well.

'Dear lady, should we not be proud of these two? Both have suffered in the cause – and uncomplainingly. What a spirited team the three of you have made! When I think of the winding trail you've followed and the buffetings you've had from all directions, I can hardly believe you've brought us to this point… Morphew is saved!'

But they knew they had not been alone. One by one they recalled the loyal helpers who had risked themselves and their reputations: Adèle Ménage, Kate Primrose, and Lady Norreys too – not forgetting the formidable Elias. Even Jem and the Captain! Each one had played a part.

'We have had such friends to call on,' said Tom. 'And your father, Will! How much he has done for us at last! I think we can say that Justice is to be served – though we despaired of it many times.'

Will responded with a look of reservation – but a smile forced its way out.

'Not thanks to the system, Tom – rather in spite of it!'

The qualification was salutary, and within a minute or two the mood of elation had subsided and the party had settled into a quiet satisfaction. It seemed the right moment for Lord Melksham to reach for his bottle. Widow Trotter, who had an inkling what it might contain, arranged the glasses in anticipation.

'I have brought you a special vintage, my friends – to celebrate your success.'

They peered at the bottle, which looked remarkably thick and unappealing, and watched him begin extracting the cork. They held out their glasses, and with a sudden popping sound the pale liquid gushed forth – in bright, lively bubbles! Widow Trotter grinned.

'Aha! Sparkling champagne! How clever of you!'

'Indeed, Mrs Trotter. Thanks to the ingenious Mr Merrett, we English can claim to teach the French good taste. This is doubly fermented – the witty liquor! Is it not delicious?'

The silky effervescence seemed to impart a joyous brilliance to their brains, and all of them agreed that the drink consummated the occasion.

The three were now braced for Lord Melksham's account of his interview with Maynwaring and the negotiation between

Maynwaring and St John that followed it. As they listened, Tom, Will, and Mrs Trotter had the satisfaction of hearing how the various pieces of the story fitted together and what a labyrinth John Morphew had been trapped in.

'As for the scene in the printing-house,' said Will, 'what we've been dealing with all the time has been a double imposition. First Harry Grice's planting of the *Curse* took our thoughts toward Bufo, and Buller's evil violence with the cane seemed to confirm it.'

'Yes – and that meant there were two victims: Emmet and Morphew.'

'I see why we were puzzled. If Morphew wasn't the killer, then the signs became unclear – even a contradiction. What began as a terrible accident was turned into a scene of murder that had no simple explanation.'

'No wonder we found the motive troubling,' said Tom, 'and why we were torn between Emmet and Morphew, as to which was the prime victim.'

A shadow of disgust passed across Widow Trotter's face.

'What games these men have been playing! – Grice and Buller were both set on their own fictions, and each arranged the scene of the crime for their own ends.'

'Yes, and what irony!' said Will. 'Both parties contributed to the deceit, and in the end it proved to be a grotesque collaboration.'

Tom nodded.

'Yes, a kind of forgery – two stories overlaid – an imposition indeed!'

Lord Melksham nodded in his turn – he'd rarely had a more attentive audience.

'And of course,' he continued, 'behind them were the puppet-masters, St John and Maynwaring… I brought them together at midnight, and it was a strange conversation. It made me distinctly uneasy: two political enemies seeking common cause! The manoeuvres were fascinating. Maynwaring was trying to keep his hands clean of Voyce and Buller, and St John was shying away from the business of Mrs Greg's letter. Of course Maynwaring knew of its contents from Emmet, but he was in the dark about the roles that George Deacon and Harry Grice had played. I have to say that when Grice's contribution was mentioned Maynwaring performed exceptionally – he hardly wavered. It was a ticklish moment. You see, all along Maynwaring had assumed that Morphew had caused Emmet's death, so he now realised that Buller's actions that night had been truly indefensible. In the end, it was that knowledge which made him press St John hard, and which sealed the rogues' bargain. The deeper embarrassments were avoided, and this worked to our advantage. Each man extricated himself, and when we left the room they both breathed deeply, as if a weight had been lifted.

Widow Trotter turned the wine-glass in her hand and looked at it. She spoke with half a sigh.

'So, away they go – the happy pair! But, my Lord, are you certain that the pardon is concluded – that there's no room for any more duplicity?'

'You are right to ask – but there I can reassure you. By great good fortune, when St John and I descended the stairs together we saw Mr Harley waiting by the door. And so I was able to see the whole business concluded. Harley was entirely happy with the pardon and swore he would sign the document this morning. It was, after all, Bufo, not Morphew, who had disgusted him. In our explanation it became clear how greatly Morphew had been imposed on, and he expressed real pleasure. It seems the publisher's fate had been worrying him.'

'But what about Joe Buller's part in this?' said Tom.

'Ah, Buller! Our histrionic constable!' interjected Will, his brow wrinkling.

Lord Melksham frowned also.

'Yes, a disgrace to his calling. I wonder what Mr Cobb will make of it?... Buller will suddenly find he's lost his protectors. He will certainly be brought to book – though what the charge will be, it's hard to say.'

Will was unable to offer an answer and kept determinedly silent. The mood in the room had darkened, and the four of them began to sense the deep shadows that were looming out there beyond their own small points of light. Away from the convivial warmth that brought people together in this life, what coldness of heart and darkness of mind drove some others!

But cheerfulness soon returned along with their reminiscences. There was genuine pleasure to be had from memory and imagination, and they indulged in both. They re-lived their various encounters and discoveries, and could not forbear picturing the scene in Newgate when John Morphew would be told of his release.

'We can only pray the poor man has survived these last two days,' said Tom.

'And two *nights*,' added Widow Trotter. 'Just think what a night in the condemned cell must be like. Let us hope word has already reached him.'

The time passed happily enough, and half an hour later they were joined by Elias Cobb and a further bottle. For some reason his lumbering tread on the stairs no longer seemed ill-omen'd, and indeed this time he arrived not to bring news but to hear it. Everyone was happy to supply him, and soon his smile spread from ear to ear. He felt he had to rise to his feet and formally raise a glass to the company.

'*My Lord!... Young friends!... Widow!...* This is a remarkable conclusion, and I want to celebrate your achievement. The story is an extraordinary one, with its intricacy of motive, its cross-purposes, its plotting and counter-plotting... What an involved adventure it has been! In the process you have shone an unflattering beam on the world of our political masters; you have exposed selfish motives and unscrupulous methods; and – to my distress – you have revealed the serious corruption of an officer of the law. On all fronts you have done splendidly!...'

Elias, rather against convention, took an anticipatory sip of his wine, and his voice gained a new resonance.

'... It was a near impossible task – but you – you happy band! – have fought through to the truth. And you have done so with courage and ingenuity – with quick wits – and not least with remarkable scientific application. This campaign has been a triumph of the detector's art! Any of you would be an ornament to the profession of *assistant constable*; and I declare here and now that I would happily employ you in that capacity!'

He drank his toast with a flourish, and sat down. Tom patted him on the back with his uninjured hand.

'Elias Cobb!' declared Mrs Trotter, 'we in turn have to thank you for the help you've given us. Without your guidance and support we would not have found our way... The pieces would never have fitted together.'

She drank in her turn, and Lord Melksham did the same.

'You are an ornament to your profession, constable!' he said.

At this point their eyes naturally turned to the silent Will, who was enthroned in his bed, not unlike a judge on the bench.

Will Lundy's brow was still furrowed with thought. He had enjoyed Elias's eloquence, and during the performance he was struck by how easily his own legal calling could be parodied. Rhetoric was a dangerous art, and with its ease of manner could come complacency of thought. It was something that in his law studies he had increasingly tired of... But here among friends old and new it could only be heart-warming and delightful... certainly the relief everyone felt was palpable, and the satisfaction genuine... the smiling faces... it was all so neat... and yet... and yet...

He looked up and saw four pairs of eyes staring at him. Several seconds passed before he forced himself to speak, and his words were faltering ones.

'But… don't you realise… it doesn't make sense… *the final piece doesn't fit.*'

A palpable shock ran through the air. Widow Trotter and Constable Cobb looked at each other, and Lord Melksham put down his glass carefully. Tom was gazing at his friend, whose head was lifted up from the pillow, his eyes searching the cornice of the bedroom.

'What do you mean, Will? Is there something we've missed?… Are you not happy with the truth we've come to?'

'Oh, Tom, I'm overjoyed at Morphew's release, and what we've achieved. There's so much to celebrate… but my mind is still itching about one thing. It won't let me rest.'

'Ah! A lawyer's scruple!'

'Yes, Tom. For good or ill, I'm a lawyer… and the more I think about the goings-on in the printing-room – and how much was going on! – I can't persuade myself that it happened in quite that way.'

'What is the *final piece*, Mr Lundy?'

Lord Melksham's voice was warm and interested – the young man deserved to be listened to.

Will took a deep breath, trying not to wince.

'I should like to ask Constable Buller for his side of the story…'

It was a simple statement, though the others were jolted by it. But within moments they saw the reasonableness of the idea – perhaps they were grasping too eagerly at a tidy explanation?

'… We are releasing one innocent victim, but must take care we are not creating another.'

'You put it very strongly, Mr Lundy,' said Widow Trotter.

'You forget that in these two days, Mrs T, I've had many hours to think. Lying here there's been little else to do... And what a pother I caused when you let me escape!'

He looked at her shamefacedly. She was about to reassure him, but Tom was anxious to hear and pressed on to the point.

'Do you have an alternative scene in mind, Will? If so, I think we should hear it.'

Will tried to compose himself. He mustn't deliver a judicial summing-up – it was too tentative and conjectural – but he knew he needed to hear himself say it.

'I've been thinking about Constable Buller – about his character and the role he has been playing – or been made to play. It is a necessary distinction. There is something about his behaviour – call it his *enthusiasm* – which strikes me. We know he is happy to serve the cause of others – at a price – but also to be exploited perhaps? It's hard to say. But by all accounts he's a fussy man – someone who is concerned about fact, about getting things right.'

'Yes, that came across at the inquest,' said Tom.

'Maynwaring called him *precise*,' said Lord Melksham.

Will smiled.

'And you remember, Mrs T, we decided that it must have been him who closed Emmet's eyes, and yet he never mentioned the dead man's stare at the trial...'

He looked at Tom.

'... Could it be that Constable Buller has scruples too?'

'But Maynwaring made much of his violent nature... ,' said Lord Melksham, but broke off, aware of what he was assuming.

'I'm sure he did,' said Will.

'But we saw him at the inquest waving the cane with a passion,' added Tom '– a sight I had to endure a second time at the Session House.'

'Yes, Tom, but with what *intent*? – Perhaps he was trying to convey the violence of the deed? Perhaps it was done in horror at the act itself?... Can we believe that on two occasions Buller gleefully repeated his own violence in public in front of hundreds of people? The man who silently closed Emmet's eyes... would he have bent over the body and hammered at the head with such power? And then have left the corpse with that terrible stare?'

No-one spoke. Each of them was uncomfortably picturing the scene.

'Let me put it to you... What if Constable Buller thought that Morphew had indeed used the cane like that?'

'You mean, that Buller believed Morphew was the murderer?'

'Yes I do... Let us think... Do we have any firm evidence against that?...'

The four of them thought hard, but no-one spoke.

'... Three times – at the committal, the inquest, and the trial – Buller told how he had found the body with the bloody cane beside it. It's only Maynwaring who questions that, and in doing so he creates a scarcely plausible – almost comic – episode.'

After a tense moment, Tom broke the silence.

'So, you're suggesting that Buller really did come upon what he took to be a murder scene – dog-headed cane and all – and naturally assumed it had been Morphew?'

'All I'm saying is that we don't know otherwise... but is it not more likely? It would make matters simpler and clearer...'

He rode another silence.

'... As things stand at present, we are invited to believe that Constable Buller found the body lying there, as left by Harry Grice – assumed Morphew had fought with Emmet, and decided to use the cane with great violence to fix the murder on him – and in the process got bloodied – left to change his coat – and then returned to the scene in order to discover it a second time – but found Morphew there (someone else evidently revisiting the scene!) – I tell you, the place was like Charing Cross!'

The sudden jocularity was unsettling, but Will carried his point. Viewed in this rapid sequence, the pictures formed a less convincing story.

'I did think the scene had something of a farcical character,' said Lord Melksham.

Elias Cobb looked uneasy.

'So what do you think *did* happen after Harry Grice had fled the scene – and before Buller arrived?'

Will turned toward Tom.

'Do you recall what Emmet had said to Harry Grice just before their struggle?'

'That he was determined to destroy Harley, and would *never* sell the letter to him.'

'Yes, but there was another threat, wasn't there?'

'He said he was going to offer it to Arthur Maynwaring – and that he would certainly pay a more generous price.'

'That shows a degree of confidence, does it not? We know Emmet was playing one side against another. And the other man with whom he would be dealing was surely Maynwaring's agent… It must have been Voyce.'

'What are you saying?' Widow Trotter asked, on behalf of them all.

'I'm suggesting that if Emmet had agreed to meet Harry Grice at ten o-clock, then he could have arranged to meet Voyce at eleven.'

Tom swallowed as he took in the implications of the idea.

'It's possible I suppose. That would mean that when Voyce arrived at the printing-house to keep his appointment, he found Emmet's body as Harry Grice had left it… and then he… did the rest.'

'If that happened,' said Will, 'things make more sense. We can imagine Voyce's frustration when he saw the corpse – Mrs Greg's letter had been within his grasp!… And we have also to ask why was he so concerned to have the death scene cleared away? To protect Buller from embarrassment? I wouldn't think so.'

Widow Trotter was looking thoughtful.

'But would Voyce have recognised the cane as Mr Morphew's?'

'I was thinking about that,' said Will, 'but it seems Morphew's cane was quite a familiar sight.'

'Yes,' said Tom. 'At the trial Walter Treadwell said it was almost a part of himself.'

Lord Melksham looked a little shaken.

'So you think the story Maynwaring told me last night was a tissue of lies?'

'What I would ask is, why did Constable Buller describe everything to Maynwaring in such detail – accounting for every action and every motive?'

'Yes, I did think it was unusual. The man had itemised his behaviour so thoroughly – and conclusively! It was almost like a signed confession.'

'Perhaps that's what Maynwaring intended it should be,' said Tom grimly.

'And then there is the violence,' continued Will. 'The fact that Buller was a violent man rests on the word of Maynwaring.'

Elias Cobb leaned forward.

'Buller is an unscrupulous time-server. But I've not heard any imputation of violence. He's certainly no Deacon.'

'But is there not something in Henry Voyce's character that would make the hammering of Emmet's skull more plausible? I can't persuade myself that Buller would risk acting like that in order to bring about Morphew's death… but I can understand why *Voyce* might want to destroy him. You see… Buller is not a *zealot* – far from it. Unlike Voyce, he isn't an impassioned prophet who thinks Bufo is about to destroy civilisation. But think back, Tom... did we not encounter, that same evening in the coffee-room, a man who was enraged with Bufo and all he represented – an individual who betrayed a righteous anger, and who might happily put an end to Bufo's printer?'

'Yes – Voyce,' said Tom 'I'll not forget the look in his eyes.'

'His eyes made me shiver,' said Mrs Trotter. 'I remember when I impounded the epigram, his hand fluttered by his sword!...'

The five of them contemplated the thought.

'... and when he left this place, he turned towards the City,' she added by way of postscript. The picture imprinted itself on their minds.

Will broke the spell by lifting himself on his arms and pushing his back against the pillows.

'This is only conjecture of course... but do you not think it's an explanation we should pursue?'

'Maynwaring is a wily fellow,' said Lord Melksham, 'and I suspect has none of the *scruples* that have been guiding us. I've been recalling last night's conversation with him. He certainly had it off pat. I felt as if, behind all he said, was a conviction that Buller himself wouldn't contradict him!'

'Perhaps Buller has agreed to the story?' said Elias. 'It would cost Maynwaring something of course, but would be worthwhile if it safeguarded Voyce's operations.'

Widow Trotter looked at her old friend.

'I think nothing really shocks you, Elias. You've seen so much – and not the best of humanity.'

'But how does this leave us?' Lord Melksham asked, contemplating what he was increasingly thinking was his own gullibility. 'Should we challenge Maynwaring again?'

'No, my Lord,' said Elias firmly. 'Before that is done, it is Buller who needs to be challenged. And at once. Whatever the truth of the business, the case Mr Lundy has made is a persuasive one. It is circumstantial at several points, yes, but it does knit together. It has the ring of truth!'

The mood was a little gloomy, but Tom's face had a glimmer of cheer.

'Ah Will, my dear friend! You continue to astonish me! And all this from your sickbed. The more I think about it, the more I suspect you may be right. Maynwaring is determined to protect Voyce at all costs.'

'Well, we shall soon find out, I hope,' said Lord Melksham.

'I'll put the wheels in motion this very day,' said Elias decisively. 'The business needs to be cleared up. Buller must be brought in for questioning.'

'Yes, we can't leave it like this,' said Widow Trotter. 'We have to put a full stop to our story!'

The swirling waters beneath the arches of the old London Bridge were notoriously treacherous, and any cautious traveller along the Thames would alight at that point and negotiate the hazard by foot. On this particular cold Friday night, with the Royal Birthday celebrations over, the dark river was churning at high speed, creating a fierce vortex that would easily overthrow a passenger wherry. A few hours before dawn the scene was deserted, and there was no-one on the bank to look down on the gloomy flood. Had they done so, they might for a brief moment have caught sight of a bundle of clothing in vaguely human shape, which was being whisked along on the surging tide. A hand seemed to be waving in a wild gesture, but it was merely swivelling in the current. Life had left the corpse a good half hour earlier. It would be a day or two before the body was recovered, and when it was found, it would answer to the disappearance of one of the City Constables, Joseph Buller, who it seemed had met a sad end – whether by his own hand or another's would never be determined. But the result did remove a final complication from the scene, and it allowed the matter of *Regina v. Morphew* to be laid to rest. Like many such convenient incidents before and since, it left everything neat and tidy, and supplied merely a fading question-mark.

Tuesday

10 February 1708

Chapter Fifty

JOHN MORPHEW'S HAND rested on the head of his new walking-cane. The Baltic amber was warm to the touch and was shaped into a pleasing oval that sat comfortably in his palm. He paused and leant on it as he looked down Red Lion Court, smiling to see the Bay-Tree Chocolate House all spruced up for its inauguration. He could hear celebratory noises coming from an open window; but just for a moment he wanted to pause and think.

He recalled his previous visit to this spot. The convivial interlude with Tom and Will had been his last moment of liberty before he was dragged away into the nightmare. But he was now free again and ready to continue life after the terrifying death-in-life of the prison. It wasn't easy. He felt shrivelled and anxious, and half a stranger to his old identity. The experience of Newgate had eaten away at him, body and mind, leaving only a core that had somehow survived because it could shrink no further. He knew he must grow himself again and begin re-building hopes for the future: he had to be busy and embrace friends, re-enter the stream of life. Morphew continued looking at the house's bright green bay-tree sign and remained there in deep thought for several minutes, after which he turned around and walked slowly back towards Drury Lane, in the direction from which he had come.

The Grand Re-opening of Mary Trotter's establishment was proving to be a spirited occasion. Drinks of different kinds were flowing free and the quality of the variously spiced hot chocolates was receiving special praise; but there were also inviting cordials to refresh the palate, and sweetened lemonade too. Peter Simco had adapted well enough to the new surroundings, although he was distinctly uneasy about the half-naked American standing by the door. Time and again he gave the figure an accusing stare, as if asking why he wasn't doing anything to help. The thing carved in painted wood was almost his own height and was lolling on a tall longbow, holding up a brass pot in its right hand. Widow Trotter had found the object at the Exchange and said it represented *Chocolate*. But Peter was hoping it would find a home outside the entrance. Looking at the exotic fellow with his feathered skirt and headdress, he was grateful that Mrs Trotter's zeal for authenticity hadn't extended to himself.

In various parts of the coffee-room there were other things to raise the eyebrows of the more conventional clientele. Not least, along the bar was a line of wooden platters onto which Jenny Trip and Mrs Dawes had arranged the food. It was not substantial fare, but consisted of savoury morsels that could be picked up and eaten while standing, without the need for plates. Further along were hearty slices of pie and pasty for the less adventurous, but it was the special dishes that were attracting curiosity. Elias Cobb had been persuaded to try a mushroom stuffed with goat's cheese and crushed walnut, but it was proving a challenge even for his agile fingers. Captain Roebuck was commending the small bean-cakes coated with mashed pea and paprika, and had to be restrained from carrying the lot away to his table – which was thought to be against the principle of the thing. If the regulars were tentative, there were others who were totally *charmed* and sampled the delicacies eagerly. Lord Tring's party were comparing the merits of the fried artichoke hearts and the crisp potato slices coated with thyme butter and tiny cubes of bacon. His voice rose above the hubbub as he declared the latter to be 'exquisite!' – an epithet bacon and potato can rarely have attracted.

Yes, Mrs Dawes had triumphed – and Widow Trotter looked on with delight as Jenny emerged from the kitchen bearing a platter of miniature meatballs. But as a pack of gentlemen surged towards the new offering with hands outstretched she began to feel a shiver of doubt. Was her new chocolate house in danger of becoming more of a high-class chop-house? Today was of course unusual, but she would have to be careful to get the emphasis right. Food for the mind – she told herself – the true stimulus of chocolate, coffee and tea. That mustn't be forgotten!

In face of the polite influx, Jack Tapsell and his friends were cowering by the fire, eyeing the goings-on with a degree of suspicion. But Gavin Leslie and David Macrae, who were seated with them, were encouraging them to sample the new food and one of the flavoured chocolates.

'Chocolate means chocolate!' grumbled Barnabas Smith, 'and it's not to be messed with. Whoever heard of *beetroot and ginger!*'

Yet another breach of decorum was evident at one corner of the room, where two *females* were making themselves at home, talking and laughing in a group. Adèle Ménage and Kate Primrose had been welcomed into the coffee-room with particular notice; and in the face of astonished whispers and raised eyebrows, their hostess made it clear they were to have a place of honour for the occasion. Morphew's release, and the part played in it by Widow Trotter and her friends, was soon common knowledge, and judgmental glances became admiring ones. Alongside the ladies, Will was seated with his back to the wall, his shoulder eased by a cushion, and Tom was there to ferry sustenance as required.

Widow Trotter made her way over, and was greeted with encouraging remarks about the quality of the food. Mrs Ménage began with an encomium on the pieces of grilled chicken marinated in lemon juice and mint…

The smile froze on Mrs Trotter's lips.

'I'm so pleased you all like the house cookery. Mrs Dawes has excelled herself, has she not? Quite the magician!'

Her face held the look of pleasure for longer than was necessary. Tom noticed a slight tightening of her cheek and smiled in his turn.

'Don't worry, Mrs T! The conversation has been remarkable too. Would you believe, when I was over at the bar I heard three gentlemen discussing Mr Locke's theory of the association of ideas. One of them was insisting that the taste of goat's cheese always brought thunderstorms to mind…'

'Hurrah!' said Will. 'Your plan is certainly working, Mrs T! Give us time and we shall shortly be more philosophical. Remember, we have Mr Bagnall's poem to come!'

The look on Mrs Trotter's face shifted to ill-disguised apprehension.

'I could hardly refuse, Mr Lundy. But I discouraged him from a full Pindaric ode. He promises it will be an extended epigram.'

'*Extended,* Mrs T? There is much danger in that word… But I promise to drop my dish of chocolate the moment you give the sign!'

Widow Trotter said she was grateful for the reassurance and continued her tour of the tables, leaving Tom and Will to entertain the female guests. Kate Primrose had been sitting quietly, taking in the display of male clubbability and enjoying the lively humour. In this place men were happy without being drunk; and everyone seemed to be taking pleasure in each other's company, making no demands and delighting in listening as much as talking. She decided there was something about a chocolate house that appealed to her.

So far, Tom and Will had not spoken to her of Emmet's death, and they were unsure what details she had been told about Harry Grice. They knew Widow Trotter had conveyed what she could to her friend Adèle; but it was a difficult topic, and they were wondering how to introduce it without opening up the wound. Not for the first time, Kate preempted them.

'Mrs Ménage has told me about John's death, and what you've found out. She says it was an accident – not a murder – and that you've had a confession...'

Adèle Ménage looked a little awkward:

'Forgive me, gentlemen. Yes, I did my best to pass on what I knew, but Kate had questions that I could not answer. The highwayman with the fork? – Marie told me he was a friend of yours, Mr Lundi.'

It was now Will's turn to look embarrassed, and he made a hesitant reply. Further inquiries followed. In the end it was thought best that Tom and Will should tell what they knew, and what they suspected. Harry Grice's story, which Kate now heard in full, was received with wide-eyed silence.

'I am sorry Mrs Greg's letter caused such trouble,' she said, '– and you say there's nothing to be done for her husband?... That's sad. But your friend Mr Grice perhaps meant well and wanted to help her. He was desperate, wasn't he! When he threatened me, I knew he was more frightened than angry. Perhaps that's why he wasn't thinking clearly. I'm lucky he was such a clumsy attacker – after all, it could have been George Deacon. I'm glad that evil man is to receive his punishment.'

Tom asked the unavoidable question.

'And what about Harry Grice, Kate? What should his punishment be?'

'Ah, the foolish man!... John had played with him, and used the letter to taunt him... They were both such fools!...'

She let out a long, extraordinary sigh, which seemed to express so much wasting of human energies. But it was also like something being released from her.

'... I can't be angry at either of them now. You say Mr Grice is going to help Elizabeth Greg as best he can? I'm glad of that... if I'm asked, I'll make no accusation against him. There's so much about this whole affair that's best forgot.'

Tom looked at her closely and was deeply impressed. It wasn't just clever men who could be philosophical.

'And what is to happen to you, Kate?' he asked. 'Or should I say *Clarissa*?'

'No no, Mr Bristowe. Clarissa is no more! Mr Quinlan says I should wipe the name from my mind.'

Tom's heart rose to think she might be leaving that life behind her.

'Mr Quinlan?'

'Yes, my neighbour in Vinegar Yard. He rescued some of my things for me, and he's offered me lodgings with him.'

'So you're back in Vinegar Yard?'

'Yes, Mr Bristowe. And I've made my peace with Mrs Purslowe.'

She looked at Will.

'From now on I'm to be *Callisto*. Don't you think that's a lovely name? It means *very beautiful*.'

By now the whole room was abuzz with lively talk, and Mrs Trotter sailed around, sampling and encouraging. Compliments were circulating freely – and not exclusively about the food. Seats at the tables were all taken, and men were standing in groups near the fire or within easy reach of the bar.

She caught Elias Cobb's eye and went over to him. The constable had just been scrutinising the new print of Mrs

Bracegirdle, and there was a suppressed chuckle in his voice as he greeted her.

'Fine feathers, are they not, Molly? Our Indian Queen and your handsome gentleman by the door are seeking to outdo one another. This place might almost be Mexico!'

'They are noble figures, Elias. I thought they could keep company… How good it is to see the place humming and to gather all my friends together like this!'

'Mrs Ménage and Kate seem quite at home, don't they! – it was bold of you to invite them.'

'They have more right than anyone to be here. Kate seems remarkably at ease with herself. She says she'll not bring a charge against Mr Grice – she wants to leave the whole business behind, and I can understand why.'

'In that case, he's a very fortunate gentleman – and a thoroughly sobered one I trust! Maynwaring's evidence has not only freed Mr Morphew, but Mr Grice too – the young man's account of his struggle with Emmet in the printing-house has been accepted – so it seems there's nothing to hold him.'

'And his post in the Cockpit looks secure…'

'More than secure, Molly! It appears Mr St John now regards Harry Grice as utterly invaluable and is anxious to favour him. Somehow the young man can do no wrong… One might almost think Mr Secretary needed him as an ally.'

'What a world, Elias! How things shift their place – so many twists and turns!'

'Let us hope Mr Grice will make the best of his fortune.'

Elias looked over her shoulder and his eyes widened. There was a sudden cry of delight, and as Widow Trotter swung round, a beaming Lord Tring seized her by the hand.

'Mrs Trotter – our lady hostess! This is a triumph! My friends and I have been thinking ourselves in a Parisian *salon* –

you have so sharpened our wits. Such a supply of dainties! True nourishment for the mind! You are a woman of *taste!*'

She met their smiling faces and was about to say something polite when she noticed the coffee-room door open tentatively, and a gaunt figure appeared. The man stood there motionless in the doorway and turned his head, only to flinch from a bare-chested exotic who seemed to be offering him a drink.

'My lords, forgive me! – Mr Morphew has arrived!'

Tom had already leapt to his feet and was walking over to shake him by the hand. Within seconds the publisher was surrounded by well-wishers greeting him as a conquering hero, though in his own mind he was something closer to a prodigal son approaching the family hearth. Mrs Trotter seated him comfortably with Will and Tom, and slid onto the bench herself. Peter was beckoned to perform the pouring, and an eager Jem was there in a trice pushing a half-empty platter towards his chin.

There was so much animation around him, and a ring of smiling faces. For a short while the publisher could only sit silently, trying to collect himself. His own face was noticeably thinner, and his eyes watchful and still bloodshot; but as the talk gathered momentum and the humour of the company established itself, they began flickering in response, and he was drawn into conversation.

After a few minutes he lifted a hand.

'Forgive me… There's such a lot I need to say to you all, but I'm sadly tongue-tied. My gratitude is too great to express – no words seem enough! You've brought me back from the dead… I don't quite know how it was done, but I warrant it's a story that will need a lot of telling…' He looked at the faces. '… And we shall have time for that, thank God! As much *time* as we need…'

His head lowered slightly as if he was weighing something in his mind.

'... How often we let it slip by without a thought – but how precious it is! Every single minute.'

Tom laid his hand on Morphew's arm and smiled.

'Mr Morphew is being philosophical, Mrs T!'

'It must be the deep-fried artichoke,' said Will mischievously.

The publisher gave a sudden disarming laugh.

'In that case, I think I might be allowed another!'

He reached to the platter and took in the picture of the two bandaged young men, both of them brimming with good humour.

'You are a remarkable pair. I know I'm not the only one to have suffered. You must tell me all the details of your adventures. But not now... perhaps tomorrow? You must both come to dinner – Mrs Trotter too! – and we can talk to our hearts' content. There are so many questions I need to ask – and be warned, you shan't rest until you've told me everything!'

The talk moved on, and Morphew soon discovered that Kate and Adèle had also played a big part – and neither of them unscathed by the experience. For the first time it struck him that he'd had a veritable battalion fighting on his side. When Mrs Ménage's name was mentioned he stopped short.

'Adèle Ménage? Can it be? Well, I've encountered your name only this morning. My pressman told me he'd had a visitor who wished to negotiate a price for a bundle of letters. But Mr Feeny saw him off the premises. Private papers are a sore point with us now, and we intend to steer clear of them!'

'My papers! They were stolen from me a week ago. And to think that you've had them in your possession!'

'Don't despair, madam – I'm sure we can do something... It was a tall, rather odd young man, a Mr *Curll*... I've no doubt we'll be able to trace him and recover them for you. Have no fear!'

The coffee-room door opened again, and this time it was the face of Lord Melksham that appeared. He paused, surveying the busy room, and offered his hat to *Chocolate*; but the figure was unresponsive, so he hung it over the man's bowl. He noticed questioning looks coming from Tom and Will, and responded with a slight shake of the head. The tables were now crowded and there was no space to sit, so Tom rose to his feet and joined him in front of the tall mirror.

'Welcome uncle! The Bay-Tree Chocolate House is proving popular, is it not?'

'I'm pleased to see it – Mrs Trotter deserves success. She's a commanding woman, Tom! I do believe she could manage anything – even the House of Commons, given the chance. I think she would keep them in excellent order!...'

Tom knew it was a far from incongruous idea, and advised him not to stir up her ambitions.

'... But before I settle in, Tom, I must give you this note from Lavinia. She was determined to come along herself, but my wife forbad it. Sophia is adamant that a coffee house...'

'A *chocolate* house, uncle!'

'... Well, a chocolate house *especially* – is a place solely for male indulgence, and is completely out of bounds for ladies – though I see Mrs Trotter has allowed an exception!'

'These are two very *special* ladies, Sir – and I shall certainly introduce you to them, After all, the three of you have been working as a team!...'

He tucked the note into his pocket.

'... But when you came in I saw you shake your head... Does that mean there is still no word of Constable Buller? Mr Cobb had nothing to report this morning.'

'No, no word at all, Tom. The man seems to have disappeared, but inquiries are still being made. It's thought he may have fled somewhere, but I am beginning to wonder if he has been disowned... and put to silence.'

It was a chilling phrase.

'You don't believe... ?'

'Yes I do – I have a bad feeling about it. But we'll see... Now I want to sample the chocolate!'

'You must take my seat, uncle – And I'll find a morsel of food at the bar for you. We have been offered a succession of delicious things – savoury fancies!... I have to say your timing has been perfect: only ten minutes later and you would have missed Mr Bagnall's poem, which I think is imminent... *Inauguratio Laureæ*. That's his title – but I do hope the thing is in our native tongue!'

'So Mr Tate was otherwise occupied?'

'Wisely so. But Laurence Bagnall will fill the breach.'

'We're not going to hear any of his *Epistle to Robert Harley?*'

'For that we must wait until the end of the week. I gather it is being printed off as we speak.'

Tom guided his uncle across to the table where Will and the others were sitting. Will rose to greet him, and Tom then introduced John Morphew. The publisher stood and took him warmly by the hand, and Lord Melksham shook his with equal ardour. The two had much to say to each other, oblivious of the apprehension that was mounting in the room, where Laurence Bagnall was reaching into his bag for his script. Tom watched and counted at least five pages, and his heart sank. But then the poet pulled out something else and Tom's mouth opened in astonishment. It was a garland of laurel... It was best not to look.

He quickly broke the seal on Lavinia's note.

Tom! – I am forbidden the Bay-Tree! My wicked stepmother has placed me under arrest. It is on the pretence of preparing for Frank's return (the tardy young man is confidently expected this evening – at long, long last!). But the true reason is, the domestic tyrant doesn't wish me to mix with wits and poets. What hypocrisy! Alas, Tom, the bay is not to be mine!... But we shall see... I have been making plans – hatching a plot, you'd say

– with Julia Norreys. Would you believe it? She has invited me to tea – and you know what that will mean… Arachne's Web! So, who can tell? This particular spinster may find herself spinning more than wool! But I did so want to meet Mr Morphew. I've heard about his ordeal and am very shocked. What you men do to each other!… But right now I expect you are all lounging around talking about poetry and saying lots of polite things.

You must call here and see the truant Frank – I long to discover what Europe has made of him – I hope it is not too shocking! And I'll expect a full report on your Bay-Tree festivities.

Till then,

Your thoughtful cousin

Lavinia Popham

P.S. Lady Norreys even suggested that you might become our – what should I call it? – I don't know what – something a little like a chaplain to a nunnery – and quite as innocent I'm sure!… That would indeed be a remarkable honour – but not without its risks – and it may meet with an insuperable objection from Mrs Manley.

Tom's imagination began playing tricks. A delicate matter indeed! He didn't know what to think, or how to respond… Lavinia really had something of the Queen Mab about her…

The room was still humming. He looked up, and saw that Mr Bagnall was now in conference with Mrs Trotter, who was shaking her head with some emphasis. The laureate of the Bay-Tree was looking anxious, and Tom began to wonder if he had indeed brought along his *Epistle to Harley* and was about to regale them with the whole of it. There was a shuffling of bodies and an expectant hush suddenly descended.

It was at this critical moment that something happened to convince everyone in the room – even the staunchest materialist – that there might be a higher power intervening in human affairs; that somewhere above, looking down on that corner of Covent Garden, was a guardian spirit with an amused glint in its eye.

As silence fell and poet Bagnall prepared himself, there was a burst of genial laughter outside the front door, which opened to admit two chattering gentlemen who suddenly found themselves facing a disconcerting stillness and a hundred staring eyes. One of the men grinned and looked around him, but the other began to blush and stopped in his tracks.

Bagnall's face radiated delight and fear.

'Mr Addison!' he said, and stared.

It was an uncomfortable moment, but Mary Trotter seized it. She stepped forward and made a friendly gesture toward the pair, who had obviously not expected to find themselves at the centre of a stage.

'You are very welcome, Sirs, and have timed your entrance perfectly! Let us find you seats for the performance – perhaps over here at the side. We are about to be given a part – only a *small* part on this occasion, alas! – of Mr Bagnall's new *Inauguration Ode*, Written in honour of The Bay-Tree Chocolate House...'

Chocolate was duly brought, and Mr Addison and his friend Mr Steele settled themselves as best they could. They exchanged doubtful glances, not entirely sure what level of threat to their reputations this might pose.

Laurence Bagnall cleared his throat, and for the next several minutes customers of the Bay-Tree were reassured that the art of poetry was not dead – it had simply moved temporarily elsewhere...

Descend, my Muse, from thine accustom'd Flights:
Descend to Earth, and ease thy wide-stretch'd Wing!
For weary art thou grown of those too daring heights;
Thou shalt of Chocolate sing

And Coffee's rich delights;
The Bay-Tree now commands th'adventurous Muse
To welcome wit, and poetry, and lofty thought,
The philosophic mind t'enthuse…

A full seven minutes later, the applause that marked the conclusion of Mr Bagnall's ode was emphatically final, and the audience returned to their talk in buoyant mood, convinced that Mrs Trotter had achieved a brilliant *coup de théâtre*. Addison behaved graciously and commended Mr Bagnall on his mastery of the burlesque, only to be met with a look of hurt puzzlement. He noticed that the garland of bay laurel remained on the chair.

Richard Steele was drawn into Lord Tring's party, but Addison turned in the direction of John Morphew. Tom surrendered his seat, but Addison assured him that he had called there in hopes of seeing both of them.

'I've come over from Will's… Word reached me of the special occasion here, and I was told that Mr Morphew's presence was to be expected…'

He looked at Morphew.

'… Forgive me, Sir, but before I say more, I feel strongly that I should convey my apologies to you – a word that is sadly inadequate, I fear.'

'From you, Mr Addison, it is unlooked for, and unnecessary. We met previously under unusual circumstances.'

'Indeed we did – painful ones. But I must say this to you, Mr Morphew… I rejoice that you are free, and have been shocked to hear of the plot that entangled you. I was this morning at the Cockpit where I heard how things have played themselves out, and how you came so close to being an innocent victim. But thankfully the matter is now settled. We are all very much relieved to have put it behind us!'

Tom glanced at his uncle before speaking hesitantly.

'You know of Constable Buller's disappearance, Mr Addison?'

'Buller? Yes indeed – a tragic case. But the man had behaved disgracefully. I think he could not live with his actions. For a constable to do what he did…'

'Has he then been traced, Sir?' asked a grim-faced Lord Melksham.

'His body was found last night, my Lord – down beyond Deptford, would you believe? The river had swept him quite a distance. A wretched business!'

There was silence at the table and a realisation that, however much could be said, nothing more would be. It was a painful ending, and one that was haunted by suspicion and conjecture; but those phantoms would soon melt away.

A sober gloom had settled on the group. Addison turned back to the publisher.

'You have done well to pull yourself clear of this, Mr Morphew – and I hope you'll now look to the future – if we have one, given the crisis we are in…'

He took a sip of chocolate.

'… I believe the *Bufo* affair has been a regrettable distraction. My colleague Mr Hopkins was full of zeal for the thing, but I confess to finding the matter distasteful in the extreme. This Bufo has talent, though he sorely mis-uses it… Do you know, Mr Bristowe, at one point I believed that you might be he – John Emmet had claimed as much.'

'Emmet said that I was Bufo?'

'Mr Emmet said a great deal, Mr Bristowe, and most of it was a tangle of untruth and malicious gossip. It took us a while to expose it.'

He turned back to Morphew.

'Hopkins and I had you released from the Cockpit as soon as we could, Sir – though Mr Maynwaring was insistent you should be held until the Saturday at least. He and his henchman Voyce wanted to be let loose on you again… But Lord Sunderland said no. I think he is tiring of Maynwaring's interference.'

Lord Melksham gave a wry smile and glanced at Tom.

'My nephew has ambitions in poetry, Mr Addison. But he has received a severe setback with this Bufo business.'

'I'm sorry to hear that, my Lord, because I would wish to encourage him. Indeed, in the course of my duties I have read his most recent effort, and I think well of it. The piece is an imitation – in places a translation – of *Juvenal*.'

Lord Melksham's face fell slightly and he felt tongue-tied. Tom's heart was pounding, and he was tongue-tied too. This left Addison with a clear run.

'One reason for coming here, Mr Bristowe, was to return this to you.'

He reached into his pocket, and to Tom's wonder and delight he took out a familiar sheaf of papers. It was headed: *Crime and Punishment: The Thirteenth Satire of Juvenal, Imitated.*

'You are no longer under suspicion, Sir! Unless I may be allowed to suspect you of being a poet. You have the makings. It's not a title I bestow readily…'

Addison held out the manuscript to him, but did not release it. And he turned to Morphew.

'… I must apologise a second time, Sir, for having prevented you from perusing this piece. You have not had the chance of assessing it.'

'I shall be happy to do so, Mr Addison. Indeed, after your commendation I would be short-sighted not to consider its printing.'

'I'm delighted to hear that, Mr Morphew… but first there are one or two small infelicities that could be set right… However, it has a directness that I like, and in the passages that are close to the Roman poet Mr Bristowe writes with rare sympathy. He seems attuned to Juvenal's noble indignation and makes it speak directly to us. Let me read you a passage... What think you of this, Sir? It has the ring of our present desperate times!

> *"The virtues are in exile: nothing's left*
> *But murder, treason, perjury and theft;*
> *A time so bad, all truth and honour fled:*
> *Is this an Age of Iron? – or of Lead?*
> *'Tis wrong the Frame of Nature to defame:*
> *No metal's base enough to lend its name.*
> *The wise are gone, and so few are the good*
> *That scarcely more were left at Noah's flood."*

How nicely shaped those lines are...'

Addison was becoming absorbed and drew the paper closer to his eyes.

'... But I wonder... would *Scheme* of Nature be better perhaps? – to avoid the awkward assonance?... The rhymes are strong, but *good* and *flood* is infelicitous, although the idea is a neat one. Perhaps with a little more work... ?'

By this point Tom was blushing like an over-ripe peach and could still say nothing. Will, who had been keeping a disciplined silence, risked a comment.

'If my friend could speak, Mr Addison, I'm sure he would tell you how eager he is to begin revising it.'

'Not revision, Sir, mere *tinkering* is called for – a little hammering out here and there, that is all. The piece does not need to be re-forged... But I sincerely hope, Mr Bristowe, that you will move on and find your own voice – and one that is wise and humane. Satire is a powerful thing, but it has its limits. Poetry should bring thoughts and ideas to life – it is not merely anger and name-calling. True humour is delightful, but abuse – personal abuse especially – takes us into the dirty alleys of the mind, away from civilised argument and open debate.'

Tom smiled at him.

'You speak wisely yourself, Mr Addison. If I am able to make it my profession I'll not forget those words.'

Tom turned his head and saw that Will was looking at him with an expression that could only be called radiant pride, and he felt Widow Trotter's hands resting on his shoulders.

'Well gentlemen,' she announced to the company, 'this might almost count as a happy ending. Such things are very precarious – so let us enjoy this one while we can… Mr Addison… would you like to try a cumin-spiced meatball? They have been pronounced excellent!'

The Epilogue

On that same Tuesday evening, the 10th of February, out west in Kensington Palace the atmosphere could not have been more different. In the antechamber the footmen had taken their positions even more stiffly than usual, hardly daring to turn their heads. A handful of hovering courtiers were glancing at each other, wondering whether to slip away or make themselves ready for the aftermath. No-one dared enter the room.

At the other side of the door in the audience chamber itself, Queen Anne was making strange sounds – sobs and shouts delivered to empty fireplaces, with only the impassive royal portraits to hear her. Even Abigail Masham was elsewhere, having been warned by her cousin Mr Harley to stay out of the way, as there would be some uncomfortable business to settle. Anne stood alone in the centre of the room, in floods of angry tears.

A terrible combination of passions assailed her. The sense of loss would have been bad in itself, but the frustration made things worse. Her own impotence drove her furiously on. The scene she had just endured had been harrowing. An audience with Mr Harley was usually a meeting of minds and hearts. But on this day there could be no such reassurance. Both of them had had to face the situation in all its starkness. As the monarch, of course, she still had a choice: she could lose the Duke of Marlborough, lose half her cabinet, lose the nation's allies, and probably lose the war – or she could lose Harley. The fact that she had wavered, protested, and stood her ground for so long was remarkable. But in the end she had to release her grip on the man to whom she had clung so tenaciously, and let him slip away. However much she protested and lamented, it simply had to be.

It was the end of April, and a beam of spring sunshine made its way into Stationers' Yard, catching the various prints and title-pages displayed in the window of John Morphew's shop. In the bright pool of light, four items – all subscribed 'London: Printed, and sold by J. Morphew near Stationers Hall' – were lined up alongside the front door, almost as if they had been deliberately arranged to tell a story.

The first was a sad and simple document – a mere single broadsheet:

A True Copy of the Paper Left by Mr. William Greg, who was executed for High-Treason the 28th Day of April, 1708.

Anyone pausing in front of the shop to browse its wares would have to bring their eyes up close in order to read the thing...

> *The Crime I am now justly to suffer for, having made a great noise in the world, the criminal takes this last opportunity to profess his utter abhorrence, and sincere repentance, of all his sins against God, and of all the heinous crimes committed against the Queen, whose forgiveness I most heartily implore... I declare the*

reparation I would make to those of Her Majesty's subjects I have wronged in any kind, and particularly the Right Honourable Robert Harley, Esq; whose pardon I heartily beg for basely betraying my trust: which declaration, though of itself sufficient to clear the said gentleman, yet... I do sacredly protest that, as I shall answer before the judgment-seat of Christ, the gentleman aforesaid was not privy to my writing to France, directly nor indirectly...

Placed alongside it in the window was a well-proportioned octavo title-page, with the lettering in slim, elegant capitals:

The Present State of the War, and the *Necessity of an Augmentation,* Consider'd.

In the matter of sales, this piece was making a considerable splash, and although it didn't carry the name of an author, it was well known to be by none other than Joseph Addison. For some it seemed odd that John Morphew, whose leanings towards Mr Harley's cause were hardly concealed, should lend his name to such a brazenly Whig essay, especially one that argued for intensifying the European War... and it was no less strange that Addison should entrust the piece to him... but perhaps there had been some kind of *rapprochement* between the two men?

Third in line, and needing no close scrutiny to appreciate its full effect, was a displayed title-page in magisterial folio:

Crime and *Punishment: The Thirteenth Satire* of *Juvenal, Imitated.* By Thomas Bristowe, Esq., Late of Trinity College, Oxford.

This piece declared itself with quite a flourish, and gave a handsome appearance. Beneath the name was a delicately interwoven crown of bay laurel garlanding a grotesquely grinning face, and beneath its protruding chin was a Latin motto: *Difficile est saturam non scribere.*

The final paper in this miscellaneous procession was considerably more modest in its pretensions. The layout was plainer, almost austere, as if its very starkness were making a point:

Public Virtue: An Epistle to the Right Honourable Robert Harley, Esq. By Mr Bagnall, Author of The Shoe-Buckle...
The Second Edition, *Revised.*

Characters

[Historical figures marked with *]

COURT & POLITICS

*Queen Anne, *the last Stuart monarch, niece of Charles the Second*
*Sarah Churchill, Duchess of Marlborough, *Anne's friend and support over many years, now angry and suspicious*
*Arthur Maynwaring, MP, *Secretary to the Duchess of Marlborough, wit and Whig pamphleteer*
*John Churchill, Duke of Marlborough, *the great general, victor of Blenheim (1704) and Ramillies (1706)*
*Charles Spencer, Earl of Sunderland, *Secretary of State and leader of the 'Junto' Whigs, Marlborough's son-in-law*
*Thomas Hopkins, *Sunderland's Deputy Secretary*
*Joseph Addison, *Sunderland's other Deputy Secretary, poet, critic and cultural authority*
*Richard Steele, *Addison's friend and soon to be his collaborator on* The Spectator
*John, Baron Somers, *former Lord Chancellor, chief legal organiser behind the Whig 'Junto'*
*Charles Montagu, Baron Halifax (later Earl), *another ambitious Whig politician being kept out of office*

*Thomas, Earl of Wharton (later Marquess), *Whig politician dogged by scandal*
*Robert Harley (later Earl of Oxford), *Secretary of State and Anne's confidant, friend of Alexander Pope and Jonathan Swift*
*Abigail Masham, *Harley's cousin, now Lady of the Bedchamber*
*Henry St John (later Viscount Bolingbroke), *Secretary-at-War, Harley's ally, almost a Tory, later a Jacobite, and Pope's close friend*
*William Greg, *traitor in Harley's office at the Cockpit*
*Elizabeth Greg, *his devoted wife*

RED LION COURT

Mary Trotter, *recently widowed, now rules in the Good Fellowship and has ambitions for the place*
Tom Bristowe, *budding poet born under Saturn, a Celadon with ambitions to be a Juvenal*
Will Lundy, *Tom's best friend, mercurial law student of the Middle Temple, future Westminster Hall orator*
Mrs Dawes, *creative in the kitchen*
Jenny Trip, *barista princess with a sharp eye*
Peter Simco, *skilful coffee-boy with a bright future*
Jeremy Jopp (Jem), *does errands and hard lifting, but in training*
Old Ralph, *sweeps and cleans*
Jack Tapsell, *Whig wine merchant*
Barnabas Smith, *Whig cloth merchant*
Samuel Cust, *Whig with a Caribbean sugar plantation*
Laurence Bagnall, *poet and critic with laureate ambitions, author of 'The Shoe-Buckle'*
Captain Roebuck, *old soldier of Marlborough's Flanders campaign*
Gavin Leslie, *down from the glens of Scotland*
David Macrae, *his friend and compatriot*

ST JAMES'S

John Popham, Second Viscount Melksham (Tom's Uncle Jack), *Queen Anne's Deputy Treasurer, an unwilling courtier*
Sophia Popham (*née Doggett*), Viscountess Melksham, *enjoys London's social whirl*
The Hon. Frank Popham, *continually expected*
The Hon. Lavinia Popham, *lively and advanced for seventeen*
The Hon. Wilmot Popham, *in trouble at Winchester School*
The Countess of Welwyn, *of St James's Square, throws a good party*
Lord Tring, *her son, very fresh from the Grand Tour*
Arthur, *the Pophams' footman, carries himself – and Tom – well*
Julia, Lady Norreys, *fine horsewoman, intelligent and bored*
Sir Charles Norreys, *her husband, unintelligent and busy doing nothing*
Alexander, *the Norreys's tall footman*
The Honourable Mr Sturgis, *falls short of his title*

THE LAW

Elias Cobb, *Covent Garden's polite constable, with semi-official interests*
Tobias Mudge, *Elias's apprentice who's shaping up*
Joseph Buller, *fussy City constable with political connections and histrionic abilities*
Sam Bennett, *rigorous City watchman*
Bartholomew Dignum, *suspicious Covent Garden magistrate*
Alderman Rivers, *City Coroner, doing his best under the circumstances*
Richard Sumner, *respectable barrister and Will's pupil-master, Lady Norreys' brother*
Roger Nugent, *tenacious Old Bailey prosecutor, worth his fee*
John Wise, *determined knight of the post*

Henry Voyce, *Arthur Maynwaring's zealous agent and 'fixer'*
George Deacon, *widely feared Ministry enforcer*
Mr Chandler, *Deputy Keeper of Newgate prison*
*Mrs Spurling, *entrepreneurial Newgate shopkeeper*

HACKNEY

Mr Justice Oliver Lundy ('Hemp'), *Will's father, Old Bailey judge and strict upholder of the Law*
Aunt Dinah, *his sister, a spiritual judge*
Aunt Rebecca, *her equally upright sister*
Daniel, *the Lundys' hard-driving coachman*
*The Revd Robert Billio, *popular dissenting minister at Mare Street*

STATIONERS' YARD, etc.

*John Morphew, *publisher-printer near Stationers' Hall, will soon become Jonathan Swift's publisher and see more arrests*
John Emmet, *Morphew's first pressman, engaged in surreptitious document supply, ambitious to have his own printing business*
James Feeny, *Morphew's second pressman*
Paul Barnard, *Morphew's compositor and Emmet's friend*
Mrs Barnard, *worrying at home*
Walter Treadwell, *friendly porter at Stationers' Hall*

THE LITERARY WORLD

*Delarivier Manley, *controversial writer, weaver of fact and fiction*
*Lady Mary Pierrepont (later Wortley Montagu), *daughter of the Duke of Kingston, poet, wit, and noted beauty*

*Anne Bracegirdle, *celebrated actress of star quality, just retired*
*Joseph Browne, *unguarded satirist in trouble with the authorities*
*Dr Jonathan Swift, *another unguarded satirist, in London lobbying for the Church of Ireland; had scandalised Queen Anne with his* Tale of a Tub *in 1704*
*Daniel Defoe, *Robert Harley's agent and influential political journalist*
*Matthew Prior, *poet and diplomat, Swift's close friend*
*Edmund Curll, *soon to become a successful publisher specialising in the illicit and sensational; known as 'the unspeakable Curll'; Pope's inveterate enemy*

ELSEWHERE

The Revd Dr Kettlewell, *Royal chaplain and noted preacher*
Harry Grice, *clerk in Robert Harley's office, a cog in the Cockpit machine*
Ned Rokeby, *law student who's not yet found his feet*
Adèle Ménage, *of Katherine Street, retired from the bagnio business*
'Bully' the bullfinch, *her trusted companion*
Kate Primrose ('Clarissa'), *of Vinegar Yard, John Emmet's partner*
Polly Gray ('Daphne'), *offering special services in Rose Street*
'Corinna', *optimistic nymph of Drury Lane who will eventually inspire Jonathan Swift*
Mrs Purslowe, *service provider of Maiden Lane, the girls' manager*
Joseph Quinlan, *clerk in the Excise Office*
Mortimer, *unfortunate street hawker*
Bob the shoe-boy, *master of his craft*
Humfrey Proby, *experienced surgeon with clean hands*
Umberto Gallini, *diversifying apothecary of Rose Street*
Mr Barson, *punctilious porter at the College of Arms*
*Dudley Downs, *Rouge Dragon Pursuivant at the College of Arms, scholar*
Major Alfred Gearey, *shinbone of the footguards*
Private Jerry Lamb, *pugilist*

Historical Note

Chocolate House Treason weaves its fictional plot into the dramatic political events of January-February 1708. The Morphew murder trial is an invention, although the printer (who was soon to become Jonathan Swift's publisher) was already sailing in dangerous political waters, and at Lord Sunderland's behest he would be arrested for sedition the following year, and on further occasions too.

In January 1708 Secretary of State Robert Harley was secretly attempting to organise a new ministry of 'the Queen's friends,' which would bring together the moderates of both parties and would exclude the 'Junto' Whigs, who were the most powerful and coherent political grouping at this time. Run by Lords Sunderland, Somers, Wharton, and Halifax, the 'Junto' was a tightly organised 'party' who met regularly to decide how to exploit their parliamentary strength. Today we would consider them the party of opposition, but in the person of the Earl of Sunderland they held one of the three great offices of government, much to the Queen's vexation. Lord Godolphin was chief minister ('First Lord of the Treasury'), and Harley and Sunderland were the two Secretaries of State, who together ran what we now think of as the Foreign and Home Offices. Anne, of course, appointed her own ministers, but she couldn't afford to ignore parliament's views altogether, and Whig pressure to include Sunderland had simply been too great. He was the son-in-law of the Marlboroughs, and Anne and the whole country needed the Duke, who at this time of European war was more indispensable than any minister. The Duchess of Marlborough detested Harley as much as Anne detested Sunderland. It was not an easy situation.

At this time Anne relied hugely on Harley and his close friend and ally Henry St John, the Secretary-at-War, both in the House of Commons. The nominal 'Prime' Minister remained Lord Godolphin, but the twin Secretaries of State, Harley and Sunderland, had the effectual power and ran their departments as competing organisations. Both employed systems of spies and informers, and to a degree so did the Duchess of Marlborough through her influential secretary Arthur Maynwaring.

In the end, at the beginning of February 1708 it was Marlborough's sudden disillusionment with Harley that brought about his fall. Harley was only days away from implementing the plans he had been secretly preparing for months, and almost everything was in place for a Harleian ministry – but he failed to win Marlborough and Godolphin round. At a meeting of the Cabinet on Sunday 8 February they refused to sit at the same table with him, and their allies walked out. By the Tuesday (the day of the fictional inauguration of the Bay-Tree Chocolate House in chapter 50) a distressed Anne had no choice but to accept Harley's resignation, and he handed in his seals of office the next day. In an unprecedented move for this period, Harley's closest allies St John and Harcourt (Attorney-General) resigned as well.

Harley's position had already been seriously weakened by two spy scandals, and during the thirteen days covered by the novel (29 Jan-10 Feb) London was full of rumours that Harley himself was to be impeached. A pair of his 'double agents,' Valière and Bara, whom he had been employing, turned out to be agents of the French, and this discovery seriously compromised his covert operations. But the more dangerous scandal by far was the case of William Greg.

On 31 December 1707, Greg, a clerk in Harley's office at the Cockpit, had been arrested for passing confidential government documents to the French. Within weeks he was tried and condemned to death; but for the next three months the sentence was suspended while the Whigs offered him his freedom and a pension if he would only incriminate his boss. But Greg resisted the pressure and continued to declare that Harley had known nothing. Greg's actual letter to Harley asking to be released from his irons (chapter 8) is dated 31 January, and I imagine it as being written the previous evening while Tom and Will are dining in Middle Temple Hall. In the end, Greg went to his death in April, and Harley – who could have faced a possible treason charge himself – lived to fight another day.

In the novel, the letter from Greg's distraught wife to Henry St John is wholly my invention – nothing of the kind is known. Its contents are intended to help explain why at the beginning of February Harley lost the vital support of Godolphin and Marlborough. His relations with his former allies (they were known as the Triumvirate) had already become strained and precarious; but Marlborough's ultimatum to Anne on Friday 6 February (the Queen's birthday) threatening their resignation unless Harley were removed, was the decisive break. My own entirely fictional suggestion is that they had learned about the contents of Mrs Greg's letter in which Harley's complicity in the treason is revealed. In the novel's imagined world, had the Whigs gained possession of the document, then Harley would have been doomed. But in the end – in history – he proved resilient. Although the General Election in summer 1708 was a Whig triumph, by 1710 the party had become very unpopular and Harley was back again, now as First Minister himself, to lead a largely Tory government. But this lasted only as long as Anne's life. In 1714, with the arrival of the new Hanoverian King George, the Tories were kept out of office for almost half a century. St John fled to France, and Harley remained to face impeachment ...

I have tried to make the documented details and descriptions as exact as possible, but in a couple of places I have made a significant adjustment to the historical facts. The Queen's annual Birth-night ball on 6 February was always a lavish occasion, but in 1708, with her husband ill and the political situation so fraught, Anne wanted a low-key affair, and so her birthday that year was celebrated not with the usual grand ball at St James's Palace but a reception at Kensington. The novel substitutes the memorable palace ball of the previous year (1707), for which Mr Isaacs' new dance, *The Union*, was especially commissioned.

In the years following 1706 many works are described as 'printed and sold' by John Morphew, but in that year he seems to have entered into partnership with John Nutt, with Nutt as printer and Morphew as publisher and distributor. I have made Morphew in 1708 sole proprietor/printer/publisher. His Tory affiliations were becoming evident, but in that year he set his name to Joseph Addison's important Whig pro-war pamphlet, *The Present State of the War*. It is subscribed: 'London: Printed, and sold by J. Morphew near Stationers Hall,' and I have taken the hint to imagine a rapprochement between the two men. Morphew's bond with Delarivier Manley was close, and in 1709 he published the second volume of her fearsomely anti-Marlborough *New Atalantis* and promptly found himself arrested for sedition. In that year he was also publisher of *The Tatler*, edited by Richard Steele, and by 1710 of *The Examiner*, the Tory paper in which Harley's friend Jonathan Swift was the government's mouthpiece. During the next four years Morphew became virtually printer to the Harley ministry.

The anonymous pamphlet which Tom picks up in the coffee-room in Chapter One, *A Modest Vindication of the Present Ministry,* had been printed the previous year and was once thought to be by Daniel Defoe. In 1704 Defoe had launched *The Review,* the first true political journal, which he continued to write single-handedly until 1713. At this time he was one of Harley's leading agents and a master-spy with his own network of informers, helping to run Harley's secret service. The *Review* was fearsomely supportive of Harley's campaign for political moderation and the Union with Scotland, for which Defoe worked tirelessly.

In the opening chapter of the novel Tom reads *The Daily Courant* for Thursday 29 January 1708, and later chapters use material from the London newspapers of the following twelve days.

The three church services draw on contemporary documentation. Details of the communion service in the Chapel Royal (chapter 14) are taken from the account given by a German visitor, Zacharias Conrad Von Uffenbach, in the summer of 1710 (he is also a valuable witness for the conduct of trials at the Old Bailey). The sermon preached in Temple Church on the Feast of King Charles the Martyr (chapter 7) draws on the words and sentiments of *The Measures of Christian Obedience,* 5th ed. (London, 1709) by John Kettlewell (1653-95), a nonjuring Church of England clergyman. The novel imagines him still alive and flourishing in 1708! The sermon preached in Mare Street Chapel, Hackney (chapter 17), was not delivered by the then minister, Robert Billio, but by his successor Matthew Henry (d. 1714). There are other contemporary sources for various scenes and descriptive details throughout the novel, far too many to be listed here.

Readers curious about what happened to the optimistic young Corinna (chapter 29) are invited to read Jonathan Swift's poem 'On a Beautiful Young Nymph Going to Bed' (1734).

A Note on the Poetry

THE EXTRACTS OF poetry quoted in the novel are a mixture of my own and contemporary pieces. The book's three main poets – all B's – Bristowe, Bufo, and Bagnall (author of 'The Shoe-Buckle') are of course, sadly, fictional.

p. 14: *He practised vices of the lighter sort,*
Coffee and tea, tobacco, wit, and port

Revised from Jonathan Swift, 'The Author upon Himself', 36-7:

And deal in Vices of the graver Sort,
Tobacco, Censure, Coffee, Pride, and Port.

---

p. 14: *Ah* H-----*! Satan's double-dealing imp,*
Foul Wharton's *cully, mighty* Somers' *pimp,*
In Spencer's *service like a rat serves fleas,*
Sign of our body politick's disease;
Whore of the Junto ...

DF

pp. 26-7: "*When dazzling* Phoebus ..."

All extracts here are from the anonymous broadsheet, *A Poem on the Queen's Birthday* (London: Printed and Sold by J. Morphew, near Stationers-Hall, 1707), with a few minor emendations.

p. 29: *with sharpened pen to scourge the offending age*

DF

p. 35: *A hackney Crew who trade on War's alarms,*
And build their Mansions as they scant our Arms.

DF

p. 54: *When Flattery sooths, and when Ambition blinds*

From John Dryden, *Absalom and Achitophel* (1681)

p. 95: *the various turns of chance below*

From John Dryden, *Alexander's Feast* (1697)

p. 123: *The Laureate's lofty Ode in* Anna's *praise*
From pipe to pipe the living flame *conveys;*
Critics, who long have scorned, must now admire
To see TATE's *verses kindling* genuine fire!'

Revised from 'An Extempore Epigram, on seeing a Pipe lighted with one of the Laureate's Odes' [1737]. The later laureate in question is Colley Cibber:

While the soft song that warbles *George*'s praise
From pipe to pipe the living flame conveys;
Criticks, who long had scorn'd, must now admire;
For who can say his *Ode* now wants its *fire*.

The London Magazine, January 1737.

p. 126: *A* Whig, *a* Nettle, *and a* Toad,
They shit, *and* sting, *and* spit *their load;*
When ground and mix'd by Spencer's *hand*
The poison spreads throughout the land.

Adapted from Ned Ward, 'The Odious Comparison. An Epigram', from *The Poetical Entertainer* (1722):

A Whig, a Nettle, and a Toad,
Are much alike, by all that's Good:
The Nettle stings, the Whig he bites,
The swelling Toad his Venom spits:
But crush 'em all, your Strength exert,
And neither then can do you hurt.

pp. 143-9: *Text of Bufo's Magic Glass is by DF*

[In 1739 Pope told Joseph Spence 'Addison and Steele were a couple of H-----s. I am sorry to say so, and there are not twelve people in the world that I would say it to at all.']

p. 236: *How num'rous, Lord, of late are grown*
The troublers of my peace!
And as their factious numbers rise,
So does their rage increase …

Psalm 3, from Nahum Tate,
An Essay of a New Version of the Psalms of David (1695)

p. 375: *Collective bodies in close Union join'd*
Remain invincible while so combin'd;
But when divided fall an easy prey:
The Whole does in its weakened Parts decay!

From Edmund Arwaker, Fable 58,
from *Select Fables* (1708)

p. 387: *… The consequence of this was such,*
Our good and gracious Queen,
Not knowing why she e'er went wrong,
Came quickly right again.

And taking then the wise advice
Of those who knew her well,
She Abigail *turn'd out of doors,*
And hang'd up Machiavell*!*

---

p. 388: *When as Q[ueen] A[nne] of great Renown*
Great Britain's *Scepter sway'd,*
Besides the Church, she dearly lov'd
A dirty Chamber-Maid ...

From the ballad, 'When as Q[ueen] A[nne] of great Renown' 'To the Tune of Fair Rosamond' (1708). Probably by Arthur Maynwaring.

---

pp. 448-9: *Curse on the authors of our present woes,*
Through whom the Nation's *desperate ills arose!...*
...And your vile dust by wicked hands be torn
From its tall urn, and made the people's scorn!

This curse is considerably developed and expanded from Ned Ward, *The Anathema: Or a Curse upon the Nation's Enemies* (1709)

---

p. 519: *pleased with the danger when the waves run high!*

From John Dryden, *Absalom and Achitophel* (1681)

pp. 675-6: *Descend, my Muse, from thine accustom'd Flights:*
Descend to Earth, and ease thy wide-stretch'd Wing!
For weary art thou grown of those too daring heights;
Thou shalt of Chocolate sing
And Coffee's rich delights;
The Bay-Tree now commands th'adventurous Muse
To welcome wit, and poetry, and lofty thought,
The philosophic mind t'enthuse ...

Lines 1-3 are from William Congreve, *To the King. On the Taking of Namur. An Irregular Ode* [1695]. The rest is genuine Bagnall.

p. 679: *The virtues are in exile: nothing's left*
But murder, treason, perjury and theft;
A time so bad, all truth and honour fled:
Is this an Age of Iron? – or of Lead?
'Tis wrong the Frame of Nature to defame:
No metal's base enough to lend its name.
The wise are gone, and so few are the good
That scarcely more were left at Noah's flood.

DF, with some hints from John Oldham,
The Thirteenth Satire of Juvenal, Imitated (1682).

CPSIA information can be obtained
at www.ICGtesting.com
Printed in the USA
LVHW110720270920
667178LV00002B/756